There once lived a man who was born a Scottish gardener's son, grew up to hold half a new continent in one hand while he burned and pillaged the ships of England with the other, and died, half mad from laudanum, in old France. He is a legend, and his name was John Paul Jones.

THE REVOLUTIONARY is his story. Half hero, half pirate, he combined the stubborn blood of Scotland with the cruelty of its old warriors, the ambition of America with its new young conscience. Driven sometimes by bitterness, sometimes by love, scourged by shame and compelled by ardor, he sailed a noose around the Old World and pulled it tight to free the New.

His love of ships drew a net across the Seven Seas: from the gentle civilities of young Virginia to the burning mists of Africa, with its terrible black cargo; from Jamaica for rum to America for steel; from muffled splashings in the dark of the night off England to the holocaust of the Turkish galleys. And slipping through the narrative of his long sea journeys, gleaming now here, now there, are the elusive figures of the women he loved: the icebound and fiery Kitty, daughter of a great plantation; golden-thighed Dolores, whose body held all the mystery of the slumbering African jungle; flirtatious Lydia, half actress, half of a Virginia flirtation, the dialogues of the theater, the wit of courts, the obscenities of sailors, and the thoughts of John Paul Jones; smell the timbers of a ship that has carried slaves, and the small, perfumed hand of Catherine the Great. He tells us the small, homely details of the events that shook the world, and he lays bare the mind of the strange hero that molded them.

By Lawrence Schoonover

THE BURNISHED BLADE

THE GENTLE INFIDEL

THE GOLDEN EXILE

THE QUICK BROWN FOX

THE SPIDER KING

THE QUEEN'S CROSS

THE REVOLUTIONARY

The Revolutionary

The
Revolutionary

Lawrence Schoonover

BOSTON   Little, Brown and Company   TORONTO

LIBRARY OF CONGRESS CATALOG CARD NO. 58–7849

FIRST EDITION

Published simultaneously in Canada
by Little, Brown & Company (Canada) Limited

PRINTED IN THE UNITED STATES OF AMERICA

FOR MY DAUGHTER
Caroline

Contents

Book One
The British Twilight

Chapter 1

HE WAS BORN of a breed of men whom no tyrant had ever been able to conquer. Something in the Celtic blood, something baffling, whether bravery or simply a rebel compulsion to hold to a dream in defiance of logic, rendered the Scotsman an enigma, especially to the British. Outwardly grave, often called dour, scorned for his thrift (till one beheld his craggy niggardly homeland), the Scot was not only calculating, as might have been expected, but exasperatingly unpredictable.

He was unpredictable because under his sober exterior there flowed an unfathomable river of faerie, deep as the mists that shrouded his barren mountains, where distances were deceptive. To him the faraway seemed near at hand, the steep ascent seemed easy. His sun shone cooler and closer and more diffuse than other men's sun, pervading his sky with a glow that softened harsh outlines; when he looked up, reality gave way to fancy, values merged, and the impossible became possible.

It was impossible, for example, that a handful of wild blue-painted Highlanders should have stood up against the might of Imperial Rome. But in ancient days that is what happened. Since they could not be subdued, the emperor Hadrian built a wall against them from Solway Firth to the estuary of the Tyne, straight across the island of Britain from sea to sea. Southward was civilization, order, law and the crushing weight of the Pax Romana that regularized the whole world. But to the north, wild, free and untamable, dwelt the Scots, dancing their sword dance among the hills and, shortly, adopting a skirtlike national costume, the kilt, like nothing which men had worn since the old Greek evzones, another breed of fighting mountain men.

But on Drummossie Moor in 1745, the year that a certain obscure Scotch gardener begat an astonishing son, Scotland lost forever her cherished independence. Triumphant English armies swept north across Hadrian's long-since-crumbled wall and won a decisive victory over the last of

3

the Stuart kings in the name of British King George II, a gross fat man whom even the English despised for his foreign German blood, his heavy German accent, his thick German neck and his despotic German temperament.

So fearful was King George of the Royal Stuarts' return that he actually banished all finger bowls from his royal table. He had observed some of his most trusted courtiers slyly passing their glasses over the water of these useful little amenities while in the very act of drinking his health. Thus the loyal toast "To the King!" became a toast "To Bonnie Prince Charlie, the King *Over the Water*," now wandering in exile, the darling of the Scots. With equal attention to all that was trifling, he sternly forbade his new Scotch subjects to wear kilts or to play upon their bagpipes. When it was represented to him by his ministers that bagpipes and kilts and finger bowls, irritating though they might be, were a far less threat to His Britannic Majesty than Scotch guns, he forbade guns too. Not even a fowling piece was permitted north of the Tweed, not even to shoot a grouse. The Hanoverians were thorough.

No Scotsman believed that this sickening loss of freedom would last for long. The Stuart prince still lived. Hatred of England still boiled in Highland blood.

The gardener's wife spun a hank of wool and dyed it red, blood red for two thousand Scotsmen slaughtered by English cannon on Drummossie Moor. "Och how!" she lamented. "Och how, for the fallen! Is it true that they slew only fifty English before they died?"

"Be quiet, woman," the gardener said. "That is all over now."

She spun another hank and dyed it green, and another and dyed it heather blue, and set up her loom and began to weave the soft warm wool into a tartan plaid.

"Jeannie, Jeannie wife," he muttered, "you know that is against the law."

"Whose law?"

"The only law there is any more."

"English law!"

"Law is law," he shrugged, "and a prudent man in these times obeys it and keeps out of trouble." But he humored her, as he always did when she was carrying a child, and the slow months passed, and the child within her grew like the cloth upon the loom. As the pattern approached completion, it became more and more alarming.

"It is tempting Providence to weave a tartan at all nowadays," he said, "but to weave the Royal Stuart is absolutely daft."

4

"It is not the Royal Stuart, Jock."

"It is much like it," he said, frowning, "and it will cause gossip."

Oh, none of the neighbors of Arbigland would betray to the gentry that a tartan was a-weaving in the gardener's humble cottage. But they would whisper excitedly among themselves; they would identify the pattern and speculate that Prince Charlie might be hiding close by, perhaps on the very estate of the gardener's employer. And what likelier prospect than that the gardener's pretty young wife should make to Prince Charlie a gift of a fine new kilt? Who knew, indeed, what other favors she might not bestow, the prince being a bonnie handsome rake and she as sprightly as the gardener was stolid and dull?

"It will embarrass my master, the laird," the gardener said, "and it embarrasses me."

A flash of color swept up from her neck, flamed for an instant on her fine-chiseled features, and then she laughed gaily. "Jock Paul, there is in your mind too much of that which makes your roses bloom so lush and fair."

"What — what do you mean?" She was always too quick for him.

"That which you gather from the laird's stables," she said, "to fertilize his plants."

"There is nothing wrong with manure," he said stoutly.

"Not in a garden, no. But in a mind?"

"Och, woman, do you mean that I have a dirty mind?"

"Did you not suggest that the bairn I carry under my heart is not yours? Not yours but Prince Charles Edward's? And all because you think I am weaving a Royal Stuart tartan?"

"By God, Jeannie, I meant no such nastiness."

"Then I'll stop teasing you, Jock."

"I only said that the neighbors might think that the prince is hiding hereabouts, whereas I know for certain that he is in Rome — or in Russia — I forget which. It was one or the other."

Bonnie Prince Charlie had flitted like a will-o'-the-wisp over the face of Europe, perpetually a fugitive since Drummossie Moor, drinking himself into a stupor to forget his troubles whenever he could find a friend to hide him, preferably in a well-stocked wine cellar.

"Do not tease me about such things. I freely admit," he said less severely, "that I do not pretend to be good at identifying Highland tartans." It was not expected of a Lowlander like Jock Paul that he should be.

"It is only the MacDuff," she said softly, "the bairn's own honest birthright."

5

"Through you."

Jeannie Paul was a Highlander, a MacDuff from Argyll, before she married the laird's gardener.

"I'll weave him a Paul tartan too, if you tell me what it is."

"If there is a Paul tartan," he said dubiously, "it probably doesn't look much like the Royal Stuart."

The work on the loom did strongly resemble it, lacking only the overcheck of yellow and white. The ground was red. Wide green and blue crossings lay over it in a stern geometric design; but the eye was led astray from the solid simplicity of the groundwork by an intricate profusion of checks of lighter blue, pale vibrant blue like a mountain mist. The gardener would have preferred some less confusing combination of colors, something more gay.

"This is a dark and somber pattern you weave," he said. "I hope it will not mark the bairn."

"The MacDuff tartan cannot mark him, Jock Paul, unless it be for glory."

Her husband chuckled. "Nothing less than a popish miracle is needed to mark for glory the son of a poor Scotch gardener." But he liked her for her spirit. "Just how do you know that the bairn will be a boy?"

"He kicks me lustily, Jock. Not like Willie, who was sluggish as if he liked his sleep; and not like the girls, who never caused me a moment of pain. No, this is a boy, with nerves like wire and steel-spring legs, for they thump me unmercifully, always when I least expect it. Aye," she smiled, "he has a hasty temper. He cannot wait to be born."

"Now fancy you knowing all that so soon," the gardener chuckled. "A wonderful thing it is to have a woman's mind."

"Just wait till you see, Jock Paul."

And, in truth, when the child was born he was not at all like his brother William, who peered down into the cradle and said, "He's a wee weak bit of a caddie, Mother."

"All babies are wee and weak, Willie."

"Was I?"

"Assuredly you were."

"Why is he so red?"

"They're red too, at first."

"I doubt if you was quite so red," his father said. "You was more —" He groped ponderously for a comparison. "Well, I would say you was more like me," and he ran his hand fondly through Willie's thick brown hair.

"Good," Willie said. "I like to be like you."

"But that does not mean," his father admonished, raising a stern Presbyterian finger, "in all fairness, that does not necessarily mean that your little brother here will never amount to anything. Though I doubt if he'll grow up to be a gardener."

Jeannie Paul rocked the cradle gently with her tiny foot, a foot the despair of Arbigland's cobbler, who had had to fashion a special last to fit her. "I too doubt if he'll grow up to be a gardener," she said. Her tone was bland, but something in it angered her husband. He called upon the best English he could muster. (Since Drummossie Moor it was fashionable to try to ape the English accent.) "And what, pray, is dishonorable in being a gardener? Did you not marry one, madam?"

"Hush, Jock, you've waked him."

"Good lungs," the gardener said. "Good strong lungs. That's something, anyhow."

"Now he's redder than ever," Willie said.

The mother reached in and drew up the child and cradled him in her arms. "Will you leave me alone with him for a while?"

"Eh?" said the gardener.

"Why?" Willie demanded.

"Oh, you men!" she smiled.

"Oh ho!" said the gardener. "I see. Come, Willie lad, this is feeding time no doubt, and the propriety of the occasion requires that you and me take ourselves to some other place with all speed."

"I don't see why," Willie said.

"Now come along, Willie."

They left the room and Willie said, "I don't think it was fair for you to name him Jock instead of me. I've got a right to that name. I'm the first son."

"You've got a braw — I mean, you've got a perfectly good name as it is. William is a lucky name. William is a king's name."

"I don't want to be a king."

The gardener snorted. "You won't be. But wouldn't you like to be the laird's gardener? Wouldn't you like to have this nice cottage all for your own, like me?"

"Oh yes."

"Well, William, that is why you're William and not Jock. I had the scheme all worked out in my mind the very day you was born. On the day you was born I went to the laird and I said, 'Sir,' says I, 'I've got a fine new son.'

" 'Congratulations,' says he.

7

" 'Sir,' says I, 'if it's not too bold, can I name him after my kind and generous benefactor?'

" 'Anything you like, Jock,' says he as if he didn't care, but I could see that he was pleased. 'I'll stand godfather to him if you wish.' Think of that now, Willie!

"So into the kirk we go one fine Sunday morning, and all the people sing hymns and pray for you, and the pastor says, 'Name this child!'

" 'William!' says the laird in his big loud voice, and I was proud. So down you go into the tank, and up you come dripping wet like a fine fat fish, for you was big and fat, Willie, and from that very moment you're William, just like Mr. Craik, the laird. His Christian name is William. And that is how your intelligent father," he said, nodding approval of himself, "looked out for the future of his first-born son."

Willie was silent a moment. "What will Jock be?"

The gardener shrugged. "What can I do? A poor man canna look out for the future of all his children. Jock must make his own way, I fear."

Chapter 2

TIME FLOWED with relentless rhythm past Arbigland, scarcely touching it, like the slow tides in the broad expanse of the Solway Firth. Blue mountains of surpassing beauty swept up from this silver arm of the sea on either side. For centuries it had separated two kingdoms, Scotland to the north, England to the south. Now all was England. Across the water the villagers of Arbigland could look towards the busy port of Whitehaven on the English shore. Arbigland had no trade.

Once a week a cutter would put across the Firth to deliver a small package of newspapers. There was seldom any mail for Arbigland; there was almost never any outgoing mail.

Prince Charlie's battle for the throne, the reckless spirit and high wild hopes of 1745, drifted further into the past each year. A generation was growing up who could not remember Drummossie Moor; a generation was dying who had fought there. But King George's memory was long and his fear of the Scots was deep. There were still no finger bowls on the royal table. Scotsmen were still forbidden to bear arms, to play on the bagpipes, or to wear kilts. And they were taxed unmercifully.

This in itself was sufficient to infuriate the poor and provident Scot. But now there was imposed another tax of a far more insidious character. Oriental in its cruelty, illegal and inhuman, it was a tax on flesh and blood. It was collected secretly, in the dark, by low and depraved agents. It was excused on the grounds of necessity, that most seductive of fallacies: that the end would justify the means. It was called "impressment," and the ruffians who hunted the human prey — and collected a bounty on each "body" they captured — were known as the "press gang." The chapter they wrote in the annals of the sea was foul with shame. They left their mark upon the language. Before the press gangs appeared, there never had been *gangsters*. Fear of them was intense.

There was another war in Europe. Great Britain was marching from victory to victory, but British losses were heavy, especially at sea. Sailors to man the British fleet were in demand, and Scotland bred the finest sailors in the world, schooled from their youth to sail and fish in the miles of lochs and firths that cut like gashes into the heartland of their country.

On the first of November, 1755, an event of almost cosmic proportions occurred. From Scotland to Asia Minor the whole earth groaned and shook. Tides rose and fell with unprecedented violence along the coasts. Tides even appeared in the Scottish landlocked lakes, a terrifying phenomenon. In far-off Turkey the whitewashed walls of Santa Sophia shivered and dropped plaster, exposing the ancient mosaics. In France Voltaire dipped his pen in wormwood and wrote a poem against God. In Portugal the city of Lisbon collapsed. Thirty thousand unsuspecting victims died, crushed in the rubble of falling walls, or burned by the fires that followed the earthquake, or drowned by the tidal wave that followed the fires.

In Arbigland, before the newspapers could bring details of the worldwide scope of the catastrophe, there was noticed only queer weather and the strange behavior of the Solway Firth. A gritty brown haze that tasted like dust lay over the town, dimming the low winter sun to a dull blood red. An enormous tide swept in, swamping the wharf, and then receded so far that thirty feet of new beach was exposed, slimy sea bottom littered with flopping stranded fish.

In the parish school the dominie watched the clock and debated uneasily with himself whether he should not dismiss his brood of students early on such an uncanny day. He was not a superstitious man, but during the night his bell had rung with no human hand on the rope; there was a crack in the wall just behind the bench on which sat Jamie Craik and the two Paul boys. He felt unnerved. "I ought to keep them till five o'clock as usual," he said to himself. "Indeed I would do so except that it is grow-

9

ing so dark." He persuaded himself that the clock might have been affected by the shock of the quake.

At four o'clock he dismissed them to let them go down to the beach to join the crowd of townspeople who were gathering up the abundance of fish that the low tide had so providentially provided. "You may hear it said by some foolish folk that the fish are unfit to eat, poisoned by a miasmic effluvium stirred up from the bottom of the sea." He smiled. "That is mere nonsense. The phenomenon we have observed is purely a manifestation of natural forces; our men of science will no doubt explain it soon in the clear and rational spirit which illuminates this modern eighteenth century, in which we have the good fortune to be born. Now be off wi' ye!"

They scampered out with a joyful whoop and ran down to the beach. When the dominie was alone, he stared hard at the crack and scowled at the bell and lashed the rope tight to a peg in the wall. Modern century or not, he was not going to hear that thing ring again all by itself. He muttered under his breath, "From ghoulies and ghosties and long-legged beasties and things that go boomp in the night, good Lord deliver us!"

Though Arbigland had no trade, it did have a tavern down near the wharf where the local fishermen could take a dram before setting out to their work, and another to warm them after their work was done. It was a respectable establishment. The laird himself patronized it on mail days to pick up his London newspaper, mingling easily with his servants and tenants, though he wore shoes and they wore boots, he a powdered wig and they their own hair. Mr. Craik was an amiable man; he was gentry, a great landowner; but his look was that of a commoner, and no one knew better than he that a laird was not a lord. He had particularly endeared himself to the townsfolk of Arbigland because he had generously acknowledged his bastard, young Jamie Craik, and given him not only his name but continuing and boundless affection. It was well known that Jamie would go to the University of Edinburgh at his father's expense and study to become a surgeon after this last year at the parish school.

Jamie Craik and Willie Paul were just of an age, both tall, and fast good friends. Jock was a head shorter and his voice, to his intense chagrin, was still sweet and high as a girl's. Try as he would (and he often tried, in secret), he could not yet coax it down to the fine deep register of his brother's and Jamie Craik's.

Willie complained to his father, "Jock makes a nuisance of himself, always following us around."

"Send him packing then," his father said.

But his mother said, "Can't you see the lad adores you?"

Most of the fish had already been scooped up and put into sacks and taken home by the townspeople by the time the boys reached the beach. Here and there one could still be seen in the distance, flopping forlornly among the slippery rocks and treacherous pools of the strange unnatural beach in the wan unnatural twilight, which was visibly fading with each passing moment.

"We're too late," Willie said.

"I see plenty of fish," Jock said. "I wonder why everybody left so quickly."

Candlelight began to shine from the tavern windows. "Maybe everybody's in there," Jamie said, laughing.

"Not so many," Jock said, narrowing his eyes.

"D'ye mean you can actually see in there?" The windows were dirty and the distance was considerable.

"There are only three or four men standing, though there may be more at the tables."

"You must have telescopes for eyes," Jamie said.

"It's past the hour for flood tide," Willie said. "I suppose they went home because the beach will be under water again soon."

"It hasn't started to flood yet," Jock said. "We could still venture out."

"Not I," Jamie said.

"I'd probably founder," Willie said good-naturedly. He was still fat, but he didn't mind. "Probably sink right in."

"I'm light! I'll go! Please let me go, Willie!"

"Go ahead. Be a fool if you want to."

Jamie shook his head. "I don't think he should. It's too risky. Not for a couple of dead fish anyhow."

"There's something else out yonder," Jock said uncertainly. "It's big and black. I don't think it's a rock."

"Probably some old hulk that sank years ago," Jamie said.

"That's what it looks like. Maybe it's full of Spanish treasure. The dominie says many of the Armada ships went down near here."

They both laughed.

"Not likely," Jamie said.

Willie said, "Jock's always dreaming up wild things to make him rich and famous."

The tavern door opened. A sharp rectangle of yellow light etched itself against the gloom and quickly disappeared as the door closed again. They had not realized how dark it had become until that relatively feeble light temporarily blinded them. When their eyes again became accustomed to the deepening dusk, they saw several men approaching the spot where they stood, led by one who carried a smoking ship's lantern. The lantern swung jauntily, and the man who was carrying it suddenly stopped and laughed. He must have turned, for the lantern blinked out as if it were hidden by his body. Then it waved gaily in the air like a signal, and the man shouted, "Many thanks, Mr. Maxwell, for your generosity."

"Englishmen," Jamie whispered.

The door did not open again. The proprietor of the tavern did not acknowledge the thanks.

"Stupid sullen Scot," the man with the lantern mumbled. His voice was louder now as he and his companions tramped closer. There were three of them besides the leader.

"When Mungo Maxwell's patrons call him generous," Jamie warned under his breath, "something is vastly awry."

"They're drunk," Jock whispered.

Willie said, "I think it's high time we went home."

"Sh!" said Jock. "They haven't spotted us. They may pass by."

But the men were already upon them. The leader saw their dim shapes, suddenly stopped short and thrust his lantern into their faces. "Oh ho!" he said. "What have we here?"

One of the men behind him muttered in a drunken whisper, "Two of them are big enough."

"God damn your eyes, shut up!" the leader shouted. Then he turned his face to Jamie, exposing a snaggly row of yellow teeth in an insinuating smile. His breath was foul and sour with drink. "Begging your pardon, young man, sir, for I recognize gentry when I sees it, I was forced to speak roughly to him. He's taken on more of your grand Scotch whisky than he can carry. Do you know why I spoke roughly to him?"

"It doesn't matter," Jamie said civilly. "I think we shall be off now."

Willie edged slowly backward into the darkness. "Good evening, gentlemen," he said.

The leader fastened a grip like iron on Willie's arm. "No, no! Hear me. I spoke roughly to that fellow there because he insulted you. He insulted three grand Scotch gentlemen, that's what he did. 'Two of them are big enough,' says he. Oh, I know you heard it. Why, damn me, you're all big enough! So he's going to apologize."

"Big enough for what?" Jock asked.

"Humble apologies," mumbled the man in the shadows behind the leader. To Jock it sounded like a sneer.

12

"Why, you young sprig, big enough to help us push our boat into the water. That's all we want. Just look at us," he whined. "Consider our predicament. Here we are, plain peaceful fishermen, minding our own business, out at our work trying to catch a few small fish to keep body and soul alive for our loved ones over in Whitehaven, and along comes this freak tide and strands us high and dry in Scotland. We couldn't push her off alone. So Mr. Maxwell entertains us for a while. But now the tide's coming in again. Just you young gentlemen give us a hand with the boat. One little push, and off we go."

Plausible, but not likely, Jamie thought. It was more likely that the man was attempting to lure them further out on the lonely beach, where whatever he planned to do could be done without interference. The leader saw them hesitate and began to talk again, fast and friendly.

"Do you gentlemen know Mr. Maxwell? A fine God-fearing upright generous man, Mr. Maxwell. He refused to take a penny from us, that he did, seeing no doubt how poor and unfortunate we was on account of us being stranded. Shipwrecked, you might almost say. Castaways."

"That was very decent of Mungo Maxwell," Jamie said, "but he is not rich, and no doubt he would still like to be paid." Jamie had weighed the situation and thought of a way to summon help.

"Eh? He wants to be paid?"

For a moment the leader's yellow smile vanished. He still held fast to Willie's arm; Willie bit back a groan of pain. The other men seemed to be closing in: Jamie could feel the shoulders of two of them touching his own. He and Willie were outweighed and outnumbered two to one. But as yet no one threatened little Jock.

"Oh, Mr. Maxwell will be paid," the leader assured them sullenly.

"I only meant to suggest," Jamie said, his plan taking shape in his mind, "that we shall be very glad to deliver the money to him now and help you push out the boat afterwards."

The leader squinted out toward the returning tide, hesitated, came to some decision and muttered, "All right. This will settle our score with Mr. Maxwell." He pulled a few coins out of his pocket and gave them to Jock. "Here. Run along and pay the tavern keeper."

"No," Jock said.

Jamie said, "Jock, you don't understand. Willie and I can easily help these good men with their boat. But you must run up to the tavern at once, and give Mr. Maxwell his money. Do you hear? Mustn't he, Willie?"

Jamie reasoned that Jock, because of his youth, would not be con-

13

sidered much of a catch and could give the press gang the slip. Jock was nimble as a goat on his feet. Probably Mungo Maxwell, a lazy and timorous ne'er-do-well, would not dare lift a finger to help, but other villagers could be reached and would come running. Jamie was not sure, however, that Jock quite grasped the situation. And Willie was not helping; Willie could not open his mouth for fear.

"Don't you see?" Jamie pleaded.

Jock said stubbornly, "I see all right, but I'm going to stay here and help push out the boat."

"Oh, Lord," Jamie breathed.

The leader of the gang lowered his lantern till it almost touched Jock's face. The flickering light fell on a thrust-out chin and flashed back green from a pair of angry eyes. Chin and eyes seemed older than the rest of the boy's delicate features.

"How old are you, sonny?"

"I'm old enough. You said so yourself."

"He's only a child, you blackguard!" Jamie said. "Let him go!"

The leader grunted, grinning. "Keep an eye on the young'un too," he ordered. "And give me back my money." He snatched it out of Jock's fist. "Your Mr. Maxwell will have to wait. You shall see our boat at close quarters, my fine cockalorum. Very close quarters."

Now Jock also found himself gripped like a vise about the arm. The men jostled them roughly towards the water's edge, Willie a helpless mass of fear, Jamie scheming hopelessly, Jock picking his way sure-footedly among the slippery rocks, apparently eager to help, for he piped cheerfully:

"Mind the sink hole there, sir; it may be over your head. Don't trip on that old timber. There's a smooth way here to the left, I think." They were drawing ahead of the others.

"Not so fast!" the leader shouted behind them. Mr. Maxwell's whisky had tangled the feet of some of the men, who were slipping and cursing and barking their shins.

The sound of the flooding tide began to roar ominously. It was a big one, coming fast.

"We've got to hurry," Jock said.

The man who was holding him — and leaning on him like a blind man on a guide — shouted to the leader, "I can't hurry. I can't see a thing. Give us your glim!"

"Soon as we catch up with you!" The leader too heard the inrushing tide.

A moment later he thrust the lantern into the hand of Jock's captor. "Now lead, quick!"

Jock felt Jamie's eyes on him reproachfully, but he strode ahead, now leading his captor by the arm. Spent waves and tongues of the advancing tide began to lick at their feet.

"The boat is just ahead," Jock said. "You'd better give me the lantern."

"Oh no, you don't!" the man said.

"Very well, sir. Then hold it a little lower. You won't stumble so much and the others can see."

The man cursed his impertinence, but he held the lantern lower. They came upon the boat; it was already afloat, rocking gently between two massive rocks.

Jock steadied his voice with an effort. "Like a ship in a wet dock," he said.

His captor said unpleasantly, "You're a cool young'un."

The others drew closer over the treacherous footing, which was now fast disappearing under water. When they were a few yards away, Jock suddenly lurched forward. He aimed a shrewd kick with his heavy-shod foot at the lantern. The blow struck swiftly home. The glass shattered with a crash. The lantern sailed out of the man's hand, flamed for an instant leaking oil and fell like a rocket hissing into the sea. Immediately darkness closed in.

"Run!" Jock screamed.

He skipped over to where Willie and Jamie had begun to struggle with their assailants. It was impossible to see, but he heard Jamie flailing and buffeting wildly about him in the dark: Jamie was on his feet. The press gang floundered and cursed, and all at once Jock heard a smashing blow and a groan that sounded like his brother's. The leader shouted, "Into the boat with them!"

Jock ran full tilt into a man and began to claw at him. "It's me; Jock! It's me, Jamie!" Jamie had recognized the small frenzied body that hurled itself against him.

"Get Willie! Where is Willie!"

Thumping noises came from the boat as the gang began to tumble into it. Oars banged into the locks. Over the hissing wash of the inflooding tide Jock heard the purposeful beat of oars being manned.

"Jock, can you see?" Jamie cried.

"No, no one, nothing."

There was no one, nothing to see. The press gang were rowing away with their prize. Jamie and Jock stood alone.

15

A voice, the leader's, came from a distance. "Well, how many?"

"Only one. The fat one."

Jock felt his ears assailed by a torrent of obscenity such as he never had heard and indeed could scarcely interpret. But the final words were clear as the voice died away over the water: "You blasted blundering fools! I wanted that young'un most particular! He had spirit."

There was gloom in the gardener's cottage that night. Supper was cold. Jock sat and stared into his plate.

"You did all a boy could," his mother said, tight-lipped.

"There were so many of them, Mother."

The gardener said, "I will go at once to the laird." His voice was empty and forlorn. In the enormity of his loss he found himself saying, "It seems to me you were very quick to save only yourself when your brother needed help."

Jock was trembling with a surge of terror which, now that the danger was past, reached round and overwhelmed him.

"That was unfair!" his mother said. "For shame!"

"I am sorry, sir," Jock said.

The gardener dropped his eyes. "I will go to the laird. I must go to the laird. Mr. Craik will get my Willie back again."

Jock had never heard his mother use the name of the Lord except in prayer. Now he heard her mutter, "God punish the English to hell ever-lasting!"

He looked into her tense sweet face, appalled. A confused conviction of helplessness, lonely and deep, gripped at his heart. In the parish school the dominie had tried to teach the meaning of justice, of fair play and sportsmanship. The dominie had spoken of "freedom," extolling its bless-ings, exemplifying it with heroic incidents drawn from the bright annals of Scottish history. But now under the shattering impact of this night's actualities the dominie's excellent teachings vanished into a limbo of ab-straction. Stillborn, they were swept away into nothingness. Only dis-belief and rebellion remained. Crystal clear and brittle as flint the fact was borne in upon his soul, to shape and twist it, that nothing was fair, nothing was just, no one was free. Only the strong were free; only the quick, the tricky, the ruthless were free. The press gang were free. But Willie, because he had been weak and afraid, was not free. Nay, at this very moment brutal English strangers were snatching him farther and farther away from home and family and all he knew and loved, bearing him helpless and unconscious over a dark tide to an unknown future.

16

Clearly, the power to win, by fair means or foul, was the only thing that was real. Nothing else mattered.

His face looked drawn and old as he stared into his plate. His eyes were oddly hard. His mother heard him say something that was horrible in a son whose voice had not yet changed to that of a man's: "God abandons the weak. The weak are helpless. The weak are slaves."

"Oh, Jock, Jock, Jock," she murmured.

"And slaves they deserve to be!"

"He's sick," his father said.

"Aye, sick. But in the soul."

Jock laughed in a way that was unpleasant and frightening to hear.

Chapter 3

WILLIAM CRAIK took a serious view of the matter. It was bad enough that an English press gang had taken the son of his gardener. It was infuriating that they had nearly succeeded in abducting his own son. Jamie had given him a faithful account of the fight on the beach. The laird of Arbigland was expecting the visit from his gardener next day. Jock walked beside his father.

"Can Mr. Craik really get Willie back?"

"Aye, lad."

"How?"

The gardener grumbled, "Don't ask so many questions."

Jock turned at the path that led to the smooth gravel walks, the trim clipped hedges and well-kept lawns in front of the laird's house, directly to the laird's front door.

"Not that way," his father said.

"It's shorter, sir."

"Shorter, is it! Shorter indeed. Remember your place, young man, or you'll get into trouble," and he took him by the shoulder and turned him into the path that led to the servants' entrance. Here he knocked respectfully and pulled off his cap and ordered Jock to do the same. The laird's cook opened the door.

"If Mr. Craik isn't busy —" the gardener began.

She motioned them in. "He's just putting on his boots. He'd have sent to fetch you if you hadn't come. I tell you the laird is in a terrible temper this morning, and Mister James has a great black eye and a fist swole up to twice its size. Come in, come in!" She led them through the kitchen and into the drawing room, where William Craik stood booted and dressed for riding in front of a roaring fire.

"It's just as warm in here as it was in the kitchen!" Jock said. He was amazed that more than one room in a house should be heated.

"Be quiet," his father said.

The laird's drawing room was the largest room Jock had ever seen. He was soon to see another that would reduce this one to more modest proportions; but now on beholding the laird's high-beamed ceilings, the carpeted floors and above all the wasteful profusion of logs that were being consumed in the fireplace, Jock was aware for the first time how vast a distance separated his father from William Craik and, even more sharply, himself from Jamie Craik. He felt no resentment against Jamie, whom indeed he admired for his fight, but the fact remained that a laird's bastard lived better and warmer than a gardener's legitimate son.

"Don't gawk at things," his father muttered roughly. "It isn't manners."

William Craik's honest country-squire face was red with indignation. "My friend," he said to his gardener, "I know what it is you feel about last night, for the same thing nearly happened to me. But I must be very candid with you. There is hardly any hope that I can be of help. The 'recruiting activity' of His British Majesty's press gang lies outside my jurisdiction." His voice grew heavy with scorn. "So likewise do activities of highwaymen and pirates. However, I'll do what I can." He turned to Jock. "Can you ride a horse?"

"Aye, sir."

The laird smiled. "I rather thought you could. Good. You and your father and Jamie and I are going to pay a little visit to Lord Selkirk. We'll see if his lordship can put a stop to these outrages. He's a good sound Scot, even if he does sit in their damned foreign British Parliament."

From Arbigland to Lord Selkirk's estate the way stretched thirty miles through narrow rutted frozen roads that climbed a ridge of rocky hills and descended again on the other side into the valley of the river Dee. Here on a wooded promontory at the river's mouth, commanding a beautiful view of the Solway, stood a spacious manor house. It was still called Castle Douglas, though the old feudal structure from which it took its name had been pulled down to make way for a modern many-windowed residence, the country seat of the nobleman named Dunbar Hamilton, fourth Earl of Selkirk, Scottish peer and member of the Parliament of "Great Britain," a name new to the history of that island which, within the memory of men still living, had comprised the two ancient kingdoms of Scotland and England. Lord Selkirk, like his house, like the still-recent Union of the Crowns, was young and inexperienced.

"Do not talk too much to his lordship," Mr. Craik cautioned. "He's only just got married, to a wee pert skillimalinkie, pretty as a rose but full of English blood. No doubt she has already started to make him over."

"I'll be dumb as an ox," the gardener said.

Behind them Jamie Craik stifled a snort of laughter with a cough; his breath was visible in the winter wind. Mr. Craik turned in his saddle and silenced him with a glare.

Jock said, "Is Lady Selkirk so formidable?"

Jamie looked down tolerantly from his immense vantage of a few years and a few inches of height. "Women always try to make over their men when they marry them," he said. "You'll see when you're older."

"Not me," said Jock.

"Oh yes, you will."

"Then I won't get married."

Jock was tired and cold. They had started late for a ride of thirty miles, and they had not stopped to eat. The early winter twilight was full upon them when Castle Douglas, shining from all its windows and with blue smoke curling from all its twelve tall chimneys, rose before them. It looked warm and rich and grand; and far from quiet.

There was a bustling of servants around the entrance, running out to hold the bridles of a large black coach-and-six that had just pulled up. Two drivers in smart cocked hats and powdered wigs sat on the box; two footmen with long pistols in their belts jumped down from a traveling seat in the rear to let down the folding steps of the imposing vehicle; they opened its heavy door and stood at respectful attention. Mr. Craik caught the flash of a many-quartered crest blazoned on the door's lacquered panel. From the dark interior there descended with careful gouty steps the portly figure of a man in satin breeches and white stockings which, from their sheen and smoothness, were recognizable even at a distance as pure and costly silk. He extended his hand to a lady who emerged, all satin and plumes, to take his arm. At the open door of the residence stood Lord and Lady Selkirk, starched, ruffled, powdered and bejeweled. From the drawing room came the music of a clavichord and at least three violins as an orchestra struck up not a Scottish air but one of Mr. Handel's most popu-

19

lar British minuets. Selkirk had gone to great lengths and expense to welcome his distinguished guests, whoever they were.

"I doubt we have come at an awkward time," Mr. Craik said.

To Jock, who had never seen a mansion with twelve chimneys or a coach drawn by six matched horses, the scene unfolding before him seemed like the bright mental picture he had formed of a theatrical performance, such as the dominie had described in school, peopled with heroic figures of impossible wealth and godlike power, a world to long for and dream about, wish to be part of. Here it was, all real.

"It's too late to go back now," Craik continued. "Oh well." He rode up to the coach and spoke to one of the footmen. "What is the name of your master?" (Craik pronounced it "maister.")

The footman eyed the travel-stained figure of the laird and noted that the wig he wore (a comfortable piece which Mr. Craik had put on for its warmth) was disheveled and completely innocent of powder. "My *maister*, sorr," he said in a crude imitation of the laird's Scotch burr, "is none of your business, and you'd better be off about your own, if you have any."

Craik's voice and temper rose. He lifted himself in his stirrups and threatened the footman with his riding crop. "Why, you sniggering, high-bendit, English prig-me-dainty, I'll bloody your breeks wi' my lash if you —"

"Softly, Father!" Jamie pleaded at his elbow.

The footman wilted somewhat under Craik's tone of command; clearly this was a land of savages, and this roaring centaur must be one of their chieftains. He stood his ground, but knew that servants were caned in France and on the Continent; apparently in Scotland too. He managed to say in a slightly more respectful voice, "My master is the Duke of Queensberry, the Duke of Devon, the Earl of Solway —"

"I know the rest," Craik said. He was not reassured. The owner of all these titles, and of many more, was a distant cousin of Lord Selkirk's, rich and influential. The best thing about him was his name: the Duke of Queensberry was a Douglas. Under ordinary circumstances William Craik would have welcomed a chance to present his grievance to so great a peer with so old and famous a Scottish name. But Queensberry's loyalties, like his estates, were divided, lying on both sides of the Tweed. Queensberry's influence on his young kinsman, who was so anxious to please him, was not likely to be of a character that would much affect the fate of Willie Paul. It seemed to Jock that Mr. Craik's shoulders slumped a little; the riding crop certainly now hung at a dejected angle.

"Still, we must try," said the laird.

The footman said, "Try what?"

"Kindly inform Lord Selkirk, your master's host, that William Craik is asking to see him."

The footman nodded and went to deliver the message.

What followed was destined to impress itself strongly on Jock's plastic young mind, like a first lesson written on a schoolboy's empty slate, looming large because there was as yet nothing else to compete with it.

A clean-cut division now took place among the four who had ridden from Arbigland to Castle Douglas. William Craik and his son were invited to sup with the gentry; the gardener and his son were taken round to the rear of the house and given a place at the servants' table. Even here in the kitchen there were distinctions: Lord Selkirk's butler presided over the head of the table flanked by the duke's English coachmen, who were guests of honor. Thence to the foot of the table ranged Selkirk's servants in strict order of precedence. Jock found himself with his father at the foot of the table; by the time the platters of food reached them, they were well picked over. In a sense, of course, the humbler servants were better off because their meal was not interrupted: the butler and several others were continually getting up and sitting down because of serving the gentry.

Jock wondered in what order Jamie and Mr. Craik might have been placed at the great table in the dining room, which was so near that he could hear voices and music. He asked his father.

"Now how in the world should I know a thing like that?" his father said. "What would it matter, anyhow?"

"He's got to be close enough to tell Lord Selkirk and the duke what happened to Willie."

The gardener stopped chewing a fraction of a second. "Aye, you're right," he said, and whispered the question to a servant who sat beside him.

The man answered good-naturedly, "Oh, him. Why, he's right where we are, I expect, right at the bottom. I was surprised they let him in at all, dressed the way he was and that boy of his with a big black eye."

"We came hurriedly, and on a matter of some urgency," the gardener said.

"I know."

"You know?"

"Aye. The English press gang. No doubt the duke will talk about that. We all hope so, for your sake."

The gardener was surprised how rapidly the news had spread. "Thank you kindly," he said.

How the kitchen was so well informed was shortly made clear. As the servants returned with the gentry's plates and scraps of their meal, they brought back also scraps of the gentry's conversation. Thus Jock was exposed, at second hand, to a flood of ill-assorted and incomprehensible information concerning great events abroad in the outside world. He listened avidly, forgetting to eat, though he was still hungry. It galled him not to be able to understand more of it.

Theater: The duchess said that the town (London, Jock guessed) was "horn-mad" about David Garrick's appearances. Garrick was a famous actor. Such a wit! He wrote many of his own plays; he even improved on Shakespeare by interpolating his own lines. Such gestures; such an air; one forgot he was short when one saw him in action on the stage. The duchess thought he would be knighted one day. Garrick had amassed a fortune for himself and bought himself a country villa in Hampton. He was behaving himself better too since his marriage to Mademoiselle Violette, though the whole world knew that Mademoiselle Violette was a German girl whose real name was Maria Veigel. The Germans were Great Britain's allies, the French were enemies, but a French name was ever so much more fashionable than a German one just the same.

Literature: Voltaire had quarreled with his patron, Frederick the Great, and gone into exile to Switzerland. Voltaire wrote fascinatingly naughty books that were always burned. The duchess thought Voltaire vaguely subversive, especially in the matter of religion, though one really did not care, did one, whether the popish religion of France were subverted! But Voltaire was certainly making one bad mistake: he was encouraging that other French exile, Jean Jacques Rousseau; Rousseau was a queer young man who wrote violent pamphlets against nobility and privilege, quite as if everybody were just as good as everybody else. Civilization was *in extremis,* Rousseau proclaimed, and only a return to the primitive state of a savage would save it.

To live in a hut, to pick one's sustenance off a bush, to cleave to one's mate in earthly fidelity and raise a brood of unspoiled little savages around a campfire in the wilderness — that was the only cure for the social ills that beset and corrupted mankind. The duke interposed that such a doctrine was damned nonsense. The duchess agreed, since she knew for a fact that Jean Jacques Rousseau had fathered five children by an ugly mistress and abandoned them all one after another to a foundling hospital in Paris.

Medicine: Inoculation against the smallpox was finally catching on. It was a pity that Samuel Johnson, who had just published his immensely readable *Dictionary* in two big folio volumes, had been too stubborn to avail himself of it. Lady Mary Wortley Montagu had long since demonstrated that this bizarre but perfectly safe procedure was a sovereign specific against the ancient scourge — how queer that it should have come from Turkey! — but the great lexicographer would have none of it and hence was so pock-marked and grotesque that fashionable drawing rooms were closed to him. Lord Selkirk smiled: "Dr. Johnson's definition of oats is 'a food for horses in England, a food for men in Scotland.' We retort, of course, that England raises excellent horses, but Scotland excellent men." The duchess graciously agreed that the great lexicographer stank of sweat and never washed his linen.

Art: Sir Joshua Reynolds was just back from Italy and Algiers. He was tremendously fashionable. He had had a hundred and twenty clients this year, all from the best families of England. The duchess herself planned to have him do her portrait. The duke said the pirates of Algiers were a damned nuisance. Frightfully expensive. One had to buy them off. Jock wondered why one should buy off pirates instead of fighting them.

Science: Mr. Newcomen's steam pumps were proving very successful, the duke said. He was thinking of proposing their introduction into the Scottish mines, which often flooded. It would be a great boon to the women and children who worked underground. The duchess wondered if Lord Selkirk had a telescope in his gardens. Telescopes were all the rage at home. Every fashionable London house had one. Lady guests always squealed with delight when they first beheld the face of the moon through Sir Isaac's miraculous invention, though, like Johnson, the moon must have suffered a bout of the pox, so pitted and cratered it was. Did Lord Selkirk remember that a great comet would soon appear — nay, reappear, since it was the same as a former one — its return predicted in accordance with a carefully calculated table of velocities worked out by the Astronomer Royal? A pity Professor Halley had not lived to witness the fruition of all his theories. The best people never doubted for a moment that Halley's comet would come back. Lord Selkirk said it would probably be too foggy in Scotland to see it.

Jock said to his father, "I wish the dominie were here to explain."

Said his father, "I wish Mr. Craik would mention Willie."

"I will study, study; learn, learn; grind, grind; work, work," Jock vowed to himself. Clearly, ignorance was doomed to sit forever at the foot of the table. It was not enough to be fearless in order to rise. One must also be informed. Ambition glittered and beckoned. One day he too would sit with peers in ruffles and lace and powdered hair, and bandy about in a casual manner all that was witty and elegant and new in this most enlightened of eras, the lucky magnificent century into which the dominie said he had had the good fortune to be born. Study, learn, work, Jock Paul. Inform yourself, and rise!

War: Mr. Craik had not ventured to raise his voice while the duchess dominated the conversation. But when the butler brought the port, when the ladies withdrew and left the men at the table to empty their glasses and fill the air with blue clouds of tobacco smoke from long clay pipes, when the mood mellowed, the laird of Arbigland spoke up. Scotland had a grievance, he said. English press gangs had begun to operate along the Scottish coasts, snatching away Scottish boys for service on English ships as if those boys were jailbirds and vagabonds. They were not. They came from good honest homes. His own had had a narrow escape from them only the night before; his gardener's son had actually been taken. That was not the way for England to win good will or cement the Union of the Crowns. What did the Duke of Queensberry propose to do about this monstrous invasion of Scottish liberties?

Civilly the duke replied that he himself was a Scot; he could understand such feelings; nay, he shared them. But one reason for his visit to Scotland was to make clear the British view and enlist Scotland's support in the war, on the success of which all British liberties hinged, Scotch as well as English. Actually, the war was going very well, though it threatened to be a long one. Britain's only ally was Prussia. Ranged against Britain were France, the ancient foe; Austria; Saxony; Sweden; and the sprawling mysterious empire of the Russias, still half sunk in the barbarism of the Dark Ages, a sleeping giant stirring in arctic wilderness, unknown and unknowable, but full of grave threat to Europe. A formidable array of enemies.

But victory was certain if Scotland would stand by her English brothers-in-arms. Nay, a British empire would emerge such as never had been seen on this planet since the Romans.

The Continental war could safely be left to Prussian Frederick and his six-foot-high soldiers, who fought like machines and struck with unparalleled ruthlessness.

But the war on the sea? That was a British affair. Britain would win it, as she had won all her sea battles since the Armada. How was it that no foe had set foot on British soil for a thousand years? What hindered them? What but the might of Britain's navies? Would the Scots, in whose blood ran the salt of the same seas, hang back, especially now with such glorious rewards in prospect? An empire in the East hung ripe for the plucking: India could be won from the French by sea power.

There was an empire in America too, vast, rich and peopled by subjects of the British Crown; but the French threatened them on the western frontier and from Canada to the north. True, the Americans were cantankerous and jealous of their liberties like the Scots, but they were showing themselves loyal and brave against the French and the Indian savages whom the French had corrupted with brandy and Popery and set against them.

The Americans needed only sea power to keep open their ports; on land they could take care of themselves. Witness their exploits. In Virginia a colonel named George Washington had marched through the wilderness to the western frontier with a tiny force, and there by a river named Ohio had fallen upon a strong French fort, killed the commander and taken prisoner all the French garrison and their savage Indian allies. It was regrettable that the Americans had no manners and always shot at commanders. But one had to make allowances for their tactics, especially since the tactics seemed to work.

In a somewhat more civilized part of the American colonies, in Philadelphia, their capital city, there was another loyal British friend, a learned doctor of science whom the Royal Society had honored with the Copley Medal for his experiments in electricity. It must not be supposed that the Americans were all illiterate backwoodsmen. Dr. Benjamin Franklin was a man of great influence and cultural achievements. He owned a printing house; he had printed *Pamela*, the first novel ever published in America. Many Americans could read. He also printed, admittedly with more profit, the American paper money. He had invented the lightning rod, which the Russians had tried to copy, only to get themselves killed by failing to ground the wires; but the device worked very well in America. He had also invented a remarkably thrifty stove, though why anyone should wish to conserve fuel in America, where there was so much of it, was a mystery to the duke.

This same Dr. Franklin was said to be working on a scheme for tenderizing meat by the passage of an electrical force through it. His interests were many and curious, but in the main they were practical; certainly he was superbly patriotic. Dr. Franklin had set up at his own expense a system of rapid transport in American wagons so that troops need not wear out good shoe leather in slow and endless marches.

Clearly, so long as Prussia stood firm and America produced soldiers like Washington and geniuses like Franklin, no one need despair of victory. But for victory, *men*, and sailors above all, were an absolute necessity.

Having assured his hearers that Britain could not lose, the duke now threatened, discreetly but forcibly: if Scotland failed to range herself on the winning side, he warned, even her best friends, like himself, could see nothing ahead but the certainty of heavier taxes, reduced representation in Parliament and progressive curtailment of freedom.

Having threatened in terms of the broadest national scope, the duke could afford to be liberal on a small local issue. It was never wise in government, as he and his colleagues conceived it, to be rigid; one must make judicious exceptions. He saw at the foot of the table, glowering at him through tobacco smoke, the bristly sand-red visage of William Craik and his son with the bandaged fist and the blue-bruised eye. In such as these, far more than in his elegant kinsman Lord Selkirk, the duke recognized the raw spirit of Scotch revolt. It would have to be appeased. Queensberry knew how.

In the servants' quarters the butler reported, "The duke said that in his opinion the press gang had exceeded their authority. He took out a gold pencil and wrote down the name 'Willie Paul' in a little black book. 'Mr. Craik,' said he, 'I shall see that your son is returned to you, instanter.' Thereupon Mr. Craik jumped up and proposed a toast, 'God bless Your Grace!' and the duke answered him very graciously."

That seemed to end the matter. The four who had ridden to Castle Douglas rode back to Arbigland with hearts softened towards the British regime.

But Willie Paul never returned.

For a long time his empty chair was placed, through habit and hope, at the supper table as usual. Then little by little it ceased to be placed there. Life without Willie became the usual way of life, as if he had died, never forgotten but less well remembered, and less often. That too became usual, as time passed and the earth spun and nations struggled and navies clashed and everything changed in the outside world. In the gardener's cottage the passage of time wrought a change too in the boy Jock Paul. His stature increased; his voice deepened into a man's; his body and mind matured and both were good.

But two things in him did not change; they were central and fundamental: one was a hate, and one was a sort of love. One was the hate of the English, flinty and deep as the roots of his own Caledonian mountains; the other his passionate ambition to rise above the servile poverty of his life. But he knew that only the fearless and well-informed could rise. It must follow, as necessary to logic, that the stupid and weak must always be underlings, slaves to the will of their betters. Since that was the way of the world, he wasted no time in deploring it. It was a fact, like any other fact.

Then a letter arrived from America.

Chapter 4

THE LETTER was from Willie, for it was in his neat and meticulous hand, and therefore he must be alive; but it did not sound like the trembling Willie of old whom a press gang could capture so easily and carry away unresisting. In America Willie had somehow imbibed a strength that he lacked before.

Arbigland rejoiced that Willie Paul was safe. The gardener proudly displayed the letter to all his neighbors. In the village kirk the pastor took as his text the parable of the Prodigal Son. It was accurate insofar as it went: "For this my son was dead and is alive again; he was lost and is found." But there the parallel ended, for Willie evinced no disposition to return to his homeland, nor had he wasted his substance, having none, in riotous living, nor had he consorted with harlots in the colonies. On the contrary, Willie had jumped ship at the first opportunity, had got himself happily and respectably married and was now fair on the way to becoming a substantial citizen of the New World.

In the parish school the dominie said when he read the letter, "'Upon what meat doth this our Caesar feed, that he is grown so great?' Do you place the quotation, Jock? I shall not insult your intelligence by asking you which play, for I've already said 'Caesar.'"

"Act One, I think," Jock said, "but 'what meat' I cannot guess. It must have been a potent brew like 'eye of newt and toe of frog,' for as I remember my brother Willie he was of all men the least adventuresome."

Jock smiled; the dominie sighed.

"I am growing older, Jock. Soon, I suppose, my little schoolhouse must be turned over to a successor. I shall have a hand in his nomination; I shall want him to be worthy of his high trust. The position of a schoolmaster is by no means contemptible. We are singularly fortunate in that respect. Scotland is the only country in the world where education is free and compulsory, where a dominie is provided to teach in every parish, supported by local taxes: the Act of 1701. Our salary is secure. Our status is respectable. Occasionally we are welcomed at the tables of gentry, especially when gentry find their sons behind in their studies. I often sup with Mr. Craik. Do not misunderstand me, Jock; you were never behind. You and Jamie Craik were the quickest students I ever had, drinking your fill at my fountain of knowledge — I had almost said wisdom, but wisdom cannot be taught — of knowledge, then, or at least of the information which Providence vouchsafes in such plenty to this blessed land and to no other. Only a dominie can experience the peculiar warmth that comes when he sees one of his students avail himself to the full of that God-given opportunity which the dominie offers to all and which all too few know how to use. You drank thirstily, Jock. Do you feel yourself educated?"

"No, sir."

"But you are, you know. When my students graduate from my highest bench, I flatter myself they can hold their own anywhere, even with gentry. I am proud of them. Jamie is at the university. He is doing well, from all reports. Soon he will be a surgeon. What will you be, Jock?"

"Known."

The dominie hesitated. "What did you say?"

"Known, sir. I will be known."

"I have always hoped you would be known as the next dominie of the Arbigland parish school. I repeat, I shall have a hand in the choice of my successor. You could do far worse, Jock Paul."

"I am grateful to you, sir."

He could also do far better.

Even Willie had done better.

Willie's letter said:

I was taken to Bristol at first with a dozen others, all English but me, for as yet the gangs did not operate widely in Scottish ports. Since then, as you know, they have carried their nefarious body snatching everywhere, even to inland cities. But I was the first Scotsman, I believe, to be impressed for this war.

It was a distinction I did not relish. In Bristol my gyves were struck off, for we were fettered like slaves at the outset, and I found myself in a tar's hat, which stank and crawled with lice, aboard of the English ship of war *Blythe*, bound for Virginia in the American colonies. The first day out, the wind coming on to blow, we were ordered aloft to take in sail, a simple maneuver that any lad born on the Solway could perform in his sleep; but I was not prepared for

28

the great height to which I had to climb, nor was I quite so prompt to leap into the shrouds as the others, who were all nimble and quick like Jock. The first sailors who clamber into the rigging always gain for themselves the lowest and safest places, this being ship's custom and making for smartness as I was told, and indeed it seems very logical if anything can be said to be logical in a sailor's detestable life.

But I, alas, was forced out to the very end of a spar, for I had and possess to this day a certain corpulence of body that I seem to retain regardless of what I eat, whether it be ship's fare of gray salt pork, very greasy and ill-smelling, or that delicious American discovery called "mush," of which I am very fond, a porridge composed of Indian corn and boiled in milk, which my wife cooks to perfection. For I must give you the good news at once: I am most happily married.

Observing the waves at a great distance below me as the ship rolled from side to side, I became exceedingly dizzy and sick, to the discomfiture of the boatswain who was working beside me: my poor stomach suddenly emptied itself and the unfortunate boatswain, being down wind of me, got it fair in the phiz. This would not have happened to him if he had been on the spar's end instead of me.

Next day the rascal belabored me with a rope's end whenever no officer was looking, for he had no authority to beat me formally; he claimed I had fouled the deck, though he knew as well as I that only he and a patch of sail had been fouled; it was blowing so hard that nothing could have carried to the deck. This demonstrated to me how dismal is a sailor's lot in life, and I determined to make my escape as soon as Providence should show me the way.

After that I was no more sent aloft, but was set to mending sails, at which I developed great skill before we reached America. Even the boatswain admired my work and would gather the men round me and declare loudly that I stitched dainty and neat as any woman alive. This was meant for an insult, and the sailors would laugh, but I held my tongue and played the oaf, pretending to be as stupid as no doubt I looked, sitting there plying my needle.

For once in my life I was content not to look like Jock, his face so lean and full of expression: there are certain advantages in having a moonface. Jock, if you read this, and I pray that you and all my dear family are alive to do so, remember the dominie who taught us when we were boys: the big round moon hides stars as she sails across the sky. And so it was with me. I cherished a plan like a hidden star.

We made for the mouth of the Rappahannock, a river which resembles one of our firths in grandeur of expanse but is nothing like a firth in other respects, for instead of mountains rising up from the water one sees nothing but endless swamps, reedy and brown, stretching to the horizon, so that it is difficult to determine where river ends and shore begins, where shore ends and sky begins. It is said that slaves being imported from Africa often jump overboard in these waters, but in a few days they invariably lose themselves in the swamps and perish miserably. I avow that I felt much like a slave at the time and that the notion of such an escape did occur to me, but Providence opened my eyes to the awful peril of the swamps and I bided my time.

At the head of the estuary the swamps gave way to swelling wooded hills, and we drew up alongside a stout stone wharf at a place called Fredericksburg, a most spacious and handsome town, with much trade, though rough and wild by our standards, particularly along the water front. I am never at ease on water fronts, a fact no doubt owing to the circumstance of my apprehension by the press gang; and even to this day, though my lot has altered and I still live in Fredericksburg, I avoid that part of town, preferring to send one of the slaves if I have business to transact there, which is not often.

Paradoxically does Providence work to shape our ends, especially in America. It is to the same wild and rough character of the water front that I owe all my good fortune.

You will be aware that it is just as difficult to escape from a British ship as it is easy to become part of her crew. This is not to say that I was forbidden to go ashore; actually I was allowed a certain amount of freedom. But they gave me only sixpence per diem to spend, and by sundown each night I was required to report again aboard ship. Had I failed to do so, the marines would have searched for me and brought me back in irons; I should have been easy to find; the townspeople would not have hidden me. The water front swarmed with footpads and wharf rats of the lowest description, eager to win the bounty that is given for turning a deserter over to his ship. This is an evil custom capable of vile abuses, for often they conspire to get young sailors drunk and detain them forcibly beyond the appointed hour; then carry them back to their ship as deserters. I eluded these scoundrels by taking long walks beyond the water front to more savory parts of town.

And now I shall tell you how patience and Providence combined to work out my deliverance. I had in my pocket a few shillings, having hoarded all my allowances. I determined to buy myself some unnautical clothes and present myself for some honest work in the back country. I had in mind the work of a bargeman on one of the barges that carry tobacco down from the big plantations in the interior. You will smile at the innocence of my plan, but I did not know at that time that this work is all performed by slaves.

I sought out a tailor shop a safe distance from the water front on a modest street just adjoining a section of town where there were many large houses of the rich. A swarthy Hebrew sat cross-legged on a bench in the ill-lighted little shop. I said I should like to talk to the proprietor. He looked at me over his half-moon Franklin spectacles and said I was talking to the proprietor. I told him I wished some new clothes, very cheap, and offered to exchange the ones I wore as part payment, pointing out that they were neat, clean, scarcely worn, and of the best wool obtainable. At that he began to shake with silent laughter, never losing a stitch, till his bald pate shone like a wet rock at low tide in the Solway.

"You bargain like one of my own," he said, "but your speech has a north-of-Britain flavor. You cannot be a Jew, so you must be a Scot."

I thought him extremely forward in manner; I was not yet accustomed to Americans. I reproached him for his saucy tongue and reminded him of his place.

"And new to the colonies," he said.

"Will you sell me a suit or won't you?" I demanded.

"I could make more collecting the bounty on you," he said. I do not know how he guessed so quickly that I was planning to jump ship.

"I am not a deserter," I said stoutly, nor was I, not yet, it still being daylight.

"You will be in half an hour," he said. "You'd better get back to your ship, young man, before I turn you over."

"I can pay," I said. "Don't you want my money?"

At this he held up the shirt he was working on. I saw it clearly for the first time. It was rich pure silk, with pearl buttons and a froth of French lace at throat and sleeves.

"I must give you to understand," he said (and though his tone was kindly, it cut, for in my turn I was being reminded of my own place, which was that of a mere suppliant), "that I deal in a rather better class of trade than the appearance of my shop may indicate. How long does it take me to make a garment like this?" (He meant the shirt.) "Three hours! How long would it take me to make you a workman's breeches and blouse? Also three hours. What shall I be paid for this shirt? Three pounds. What would your work clothes be worth? Three shillings. Three miserable shillings. As for the present clothes you wear, they are not only worthless but dangerous. They would lie around the shop till somebody discovered them and hauled me up before a magistrate as a receiver of stolen goods. Could I truthfully say I was not? So what must I charge you for your paltry three-shilling breeches and blouse? Why, three pounds, not a penny less."

"I'll pay!" I cried. "I'll work out the difference."

He began to laugh again. "What could you do for me?"

"I am an excellent sailmaker."

He eyed me suspiciously. "You are?"

"I am."

"And the sailmaker thinks he can become a tailor?"

"I'm sure I can. I should certainly try."

"How would you stitch a buttonhole?"

I hadn't the slightest notion.

"Just like a grommet," I said firmly.

He seemed to pause at that, but he said, "You know nothing," and my heart sank, for it was growing dark outside and to reach the ship before sunset would now be impossible. "You know nothing; I promise nothing. Sarah! Sarah! Come here!" Answering his summons came his wife, as if she had been waiting behind the door for his signal, carrying a basin of hot water, looking only at him, not even glancing in my direction, as if I did not exist. "Ach, Samuel," she said — and the "ach" sounded just like Scots — "again you work so late! How are they tonight?" She gently took the shirt and the needle and thread from him, and laid them aside on the bench.

He immersed his hands in the steaming water and rubbed them slowly together. "They will be better."

"You always say they will be better; better they never get."

"They are better, Sarah."

As I looked more closely, I observed the tailor's hands to be frozen, as it were, in the posture of work, as if they still held the needle and shirt. His joints were stiff with arthritical swellings. Only slowly, as the heat of the water relaxed them, could he move his fingers again. During this time his face worked, as if there were pain.

"Maybe I shall sew less in the future, Sarah?"

His wife looked at me, and after some time she slowly nodded her head.

"Yes, this one can be trusted." I felt that I had been subjected to a test, and that I had passed.

Thus I became apprenticed to the tailor, who concealed me in a garret like contraband while the marines searched for me in vain. At length the *Blythe* sailed away and it was safe for me to venture out. For two years I remained with this kind master, studying assiduously to perfect myself in the tailoring craft and making myself agree-

32

able and useful to him in many ways, with so much success that he soon entrusted the writing of letters to me, his hands having grown too stiff to hold either needle or pen, poor man. From his letters I learned that Samuel the tailor was also a moneylender and provisioner of ships on a large scale. Sometimes in his latter days, as he would sit dictating letters to shipmasters, to debtors who owed him large sums, or merely some small notice to a newspaper advertising his tailor shop — treating each matter, great or small, as of equal consequence — I would ask him, How is it, sir, that you keep your activities separate one from another? There is nothing illegal in any of them. Willie, he would answer, it amuses me. This attitude shocked me: Sir, I would protest, life is not an amusing matter. All he would answer was, Isn't it?

He died last year a helpless cripple, and I mourned him, wishing I had known him longer, wondering from what hidden source had sprung his kindliness and his bitterness; but I doubt if a lifetime with Samuel the tailor would have sufficed to explain him. Sarah his wife departed to Spain to live with a married daughter. "Willie," she said, "you shall have the shop. Had we had a real son, how much more should he not have had!" Then she wept, God knows why, and turned her back and went aboard the ship.

With Samuel's death all his enterprises collapsed, excepting the tailor shop. This I continue to operate, leaving the sign SAMUEL DA SOLA, MASTER TAILOR, above the door out of respect for his memory and also because WILLIAM PAUL might still be of interest to the marines of the *Blythe* if ever she should come back to Fredericksburg.

It is not quite accurate to say that all of the tailor's enterprises collapsed at his death. Recently some of them show signs of resuscitation. Gentlemen to whom he used to loan money have lately applied to me for the same, money being somewhat scarce on account of the recent course of the war, and as often as I am able I oblige, charging no more interest than did Samuel, which makes for a lively game. Shipowners also who formerly dealt with him have approached me of late, and could I but overcome my aversion to the water front, no doubt I should be able to augment my income in that direction also, for, though Samuel kept no records, I felt it my duty to do so (lest he forget), concealing the information in my sea chest, so I know all his sources of supply. Meanwhile, the tailor shop prospers and I have bought some land, which is cheaper than it was, on which I raise tobacco, for I do not wish to be known only as a tailor, and a country estate is always a source of satisfaction to a wife.

With every good wish for health, long life and prosperity to all members of my dear family in Scotland, and with a special notifica-

33

tion to Jock that I freely relinquish to him my prior right to the post of gardener to the laird of Arbigland when in sad due course that post shall become vacant,

I subscribe myself from my plantation at Fredericksburg, Virginia,

Your affectionate brother and son,

WILLIAM PAUL

So, pompously, Willie from the New World.

The laird of Arbigland read the epistle and sputtered with anger.

Chapter 5

YOUR BROTHER makes very free with my patronage, Jock," he said. "He relinquishes to you 'prior right' to the post as my gardener. That is most generous. Does it occur to your brother that he cannot dispose of something he does not possess and to which he has no claim? Is the comfortable Virginian aware that times may have changed in his homeland and a Scottish laird may not be able to afford a gardener at all nowadays?"

Gloomily the laird contrasted Willie's prosperity, which had been achieved so casually, with his own war-stricken fortunes, which were now approaching their lowest ebb.

Scotland, nursing old wounds, had been slow to support the English war. Scottish taxes soared. Scottish landowners found themselves in debt, their debts mercilessly collected, credit denied them, their estates put up for forced sale and sold out from under their noses at distress prices; acres of ancestral farm lands that their tenants had cultivated for centuries were turned into deer parks and hunting preserves for a new English gentry, while their evicted tenants went underground into the mines, or became vagabonds and were whipped, or smugglers and were hanged. To save themselves from utter ruin, old patriots like the laird of Arbigland must turn perforce from agriculture to some other means of livelihood. The sea was always at hand. Mr. Craik compromised his scruples to a degree that shamed him in his own eyes, but he was actually less drastic than many in his position were forced to be.

"I know a merchant across the Solway who might give a great deal for a peek at the tailor's records that Willie concealed in his sea chest. It might be worth a partnership to me. Will you help, Jock?"

34

Jock frowned. "Is the merchant English?"

"He isn't so bad as most of the breed."

"I'd rather dig coal."

"Would you? I doubt that. You strike me as ambitious. You could never get out of the mines; they break a man. But on one of the ships of John Younger over in Whitehaven you might rise far, particularly if Willie's chest contains what I think it does. Old Samuel the tailor did not get rich just because he was a Jew or just because tailoring happens to be profitable in America. Remember, he also was a ship's provisioner. Now, to have friendly American ship provisioners is invaluable to an English ship-owner. Somehow, no one asks how, they can offer prime ships' stores at rock-bottom prices; it is generally supposed that many Americans manage to evade their taxes, which, like ours, the British impose more harshly every year.

"But Americans are a canny, elusive lot; I think they get it from the Indians; it is hard for an Englishman to make contact with them. But Willie is a Scot, he is already there among them, and in his chest is a written record of all his late master's sources of supply. Willie has no use for this information; he doesn't even go down to the water front. It might, however, be valuable to me, *and* to you."

Jock looked dubious. Mr. Craik's proposal seemed almost like an invitation to steal.

"I am not suggesting that you rifle your brother's closet in the dead of night and make off with a parcel of stolen papers," he said, smiling. "Nothing so romantic. I know you, Jock; your mind is quick to leap to extremes. Merely ask Willie for what you want; I have no doubt he will give it to you."

"I'd still rather dig coal."

"Then I'm afraid you must also tell him how straitened my circumstances have become, and that if I cannot discover some means of improving my fortunes I shall be forced to curtail my expenses even further than I have; anything like that would necessarily affect the people I employ, even my gardener. I do not think Willie would like to see his old father dispossessed."

There was a hardness in Craik's voice; Jock smiled wryly to hear it. It proved to him that everyone, even so kindly a person as the laird of Arbigland, had only to be pushed to a certain critical point and the animal instinct for preservation of self would come out; the strong attacked, the weak ran; the lion charged, the fox scuttled into a hole; but the result was the same: every creature preserved itself, at no matter what cost to another.

35

Craik's threat confirmed the cynicism already so deeply rooted in Jock's heart.

But where his father was concerned, and even more so his mother, Jock could not be cynical; logic seemed not to apply to them.

"No," he said, "Willie would not like to see his old father dispossessed. It may have occurred to you, sir, that neither would I."

"Of course you wouldn't," said Mr. Craik. "I just didn't want to put it that way."

"Naturally I shall go."

"You won't be a passenger, you know. You can accomplish more if you sail incognito and set up your agency on the other side as if it were quite by accident."

"I am not afraid of work."

John Younger, Esquire, member of the Honorable Board of Trustees for the Town and Harbor of Whitehaven, merchant-trader, and head of the shipping firm that bore his name, was not in the habit of granting personal interviews to men who presented themselves for work as common sailors. He would not indeed have refused. In the present critical shortage of seamen he would gladly have divested himself of his dignity, willingly stood all day at the gangplank of one of his ships and received a line of applicants with formal liftings of the hat, as if they were visiting aldermen; but there were no applicants, and had not been any since the early days of the war. The Royal Navy itself was so desperate for men that it had to be satisfied with the offscourings of city slums and water-front stews, captured and herded aboard by the press gangs. Even more difficult was recruitment for private firms of the merchant marine, for merchant-traders did not share in the press gangs' human harvest but must gather their crews by any means they could contrive, offscourings of the offscourings, dregs of the dregs. Nor could they offer tempting wages, for taxes had risen, supplies were expensive and scarce, and profits had withered dismally. All this in addition to the usual hazards that plagued a trader in wartime, for one never knew when a ship would be captured by the Spanish or French. Such losses were covered by insurance, of course, but insurance grew costlier every year. If any one of these factors could be mitigated, an honest trader might at least be certain of staying in business; instead, they all grew more formidable together. John Younger felt himself squeezed and threatened on every side. It was especially galling because he knew that England was winning the war. To suffer private defeat when your country triumphs is exasperating.

36

These thoughts ran in his mind when he greeted his Scottish neighbor from over the Solway, who brought with him one of the likeliest young men he had ever seen and a proposal so tempting that he wondered what was wrong with it. He had lived too long on the Scottish border not to admire and beware of the Scots. He therefore resolved to appear casual in accepting the laird of Arbigland's proposal.

"There is no question that a berth can be found for Mr. Paul on one of my ships," he said. "No trader would deny the shortage of hands. But is he experienced?"

"Any man born on the Solway is experienced in the sailing of boats, Mr. Younger."

"The sailing of ships is rather different, Mr. Craik."

"Only in the matter of size, Mr. Younger. A ship is naught but a braw big boat."

"Shipping him as an officer the first trip over would cause comment, Mr. Craik." Mr. Craik noted the remark. Younger was actually willing to take Jock on as an officer. It was significant.

Jock said, "I know I have much to learn, sir, but I hope soon to prove that I can make an officer."

Younger smiled amiably. The applicant, at least, was sound. "As for your further suggestion, Mr. Craik, that Mr. Paul act with his brother in the colonies as a provisioning agent — I do not know, I do not know —"

"It is perfectly legal, Mr. Younger, and thoroughly practicable. It stands to reason that a colonial provisioner over on the American side can procure local stores at better advantage than an English one."

It was perfectly legal, Younger knew; and if it wasn't, the colonial provisioner, not the British trader, would be in trouble with the law.

"No doubt, no doubt, Mr. Craik. I should be happy to see it arranged, if Mr. Paul can arrange it."

"I shall certainly try," Jock said.

"The question of your partnership in my firm, however," Younger said to Craik, "ought surely to wait till we see whether the colonial arrangement is profitable." But he smiled so engagingly that Craik took a mental step backward. John Younger seemed oddly anxious to welcome an outside investor.

"At the outset I should be quite content to accept only a commission," Craik said.

Younger stifled a look of disappointment; he had, after all, appeared too anxious. Necessity pressed him hard. Confound the Scots anyhow!

"I did not say a partnership was impossible, Mr. Craik."

37

Between the two sat Jock, the pawn.

"You can sail at once, Mr. Paul?"

He would have liked to answer Yes for himself, but Mr. Craik said, "Of course he can."

The gardener grumbled, "My sons desert me, first Willie, now you. If you're ashamed of being a gardener, and such I suspect is the truth, is there nought else honest and steady to which you can turn your hand?"

His mother said, "Why did it have to be an English ship?"

Jock said, "Perhaps it will be only for a short while."

It would have worried them needlessly to say that he knew that a gardener's position was not as secure as it seemed. As for his hope of setting up an agency in America, Craik had forbidden him to mention that until it should be accomplished. In any case, Jock knew that his father would call it a wild impractical scheme. As he held his tongue and prepared to depart, one thing surprised him in both his parents: their fierce and inborn pride, which he now saw clearly for the first time. Not once did they complain or even seem to notice that Willie, who could so easily afford it, had failed to share his good fortune with them. Not even so much as a shilling had he sent them from America. In the same spirit of silence and reserve neither of them actually forbade Jock to go to sea. He sensed why. They knew he would go anyhow. Rather than beg him to stay, and be humiliated by his refusal, they did not beg. There was a lesson in that.

On the eve of Jock's departure his father returned home from work carrying a mahogany sea chest on his shoulder, a gift from Mr. Craik. "The laird sends you this handsome thing, with his blessing."

"Sir, do I have yours too?"

"Och, son, d'ye think I withhold it?" and the elder Paul blew his nose furiously.

"I'd hoped you would not."

"But I dinna have to be enthusiastic."

Dry-eyed, his mother packed the chest without a word. It was barely half full when she finished with all that a sailor would need, which indeed was virtually all he possessed. Slowly she closed the lid and murmured, "Oh, Jock."

"What is it, Mother?"

"How little we can help!"

"It's I who ought to help."

Either she did not hear him, or she did not understand. "You have made up your mind to leave our little world, and look —" the chest —

38

"you leave it almost as naked as when I brought you into it." He had never seen her cry, but her eyes were suspiciously bright.

"I'll travel farther light," he said, smiling. "Yon chest shall be full to the brim when I come back."

"Just promise to come back."

He fancied himself indistinguishable from a seaman as he strode down the long Whitehaven quay. Nothing about his dress set him apart from the crowd of sailors working about their ships or lounging in front of the taverns: his trousers, shoes and shirt, like theirs, were work-worn, sturdy and old. Like theirs, his hair was tied back in a short pigtail to keep the wind from blowing it into his eyes. Any middle-class workingman from the shores of the Solway looked very much the sailor superficially. But everything about him marked him as a landsman: his gait, his fresh complexion, the shiny new sea chest, the eager way his eye took in the quayside scene, which was all so new to him.

The quay ran like a street along the water front. On one side stood warehouses, shipping offices, taverns and other places of refreshment where sailors with money in their pockets could slake their thirsts and satisfy hungers pent up through long months of loneliness at sea. A score of ships were tied up at the wharves that jutted out into the Solway; their bowsprits overhung the cobblestoned quay, and those of some of the larger ships projected almost to touch the line of buildings on the other side. In peacetime, Jock knew, the Whitehaven quay was a polyglot maelstrom where ships from a dozen nations tied up and spewed forth their crews; but this was wartime. Lacking were the French, with their dandified airs; the Spaniards, poor and proud; the Russians, whom nobody understood. All these had once stopped at Whitehaven and contributed to the town's prosperity, but now they were England's enemies. In Whitehaven now there were only British ships, a few from the navy of Frederick the Prussian, who was England's only ally, and a colonial craft or two. The American ships smelt good, of fresh pine from the trees they brought over from New England for masts for the king's navy. He heard some Americans speaking as he passed by; the accent wasn't Scots and it wasn't English: it was more like the pastor of the kirk in one of his high Presbyterian moods. He supposed Cromwell might have talked that way. Other smells were good too: coffee and tea and cinnamon and cloves from the vast and distant stretches of ocean around India, where England was filching an empire from the French. Some smells were sickening: vinegar and salt being vainly applied to purge the black sweat from the timbers of a ship in

39

the African trade. He had heard men who knew assert that a slaver could be smelled five miles down wind. Glancing up, he read the name *Two Friends* painted on the bow of the ship that was the source of the offensive odor. He hurried by.

Ships' names had always puzzled him. He guessed that they must be named out of hope. In the same hope, the dominie had taught him, the ancient Romans named their sons: Fortunatus, if they had suffered misfortune, Felix if they had been especially unhappy that year; always the opposite of what was feared, that the gods might be appeased and grant what was longed for. How else explain how Willie had been impressed on the *Blythe?* How explain *Two Friends*, the slaver?

He asked a girl at a tavern door, "Do you know where the *Friendship* lies?"

"That your ship, Scottie?"

"Aye," he said.

She eyed him speculatively. "The *Friendship* doesn't sail till tomorrow."

"I know that."

He also knew one would have to be mightily parched to slake one's thirst at so public a font.

"Why go aboard before sailing time, Scottie?"

That was hard to answer. He knew that only the rawest of newcomers to the sea would board a ship before the last possible moment.

"I — I just want to see what she's like."

The girl laughed, exhibiting a sparkling array of remarkably even white teeth — she could hardly have been more than seventeen — and smoothed down her blouse, a sheer China silk affair that some sailor must have given her in a spasm of gratitude after the long run from the East, tight over the breasts that Jock had to concede were high, wide, handsome and knowledgeably presented for his inspection.

"In the matter of friendship," she pronounced, "I might be able to show you what she is like."

"I dinna think I can afford the demonstration," he said.

"I'll wait till next trip when you're paid. Honest I will. Come on, Scottie! If you're really broke, I'll stand you the drinks. Then we'll see how you feel about going aboard."

Perhaps it was time to change the subject. "How do you know I'm a Scot?"

"It sticks out all over you like —" She employed an extremely salty expression. Jock followed her glance to the bowsprits up-angled over the quay.

"I think I shall find my ship," he said.

She spat on the cobblestones and screamed after him, "Stingy Scotch bastard! Stingy! Stingy! Stingy!"

One thing you had to grant the English: they were superb navigators. Captain Jeremiah Benson, stomping the daily-scrubbed, daily-drenched planks of his diminutive quarter-deck, grim and complaining like his old-fashioned Christian name, viewed every hostile wind as a personal affront, from which every mile of headway that cunning and seamanship could contrive must be wrested. He got the most out of every breeze; he got the most out of his cranky ship; he got the most out of his crew. All were second rate. To Jock it was instructive to see so much made of so little. Against contrary winds, with a listless crew, with patched sails and rigging frayed like the fur of some mangy dog, the little *Friendship* beat steadily, stolidly, westward across the gray Atlantic. One need not like but one had to admire the resolution of the man who bore the whole weight of the ship on his own hunched and bulky shoulders.

The captain was aware that Jock was something more, potentially at least, than just another green forecastle hand. The day the ship sailed, Benson took occasion to drop him a friendly word in a moment when the confusion of sailing covered the act of singling out a common sailor for special notice.

"Your position on my ship is anomalous, young man," he said. "But do not presume that it confers any special privilege."

"I do not, sir," Jock said.

"On the other hand, there would be no point in falling overboard your first time aloft, would there?"

"Sir, I'll cling fast enough."

"Watch that you do," Benson said, and passed on a pace to reprove a sailor who was as new as Jock but apparently even more green: "Can you tell time, fellow?"

The man straightened up; his young face was pale and intense; he looked scornfully at Benson. "Yes, I can tell time."

"Tell me how the hands of a clock rotate."

"Fast," said the man staring out at the horizon. "Faster than anyone conceives."

Benson eyed him. "Perhaps you will be good enough to demonstrate by means of your finger in the air, if that is not asking too much, in which *direction* the hands of a clock rotate."

"This way, monsieur."

"Sir."

"This way, sir." The man traced a clockwise motion with his hand.

"Excellent!" Benson said. "In the future try to remember that that is also the way to coil a rope. Clockwise." He kicked at the coil that the sailor had laboriously wound in the wrong direction. It leaped and stirred like a startled snake. Internal tensions were suddenly released. It twisted itself into an astonishing tangle, then relaxed and lay still on the deck.

Red-faced, the Frenchman bent again to his task. After some search he found the head or the tail of the snake and set about painfully to disentangle the mess. *"Parbleu,* there is no flexibility in these English. Even their ropes rebel at change."

Jock laughed. "Do French ropes coil both ways?"

"My friend," said the Frenchman, "I do not know."

"Cela saute," Jock essayed, a little struttingly, *"aux yeux."*

"But you speak French!"

Jock coiled his own length of rope rapidly, skillfully, clockwise. "Oh, I was taught a word or two by the dominie in the parish school."

The Frenchman smiled, "A word or two. *Ça saute aux yeux.*"

"It sounds different when you say it."

"My friend, I understood what you meant to say: 'That is self-evident.' No?"

"Aye," said Jock, less struttingly.

"What you actually succeeded in saying, however, was, 'Whilst engaged in their pleasures, the persons exploded.' A delightful conceit. A most beautiful end. May it happen to all of us."

A rope's end whistled around Jock's ears and descended painfully between his shoulders. In a trice the boatswain stepped over to the Frenchman and dealt him a similar blow. "Stow the talk and get at your work, you two!"

Paler than before, the Frenchman muttered as soon as the boatswain was out of earshot, "One day I will run that brute through with my sword."

"They'd only hang you, Frenchie. Do you have a sword?"

"I used to have."

In the forecastle, where the ship's sleeping quarters were located, Jock, who had come aboard early, had surveyed the bunks with care. He was first and he had his choice. They were arranged in a double tier on either side of the ship, firmly fastened to the bulkheads. Those to the fore near the bows would pitch most and were likely to be wettest. Those aft were more comfortable, with less motion and more headroom, dryer, and above all closer to the single door that led out of the dark stifling place. One got ahead of the others in the race to the shrouds to make or take in sail at the shout, "All hands on deck!" And to get ahead of the others was to get the best place aloft. Yet he knew he did not wholly have his choice, since the boatswain's bunk was the best of all, directly next the door; and, presumably, a couple of other desirable ones must be reserved by custom for leading seamen who had made previous voyages on the *Friendship*.

He therefore pre-empted the best of those that remained, placed his mahogany sea chest firmly on top of it in token of ownership and prepared to fight for it if necessary, which he deemed very likely.

Oddly, nothing happened. He did not have to fight. The others had come aboard, some sober, most of them drunk, and thrown their gear casually into whatever bunks remained. He did not understand it, but it was the first of all the delights of life at sea, delights that were never to fade for Jock Paul so long as he lived.

The Frenchman had taken the bunk above him by throwing upon it a lumpy sack made out of patched and discarded remnants of sail. "I saw your chest," he said to Jock, "and communed with myself. I said to myself, 'The owner of this exquisite object has a soul. Over him and no other shall I sail to the land of the beautiful savages.' Permit me to introduce myself. I am Henri Armand Marie Hippolyte Victor de Beaujeu, Marquis d'Hauteville in Poitou."

"How do you do," said Jock. "I am Jock Paul."

A simpering voice from a bunk far up near the bows, mimicking the Frenchman's accent, said, "How d'ye do, Marie."

A fiercely unshaven old sailor, puffing a foul-smelling pipe, snarled, "Shut your mouth!" and calmly went on with a project that seemed to require great skill and concentration of mind: the construction of a cat's cradle of string, which grew and changed shape ingeniously under his fingers. Another sailor plaited a belt of rope yarn; another sewed on buttons.

Jock said to the Frenchman, "Which of all your names shall I call you by?"

"It doesn't matter," said Henri Armand Marie Hippolyte Victor. "At home my friends called me Henri."

"Let it be Henri, then. Are you really a marquis?"

"I was."

"What happened?"

"How can I tell you that in front of this *canaille*?"

"*Canaille* means distinguished company," Jock volunteered to the fore-

43

castle at large. To Henri, "Be careful of what you say. Have you ever been to sea before?"

"Alas, can you ask me that when you saw how I coiled that miserable rope *countaire* clockwise?"

"You deserve a better bunk," Jock said thoughtfully. "Permit me to offer you mine, and I shall take yours."

"Monsieur, I cannot accept, I do not understand, I must refuse!"

"Please."

"Monsieur, you are a gentleman. My heart swells. My eternal gratitude!"

The old sailor paused at his cat's-cradle activity, snickered, eyed Jock appraisingly and went on with his cat's cradle.

The lower bunk was unquestionably preferable. It was so much faster to get in and out of. But it could be rendered untenable by a seasick-prone occupant above.

All the way to America Jock reveled in the security of the upper bunk, while every night the poor Frenchman fought against nausea, and lost. Jock would turn on his side and, smiling, face the hull of the ship, beyond which, thin inches beyond, whispered and beckoned the clean and curling sea in a deep elemental harmony. Practical men of science, sons of the enlightened eighteenth century with a military end in view, the designation of ice-free enemy-Russian ports, had measured the temperatures of the seas; doctors had measured the rhythmic rise and fall of the heat in human blood. It was noted with awe and disbelief that the two were strangely alike. Man's blood and the ocean's waters both reached their coldest at three o'clock in the morning, their hottest at one in the afternoon, a singular parallel for which no cause could be assigned. Jock sensed the cause through instinct. It was kinship, a primal kinship old as the planet, to which he was simply more sharply attuned than other men. It fashioned his life, like a love. No duck ever took to water, no eagle to the air, no vampire to blood, as Jock took to the sea.

Chapter 6

EXCEPT FOR one minor incident, which shed a few drops of blood, not his, Jock encountered no difficulties with the oddments of humanity who were his shipmates in the forecastle of the *Friendship*. They kept very much to themselves, each man, individually, alone. He had, of course, expected the Atlantic run to be longer than, but otherwise much like, the trips he had occasionally made on Solway fishing boats when his family had needed money, where every hour was crammed full of friendly concerted labor. Quite the contrary was now the case. Deepwater sailors, he discovered, possessed many moments of leisure, to squander or use to advantage as the fates that had fashioned their natures decreed. Most squandered, silent and withdrawn. He wondered why.

The leisure was easy to explain. Thirty men on a one-hundred-and-forty-eight-ton vessel, only ninety feet long and thirty feet broad, were more than enough to keep her tidy in good weather, barely sufficient to handle her in a blow. But good weather was the rule, bad the exception. Nine days out of ten, therefore, the ship had more crew than she needed, and much of the work that the boatswain contrived for them was repetitious, unnecessary and purposely time-consuming. To take long at a thing that is consciously designed to take long is easy. The men availed themselves of this pleasant fact to the full.

They spun yarn, in the literal sense, picking old ropes to pieces and fashioning new ones from the fragments on an awkward spinning wheel, a job that could be done faster and better in establishments ashore; why did they not "spin yarns" in the figurative sense, those endless stories of exploits they had had, or pretended to have had, on other ships on other voyages in fabulous ports all over the world? They did not.

The incident that shed blood took place on a squally night when all hands were suddenly ordered aloft to take in sail. Jock liked the heights. Some sailors did. There was even a term, "skylarking," to describe the dangerous antics that certain effervescent sailors delighted in, swinging like monkeys from line to line high up in the rigging, sliding down perilous curves of bellying sails on the seat of their pants, perching like happy sea gulls on swaying spars. It was all very reprehensible and undisciplined, but they did it, some of them, for the sheer exhilaration it gave them. Others, as Willie had, suffered agonies of dizziness aloft. Most, of course, made haste to climb up simply to get first to the safest and lowest places. Jock, as he always did, had exerted his utmost to climb to the highest.

The sailor who followed Jock up the ratlines was the one who had mimicked the Frenchman's accent. In the darkness he followed too far. Suddenly, dimly outlined against the sky, he saw at a level with his eyes that dizzy perch where the lookout stood, the roundtop. He realized how high he was, and panicked. He grabbed hold of Jock's foot.

45

"Confound you, fool!" Jock yelled. "Do you want to pitch us overboard?"

The fellow hung on.

Jock tried to kick the hand loose, but it clung tight. At that height, where the angular motion of the ship was multiplied by the great distance from the deck, like the end of a whip moving faster than the handle, balance becomes an intensely individual and delicate bodily function. To touch someone else destroys it, in him and in you, to your mutual peril.

Since Jock could not kick the hand loose, he scraped his foot hard against the shroud. The violent contact with the taut rough rope removed a fair patch of skin from the back of the man's hand. Pain made him let go; pain made him cry out; but pain brought him to his senses.

"Don't do that again!" Jock shouted. "Ever! To anybody!"

Next day the offender got no sympathy, and Jock got no blame. The offender complained, "Jock Paul is a bully!" The others said, "It'll heal." Jock said, "I probably saved the idiot's life. I certainly saved my own." All went about their business, not taking sides, and the incident passed.

"I suppose I made an enemy of that blundering idiot," Jock said. "I'm surprised he does nothing to retaliate. In his place I should."

Jock and the Frenchman had been put to work at the interminable task of calking and painting the longboat, which was rotten and leaky in a dozen places.

"No doubt he has pleasant dreams of slitting your throat," the Frenchman said. "But he will make not a move. You expect an attack in the dark, no? One night, as you lie asleep in the bunk above me, out of the blackness a knife will descend and bury itself in your heart. Or a fid will come crashing down and bash out your brains, those busy agile prefiguring brains of yours, for such they are. Or you stand by the rail in a moment of reverie; the moon is rising; she spreads her garment of silver over the sea; her beauty intoxicates you; you are lulled; you drop your guard. *Whoosh!* comes a lurking body against you. *Splash!* goes Jock Paul into the beautiful sea, ripping one ever-so-tiny hole in that lovely moon-silver garment, which instantly repairs itself, and down goes my friend to the depths. Finish. Forgotten. For the fishes. No?"

"My mind has dwelt on such possibilities."

"They are impossibilities. They are not in the nature of things."

Jock laughed.

"Do you flatter yourself that you are the only enemy the blundering idiot would like to eliminate? Oh no, not at all. There are so many others.

The old man who told him to shut up. Everyone who said, 'It'll heal,' instead of saying, 'How put upon you are!' The boatswain, who enslaves him. The captain, who enslaves the boatswain. John Younger, who enslaves the captain. King George, who enslaves John Younger. Upwards and downwards, all who are in authority and all whom authority deprives of their natural rights: they too are enemies; them too he would eliminate. All who are governed yearn in their hearts to be free, which would be a very good thing if it could be accomplished. But it cannot. And so they are slaves. The blundering idiot who gripped your foot and whose hand you so cleverly wounded dares not make a move to retaliate upon you, much as he would like to see you dead. For to do so would threaten his own existence. Who knows what he is hiding? Who knows what all our spiritless crew are hiding? They hide much. Crimes ashore, robberies, desertion of sweethearts, desertion of wives, drunken slayings, pistol-point thieveries, bastards begotten and forgotten, adulteries, incests, coin-clippings, smugglings, jail breaks. Can their lives bear the scrutiny that murder at sea, your murder, would subject them to? No. A poet of yours says, Conscience does make cowards of us all. My Rousseau says, Man's first law is to attend to his own preservation. Shackles stronger than steel restrain men's hands; fear seals their mouths. And so our crew of slaves arrive at a point of armed neutrality, impotent, safe on the bosom of the all-encircling impersonal sea, which keeps them alive and obscure to savor an early taste of the tomb. Only ashore do sailormen brawl. At sea they are quiet, tolerant one of another, as corpses are tolerant of the corpses who lie next to them in the churchyard. Do you follow me, Jock Paul?"

"I hobble along."

"Do I not seem to you, as I seem to myself, to speak, as Socrates said, like one touched of the gods?"

"I think you're most frightfully gloomy."

"I am realistic."

"So am I."

"But not gloomy? That is because the shackles you wear have not yet bit to the bone. But they are there; I see them. Even now they are working, working, working, deeper and ever deeper into your narcotized flesh. One day they will rattle a funeral knell about your dead bones, which will be all that remains of Jock Paul: tyranny's shackles and dead white bones."

"Come, Henri; calk your seam. 'Tis a beautiful day."

"Do you know why I go to America?"

"I should guess you are fleeing the law."

47

"The law! The law slew me. Picture to yourself what it is that it is, the *lettre de cachet.*"

"I cannot."

"Because you have nothing to lose but your chains. My Rousseau says, 'Man is born free, but everywhere he is in chains.' Those are the very first words of the immortal *Contrat Social.* The *Contrat Social* will replace the absurd Christian Bible; Rousseau's radiant dictum will replace 'Servants, obey your masters,' and all the rest of such clerical nonsense. I tell you that kings, *kings,* have forged the shackles we wear, to their everlasting shame and the shame of our free natural selves. Who is free? Not we of the *Friendship.* Friendship! I spit! Not he who is captain. Nor he who is owner. Nor even King George. No civilized man is free.

"I was born to an ancient marquisate in Poitou. I happened to be Protestant, born to that superstition as I was to my estate. I had a grasping Catholic neighbor; he was born to his superstition also, as I was to mine. I no longer hate him. Long since I have passed beyond the narrow confines of creeds. It was his luck and my misfortune that just at that moment the anti-Protesant wind in France began to blow: we Huguenots fell into disrepute. My Catholic neighbor, coveting my lands, bought a *lettre de cachet.* Yes, they can be bought in France. And now I shall tell you what is a *lettre de cachet.* A *lettre de cachet* is a document signed by His Most Christian Fat Majesty Louis XVI which states that so-and-so — a blank is left for the name — is an enemy of the state. Your enemy purchases this formidable document. In the blank space he writes your name. The thing is done. A gendarme arrives at your door. 'Monsieur le marquis,' he says, 'my duty compels me to take into custody your person.' He shows you the letter. He is very respectful. You probably know him; perhaps he is the son of one of your peasants. You read the letter. You read your doom. There is nothing to be done. You are imprisoned without trial, sentenced for life to jail or to the galleys, or transported. My own fate was mild; my neighbor was covetous, not cruel; he bore me no personal grudge. I was merely banished from France in perpetuity with confiscation of all I possess in this world; the provision for confiscation never varies. Oh, Jock! My rolling vineyards, my green, my beautiful acres, my precious chateau! I knew every stone! I loved every morsel of earth! Gone, all gone, vanished, snatched away between one little setting and rising of the sun! That is the *lettre de cachet.* I threw away my sword lest I fall upon it and end a life which, in that hour, seemed too futile to live. But I had my books. I had my Rousseau. I was young, and soon I no longer wished to die. Rousseau? My neighbor did not covet Rousseau. They burn his books in Protestant

48

Geneva; they burn his books in Catholic France. I fled with my books, I arrived in England, an enemy alien but not proscribed, since at home I was already proscribed. Now, for one voyage I am a sailor, coiling ropes in the wrong direction. Nobody burns books on the *Friendship*. Ha! Who knows or cares what makes the lumps in my sack! They are books. With my books I sail to America. There I shall be free. Do you know who is free? The Indians! Do not laugh. Reflect. Read Rousseau. The Indians are free, the beautiful savages of America, who own neither money nor fleets of ships nor manor houses nor fixed abode nor fiscal shares nor corporate stocks, who obey neither princes nor kings nor czars nor governors of any kind, but live in glorious natural simplicity in God's fertile and provident wilderness, golden sons of the golden sun. To them I sail! With them I shall make my life. — Have you read Rousseau, Jock Paul?"

Jock looked at him. "I think I should."

"Do, do! But not in translation. Shall I tell you what are translations?"

"I have heard that they are like women: if they are faithful, they are not beautiful; if they are beautiful, they are not faithful."

"*Parbleu!* No Englishman could have said that."

"I am not an Englishman just because I speak English."

"English is excellent for the sailing of ships and the ordering of mutton chops in a tavern; but for logical disquisitions, for delicate shadings, for exquisite subtleties — alas. Quite inadequate. How fortunate for you that I have no English translation of *Le Contrat Social*. You shall drink at the crystal font of Rousseau in the pure French original. What a privilege to teach you! Before we reach America I shall transform you into a liberal philosopher; into a polished gentleman — nay, you are that already. You gave me your bunk. And you shall speak elegant French. Already you have the foundation, laid — how incredibly! — by a parish schoolmaster in barren Scotland. What a formidable country. I salute the Scots. Who would have conceived possible such a miracle of good taste! Will you be my pupil, Jock?"

"I have always striven to learn all I could that was useful," Jock said soberly.

"Then it is agreed!" He held out his hand; his eyes were bright with Gallic emotion. "We seal our compact!"

Jock grinned and shook the proffered hand. "But it strikes me as strange, monsieur le marquis, that you, who are about to transform yourself into a red Indian, desire to transform me into an elegant gentleman."

Henri said bitterly, "It is my legacy to the civilized world."

Chapter 7

AN ODDITY of seafaring, well known to old sailors but new to Jock, now strongly impressed itself upon his senses: land has a smell. As the *Friendship* gradually approached Virginia, the clean sea air underwent a change. It was not altogether pleasant. The winds that had swept across the gigantic American continent had drawn into themselves part of its substance: dust of its earth and particles of its vegetation, mold of decay and seeds of rebirth, the pine-sweet scent of trackless miles of primeval forest, the strong wild odor of millions of prowling animals, the smoke of man's fires. It was the heavy and complex odor of life, carried by the winds far out to sea, where salt would cleanse and purge it. It was like opening the door of one of Mr. Craik's hothouses, difficult to breathe for a moment until you got used to it.

For twenty hours Captain Benson had sniffed the land wind. His logbook placed him three hundred miles east of where he knew, by his nose, he actually was. Still, it was not a bad landfall. Sooner or later he would sail straight into the estuary of the Rappahannock; he was sure of his latitude by the elevation of the sun, which a sextant could accurately measure. But as for his longitude, when he would get there, that nightmare of navigators, no one had ever yet devised a means of measuring it and no one probably ever would; for to do so would require some accurate means of keeping time at sea. On the unstable platform of a ship, pendulum clocks were useless, and sandglasses, precise though they were, were at the mercy of cabin boys, who constantly fell asleep and neglected to turn them, or "cheated on the sand" and turned them too soon so as to shorten their watches and get themselves back into their bunks. Longitude! The captain loathed the word. Surer than longitude was the smell of land, the change in the color of the sea from clear blue to dirty blue, and the change in the feel of the deck underfoot. These were tidal waters charged with the brown silt of the Rappahannock; these were waves whose motion already was hampered by the presence of shallowing bottom a few fathoms down, inching closer to the hull from underneath as the *Friendship* drove closer to the shore. At length, to left and right, the low beaches of the mainland took solid shape emerging from the mists of the horizon, and the ship sailed into the broad jaws of the estuary. She no longer pitched or rolled; for the first time in two months her masts stood straight as rooted trees; to walk her decks was now curiously like walking the planks of a wharf: the knee bent to receive the upsurge of deck that did not come; the body balanced to compensate for a roll that was not there. Here, Jock learned, was the explanation of that rolling gait of sailormen newly ashore. They weren't drunk after all, not in the first few moments, at least; they were simply getting their land legs.

In the general change that marked the transition from deepwater to shoreside discipline Captain Benson's attitude towards Jock had thawed.

He said, in a friendly tone, "I suppose we'll be losing you now, young man."

"If I do what I hope to do, my association with you and the *Friendship* will be a long one, sir."

"Only as a landsman, I'm afraid. To tell the truth, Jock, I don't care much for landsmen. I'm tempted to clap you in the brig and keep you aboard."

"What have I done?" Jock demanded.

"Rather too well," the captain said shortly. "Oh well, never mind. You've got your orders and I've got mine. But if it should happen that this mission of yours doesn't quite come off," and he winked broadly, "I dare say I could find a berth for you on the *Friendship* again."

"I thank you kindly, sir."

"I'm not thinking of a bunk in the forecastle, you know. I am thinking of the cabin. Bear it in mind. For the moment, I suppose you must meet your brother."

"I don't even know if I shall remember him. It's been a long time since I saw him."

"He'll be expecting you, I imagine."

"I don't see how."

"The *Friendship* enjoys the distinction of being John Younger's slowest ship. If I know John Younger, he'll have sent word ahead of your arrival by packet, beating us by at least two weeks."

At the quayside, at the moment when every man aboard was heavily engaged in the complex but well-ordered confusion of making the ship secure, Benson again approached Jock and quietly detached him from a group of others. "Go to the Frenchman's bunk," he ordered, "and get his sack of books and put it in the arms closet in my cabin. Here is the key. Return it to me when you've locked up the sack."

Jock looked blank. The captain deigned to explain. "I never saw a man with 'jump ship' so eager in his eyes. I cannot afford to lose even him. He won't run away if I temporarily impound his beloved books. It is kinder than locking him up. Do not salute. Go, do as I bid you."

"Aye, sir," said Jock.

"And now," Benson said when he returned the key, "I think you had better go ashore and see if the coach yonder isn't your brother's."

Among the drays and wagons in a crowd of barefoot black slave workmen, of tattered peddlers, pimps and petty merchants, of women with high-pitched voices and low-pitched blouses, all of whom for their several reasons had gathered to greet the *Friendship,* Jock descried a soberly handsome coach. On the box sat a sleek Negro in livery, respectfully at attention. Beside the coach stood a very fat man, fatter by far than Jock had remembered him, with a plump little rosy-cheeked woman who clung tight to his protecting arm, eying the noisy water-front scene with some apprehension.

As Jock approached he could hear the man saying, "Courage, my pet! If he does not find us, we will go aboard this craft and find him. Yes, by gad, without hesitation!" He flicked an imaginary speck of snuff from the immaculate ruffles of his jabot, took a firm grip on a cudgel-like walking stick and leveled a militant gaze on a sailor who, with a mahogany sea chest on his shoulder, was bearing rapidly down upon them on a head-on collision course.

"Oh, I shouldn't care to go aboard, Willie, even to welcome your brother. This is a frightening place."

"Tut, tut, my dear. Merely a water front. Nothing at all to be frightened of." Apprehensively he glanced around.

"It's so hard to remember," she said fondly, "that you were ever one of these rough sailors. What — what will Jock be like? I mustn't let on that he frightens me, even if he does frighten me, must I, dear?"

"Good heavens, no. But I don't think he will. He's a very small lad, very pale, very slender — well, fellow, what are *you* grinning at?"

The sailor, bronzed by the sun almost to the burnt-umber of his sea chest, had paused beside him and was smiling down into his face from a two-inch vantage of height.

"I think," said Jock, "that I've found my brother. Are you not Willie Paul?"

"Upon my soul, it's Jock!" Willie cried, dropping his walking stick and clutching Jock's hand, which he began to pump with the vigor of a man determined to fill his pail no matter how deep the well. His broad face beamed, his ruffles heaved, his honest eyes bulged, and his whole body

52

shook with the exuberance of his welcome. Jock knew that the Americans habitually greeted one another with a handshake, like the Indians. The custom was still considered bizarre in Europe and a little barbarous. He was glad his own brother introduced him to it. It was extraordinary, of course, but he had learned from Henri that Frenchmen kissed each other on the cheek, Russians on the mouth, Arabs held hands like lovers though they maintained well-stocked harems of thoroughly bedded wives, Eskimos rubbed noses, and Negroes in their African jungles cracked knuckles in each other's faces in welcome. The handshake was as good as any. "Bessie, my pet, this is Jock." Willie laughed heartily. "My little, pale, younger brother. Look at him. Och, Jock, we are glad to see you. Jock, you may kiss your sister-in-law."

She said, "Oh, Willie, for goodness' sake!" But, flushing, she held up her pink plump cheek. Dutifully Jock bent and kissed it. "We honestly didn't know what to expect," she said, "a little boy or a bearded pirate with rings in his ears."

"I guess I've outgrown the boy," Jock said, "and it isn't likely I'll ever grow into the pirate."

Willie said, "You must be extremely tired after your voyage. I assure you I know what it's like. You have my deepest sympathy, and Bessie's too."

"I am not in the least tired."

"The nervous excitement of landing has temporarily buoyed you up."

Jock was not nervous either, but he saw how uneasy his brother was in their present surroundings.

"We must get you out of this district at once. Give your chest to the man. Come now, into the coach with us!" The slave had already opened the door. "You first, my dear," and Willie handed Bessie up the little step; the soft springs of the coach sagged comfortably under her weight. "Now you, Jock; and now —" with an effort that started with a lunge and ended with a wheeze — "me!" and the springs sagged down to the axles. He slammed the door with relief. The little vehicle under their combined weights labored for a moment like a heavily laden ship. "Well, Patrick? Home! Quickly!" He thumped with his walking stick on the roof of the coach above their heads.

"Patrick?" Jock asked.

Willie chuckled till he shook. "The good Lord only knows what their real names are. This one was called 'Lion Rampant' or something of the sort in Africa. But a decent Irish captain so enchanted him on the voyage to America that the fellow adopted his name as a token of renunciation of heathenism and a tribute to civilization. I am very lucky in Patrick,

53

though I paid forty pounds for him. He's a full-blooded Fulani, far and away the most intelligent of all the breeds. You can't work them in the fields, of course; they die for some reason."

"It's a very handsome tribe," Bessie said. "The women make excellent maids, soft-spoken, eager to please, quick to obey, and many of them are really beautiful."

"They give a delightfully decorative touch to the household," said Willie, and added with pride, "Just wait till I show you my household. Not the town house, of course, I keep that simple, for business reasons. I mean the plantation. I shall invite your Captain Benson there one night when he gets the tar smell out of him."

Jock looked uncomfortable.

"My dear fellow, I didn't mean you. The taint of tar is the merest whiff after a single voyage. We'll eliminate all that in a day." He paused and took in Jock's measurements with a practiced eye. "Well, perhaps two or three days. The clothes I prepared for you will require certain alterations."

Bessie dimpled. "You know very well that you'll have to start all over again from collar to garter buckles."

Willie sighed, and agreed. "I believe you are right, my dear. I skimped everything. The shoulders especially." Then an idea struck him, and his face brightened. "But there need be no loss! I'll take off the satin collar and give it a higher one; a pair of clerical bands will hide the patching in front. I'll put on some dull bone buttons instead of the pearl ones. I'll take the flare out of the cuffs and give them that tight Presbyterian look, very black, very edifying. I'll broaden the breech seat and square up the coattails. Then I shall present it for the inspection of the Reverend Gordon Eusebius McKorkle, who has wanted a new suit for a long time. But a great many other customers were ahead of him, and to be quite candid about the matter, their trade was more profitable."

"I'll pay you, Willie, as soon as I can."

"Of course you will, Jock. D'ye think I'd rob you of your self-respect? On the other hand, I'd be hurt if you thought I'd press you. If I can wait for the Reverend Gordon Eusebius McKorkle, be assured I can wait for my own brother."

"Perhaps you won't have to wait long."

Willie nodded and turned his head a fraction of an inch toward Jock. At the mention of money, Jock noticed, his brother's face, so large and placid, could take on a remarkable degree of animation. "I suppose you refer," Willie said, "to the possibility of setting up an agency for the

54

provisioning of the Younger ships. Younger wrote me, oh, ever so guard-edly, that something of the sort was in the wind. I have often considered it myself. There is no question that the right man could make it feasible and profitable. But I am not the man. My own talents, if I have any, lie in another direction. I am far too happy making gentlemen's clothes and raising tobacco to venture into anything so violent as dealing with sailors, even super-sailors like captains and ship chandlers. No, Jock, 'tis not for me."

"I could make the contacts, Willie, and you could run the office. You have all the information."

"No, Jock, I've all I can do as it is."

"Willie mustn't spread himself too far," Bessie said.

"What say, my pet?" Then he laughed. "By Jove, that's a good one. Spread myself, eh? Ha, ha! I know what you mean, you minx! Jock, when you marry —"

"And you ought to, you know," Bessie said.

"Marry a wit, the way I did. Sharp as a razor, by gad. She means I've spread too far already. My spreading waistline, get it, Jock? Oh, I see you do."

"All he can think of is those silly old records in your sea chest, Willie."

"I'm not so sure they're silly, pet. I've read them all over again these last few days, soon as I saw how great store the firm of John Younger sets by them. The old tailor certainly knew everybody of any consequence here-abouts: Dandridges, Pendletons, Washingtons, Henrys, Fieldings. Most of them buy their suits from me still. But his largest dealings, outside the tail-oring field, seem to have been with a certain Colonel Fielding." He looked inquiringly at Jock. "Colonel Robert Fielding?"

Jock shook his head. "I'm afraid I never heard of him."

"He's extremely wealthy, and benevolent to a degree. High Church of England man. Contributed the new organ in the Anglican church here. I tried to find out what it cost, but I couldn't. It must have been frightfully dear."

"That's how he is," Bessie said. "He hides his light under a bushel."

"He doesn't buy his suits of me," Willie said wistfully, "and he owns seven thousand acres, all of it worked. Makes Bessiwill look like a truck garden."

"Bessiwill?" said Jock.

"My plantation. 'Bessi-' for Bessie, '-will' for Willie. Bessie named it. Ob-serve how wittily she has combined our two Christian names. Yes, sir." Bessie dropped her eyes modestly.

55

"Willie has accomplished what no Greek god ever did," Jock said, his face perfectly straight. "To have wooed Aphrodite and Calliope and won them in one and the same charming lady!" He looked at Bessie, who blushed, and instantly relented. There would be another time, if Willie pursued the allusion, to inform him that Aphrodite was the goddess of love, Calliope the muse of music. For Willie had just said helplessly, "What say, Jock?"

"There was a French nobleman aboard, Willie, a victim of politics who had lost his estate, a refugee. He and I whiled away many dull hours reading together a great pile of books of his. I'm afraid I'm still under his spell. I meant merely that Bessie Paul is, as you say, a great wit." Quickly he went on. "Why doesn't Colonel Fielding buy suits of you if he did of Samuel da Sola?"

"Now that is something I do not understand. He and the tailor grew cool. I suspect they fell out over some matter of which I know nothing. The tailor's records show evidence of collaboration in the shipments of great quantities of rum. But, my word, lots of merchants deal in rum."

"Maybe it was trade rum," Bessie said.

Willie was glad to be in a position to tell Jock something he did not know. "Trade rum is a vile cheap drink, part rum, part water, part spirits of Indian corn, raw, smelly, disgusting. I can hardly believe it of Fielding. But yes, Bessie, the disagreement may possibly have been over trade rum. Da Sola's records are mostly figures, almost no written notes at all. I think it was his hands; writing was so painful to him in his last days. At any rate, you must meet Colonel Fielding, Jock. He would be the best possible source of supply for your agency."

"You are kind to me, Willie."

"Tut, tut, lad. Once you kicked a lantern and tried to save me from a press gang. It didn't work, but you tried. I shall never forget that. And besides, perhaps I'll have a chance to get back the colonel's custom."

"We'll invite them to a supper at Bessiwill," Bessie said.

"Them, my pet?"

"His daughter, too."

"I had quite forgotten Catherine."

"Willie always forgets the ladies," Bessie said proudly. "Could there be any greater compliment? Colonel Fielding is a widower; his daughter keeps house for him."

"By all means invite her," Jock said.

"Oh, Willie, I hope they'll come!"

"Come, my pet? Colonel Fielding is the soul of condescension, a thoroughbred gentleman; there isn't a snobbish bone in his body. Everyone says so. I'm sure they will come. Now tomorrow, Jock, I shall set about your new suit, and this time I'll make it right."

Chapter 8

THE SUPPER at Bessiwill opened with a grace at table. "We return thanks, O Lord," intoned Willie, his head bowed over his plate, his pudgy hands clasped, his eyes for the moment shut, "for Thy manifold mercies that we, who are less than nothing, be now by a singular Providence set in the way to labor to make ourselves something, working Thy will in a new and larger land. For this Thy mercy and these Thy gifts we bless Thy name." On which he opened his eyes on a slab of steaming nut-brown mush swimming in a pool of sugar-cane syrup, and genially beamed upon his guests.

Bessie in fluttery ribbons and pink starched lace smiled round the table with satisfaction. Everything had gone right; nothing had gone wrong. Colonel Fielding and his daughter had accepted her invitation, arriving in a trim little pony chaise, very fashionable, very shiny. Captain Benson wore a sword and did not smell of tar. Jock looked lean and smart in a suit of the latest cut that Willie had lovingly fashioned for him, at considerable pain, though Willie would not admit it. Willie was troubled with a whitlow on his sewing hand; the doctor had prescribed a course of tar water, and in time the nasty little infection around the cuticle at the edge of his nails had grown better. It was not gout, the doctor said, but it was very much like the gout. Willie would do well to eat less, or exercise more. What nonsense, Bessie thought; she loved him as he was.

Jock neglected the mush, which Bessie and Willie consumed with evident relish; it was far too sweet; but both he and the captain wolfed down their salads. Bessie said, "Do take more!" and they promptly did, Benson with awkward apology. "You cannot conceive, madam, how curiously a sailor will lust after green stuffs. Once in the China Sea I spoke a ship with a mighty suspicious look about her: false ports that obviously hid secret cannon, stunsail yards all in place for a burst of speed, for which there seemed no reason; a privateer in disguise, I am convinced to this day; but so starved was I for fresh vegetables that instead of running away from

57

her, as easily I might have, I drew close and hailed her. Can you guess what I asked for, Mrs. Paul? Onions! I lusted after onions. They had aplenty, being just out of China; I heaved them a line and they slung me some bushels of fresh white beautiful onions, demanding in return some casks of salt pork, of which I, in my turn, had enough and to spare. The exchange being made, he saluted properly, I returned his salute and we separated friends. My crew and I fell upon those onions like starving men, eating them like apples. By a coincidence three of my crewmen who had shown signs of scurvy found their spirits so roused that they threw off their lassitude and returned to their duty. It often happens so. That is why, madam, I forgo the delights of your excellent — mush, is it? — in favor of this salad."

"How charming," said Bessie, smiling, and thought, "How thoroughly peculiar!" To eat onions like apples! But Jock was displaying the same voracious appetite until, catching the eye of Catherine Fielding, a deeper hunger took over; he bethought him what onions could do to the breath, and nibbled abstemiously at his greenery, waiting for the roast. About this girl, whom the colonel had genially presented as Kitty, clung a dark and pervading aura of such highborn perfection of beauty that to approach within three feet of her with onions on one's breath seemed almost as sacrilegious as (so Henri had taught him when they read of the classical world) would have been the approach of a Roman high priest to an altar of Venus after witnessing shackles, blood, or a slave, or anything common and mundane. Just by her presence she made you ashamed of your grossness, made you resolve to be better than you were. Especially when, as now, she smiled at you across a table with candlelight in her eyes. Bessie, her soft heart swelling at the prospect of making a match, squirmed with pleasure. Willie, accepting a fat slice of roast from the Fulani servant, suppressed a belch, dug in, and breathed, "By gad!"

Colonel Fielding's glance moved coolly round the table.

"From the speed of your crossing," he said to Benson, "I'd guess that the winds proved favorable for this time of year."

It was early spring: a chill lingered in the Virginia air; on Willie's hearth blazed a profusion of big sweet-smelling logs such as Jock had not seen since William Craik's, a world away in time and space, in Arbigland.

"It always strikes me as odd," said Captain Benson, "that the weather at home and the weather here are so much alike. Fredericksburg lies full seventeen degrees south of Whitehaven. By rights it ought to be tropical here in comparison, but as a matter of fact it isn't."

"One of the American scientists," said Fielding, and Jock noted that this

Tory High-Anglican gentleman said "the American," not "our American," as if disclaiming kinship, "has constructed an ingenious map or chart of what he denominates 'The Gulph Stream' running like a river from the Floridas clear across the Atlantic, carrying its waters to warm the British coasts. A novel theory. What do you think of it?"

"I do not subscribe to it, sir."

"But a strong current unquestionably sets west across the southern Atlantic. Could it not be that it impinges upon the shores of the Mexican Gulf, warms, turns, and thence runs east again towards Britain?"

"That is a route taken by certain ships in the African trade," Benson said, "but it's wind that makes it easy, not an ocean stream. Are you interested in shipping, Colonel Fielding?"

"Good gracious, no, Captain."

To Jock, the suave and self-possessed expression on Fielding's face seemed mightily interested.

His daughter said, "Father's a dry landlocked planter."

"I concede, my dear," he said, "that no Negro was ever so tightly chained as am I to my acres."

"But some of our neighbors own ships," Catherine said. "We hear them talk about shipping."

Spaciousness, acreage and vast expanses seemed to Jock to typify this new world. Willie's plantation house stood atop one of those grand rolling Virginia hills, actually as high as many a Scottish mountain; but so gentle was its ascent and so multitudinous were its companions, sweeping in green gigantic undulations away to a distant horizon like smooth sea billows deceptively large after a storm that is past, that it seemed no bigger than a fair-sized hill. Spacious too was the pillared white mansion of Bessiwill, but it did not seem big until, after minutes, the horses would wind up the long gravel approach to its portico, which then loomed and dwarfed man, horse and vehicle. It struck Jock with some force, and with deep implication, that the Scottish gardener's cottage where he and Willie had been born was probably not so large as some of the slave cabins clustering behind this American tailor's mansion, certainly smaller than the kitchen house attached to the rear. On the horizon to the west rose like a wall the blue ridge of a distant chain of mountains. Beyond the mountains, unmapped, unsettled, unknown, all was Indian country.

After the roast an American turkey, and after the turkey a pie, though it was like no pie that Jock could remember in Scotland. Instead of a deep hot stew with a crust underneath, a main dish, this was a sort of enormous round tart with a crust on top, cold, stuffed with sweet filling things that

59

Bessie said were raisins, pecans, oranges, citrons, yams and quantities, but quantities, of sugar. And after the pie, the port. After so rich a repast Jock would infinitely have preferred a good strong tot of dry Scotch whisky, but Willie was trying so hard for his sake to please Colonel Fielding and Colonel Fielding was so ostentatiously English in his taste for drink that Jock was silent and sipped his cloying port.

"Such sweetness," he said softly into his glass, "added to such sweetness!" It was as near as he could bring himself to protest; he said it smiling. Suddenly he was aware, with an acute accompanying twist in the region of his stomach, such as one feels who is hungry, which he certainly was not, or one who slips and falls from a great height, which he never had, that the girl across from him had accepted the remark as meant for herself and seemed not displeased. She lowered her eyes; her lashes caught glittering flecks of candlelight and cast fringed shadows on the delicate curve of her cheeks. Her shoulders were satin smooth and baby bare in a new Continental style that was probably no novelty to Willie. Indeed, Willie must know exactly how to sew it, for as Jock now looked at Bessie he saw that she was gowned in very much the same way. Only on Bessie, though it revealed as much, nay more, there being so much more of her, it held no promise and quickened no pulse but Willie's. Bessie was glancing from him to the girl, from the girl to him, her heart fluttering with excitement and full of deep schemes for a campaign of cooperation: Kitty and Jock must assuredly see more of each other. Colonel Fielding seemed not to notice the subtle warming of the atmosphere; Willie genuinely noticed nothing but the deep ruby depths of his port. "If only that Doctor Read would prescribe this instead of tar water!"

A female slave with delicate features and graceful limbs, probably one of Bessie's Fulanis, brought tea for the ladies who, Jock was afraid, would now withdraw as Henri had told him fine ladies always did, leaving their men to tobacco and wine; but perhaps American manners were looser, or perhaps Kitty wanted to stay. At any rate the ladies stayed, to Jock's delight and Captain Benson's unfeigned surprise.

Benson stuffed a plug of heavy rum-cured tobacco, black as coal, into the bowl of his pipe and looked pleadingly at Bessie. "My goodness, we don't mind," Bessie said.

"I grow it," said Willie. "My guests should smoke it. It sets a fashion. It's good for trade. Where would America be if nobody smoked our tobacco?"

"Where indeed?" said Colonel Fielding. "I grow it too."

The table was wide, the snow-white linen thick with embroidery. To drop a fragment of glowing tobacco would burn a disastrous hole. Captain

Benson took a bearing on the nearest candle, gauged its distance to a fraction of an inch, extended the long whip-stem of his pipe till the bowl touched the flame and sucked it in with a triumphant gurgle. Then out of his mouth he propelled a vast storm cloud of thick blue smoke and leaned back with a beatific smile. "I thank you, ma'am," he said. The linen was safe; not a spark had fallen.

"You've a good steady hand, Captain," Colonel Fielding said.

"To tell the truth, sir, I'm a deal steadier at sea. At sea things shift about and you know where they're headed. On shore you have to get used to things staying put."

"Do you smoke?" Catherine said to Jock.

"Never knew a sailor who didn't," the captain said.

"It's quieting to the nerves," Jock said, "when they're jumpy."

She said, "Are yours?"

"Naturally they're jumpy," Willie said. "It was his first trip, and I don't mind saying I hope it was his last."

"I don't," the captain said bluntly. "Jock came aboard through the shore office; I thought to myself, Now here is a proper swab, and all I can do is put up with the lubber. You have to, you know, when the shore office orders you to. But pretty soon he was steering like a Solway pilot and sneaking sights at the sun when he thought I wasn't looking — with my best sextant if you please! — and reading French navigational books that a madman had brought aboard —"

"I didn't know you knew I borrowed your sextant," Jock said. "I didn't injure it."

"No, you polished it; and set it back to the mate's calculation, which was off."

Jock laughed. "I did polish it."

"I know he has other plans," the captain said, "but if he wants to ship again as an officer, I've told him I'd welcome him."

"Would you trust him to navigate?" Fielding asked absently.

"I would, sir."

"I see," Fielding said.

He and the other men held up their pipes to Patrick, who appeared with a lighted taper. Soon a more delicate tobacco aroma arose to compete with the captain's rum twist, but failed.

"Jock's other plans," Willie said, "are of a character which in my estimation affords him a brilliant future and will in the end prove more profitable to all concerned, including you, Colonel Fielding, if you come into the venture, and you yourself, Captain Benson, since it affects the earnings of the Younger Line." For twenty minutes Willie plumped for the provisioning agency. Patently, in matters of business, Willie could speak with persuasive conviction.

"I take it we can agree," he concluded, "that American ship stores, locally produced and not subject to tiresome examination by Crown health officials, are fresher and cheaper than government stores." He did not mention, though all understood, that such stores would also escape the scrutiny of the Crown tax officials.

"They'd have to be just as good," Captain Benson said nervously.

"My dear Captain," Willie said, "they could hardly be worse. I ate salt pork on the *Blythe* that had rotted in storage a year before it was finally released for consumption."

"I'll back my bread and flour and beans and Virginia pork against any in the world," Fielding said, "and I'll personally warrant full measure."

"That would be as gratifying as it is unusual," Benson said.

"I know it's unusual. But that's how I deal. Actually, I shall welcome an opportunity to bring my plantation up to full production. No one denies that the Spanish and French privateers — pirates would be a better name — are heavily injuring American trade, even in tobacco."

"It isn't only foodstuffs that are needed," Jock said. "There's canvas and cordage and ironmongery."

"Those obviously I cannot grow," Fielding said, "but I can get them from New England or from Jamaica, reasonably, I assure you."

Willie was glad to see negotiations proceeding so smoothly. "Colonel Fielding, if you can best the canny Yankees at their own game, I doff my Scottish bonnet to you."

"It is not widely appreciated," Fielding said, "how far the godly New Englanders will go for a steady reliable supply of strong cheap rum. Their frigid winters, no doubt."

Willie laughed, but at Bessie's glance he said innocently, "I'm afraid the only strong *cheap* rum I ever heard of was trade rum."

Colonel Fielding flushed purple. He roared, "Damn me, sir, if I were not a guest under your roof I should send you my card!"

"Good gracious me!" Willie set down his glass. Pistols or swords on a cold spring dawn were nothing his comfortable soul had ever yearned for. Moreover, Colonel Fielding had a look of such deep and genuine outrage on his furious features that Willie was willing to concede that never would such an honest man sully his integrity with such a shabby product. "I assure you, Colonel Fielding, I was making a jest."

"A very poor one, sir."

"I am deeply apologetic."

"Sir, I accept your apology."

Jock, who had half risen from his chair during the interchange, relaxed; the pink returned to Bessie's ashen cheeks; Catherine smiled again. Willie said shakily, "Patrick, fill Colonel Fielding's glass." Patrick, decanter in hand, hastened to the colonel's elbow; he filled his glass and then all the others. "I drink your good health, sir," Willie said.

The colonel gallantly returned, "Sir, I yours; and complete success to our venture!"

Jock wondered, as he joined in the drinking of the toast that drowned the memory of the little contretemps which might have been so serious, whether Colonel Fielding's ingenious mind, a mind one had to respect, also envisioned the shipping of rum to Jamaica. That would be coals to Newcastle with a vengeance. It was not a point he cared to raise at this moment when peace was so happily restored.

"It looks as if the *Friendship* can't have you as mate," Captain Benson said. "Ah well, good luck to you, Jock."

Just then at the rear of the house Willie's hound-dogs set up a furious commotion, snapping and barking and straining at their leashes till the noise of their chains could be distinctly heard. Willie kept hounds because every other gentleman did, and when they did not hunt game they hunted runaway slaves. But no slave of Willie's had ever run away, and Willie, no hunter, kept off horses as much as he decently could, riding only to such inaccessible spots of his plantation as had no carriage roads, a defect he planned to remedy. The hounds were accordingly unworked and grew sleek and fat like everything else at Bessiwill. But they could be aroused.

"Upon my soul, what is that?" Willie cried.

Patrick said quietly, "Master, a stranger is here."

"Preposterous," Willie said.

"Master, shall I go and see?"

"Why yes. Yes, I think you should. Take a stick. Take a gun. Take reinforcements." The slave disappeared and Willie mused, "It can't be Indians. They're way over the mountains. Did you invite anyone else, my dear?"

Bessie said, "If I had I'd have told you, and they certainly wouldn't be coming in by the kennels."

Presently Patrick returned. "A stranger dressed like a sailor, speaking un-Englishly, demands to see Mr. Paul. He has a pistol."

Willie gulped.

"You stay right here," Bessie said, gripping his arm.

Captain Benson growled, "Confound that Frenchman. He jumped ship after all. I'll take care of this."

"He said the pistol was for Captain Benson," Patrick said.

"I'm afraid I'll have to go, my dear," Willie said, and reluctantly rose.

"Master, he said he demanded to see Mister Jock Paul."

"You shall not go out in the dark and confront a desperate deserter who's armed with a pistol," Willie said positively. "We shall barricade the establishment and shoot the dastard down."

Patrick said, "He is sobbing."

"Poor Henri only wants his sack of books," Jock said. "Will you release them, Captain Benson?"

"I certainly will not. He has deserted, and I want him back. If he succeeds in escaping, I shall sell his books and try to hire a replacement."

"I'd purchase the books, Captain, if —" He looked at his brother.

"Good heavens, yes, Jock. I'll advance you the money. Buy the blackguard off." In moments of emotion Willie could lapse into pure Scotch. "Ca' canny, laddie!"

"Oh, I'll by careful," Jock grinned, and went out.

Catherine looked at her father. "Father, will you help?"

"My dear, I think you really wish me to."

"I do."

"Jock won't get shot," the captain assured her. "The Frenchman clings to him, leans on him, adores him."

"If this man escapes —" she said.

"He will," Benson grumbled. "Jock won't stop him."

"— could you find a replacement for Captain Benson?"

Fielding chuckled. "When Kitty's eyes take on a hue like pansies washed in morning dew —"

"Father, I'm serious."

"— I never can resist her. Very well, my dear, I shall find a replacement. I know of a very good man who'll be happy to sail with Captain Benson."

"He won't have to be very good to be better than the Frenchman," Benson said. "Good Lord, counter-clockwise!"

Jock returned.

"He overpowered me and fled."

"How does it happen," Fielding said, "that you hold his pistol in your hand?"

Jock looked at it. He did not smile.

"I promised to keep his books safe until he should return. He hurled the

64

pistol at me and took to his heels towards the forest to the west. He said he would have no use for firearms among the beautiful golden savages."

Chapter 9

A PERIOD of intense commercial activity now ensued. It was vastly agreeable to Willie, who rubbed his hands, peering over Jock's shoulder as Jock labored through sheaves of accounts, clucking, "Lad, lad, ye're making rich!"

"It is Colonel Fielding's doing. The man is a wizard. I wonder how he does it."

Ships' stores were arriving in quantity as if by magic, fresh, sound, full measure and always on time. Items difficult to procure were streaming in from New England, from the West Indies and from Colonel Fielding's own fertile plantation, which had now come into full production. The number of his slaves had likewise increased to take care of increased demand. From Jamaica, Fielding had laid his hands on a prime source of excellent rum, a most valuable commodity. Not only John Younger's line but other shipping firms and even some men-of-war, the Crown's own naval craft, slyly availed themselves of Jock Paul's unnamed, uninhibited, tax-free and increasingly sought-after provisioning agency.

"It is permissible to wonder at a wizard's art," Willie said. "It is daft to pry into it."

"I won't. But there's certainly a vast amount of rum involved. He never demands cash for any of the stores. Only rum; while I sell for cash."

"Cash is harder and harder to come by now that the Crown has forbidden America to print money."

"I suppose so."

"And it's good rum, Jock, that you're using for money. I never tasted better."

"That's true enough."

"And to think I nearly got myself shot or my gullet slit for suggesting that Fielding might be mixed up with trade rum! I tell you, I scolded poor Bessie for that mean unfounded suspicion. She forgave me, the dear."

Jock laughed, "Willie, I think anybody would forgive you anything."

"I protest, brother, that I should prove a most formidable antagonist once I were thoroughly aroused."

"I shouldn't care to cross swords with you."

"Jock, you are pulling my leg. Fundamentally I suspect you are quite heartless."

"Not quite."

"Kitty? Bessie loves her."

"So do I."

And at another time, "Willie, I ride your horses, I set up my agency in your shop, I live in your plantation house, and never a penny will you accept from me."

"You make regular contributions to Mr. Craik," Willie said, "you make dutiful contributions to Father and Mother, which I never did — I always wished to, but there was always some pressing improvement for Bessiwill, especially those roads, very expensive roads —"

"I owe you a lot, Willie."

"Nothing."

"Is it that fool lantern I kicked?"

"The fact is, Jock, you give me class. Colonel Fielding buys his suits from me again."

"He and Kitty," said Bessie with pride, "never visited at Bessiwill much before you came. But now!"

"Fielding's taken a great fancy to you, Jock," Willie said. "By gad! To see you and the old boy in your shirts on the lawn tearing each other's jabots to pieces with those foils!" Colonel Fielding, to keep in practice, he said, had invited Jock to fence with him for sport. "Patrick must have picked a peck of the best French lace off the grass after that last bout. Fair set my blood to racing, just to watch you. Pity my hand won't let me use the rapier any more." Bessie smiled. If Willie had ever learned to use the rapier, it must have been before he met her.

"When Fielding offered to teach me something I didn't know," Jock said, "I'd have been foolish not to avail myself of his kindness." Till now Jock had learned to handle only a heavy cutlass, like any other sailor. To change from that slashing weapon to the feather-light sword of a gentleman, which was designed to pierce the heart, not to split the skull, was a fascinating experience. "It will take some time to equal Fielding's art," Jock said, "but I'll beat him before I'm through."

Bessie said, "I've grown to know Kitty quite well in the time I've had to chat with her while you and the colonel were at your sport. She's such a dear. Confidentially, I suspect she thinks her father is monopolizing you."

66

"Ha!" said Willie. "The daughter is jealous of the father. A neat reversal of the ordinary."

Bessie said, "You are seldom alone with her. I think she'd rather walk with you in the garden. The roses are just coming into bloom."

"Big moon, too," Willie said. "Tell me, Jock, is it better to lead a beautiful young lady down a garden path and lose your heart, as I did, or fence with her father and wilt your linen and learn to save your life with a rapier? Personally, I'd choose romance."

Bessie rewarded him with a glowing glance; but Jock said severely, flushing a little, "I dinna need instruction to lose my heart; to learn to save my life I may." His speech betrayed how shaken he was.

"Lad, I did not mean to offend you."

"She's a precious girl," Bessie said, "and Jock we do wish you well with her."

"I must grow very rich to be worthy of her," Jock said.

"That's not really important," Bessie said.

Willie said thoughtfully, "It just might be."

"Well, it's not the most important," Bessie said. "Of course, she's used to all the luxuries and she's courted by every bachelor in Fredericksburg, but it seems they don't kiss like Jock."

"Eh?" beamed Willie.

Jock flushed redder. "I protest I kissed no more than her hand!" He added miserably, "I dared no more."

"She'd have permitted you," Bessie said.

"Did she say so?" He was very eager.

"*Say so?*" Bessie laughed. "You silly! Of course not. But I could tell by the way she spoke of you, and a certain look in her eyes. There are ways and ways and *ways* of kissing a hand."

"I meant it," Jock said simply.

"Upon my soul!" said Willie. "You made good use of a walk or two in the garden."

Bessie shot him a warning glance not to tread too heavily.

"I meant it with all my heart," Jock said.

"Well," Willie said, "I don't see why you're not just as good as anybody. Maybe we didn't come from much in the old country — my pet, I mean we were not wealthy; there is frightfully good blood in us Pauls — but this is a new country and here a man can make his own way and become whatever he wants to. Look at me. Here I can be a gentleman, almost a gentleman anyhow; I can certainly make a gentleman's fortune. And so can Jock, by gad!"

"I propose to."

"She'd have you anyhow," Bessie said.

"Would her father?"

Bessie could not reassure him quite so readily on that score. The Fielding name was very old, and so was the Fielding fortune.

"He certainly likes you," she said.

For some time thereafter Jock worked as long and hard as any of Fielding's slaves, which was long and hard indeed, spending his days on the water front soliciting likely customers, his nights auditing the agency's growing list of accounts, sharply as only a Scotsman can, lest a single farthing be lost or a bargain struck that might be made more profitable. The vision of wealth beckoned him on like a Grail, and behind the vision, Kitty.

She and her father came to Bessiwill again shortly. Jock thought Kitty might be a little out of temper. She was very quiet and her color was certainly higher than usual. It was always a warm and perfect ivory-pink. But then, Bessie's roses in bud were perfect too. Now as they opened to the sun they were even more perfect. So "perfect" was not a superlative after all, not for a flower, not for a woman whose enchantment could grow till it wrought injury, cruel as the sun which could blast the eye or a rapier which could rend the heart.

Fielding was so cordial he was almost jovial — joviality was a little-seen facet of him — and he did not bring his foils. Jock was glad of that. This time he did not want the colonel to take up the whole afternoon. He wanted to walk with Kitty in the garden and tell her, if he dared, how it was that flowers could be more perfect than perfect.

She smiled as Jock approached her and held out her hand.

Her father grasped it, not as one takes a hand in greeting. Jock saw a queer mental picture, which he instantly blotted out with a spasm of self-reproach, of Colonel Fielding baiting a trap with a lure for a hungry animal.

"One moment, my dear," Fielding said. "Jock and I are going to have a chat."

"I thought Jock and I were going to."

"I thought perhaps Kitty and I might take a little stroll," Jock said. "Bessie's roses are lovely."

"That can wait," Fielding said, "though as you say, they are positively outblooming themselves."

"I'd really rather see the cockfight in the town, Jock," Kitty said.

It took him a moment to accustom himself to that; then he rather liked

68

it. It would give him a chance to be longer alone with her, to shepherd her among the odd characters on the water front which Willie feared so much. She would lean on him, depend on him, and he would protect her. Actually, he assured himself, she would be in no danger because he was acquainted with all the odd characters, and they respected him or had something to gain from him. But he admired her spirit. And ladies did occasionally go to the cockfights for the thrill of it, much as they watched the slave auctions.

"I'd love to take you to see one," Jock said.

"And so you shall, so you shall," said Fielding. "After we've had our chat."

"He wants you to be first mate on a silly old ship that belongs to a neighbor of ours," Kitty said petulantly.

Jock warmed with pride and hope. Kitty did not want him to go.

"Let *me* talk to him, my dear," her father said, softly but in a tone of iron command.

Dutifully, like a sweet unwilling child, Jock thought, she lifted her long full-flowing skirts with a practiced hand exactly the couple of inches a highborn lady should, and rustled up the white steps of Bessie's white portico, twinkling a pair of tiny feet and silky ankles that one had to be very well-bred not to stare at.

Bessie met her at the door. "Tea is just ready," she said.

Jock did not catch Kitty's answer; perhaps she did not reply.

Fielding was saying, "I told Kitty I wanted you to do me this little favor, but naturally I couldn't tell her everything."

"I don't see how I can leave the agency just at this moment," Jock said. "There's a terrific amount of work, and I'm trying to keep things humming."

"Tush," said the colonel. "You're working wonders, but a few weeks away won't ruin the business. My own auditor will see to the office; the customers won't wander off."

"What if they do?"

"I'll lower prices and they'll swarm back like flies."

"That would cut into the agency's profits."

"I'd lower *my* prices to *you*, Jock."

"Then you'd cut into your own profits."

"Not if you sail as mate on my ship."

"I thought Kitty said that the ship belonged to a neighbor."

"I do not think you know me very well," Fielding said. "I shall try to explain certain things to you, man to man, nay, gentleman to gentleman.

That is always much better in a matter like this, which requires a broad and civilized interpretation of the very highest moral values."

Jock nodded, as he might at a tiresome sermon; yes, yes, the very highest moral values. Suddenly his eyes narrowed: broad and civilized interpretation of them?

"What do you mean, sir?"

"Bessie's flowers really deserve closer inspection," Fielding said, taking Jock by the arm. "Let us have a closer look at them, safe from female ears, which I must tell you possess keen powers of perception, if you do not already know it," and he led him into the garden among the roses. "I don't suppose there is anything half so beautiful as a rose," he said, picking one. In his ruffles and velvet, his aquiline nose lightly brushing the petals of a flower, he looked the very archetype of the eighteenth-century gentleman, sensitive, civilized, enlightened.

The ship, the *Misericordia*, he said, only partly belonged to him. Several other gentlemen were involved; honor, naturally, forbade him to name them; he merely owned the controlling share. "It was too good a venture not to let some of my neighbors in on the bounty," he said, "and letting them in puts a stop to gossip at the source." He said, "I do not like the look on your face, Jock Paul. Do you think it illegal to accept a commission as mate on the *Misericordia*?"

"I don't know, sir. I don't see how it could be."

"Do you take me for a smuggler?"

"I wouldn't mind that. I wouldn't mind evading British taxes."

"Such a remark hardly does me justice. Everything, *everything* I do is completely legal. I merely trade sharp when I trade."

"On the contrary, you have been most liberal supplying my agency."

"I have liberal resources. I require at present only a competent mate, my last having met with an accident in Africa. The mate's post, I may say, is worth more in a single voyage than the entire profit of your agency in ten years."

This was the cycle, Fielding said, of his liberal resources. No snowball ever built up so fast:

First, from Fredericksburg, with a cargo of money and trinkets, the *Misericordia* sailed for Jamaica.

Second, in Jamaica she took on a cargo of trade rum and sailed to Africa, where trade rum, vicious as gold, was much in demand, and bought slaves at low prices, eked out with the trinkets and a minimum of cash.

Third, from Africa the *Misericordia* brought her cargo of slaves to Jamaica, whence they were quietly transshipped and sold by recognized slavers, a perfectly legal but somewhat objectionable class of merchant, throughout the American colonies.

Fourth, at Jamaica, having disposed of her slaves, the *Misericordia* took on a cargo of honest, good, reputable rum and sold it in New England for cash.

Last, thence back to Fredericksburg to repeat the cycle, with no one the wiser, everywhere a huge profit, every gentleman's hands clean as a hound's tooth and his purse good and heavy — Well, Jock?

Jock had no more scruples about slavery than anyone else. Benjamin Franklin advertised slaves for sale in his Philadelphia newspaper; all southern gentlemen owned them; gentlemen in New England often did too, but for the most part the Yankee colonists lived longer and worked cheaper than Negroes; the Bible laid down rules for slaves' management; every civilized nation throughout history had accepted slaves as a normal element of national economy; no civilized eighteenth-century nation forbade them. Only a few feather-brained visionaries, like Jean Jacques Rousseau, who spent most of his time locked up in a lunatic asylum, believed slaves should be set free. And Jock had long since made up his practical mind that the weak and ignorant must defer to the strong and informed. Nothing existed or ever had existed on the face of the planet to cast a shadow on Colonel Robert Fielding's secret trade in slaves, save only some obscure words of Jesus Christ, which had wrought no reform in eighteen hundred years and were subject to various interpretations, and the more personal consideration which moved Colonel Fielding just at that moment: slaving was not quite respectable socially.

"I have been speaking to you, Jock, as gentleman to gentleman. I assume I can take it for granted that you, on your sacred honor, will breathe nothing of this to Kitty."

Jock blurted out, "Good God, sir, I love her!"

"Good lad."

"I'd rather die than — embarrass her."

"Say it, Jock: shame her?"

"Well, yes, sir."

"So would I. Never doubt that."

"Neither in this nor in anything will I ever shame her, if she will have me."

"I do not conceive that she regards you with absolute indifference."

"Have I your blessing, sir?"

"My boy, what a delightfully proper question! Here is my hand."

Jock clutched it eagerly.

71

"I am naturally pleased that you have decided to sail as *Misericordia*'s mate," Fielding said, idly stripping the petals from the rose to savor the queerly erotic odor that exuded from the crushed stamens. "I am not quite sure how your agency would have made out if I had been forced to cancel my supplies. I understand you make a very generous allowance to your father and mother in Scotland, and to a certain William Craik. How pleasant to know that all that will continue."

Jock laughed harshly. Weak as water where Kitty was concerned, he was quite unmoved by Fielding's late and superfluous threat. He knew where he stood; a dangerous, dirty and highly remunerative position was being offered him. But in making the offer Fielding had been forced to place his own reputation in Jock's hands. "I have no fear," he said coolly, "that your auditor will neglect my personal remittances, since you, sir, honor me with an enterprise of such a delicate and confidential nature."

Fielding flushed slightly. "You have a nasty habit of seizing the upper hand, young man." But then he shrugged. "Perhaps it is a good sign. I dare say you will have plenty of occasion to exercise your talent in Africa."

Kitty appeared at the door, having apparently had her fill of Bessie's tea. Colonel Fielding's manner melted.

"Where in the world," he said fondly, "could my little daughter have got the gumption to watch a cockfight! Her mother was so timid she couldn't even watch a chicken killed for supper."

The satin shoe, from which Jock manfully tore his fascinated eyes, was now thrust into his hands as he made a stirrup with interlocked fingers and lifted Kitty up to her saddle. He marveled at her lightness; he envied the horse. The hand he had dared only to kiss rested for an instant on his shoulder; he felt its warmth and wished it would linger. Kitty smoothed her skirts, which rustled and mantled the animal's flank, and smiled down at him. How anyone could sit comfortably on a sidesaddle mystified Jock; to sit gracefully on such a contrivance and look beautiful in such a position only deepened the mystery. He swung himself up to his own mount.

"Sidesaddles must have been invented by the devil," he said, "to torture poor unsuspecting ladies. It's a pity you can't ride like men."

"Would you like us better that way?"

"You'd be a lot more comfortable."

"But think, Jock, how we'd look."

He began to. It startled him.

"What a naughty man you are!"

72

"I did not mean to be brash, Kitty."

She laughed and flicked her horse with a little ivory-handled whip. "I'll race you to the cockpit!"

Some of the better eyebrows of Fredericksburg were raised disapprovingly at the madcap spectacle as Jock and the colonel's daughter, her skirts aflutter, her ankles exposed, her curls streaming, thundered over the cobblestones in the direction of the water front.

The pit was a circular stage twenty feet across, mounted a few inches above a flagged floor and covered by an awning to shield the spectators from the sun. A barrier, elbow-high, convenient to lean upon, kept the birds from escaping. A thin matting of straw, which facilitated cleaning after the fights, covered the stage. The ringside benches were already full when Jock and Kitty made their way slowly through the crowd of expectant spectators, but a gentleman with a vaguely nautical air about him recognized her, raised his hat and, bowing very low, offered her his place.

"Thank you, Captain Newton," she said.

The obliging gentleman then said in a low voice to the man next to him, "Give up your seat. Mr. Paul is with her."

"Why should I?"

"You'll find out."

"Oh, very well."

"Thank you," Jock said.

He had recognized a number of his customers among the crowd and nodded to them, but Captain Newton he had never seen. "That was very kind of him," he whispered to Kitty. "Who is he?"

"He's a psalm-singing insufferable bore, but he knows Father and so he tries to be polite. He wouldn't if he didn't know Father."

"What is he captain of?"

"The *Misericordia*."

Two Negroes brought out a couple of gamecocks and set them in the pit. They were beautiful birds with elegant combs, furiously crimson and furiously stiff. Screaming, they hurled themselves upon each other, aiming for the eyes. Kitty bet on the bird with the silver spurs; Jock pondered a moment and bet on the other, whose spurs were iron. Jock won, and the man came round with a two-guinea chit, which Jock might cash on leaving or use to bet with on other fights.

"I only bet a guinea," Jock said.

"The odds were two to one, sir."

"How did you know you'd win?" Kitty asked.

"It was luck."

"I think you knew."

"It seemed to me the losing bird had longer spurs."

"They're always the same length. That's the rule. It wouldn't be fair otherwise. But suppose he had? Wouldn't that be an advantage?"

Jock's eyes had deceived him. He stored away in his mind a little lesson that might not be little if applied to cannon or swords: shining metal looks more formidable than dull metal of the same size.

"If a fighting cock needs longer spurs than his enemy," Jock said soberly, "he can't be much of a fighter."

But he lost his chit on the next fight and Kitty won, clapping her hands with delight. Jock neglected to watch the bouts, turning his head to admire her. Her color heightened, her eyes dilated and deepened in hue, her nostrils quivered with quick short breaths that sent her hand fluttering to her breast as if to free herself from something of silk or lace that restricted her breathing. Jock cogitated on what it might be and where, underneath, it might lie, and found his own temperature rising; but another cock died and Kitty regained her composure.

"We both won that time," she cried.

"Did we?"

"We bet on the same bird."

"Why, so we did."

"Oh, Jock, you weren't even watching."

"Yes, I was."

She leaned against him — in the noisy jostling crowd it was easy to do so without attracting attention — and gave his hand a little squeeze.

"I don't mind being watched."

The last bout was the "battle royal," an event greatly favored by the rear benches because it was the biggest, bloodiest and most spectacular. Sixteen fighting cocks were placed in the pit at the same time. Only one would emerge the victor. Rules of the battle royal required that each bird fight to the end, literally to victory or death. In ordinary bouts a gamecock might save his life by simply refusing to fight. So also a man might, at the very last moment, walk away from a duel and save his life, if not his honor, by showing the white feather. For a gamecock to show the white feather was a purely physiological phenomenon: his hackle would automatically rise, and there, growing beneath the colored plumage of his neck, the white underfeathers would stand exposed to view. To jeers and catcalls his red-faced owner would swoop him out of the pit to safety and rest, to fight again another day. But there was no escape from the battle royal, not even for beaten, dead-tired birds whose bodies cried "Halt!" by

74

an uncontrollable physical reaction and whose brains were too innocent to feel shame.

The battle royal lasted a quarter of an hour, and the death rate was therefore, on the average, one per minute, which should have satisfied even the rear benches; but at the beginning little could be seen or enjoyed. There was such screaming and squawking in the cockpit, such a mass of flying feathers, blood, and shreds of mangled combs, such gouging of eyes and such sinking of spurs, that the spectacle seemed some boiling witches' cauldron of confusion rather than a battle. To the shrieking of the birds was added the shouting of the spectators, which grew in volume, jeering the fallen, cheering the survivors, as the noise of the birds diminished through death and fatigue.

Kitty cupped her hand and cried in Jock's ear, "When the ranks thin out, we'll know how to bet!"

"Aye!"

But "ranks" was not the word. They formed no ranks. Only men had brains enough to fight in concert. Birds fought for themselves alone. Time after time Jock chose some likely gamecock which had slain an opponent and had been joined by an ally at the moment of the kill, only to see his choice and the ally fly at each other's throats as soon as the common enemy lay dead. There was a lesson in that perhaps. One day he might ponder it. But not now. Excitement of the sport had communicated itself to him, heightened by Kitty's presence and her heedless, violent, utter surrender to the fighting birds. "If these were gladiators, I'd know how to bet," he said. "They'd make human sense. The brain of a bird I cannot fathom."

She did not hear him, and he had not actually expected an answer. He was wondering whether he would have enjoyed watching gladiators. He thought he probably would. The Frenchman had said they were respected in their day, nay, lionized, especially by the ladies. On balance, making allowance for the barbarity of classic times as opposed to the enlightened eighteenth century, it would probably be more sport to watch fighting men than fighting cocks.

But the birds were undeniably exciting. Now, as their number grew fewer, it was easier to guess which might stand alone at the end. The bet-takers began to circulate among the crowd, accepting wagers. They were marvelously proficient, knowing most of the spectators by sight, communicating largely by a complicated system of sign language, scarcely ever having to speak, handing out the chits, keeping one eye constantly on the battle, nodding, smiling, perfectly poised and unerring. It was an experience and an education to watch them.

75

Suddenly Jock was aware that Kitty had signaled something to one of them. At once the man was at her side and Kitty showed Jock a ten-guinea chit, odds ten to one against.

"Which bird?" Jock asked her. He could hardly make himself heard above the rising din.

"Over there!" she cried. "With the purple crest!"

"You, sir?" the bet-taker asked.

Jock hesitated, swallowed hard. There were six fighting cocks left in the pit. He wondered whether a purple crest meant waning strength and a failing heart; on the other hand, it might mean a heart so strong that the crest was pumped full, fair to burst with fighting blood. If Purple Top won, he, Jock Paul, would win a hundred guineas, a formidable sum. If Purple Top lost, he, Jock Paul, would lose only ten: not so formidable, but he had only five in his pocket. He would have to borrow from Kitty.

Intolerable.

He looked up to refuse, but the man was gone and Kitty was handing him his chit. "I said Yes for you," she said.

"I didn't pay for it."

"He knows me; he'll be back to collect if we lose."

Suddenly Jock went coldly, inhumanly calm. While the others screamed and stamped their feet and whistled and cursed, while Kitty clutched his arm in a paroxysm of excitement, while one by one the fighting cocks slaughtered each other, Jock alone was calm.

He wanted so desperately to win that his mind rejected the possibility of losing. Till now he had soberly calculated the odds; he no longer did so. Now that the battle was joined and he was part of it, now that the outcome was of great personal importance, it became a mental impossibility for him to envision any end but victory. In retrospect the experience would be somewhat eerie, a little daft.

Never once as he watched the fight did he lose contact with reality: one by one the birds were dying; he knew exactly which ones; he knew exactly where they were falling; he knew how they met their death; he knew Purple Top was still on his feet. He saw the bet-takers still circulating: bets could be made up to the very last pair. He heard Kitty cry, "We're lucky! Their odds won't be so good!" and knew what she meant: as each bird managed to survive nearer and nearer to the finish, the odds would narrow, and anyone who bet on the last pair would get only even odds.

But the eerie thing, the daft thing was this: superimposed on the actual picture of the fight which he saw taking place before his eyes there came a mental picture, just as sharp, just as real, of Purple Top standing alone in the pit and all his enemies dead around him. So strong, so convincing was this prevision of victory that it blotted out everything else. In his mind's eye there was a blind spot. That blind spot was Defeat.

Thus it was utterly impossible for him to imagine losing, and he sat perfectly composed while everyone else, prey to normal suspense and uncertainty which he did not, could not, feel, made a great deal of commotion and uproar.

Presently the two pictures merged into one: Purple Top did actually stand alone, victorious.

Kitty sank limp against his shoulder. "We won, Jock! We won!"

"Of course we did."

She looked at him. "I must say, you're very cool about it. One would think you knew all the time."

He frowned uneasily. "Somehow I did."

"But you couldn't have."

"I did though, Kitty."

"That's rather frightening," she said. Then she slipped her arm through his and said, "No, I think I'll just let you take me to all the cockfights from now on."

A week prior to Jock's departure Colonel Fielding found business that took him conveniently out of town, avoiding any connection with the *Misericordia*. "It's a pity I can't see you off, Jock. I'd looked forward to drinking a stirrup cup with you and Captain Newton in the cabin."

"That would have been a pleasure, sir. Do you go aboard the *Misericordia* often?"

Fielding said, "The truth is, I boarded her only once, two years ago, when I bought her in Tobago. I can't be too careful in these matters, you know, though of course her reputation is perfectly clean. I've seen to that."

"I've looked her over a couple of times on the quay."

"Well? Are you satisfied?"

"She's a beautiful ship. I wonder if you ever noticed her odor."

"How could I? I never go near her." But Fielding looked concerned. "Is it bad?"

"Not bad, but it's there."

"We can't have that. I shall speak to Newton. No, you shall speak to Newton. No, he is so used to it he'd say it wasn't there. Get rid of it yourself, before you return."

"I'll try. I took occasion to introduce myself to Captain Newton the other night in the Turk's Head."

Fielding smiled. "A very logical place to find him, I should think."

"A good many of my customers drop in there, for a glass or a chat during an evening. I found that the captain already knew me."

"Yes, I know. I pointed you out the other day and told him about you. Under the circumstances I couldn't very well have him over for tea to introduce you formally."

"I understand."

"You'll find him an amiable fellow."

"He was extremely amiable in the tavern. In fact, I had to take him in tow after his fourth bottle and pilot him aboard. I was a little afraid he might get too talkative."

"No," Fielding said, "Newton drinks, but he doesn't talk. Your reputation is quite safe."

"I wasn't thinking entirely of my own, sir."

"Mine? Thank you, Jock. That is really very good of you, and most tactful."

Jock looked at him.

"Oh," Fielding said, "I see. Not mine. Hers. That is even more important."

"Yes, sir."

"She didn't want to come with me on my trip," Fielding said, cocking an eye at Jock.

"Are you taking her?"

"When she doesn't want to come? My dear fellow. Of course not. What an extraordinary suggestion."

Willie said, "My pet, can't we walk in the garden too? I should very much like to. Moon's bigger than I ever saw it. I told Jock it was big. They shouldn't have it all to themselves."

Bessie smiled. "I think we'd be selfish to intrude. In a few hours he'll sail."

"Aye, so he will, and I'm sorry. I've liked having him here."

"We both have."

"Odd, isn't it, how Colonel Fielding lets Kitty stay alone in that big house? Of course, he lets her do anything she pleases; but he spoils her, if you ask me. You know what people will say. A self-willed girl like that might take it into her pretty head to do almost anything."

"Now, Willie."

"It's my romantic nature, pet. Such a night, by gad! 'On such a night stood Dido with a willow in her hand upon the wild sea-banks and waved

78

her love to come again to —' hm, hm, it wasn't Fredericksburg; Carthage, I think it was, some such place. Dominie taught us in school. Never did understand how Dido could have waved a tree; don't even see why it had to be a willow. Love-language of some kind, perhaps, like the language of the flowers. 'Pansies, that's for thoughts.' Jock would know. He actually likes Shakespeare."

"Kitty isn't alone," Bessie said. "Mrs. Dandridge and her little girl have come over to stay with her while the colonel is away."

"Oh," he said, "Then it's all right. Very good family, the Dandridges."

Bessie gave him his tarwater.

"One day I vow that I shall heave this abominable stuff through a window."

"We mustn't have your whitlow nagging at you again, now must we?"

"Good gracious, no!" and he quaffed down the draught.

In the garden where Kitty and Jock walked arm in arm the brilliant moonlight flooded down. Some quirk in the nature of the light from the beautiful orb stole the red from the roses, leaving them ghosts of themselves, pallid-white or spectral-gray or mourning-black under the thieving moon.

"It's a sad night, Jock," she said.

He said, "I think I don't really like the moon."

He slipped his arm from her arm, to encircle her slender waist. She let herself be drawn close and measured her steps to his, so that their bodies moved together as one. The gravel path crunched softly under their feet. There were long silences.

"Tomorrow night will be a great deal sadder for me than tonight," he said.

The moonlight that robbed the roses lent an ethereal air to the exquisite woman beside him. Tomorrow she would be far away; tonight, in this bloodless moonlight, she seemed to assume already the pale quality of remembrance. It was too soon, too soon. He did not want to lose her. She found herself suddenly in his arms; he felt his kisses returned; her arms clung round him, answering his embrace; her hand slipped up the back of his neck, pressing his lips harder against hers. Perfect in feature and form he had always known her to be, but so were statues, and statues were cold, cold as moonlight.

Now, to feel her pliant, human, warm against him, for him, seemed an act of supererogation on the part of the angels who had lavished upon her their treasures of beauty, beauty a man might yearn to possess

79

but beauty beyond anything a man deserved. Mouth on his, she whispered, "I'll be lonesome while you're away. Will it be long?"

Jock knew it would be; he did not answer.

"A voyage to Jamaica and back oughtn't to be long," she said.

It would not be only to Jamaica and back. It would be to Africa and back. He could not tell her that. He said, "It will be long, dismally long for me."

"Jock, why don't you like the moon? I do."

"I like the stars better."

"Why?"

"Stars have color."

"But with only the stars," she said softly, "it would be terribly dark, wouldn't it?"

"Not terribly."

"You naughty, naughty man." Her laugh was low and infinitely enticing. It tugged at him physically, like an undersurface current sucking the ship the wrong way. He was afraid of himself, what he might do, and yet still more afraid of a reproach from her; how base she would think him if she could see into his thoughts. He sighed; but the sigh served only to press their bodies more closely together. Through the lace of her bodice, through his waistcoat, jacket and shirt, as if moonlight could steal not only color but the actual substance of clothing, as if naked against him, he could feel her breasts.

He said, as dispassionately as he could contrive, "The truly bad thing about the moon, Kitty, is that it shines so bright that it hides the stars. Stars stay fixed and you always know where you are, but the moon is impossible to steer by."

"Oh, dear," she said drawing away, "you're navigating already."

"My dear, dear love, I love you so!"

She pouted. "You do not seem to."

"Kitty, your father has given me permission to ask your hand."

"I know," she said in a smaller voice.

"Will you marry me, Kitty, when I return?"

"I would," she said, "if you really wanted me."

"Dear God, how sair I do!"

"I will," she said.

He said as they retraced their steps, "The cruel thing about the moon is that it brings floodtide to float the *Misericordia* out to sea."

She was gayer now. "I promise to curse all full moons till the one that brings the *Misericordia* back."

He would have to say something, if only a hint, about the length of his voyage. "There will be cargo to load and a certain amount of trading to be done in Jamaica, Kitty. That always slows things up a little."

"What in the world," she said primly, "do I know about trade?"

Chapter 10

BRITISH-BUILT, captured in her early youth and converted by Spaniards into a privateer, then sold in her middle age to Colonel Fielding, the Virginia planter: such was the checkered obscure career to date of the *Misericordia*. She was still a beautiful ship, a sailor's ship. Her 'tween-decks stank, and her bilges were foul with run-off vomit and sweat from countless suffering human cargoes she had carried from Africa to bondage in the New World. But her built-in excellencies remained: her swift and slender hull; her rakish masts, canted like a schooner's, of lithe New England pine, which, whiplike, would bend but never snap; her immense spread of sail. *Misericordia* was dashing. *Misericordia* was impudent. In her privateering days many a sturdy frigate captain, counting her gunports and reckoning her an easy prize, had watched her sail, as it seemed, point-blank into the eye of the wind as if self-propelled, and, as a consequence, shown her a prudent pair of heels, muttering, "The devil is in her!"

Misericordia would hug the wind tight as a lover, streaming a bow-wave of hissing white spume from her copper-sheathed prow, a golden knife-edge slicing the blue of the sea into a froth of cream on either side. To a practised nautical eye the length of her twin bow-waves was instructive, and frightening. They were long, hence *Misericordia* was fast. But there was another factor. As *Misericordia* sped into the wind's eye, the starboard bow-wave and the larboard bow-wave looked identical in length. At exactly the same distance astern, or so nearly that the eye could detect no difference, they would disappear. From this it was clear that the ship was sailing almost directly against the wind, a formidable, unusual and dangerous characteristic, bespeaking maneuverability that few ships could match. One had to be very brave, or very inexperienced, to approach her.

In her privateering days, too, her Spanish captain, with a flair for the elegant, had mantled her quarter-deck with teakwood planking: Jock Paul and his second officer now trod a deck of obsidian black and obsidian smoothness.

Misericordia was not, probably, her original name. Under the golden letters that the Spaniards had nailed on, painted out and forgotten was probably a beefy British name like *Bristol Pride,* or *Speedwell* or *Fleet.* Wryly, with a view to the trade in which she was now engaged, Fielding had let the name *Misericordia* remain.

In the great cabin, in a bunk above which the stubborn imprint of a Spanish crucifix, now removed, could still be seen on the fading tapestry, John Newton lay drunk.

From Fredericksburg to Jamaica, Newton had captained the *Misericordia* competently; but once in Jamaica, his trade rum aboard, he had shut himself up, as if with a long-yearned-for love, to his bed, his bottle, and his solitary vice. His meals, untouched, went back to the cook, who shook his head and sighed. He rang his bell more and more often for more and more bottles of rum, the vicious brain-searing trade rum for which he lusted, till it seemed to Jock that surely he would drink himself dead before they reached Africa.

"Is it always like this?" Jock asked.

"You'll see," the second officer answered.

"It would be awkward if he should die."

"Would it?"

"It certainly would," Jock said impatiently. The second officer was the thin-ribbed man Captain Newton had elbowed so forcibly at the cockfight.

"He won't die, Mr. Paul," the second officer said.

Under the moon that had shone so full on Willie's garden and stolen the red from the roses and wrought other marvels of magic, now rising late and yellow and old, chased by the hot early sun of the tropics, the *Misericordia* sped east over the mighty bulge of the Atlantic towards the Bight of Benin in the Guinea Gulf, an eerie place for Jock because there, and only there on the face of the planet, existed a spot that possessed neither latitude nor longitude. With frantic speed and straining sails the *Misericordia* was dashing over featureless seas to navigational Nothing, where all instruments measured Zero, and where, if anyone were to believe the reports that filtered out to the outside world, a man's character too might sink to Zero. "The Bight of Benin, the Bight of Benin; few come out though many go in." A jingle and nothing more, thought Jock; an exaggeration.

One sweltering day the drunken grunts and ribald songs that had issued for many days from the great cabin were suddenly interspersed with doleful hymns, sung in a shaky monotone like a travesty of a chant of the Old Religion, as if the poor captain were experiencing some painful and private purgatory, intensely his own. He was. He was sobering up.

"What is that, Mr. Webb?" Jock asked.

The second officer said nonchalantly, "The usual. Pretty soon he'll be calling for his chalice, and then he'll walk out of his bloody cabin, dry as a bloody harmattan and a stone-weight lighter. You'll see."

Among the curiosa that the Spanish privateer had left behind when the *Misericordia* was sold was a Catholic chalice, used in the Roman Mass.

"He always drinks his last bottle out of that popish cup," the second officer said, snickering. "Eases his conscience, he says."

"I wonder why."

"Who knows?" And the shrug of Thomas Webb, second officer of the *Misericordia*, eloquently added, "Who cares?"

"What a strange man Captain Newton is."

"Maybe you'll be strange too after a few voyages in this trade."

Jock said with perfect conviction, "I do not conceive that this trade differs in the slightest degree from any other trade."

Webb touched his forelock respectfully. "Mister Paul, sir," he said, "it is going to be a real pleasure to work alongside of you. Captain Newton now, he worries about these things."

The captain emerged from his cabin a few days later, faultlessly attired and steady of foot, but ghastly pale and thin as a prisoner just out of jail, blinking in the sunlight as if it hurt his eyes.

"Where are we, Mr. Paul?"

"Approaching Lagos, sir."

Newton nodded complacently. "God has blessed us with favorable winds," he said. "We don't usually reach Lagos so quickly."

"They were the usual winds," Jock said.

The captain looked at him oddly.

"I don't see how they could have been. Of course, I have not yet read your logbook. I shall tonight. But the usual winds are head winds on the southern passage."

"We are not on the southern passage, sir. I took her north to catch the westerlies. It was faster."

"That was wrong. That was dangerous and contrary to my explicit orders." In better health, or with a better personal record, the captain would have angrily upbraided his new first officer. "Perhaps I ought to remind you, Mr. Paul, that the northern route swarms with enemy ships. It is providential that none of them attacked us. They didn't, did they?"

"They did not, sir."

83

Thomas Webb was standing by, showing all his snaggly tobacco-stained teeth in an insolent grin, prepared to enjoy the discomfiture of his captain, who was obviously about to hear for the first time what had happened in the world while he lay drunk.

Jock said, "Mr. Webb, I think you failed to give me the report on those chains that I asked for."

"Eh?"

"Do not say 'eh' to me."

"Chains, sir?"

"How many extra pairs of manacles were put aboard in Jamaica? There should have been fifty, both wrist and ankle. I do not want us cheated. Report any shortage. How many were left over from the last trip? Are they in good condition? Are they rusty? Did the vinegar rust them? Rust rots iron. If they are rusty, have them scraped and oiled. See to this personally, Mr. Webb, and report to me."

"You want me to count all those gyves myself?"

It would take hours.

"I think that is what I requested, several days ago."

"Oh, all right."

"I beg your pardon?"

Webb amended his reply. "Aye, aye, *sir.*"

"Thank you, Mr. Webb."

The second officer saluted, scowling, and shuffled off the beautiful teakwood quarter-deck, muttering under his breath, "Damned Scotch kiltie wants man-of-war routine aboard a bloody slaver!" But he counted the chains.

"For a man who fails to obey his own superior you are somewhat rigorous towards your subordinates," Captain Newton observed.

"Webb wanted to gloat, sir. I sent him away so he couldn't. When the captain is temporarily incapacitated, I do not think it beneficial to ship's discipline to permit an officer to indulge in sneers."

"I suppose I should thank you," Newton said wearily. But it seemed to the captain that young Mr. Paul must have been born with very cool blood in his veins, if any.

"During your illness, Captain Newton, some important events have occurred. You were not in a position to appreciate their gravity at the time."

They had learned in Jamaica, Jock said, that old King George II was dead, and King George III now sat on the British throne, first of the Hanoverians to speak without a German accent. English born, English bred and English in outlook, George III was determined with all the force of

84

his powerful personality to bring the long, costly (but very successful) war to a close. The newspapers were enthusiastic. Canada and India were won and incorporated into the British Empire; France was humbled; Spain, in her impotence, was tractable, Gibraltar was permanently safe for Britain; Prussia, triumphant like England, was willing to pause; and beyond the Urals, Russia, digesting large areas of ravished Poland, had turned her enigmatic face eastwards against Turkey, her interest in Europe waning. The whole world was ripe for peace. "True, sir, no treaty has yet been signed, but everything points to one soon. Meanwhile, all the old enemies are very polite to one another, avoiding incidents that might upset the peace that everyone wants. It seemed to me safe, therefore, to strike north and catch the steady westerlies instead of beating against head winds all the way to Lagos on the southern route."

"Did we meet any ships?"

"Several. But they did not close."

The captain nodded and thanked him gruffly, surveying the ship with eyes that saw better now. *Misericordia* was taut and clean and smelled fresh.

"What is that odor, Mr. Paul?"

"Vinegar, I expect. I scrubbed her inside and out after we left Jamaica. She didn't smell healthy."

Newton's mouth twisted into a grim smile. "Oh yes. I did that once. Once Hercules cleansed the Augean stables, too. If I remember, though, he did it only once. Didn't he have to divert a river?"

"Yes, he did."

"You must have needed quite a river of vinegar."

"It took a lot."

"She does smell better," the captain said. "Clean."

"Yes, sir."

"Jock, do you drink?"

"Sometimes," Jock said.

"A great deal?"

"No, I don't think so."

"You will."

"Why on earth should I?"

"Take my word for it," Newton said.

Chapter 11

WITH THE thoroughness and forethought that ran so deep in his nature, fortified by the conviction that only the well-informed succeed in life and rise, Jock pestered the captain for information concerning the slave trade.

"It will be helpful to the venture if I learn enough to speak with a reasonable air of authority," he said.

"Every trade has its peculiar vocabulary," the captain said. "To learn it is to learn the trade itself in an easy, quick and fundamental manner. You speak French, I understand; therefore no Frenchman will ever outwit you. You also speak the language of the sea; so to you the sea is understandable; it seems, for example, quite natural to you that the command 'Hard-a-larboard!' instantly swings the ship to starboard, though that is the exact opposite of what a landsman would expect. As for me, it may surprise you to know that when I was young I was destined for the Church: 'theandric,' 'antinominianism' and 'Homoousian' were terms I could discourse upon for long and happy hours, though of late I have had little occasion to use them. They and so many others, all beautiful, all soul-stirring, are part of the trade vocabulary of the Church." He paused, his brow furrowed, thinking back. "Another trade occupies me now," he continued, "and my ecclesiastical vocabulary is, as it were, silted over and buried.

"The technical vocabulary of a seasoned slaver is small and easy to acquire. That is because the trade itself is so simple. No special aptitude is required to buy and sell a helpless human being."

"You make it sound extremely objectionable," Jock said. "I do not see it in that light."

"I am aware that you do not; neither does Thomas Webb; that is why both of you will go further in this business than I. You have only to learn a few terms of the trade, Mr. Paul, and put them into action, and a bright future is yours, or at any rate, a rich one: 'dantica,' 'dash,' 'resident factor,' 'barracoon.' Consider the *dantica*. The caravans that come down to the coast from the highlands bring with them chained and clanking files of natives for sale. It must be understood, Mr. Paul, that we ourselves need not venture into the interior to capture slaves. That is done for us by the natives

86

themselves, in tribal wars or outright slaving raids. These caravans are always welcomed at a great and joyful celebration, the *dantica*, where there is much firing of muskets, like ships saluting each other, many speeches of greeting and a good deal of mutual gift-giving. There is also feasting, and there may be some convivial drinking, unless the caravan is Moslem. The Moslems do not drink; they 'make kef,' which is to say, they chew a weed that transports them into a state of delicious benignity — after the trading, naturally. Arab caravans avoid the coast at this time of year. That is perhaps fortunate for you. I should not like to see you making kef, Mr. Paul. The *dantica* always precedes the humdrum business of actually auctioning the slaves.

"Then there is the important detail of the 'dash.' You are not a politician, Mr. Paul? No, I thought not. It would be easier to explain the 'dash' to a politician, who would deem it normal. The 'dash' is simply a bribe. You 'dash' everybody: overseers, guards, guides, and of course the resident factor. The Portuguese governor also requires a 'dash,' though on his exalted level it is called a gratuity. To fail to 'dash' the governor invariably brings inexplicable delays in obtaining clearance papers for the ship.

"Now: the resident factor, and his barracoons. The resident factor is a middleman, usually a European, a wholesaler who purchases slaves on his own responsibility from the caravans. There are tales of resident factors who made their own raids into the interior, seeking to avoid the caravans' profit; there are no tales that they ever returned. In barracoons the factor herds the commodity of our trade till some likely ship takes them off his hands. Barracoons must be seen to be fully appreciated. To call them stockades is not enough. At the height of the trading season, and this is the height, they are so full that no ground is visible. It is possible to walk from one end of a barracoon to the other without once sullying the foot with earth, stepping only on kinky heads and shiny shoulders wet with sweat of massed men, women and children. A ship, by contrast, is commodious. On a ship they can lie down.

"That is all you need to know, Mr. Paul, of the trade which I believe you have stated differs in no wise from any other trade. It is merely more profitable. There is, I confess, one curious local word, the *customs*. But if God still hears my prayers, which is not very likely, you will never be required to learn the meaning of that word."

"Customs?" said Jock. "Some duty perhaps, some export tax? Some little additional gratuity to the Portuguese governor?"

"The condition of my stomach," the captain said, "is not yet sufficiently recovered to enable me to discuss the Ashanti customs."

"Who are the Ashanti?"

"The delightful tribe which supplies the entire Slave Coast with slaves. Have you ever seen a gorilla, Mr. Paul?"

Shortly Lagos, on its marshy island, rose steamy and green on the horizon; and beyond it, as the ship approached, stretched a smooth blue lagoon, a perfect roadstead big enough to shelter a hundred ships. On the mainland, dark and forest-clad, a range of long smooth hills billowed interminably eastward, up to a blazing copper sky. The heat was astonishing.

Chapter 12

AS THE *Misericordia* drew in towards the anchorage, a heavily laden ship under full sail made a hasty departure. The Bourbon lilies fluttered from her masthead. Captain Newton instantly ran up the Union Jack and glared at her through his spyglass.

"I wish we were to windward of that big Frenchman," he said. The Frenchman was showing his teeth; his ports were open, and all his guns shone darkly in the square openings that traced the long line of his gun-deck.

Jock gauged the distance. He knew what *Misericordia* was capable of. "We can still get to windward of her, sir."

"No," Newton said, "no, we'd better not. We'd only arouse his suspicions. If we're as close to peace as you say, he'll probably behave politely and pass on."

The *Misericordia* held her course, and so did the big Frenchman. Presently he dipped his flag in salute, Newton promptly returned the compliment, and the vessels drew near; they would pass each other at a distance of about a hundred yards. Framed in the shadows of the open ports, there could now be distinguished the tense faces of gunners and the glowing points of light that meant slow matches burning and ready in their hands. But Jock knew that the *Misericordia* presented a similar threatening aspect to the Frenchman.

"Even if the war were at its height," Jock said, smiling, "I doubt if yon ship would start a fight. He is full, we are empty. We'd kill enough of his cargo in a single broadside to take all the profit out of his voyage."

Newton snapped shut his spyglass. "You evince deep understanding of this trade, Mr. Paul," he said. Jock did not feel that the captain was complimenting him. "You are undoubtedly right. There is a certain sense of brotherhood among slavers, much as, I am told, there is among thieves. It must be remembered, however, that thieves do fall out from time to time. There were three crosses on Calvary. Those to the left and right were occupied by thieves. Their last words to each other were words of bitter altercation."

Jock flushed. It was not fair for the captain to preach him a sermon. If Newton didn't like the slave trade, why didn't he get out of it? "My conscience is perfectly clear," he said.

"How very fortunate for you," the captain said, and went on to explain. "Had we cut across his bows, Mr. Paul, and got to a better fighting position to windward of him, the French captain might have said to himself, 'The English ship is going to engage me and try to snatch a cargo on the cheap.' It is by no means unknown for an empty ship to attack a full one, smash her to pieces and steal what remains of her cargo, thus avoiding the unpleasant necessity of buying slaves ashore. So thieves, you see, do fall out, to this day."

"But that's piracy!" Jock gasped.

Newton sighed. "One thing leads to another."

Presently the Frenchman was passing abeam. Her captain and his officers stood on the quarter-deck. They had apparently just come from a farewell dinner ashore; their ruffles and stockings were clean and white. Simultaneously they raised their lace-edged cocked hats and bowed. The French always managed to show a deeper, more elegant fringe than the British. Jock, Webb, and the captain raised their hats in acknowledgment and the ships drew rapidly apart. A suffocating stench, like an invisible wake, streamed after the Frenchman and engulfed the *Misericordia* for a moment.

Newton sniffed the polluted air. "Ibos, I suspect."

"How in the world — ?"

"Stronger than the other tribes," the captain said. "The staple of the trade."

"How long have you been in this business, sir?" Jock asked.

"Long enough to know it stinks."

In the anchorage a trim little launch manned by two banks of native rowers cut swiftly out from the landing and came alongside the *Misericordia*. Seated under a faded awning that had once boasted an awesome combination of yellow, pink and purple striping, there sat in a wicker chair and permitted himself to be fanned a shriveled swarthy man in negligent European dress.

"We have here," Captain Newton said, "the barge of Duarte Bombarda, the resident factor of Lagos. He would seem to have had a fatiguing day, entertaining our Frenchman in all probability."

"Is his name really Bombarda?" Jock grinned.

"Bombarda is a genuine Portuguese family name and Bombarda is what he calls himself. It may be rightly his; I have never inquired. It may strike your Scotch ears as odd."

Bombarda also struck Jock's Scotch eyes as odd.

The launch crunched against *Misericordia's* side, and a yell of anger, followed by the hissing of a whip and a grunt of pain, floated up to the quarter-deck. "Bombarda must have missed his footing," Newton said.

Sweating with exertion and short of breath, the resident factor climbed awkwardly up the Jacob's ladder and paused, surveying the *Misericordia* and her officers with bloodshot eyes. In the lobe of his left ear a diamond sparkled; in his right fist there was the whip. Newton stepped forward to give him a hand over the rail.

"For a moment I feared you might have suffered an accident," the captain said. "Welcome aboard, Senhor Duarte."

"Accident!" shouted the factor. "It was not an accident. I have stubbed my toe. My foot will rot off. God damn your ladder. God damn you too."

Jock stiffened, but Newton calmed him with a knowing glance. Webb whispered to Jock, "He's only a little drunk. It's worse when he's sober. Then he's polite and you have to be on your guard."

"I shall have the ladder weighted, so that next time it will not swing," Newton said. "Will you join me and my officers in a drink, Senhor Duarte?"

"In the sun? No, by God."

"Certainly not. In my cabin."

"I will," said the resident factor.

"I think you know Mr. Webb?"

Bombarda grunted something unpleasant. Webb grinned and saluted.

"And this is my new first officer, Mr. Paul."

"Ah," said Bombarda, squinting at him. "I knew your predecessor, Mr. Paul. I liked him."

"We all did," Newton said.

Bombarda said, "He met with an unfortunate accident. You have probably heard."

"Mr. Paul is new to Africa," Newton said, "and no doubt he will learn all that in due time."

"I shall drink to Mr. Paul and his predecessor," Bombarda said, with such concentrated venom in his voice as Jock had never heard; but to whom the hatred was directed Jock could not at the moment guess.

In the cabin the hate was clarified. Duarte Bombarda solemnly raised his glass. "To your predecessor, Mr. Paul. The Ashanti ate him, piece by piece, till he died." He drained his glass. "This is excellent rum, Captain Newton." He fanned himself with his hat. The rum seemed to revive and freshen him; his manner grew less abrupt. "The accident at the foot of the ladder was not your fault, Captain Newton. One of my rowers is clumsy. A new man. Is it a thing of no consequence to stub the toe of the resident factor? It is not. I have promised him a lesson. To escape punishment the coward, of course, claims to be sick. Sick, ha! Sick he is not, but sick he shall be. Yes." Bombarda held out his glass. Newton filled it.

"Eminently just," Newton said.

"I am always just," Bombarda said, scowling into the clear-coffee depths of his rum. "No," he amended, "I am not perhaps strictly just. To be *strictly* just I should eat an Ashanti. Alas, I cannot. So I must dispense my justice in other ways."

"*You* were not eaten," the captain said.

The hate growled in Bombarda's voice again. "A white man was."

Jock's throat constricted; he could barely sip his rum; in his glass it had turned to white man's blood. The African trade presented unexpected aspects.

"How many can you take this trip?" Bombarda asked.

"How many do you have?"

"How many can you take?"

Quantity, Jock rightly reasoned, as in any other trade, affected price.

"I should like to see the barracoons," the captain said.

"Then I must see your ship."

Newton smiled. "Haven't you already? My ports were open."

Bombarda set down his empty glass and laughed. "For a man who pretends to dislike his profession," he said to Jock, "your Captain Newton is a miracle. He is my shrewdest customer; I delight in him; I love him. When the *Misericordia* sails into my beautiful stinking lagoon, I say to myself, 'Here comes the whetstone to sharpen the wits of Duarte Bombarda, the resident factor of Lagos.' This time, Captain, when you and I have finished our pleasant trading, six hundred filthy devils will depart forever from Africa."

91

Newton raised his eyebrows. "Six hundred, Senhor Duarte? I took five hundred last time."

Bombarda waggled a finger at him. "Ah yes, Captain. But I did look through your open ports, and there in the gun deck I saw the extra manacles. You approach me this time to propose a larger purchase at a quantity price, no? I delight to oblige. The more of the fiends I dispatch into servitude the better I am pleased. Manacles on the gun deck! What a novel expedient. Who else would have thought of it? Not that stupid Frenchman. His gun deck was clean as a man-of-war's. Such a waste of space. I had to drink brandy with him. I detest brandy. No, he could not have thought of it. Only Captain Newton, who pretends to dislike his profession, could think of it. Is my Captain Newton a Jew? No, he was raised to the Church — the wrong Church, of course, but better than juju. Is Captain Newton a Scotchman? No, he is English as mutton. I mean no offense. I love mutton. Is he Portuguese? The saints forbid! So, since he is none of the clever races, he is — what?" The resident factor shrugged eloquently; his hands waved in a Latin gesture of utter helplessness. "So — he is a living miracle."

Newton said, "Yes, with the additional quarters on the gun deck I think I can accommodate about six hundred this trip. But I wonder if you have that many, prime. The Frenchman was low in the water. He must have taken a great many."

"You shall see my barracoons," Bombarda promised confidently. "I am plentifully stocked. There has been a great war in the interior."

"They are Ibos?"

"Yes, but I don't know how you know."

"I sensed they might be Ibos."

At the foot of the Jacob's ladder the launch waited for Bombarda. One of the rowers lay slumped on the floorboards, motionless. Subdued, excited voices, muttering in Ibo, floated up. "Chima is going to die, they say," the captain translated, answering Jock's glance. "Perhaps it is just as well. Chima, whoever he is, will escape Bombarda's justice."

The whip whizzed again, but this time there was no grunt of pain. They heard Bombarda snarling as he clambered into the boat, "Malingerer! Filth! Fraud! I shall teach you to stub the toe of Duarte Bombarda!" Then, cheerily to the captain, "Till tomorrow, my dear Captain!"

"Till tomorrow, Senhor Duarte!"

Newton said in a low voice to Jock, "I did not think it necessary to tell Bombarda that the extra accommodation on the gun deck was decidedly not my idea. He seemed to fancy the notion."

"I am sure there will be peace, and that it will prove safe," Jock said.

"I hope you are right."

"It will mean a twenty-per-cent gain."

"Wastage usually amounts to just about that — sickness — deaths — the births aboard never make up the deficit — the babies almost always die, too."

"In that case I calculate this trip ought to average exactly one hundred per cent, that is to say, as if there were no wastage at all."

Newton looked at him. "Bombarda did you the honor of classing you with the clever races, Mr. Paul. I am inclined to agree with him."

Jock was a little taken aback. "But he called *you* a miracle, sir."

"Would you have preferred that?"

Jock did not answer. He did not know. In both Newton and Bombarda the slave trade seemed to have aroused intense emotions, different in character but equally strong, which he did not understand and simply could not feel.

"I noticed that you neglected to finish the toast to your predecessor, Mr. Paul."

"I think I shall drink it now," Jock said, somewhat testily.

"Pray do. It is still in the cabin. I shall not join you, if you don't mind."

The proper reply was, "Thank you, sir." "I do not mind in the least," was what Jock said, and he entered the cabin and drank the toast alone; it tasted like any other rum.

The factory of Duarte Bombarda — for such was the designation of the resident factor's establishment — greatly surprised Jock by its spaciousness. He had expected he knew not what; perhaps a slovenly version of Willie's plantation in Fredericksburg. But the factory was far from slovenly. Many an English lord of the manor might have envied the acres of lawn, the gardens and well-trimmed hedges that surrounded Bombarda's house. Jock wondered what it must cost to keep up such a place, remembering that the laird of Arbigland could afford only one gardener. But on reflection he realized that it cost nothing at all. Nowhere in the world was labor so cheap as in Lagos.

Bombarda himself had come with his launch to escort them ashore, protesting that the *Misericordia's* boat had no awning and that under no circumstances would he permit his guests to expose themselves to the African sun. The landing had been covered by pink mats, rolled down for their special use, rolled up immediately after they had walked the few steps to where sedan chairs awaited them. African chieftains provided mats for distinguished visitors, much as red carpeting was provided in Europe for royalty; Duarte Bombarda provided mats for his customers.

Jock knew that sedan chairs were fashionable in England and on the Continent, especially in France, for Henri had told him much about the delights of this effortless mode of travel. But he had never seen one before, neither in America nor, of course, in Scotland. In fact, the mental picture of a sedan chair jogging over the heather-clad Scottish hills was so incongruous that he almost burst out laughing as he stepped into his chair. It had a pink roof, and he discovered that, if he wished, he might close the pink curtains with which it was provided to keep out the insects. Presently two stalwart Negroes placed themselves fore and aft between the poles and picked up the chair. Jock found himself being borne, smooth as a ship in harbor, over the walks and among the hedges that led to the little rise on which stood Bombarda's residence. Bombarda, Webb and Captain Newton were each being carried in a similar chair. It was certainly better than walking in the sun. It was certainly a pleasant way to live. He leaned back to relax and enjoy the ride, as the carriers sweated and labored up the slope.

But Jock could not quite relax. Bombarda's landscaping irritated him; it was all wrong; it did not make sense; it was neither formal like a city park nor casual like a country estate. "If you wanted to be a landscape gardener, you should have stayed in Scotland," he muttered to himself. "This is Africa." But the African arrangement of the hedges, clumps here and clumps there, was undeniably bizarre. The carriers seemed to avoid them. This caused Jock to scrutinize them only the more closely.

All at once everything was clear. Bombarda's landscaping made sense after all. Behind each hedge, painted as green as the foliage, pointed squarely at the lagoon where the *Misericordia* lay at anchor, was a cleverly concealed cannon. Beside each cannon, neatly piled, were round shot, also painted green. Green cannon balls are not seen every day of the week. The pattern of the hedges, too, made sense. No hedge was squarely behind any other until higher up the slope so that the shot would clear. Bombarda's factory could evidently fire a broadside equal in weight to that of a dozen frigates at any moment. No ship in the anchorage would have the slightest chance against such a powerful secret fortress. It wasn't landscaping, thought Jock, but it was superb engineering.

Gently, for a jolt would have been unthinkable, his carriers set him down before the heavily screened verandah of Bombarda's residence. A smartly liveried major-domo who, except that he wore no shoes, might have headed the staff of servants in the finest household in Fredericksburg, was stirring a large bowl of punch. Beside him a girl, so fair that Jock thought she was white, was adding lemons and limes. Yet Senhora Bombarda, if a Senhora Bombarda existed, could hardly have been employed at such a task. In any event, the major-domo would not have spoken to her so sharply as now he did. The girl, whose face had been extremely sad, now managed to smile, as at an order. The other sedan chairs drew up, and Bombarda welcomed his guests into his house. His house, he said, with all it contained, was at their pleasure, nay, was actually theirs. He spoke so sincerely and bowed so low that Jock thought he meant it; but the captain answered with some polite conventionality or other, and Jock realized that Bombarda was merely transliterating an empty Portuguese formula of greeting. Presently, the punch having been brought to its peak of perfection, the major-domo retired to supervise (and to quiet) the noisy activities in the kitchen, where a dinner was in preparation; the girl had disappeared; and Bombardo, with a silver ladle, filled crystal glasses with punch and served one with his own hand to each of his guests: "Captain Newton? Mr. Paul? Mr. Webb?" Instinctively Webb saluted. Jock found himself saying, "Thank you, sir," most respectfully. Even Newton behaved as if in the presence of a superior. The grand air came naturally to Bombarda. One wondered who he was, but no one knew. Jock had asked, and Newton had shaken his head. "On the Slave Coast such questions are not diplomatic. Some Portuguese grandee, perhaps, exiled, in disgrace, God knows. Maybe he murdered his wife. He is not incapable of murder."

"You keep a happy household, Senhor Duarte," Jock said. "On a first visit one is pleasantly struck by your superb service and the smiles that surround you."

Bombarda said fiercely, "Mr. Paul, I demand smiles." And then, his trader's mind at work, more suavely, "It pleases the customers."

"When I was a boy in Scotland," Jock said, "I learned something of the gardener's art. I have been much impressed with yours."

Bombarda stared at him.

Newton smiled. "You will discover, Senhor Duarte, that my first officer has extremely sharp eyes. When no one else can see through a fog, I depend on Mr. Paul for a lookout. He has spotted your guns."

"That is most unusual so soon," Bombarda said. "Only last week I had everything freshly painted. But what would you do, Mr. Paul? Consider my position. Behind me lurk a thousand bloodthirsty savages. They hate me. I return the compliment. Before me in the lagoon come armed ships of all nations, and not all my customers are so trustworthy as Captain Newton.

Many of them are as savage as the cargoes they buy. Do not merchants in Scotland protect their warehouses by certain deterrents to thieves?"

"Aye, that they do," said Jock.

"And Scotland, by all accounts, is a civilized country. How much more alert must I not keep myself in Africa, which is not civilized. *Maria Santísima!* How unholy uncivilized Africa is!"

"You would seem to have civilized your portion of it at any rate," Jock said. The regal mats, the sedan chairs, the truly excellent punch — never had he been received with such distinction.

The resident factor's dinner was long, delicious and full of strange dishes that Jock had never tasted before, pleasantly peppery and obviously designed to create a thirst. The major-domo stood by with a crystal decanter to refill their glasses. Glancing at this factotum, Jock got the notion that his smile, which never faded from his big black face, was decidedly strained. Bombarda growled something in a low unintelligible voice. The major-domo's hand shook as if he were suddenly seized with a bout of fever; the wine in the decanter danced; he answered his master in a flood of pleading, excited Ibo.

"I had thought to provide you with a prettier face than this," Bombarda said, pointing his knife at the major-domo as if he would willingly skewer him. "But Dolores has taken it upon herself to desert her post. She is only half trained and still restive. She cannot have gone far. You must content yourselves with being served by this gorilla here."

"It's quite all right," Newton said. "He is quite acceptable."

The major-domo, sweating with fear, looked as if he could kiss Newton's hand. Jock got the idea that the captain might have saved him a whipping. He wondered who Dolores was, and must have looked it.

"Do I see interest in your eyes, Mr. Paul?" Bombarda asked, his smile oily and insinuating. "Alas, my friend, I cannot accommodate you. Dolores is not for sale."

Something in Jock's face made Bombarda pause.

"Do not look at me like that, sir!" he barked. "I will not be misunderstood! I would rather copulate with a swine — yes, by the Great Holy Mother of God, with a swine — than copulate with a Negro!"

"It was not my intention to offend you," Jock said quietly. "In fact, I did not say a word."

"You did not have to. You looked."

"You need not take offense and you need not be offensive," Captain Newton said, pushing away his glass, his eye level and steady upon Bombarda.

96

Bombarda wiped his forehead. "Fan me," he said to the major-domo. Calmer, he said, "I call her Dolores because no one can pronounce her Ibo name, which is Nwa-Eji-Gbo-Agha: it means, 'She-Who-Was-Given-To Avert-War.' But that is only her Ibo name. What her Fulani name is I do not know. She will not divulge it. It does not matter. Dolores is not, of course, an Ibo. You can tell at a glance: her long limbs; her narrow feet; her heel — the heel is always significant; Fulani heels do not protrude — her slender hips; her rounder, higher breasts; everything is different, finer; also her wavy hair and delicate nostrils; oh, totally, basically different."

"Was Dolores perhaps the woman I saw with the lemons and limes?"

"Yes."

"I thought she was a white woman."

"She is black as purgatory," Bombarda said savagely. "I sell thousands of Fulani."

"Concede, Senhor Duarte," the captain said smiling, "that they are the lightest of the Negroes and are often mistaken for whites. There is, indeed, a legend among them that they *are* white, or at least that originally they were before they intermixed."

"That legend is nonsense," Bombarda said.

"She goes by a curious name," Jock said idly. He must not let it appear that Bombarda's enumeration of Dolores's physical attributes, which had certainly been explicit, flattering and to judge from the glance he had had of her, thoroughly deserved, had stirred him. The resident factor had been dealing in the technical terms of his trade — one grade of stuff is finer, lighter in color than another — and on such a basis Jock, as a fellow trader, must keep the conversation.

Bombarda leaned back in his chair. It was not, Jock noticed, like the other chairs, but high-backed with a faded crest in the fabric over his head. Bombarda smiled broadly. Quite by accident Jock had said just the right thing. Bombarda launched into his favorite theme: war and death, death by the thousands, death with unspeakable suffering, among the natives of the interior. These deaths never affected his trade. The tribes never exterminated one another. The jungles contained too many for that. Actually, instead of wiping each other out, they had learned to curb their killing because on the Coast in places like Lagos there were dealers like Bombarda with yawning barracoons. After every war the captives streamed in. Wasn't slavery better than death? Even for a white man? The Romans had thought so.

"Of course, Rome fell," Newton said.

Bombarda said, "All nations fall. So will Britain."

"Oh come, come, senhor!"

Bombarda said, "I who live in exile in African darkness, in the midnight of Portugal's greatness, which once was a mighty empire, have learned to see things that are hidden from others; but my eye is a spiritual eye, unlike the mere sharpness of physical vision enjoyed by your first officer, who detected my cannon." Bombarda was not drunk; he was not even boasting; he was comfortable, relaxed and speaking the truth, at least as he saw it. "What do I see in your British victories, in the long war which is drawing to a close — "

Newton glanced at Jock, who raised his eyebrows as much as to say, "You see? They know it even in Africa."

"Oh, it is closing, Captain Newton; I hear it from every source."

"Peace is always a blessing," the captain said.

"Humph!" said Bombarda. "I shall tell you what I see in your glorious victories, in this blazing high noon of your greatness. I see a twilight, creeping, insidious, the twilight of Britain."

"It certainly would not appear so."

"Twilight is never apparent at noon, but it never fails to follow. That is what the Ibos, your cargo, my dear Captain, have also just experienced.

"They were the most powerful tribe in Africa until last week, excepting, of course, the Ashanti. The Fulani stood in particular dread of them and were particularly menaced by them. The Oba — that is the Ibo king, Mr. Paul. His palace courtyard is most interestingly paved. The cobblestones sound hollow when trodden upon. They are skulls. This Oba of the Ibos, sitting in Benin among his cobblestones, dispatched an ambassador to the Sultan of the Fulani, where, being received, he chewed off the head of a chicken and spat it into the sultan's face, thus declaring war. This behavior was offensive, by African standards."

"I should think it would be," Jock said.

"The insult was the chicken, Mr. Paul. A chicken is a bird despised for its cowardice. Its blood now defiled and weakened the sultan, since in Africa blood is supposed to impart the character of its original owner on contact. Thus an African would bathe in the blood of a lion — in fact, they all do — but sedulously avoid the blood of a chicken."

Jock was glad he was no longer eating dinner. Duarte Bombarda's conversation was not one to stimulate the appetite.

"Now a curious thing occurred," Bombarda continued. "Instead of taking offense, the sultan received the Ibo ambassador very courteously, spoke softly to him and dwelt on the blessings of peace. Instead of causing the war drums to be beaten, he summoned Dolores. It is rumored that she is one of

98

his daughters; of course one cannot know, but in such cases they are always of noble birth. He offered her up as tribute to the Oba of Benin. All the native kings are plentifully supplied with wives, especially the Fulani, who are nominally Moslem; so the girl of herself was of no great value, beautiful as she is. But for the proud Fulani to offer tribute is unheard of in my knowledge of the Coast. Still, offered she was, and the ambassador took her to Benin for such use as the Oba, who is seventy years old, might care to make of her, or could."

Jock smiled. "If I were an Oba, even seventy years old, I think I'd have welcomed the tribute, which is decorative, to say the least. But apparently the Oba did not want her, or you would not have acquired her."

Bombarda shook with silent laughter. "Mr. Paul, I have acquired not only her but also the Ibo ambassador who fetched her and fifteen hundred more Ibos as well. You see, 'She-Who-Was-Given-To-Avert-War' did not avert war. The Ibos attacked anyhow. There was a tremendous conflict. Even the lions fled the scene, though they came back later, I understand, to clean up. So furious were the Fulani at the Ibo breach of faith that they fought like fiends, and the Ibos were defeated. On this the Fulani sold their captives to the Ashanti, and the Ashanti, good fellows that they are, obligingly sold them to me, Duarte Bombarda, the resident factor of Lagos, who always deal honestly. I take some pride in my barracoons; they are clean; they are large; but you must believe when I tell you that for some days after the Ibo defeat they were uncommonly crowded. They are now, I am happy to say, again in most excellent condition. You wanted to see them, Captain? I shall be delighted to conduct you. We should be about it, I suggest, while there is still daylight. I am not one of those factors who exhibit their merchandise in the dark."

"You know I would not inspect them in the dark," Newton said.

"What became of the ambassador?" Jock asked.

Bombarda scowled. "I thought to make a rower of him and keep him. He had a remarkable physique. But he is no good, a disappointment. I shall get rid of him."

"Sell him?" Jock asked.

"Yes, if anybody will buy him after I teach him not to stub a white man's toe. Not you, Captain Newton. You would not buy him. He will not be worth much."

Jock wondered whether the resident factor of Lagos would perhaps personally witness the punishment. He suspected he would. That seemed unnecessary; a merchant should not stand by and gloat over the destruction of a disappointing piece of merchandise. Why could not Bombarda, why could not Newton, view this trade like any other trade? But then, in all fairness, he asked himself whether he viewed the Fulani girl as if she were a piece of merchandise. There are advantages to the practical logical mind: he had to admit that he did not so view her. Africa was lush, hot, and he was far from Fredericksburg and Kitty.

Objectionable animals, like pigs, have always been housed on the outskirts of any well-ordered establishment in which they constitute an element of its economy lest their squalor and smell offend the inhabitants, while nobler animals, like horses, are stabled close; and thus it was with the barracoons. They were situated on the outskirts, well to the rear of Bombarda's residence, over the brow of the hill on a gentle declivity that sloped down to the marshes of Lagos Lagoon. Fortlike, with watchtowers every twenty paces, they were big enclosures open to the sky, formed of stout stakes driven deep into the earth and pointed on top. The brush had been cleared for fifty feet beyond the stockade. Escape would have been impossible even for a man unencumbered by chains. All the captives were chained, not individually (which would have tempted some of the bolder spirits) but in strings of a dozen. "There is always at least one in a dozen," Bombarda said with satisfaction, "who will, for a price, inform on anyone who might try to escape. In this they are almost human." An armed guard unbarred the gate and let them in.

In the slanting sun of the late afternoon, which shed a ruddy light over the massed humanity within — gold on black so that they looked like beings of precious bronze, and precious they were, more precious than bronze — Jock saw turned towards him a sea of living faces, each face alert and questioning, wide-eyed. There was no hatred in their glance, certainly none such as glared from Bombarda's eyes as he held to his outraged nostrils a lace handkerchief heavily scented with camphor. "I have tried everything," he complained, "attar of roses, frangipani, thousand-flowers-water: camphor alone is effective." He offered the handkerchief to Jock. "Permit me," he said.

Jock grinned. "I shouldn't think of depriving *you*, senhor."

"My dear sir, do you imagine I came unprepared?" and Bombarda whipped out another from his pocket.

"I don't mind the odor," Jock said.

Neither, apparently, did Newton, whose face was stern as if he were drinking bitter beer.

"In that case let us proceed," Bombarda said. He drew their attention to the salient points of the merchandise. "Observe the cleanliness, the order, the excellent sewage disposal: the barrels are emptied every day. Observe the brimming cooking pots. They are always full. All they wish, whenever they wish, I permit my Negroes to eat. Regard them. Are they thin? Are they weak? Are they palsied, feverish, spotted, sick? No. They are sleek, fat, happy, strong, and the wounds left from the recent war will quickly heal. Prime stock. Prime condition. If you do not believe me — ha! ha! ha! — point me a pale one, Mr. Paul, point me a pale one!" Jock was new to the trade; the factor's well-worn joke produced its effect and he laughed heartily. Newton, who had heard it before, did not even smile. His face was sterner than ever, and there was a curious glint in his eyes which Jock had not observed since Newton had come out of his long bout with the bottle. Yet the captain had drunk very little at dinner, and could not possibly be intoxicated. The factor continued to pilot them through the barracoons.

Jock noticed that no escort was provided. He, the captain, Webb and Bombarda walked alone and unarmed, four in the midst of perhaps five hundred, which was the present population of that particular stockade.

"They seem happy," he said, pretending a casualness that he did not feel, "and they seem tame."

"They are tame," Bombarda said. "I have tamed them. All in a week I have tamed them. Nay, sir, I have *trained* them. Did you ever train an intelligent dog, Mr. Paul?"

Jock thought back to his pets in Arbigland and the sheep dogs, almost human in understanding, of his neighbors.

"Why, yes, Senhor Duarte. I have trained dogs, and horses too."

"Not horses. *Dogs!*" Bombarda spat out the word. He glared at his dogs and wafted his camphor handkerchief under his nose. "And how did you train your dogs, Senhor Paul?"

Jock said, "Like everybody, I suppose: reward for obedience, chastisement when they wouldn't behave."

"An excellent word, Senhor Paul. Chastisement. I too chastise, to the end that all shall be orderly, disciplined, and well behaved. Those are the qualities one expects in a good dog; those are the qualities one expects in a good slave; those are the qualities which I, Duarte Bombarda, inculcate in my living — I do not say human — merchandise, to civilize and make them profitable. Yes."

"Ask him how," Newton said hollowly.

Bombarda showed all his teeth in a smile of commercial ingratiation. Was there actually such a thing, Jock wondered, as a laughing hyena, and if it laughed did it show its teeth like that?

"The Negroes," Bombarda said, "are unacquainted with firearms. I acquaint them." He waved his handkerchief to encompass the surrounding stockade. "You have seen my towers? In each tower stands a guard with a primed musket. From time to time, almost daily in fact, there occur infringements of my regulations. The malefactor is separated from the others, firmly chained to a stake in the ground. I enter. I look up to the sky. I cry to the malefactor, 'Behold the juju of the white master! Descend, death-thunder from the heaven!' On which a guard in one of the watchtowers, having screened his musket so that neither fire nor smoke shall be visible, takes aim. There is a mighty roar. Simultaneously, as the forests echo, the malefactor falls dead. The effect is theatrical. No one has approached him. No arrow, no knife, no spear has wounded him. The speeding invisible bullet has slain him from a great distance. It is strong juju, a miracle. 'Learn to obey the white master!' I say. There is never the slightest difficulty with them after that. So we are really quite safe here, though unarmed, Mr. Paul." He pointed to a little girl, too young to be chained. "Observe that pretty child. She must have Fulani blood in her. About twelve, I should say, judging from the pectoral development. She will fetch a fancy price. Are you satisfied with the training I have described, Mr. Paul?"

"What are the infringements of your regulations that usually give rise to this training?" Newton asked.

Bombarda smirked. "Whatever I care to dislike that day. What does it matter so long as the training is accomplished?"

"Your training is stern," Jock said objectively, "but it is unquestionably effective, and I dare say a good many lives are saved by such measures, since they neither fight among themselves nor revolt against their white masters afterwards."

"Precisely," Bombarda said. "How quickly you apprehend these critical points."

"Wrestle, wrestle, wrestle," Newton muttered. "Once I wrestled too."

"I beg your pardon, Captain?" Jock said.

Newton said, "With your conscience, and lose. I lost." He looked feverish.

"Are you feeling quite well, sir?" Jock asked.

"I thought I heard something just now," Newton said. "Senhor Duarte, do you permit drums in the enclosure? They can speak to the forests, you know."

A thought new to Jock suddenly lighted like a flash of gunpowder in his brain. The captain was right. Drums in the stockade might beat out a message to tribes in the forests who, answering the call for help, would swoop down upon the compound and wipe it out. Jock had heard of Africa's talking drums; in fact, their fame was so widespread that he wondered if it might not have been exaggerated.

"Any beating of drums," Bombarda said positively, "would constitute a most grave infringement of the regulations. They excite emotions that are difficult to handle. You hear no drums, Captain Newton."

Newton said, "Listen."

Bombarda paused and cocked his ear; the rest stood silent, listening. Muffled but distinct, the sound of a drum could be heard from the far end of the barracoon where there stood a poorly thatched hut like the shelters that farmers build for cattle. Each barracoon was equipped with such a shelter. In them women gave birth, and, occasionally, someone died. All other natural functions took place under the open sky, but a measure of privacy had to be provided for the Negro for the beginning and the end of his life, for he believed that at such a time the soul was loosely attached by a slender vine to the body and liable to be pounced upon and eaten by malignant spirits.

Bombarda listened and scowled. "It is not a birth," he said. "That is a faster beat. This is for a sickness, but it is not to cure a sickness. Do you recognize the beat, Senhor Captain?"

"Confound you, Bombarda, how can you permit it?"

Bombarda shrugged. "What can I do?"

"Stop it!"

"Why?"

"Because they are killing."

"Someone in the barracoon has incurred the displeasure of the others," Bombarda said to Jock. "They are taking their own way with him."

The captain said, "They are conjuring his life away, and you know it."

"I dislike these practices, but it will satisfy them."

Newton said angrily, "I will not permit it!" He strode off in the direction of the hut.

"Your captain is unpredictable," Bombarda said.

"We'll have to follow him," Jock said.

"I'm afraid so."

In the shadows of the hut a suffering Negro lay supine on the earth, surrounded by chicken feathers. He was dripping with sweat and he moved convulsively. His eyes were rolled back under the lids, and the whites glinted like polished bone. He shook and he twitched. In the corner a native beat a drum with his hands. Over the sick man, rattling a monkey skull full of dried seeds and waving the yellowed branch of a feather palm, there

103

stood a figure whose face was hidden by a red-toothed mask. Beside the sick man crouched and wept Dolores. Never had Jock seen any living thing so utterly consumed by terror as the creature who lay among the feathers. Newton, gesticulating and shouting, hurled curses in English at the masked figure, who paid no attention to him. Bombarda caught the captain by the arm. "In God's name, calm yourself and let this alone."

"In God's name I will not!"

"It is only Chima, the ambassador whose mission failed and lost the war. His Ibo countrymen naturally resent the failure of the ambassador's mission, since it landed them in my barracoons. It would be dangerous to interfere."

Newton shouted, "Blasphemy! Murder! Shame!"

"Foolish man, it is their law."

"You set them at this. Chima stubbed your damned toe!"

Bombarda said to the medicine man, "Onumba, retire." Sulkily the masked figure withdrew.

He said to the sick man, "Chima, get up." The sick man whimpered, voided his urine like a terrified dog and lay as before. Bombarda spat on him. "Pig!"

He said to Dolores, "Go to the residence," but Dolores crouched and wept as if she did not hear him. He kicked her.

Chima at once stood up and bared his teeth, which were filed to points, and lunged at Bombarda. In a second he would have fastened his fangs in the factor's neck, but the medicine man, bleating like a sheep, rushed in between them, frantically waving the withered branch of the tree. Chima fell back, shielding his eyes with his hand.

Newton's reaction was quick and rash. He seized the tree branch and broke it over his knee and doubled the fragments and broke them again and ripped off the leaves and hurled the shreds to the ground and stamped on them. The branch was very old; it destroyed easily.

Bombarda turned pale.

Everyone in the hut except Dolores, who was a Fulani, fled terrified.

Bombarda said, "Captain Newton, you are a fool. Quickly! Into the open, where the towers can protect us!" But so great was the sacrilege and so deep was the terror of the Negroes that the white men were not attacked. Rapidly they made their way to the gate; ponderously the mighty timbers closed after them; iron bolts thumped into place. Then from the barracoon a howl arose like the howl of a pack of wolves. It was mournful, hungry and sustained. Involuntarily Jock glanced behind him, but no one was there except some competent Portuguese guards of Bombarda's household, looking a little scared but standing their ground with muskets at the ready.

"I suppose you know what you have done," Bombarda said, glowering at the captain.

Newton replied, "I was beside myself. I could not help it."

"I should not care to be aboard the *Misericordia* when she sails with that cargo," Bombarda said sourly.

He wiped the sweat from his face and grunted something in Ibo. His major-domo gently fanned him. Jock saw the angry glint fade from Bombarda's eyes; his face relaxed and presently the trader's smile asserted itself again. After all, Captain Newton was in Lagos to purchase six hundred blacks: a merchant must permit an important customer his little eccentricities. Another Ibo order set punch before his guests, and among the African words Jock caught the name Dolores.

"That was most embarrassing, my dear Captain, but *most* embarrassing," Bombarda said, his voice under control, an apology for his petulant remark implicit in his tone. "To desecrate the Sacred Ofo was certain to cause trouble. But we shall smooth things over. Pay no attention to the howling. Like a storm at sea it will howl itself out. Nay, there are measures we can take to hasten the process. Once they are taken, depend upon it, the cargo you carry to America will be as docile as a flock of sheep. Do I detect in your handsome open face, Senhor Paul, that 'Ofo' is a term strange to you?"

"I am learning, Senhor Duarte, that in certain respects the slave trade differs from other trades. In Captain Newton's gloss of trade terms 'Ofo,' I think, did not occur."

"Captain Newton's militant evangelism warms my heart with admiration for his faith," Bombarda said. Looking into his earnest face the captain, mollified as Bombarda wanted him to be, had no doubt of Bombarda's sincerity. "But we of the Older Religion," Bombarda continued, "are perhaps more patient, or perhaps" — his hands waved in deprecation — "perhaps we are more lazy. Above all we are slower. We have endured such heresies, such blasphemies, so much, so long, that at times I suppose we appear to you to temporize with superstition; but temporization is only on the surface, as one temporizes with the vagaries of children waiting for them to mature, knowing that eternity is long and salvation is for eternity. You will ask me, Senhor Paul, why I permit the Ofo in my barracoons, I who count myself a Christian. Alas! Why do I permit the eating of monkey soup? It is difficult to wean them away from their savagery in the few weeks that I have them in custody.

105

The Ofo, that foolish, dried-up branch of a feather palm, it is their most sacred symbol. Scholars of these things have compared it with the Hebrew Star, the Moslem Crescent, even the Christian Cross. It is greatly revered. Oaths are sworn upon it. It figures in rites of worship. It is possessed of miraculous powers. Huntsmen return laden with game when blessed by it. Crocodiles disappear from the river under its spell. Cattle and wives produce multitudinous offspring. The dying are comforted when it is wafted over them, secure in their belief that their souls will not be eaten by devils, and the mortally sick are cured of their sickness. Its powers can also be turned in the other direction, to destroy, as was happening tonight. Only a medicine man is permitted to touch the Ofo. That was the sacrilege committed by Captain Newton, virtually inexpiable in their eyes, for he not only touched it but in his commendable zeal he actually smashed it to bits." Outside, the wailing from the barracoons continued. "You did, you know, my dear Captain."

Newton said stanchly, "I was never more certain in my life that I had done the right thing."

"No one disputes that; but neither, I submit, ought we to seek the crown of martyrdom as a consequence. That glory is painfully acquired in Africa."

Jock said, "A man would be daft to die for a slave."

Newton said, "Ritual murder in the name of a heathen juju — that was what incensed me. I was wrong. I am sorry."

"Surely you cannot believe, Captain Newton, that I would punish Chima for stubbing my toe in so devious, so unchristian a manner."

"I thought so."

"I shall be far more direct in Chima's punishment. Muskets. The towers. Punished he shall be."

"Hasn't he been punished enough?" Jock said.

"Not nearly."

Jock asked, "Is the medicine man, Onumba, a member of your household?"

Bombarda smiled. "Of course he is. How else would I keep order? He is greatly revered and most valuable. He approached me the day he was captured and disclosed his sacerdotal character, knowing that I would respect it. All wise factors on the Coast do the same. I permit him wide latitude, many privileges. He will not be sold. He eats first, has his choice of the cooking pots. He has his choice of wives also. They change with amusing rapidity."

"Who will be next, I wonder?" Jock said idly.

"I beg your pardon?"

"His next wife."

"Anyone he desires, I suppose. Who cares?"

"I was just wondering if he might not choose Dolores."

"Good heavens, no; I shouldn't think so; she is a Fulani, he is an Ibo."

"I was merely trying to acquaint myself with native ways," Jock said.

Bombarda nodded. "Of course. Very wise."

"Why was it necessary to kick her in the stomach?" Jock asked.

"I did not kick her hard. The Negro can withstand extraordinary abuse, far more than a person."

Newton, now keenly aware of the enormity of his act, seemed to regret it and went to great lengths to propitiate Bombarda, hoping Bombarda could somehow minimize its effects. The prospect of a belligerent cargo all the way across the Atlantic frightened him. "Senhor Duarte's quick action introduced a new element into the unfortunate confusion I was causing," he said. "The instant he kicked her the heathen spell was broken, Chima lost his fear of the Ofo and, Lazarus-like, stood up as one from the dead."

"It seemed to me he had taken a fancy to Dolores," Jock said. "That was a hard kick. In Chima's place I too should have stood up."

"What an extraordinary remark," the captain said. " 'In Chima's place!' "

"There will not be a scratch, not a bruise upon her," Bombarda hastened to say. "You shall see for yourself. Examine her. I shall make it easy."

"Oh, I'll take your word for it," Jock said.

But Bombarda was old in the ways of the Coast and had dealt with hundreds of buyers, many of them as young as Jock Paul. "No, no!" he protested. "You must see. I take pride in my reputation. I will not have it said that the resident factor of Lagos conceals blemishes in his merchandise." Bombarda gave a somewhat lengthy order to his major-domo, who grinned broadly and padded off the verandah on his big hard feet. Shortly Dolores appeared in his place and took up the decanter and served them. She was stark naked and no bruises were visible. Captain Newton eyed Jock narrowly.

"They'll be naked on the ship, Mr. Paul," he said. "You had better get used to it."

"Yes, sir," Jock said. His hand was a little unsteady as she filled his glass. "Doesn't she mind?"

"That is a difficult question," Bombarda replied. "The Ashanti don't mind. The Ibos don't. They go naked anyway. But this girl is a Fulani, a Moslem. Ordinarily, yes, a Moslem would mind. But it must be remembered that when she became Nwa-Eji-Gbo-Agha, 'She-Who-Was-Given-To-Avert-War,' she became tribute, dead to her tribe, money that is spent.

She does not exist, even to herself. Therefore the answer is No, she doesn't mind. She doesn't mind anything."

"She was weeping for Chima," Jock said.

"Perhaps," said Newton, "some human feeling remains."

Bombarda raised his eyebrows. "Human? I shall never understand you English. All my customers I understand, but my English customers I do not understand. It is a gap in my intellect. Alas."

"What have you done with Chima?" Jock asked.

"Caged him," Bombarda said. "They would have torn him to pieces by now for losing the war. Tomorrow I shall have him shot. Death-thunder, *boom! boom!* big juju. I maintain discipline. Yes."

"I want to buy him," Jock said.

"*Santísima,* why?"

"Don't buy him, Mr. Paul," Newton said. "We couldn't take him aboard the ship, you know. They'd murder him, or us, or both. Remember, his mission failed and the Ibos lost the war."

"I could leave him in Africa," Jock said.

"For Senhor Duarte to murder?"

Bombarda flushed hotly. "Senhor Paul, you shall have your Chima!"

"For how much?" said Jock.

"Nothing! Upon my soul, on the soul of my mother, for nothing. Do I paste on your glass a sixpence tag? Do I post in your room, 'For the bed, a shilling'? Is there a price on hospitality? How measure it? You have asked for Chima. Chima you shall have."

"I am very grateful to you, sir," Jock said. "Will you take care of him after I leave? Return him to his own people?"

"They scarcely exist, after the war."

"Or sell him to some kindly master?"

"I think," Bombarda said, rubbing his chin, "that with Onumba's assistance I shall find a means of making it safe for you to take him with you on the *Misericordia.*"

"That would be gratifying," Jock said. It seemed to him illogical that ambassadors should be shot for losing wars.

"That would be a miracle," Newton said. He was uneasy.

In an amiable atmosphere he and the resident factor of Lagos arranged for the purchase of six hundred slaves. The price was about as usual, that is to say, a pound per head plus the trade rum and trinkets. Both seemed content with the bargain which, as always in this if in no other trade, assured both an ample profit.

With the commercial details ended, Bombarda sent men to unload the

Misericordia of her rum, and Webb saw to the victualing and watering of the ship. Actual loading of the living cargo was delayed, as was customary, until just before sailing: one day less at sea meant one day's less wastage.

About ten o'clock that night, when the heat of the day was abated, Bombarda set out a cool delicious supper of salads and fresh white meat of some African fowl. Jock's sailor-hunger for greens and unsalted meat was still strong. He ate voraciously, but Newton's face was pale and drawn and he ate very little. Jock detected the odor of trade rum about him and feared that the captain might be off again on another bout with the bottle. Newton left the table early and retired to his room.

Bombarda shook his head. "Your captain, Senhor Paul, he has a schism in his soul."*

"Perhaps."

"Half wants one thing and half another, no?"

"I do not know."

"You do not wish to discuss your Captain Newton? But he is fascinating, Senhor Paul, absolutely fascinating."

"He is my commanding officer, he is a gentleman, and he isn't here."

"Ah so. Yes. I see. I am overrun with gentlemen tonight, English gentlemen. The French gentlemen are so much easier. You always know what will please *them*."

"I am a Scot, Senhor Duarte."

"I have never met a Scot. But you speak English."

"You speak Ibo."

"Naturally. And Ashanti, Fulani, Hausa, many of the African dialects. What of that?"

Jock looked at him.

"I see." Bombarda reddened. "Thank you for not saying it. No, speaking African does not make me an African. No, by God!"

"I did not call you an African."

"I did not call you English. Forget that I called you English. *Santíssima!* Here is a gentleman I understand. In his soul there is no schism. He knows what he is. That is so rare. We are friends, no?" He held out his hand.

Jock grinned, grasped it. "Friends."

---

* The schism in the soul of Captain John Newton ultimately resolved itself in favor of humanity. He renounced the slave trade, gave up the sea and studied for the priesthood. After some preliminary difficulties, his past was forgiven and he was ordained by the Bishop of Lincoln. Newton's letters and an inspiring collection of hymns, written in his later years as a reputable Anglican divine, are still extant.

"Dolores! You will fill my friend's glass, and mine!"

She was the only servant now in the room. The bottle she carefully decanted was very old and the liquid that presently filled their glasses was darkly honey-colored, rich, warm like her skin.

"This," Bombarda whispered in a conspiratorial tone, glancing in the direction of Newton's room, "this is no ordinary wine. This I save for my friends. It was born in the valley of the Duoro. It grew old in the cool caves of Miranda. In the Azores it was fortified with brandy. Attend me: cool, mature, fortified. Africa requires those qualities in a wine. Anything else goes sour." He nodded towards the captain's room and looked inquiringly at Jock.

"He'll be all right in the morning," Jock said. "Captain Newton is thoroughly dependable at sailing time."

"Goes sour," Bombarda continued, as if to his glass, "because not fortified. But this is glorious wine. Regard its tawny depth. Savor its smoothness. Feel its fire!"

"Delicious," Jock smiled, following Bombarda's eyes, which now rested on Dolores.

"Africa can be enjoyed if a man, like a wine, can be cool, mature and, above all, fortified."

Jock chuckled heartily. "Senhor Duarte, I follow your not-too-difficult spoor. What is it you want of me?"

"Want of you, senhor?"

"In return for the girl."

"For the girl?"

"Come, come, Bombarda. You have everything; I have nothing. What can I possibly possess that leads you to offer this — what shall I call her — this spotless lamb for the sacrifice? For I observe that you were correct; not a blemish visible."

"It does not seem to me that you have examined her very closely," Bombarda said.

"Oh, yes, I have."

"And you desire her?"

"Any man would."

"Well then — ?"

"Unless his heart were full to bursting with someone else."

"Oh, the devil!" Bombarda grunted. "You're in love. The worst kind of love. The tyrannical kind that reaches half around the world like a chain and fetters you, faithful even in Africa. Is that it?"

Jock sipped his wine and did not comment, but his face went stern and a little red.

"I see how it is," Bombarda said regretfully.

The howling from the barracoons, which had subsided to a drone, suddenly rose to a frenzied pitch and then stopped abruptly in absolute silence. Nothing could be heard in the room but Dolores's breathing, no motion seen but the rapid rise and fall of her breasts and an expectant tensing of lithe muscles under her honey-colored skin, like a panther about to spring. In that instant of silence, in the light of the candles, her eyes went yellow as a cat's, like molten gold.

Bombarda held up three fingers and ticked off two of them. "One: the sudden noise — that was the entry of the sacrifice. Two: the sudden quiet — that was the chaining. And now, my dear Senhor Paul, you must excuse me for a moment."

He cast on a cloak, though it was far too warm for a cloak, clapped on a cocked hat and fluffed out the ruffles at his throat as if he were about to meet an important personage. "One must look one's best when one calls down death-thunder, *boom! boom!* big juju! I shall not bore you long alone with Dolores," and he laughed and strode off in the direction of the barracoon.

"You promised *me* Chima!" Jock shouted angrily after him.

Bombarda called back cheerily, "I never break my word."

Dolores, while she had been serving, had neither cringed like a slave nor seemed ashamed of her nudity. Only twice had she shown any emotion at all; once in the hut, where Chima lay near death for fear, when she wept for him; and now again, when Bombarda went out in the dark to commit his disciplinary murder.

Bombarda had said she considered herself nonexistent, and perhaps she did, but where Chima was concerned she did not behave like one who is nonexistent.

She was not weeping now. She approached close to Jock and held up three fingers exactly as Bombarda had done. As he had, she ticked off two. She held up the other expectantly.

"Chima?" Jock asked her. He was incredulous.

She answered in Fulani, which of course he did not understand.

"Chima?" he asked her again.

She shook her head violently; no, it was not Chima. Perhaps it was no one. Some of her sleek wavy hair brushed his cheek as she shook her head; it was soft and fresh smelling. It was not in the least like the wool of a rancid goat. She was looking into his face with eyes as radiant as they had been hopeless when she wept in the hut.

All at once Jock heard Bombarda chanting in Ibo in the midst of the barracoon. Instantly three muskets, fired almost simultaneously, thundered in answer. From their noise Jock judged they must have been double-charged. An animal roar of delight flooded up from five hundred throats, with Onumba's powerful voice in the lead, a sort of rhythmic barking chant, awesome, spine-tingling, evil.

Dolores flicked down the third finger and uttered a grateful protracted "O-o-o-o-o!" and prostrated herself at Jock's feet. She clutched his knees. She licked his shoes.

"For heaven's sake, get up!" he said, but the words meant nothing to her. He reached down and drew her gently to her feet. Although he had failed to establish the slightest degree of verbal communication with the girl, it struck him — and the comparison was so grotesque he almost laughed — that she responded to his touch in exactly the same way that a very superior vessel responds, "answering" the least pressure on the helm, as if sub-mission were built into every timber, pliant, quick to understand, anxious to obey.

Looking at her he said, " 'Timber' does you something less than justice, Dolores," and was guiltily glad that Kitty Fielding could not hear and that Dolores could not speak English. But she understood her name. His smile, which the comparison with a ship had evoked, she applied to herself. She smiled back. Thus Bombarda found them.

"It would seem that you have not been too bored," he said, casting off his cloak, hat, sword, loosening his jabot. He was in high good humor.

"Apparently you didn't shoot Chima," Jock said.

"She told you?"

"In a way."

"Dolores makes herself understood."

"She licked my feet for joy."

"Naturally. You saved her precious Chima. You were quite right, Senhor Paul. You read the blacks quickly. She has taken a tremendous fancy to Chima."

"Did you shoot anybody?"

"Three. Onumba picked me out three minor leaders. Together they equalled one ambassador."

Jock swallowed tightly. "I must suppose that you know what you are do-ing."

"Do you question it?"

"It seems a pretty strict way to run things."

"It was one of the most successful lessons I ever administered," Bombarda said. "Usually it is rather humdrum, but this time there was an element of artistry. Captain Newton had complicated the situation with sacrilege, you see. That had to be overcome, through Onumba, the local clergyman as it were. I gave him a 'dash' — I'm afraid I shall have to charge it to your account, Senhor Paul. Three fat pigs and that pretty little girl we admired today in the barracoon. Onumba had noticed her too."

"Isn't she rather young?"

Bombarda shrugged. "So were the three little pigs."

Jock kept down the resentment in his tone. "I'll pay Onumba's 'dash.'"

"The great beauty of the thing," Bombarda continued with relish, "was this: just as the men fell, when all eyes were on them, Onumba discovered a prodigy. He shouted, 'The Ofo! The Ofo!' and down from heaven came floating a withered frond of a feather palm. Onumba recognized it immediately. It was the same that Captain Newton had broken to pieces, miraculously put together again."

"Of course," Jock muttered. "Poor people."

"I beg your pardon, Senhor?"

"Oh, nothing."

"Perhaps I am getting old," Bombarda said, "and hearing things that are not there. I could have sworn that I heard you sigh, 'Poor people.'"

"Well, suppose I did!"

"Senhor Paul, Senhor Paul, not *people*." Bombarda seemed almost to plead.

"They fall in love like people. They die like people when bullets hit them."

Bombarda said, "I beg you not to make the same mistake as Captain Newton. It is fatal. Apes too fall in love. Their courtship is startlingly human in aspect; the very generative act is ventro-ventral. As for dying of bullets, so do pigs, so does any animal. No, no, Senhor Paul. You are sterner stuff than your captain. You know what you want; I know what you want; you want what every gentleman wants. You want money, position, power. You want to rise in the world. Do not answer. I see it in your face. I see a lady in America, a great lady, beautiful, rich, in her veins blue blood, an aristocrat. You are a gentleman, but you are not an aristocrat; to that one must be born. That is why you are in this trade. But in this trade you are new, you wonder, you hesitate. Do not. In this trade there is money, and money can accomplish anything. Stay with it for a while. Grow rich. Then, when you are rich, behold, everything else will fall into your lap, especially in America, like the miraculous new Ofo from heaven. But do not tell this to the aristocratic lady in America. She doesn't know, does she?"

"Good God, NO!"

"There is no reason why she ever should. Make a voyage or two in the *Misericordia*. Captain Newton will not last long. Rum or religion, one or the other will claim him. Then you will be captain; you are not soft like him. And when you are captain — did you ever consider a partnership on the Coast, Senhor Paul?"

Jock was wary. "That is surely the last thing that ever entered my mind, and I don't see why anybody should offer me a partnership."

"Did I not intimate, my friend, that I wanted something from you?"

"Ye-es."

"That was it. Consider it."

"One would like to know why one is suddenly made such an astounding offer on such short acquaintance."

Bombarda rubbed his chin reflectively. "Say I am getting old," he said. "Say I am weary. Say I observe the men I deal with. Say I dislike cowards, who turn green when they learn how the natives have to be handled. Say I dislike lechers who spend their first nights wallowing with females in the barracoons. Say I like young men with ambition. Say, above all, that I admire a gentleman who refuses to talk behind his drunken captain's back. Such men are trustworthy."

Jock looked at him, waiting. It wasn't enough.

Bombarda smiled craftily. "You are difficult to flatter, Senhor Paul."

"All these qualities are available from other men, Senhor Duarte, men of fortune who could invest in a partnership, which I cannot."

"You are disturbingly fundamental," Bombarda said. "Very well. I shall be equally fundamental. There is danger of another native war, Senhor Paul; the Ibos are not entirely wiped out. The remnant will re-form, gain allies. Alliances among the tribes are shifting and unexpected. This time the coalition may be directed against the Coast, against the whites, against me. There have been hints and murmurs. I require a partner conversant with guns, a fighting partner, who will help me defend the compound in case of attack and lead a furious expedition in reprisal. You are not afraid?"

"No," Jock said simply.

"And as for your lamentable lack of fortune," Bombarda smiled, "it is precisely because you have no fortune that I can trust you. You will not conspire against me; you will not 'dash' the governor to exile me from the Coast. Ha! Exile from exile! Yet with a fortune, how easily it might be done. In short, until you are as rich as I am, you will be trustworthy, loyal, my junior partner. After that, we shall see."

He was certainly fundamental, Jock thought.

"You are not offended, Senhor Paul?"

"Not at all. I should reason the same if I were in your position."

Bombarda sighed, settling back comfortably. "It will be a peaceful life for my latter years. I shall retire to Goa, I think, in India, among Portuguese, where I belong. One grows lonesome for the music of one's own beautiful tongue after hot humid years of this Ibo, this Ashanti, this Fulani — faugh!"

"Wouldn't it be better simply to go back to Portugal?"

Bombarda scowled. "That is a subject I never discuss."

"Very well," Jock said.

"One day perhaps, when you are a rich factor, I shall discuss it."

"It doesn't matter."

"You will be rich, you know."

"I am not sure I shall make another trip in the *Misericordia*, Senhor Duarte."

"So much the better; get a bigger ship; and get rich the faster."

"I do not think I shall make another trip at all."

Bombarda chuckled. "You will. You will. Decide nothing tonight. Decide nothing till you reach America and total up your gains. Then remember the resident factor of Lagos. The offer will still hold."

Black faces shone darkly in the filtered light outside the verandah screens. Onumba brought in Chima, who uttered a sound like a whimpering pup and groveled at Jock's feet. Bombarda eyed the Negro disdainfully. Chima set Jock's foot upon the nape of his neck and muttered something to the ground.

"What does he say?" Jock asked.

Bombarda said, "He says that he is yours, and all he has or ever shall have, so long as he lives. In a moment he will bite himself to prove it. Touching?"

"Tell him to stand up."

Bombarda spoke to him, and Chima stood up; but not before he had slashed two deep gashes in his right forearm with his needle-filed teeth, which dripped red as he smiled broadly at his new master.

"Good Lord!" Jock said, horrified. "Tell the poor creature to bind up that hideous mess."

"I shall, if you wish to insult him." Bombarda coolly sipped his wine. "Note Dolores, by the way."

Sadly, reproachfully, she was looking at Chima. It was impossible for Jock to fathom the thinking of these two, but he sensed that Dolores was offended and that Chima expected praise.

"How would I insult him?" Jock asked.

"My dear senhor! He is merely informing you that he is ready to shed his blood for you. It is the rite of voluntary servitude. Chima forgets that he is already a slave. But you will never have to chain him now. When a warrior thus humbles himself, he becomes 'Osu,' outcast, one dedicated, as to a god. You are now a god, Senhor Paul. I doff my hat. Chima and his descendants are now barred from the life of the Ibo tribe, ostracized from dances, sports, funerals, births, wars; he cannot live, eat, sleep, drink or even walk with his fellow tribesmen. Nay, should he provoke a free Ibo by most deadly insults, the free Ibo will not fight him but will take to his heels lest he inadvertently shed one drop of Chima's dedicated blood; for if he should, he, the freeman, will be forced to purchase another man and dedicate *him* to you, or risk the penalty of becoming 'Osu' himself. I trust this is clear."

"It sounds like the old treatment of lepers."

Bombarda shrugged, and Chima bled, motionless, smiling.

At a word from Bombarda, Chima and Onumba retired.

"I hope you told him to bind up his wounds."

Bombarda replied, "Certainly not. He will now pound mud and dung, which Onumba has chanted over, into the gashes so that the scars will swell up into beautiful, smooth, high welts as perpetual token of your ownership. He will display them with pride and mention your name as he does so."

"Strange, strange," Jock muttered.

"Only at first."

"Are there 'Osu' in your household?"

"I am not so honored," Bombarda said with crushing sarcasm. "I do not rescue Negroes. I sell them."

"And shoot them," Jock thought, "as object lessons." And yet, after the confusing display he had just witnessed he did not know whether, in logic, he had the right to condemn Bombarda. Savagery ran deep in these weird black children of the forests. How deal with savagery? Perhaps Bombarda's was the only way.

Never had the gulf between white man and black, civilization and the jungle, yawned so deep. He sympathized with Newton. He yearned for Fredericksburg. He did not count himself well informed in the ways of the slave trade, which differed more and more from other trades. Slavery was not wrong, he assured himself, but there was much unpleasantness in its early stages which disturbed him. How much more comfortable to be on Willie's side of the matter, across the Atlantic, dealing with slaves only after they had become civilized. He held out his glass to Dolores, but withdrew it before she could fill it, remembering how Newton had warned that the slave trade would drive him to drunkenness.

Bombarda watched him closely, nodded, satisfied. "You do not make the captain's mistakes," he said. "I congratulate you."

"I suppose Dolores will want to marry my Chima," Jock said idly, "and come with him to America. They will make a handsome couple. I had better buy her, Senhor Duarte. What are you asking for her?"

"You persist in employing human terms," Bombarda said. " 'Marry' indeed! Say rather, 'mate.' "

Jock grinned. "Whatever you care to call it, senhor. *Fundamentally* it's the same thing, isn't it?"

"What makes you think she will want to go?"

"She loves him. Or does a Fulani also refuse to associate with an Ibo who is 'Osu'?"

"Oh no, it isn't that. But I think she'll surprise you tomorrow."

Competent, sober, serious, grim-faced, Captain Newton stood on the quarter-deck of the *Misericordia* and watched the shackled strings of Negroes, twelve to a string, file up the gangplank and disappear down the hatchway into the hold. Webb attended to the stowing of the cargo, quartering them by strings, first on one side of the ship, then on the other, so that their weight would be evenly distributed. *Misericordia* settled slightly in the water as she took on her living load. Jock stood at the gangplank, counting. Bombarda stood beside him, a salesman to the end, praising his merchandise. "Prime! Prime! Behold, their war wounds are already healed. Healthy! Strong! Well fed! Never before did I ship such a magnificent cargo."

Presently chains were heaved, clanking, onto the landing. This meant that the slaves were now fettered in *Misericordia*'s own irons. The chains with which they had gone aboard were Bombarda's property and were being returned to him. Now he too began to count, to count chains.

Jock laughed. "There is no need of us both counting, Senhor Duarte."

"Forty-three" — *clank!* "Forty-four" — *clank!* Bombarda ticked them off. "When there are fifty, your cargo will be complete."

Newton called from the quarter-deck, "He loves his chains, Mr. Paul. Let him count his chains from here to eternity."

Bombarda said stiffly, "Your captain has a disagreeable habit of speaking in allegory when the mood is on him. Come, Senhor Paul, neither of us

117

shall count, neither slaves nor chains. We are friends, no? We do not cheat, no! There is cool punch on my verandah. Drink me a stirrup cup before you sail."

"Mr. Paul, are you counting?" the captain called sharply.

"Yes, sir," Jock answered; and to Bombarda, "I must remain at my post till they are all aboard."

"Quite so," said Bombarda.

Jock noted that Bombarda did not count, or did not appear to count, the chains after that.

As the last string of twelve marched up the gangplank, Newton came to the rail.

"All accounted for," Jock reported.

The captain said, "Thank you, Mr. Paul," and bowed to Bombarda, distantly, formally. "Senhor Duarte, adieu."

"You will not have a stirrup cup with me, Captain?"

"Thank you, no."

Bombarda gave Jock the cargo manifests, the receipt for the trade rum, the receipt for the trinkets, the receipt for the governor's "dash."

"You have read this, Mr. Paul?" Newton asked, scanning the papers.

"Yes, sir; all is in order: six hundred blacks, six hundred pounds; and the rum and oddments at the usual rate."

Newton signed them.

"What is this page, Mr. Paul? 'One black, answering to name of Chima, gratis; three little pigs, three pounds; one black child (female), ten shillings.' A very high price for pigs, Mr. Paul."

"That is my personal account, sir, a purchase I made last night while you were sleeping."

"A queer account, and a miserable one," Newton sighed. "But God forbid that I should judge any man. You will sign this page, Mr. Paul. It will be deducted from your share of the profits: three pounds, ten shillings."

"Yes, sir," Jock said. Flushing scarlet, he signed the page, which now became an official record.

"It is not what you think!" Bombarda cried, but Newton had already turned away. "When is the tide, Mr. Paul?"

"About an hour, sir."

"When is the tide, exactly?"

"One hour and ten minutes from now, sir."

"That will just give me time," Newton said. He strode away, back still turned, and went down into the hold by the same hatchway as the Negroes. Presently, from the bowels of the ship, his voice could be heard, haranguing them in their native tongue. Jock looked at Bombarda, who laughed heartily.

"He always delivers them a sermon on the blessings of slavery and civilization before he sails. Come, friend Paul, our punch grows warm and so do I."

"I wish I knew what he is saying," Jock said.

"It is always the same, and his accent is so amusing that the blacks always laugh at him."

"At least he gets them in a good humor, one way or another," Jock said.

"And why should they not be good-humored?"

Was it not preferable, the captain was preaching, earnestly sweating, down in the hold, to be a white man's slave than to dwell in darkness, perpetually at war? America was a beautiful land, more beautiful than Igwe, the Ibo heaven. There were no evil spirits to devour their souls in America, neither at birth nor at death nor in dreams. There was food in plenty, free, supplied by the white masters, and it did not have to be hunted. Stone dwellings, too, big as the palace of the Oba of Benin, awaited them. They were to wear soft shirts of red cotton, like the Oba's robes and leather breeches that never wore out, nay, some of them might even wear hats and shoes. There would be skirts for the women and molasses for the children on bread white as bone. In America there were no Ashanti to frighten them with 'customs' — in America no one, absolutely no one, was ever eaten alive. American white masters did not permit that. That was because America was civilized and Christian.

"He can preach for hours on the benefits of Christianity," Bombarda said, "and Protestant though he is, he makes it sound more attractive than juju."

"Does he tell them they'll have to work?" Jock asked.

Bombarda answered, "I have to work. You have to work. Everyone has to. That is a detail."

Perhaps it was, Jock thought. It was certainly true.

From the ship in the lagoon they could hear massed, muted laughter. "They are cheering," Bombarda said. "You will have a happy voyage."

"It would be valuable if I could speak Ibo," Jock said, musing.

"Eh, my friend? You are thinking of more voyages? You are considering my offer?"

"I was thinking of Chima."

"Oh, he'll teach you Ibo while you are teaching him English. Ibo isn't difficult."

"Is Fulani difficult?"

Bombarda laughed. "To learn Fulani, Senhor Paul, you must wait till your next trip to Africa. Chima has informed Dolores that he departs with his master across the sea, to America, to the moon, anywhere. Dolores, remembering that she was a princess, was furious that he should desert her for you."

"But I offered to buy her for him."

"And I would have sold her. But her love has changed to hate, as often happens even among humans, and she has informed Chima that she spits in his face. You can still buy her, of course, but you will have to chain her securely. She would scratch his eyes out while he was asleep."

"I don't want any trouble on the ship," Jock said. "I'll leave her here. It's a pity, though."

"Much the best decision," Bombarda said.

"I rather hope you do not give her to Onumba," Jock said. "Onumba without his mask is almost as repulsive as with it." He made the remark in spite of himself. He was firmly determined never again to set eyes on Lagos Lagoon or its resident factor, and he wondered why he should have mentioned Dolores as if he cared. "I don't really care," he said.

Bombarda said, "No, I don't think I'll let her mate with anyone. She is more decorative virgin. I'll keep her around the residence to fan me and serve my punch. Shall I teach her English, Senhor Paul, so she can teach you Fulani when you return? She has lapsed again into nonexistence, you will note, and she would oblige."

"I shall be very candid with you," Jock said. "It is extremely unlikely that I shall return."

Bombarda raised his glass, smiling. "Your health, Senhor Paul!"

The stirrup cup was drained. "Yours!" Jock said.

A strong tide sets through the inlet between Lagos Island and the mainland, filling and draining the great roadstead of Lagos Lagoon twice a day, flooding in the sharp salt waters of the sea and, at the ebb, cleansing away the fetid debris of the marshes: decaying vegetation, floating carcasses of dead snakes, rats, crocodiles, turtles and the litter and garbage of man. Borne along on this ebb tide of filth, the *Misericordia* departed. Bombarda, from his sedan chair, waved a cheery good-by with a large silk neckerchief which was red as blood.

After some preliminary fright caused by the motion of the ship and some sporadic seasickness (which was promptly punished and cured by withdrawal of food), the cargo became docile, sluggish as animals in hibernation. The crowding was incredible. At night from stem to stern they lay like black logs of firewood, one long neat layer of parallel bodies so closely packed that no deck was visible between them. Yet so deep was their savage horror of being alone in new and unknown surroundings that they welcomed each other's contact and huddled together, in spite of the great heat.

Chima, by some secret means of his own, probably with his teeth, kept open his wounds, till Jock begged Newton to tell him that his new master desired no larger welts; on which Chima bound them up with spun yarn soaked in tar, and they healed with remarkable speed. To make himself understood Jock learned, perforce, a few words of Ibo and Chima some English. Their mutual vocabularies grew. Chima's first word was "master." His first sentence was "I love you." Jock was amused to remember that the last person to teach him a foreign language had been a French marquis, whose discourse had been elegant and doctrinaire and had dealt with philosophy: man was born free. By now poor Henri must be living, if he still lived, in the forests of the New World with the "beautiful savages" he had praised in the drawing rooms of his chateau.

Every day Captain Newton descended into the ship's hold and harangued the Negroes, wearing his hat, wig and dress uniform, half to impress them with the finery of the white man's attire, half, Jock suspected, as a private penance of his own, for every day the atmosphere below deck became more foul. Near the end of the voyage his sermons had advanced to the point where he would read them the Bible. "I am always thrilled with their grasp of God's Word," he told Jock. But Chima told Jock, "When an Ibo is conquered, the Ibo gods are conquered also." Jock did not tell the captain this, since it seemed to place Newton's missionary success on a crude and nonspiritual level.

But at the beautiful story of the Nativity and the God-Man Jesus sacrificing himself for others, the Negroes listened spellbound, faces alight with complete comprehension, eyes glistening in the shadows for joy. They clapped their hands, snapped their fingers, stamped on the deck with their feet till the ship was full of the rattle and clank of iron chains, shouting, "Tell us again! Tell us again!" like children demanding the repetition of a story; and, if Newton should so much as change a word when he told it again, they would correct him. Jock was astounded at their zeal and their understanding. Was Newton right? Was it the power of the truth of God's Word? He asked Chima.

It must be the truth, Chima answered, since the Christian God had them in His power. This, too, was nothing that Jock felt he ought to tell Newton.

One day, shortly before anchoring at Kingston, Newton took a large bucket of water below and baptized the entire cargo.

"You must be baptized too, Chima," Jock said. Newton, in his zeal for the six hundred, had missed Chima, who was self-effacing as Jock's shadow.

"Were you baptized, master?"

"Why, of course I was."

"Then so was I," Chima said with utter conviction.

Jock did not press the matter. Presumably, in the course of time, the slaves would be properly instructed and Christianized by some qualified clergyman. To be forcibly herded into the fold by the captain of a slaver seemed grotesque.

The morning the *Misericordia* furled her sails in Kingston Harbor, Captain John Newton came to a critical decision in his personal life and he did a curious thing. He lugged a case of trade rum from his cabin to the rail and with his own hand threw the bottles into the sea. Not one had he opened all the way from Africa. Not a drop had he touched.

"Mr. Paul!"

"Yes, sir?"

"Mr. Paul, I am leaving the ship."

That seemed only logical. The buyer's barge was already rowing out to them. The cargo, minus some dozen deaths (an excellent record), would be landed as soon as the purchase papers were signed. The captain would go ashore in the barge as usual and complete the formalities.

"I understand, sir," Jock said.

"I do not think you do. I am *leaving* the ship, Jock."

It was the first time Newton had ever addressed his first officer by his Christian name.

"I can endure it no longer. I am leaving the ship. I am leaving the sea. I am leaving the slave trade."

"But, sir, you cannot!"

"I did not think I could. But I can, with God's help. With the help of God I *can!*"

He spoke with intense emotion.

"But your pay and your share of the profits! Will you receive them if you give up your command?"

"I do not know and I do not care." In the captain's face there was beatitude, or Bedlam. Jock knew not which.

"But the landing of the cargo, the loading of the rum, the signing of the bill of sale?"

"I shall have to arrange for that, I suppose. But it's for the last time, Jock. Then, thank God, I am free."

"I wish you would stay on, sir."

"And I wish to God that you would not."

"Why are you doing this, Captain?"

Newton looked at him.

"I will tell you, and some day I pray that you will remember and understand. What does the word *Chima* mean in the Ibo tongue?"

"I thought it was only a name. Does it have a meaning?"

"It means *God Is Aware*. God *is* aware, Jock Paul. Think on those words. That is my answer."

Chapter 13

JOCK REMAINED aboard that night, though many of the crew went ashore to celebrate or carouse on Kingston's well-peopled water front. The harbor lights beckoned, the offshore breeze was full of the scent of land. He was anxious to stretch his legs and feel underfoot the welcome solidity of firm unyielding ground, ground whose position did not have to be anticipated by muscles long trained to "answer" the changing position of a deck.

At the beginning of a voyage captains were always the last to board a vessel, and at the end always the first to leave; so Jock was now left in command. Newton had gone ashore in the buyer's barge to execute the formalities that would dispose of *Misericordia*'s cargo and substitute therefor a cargo of first-quality rum, rum that was just as black and just as strong as Negroes and acceptable to the taste of the New Englanders for whom it was destined.

The night passed and the next morning; evening came. No one appeared to claim the cargo. *Misericordia* might have been in mid-ocean instead of snugly anchored in Kingston Harbor. Nonplused, Jock put the ship back on sea rations, sea routine, watch and watch. The crew, their money spent, returned to find their leaves cancelled and, grumbling, went about their regular duties as if *Misericordia* were a thousand miles from port.

Meanwhile, an old Negro died and Jock buried him, weighting the body with double weights since the harbor water was shallow; and a baby was born. He had expected a price of fifty pounds for the mother, who was obviously at term. During the night the baby disappeared. Chima said it had probably died. The mother, sick and despondent, deteriorated in value. Jock was concerned for the condition of the cargo.

"Confound that man! What is he about?"

Webb shrugged. "He was turrible distraught when he went ashore, Mr. Paul."

"You do not know where he is?"

"No, sir."

In the roadstead ships of many nations were anchored, some of them quite close, flying their national colors: Spanish, Portuguese, German, French, all the old enemies, all the old friends. Their ports were closed and their sails were snugged up tight. Their appearance was leisurely. None of them looked anxious to leave in a hurry.

"I heard in a tavern," Webb said, "that the war is over. Peace, with a treaty and all, has been signed at Paris. Everybody drinks with everybody else now; everybody's friendly."

"Who won?"

"Why, we did, sir."

"Who?"

Webb remembered that he was speaking to a Scotsman.

"England won," he said.

"Then everything's all right, I suppose," Jock said. At least, Willie and Bessie and the American colonies would not pass under foreign domination.

Webb scratched his head, "Yes, everything's all right, only up in New England they've begun heaving tea into the harbors. The king's put a tax on tea, and the New Englanders say they won't pay it."

"Well, wars cost money," Jock said. It was odd that the king had decided on a tea tax instead of a rum tax, which would have raised more revenue. But it wasn't a sailor's affair.

"It's high time we loaded our rum," he said. "They're not throwing rum into the sea too, are they?"

"Oh, they wouldn't do that, sir. But I don't know how you'll load the rum till you unload the slaves."

"Aren't they sold?"

"No, sir."

"Didn't the captain dispose of them? He went ashore expressly for that purpose."

"I know the buyer here, a Mr. Geoffrey Tubman, very friendly, very liberal. I met him —"

"Where did you meet him, Webb?"

Webb said defensively, "I met him in the drawing room of Madame Louise's. He told me that Captain Newton went into a church, prayed for three hours, and then came out and took a packet back to England."

Jock frowned, paused. Newton must have taken the packet on a sudden impulse, discovering that it was about to sail. He had left all his personal belongings aboard the *Misericordia*.

"What did Mr. Tubman say to that?"

"He laughed very heartily and gave me a guinea and said, 'I look forward with keenest anticipation to making the acquaintance of Captain Paul.'"

"He said 'Captain'?"

"He did indeed."

"Meanwhile," said Jock angrily, "your friendly liberal Tubman lifts not a finger to see me, and *Misericordia* wallows port deep in the water, crammed to the gun deck with precious cargo, while Tubman waits for time and heat and scurvy to take their toll and frighten me into lowering prices! We shall see about that. Get the longboat into the water, Mr. Webb!"

"Are you going ashore, sir?"

"To meet Geoffrey Tubman."

"He is still at Madame Louise's."

"Then I know where to find him."

Any prosperous Jamaican, or seaman (if he were an officer), could have directed you to Madame Louise's, which was located a block from the water front, brightly lighted, police-protected, and pompously equipped with a doorman of commanding stature, to usher you in with a bow, and usher you out with a boot if you quarreled, or haggled over price, or threw bottles, or used coarse words to Madame Louise's ladies. "Sir, my ladies are *ladies!*" she would remind you, daring you to doubt it, boring you through with colorless eyes sunk deep in rolls of perfumed, powdered fat. She employed no runners to meet you at the docks; word of mouth and the competence of her ladies made her reputation. Every week a physician arrived to inspect for the French disease. Discovered, the offender was ruthlessly expelled, no matter how pretty, popular or profitable. She held a controlling interest in a tavern across the street, and she could have retired, if she had wished, from her original house. "But my ladies need me," she would croon. "Most of them are foreigners, the little dears, working to make their dowries." Some of them were. "And every one is white!" was her proudest boast. She was militantly, defiantly genteel.

But her rum was weak, her beer was watered, her wine was tasteless, cheap. "I discourage tippling," she would pronounce with an air of saving your soul. Pressed, she would confide, "Did you come here to drink? When a gentleman is in his cups, he disappoints my ladies. They hate to be disappointed, they're that anxious to be loved."

Nevertheless, for reasons she never could fathom, her taproom was popular in spite of high prices and poor liquor. Her customers — "patrons," she was careful to call them — would sit at the tables chatting among themselves, greeting old acquaintances after long voyages, making new ones, drinking, smoking, boasting of amours in foreign ports, as if oblivious of the fact that a houseful of willing females waited in the drawing room to be looked over, picked out and escorted upstairs to "work." Men. The longer she catered to them the less she understood them, but she had learned not to force her ladies on patrons in the taproom, for that would not have been genteel and would have lowered her standards.

The doorman opened the door; Jock and Webb entered; Madame Louise advanced with an air of a duchess and bade them welcome. "Good evening, Mr. Webb! Oh, you rascal, you; so soon again! Little Virginia talked of you all day long. 'Madame,' she said, 'I never met a man like Mr. Webb in all my born days!'" Meanwhile her small shrewd eyes had taken in Jock from head to toe: men who dressed so smartly and looked so stern were always captains to her until they proved otherwise. "I do not think I know Captain — Captain —"

"Captain John Paul of the *Misericordia*," said Webb.

"I was sure you were a captain, Captain Paul," she said, smiling. "I can always tell. It's that air of authority, that look of command. But this time I thought, 'No, this young officer just cannot be a captain. The handsome ones are never captains.' But I was right all the time, wasn't I? Come into my parlor, gentlemen. Virginia isn't engaged at the moment. In fact, I suspect she is saving herself for Mr. Webb again. She was in bed all day. Good heavens! What am I saying?" Jock was grinning broadly. "It wasn't *that*, Captain Paul."

She was edging them towards the open door of the drawing room, which was lighted with wax candles in elaborate sconces between large French glass mirrors. The room was heavy with the scent of perfume lavishly applied, and full of the hum of men's and women's voices. Except that there were no chairs, lest the gentlemen grow too comfortable and linger too long over unprofitable preliminaries, and except for the dresses of the ladies, which were transparent, cut astonishingly low, obviously unencumbered by anything underneath and designed for instant removal, the scene might have been any fashionable drawing room. "Virginia will introduce you to my ladies, Captain Paul. What a bevy of beauties, and every one of them white as sugar. But what a variety! Blue eyes, black eyes, blond hair, red hair — all natural too, you naughty naughty captain you, as you will see for yourself. Madame Louise does not cheat. What *is* your preference, Captain?"

Jock said, "I am not looking for a woman."

Madame Louise was mildly startled. "My! I had no idea! Of course, some gentlemen do prefer — but I am afraid I am not prepared on such short notice — the police are strict in these matters — I myself always try to see all sides of a question — the price would be very high —"

"Captain Paul is looking for Mr. Geoffrey Tubman," Webb said.

"Oh," said Madame Louise. "In my profession, Captain Paul, I sometimes encounter unusual requests, even from captains."

Jock grinned. "All I want is Geoffrey Tubman."

"The girls would be more agreeable," she muttered. "You will find him in the taproom."

In the taproom alone at a table sat Geoffrey Tubman, smoking a Cuban cigar and drinking with relish glass after glass of cheap Geneva gin, which he sweetened with sugar and stirred with a Chinese toothpick, one end of which was shaped like a miniature spoon. He was pathologically corpulent. One was reminded of the cartoons in the English weeklies that pictured all manner of scientific freaks: the two-headed calf born on the occasion of the last return of Halley's comet; ladies in amusement parks with breasts and beards; the man whose belly was so large that he carried it on a wheelbarrow whenever he walked, since without it he could not walk at all. One wondered if Geoffrey Tubman ever ventured beyond the taproom, and if so, how he fared with Madame Louise's ladies. On his face was a sheen of oil that reminded some nautical patrons of whales. He nodded to Webb, looked appraisingly at Jock.

"You know him?" asked Madame Louise.

"Yes," Webb said.

"Then you shall introduce Captain Paul," she said. "I am needed in the drawing room."

"He would seem to dine well as a rule," Jock hazarded, wishing to learn more about him, searching for a weak point.

Madame Louise said primly, "I never gossip about my patrons," and went off to the pleasant atmosphere of the drawing room.

"There's never any gossip about Tubman," said Webb. "Even the girls won't have him. He hates and laughs at everything. They return the compliment."

"I doubt if he laughs at money," Jock said.

Tubman watched them approach, a half smile on his face, his eyes half shut like a Buddha's. Yet he was swarthier than an Oriental, and the closer one drew to him the stronger grew the impression that a fraction of his blood was as African as the cargoes he traded. He did not rise to greet them. "Sit down," he said.

"Why are you acting so oddly?" Jock asked. His tone was amiable but his face said clearly, "No nonsense."

Webb said, "Mr. Tubman, this is Captain Paul, the new commander of the *Misericordia*."

"It would seem that Mr. Tubman knows us already," Jock said levelly.

Tubman puffed his cigar, eying him speculatively. "You are not at all like Captain Newton," he pronounced at length. "My compliments, Captain Paul. Some gin?" He snapped his fingers. A waiter produced glasses. He decanted the stone bottle of Geneva. "Sugar?" He seemed to possess the savage's craving for sweets; his finger snapping was pure Guinea Coast. How many generations in Jamaica — how much white blood — were required to water down the inheritance of tribal traits? Four at least, Jock guessed. He doubted if Tubman had quite achieved the fourth.

There was an interlude of small talk, and Jock became aware that for all his appearance of nonchalance, Tubman was still the merchant at heart, maneuvering to buy, to buy cheap. "I had this from an East Indian captain," Tubman said, exhibiting the gold toothpick. "How delightfully economical, the Chinese! The mandarin aristocrat picks his teeth and cleanses the wax from his ears with one and the same delicate invention. Would you care to examine it, Captain Paul?"

"My drink wants no stirring," Jock said.

"Sugar would round out your angles, Captain Paul. I prescribe it. One lives so much longer, especially at sea. But of course, you have just begun to live."

"Mr. Tubman, I put the first question. Your disinterest in my cargo is strange, or else singularly sly."

"There is no reason to be rude," Tubman said.

"There is no reason not to be direct," said Jock. "I sell, you buy; my cargo is prime, you want prime cargo. Our interests should be the same. Why do you artfully scheme to lower its value, to our mutual loss?"

"You are certainly direct," Tubman said. "But you are grossly misinformed. I heard only tonight that Captain Newton had deserted his ship and that you were in charge. I waited for him in vain to make over the cargo to me: six hundred blacks in good condition after a swift and prosperous voyage. The stupid man."

Tubman was well informed.

Tubman continued, his tone reproving, "Old men die, babies get born and their bodies are not found. Still on the ship, no doubt, to infect all the rest with disease. Very careless. Why did you not seek me at once? Who knows how little they must be worth by now? Who knows how much less by morning?"

"Why didn't you seek me?"

"My dear Captain Paul, I never heard of you till today and then quite by chance. But come, we know each other now. I offer you thirty pounds."

Thirty pounds per head. The going price was forty.

Jock said, "No."

Tubman's shoulders moved in a slow perspiring shrug. "Then, Captain Paul, I shall not deal with you, and your cargo can die and rot for all I care; the fault will be yours."

"There are other buyers in Kingston," Jock said.

Tubman said, "Are there?"

"I'm afraid there aren't," said a voice. It had a lisping accent, and its owner, lank hair tied back in a yellow bandanna, had entered unobtrusively from another part of the house and taken a stand directly behind Tubman, who jumped as if a pin had stuck him. "I could not help overhearing," the newcomer said blandly. His smile exposed a diamond, neatly set in a front tooth under a thin moustache of Spanish cut and curl.

"Jesus!" Tubman gasped.

"In a sense," the newcomer said, evidently enjoying Tubman's discomfiture.

Tubman's hand fumbled in a pocket of his waistcoat, but the intruder, lithe as a cat, closed on his wrist with an iron grip, and presently there clattered to the table with a pure metallic ring a neat little pistol, whose short double snout was blue as Tubman's face.

"How did you get out of jail?" Tubman roared.

Madame Louise peered in at the door. But the patrons scarcely looked up from their tables. No bottles had been thrown; there was no uproar.

Everyone carried arms of one sort or another. Till they were used, it was no matter for the police. Her pale unblinking eyes swept the taproom and seemed to approve the clientele. Tubman was not the brawling sort; as for the newcomer, she knew he did not dare to brawl.

"I got out the same way you got me in," the newcomer said calmly, holding tight to Tubman's wrist, twisting with a force that kept Tubman in his seat and made him cringe with pain.

"You deserved jail; you deserved hanging, you filthy pirate!"

"But here I am, Señor Tubman," he said suavely, "free as a bird. Would you care to read the governor's disposition of my case? You do read, Señor Tubman?"

"You dirty Spaniard!"

"Do you think you ought to break his wrist?" Jock asked. He reached over and shook the priming out of the pistol and returned it to Tubman. "There is no reason to be rude, Mr. Tubman."

Tubman glared at him. Webb grinned, and the newcomer relinquished his grip. Tubman rubbed his injured wrist.

Jock said, "Perhaps you will introduce your friend, who seems to agree that you are the only buyer in Jamaica."

"Don Jesu de Silva," Tubman grumbled, while the Spaniard bowed to Jock, "late of the government jail on a piracy charge, released heaven only knows how."

"Through no good offices of Señor Tubman, I assure you," Don Jesu said. "Señor Paul, your servant."

"You might as well sit down," Tubman said. "One feels easier without you behind his back."

Drawing up a chair, the Spaniard said pleasantly, "Señor Tubman's eloquent testimony before the governor very nearly placed a rope around my neck, but I was able to persuade his excellency that I and all my crew were innocent as babes and that my letters of marque during the late war were not forged but perfectly genuine. He even recognized his own signature on them."

"How big a bribe did you pay to open his eyes?"

"Señor Tubman is commercial," Don Jesu said, waving aside the question as unworthy of notice. "And you, of course, are Captain Paul?"

"Your servant," said Jock.

"Captain Newton spoke highly of you, señor. I was instrumental in apprising him of a packet that was about to sail for England. He was eager to depart and grateful for the information."

"His disappearance was awkward for me," Jock said.

"But a blessing for me! He had something I greatly desired, a certain chalice which he habitually profaned, to his own detriment, and which I shall restore to its proper setting. He gave it to me."

"I'm afraid the captain's popish cup is ship's property," Jock said. "I am not at liberty to deliver it."

"My dear Señor Paul, I already have it."

"How can you? He took nothing ashore."

Tubman muttered, "He didn't have to."

Don Jesu's diamond fairly scintillated.

"I set a strict watch," Jock said, "I don't see how —"

"I did not feel I ought to draw the attention of the watch to my visit," Don Jesu said.

"You boarded my ship undetected, you entered the great cabin and made off with the captain's chalice?"

"I did, alas," smiled the Spaniard. "But recollect that Señor Newton, believing it to be his own, had given it to me. In truth, since it was blessed, it belongs to no man, but to God. I shall return it."

Tubman said in his thoughts, "When you meet God, which you won't."

"I see I shall have to set a stricter watch," Jock said.

"It wasn't Don Jesu's first act of robbery at sea," Tubman said.

"At least I have never borne false witness," the Spaniard said, his eyes narrowing as if he were sighting along a gun barrel.

"None of my testimony at your trial was false," Tubman retorted.

"Wholly unsubstantiated," Don Jesu said airily. "Figments, imaginings. Do I not tell a truth now, no matter how unpalatable to Señor Paul? This gentleman, sir, this excellent merchant, this indescribable Geoffrey Tubman — he is indeed the only buyer of blacks in Jamaica, since all the others dare not offer a penny more than he. *Verdad, mi señor?* Once one did, and his barracoons instantly burned to the ground."

"I have been moderately successful," Tubman said, "and my colleagues naturally look to me as a sort of senior partner."

"I see," Jock said.

"Has Señor Tubman already made you an offer on your cargo?" Don Jesu asked.

"Thirty pounds," Jock said, "but rather than take it I'll sail on to Virginia and dispose of my blacks there."

Tubman replied, "That is a vain and useless threat. Please to remember that I am intimately connected with Colonel — you know the colonel I refer to. His greatest fear is that gossip will link him with the slave trade. His reputation is valuable, and he has a daughter. Once you appear in

Fredericksburg with a cargo of slaves, he will disown you, the ship, the profits, everything. No sacrifice will be too great to protect his name, and especially the name of his precious Kitty." Tubman wrinkled his nose at the mention of her; Jock could have strangled him, but he controlled his temper, recognizing the validity of Tubman's cold logic. "No, I do not think you will sail on to Virginia with your cargo."

Don Jesu said, "But Señor Tubman, thirty pounds! For shame! Twenty-nine or thirty-one, not thirty! Remember what happened to Judas."

"It was hardly the same sort of transaction," Tubman said.

"Didn't Judas hang himself?" Jock said.

"Don Jesu will not hang himself," Tubman said. "There will be willing hands to help."

"Perhaps I shall not be hanged," Don Jesu said musing, as if it were a new and interesting possibility. "I am thinking of new ventures. The late war's end, this dull new peace, the inactivity — look at the ships in the harbor, with no mission to stir the heart or spur the soul: perhaps I shall lapse into legal trade. What would you think, Captain Paul?"

"I'd think it no disgrace. English gentlemen trade."

"I'd think it a miracle," Tubman said.

"Thirty pounds, when the going price is forty! Señor Paul, I, Don Jesu, Marqués de Silva y Villanueva, I offer you fifty per head for your cargo."

"It isn't worth it," Tubman said.

"Quite by accident I have observed it," Don Jesu said. "It is."

"This man is bankrupt!" Tubman said. "It is impossible not to be bankrupt when you buy a pardon for piracy in Jamaica!"

"Are you bankrupt, Don Jesu?" Jock asked smiling. He had ordered a drink for the Spaniard, whom he liked because the Spaniard so obviously liked him. Moreover, the feat of stealing aboard a well-disciplined ship and making off with a valuable object was not to be despised. The man was undeniably interesting.

"I am not bankrupt," Don Jesu said.

"Then governors' pardons have woefully fallen in price," Tubman said.

"And if I were, I have no doubt that I could easily raise money on my personal credit. Many of my friends are, so to speak, gentlemen of fortune."

"There is no denying that," Tubman said. The Spaniard had shaken him. In his mind's eye he envisioned the ship of the pardoned pirate standing offshore some moonless night and lancing a few mischievous red-hot shots into his barracoons, burning them down and retreating unscathed into the misty Atlantic: a pleasant exercise in gunnery for Don Jesu's crew, who must be as bored as their master with inactivity, and a gentle reminder that Don Jesu resented Tubman's testimony at the trial. What an error of judgment that testimony now appeared to have been.

Tubman forced a smile: "Captain de Silva has the advantage of me since he has, ahem, already inspected your cargo. I shall meet his price, Captain Paul."

Jock said, "He offered it first. Captain de Silva, I am grateful to you, and you shall have my cargo."

"I'll give you fifty-five," Tubman said, beginning to sweat profusely. The Spaniard's ship, in his mental picture, had now been joined by a dozen of his friends, those gentlemen of fortune. Now that the war was over, the islands would swarm with them. No longer would legitimate hostilities between nations afford them a vestige of respectability and endow them with letters of marque. Unemployed, they would sink from privateers to outright pirates. Their money spent, they would prey on ships of any flag indiscriminately. Too late Geoffrey Tubman realized that that was why the governor had been so quick to pardon Don Jesu: the fraternity of pirates, Don Jesu in their lead, had exacted and received a sort of tribute to keep them passive. No doubt the English exchequer justified the payment by calling it a retirement pension. There was ample precedent for such things.

"Don't you think your blacks are worth more than fifty-five?" the Spaniard asked slyly. "What *are* they worth, Captain Paul? I can pay." He seemed greatly amused at Tubman's fright. "In gold."

It was not Jock's intention to play off one against the other. He disliked Tubman intensely, but he did not wish to make an enemy of him for Colonel Fielding's sake; and as for the Spanish gentleman, he was clearly untrustworthy.

"Captain Paul does not wish to be paid in gold," Tubman said.

Don Jesu raised his eyebrows. "No?"

"No, actually I don't," Jock said. "It hasn't been the arrangement heretofore."

"How curious," Don Jesu said, genuinely interested. "What in the name of all the saints *do* you wish to be paid in?"

"First-quality rum is the usual medium," Jock said. "Then later on, of course, we exchange the rum for other commodities."

"That seems a very indirect procedure," Don Jesu said, puzzling it out.

"I don't suppose you happen to have a shipload of rum for Captain Paul," Tubman said. The sarcastic note had crept back into his tone, but faintly: Don Jesu just *might* have a shipload of rum.

133

"Señor Tubman is raking me, Captain Paul. Rum! How long would it last among the extremely bibulous gentlemen who make up my crew? Gold I can lock away from them; rum — alas!" He shrugged. "I take it, Captain Paul, that you reject my offer?" There was not the slightest resentment in his voice; but if he honestly wanted to reform and engage in some decent trade, Jock felt he ought not to discourage him.

Jock said, "I am instructed to take payment in rum, and we are used to Mr. Tubman's brand; but since you have gone out of your way to be kind and to act, as it were, as an intermediary between Mr. Tubman and me at a moment when we were frankly at loggerheads, it seems only fair that you should be paid an agent's commission of, say, ten per cent. That would be — let me see — thirty-three hundred pounds, wouldn't you say, Mr. Tubman?"

"Over and above my fifty-five per head?" Tubman thundered.

"I can hardly deduct it myself."

"*You* are the pirate, Mr. Paul."

"Payable in rum?" the Spaniard asked. "I should like that."

"Certainly," Tubman agreed. In his mental picture the vengeful ships ceased fire. His barracoons rose from their ashes. He had got off cheaply.

"Wonderful are the ways of honest trade!" marveled Don Jesu de Silva y Villanueva. "To think that nobody gets hanged for it!" He flashed his diamond smile, saluted them profoundly and returned to the other part of the house from whence he had come.

"You'll pay him, I suppose," Jock said.

"I'll have to."

Over the horizon of Tubman's fears the pirate ships still hovered, threatening.

"You can take possession of the cargo tomorrow morning," Jock said.

"Not too early, I hope."

"Dawn ought to be just about right."

Tubman sighed. "Oh, very well." Wastage was chargeable to *him* from now on. It had not been a profitable evening.

"I'd like the rum aboard by nightfall."

"You are in an extraordinary hurry to clear port, Captain Paul."

"Yes, I am."

"One would have thought that you would stay and refresh yourself for a day or two —" His pudgy hand embraced in a wave the amenities of Madame Louise's establishment. "Most captains do. It does smell good. Ought to be quite a change."

"It is not my intention to insult you, Mr. Tubman, but I know of a rose garden in Virginia that smells a great deal better."

Wearily Tubman shrugged.

Nothing Jock could do could insult him any more.

But didn't the impetuous young Scot, who bargained so shrewdly, realize that spring was past and roses no longer bloomed?

Chapter 14

YOU HAVE MADE an excellent beginning," Colonel Fielding exclaimed, "and I hear that the ship smells like a vintage French liqueur! Superb! How did you manage it?"

"When we left Jamaica," Jock said, "I scrubbed her with salt and scattered roasted coffee into the bilges. The only really foul spot was in a well around one of the pumps: an odor persisted there. We found a small body in an advanced state of decay stuck in the suction hose."

"Some animal?"

"No, I'm afraid it was a child."

"Glad you found it before you reached port. A thing like that could have caused gossip. You chucked it overboard, I presume."

"I stopped ship and read the burial service over her," Jock said. "It was a little girl."

"Oh well, no harm done. That couldn't have taken long. I'm glad you kept everything tidy. *Misericordia* smells like an East Indiaman now, respectable as a bishop." He rubbed his hands.

They were drinking a friendly glass at the Turk's Head, Fielding having ventured no closer to the ship.

"Newton was always unpredictable," Fielding said. "I only kept him on because he was a good trader. Now it seems I have just as good a trader, nay, a better one. It was a shrewd maneuver to get over fifty pounds per head in the present market. I must say, though, your commission to that piratical Spaniard was pretty liberal."

"I couldn't have managed Tubman without him. Tubman wasn't a bit impressed by my threat to bring the cargo here."

"It's a good thing you didn't, or you'd have had me to deal with," Fielding said unpleasantly.

"That's why I dealt with the pirate."

Fielding glanced at him sharply. "Don't you like your work, Captain Paul?"

"I like the pay and the profits."

"Both will increase," Fielding said genially, "and there's no reason why you shouldn't continue on as captain."

"I don't think I'll make any more trips," Jock said, wondering what sort of excuse Fielding would accept. "I ought not to be gone so long. I lose touch with my own agency business."

"You certainly are out of touch. Have you read your letters from Scotland?"

"No, I reported to you first."

"When you read them," Colonel Fielding said, "you may think better of leaving the *Misericordia.*"

"What has happened in Scotland?"

"My dear fellow, it's happening in the whole world."

"Are my parents alive and well? For obvious reasons I could not write them from Africa."

"Alive, well, happy, and prompt in signing receipts for your remittances, which were sent to them regularly by my auditor. Your brother Willie doesn't write them much."

"He never did."

"My auditor took the responsibility of keeping them apprised of your health, merely saying you would write soon but that you were terribly busy just at the moment."

"It was kind of you to arrange that."

Fielding said, "We're working together, aren't we?"

But the news from Scotland was very bad. Her victorious war had loaded England with monstrous debts. Huge chunks of the earth's surface — Canada, India — and millions of new subjects had passed under the dominion of the British Crown but remained undigested and unprofitable. Trade stagnated. Jock had seen the idle ships in Jamaica, an indication of what was happening all over the world, not only to British vessels but to vessels of all nations; for if the victor does not prosper after a glorious war, how can the vanquished?

There were ominous items in the newspapers that King George was frequently indisposed. No hint had as yet leaked out that His Majesty's trouble might be mental; but for long periods he seemed unwilling, or unable, to affix his signature to parliamentary acts. Then, in a frenzy of activity, he would sign everything at once.

The prime minister was equally erratic. By a singular coincidence, which boded no good for the mighty, swollen and vastly complex empire, he was just as mad as his master. Seldom in history has Fate visited with lunacy the two most powerful men in the world. Both would recover from their attacks, but at that critical stage in the world's affairs much damage was done and the seed of future trouble sown, trouble that soon was to burgeon and grow beyond the most dire imaginings.

Lord Sandwich, head of the British Admiralty, might have steadied the empire whose unchallenged fleets must now regulate the trade and patrol the oceans of the whole world. But Lord Sandwich was an idler and a gambler, who distinguished himself only in trifles. He gave his name, which would otherwise have been forgotten, to some beautiful Pacific islands, and to a kitchen discovery that enabled one to continue at the gaming table without pausing for food: he ordered a servant to cut a piece of meat and place it between two slices of bread, which he promptly devoured in one hand, the other being free to hold the cards. This momentous invention, the "sandwich," became fashionable and contributed its share to the indigestion of mankind and to the postwar depression that gripped the world.

Under this trinity of two madmen and a fool things were bound to go wrong. Taxes rose, administration faltered, and trade stood still.

One of the financial casualties, one among many in a dozen countries, was the Scottish firm of John Younger, which went bankrupt. Mr. Craik wrote, "I am glad I did not invest."

The commercial tie between Jock and the laird of Arbigland was severed now, and though Craik's letter was friendly, his tone was gloomy, complaining of the hard times and high prices in Scotland. He did not advise Jock to return, and wished him good luck with his agency in the New World.

But Jock's agency was also hard hit, and except for his share of the *Misericordia* venture he would have been unable to continue his remittances to his mother and father just when his parents needed them most.

Even Willie complained. "Mr. Henry ordered a cotton shirt, Jock," he said. "Think of it — cotton!"

Bessie said, "I should think any man with six children to support would have to wear cotton shirts."

"It isn't like Mr. Patrick Henry," Willie said.

"The sempstress told me that Dorothea Dandridge is wearing an old petticoat of her mother's, cut down," Bessie said.

"It must need a great deal of cutting down," Willie said.

"Not so much. Dorothea's getting quite big."

"I didn't notice."

"He really didn't, Jock," said Bessie.

"Why should he? He isn't a ladies' tailor."

"You don't have to be a ladies' tailor to observe that the Dandridge girl is going to be a beauty."

"Are the Dandridges still staying with the Fieldings?" Jock asked with unconvincing indifference.

"You needn't beat around the bush," Willie laughed. "You don't give a hoot whether the Dandridges are in town or not. You're thinking of Kitty, I can tell."

"Kitty spoke of you many times while you were in Jamaica," Bessie said. "We must have her and the colonel to dinner."

"Indeed we must," Willie said. "She's a catch, Jock lad, especially in times like these."

"So is Jock," Bessie said stanchly.

Jock said, "She would be at any time."

It was certainly easier now, Bessie thought with satisfaction, to attract dinner guests of the social stature of Colonel Fielding and his daughter than it had been before Jock came. Jock conferred a sort of distinction upon Bessiwill, the plantation house that people tried to forget had been built by a tailor. It was difficult, even in America which was less snobbish than the mother country, for some gentlemen to sup with a tradesman who only that afternoon had measured them for breeches, with pins in his mouth and a tape around his neck. It was not so difficult when that trades- man had for a brother a young unattached man of exceptional good looks who showed unmistakable signs of rising in the world: everyone knew that Jock's provisioning agency had prospered — at least till the present hard times, and even now it was solvent — and that Jock was already captain of a ship just back from a successful trading voyage to Jamaica. Respectable widows with marriageable daughters began to gossip over their tea — though it was more often coffee nowadays since the trouble up in Massa- chusetts — that Bessie Paul was quite charming actually, even if her hus- band did do a little tailoring on the side, and it might be worth while to make her acquaintance. Beyond doubt Bessiwill and its surrounding planta- tion were handsome. Willie's holding of acres and slaves was substantial, above reproach. If only he would give up tailoring. "He's a Scot," some would say. "He doesn't know the difference, just as long as he grows richer and richer." Somehow that did not dampen the widows' interest, for Jock, his blood brother, was equally a Scot, equally promising and providentially unattached.

Bessie indeed could have filled her long table with social leaders, but for Jock's sake, knowing his heart, she invited only the colonel and Kitty. "I'll take out all the leaves," she told Willie, plotting happily, "so the table will be small and intimate."

He agreed at once and fell in with her mood, but the seating pattern, like the pattern of a well-planned suit, troubled him. "Will you place Kitty and Jock across from each other so he can look at her, or will you seat them next to each other so he can, well, be near her?"

"I shall certainly seat them side by side," she said, secure of her ground. "He's been away from her long enough. I never knew a trip to Jamaica took so long."

"Neither did I," Willie said. "But Jock says it's the hard times, the endless haggling, searching for bargains to sell at a profit."

So Kitty and Jock sat side by side, while Willie's Fulani table servants served smoothly and unobtrusively. Jock thought, with a rising heart, intoxicated by Kitty's perfumed nearness, that this was the best of all possible worlds, or would be if he could be certain he need not return to Africa. The colonel discoursed optimistically on the state of the world and speculated on the nature of the king's illness and looked for an early upturn in trade. Bessie dwelt on the asters in her garden — she had planted a whole border of them this year — which would soon be coming into bloom. Kitty said, "Jock, I counted all the full moons. You said they made tides and brought ships back into the river; but that didn't work and I stopped counting. Maybe full moons are so attractive in Jamaica that one simply remains there."

Bessie caught her teasing tone and said, "I'd wager Jock didn't once look up at a full moon all during the time he was trading in Jamaica."

"Actually, I didn't," Jock said. *Misericordia* had spent exactly two days in Kingston Harbor discharging slaves and loading rum. It had been the dark of the moon. It was still the dark of the moon.

"I doubt whether Captain Paul plans to bore you with tiresome commercial details, my dear," Fielding said amiably. "Jock, will you stay for the port and a smoke? You don't look like a man who wants either."

"Fathers have horribly heavy hands," Kitty said, "when they decide to marry off their daughters." But she did not seem displeased.

139

"I'd thought it might be pleasant to look at Bessie's asters," Jock said. "Remember, I'm a gardener's son."

Fielding said, "You'd never guess it now."

Bessie said, "It's black as the pit in the garden, Jock. Take care."

Willie said, speaking from old memory, "Jock can spot a trap a mile away on the darkest night," and thought of the press gang's boat.

Kitty said archly, "What a comparison! And who said the trap would be a mile away?"

Together they went into the starlit garden, while Fielding and Willie drank the port and Bessie, because there was nothing else to do, remained with them, a little uncomfortable since she was the only woman and feared that her presence might hamper the free flow of exclusively male conversation.

Shortly her upstairs girl appeared and whispered in her ear. The girl said that one of the kitchen boys had told her that Captain Paul's body servant, new to service, Chima by name, was roaring drunk and creating a disturbance. Bessie excused herself, glad to leave the men to their treasured indelicacies. As if the ladies did not know the same words! Still, it was nice that they didn't use them in a lady's presence. She went out to investigate.

There can be no doubt that great masses of honest people think differently from other great masses of honest people concerning an identical situation. England, the mother country, was close to the heart of the colonists; but how remote, how mysterious, how utterly unimportant to their slaves. In a similar fashion Africa, unthinkably dark and vague to the colonists, was the mother country of slaves, of their culture, nations, tribes and family connections.

Even with blacks who were born in America the African ties were remembered; with the newly captured, the first generation, they were ever present, no matter how devoted a slave, through love or good treatment, might grow towards his master. To the continual astonishment of the colonists, who seemed to assume that a black's existence began, full grown, on the auction block, a slave would discover a father, a mother, sometimes a child, after years of separation, living by the mercy of the tribal or the Christian God, on the very plantation to which he had come after, perhaps, a dozen sales.

In Willie's comfortable slave quarters behind the house a cousin had recognized Chima and welcomed him with a rattle of joyous finger-snapping that sounded like a collapsing egg crate and a fang-filled grin as formidable as Chima's own, plying him with Willie's brandy, stolen from Willie's unguarded cellar, and congratulating him on having fallen to so considerate a master as Willie Paul. Brandy was totally new to Chima and affected him with the shock of a sudden religious conversion. His master was *not* Willie Paul, he declared, but Captain John Paul, whose station was as superior to the tailor's as were *ogalanya*, the noble and fearless warriors, to *omise*, the despised class of laborers, collectors of the night soil. Thus, each extolling the merits of his own master, their voices rose, till Chima stumbled off in a dudgeon and was sick among the asters, where he lay for some time disconsolate.

In the garden, lighted by stars scattered prodigally through all the dimensions of the overwhelming profundity of the sky — which is never so dark as the earth beneath — there was abundant illumination for Jock's vision, which was naturally keen and trained by long watches at sea. Plainly beneath his steps he could see the ribbon of the gravel walk; he saw the foliage of the flowers, the boles of trees, the tracery of trellises; and beyond, the blocked-out masses of stables, kennels and slave cabins — a picture colorless but complete in subtle shades of darkness.

But to Kitty, whose eyes were accustomed to brighter light, the night was pit-black. She leaned on his arm, and once when she stumbled a little she felt his arm slip round her waist, supporting her; and thereafter she was content to surrender to his surer guidance.

She had surrendered a great deal, he was happily, proudfully aware. She had promised to be his wife when he should return; and now that he had returned she had not abjured her promise. On the contrary she had confirmed it with touching sweetness by her little joke at her father's expense — "when fathers decide to marry off their daughters." She was willing to link her life with his and give up the proud name of Fielding for the unknown name of Paul; to lose her aristocratic English lineage in an alliance with a descendant of Scottish gardeners, farmers, craftsmen, gunsmiths, tavern keepers and stolid pot-wallopers.

Jock knew little about his forebears, but obscure respectability was all they could claim; not one had ever risen to distinction, not even so high as a gallows. In the star-spangled night with its myriads of eternal fires as witness, with darkness to conceal his emotion, he swore a secret oath to become rich, reputable, renowned, worthy of the sacrifices she had made through love of him, and to raise the name of Paul to the level of Fielding; and then, God willing, beyond. The ambition he had always cherished to rise in the world was now goaded, whipped, spurred into frenzy, for now, quite suddenly, it was no longer selfish.

141

"What are you eating, Jock?" Her voice came clear and laughing, but it seemed from a very great distance. He clutched her tighter, lest he lose her.

"Eat — what?"

"That awful grinding." She laughed. "For goodness' sake, don't break me in two!"

He realized that he must have clenched his teeth in the passions of his resolve until they actually audibly gnashed. He relaxed the arm around her waist, feeling sheepish and abashed.

"A woman has ribs — here —" she said, running his hand over the place. "It's a lucky thing I don't wear stays; you'd have cracked them too. What in the world were you thinking about just now?"

The oath was still upon him; candidly he avowed it: "Wealth, position, fame — oh, my dear, my dear — !"

"Oh," she said. It hadn't felt at all like that. "It doesn't matter. Father will help us at first."

"You are giving up so much; but can't you see that it's exactly for that reason that I mustn't accept a farthing from your father?"

"Are times really so hard, Jock?"

"They'll be better."

"Till they are I can help; I have something of my own."

"I don't want that either; all I want is you."

Her laughter was throaty. "Just me? Stripped of *everything*? Oh, Jock, shame on you. Still, I suppose, a bride —"

"Kitty, I didn't mean it that way at all." But her intimate teasing had had its effect, and he crushed her to him.

In a moment she whispered against his lips, "I cannot see you, but I feel that you did." She drew away from him slightly. "I shan't mind if you want us to live as if we were poor, not at first anyway. But I know it won't be for long. Father never misjudges his men, and he says you were born to be wealthy. He speaks of your success in Jamaica. He admits he doesn't know how you did it — but of course Father can't be expected to know all the details of his businesses. But already you've managed to make better deals than Captain Newton ever did, and Newton had ever so much more experience than you. Father is almost as happy to have found Captain Paul as I am, and I'm even more happy because Father is."

"You love him a great deal, don't you, Kitty?"

"More than anybody, I think. Shouldn't I?"

"Of course you should. I shall try never to disappoint you, or him."

Something in Bessie's border of asters grunted, moved and got up. It stumbled towards them, apelike in silhouette, its hulking shadow monstrously exaggerated by proximity and darkness. It stank sickeningly of brandy — brandy drunk, gone sour, and regurgitated. It lunged unsteadily against them. Kitty screamed and drew back. Jock pushed it away with his hand, and Chima collapsed. Recognizing him, Chima groveled back and clasped his knees.

"What are you doing here! Go back to the quarters at once!"

"What *is* it?" Kitty gasped, holding her skirts away from the creature.

"It's only Chima, a manservant I bought in, ah, Kingston. I'm afraid he's been drinking. I'll have to punish him."

"Only new imports behave like this when they drink," Kitty said with disgust.

"New, yes, new," Chima said. "I didn't know. In Africa —"

"Chima, be quiet!"

"Yes, master."

But the terrible need of the terribly intoxicated to justify themselves overwhelmed Chima, and he blubbered: "I celebrated with my new-found cousin; he praised his master; I praised my master more. I said, 'My master is greater than any master, braver, kinder, nobler. My master defied the Ofo. My master saved me from thunder juju.' Did he believe me, my stupid cousin? He did not. 'My master brought more black men than any white man ever, and kept them in health on a gundeck. My master subdued Onumba and dashed him with a black girl, his own property, very young, very valuable, bought and paid for —"

"Chima! Silence! Not another word!" Jock commanded him in Ibo.

In Ibo Chima's litany of praise continued for probably sixty seconds, a long full harrowing minute. Between Chima's drunken gasps for breath Jock tried to make himself heard, commanding, entreating, threatening.

"This is the woman I love."

"She is blessed above all women."

"She is going to be my wife."

"God send you ten thousand children."

"She must never find out that I bought and sold blacks."

"God curse the man who tells her."

"You told her."

"I shall never tell her, nor shall my cousin, nor anyone else, or I will kill them."

Kitty said, spitting out the words as if they defiled her tongue: "Only *slavers* speak African, Captain Paul. Thank you for letting me know how it happened that you lingered so long in Jamaica. Father will be interested to discover that you used his time to fatten your own purse. He hates slavers."

She paused. Then with hate-filled finality, she said, "Captain Paul, I *loathe you.*"

Bessie approached them. Observing how dark it was, she had not ventured out until one of the kitchen staff had found and lighted a lantern. In its smoky glow Kitty's face shone white as a marble Fury.

"The detail concerning your black mistress was particularly enlightening, Captain Paul. You almost make me loathe myself."

Superbly erect, she swept by Bessie Paul without a glance at her.

"The colonel and his daughter left with astonishing suddenness," Willie said, confused. "Kitty was in a frightful pet. Lovers' quarrel, I suppose?" He tried to smile hopefully.

"I don't think so, Willie."

"Fielding was trying to calm her down, trying to smooth the thing out, whatever it was that made her angry. They're not angry at us, are they, Bessie? Bless my soul, I hope not."

"Kitty wouldn't speak to me. I get the feeling they won't come here again."

"Jock wouldn't speak to me either. I asked him what had happened."

"What did he say?"

"All he said was, 'Go back to your confounded tailoring. It's so exquisitely respectable,' and slammed the door of his room in my face. Didn't make sense."

"Willie, Jock's man was in the garden."

"Did you ask him what was the matter?"

"Of course I did."

"Wouldn't he talk either?"

"He made sewing motions with his finger around his mouth. He was drunk."

"The new ones are always queer for a while."

"The kitchen boy helped him back to a cabin. He talked loudly with another slave for a minute or two and then everything quieted down."

"What were they saying?"

"The kitchen boy didn't know; he's a Fulani and he can't understand Ibo."

"I'd hate to lose Colonel Fielding's patronage," Willie muttered. "He's helped me in all sorts of ways — the fine acquaintances I've made —"

"Don't you care what's happened to Jock?"

"Of course I do. But Jock always lands on his feet like a cat."

He pondered heavily.

"I think Kitty is merely angry at Jock," he said at length. "The colonel, on the other hand, is not angry at Jock or at us. If he were, he would not have tried to smooth the thing over. He is quick to loose his sword, so to speak, at the smallest slight to her. Everyone knows she's the apple of his eye. Ergo," he pronounced, the syllogism complete, "it was merely a lovers' quarrel. You know how lovers quarrel."

"We didn't," she said.

"Oh, I'm not Jock," Willie said in mixed admiration and irritation. "I'd be a nervous wreck if you were."

Chapter 15

ALL THROUGH the night Jock sat alone in his room, unconscious that he was sitting in the dark. Kitty's face was still before his eyes, beautiful, flaming with fury. Kitty's voice was still in his ear, burning with scorn: *I loathe you, I loathe you, I loathe you,* regular as a Lagos drum (Lagos had brought this agony), regular as a ship's pump (he saw again the small black body lodged in the suction hose — damn black bodies!), regular as the beating of a heart. Nay, the horrid sound *was* his heart, pounding furiously. Did he have a heart? Do hearts break? "Yes," said his heart.

"The heart," retorted his mind, "is a material organ whose function is to circulate blood throughout the members of the body. It is an excellent pump, superbly engineered and extremely efficient. That is all we know about the heart and all we need to know. Enlightened scientists of our modern eighteenth century discredit the ancient myths which designated the heart as the seat of emotion. It is sentimental twaddle to speak of hearts as 'breaking.' Hearts do not break."

"But they ache," Jock said to the darkness.

A fleeting remembrance of a Biblical personage brushed close to his consciousness and flickered out: the man in the land of Uz whose name was Job, sitting among the ashes, smitten with loathsome boils and scraping himself with a potsherd, utterly abandoned and alone. It was not an age when Biblical references occurred readily to anyone; reason and common sense were in the ascendant; it was an ebb tide of faith; science, with a growing paraphernalia of clever instruments, was at the flood. But during that wakeful painful night Jock sensed a kinship with Job, Job's loathsomeness and loneliness.

Reason and common sense indeed might have lighted a way out of his darkness. It would have been possible to make a simple avowal of truth: "Yes, Kitty, I did buy and sell slaves; I am a slaver; so are half the fine gentlemen of Fredericksburg; so is your father, who employs me." But he had not spoken thus in the garden and he knew now that he never would. He did not ask himself why he could not take this easy way out, for he did not wish to face the fact that reason and common sense would provide no answer. Only the heart could do that, the mythical, illogical, discredited heart.

At breakfast time Bessie knocked timidly at his door, asking if he was all right.

He was quite all right, he answered in a hollow voice that was completely courteous and completely frightening. She hurried to her husband.

Willie's voice was next. "Jock, lad, are you coming down?"

"Directly," said Jock.

As the long night hours had worn themselves out, thinking had become easier and more rational. He still loved Kitty desperately. It was not in his nature to cast away anything he cherished. It was not in his nature to go down without a fight. With morning had come a scheme to win her back.

Blank denial.

And included in the scheme was a powerful confederate, as deeply enmeshed as himself: Colonel Fielding, her father.

Composed, but pale, he left Bessiwill and rode towards the water front.

"He didn't eat his breakfast," Bessie said.

"He looked gaunt," Willie said. "I'm afraid it was worse than a lovers' quarrel."

Bessie said, "He looked haunted."

Knowing the colonel's dislike of being seen in the vicinity of ships, Jock looked for him first at the Turk's Head. He was told that the colonel indeed had been there, and had asked for him. Jock smiled to himself; it was a good omen; he felt sure of his confederate. He found Fielding outside the provisioning agency, pretending to enjoy the air.

Inside, having sent away his clerk, Jock waited for Fielding's opening, wondering what turn it would take. When it came, it was formidable underneath its icy politeness. "I shall be interested to hear how you propose to extricate yourself from the predicament you find yourself in, Mister Paul." No word of how Jock might feel; no hint of encouragement; a significant dropping of the "Captain." Fielding apparently considered *himself* in no predicament.

Jock wondered what the papers were that the colonel was tapping ostentatiously with his beautifully polished nails, and recognized with a start that they were the ship's manifests: these were the records signed by John Paul that disposed of five hundred and seventy-eight living black humans. No doubt the other sheets were the records of purchases, and one of them covered Chima, one Onumba's "dash" — three little pigs and a little black girl, signed for, duly received by, John Paul. Clearly Colonel Fielding did not enter a conference unprepared. This was not the willing confederate Jock had expected.

"Well, Mr. Paul?"

Jock fenced. He knew the danger of allowing himself to be placed on the defensive.

"It is maddening, Colonel Fielding, to find myself suddenly an object of loathing by the woman I love and who, until the unfortunate episode of last night, I had every reason to believe returned my affection. You yourself, sir, gave me leave to woo her."

"It would appear that she has changed her mind. She no longer wants you. If my daughter's affection has cooled, Mr. Paul, it is neither my wish nor is it in my power to rekindle it. I shall always allow her the greatest latitude in making the choice of her own husband — so long as he is a gentleman. We shall speak no more of my daughter."

"You are a gentleman, Colonel Fielding. If you are, then so am I."

"A gentleman always remembers to be discreet," Fielding said, tapping the papers.

"Sir, I have done nothing you have not done ten times over."

"You signed these."

"Someone had to sign them. You cannot clear port without signing ship's papers."

"I am aware of that elemental requirement, Mr. Paul. I merely draw your attention to the fact that your name, not mine, is the one that appears."

Jock's anger rose. "I do not conceive, Colonel Fielding, that you will exhibit the *Misericordia*'s manifests among your fine friends with the purpose of demonstrating that John Paul is a slaver. Has it escaped your memory that you are the owner of the ship?"

"By no means. Part owner, at least. There are several other gentlemen in the venture."

"So if you disgrace me you disgrace yourself."

147

"Not at all. When a landlord owns a house and the tenant turns that house into a brothel, the landlord stands blameless. I assure you that I feel myself on the firmest of legal grounds."

With a sinking heart Jock realized that Fielding's position must indeed be firm. A man like Fielding would certainly long since have made the legal maneuvers that would clear his name in case the true nature of *Misericordia's* traffic ever leaked out.

Fielding, now launched upon the offensive, quickly consolidated his gains, speaking in a softer voice that was somehow more ominous. "It is not my intention to disgrace you, Mr. Paul. What would I gain by ruining the name of a very young, very capable, very personable man? What pleasure could I possibly derive from witnessing the collapse of your provisioning agency — do not deceive yourself; your customers would leave you. And poor Willie. He would lose Bessiwill. No doubt he'd be glad to be rid of it when decent people refused to speak to him. He and Bessie would have to live over the shop again, I suppose. That would not be good for Willie. It has seemed to me lately that his health has declined."

Jock listened to the smooth and frigid voice, controlling his anger. Some of this, a little, might be exaggerated. Most of it was horribly true, especially the reference to Willie's inevitable ostracism. Willie would be ruined.

"I remember also your father and mother, so far away, so dependent on their son in these hard times for their sustenance. Do you suppose that I relish the prospect of their actually going hungry in addition to the shame that they would feel?"

"Damn you, sir, why are you threatening me?"

"I dislike the word. I am simply informing you, John Paul" — and now the cynical tone was dropped and the truth rang clear in Fielding's voice and his taunting face was stricken — "that I am a father with a love so deep for my child that I should happily commit murder for her. Kitty must never find out, she must never be told, she must never even suspect that I deal in slaves."

Fielding had laid bare the one weapon that Jock knew he could not use; Jock knew he would never tell Kitty; he was silent, waiting.

Fielding said, "I think I should die."

"That would be an excellent solution," Jock said.

Intimation of victory suffused the colonel's thoughts. He had not miscalculated. Love — the silly boy — would seal this young man's lips. "Death solves nothing," he said. "There is a better solution, more comfortable for me, and for you immensely more profitable."

"I shall be interested to hear how you plan to extricate yourself from the predicament you find yourself in, Colonel Fielding."

Fielding nodded, restraining his smile of approval that he felt taking shape on his lips, repressing the "Bravo!" that leaped to his tongue. His finely cultivated instinct for sportsmanship — and the colonel's was strong — applauded the younger man, so deeply hurt and so patently helpless, foundering in a storm of greater experience and damning evidence but still able to make a brave gesture of turning the victor's own words against him, as if Fielding, not Paul, had lost the encounter. In the moment of Jock's defeat Fielding wished wistfully that they were on the same side. What a son-in-law John Paul would have made! But since Kitty was involved, there could be no question of that now; he must remain the enemy.

"How fortunate you actually are, though you do not recognize it! What would I not give to possess your youth and your prospects!" Fielding, having slain the dragon, must now resurrect it so it would fly away and leave him at peace. Having appealed to Jock's innate sense of decency, he recognized it was now time to appeal to Jock's ambition, which Fielding knew ran deep. "The old survive in this world through caution — documents like these, John Paul." The ship's manifests threatened, just out of reach.

"I have learned that it is just as degrading to be called a slaver as to be one," Jock said bitterly.

"Proved is a better word. You see, you cannot prove me a slaver."

"I would not stoop to try."

Fielding, secure, could smile at the scorn.

"That is why I would give so much to possess your youth. You do not need to buttress your life with documents. You can commit one, two, a dozen errors of judgment and strike out again, nothing lost, on a brave new course. How often it happened to me in my youth, till time ran out and my fund of years depleted, like money in the bank. Depend upon it, sir, you can be sure of one thing when you talk to an old man: once he was young. He remembers, and he envies you."

"You can never be sure when you talk to a young man that he will live to be old."

"Are you sure you want to?"

"Frankly, I don't care."

"Do you know what you do want?"

"I knew last night."

Fielding shrugged. "That is now impossible."

149

"It is not necessary to take that line, sir! Your daughter has made it abundantly clear that my very presence defiles her."

"For me, but not for you, she is the only girl in the world. Ponder that. This will pass, John Paul, this will pass. It always does."

"Does it?"

"For the fortunate young, it does."

"As far as she is concerned, I might as well be exactly what she thinks me."

"The important thing," Fielding said, "is not to let the next one know."

"There will be no next one, sir."

"Youth, youth," sighed Colonel Fielding, cynically but not unkindly. "Youth thinks it will never change. It thinks the world will never change, whereas the world is always changing, changing wildly before youth's beautiful dream-blind eyes. Golden opportunities lie open to it; it has only to reach out and grasp; and in a few years, before his hair is as white as his three-guinea wig, the young man is a rich gentleman no matter what his past may hide."

"At the moment I wish only to hide myself."

"I have felt that way."

"I should think you would. For shame?"

"Good heavens, no. For time to think and act and heal."

It was only natural that Jock should wish to absent himself for a while, Fielding said. He himself had often in the past made long trips to which he never referred afterwards. One always wished to put distance between oneself and a locality where unpleasantnesses had occurred. On the other hand, there was no reason to sink into the mire. The ocean's thousand desolate shores were strewn with wrecks of men no less than with wrecks of ships that had failed to weather the storms to which all ships and men were subjected. There was danger of forgetting, in self-centered, self-pitying extremes of emotion, that one still owed a duty to those who still loved one. If Jock wished to withdraw for a while — and what could be more logical? — from a scene that had caused him pain, he, Colonel Fielding, would understand and aid him.

Jock cared very little how he withdrew or what demon showed him the way.

"I know of a ship, no matter how, engaged in a certain trade, the most lucrative in the world, to which you are not a stranger, in which indeed you have acquired notable success —"

"I have considered it," Jock said. "No compass is needed to point a dog back to his vomit."

"Splendid, my boy, splendid! But I do wish," he said, "that someone would teach you to employ more appetizing metaphors."

"I call things what they are."

"A very ill-bred habit that you should break yourself of."

"This would be another of your little ventures, I suppose."

"After the *Misericordia* I should hesitate a long time before employing you again in any venture of mine. No, the ship *Two Friends* belongs to a business acquaintance in Kingston, a man who, as it were, is branching out, having recently made the discovery that the middleman can be placed at a disadvantage." Fielding smiled engagingly. "He has formed a high opinion of your trading methods and would rather employ you than compete with you."

"Tubman?"

"Yes."

"I had forgotten him."

"He did not forget you, Captain Paul."

The "Captain" again.

"It would appear that I have another command."

"I said you would agree to take the *Two Friends* on an arrangement that guaranteed you fifty per cent of the profits. You will, won't you?"

Chapter 16

STANDING ON the quarter-deck of the *Two Friends*, with Africa dim on the horizon, Captain Paul coldly weighed his prospects in life. Rational he had been born, he assured himself, and rational he had lived until he met Kitty. Now he was himself again. Cold logic etched the mistake he had made deep in his mind: he had climbed too high with muddy boots and the mud had caused him to slip and the slip had caused him to fall.

It was a foolish mistake for a sailor. Sailors climbed barefoot, stripped of clumsy shoes, especially of shoes with treacherous mud still clinging to them, stripped of everything that might impede their race to the heights. Next time this sailor dares to aspire above his station, Jock vowed, he will climb on rungs of pure gold, with all the mud washed clean away and forgotten. What but gold had washed the colonel's boots?

Stripped. The word gave him a wry satisfaction. John Paul was unquestionably stripped, divested of everything that might obstruct the accomplishment of the single objective around which his life now revolved. During his talk with Colonel Fielding, Jock's acceptance of the *Two Friends* had come instinctively at a moment of desperation; now he must rationalize it:

"I couldn't very well tell Kitty what her father was. I *couldn't*. And the sly old rascal knew I couldn't."

With Kitty lost, a different set of values took over the management of his life, as if a person with boundless authority had gone through his warehouse and marked down the price of each item of merchandise, including himself. In his mind's eye, mercilessly clear, he saw the price tags: *John Paul (beloved of Kitty) Sterling Quality, Very Rare.* That was crossed out, and in its place: *John Paul (loathed by Kitty) For Quick Disposal. No Reasonable Offer Refused.*

To do the colonel justice, he had behaved most handsomely after Jock's acceptance. He had continued his patronage of Willie, introducing him to a number of new customers, gentlemen of impeccable standing in the community with conservative political views. "Tension with England is increasing every month," Fielding said. "Your brother must not get caught on the wrong side if things really get serious, must he? Willie must have a good solid clientele. These erratic frontiersmen like Patrick Henry" — he brushed them aside with a wave of his elegant hand like annoying flies — "self-made, no background, they won't help Willie a bit if the king should ever decide to send troops. I wish to help Willie."

"I trust you won't tell him of my present employment."

"My greatest desire, sir, is to tell no one."

Without loss to Jock, Fielding had also agreed to take the provisioning agency off his hands. Jock deposited the entire purchase price with Willie with a request, to which Willie agreed, that the monthly remittances to their parents in Scotland be continued.

"Of course I'll continue them, Jock lad. I'd add some of my own too except for the fact —"

"I know, Willie; the new roads."

"Transportation is frightfully expensive," Willie said, pursing his lips.

"I think I'd like a receipt, Willie."

"A *receipt?*"

"Just to keep things neat."

"Upon my soul!" Willie penned the receipt, looking offended. He wrote slowly, painfully. His joints were stiffer, more gnarled every day. Bessie had increased the strength of the tar-water infusion. "Of course, Jock, if you don't trust me."

"I may be gone for some time. It will be a source of comfort once in a while to glance at something tangible that assures me that Father and Mother are taken care of."

"I was afraid you didn't trust me," Willie said peevishly. "What shall I do when it's gone?"

Jock laughed. "I shan't be away *that* long. And if I am, I'll send you more."

Willie did not ask where Jock would be or what he planned to do. Bessie had forbidden that: "When a hound gets hurt, he goes off by himself and licks his wounds till he heals."

"Oh, Jock always lands on his feet."

To be stripped to the bone is a profoundly simplifying experience. One by one the various aspects of his life that had divided his energy and competed for his attention now fell away. Even trading was now reduced to the essential. Formerly his cargo had had to pass through a series of conversions, lest its original nature become known. Now he could call it by its true name: slaves; and he would be called by his true name: slaver. It wasn't pleasant but it was certainly direct, and this time he would take payment in gold: gold, the rungs of the surest ladder on earth, the quick way up.

Fielding indeed had gone so far as to offer to buy Chima, but Jock would not sell him.

"I shouldn't think you'd care to have around you the Negro that caused all the trouble, reminding you of the past."

"Neither should I care to have him killed," Jock said. "He's the only one who knows."

"I would not have destroyed such a good piece of property," Fielding said. "But I admit I'd have sold him overseas, the way I did his cousin."

"You bought his cousin?"

"Willie was delighted to sell the cousin; I paid eighty pounds for him. His cousin knew too, you remember."

The thoroughness of Fielding's resolve to stop gossip at its source struck Jock as mildly commendable. If the man possessed a single redeeming feature, it was fierce blind love of his daughter. Jock could understand, though no longer feel, that love. Distance, passage of time, the fragmentation of all other values had had their effect on the value of Kitty also. Jock seemed to hear the colonel's sophisticated voice, "It will pass. It always does." For the first time Jock began to believe it. Meanwhile, the fragments of life were stirring, joining together again in a simpler harder shape, but whole.

153

Two Friends was broad in the beam, shallow of draft and much given to yawing, a miserable sailer. To keep her on course required twice as much work at the wheel as was needed for the beautiful *Misericordia*. Jock despised her. Once she was caught broadside between two seas which foamed across her, green and deep, and carried away everything in her waist not actually bolted to the deck — the chicken coops, the pigsty, the spare anchor which men had been working on, pounding it with hammers to remove the rust. Jock was reminded of a clumsy fishwife, spilling the contents out of her fat lap. But he liked her a little better after that: he too had lost an anchor. After the accident the men supposed they might look forward to easier work. No sailor liked to pound anchors, and the officers who put them to such work were heartily cursed and grudgingly admired: man-of-war discipline aboard a bloody slaver! They were not to have their ease, however, for Jock set them to shaking the gunpowder. Gunpowder, like champagne, had a tendency to settle, the heavier components seeking the bottom, the lighter the top. A cannon charged with such stratified powder would either fizzle harmlessly like a squib, or explode. Quick-burning and slow-burning components had to be thoroughly, intimately blended. Shaking the casks (each about a hundredweight), with rivulets of sweat tracing white streaks through the grime of their faces, his men murmured among themselves and asked one another, smirking at their own below-decks humor, whether the captain's precious powder butts were not just the right size to be stuffed, as they said, where they ought to be stuffed so the captain would have them with him always. Yet they were in a better humor than might have been expected. Captain Paul was paying them well. He had also unbent, that rare thing in a commander, to explain why the job was necessary. Many of them had lived with gunpowder all their lives; but Captain Paul was the first officer to take time to explain why cannon sometimes missed fire and sometimes blew up, killing the gun crew. They liked a man who knew their jobs better than they did themselves.

When he remembered the sleek obedient *Misericordia*, Jock called the *Two Friends* many insulting names — tub, pot, scow, barge. But awkward as she was, he recognized her good points: the broad expanse of her deck would provide a magnificent platform for cannon. Her spacious interior would carry upwards of a thousand blacks with little more than the usual crowding and little more than the usual wastage in transit. Numerically he would be ahead. If he managed to deliver them alive, Tubman could fatten them up in Jamaica. Jock had transformed the *Two Friends* into a floating warehouse and a floating fortress combined.

154

As the coast line of Africa rose and took shape on the nearing horizon, Jock was aware that its aspect was different from when he had seen it first. Gone were the lazy miasmic mists that had shrouded the uplands and stagnated over Lagos Lagoon. The sky burned with a reddish glow, the sun blazed like iron in a blacksmith's forge, and the bay looked like cheap red wine. Redness was everywhere. The air was furnace-dry; he opened his mouth the better to breathe; when he closed it, his teeth gritted on sand.

This was the season of the harmattan, that hot dry wind from which a thousand miles of Sahara had wrung every atom of moisture, flowing southward another thousand miles over tropical forests, parching them, narcotizing them into the only winter sleep that Africa knows, ripening their fruits and scattering their seeds, the year's dead end. No rain would fall till that wind reversed itself and the seasons changed.

The heat was more fierce than before, but it did not feel oppressive, being dry. And a white man, looking up through the hot red air, might enjoy a curious illusion of cold, for all around him, drifting far out to sea, glinted the snow-white seeds of the bombax trees, upborn on flashing cotton-silk wings. It was the season when caravans came down to the Coast to trade, when the torpor of the rainy months lifted, and blood flowed faster in animals and men. Chima said that the natives called it the Witch Doctor Wind. Even the lepers suffered less during the harmattan season, their sores drying up, their bodies becoming invigorated; and many found new hope of cure, only to have their hopes dashed when the rains returned and their tissues again began to slough away. In the forests and backlands away from the Coast this was a season of ceremonial dancing, wild celebrations, tribal initiations, elaborate marriages and fiercely fought wars.

Jock eased the ship through the inlet and into the lagoon, half expecting to sight the outlandish awning of Bombarda's barge rowing out to meet him.

The barge of the resident factor of Lagos was nowhere in sight.

Anchored a cable's length away rode a beautiful slim black ship with rakish masts. Though she was motionless, Jock sensed the speed in her. She displayed no flag; it was impossible to determine her nationality. If she had ever had a name, there was no evidence of it now. Jock scrutinized her through his glass, which was a good one, bringing her so close that the grain of her timbers was visible; but where her name should be was nothing but clean black paint. Ships put in to Lagos for only one cargo. Lagos offered nothing else. Patently she was a slaver. It was strange that she should conceal her identity in so perfectly legal a trade.

Dark-visaged sailors with Spanish mustachios stood idly along her rail and stared back at Jock with curious eyes. An oddity in her rigging struck him. Ordinarily a ship that anchored in a protected roadstead with a probable wait of days or weeks ahead would furl her sails: that is to say, each sail would be firmly secured to its spar by a dozen tight loops of rope, the trim harbor dress of a vessel in port for a protracted stay. But the sails which Jock saw through his glass were merely clewed up. One pull on a single line would release them, like the trigger of a trap. This stranger could put herself under full sail in a matter of minutes. Her ports were closed, but through the glass Jock saw the covers swinging on their hinges in the gentle swell. A word of command would send those shutters banging up, and through the square holes thus disclosed in the sinister black hull would stare the ugly muzzles of cannon.

"Our neighbor yonder has a guilty conscience," Jock muttered to himself. "Let's see who he says he is."

He ordered the Union Jack run up.

In a trice the stranger also displayed the British flag.

"If I had rung up the Ottoman Crescent I dare say he'd have answered with the same," Jock said. "I suggest you prepare the ship for action, Mr. Webb. I don't like his looks, and I intend to find out who he is."

Webb, who had followed Jock aboard the *Two Friends*, said, "That will be difficult, sir."

"Not if I pay him a visit."

"But then we'd hit you, sir, if we fired on him."

"I don't think you will have to. Look at his sails."

But in the absence of Bombarda, who habitually met all incoming ships, the appearance of the stranger was disturbing.

As the *Two Friends'* boat slipped into the water and made its way across the distance that separated the ships, a figure appeared on the stranger's quarter-deck and leveled a spyglass on Jock. Suddenly the figure began to wave its glass wildly; it ripped off the yellow bandanna from its head and whirled it in greeting. Under the fiercely pointed mustachios flashed a quick white grin, the brilliance of which was enhanced by a diamond set in a front tooth. Surely there could exist in the world only one such diamond smile.

"Don Jesu!" Jock shouted, laughing and waving back heartily.

"Señor Paul!"

A Jacob's ladder clattered down as Jock's boat came alongside, and Don Jesu cried, "Come aboard! Come aboard!" Jock stepped on the Spaniard's deck to receive the honors of a visiting admiral, finding himself between two ragged lines of scar-faced slovenly friendly rascals who appeared to constitute Don Jesu's corps of officers, pistols in belt and cutlasses slung bare without scabbards in the manner of men who never put up their weapons. Jock returned their salute and was instantly all but suffocated in Don Jesu's embrace. "What a joy to set eyes again on my friend, my mentor, my Virgil in this *purgatorio* of trade! Welcome, my initiator into the mystery of the honest livelihood! Come into my cabin and drink with me a goblet of wine; it is still cool from Señor Bombarda's most excellent cave."

"I expected him to meet my ship," Jock said. "He met yours?"

"Mine met him," Don Jesu said, "with a beautiful broadside."

"Why?"

"This resident factor of Lagos," Don Jesu spat out the words, "this traitor to his class, this man dead to all honor, sits sulking and skulking behind craftily hidden cannon; the great fat rabbit is safe in his hole. Alone I was not quite strong enough. But now comes my friend to reinforce me; together we shall blast him to hell before he has time to mumble a confiteor, eh, friend Paul?"

"I don't see why that should be necessary."

"Not *necessary!* He demands an unfair price for his Negroes, taking advantage of my known inexperience in trade."

"What does he ask?"

"In English money, one pound ten shillings per head."

"That is only a trifle more than I paid him. Perhaps there is a scarcity."

"He insists that there is, brought on by some native war in the interior."

"Well then, the law of supply and demand —"

"*Madre de Dios!* Does there truly exist such a law? He spoke to me of it; I pretended to understand; an angel must have guided me. 'Precisely,' said I. 'You have the supply and I demand it!' To think that I, Don Jesu de Silva y Villanueva live within the law!"

"That isn't exactly how it works," Jock said.

In the great cabin, where Captain Newton's gold chalice, shining like a shrine, had been reverently placed in a niche above Don Jesu's bunk, Don Jesu related the swift events that had led to the present deadlock between him and Bombarda, a story old as greed, old as gunpowder, and common as death on the Guinea Coast.

Most slavers were willing to pay for their cargoes in Africa, contenting themselves with the enormous profit they earned for every black man they managed to deliver alive on the American side of the Atlantic. The English and Americans were particularly honest in their dealings with African

157

suppliers, not only because commerce of any kind was no disgrace in the English-speaking world but also because Great Britain, by the treaty that had won her so much of the earth's surface and population, had also exacted a monopoly of the African slave trade. This monopoly naturally was unenforceable. The Guinea Coast was too long, too wild, too sparsely patrolled. African factors, scanning their marshy lagoons for the British frigates that seldom were there, habitually emptied their barracoons into the holds of any ships of any nationality that happened to appear in their waters.

But the treaty right remained, and the hard fact remained that in spite of all connivance, all smuggling and downright thievery, more than half of the slaves exported from Africa were carried in British bottoms. Thus England and her colonies could afford to pay for their cargoes, law-abiding and standing on their rights, enjoying the low prices that monopoly always brings.

Other nations, to whom the trade was prohibited, inevitably paid a premium, for the African factor would always protest that the British navy would punish him if the transaction were discovered. The result, as in all prohibitions, was an almost overpowering temptation for non-British buyers to go to the other extreme and pay nothing at all: simply attack the factor's establishment, raid the barracoons and make off with a stolen cargo. Not only barracoons but ships as well, fresh-laden, full of slaves and setting sail for America, were in danger of being raided, their cargoes transshipped and the vessels themselves sunk to the bottom, the crews slaughtered lest the deed become known. This situation was conducive to grossly un-British instability on the Guinea Coast and was reflected by increased violence among the natives of the interior, as if chaos, like a sickness, were infectious.

The Ibo tribe, scattered but not exterminated the previous year, had now regrouped and formed alliances with some neighboring tribes; this coalition was waging a fierce war in the jungles against the Fulani.

"At least," Don Jesu said with a shrug, "that is what the great liar Bombarda told me."

"I wonder why the natives fight among themselves," Jock said. "Africa is so big."

"For the excitement, of course," Don Jesu said. "Even a white man fights for excitement if there is nothing else to fight for. Sometimes," he lowered his voice, "I have permitted my gentlemen to take a prize just to lighten the tedium of an uneventful voyage, even when I knew she wouldn't be worth the gunpowder I spent on her. The thing was to win, even if what we won was worthless. Can you understand that, my commercial friend?"

"Yes," Jock said, thinking of the cockfight, "I can understand the exhilaration of winning."

"Fighting is easier to understand than the law of supply and demand," Don Jesu said, "as the resident factor found out."

Bombarda's instinct, highly trained and accustomed to gauging the character of his customers by the aspect of their ships, had warned him at first sight that the sleek black stranger in his lagoon boded him no good; he would have welcomed a British frigate. He could not know, in his hot little corner of the world, that the British admiralty had ordered the British fleet to blockade some American harbors and compel some hotheaded American colonials to pay their taxes on tea, which, like slaves, was another British monopoly; so while Boston was invested, Lagos was forgotten. Bombarda, not daring to go aboard Don Jesu's ship and place himself in Don Jesu's power, had nevertheless met him civilly on the landing and "dashed" him with a boatload of wine, explaining as best he could the lamentable shortage of prime blacks and the consequent higher price he must ask. Having accepted the wine, which Jock was drinking, Don Jesu had swung his ship broadside and sent a thundering volley of cannon balls into Bombarda's establishment. Instantly the whole area on the hillside surrounding Bombarda's residence had answered the fire.

"And there," Don Jesu said ruefully, "the matter stood, deadlocked until you came. But now we have him! Two ships can reduce one land fort; two ships' companies can overwhelm him!"

"Suppose his barracoons are really empty, or nearly so. What will happen when we take the fort? Shall you and I then fight each other for half a cargo of slaves?"

"Fight you? Not I, my friend."

"Your gentlemen would demand it," Jock said.

"Hm-m," reflected Don Jesu uneasily. "You have great understanding."

"That would be a most unskillful, not to say ignorant way to trade," Jock said, like a schoolmaster reproving a slow student. "First we must determine the supply; then we shall choose the best means of demanding it."

"I am glad that you came," Don Jesu said weakly. "It shamed me not to be strong enough alone."

"Would you agree to parley with Bombarda?"

"Oh yes. We shall parley from strength. I think it would be simpler to blast him, however." But Don Jesu let himself be led by the merchant of greater experience. Late in the afternoon, when the setting sun shone in the eyes of Bombarda's gunners, two boats rowed towards the landing, displaying large white flags of truce and carrying the captains of the two ships. The sulphurous fumes of slow matches, lighted and ready, mingled in the hot air with the beautiful feathery seeds of the bombax trees. Jock Paul and Don Jesu were coming to trade with the resident factor of Lagos. Bombarda greeted them at the landing as if nothing were amiss.

He was somewhat thinner, Jock thought, with little lines of worry creasing his forehead; the look of apprehension was natural enough in view of Don Jesu's attack, but the loss of weight was less easily explained and could not have occurred in a day: a trouble of longer standing, deeper and more insidious than Don Jesu, was wasting Duarte Bombarda. "Welcome to Lagos," he exclaimed to Jock. "I spied you on your quarter-deck, and I said to myself, 'Senhor Paul has risen in the world, a captain's uniform, his due, his due!' "

Jock said, "I believe you have already met my good friend, Captain de Silva?"

"Closely, warmly, Senhor Paul. Some accident of the great heat, I suppose, must have set off his cannon today."

"That's exactly what happened," Don Jesu said. "They exploded spontaneously, all by themselves."

"The air is very dry at this time of year," Bombarda said, "and powder takes fire easily. The same thing happened to me. The extreme heat, aggravated no doubt by the shock of your balls falling all around, set off my guns by a sympathetic reaction. How fortunate no one was hurt."

"It mustn't happen again," Jock said sternly. "We have come to trade. Between us we can carry upwards of fifteen hundred head, a thousand for me, five hundred for —"

"Six, seven, eight," Don Jesu said.

"Captain Paul's figure is closer to the mark," Bombarda said. "Crowding kills them."

"Then I'll load more to start with."

"You would only find yourself victim of the law of diminishing returns," Jock said.

Don Jesu muttered, "Laws, laws, laws!"

"In any case," Bombarda said, "I could not fill even the smaller ship. My barracoons are empty. Nay, not literally empty but virtually so. A scant three hundred, no longer prime, huddle together in a single enclosure, lonely and frightened. The savage in loneliness is a sorry sight; he whimpers and pines and loses his gloss and refuses food. Negroes and wolves must live in the pack to thrive. It is strange, strange; but every factor knows it. No, I cannot supply you."

"You would, of course, be willing to show us your barracoons," Don Jesu said suspiciously.

"At any time, Senhor Captain."

"I am convinced," Jock said. "It is not necessary for me to inspect your barracoons."

"Perhaps Senhor de Silva would like to see them?"

"They are always instructive," Jock said smiling.

"I do not think I should care to inspect them alone," Don Jesu said. "If Señor Paul is convinced, then so am I. But what is to do? How are the ships of two honest merchants to be filled with merchandise, bearing in mind the law of supply and demand and the law of diminishing returns? Por Dios, gentlemen, I discover that lawful trade is a formidable undertaking, hedged round with obtuse and unexpected restrictions."

"We have not yet found the supply," Jock said thoughtfully. "There is no doubt in my mind that it exists. Someone is keeping it off the market. Fortunately I know a man I can send into the interior to scout it out."

"Me?" Don Jesu said, flashing his smile. "I should like that."

Bombarda, in his specialized knowledge, took a little revenge for the Spaniard's unprovoked attack. "Senhor," he said, emphasizing the minute but scathing difference between the Spanish and Portuguese forms of address, "you wouldn't last the space of an Ave."

"Then who?" Don Jesu asked.

"Chima," said Jock.

Bombarda sighed. "I myself should have sent out a spy long since, but present conditions are peculiar. Even my major-domo refuses to set foot in the forests."

"How long has this lasted?"

"A month, two months, it is hard to say. So little leaks out of the interior."

"Who is Chima?" Don Jesu asked.

Jock chuckled. "A body servant of mine. He used to be an Ibo dignitary, a sort of ambassador."

Chima entered the forest with the confident familiarity of a householder going out to inspect his own garden. He had been born in this country; it was Ibo territory; he knew every feature of it down to the individual water holes and trees. It was dark and the night was moonless, but the air was clear and he could tell his way by the stars. Other senses guided him, familiar smells and the hushed night sounds of insects, birds and animals. All was at rest. No danger signals impinged upon him. No vultures circled against the sky, hence there were no bodies, hence the Fulani had not penetrated into Ibo land. Indeed, that would have been unlikely in view of the coalition; the fighting must be far away in Fulani territory. He smelled smoke, but it was live, not the stale odor of hastily drowned campfires: members of his tribe were camped in security around some cheerful open blaze not far hence. Chickens and pork had been cooked in it, family food, nothing more potent, nothing that warriors might eat in a ceremonial feast to propitiate a demon after defeat or praise a god after victory.

Chima had accepted his mission as he accepted all other commands from his master, cheerfully, intelligently, obediently. A white European would have called it selfless devotion. A Moslem Fulani would have given it the name of kismet, fate. But these explanations fell short of Chima's exalted desire to do his master's will, for Chima was more cautious, more alive, more aware than ever before; he did not consider himself "fated" to do or experience anything. When Chima bit his arm and the blood flowed out in the act of voluntary servitude, his action possessed both a negative and a positive aspect: negative in that he surrendered his caste and became Osu, outcast, among his tribe; but positive in that a portion of Jock Paul's soul had slipped into his own black body and made therein a home; hence the wounds had had to be kept open as long as possible, that more of the essence might slip in and as much blood as possible be let out to give the essence more room in which to dwell. Far from being selfless, Chima now possessed a double self, and in the whiter, greater, stronger self would center all his thoughts and actions so long as he lived. He must manage to live long, for when he died a part of Captain Paul would also die. He must be careful to cover his spittle and excrement, to bury his nail parings and the hairs that came out when he scratched his head, lest an enemy secure them and cast a spell by means of them, not to Chima's own detriment, since no one would touch the detritus of an Outcast, but because through him his master might become subject to evil influences, might be changed in some manner, or hurt. It was doubtful if Captain Paul could actually be killed, as someone unquestionably was killing the resident factor, since Captain Paul still possessed the greater part of his self; but he could be made sick. Heavy with these responsibilities, but glorying in them, Chima did not succumb to the temptation to throw away the sailor shirt and trousers which impeded him as he trotted tirelessly through the jungle in the direction of the smell of smoke.

He came upon them, a band of Osu, in a clearing on a hillside, the lowest caste of the Ibos. Unlike Chima they had been born to servitude and ostracism, not entered into it through an act of voluntary servitude. There were strong men among them, yet they were not permitted to fight, high-breasted fecund girls, yet they were not permitted to marry among the noble or warrior classes. Old prejudices rose in Chima, for he had been born a noble and he looked on them with revulsion; but then he remembered that these Osu were the only Ibos who would not flee terrified from his presence, and in a jumbled prayer he thanked Igwe, the supreme Ibo deity, the God of the Christians and that little part of the self of Captain John Paul which dwelt in him for guiding his steps aright through the forest. Here he could learn the truth. Here he could accomplish his mission.

A white-haired elder approached him, asking the ritual question, the answer to which was already known: Chima's history was famous throughout his tribe, his mission to the Fulani king, the chicken, Onumba's curse, his sudden release by the white man, the three who were murdered in his stead, his degradation to Osu, his mystic elevation to union with John Paul.

"Who are you who seek community among the Outcasts?"

Chima gave an answer that would have sorely mystified his white master: "I am John-Paul-Chima," he said, the greater name first.

"Be welcome, John-Paul-Chima," the elder replied.

They sat him beside the campfire and welcomed him into the caste. They fed him pork and chicken.

"I did not know Osu ate so well," Chima said. The Osu as a caste were forbidden the market place and must content themselves with leavings.

The elder replied, "We celebrate with our victorious nation, who slay the Fulani," for the Osu, though forbidden to bear arms, still thought of themselves as Ibos and shared with the rest of the tribe, who proscribed them, the tribal victories.

"Do we slay them all?" Chima asked.

"Nearly all. The war is fierce."

"Do they slay us all?"

"Nearly all."

"And the others? Those who are not slain?"

Chima knew that the Osu's answers were true. Those who have nothing to lose have nothing to hide.

The elder said, "The new war is like no other. The Ashanti, contrary to all that has been in the past, impound those who are not slain, like grain saved up for a famine."

"They impound both Ibo and Fulani?"

"Both."

"This is new."

"Both Ibo and Fulani sell their prisoners to the Ashanti, as has always been; but the Ashanti impound them like grain saved up for a famine."

"There is no famine."

"There is created famine, for famine prices."

"This too is a new thing."

"The Ashanti king is new."

The venerable king of the Ashanti, Osai (King) Tutu, had died; and in his stead, now resting his arm on the Golden Stool — no one would dare sit on it, not even the king, since it had come down from heaven and it embodied the soul of the Ashanti nation — reigned a new king, Osai Apoko. The old king had sold prisoners of war, bought from both sides, in the traditional way of the old times as soon as he procured them. But Osai Apoko was a modern man, imbued with new ideas: he impounded them to force up prices.

"The factor Bombarda," the elder said, "raided the Ashanti compounds some months past and was beaten off. There is great hatred now against the factor Bombarda."

"What is done?"

"We do not know, but the factor Bombarda sickens."

"What will be done?"

His own name met him in response, "Chima" (God knows).

"How many, unkilled, are imprisoned behind the Ashanti stockades?"

"Though the war is fierce and most fight to the death, yet not all do so, and the prisoners now number in thousands. Never in war have so many thousands been prisoners."

"Where are these thousands?"

"Why do you ask?"

"Why do you hesitate?"

"You are new among the Osu."

"But I am Osu."

"Osu, beyond this place, over the hill a half day's journey, there are the thousands."

"There was a smooth-limbed girl, a Fulani —"

"Nwa-Eji-Gbo-Agha, 'She-Who-Was-Given-To-Avert-War'; very fair. We know."

164

"What has become of her?"

"The dying factor perfumes her with precious oils and lusts after her."

"I was greatly in love."

"He lusts only with the eyes, for in his body he spurns her to humble her, her who can never be humbled, being already nought."

"I was greatly in love."

"We know."

"We are greatly in love."

"Who are we?"

"We are John-Paul-Chima."

"Take heed lest one of your souls come to harm with the body of the soulless one."

"We are greatly in love."

"She who is empty will empty him who is full."

"We are greatly in love."

"There is danger."

"Even so."

"Even so ye are greatly in love?"

"Yes."

"There is danger."

"We do not care."

"There is danger."

"We are beyond caring."

"There is danger."

"Be it so."

Captain Paul betrayed some impatience with Chima's verbatim recital of this news when Chima returned. The African rhetoric, repetitious as jungle drums, irritates before it enchants, and enchants before it enchains.

"It took him a long time to get it out," he said, "but at least I know now where the supply is." Jock did not tell Don Jesu and Bombarda that Chima had mentioned Dolores, not wishing to admit that Chima had sensed his interest in her. Besides, there was too much to do. Dolores would have to wait.

Dolores, eying them with languid yellow eyes as she served them wine while they planned an expedition in force against the compounds of the Ashanti, would have waited eternities for anything or for nothing. Bombarda and Jock were accustomed to her flawless nudity, but Don Jesu's eyebrows fluttered in astonishment. "*Sangre de Dios!* Do you always live so?"

"While I live," Bombarda said.

165

"This I understand," Don Jesu said amiably. "This I enjoy. This is how you negotiated with Tubman in Jamaica. When you go into action, Captain Paul, the mystery of trade disappears, the essential stands clear like a prize downwind, ripe to be snatched. Shame on you, *amigo mio!* Why do you confuse my mind with incomprehensible laws in which you yourself do not believe?"

"The laws are perfectly valid," Jock said. "They are simply generalizations which have to be backed up by force once in a while to make them apply."

"Let the angels record," Don Jesu intoned with mock piety, "that Jesu de Silva y Villanueva now backs up and enforces the laws."

"Confound you, cease your blasphemy!" Bombarda said. He looked feverish and drawn; he fanned himself in his sedan chair; beside him Don Jesu and Jock walked at the head of a column of armed men. They numbered nearly five hundred: Jock's crew, Don Jesu's crew, Bombarda's gunners and guards. Trotting ahead, bursting with pride, with a white man's pistol in his belt and on his head a sailorman's hat that glistened with fresh tar, Chima was leading them towards the Ashanti compounds.

Bombarda, in his measureless hatred of all blacks, had readily agreed to the expedition. Don Jesu, together with all his men, liked fighting on any pretext. It had thus been possible for Jock to persuade them that the white men must stand together to present a show of force against the Ashanti, to pry loose the merchandise that was essential to all their careers and to set flowing again the lifeblood of their trade.

They were not attacked; but Chima reported, "Bushes have rustled; bird sounds arise where no birds are, and the sounds repeat themselves until they fade in the distance; we are observed by Ashanti scouts, and word of us is already in their camp."

"Let them observe all they like," Jock said. "It isn't as if our visit were a secret."

Bombarda swore darkly.

Don Jesu said, "My gentlemen like to sing before going into action. If no law prohibits a song —"

Jock laughed. "Go ahead."

"And a swig of rum, to sweeten the notes? Frankly, their voices are horrible."

"Don't waste the rum," Bombarda said. "It is a prime article of trade with the Ashanti."

"Just don't give them so much they can't shoot straight," Jock said.

"*Por Dios!* Must they also fight sober? The shock would kill them."

"We don't want to fight at all."

"I do," Don Jesu said, grinning.

"I do," said Bombarda, yellow, sweating.

"We are going to trade, not fight."

Don Jesu shook his handsome hawklike head. "Assuredly there *is* a difference; how strange that I cannot see it." How often he mocked and how often he was sincere Jock could not tell. The porters broached a hogshead of trade rum and Don Jesu's men broke into a song; Bombarda's men, mostly Negroes of various tribes with a sprinkling of Portuguese officers, beat out the rhythm with hands and feet and sticks; Jock's men looked on, British-Americans, apart, amused but sympathetic. The din was deafening, lighthearted, happy-go-lucky. Then they ate and resumed their march. They had now passed the line of hills which constituted the horizon as seen from the sea and entered upon flatter, higher terrain, still wooded but not so densely. They had started early and calculated the duration of their journey so as not to be caught in the dark. The afternoon sun was still three hours from setting when they came upon the Ashanti barracoons. Bombarda's practiced eye surveyed them. They were the biggest he had ever seen.

"Four thousand at least!" he muttered.

Ashanti guards walked up and down. Mingling with them was another sort of guards, who wore turbans and carried long muskets.

"Arabs too?" Bombarda exclaimed. He acted stunned. "The caravans deliver to the Ashanti, not to me? The indignity! If I had known! If I had suspected! We should have brought cannon. My head is splitting. I should have guessed, and if I had guessed I should have brought cannon."

"Cannon would have been easy," Don Jesu said. His eye too was practiced; he took in the vast extent of the camp, the multitudinous guards, and looked at Jock reproachfully.

"We are mobile, strong enough to parley," Jock said stubbornly, "and we did not come to fight."

Two structures, profoundly different, products of cultures that were worlds apart, stood side by side. One was an Arab tent, for even where wood was plentiful the Moslem set up the desert dwelling of his ancestors of the treeless Sahara; over it fluttered the Crescent banner. The other was a new-built circular house with walls of slender peeled branches, beautifully woven, topped by a conical roof of fresh green thatch that still must smell like a new-mown field; it was the regal version of the characteristic beehive African hut.

"The Osai Apoko keeps some state," Bombarda observed, impressed by the symmetry and solidity of the chief's temporary dwelling. There was a patch of green in front of it, looking from a distance like carefully kept turf: it was a finely wrought and brilliantly dyed mat of rushes. "Even in camp the Osai Apoko does not step on the ground."

As they drew closer, Jock could make out the complexion of the Arab guards.

"They are nearly as black as the Negroes," he said, perplexed.

Bombarda snorted. "They are Negroes. Not one of them can boast a white ancestor for ten generations. That's what comes of trading in Africa."

Jock looked at him questioningly.

Bombarda's eyes blazed. "I said *for generations,* Captain Paul. Perhaps *you* will accomplish it sooner."

"That remark wasn't required," Jock said.

"It didn't even make sense," Don Jesu said. "Señor Paul might take dozens of black mistresses and father a whole tribe of brown little Señor Pauls and it wouldn't even tan him. Come, come, *mis amigos;* are we to quarrel after all?"

"My head is splitting," Bombarda said listlessly. "I meant only that these Arabs have dwelt among the tribes for hundreds of years and have lost all but a vestige of their original blood. Even their Arab speech is corrupt. They cannot read their Korans, but carry them about like charms. I regret that I snapped at you; I fancied that you looked at me in an insulting manner, Senhor Paul."

"I certainly didn't mean to."

Presently they were within hailing distance. Bombarda shouted a greeting in the Ashanti tongue. For answer a slave of Apoko's rushed out and rolled up the green mat, insolently turning his back and waggling his feathered headdress as he took the mat into the dwelling.

Chima's low brow furrowed in deep perplexity. It was not Ashanti magic that was wasting the factor Bombarda. Those who would kill with spells welcome the nearness of their victim, since nearness increases the power of the spell; they smile and conceal their intentions, they do not gratuitously insult. Who then?

"Apoko still bears me a grudge for that little foray of mine," Bombarda grumbled. "He shouldn't; he won, and gained great renown. We are not to be received."

In the stillness that followed, a tall swarthy man of distinguished carriage, dressed in white woolen robes and wearing a green turban, stood forth from the Arab tent and said something in a low voice that did not quite carry to the white men. After some moments Apoko's slave came out again with the green mat and replaced it.

"Everything is now changed," Bombarda exclaimed, shaking with delight. He began to laugh. "We shall be received after all."

The change was not evident to Jock Paul or Don Jesu.

"My friends, the Osai Apoko has overreached himself. We have come upon a camp divided against itself."

Clearly Osai Apoko was sulking, hurt in his pride and showing his ill temper as openly as a child. Equally clearly the leader of the Moslem caravan, a mature trader who often had dealt with Bombarda, was disturbed by the interruption of trade which he found this year on the Coast and welcomed the white men's appearance. This division in the camp, which caused Bombarda to laugh in spite of his headache, had to be explained to Jock and Don Jesu.

"Like the Osai Apoko," Bombarda said, "you gentlemen are somewhat inexperienced." The Arab caravans habitually brought down to the Coast products of the back country: ivory, furs, salt, and a few special items suitable for "dashing" purposes such as silver-mounted saddles and white slave girls, absolutely unprocurable locally. In return the Arabs asked for muskets, powder, cloth, kitchen pots, matches, sewing needles and minted gold, which were all products of European manufacture available only from the Coast factors. By hoarding up slaves and damming the free flow of Africa's most essential commodity, the Osai Apoko had seriously disrupted the basic economy of a region as large as all Europe.

Behind the tent of the Arab, who continued to stand imperturbable, facing the white men, a strong contingent of his turbaned guards moved inconspicuously into line of battle. A similar movement took place among the Ashanti warriors behind Apoko's dwelling. The white men, answering the threat, immediately ranged their own followers in line against them. The armed forces were about equal, though the whites were better armed. "For God's sake," Bombarda cautioned Don Jesu nervously, "make sure your crew do not fire!" Don Jesu grinned, "Señor, I will try." Motionless for perhaps five nerve-racking minutes, a thousand ready weapons — muskets, pistols, arrows, knives, spears — a thousand mute tongues, stood ready for trade or war across forty paces of neutral ground.

"I like this," Don Jesu said.

Jock said, "Don't like it too much."

The green mat was empty. The Osai Apoko remained invisible.

Bombarda said, "I shall have to go closer."

"We'll come too," Jock and Don Jesu offered in unison.

"No," Bombarda said. "We must not appear eager. Not until the Ashanti king shows himself."

He ordered his carriers to bear his chair to within a few feet of the Arab tent. The Arab leader advanced a little to meet him.

"Salaam, Duarte Bombarda," the Arab leader said, and in the conventional Arab greeting "Salaam" faintly echoed six thousand years of man's never-achieved yearning, for the word meant "Peace."

"Peace upon you my friend, Hakim, Son of Nasr, Son of Din, Valiant in Faith," Bombarda replied. "Peace is our prayer and our hope."

"As it is mine."

"We have come not to fight but to trade."

"As do I. But there is a difficulty. You strangled trade when you treacherously set your men to attack the young king of the Ashanti and steal his Negroes, paying nothing for them."

"A devil tempted me. I was not myself."

"He will understand that."

"In my heart I have already 'dashed' him, making restitution."

"He will demand proof of that."

"Convince him of my sincerity."

"He will not parley with you."

Nothing must be hurried.

"I have prayed often for your health, friend Hakim, Son of Nasr, Son of Din, Valiant in Faith," Bombarda said.

"My health is as God wills," Hakim answered, "both good and bad."

"For the good, blessed be God; and for the bad, may the spirits of evil be propitiated," Bombarda said, "which, with my prayers and my 'dash,' shall happily come to pass."

"It is forbidden a follower of the Prophet to partake of intoxicating beverages," Hakim observed, running a tongue, almost black, over full thirsty lips.

"It is equally written, 'Stand strong for the glory of God,' for which strength the body must be kept in vigorous health," Bombarda replied; and at his signal two men came running forward with a case of bottled strong-waters, flavored with saffron and molasses but fundamentally nothing but brandy, the strength of which would have curled Jock's Scottish hair.

"Medicine is not forbidden," the Arab said placidly.

It seemed to Don Jesu and Jock, observing out of earshot, that the negotiations were proceeding favorably, for there was action on the green mat. A slave appeared with a low object heavily draped in black and set it in front of the Osai Apoko's dwelling; the Osai himself had not yet come out, but his feathers could be seen in the shadows within.

"If the Osai will not parley with me," Bombarda said, "with whom will he parley?"

"He will not parley with the Spanish pirate."

"That is understandable."

"He will parley with the other white leader, whose word can be trusted."

"Captain Paul would be at a disadvantage, speaking no Ashanti."

"He is known to speak Ibo."

"Haltingly."

"The Osai Apoko will admit to the parley his manservant who shares his soul."

"Do you believe these myths?" Bombarda asked, impatient and irritated.

Hakim answered smoothly, "With God all things are possible, and if the king of the Ashanti believes them, who are we to place obstacles in the way of peaceful trade? For it is written, 'The prudent man knows how to make of stumbling blocks stepping stones.' Let us prosper together."

"I shall send Captain Paul to parley with the Osai," Bombarda said.

"What does Captain Paul desire, that my 'dash' may be found commensurate with his wish?" Hakim asked.

Bombarda shrugged. "It is difficult to fathom the secret desires of Captain Paul; they are many, complex and contradictory."

"I suspect one would make no mistake with something all young men desire," Hakim said gravely. "Meanwhile, accept this for yourself with my prayers."

In the privacy of his traveling chair, as it jogged back to the waiting white men, Bombarda touched with the tip of his tongue a speck of brown powder that had leaked out of the small packet wrapped in yellow oiled cloth which Hakim had pressed into his hand: it was bitter as wormwood; he recognized the taste. "I hope *that* is all that is wrong with me," he muttered to himself. Hakim, observing his yellow countenance, had made him a truly noble gift, far more generous in Africa than it would have been in America where the substance was common: it was the powdered bark of the quinine tree. The prospect that his trouble might be nothing more deadly than malaria, which was deadly enough, cheered Bombarda. "I have been in Africa so long," he murmured, "that I am prey to fancies unworthy of a Christian!"

"Is it time to shoot?" Don Jesu asked eagerly when Bombarda's chair was set down.

"No, Don Jesu, it is time to hold your fire, and your tongue!"

Don Jesu swore under his breath, "Filthy fat Portuguese pig!"

Bombarda replied with remarkable tolerance, "If Christian curses were all I had to fear, I might indeed grow fat again." He paused for a moment, staring fixedly at Hakim's little yellow packet, feeling better than he had for days. It could so easily, please God, please all the heavenly host of saints, be nothing more sinister than malaria!

"Is the parley at an end?" Don Jesu asked, softened by Bombarda's soft answer. "It seems to me the compounds still are shut and the Ashanti chief still refuses to trade."

"Things are progressing more swiftly than meets the eye," Bombarda said. "On the green mat, veiled from our gaze, the Osai has set out his Golden Stool to signify his willingness, in principle, to parley. Unfortunately he will not parley with me."

"I'll parley with him!" Don Jesu said threateningly.

"In this trackless wilderness, so seemingly far from the sea," Bombarda said smiling, loading his words with venom, "your fame has already run before you."

"*Por Dios!* The feathered savage has heard of me?" Don Jesu's diamond sparkled.

"He has indeed. The Osai Apoko declares he will have no parley with a bloody Spanish pirate. In certain respects the moral standard of the feathered savage is curiously high."

Don Jesu's diamond went into sudden ignominious eclipse.

"But the Osai Apoko will parley with Captain Paul," Bombarda said.

Walking slowly across the level sward, thick-tufted with steely grass that crunched like breaking needles underfoot, Jock felt ill at ease and ill prepared for the ambassadorship that had been thrust upon him. Answerless questions drifted through his mind like the bombax seeds that drifted through the air, confusing the eye that attempted to follow, but he could not focus upon them. Why had he glibly assumed that the slave trade differed in no wise from any other trade? What was he doing here in this hot red alien afternoon, where air tasted like sand, where customers presented themselves in the guise of Arabs and savages, where commercial associates were pirates and degenerate Portuguese exiles, and the commodity was black men's bodies? What was he doing here, he, the Scotch tradesman from Arbigland, whose only desire in life was to rise in the world and "make rich"? (How the Scotticisms of childhood returned in times of stress! How simple a provisioning agency had been!)

Chima, walking beside him to interpret the Osai's speech if the Osai should speak too fast, looked up and saw on his master's face a look akin to fear, and shuddered. But the look passed swiftly, like a driven cloud that obscures only for an instant the shining orb of the sun: Captain Paul's stride lengthened, his jaw set, and his countenance assumed an appearance of serene, oddly careless confidence. Chima's strength returned; his needle-sharp teeth grinned at the Osai Apoko, who had just made his appearance upon the mat, squatting amongst his feathers and resting his arm upon the black-veiled Soul of the Ashanti Nation.

For the second time in his life — though he could not recall the first — Jock Paul was experiencing an eerie, overpowering phenomenon. In the face of a challenge of great magnitude he had suddenly become incapable of envisioning any outcome but success: obstacles faded away, dangers simply ceased to exist.

"Welcome," he said, smiling down on the Ashanti king, who drew in his breath in astonishment. No one had ever before "welcomed" the Osai Apoko to his own seat of power. It was as if some eccentric stranger had airily waved King George III onto his own throne and said pleasantly, "Won't you be seated, Your Majesty?" Naturally it carried a certain shock value.

"Welcome, Captain Paul," the Osai Apoko said and, having said it, believed it. His face was intensely black, and smooth with the gloss of youth except where the tribal scars, inflicted at puberty to prove his strength, rose in blue welts on either cheek: they were always more prominent in a king, since a king must be stronger and braver than his nation and hence suffer more at initiation. His deep-set eyes were bright and intelligent. He smiled frankly and openly, the broad expanse of glistening teeth contrasting sharply with the blackness of his features. Yet Jock got the impression that these pleasant features, now smiling so cordially, were capable of going to the other extreme. He would not have liked to witness that.

A kind of artless sincerity inheres in the speech of one whose skill in a language is small, as Jock's was in Ibo: things are pared down to their naked essential, unadorned and unqualified. The Ashanti king's knowledge of Ibo, in which they were parleying, was only a shade broader than Jock's. To Chima's chagrin, Chima found himself virtually superfluous. Captain Paul and the Osai Apoko concluded an agreement which, for sheer magnitude of commercial value, would have been elevated to treaty status by a British agent. But it was done orally, with instinctive trust on either side, between the time that the lower rim of the setting sun touched the horizon and the time that the upper rim disappeared beneath it.

Item: Captain Paul and the Osai Apoko had never yet harmed one another and therefore ought to be friends.

Item: Friends were good to have, and enemies were bad to have.

Item: Trade was good, and cheaper than war; though war was more glorious.

Item: Three friends possessed articles of trade which could be exchanged to their common advantage. These three friends were Hakim, the Osai, Captain Paul.

Item: The factor Bombarda was no friend, but a criminal; he deserved death.

Here Chima interposed with the explanation that Bombarda was bewitched, by enemies unknown, and could not be held accountable for his acts. Apoko disclaimed responsibility and stated that Bombarda was getting what he deserved. Hakim, who viewed the parley as an evidence of Allah's eternal providence, remarked, "If Bombarda's acts are such as destine his own destruction, nothing can prevent it and we should be wrong to interfere." The point was not cleared up and the matter was left in abeyance.

Item: The Ashanti king would open his compounds and deliver slaves to the Coast on condition that Captain Paul receive them, not the factor Bombarda, though Bombarda's barracoons might be used if Captain Paul so desired.

Item: Hakim would also deliver to Captain Paul.

Item: Thus everything would be as it always had been, trade flowing freely to the Coast in the usual manner, which was easier for everybody to understand and permitted time for "dashing," celebration and pleasure.

Item: Pleasure was good.

Apoko now stood up and the Golden Stool, which had heard and witnessed the parley, was removed, still veiled, to the dark interior of the dwelling.

"Caution your associate Don Jesu, who steals even the name of your God, not to be alarmed when he hears gunfire. On occasions like this it is customary for everyone to discharge muskets for joy: the *dantica*."

Jock could not let the slur pass unchallenged.

"Don Jesu bears the name of God, but he is not struck down, therefore God is not angry at him."

"Then he cannot be all bad," Apoko said.

"He will answer your salute volley for volley," Jock promised, "and so shall I."

"Let him take heed that he fire into the air, and give him this from me." The Osai removed from his neck one of the numerous objects that decorated it and handed it to Jock. It was, he explained, a chaplet of knucklebones; the newly boiled and whiter ones were trigger fingers of some of Bombarda's men who had made the attack on the Ashanti compounds.

Jock said, "I am sure Don Jesu will understand."

"And this is for you," Apoko said, taking from his neck a little leather bag full of some foully odorous substance. "It is a powerful charm; while you wear it your blood will never be shed; not even the insects will sting you."

Manfully Jock put it on. "I thank you and I believe you." However fragrant the talisman might be to an Ashanti, it was nauseatingly offensive to Jock's nostrils.

He wondered what "dash" he might make in return; he had little on his person; he sensed that it would appear forgetful if he should send Chima back for something of value. His hand hesitated towards the pistol in his belt.

Some of Apoko's guards muttered ominously. Apoko quieted them with a growl in Ashanti. "I have told them," he said, "that Captain Paul is not mad. He merely wishes to 'dash' me with his beautiful pistol. He does not realize that a pistol is more acceptable to an Arab than to an Ashanti king."

Jock felt the tremendous pride of the man; the king who would not defile his feet by stepping on the ground scorned to accept any weapon, no matter how powerful, since it might imply a need to protect himself, him who had a nation behind him. He remembered that European kings never touched money like common men. Could a man rise so high that he made it a point of honor to show contempt for things everyone else wanted?

The Osai waited, smiling. Suddenly he came a step closer and wrinkled his nose, sniffing at something. It could not be the talisman.

"Do you eat fire and breathe smoke, like some white men?"

A sense of unreality settled upon Jock. With great difficulty he suppressed an impulse to laugh and maintained a straight face.

"Why yes, as a matter of fact I do."

"I wish to do the same!"

Jock was tempted to thrust his hand into his pocket, draw out the tobacco Apoko had smelled and say, "Have a cigar!" But the matter could not be so lightly treated. If the king smoked it and became sick, as was very likely, the consequences might be disastrous.

"Why do you hesitate, Captain Paul?" The Osai Apoko looked offended.

"Because there is danger in the first time."

"I am not afraid of danger."

Jock handed him the cigar. Apoko took it and waited for it to take fire spontaneously.

Jock said, "Let me show you how, but remember that the fire spirit in the tobacco rebels the first time you confine him; he chokes you if you breathe him into your lungs; do not swallow him or he will burst out of your stomach; you will vomit and everyone will say I have poisoned you. The second time you smoke, the fire spirit is weaker; he does not fight so hard. And the third time he is completely subdued. Then you will enjoy such pleasure in smoking as passes your fondest dreams, pleasure greater than women, pleasure greater than rum."

"If this be true," said the Osai Apoko, "it is worth all the preliminary pain." He touched his tribal scars. "I am not afraid. Show me how."

"It will have to be lighted."

One of Apoko's slaves who had been kindling the cooking fires came running with a torch and thrust it close to Jock's face; it singed his eyebrows and the heat hurt, but thousands of glittering eyes were staring at him and Jock dared not draw back from the fire spirit. But never had he lighted a cigar so quickly. He puffed out a great cloud of smoke.

"In America," he said, "it is considered a mark of close friendship for men to smoke tobacco together."

"So shall it be between us," Apoko said.

In the gathering dusk the spark was seen to pass back and forth between them, glowing brighter each time it paused before each face, while smoke breathed from their mouths like words taking visible form. The Ashanti spectators screamed with delight; the white men cheered and applauded. On Jock the sense of unreality deepened, mingled with pity.

"I become aware of the onset of the pain you mentioned," Apoko said. "You must leave me now." His brow was beaded with sweat; his throat muscles worked; clearly he was nauseated, but he was fighting it back and his expression did not change. "Next time it will be pleasure?"

"Yes; or at least the next. I have many more cigars. You shall have them all."

"I shall treasure them."

He accompanied Jock to the edge of the mat and then, somewhat hurriedly, retired out of sight.

Jock returned to the white men to find Bombarda in an agony of suspense. "I saw what you did! The moment he gets sick he will think you bewitched him. They will fall on us like tigers. You choose a bad moment for hostilities, Captain Paul. It is never wise to fight the natives at night."

"Somehow I don't think he's going to get sick," Jock said. "The man has iron command of himself. I thought him rather admirable."

"Faugh!" Bombarda said, spitting on the ground. " 'Man,' 'admirable.' Human terms. You grow soft as Newton. Soon you will be preaching to them."

One of Bombarda's black chair bearers carefully gathered up the handful of earth which Bombarda's spittle had wet and dug a little hole with a stick and buried it. Bombarda crossed himself. "Thank you," he said in a low changed voice.

"King Apoko sends you this," Jock said to Don Jesu, "with a friendly caution not to be alarmed by his gunfire; it's only a salute and we must return it." He gave him the chaplet of bones. "Some of these used to speak Portuguese," he said, glancing at Bombarda.

"My foray was an error of judgment," Bombarda shrugged. "I'll be stronger next time."

"Till then we can trade in peace," Jock said, and sketched the terms of the agreement he and Apoko had made.

Bombarda smiled craftily. "One would think you had been on the Coast twenty years, like me! I could not have done better myself."

Don Jesu said, "I don't think you could," and fingered the necklace of knucklebones. "I wonder how many of the skins that used to cover these were black and how many were white. They are all white now."

"You too are soft," Bombarda said.

Shortly the Osai Apoko appeared on his green mat again, composed and smiling and unbewitched. Whatever pains the fire spirit might have caused him were not apparent. Hakim sat placidly cross-legged in the Eastern fashion before his tent, and all around campfires and cooking fires began to blaze, cauldrons began to boil, and the festive odors of monkey soup, roast elephant leg, spitted whole buffaloes and (for the Moslems) curried rice and broiled lamb filled the air. A blast of gunfire rang out, answered spiritedly from the white men's side: the *dantica* had begun in earnest.

After the feasting came an exchange of gifts: the hardset lines melted and became less rigidly defined as men crossed back and forth over the neutral ground in easy comradeship, except that the Osai never stepped beyond his green mat.

"He lives under curious restrictions," Don Jesu observed.

"Not at all," said Bombarda. "When he leads his nation into battle he wears shoes."

Captain Paul, with a troop of servants behind him, placed before the

Osai's dwelling a dozen demijohns of trade rum, a heap of copper wire for jewelry purposes, and all the cigars he had brought with him on the expedition; and received in return the smiling assurance that the Osai's compounds would be opened at once: Captain Paul had only to give the command. "I think it will be better if they follow us at a distance till we get to the Coast," Jock said.

"You are not equipped to escort them?"

"Frankly no; we haven't enough men."

"I knew you had not. I was told you would not admit it. I said that you would. I shall escort them for you, under guard."

"On the Coast I will pay you."

"I never doubted it."

To Hakim, Jock presented an American rifle. Hakim looked at it askance. It was a grim unadorned thing without plating or engraving. Hakim fancied the exquisitely chased firearms of Italian make, full of niello work and florid as a Byzantine mosaic.

"It is better than it looks," Jock said. "It is unlike a smoothbore."

"Show me."

"It can hit a target the size of a dish at a hundred paces."

"You vaunt."

"I swear."

"We shall see."

Two turbaned guards, with a white girl between them, measured off a hundred paces and held the target fast.

"Her head, I should say, is about the size of a dish. Shoot her head."

Jock gulped.

"Rather too large, I think. I meant a small dish, like a rice bowl. Let her hold a small dish above her head."

It was supplied.

The girl held it aloft.

Jock shattered it.

"Take the girl," Hakim said. "I accept the rifle."

"I accept the girl."

Hakim smiled. "You have praised your 'dash.' I praise mine. She is a Circassian. You will be aware that the Circassians, a Russian people with no wealth but their cattle and sheep and daughters, sell all indiscriminately to the Turkish merchants, from whom I bought her. I think you saved her life on purpose."

"I did," Jock said.

"It is astonishing that you could," said Hakim, touching the rifle barrel with awe. "It would be astonishing if she were not grateful."

Jock took her by the arm and conducted her to the white men's camp. "What shall I do with her?"

Bombarda snickered.

Don Jesu said, "Shall I show you?"

Bombarda received no "dash" at all and, glowering, held his peace. About them closed down the quick equatorial night.

"It is time to decamp," Jock said.

On the other side the Ashanti warriors were grouped in a senseless monotonous dance, all feathers and writhing hot bodies, gleaming like boneless things in the campfire lights, to the drum beat of queerly tuned drums; there must have been scores of them, beating out well-defined notes, in rhythm but always in tune, like antiphonal voices with something to say. Hakim was drinking himself solemnly drunk with "medicine." Don Jesu's men were roaring over a broached hogshead of trade rum.

"It's not an ordinary sort of dance," Bombarda said complacently. "If you understood the drums, you would hear no note of menace. Wouldn't you like to inspect the target you didn't hit?"

All but her face was heavily robed in the decent Mohammedan fashion, like a badly wrapped bundle.

"Her face looks well worth the rifle," Bombarda persisted. Jock speculated that the resident factor was enjoying himself.

"There is plenty of time," Jock said. "I'm as curious as you, but —" He nodded toward Don Jesu's men.

"I'm afraid they couldn't stand it," Don Jesu sighed. "Forward, *mis amigos*, into continence and Lenten restraint. *Qué lástima!*"

"Put her in here with me then, lest she cause trouble," Bombarda said. "The chair was made for me when I was fat."

"Captain Paul is a proven dead shot," Don Jesu laughed. "This time the target won't be a hundred paces away. You are still bigger than a rice dish."

"Humor him," Jock whispered. "He didn't get anything at the *dantica* and his feelings are hurt."

"Maybe I'll trade him Dolores for this Circassian," Bombarda's voice floated happily out of the chair.

"Would that be an example of the law of diminishing returns?" Don Jesu asked in mock innocence.

"Confound you, I don't give a hoot in hell for either of the girls!" But Don Jesu saw him bite his lip.

179

"*Por Dios!*" mused Don Jesu. "What a trader the factor must have been in his prime!"

Before their men got out of control, Don Jesu and Jock marshaled them into file and marched them towards Lagos; Bombarda's men followed rather than be left behind at the mercy of the Ashanti; Bombarda himself drew the curtains of his sedan chair.

Following the passage of some hours, bearing courteously in mind the fact that white men were always clumsy and slow in the jungles, the Osai Apoko opened his stockades and dispatched his strings of prisoners. The jungle thudded and shook under the lock-step impact of their feet. Not having white men's chains, the Ashanti escort tied their captives body to body, neck to neck, by means of thirty-foot creepers, a variety of climbing vine that grew in the forest, peeled for the purpose.

Some of the prisoners had heard of white men's chains and hoped they would live to wear them: the creepers were slippery, the loops around the neck would tighten and strangle anyone who might falter, or faint, or break step, and the body of such a one would be instantly removed from the line and cast aside.

This kept excellent order and insured delivery of only the best.

Chapter 17

AT LAGOS LAGOON on the Coast the pent-up stream of trade flowed again in its normal channel like a flash flood after a drought: the Ashanti delivered their prisoners of war, who poured into Bombarda's barracoons, receiving in return their value in rum, cloth, broken mirrors, knives, hatchets, copper wire, beads, little bells and a musical box and a bucketful of cigars. The Negroes departed, pleased with their acumen and Captain Paul's fair play.

The Arab caravan delivered burroloads of that queer commodity salt, which is taken for granted in areas where it occurs but famished after in areas where it does not, bars of it, big as gold bricks — in many localities such salt bars were used as money; also pepper and Russian furs, Oriental rugs and cut jewels: the concentrated wealth of the Eastern trader whose transport is light, whose wits are sharp, and whose merchant blood dates back to the Phoenicians. The Arabs received in payment minted gold, matches, English cloth, needles to sew it, muskets, gunpowder and balls. Hakim had in his train another white slave. Onumba saw her and whined for her. Bombarda kicked him and refused. Hakim remarked, "Next time, perhaps."

Praising God, calling "peace" on Captain Paul, the Arabs departed their separate ways. Trading on the Coast had been profitable in spite of native wars and the greed of the Osai Apoko, whose inexperience Captain Paul, with the help of Allah, had so masterfully managed. "Well he deserves his Leyla," Hakim mused. "I was loath to part with her."

The Circassian girls enjoyed a high reputation for physical beauty. Reared in the knowledge that one day they would be sold, they were proud and aware of their charms: at an early age they learned to stain their palms and the soles of their feet with henna, bright as the beard of the Prophet, to remove all hair from their bodies (hair being a disfigurement to the masters likely to purchase them, since such purchasers were usually Algerians or Turks, Eastern peoples, scantily supplied with the same themselves), to outline their eyes with kohl, exaggerating the brilliance that youth and their blood already insured, and to perfume their bodies with rose and vanilla and musk, so that being in the presence of such a girl was like standing in a garden of flowers. Hence Hakim's reluctance to part with her.

But Hakim was an Easterner, and Jock's proclivities lay with the West.

Leyla emerged from Bombarda's chair, to the factor's great regret and her mild surprise, as virgin as when she entered.

"She is exquisite," Bombarda said. The feeling of well-being he had experienced drained away with every step nearer home; and now that he was back on the Coast he was yellow again and ill-tempered. "Something is amiss with me. I do not desire her."

He had dwelt so long on the Guinea Gulf that to him, as to a native-born African, Leyla was beautiful: for owners like him she had been born, trained and sold.

Jock examined his property, which looked back at him anxious to please. The lot of a slave which did not was hard, and she knew it. She was stockily built, short-necked, small-breasted, straight-haired. Her cheekbones were prominent, her chin line was strong as a man's.

Don Jesu knocked impishly, though the door was open. "May I come in?"

Jock chuckled. "There's certainly no reason why you should not."

"I confess I am dying with curiosity."

"Behold her."

"O-o-f!" said Don Jesu. "What a sinful waste of a rice bowl."

"Concede," Jock laughed, "that the poor child has beautiful eyes, very large, blue as smoke."

"Only a poet would see them. No wonder they bundled up everything else."

"And she's trying to be agreeable."

"She *is* white," Don Jesu said, "if that's an advantage; I wouldn't know, would you?" He cocked a Mephistophelian eye at the door.

Dolores had passed slowly by, looking in, her yellow gaze fixed on the Circassian like a cat's on a bird.

"The factor considers Leyla exquisite," Jock said.

"Fevers and local ideals of beauty must be infectious."

At the sound of her name the girl ventured a step forward, smiling brightly.

"No doubt Dolores had a message from Bombarda," Jock said, forcing indifference into his tone.

"How thoughtful of him to send her instead of his ape of a major-domo," said Don Jesu.

"She is nothing to me," Jock persisted.

The savage kicking he had administered to Onumba seemed to have relieved some of the tension in Bombarda. "The filthy black rascal was beginning to annoy me," he said. "He ate the pigs; and the little girl — you remember the little girl, Senhor Paul?"

"I always remember what I pay for. Captain Newton charged her to my account. The transaction occasioned me considerable trouble when a lady in Virginia discovered it."

Bombarda said, "I had trouble with a lady in Portugal once in circumstances that were similar. Well, the little girl died as a result of too much attention."

"I shouldn't have thought the old medicine man capable of it."

"He hired her out and took fees for her."

"I'd have kicked him too."

"Oh, I didn't kick him for that. What irritated me was his desire to replace her with one of Hakim's white slaves. White, do you hear, Senhor Paul?"

Jock shrugged.

"Perhaps the African sun has rendered you color-blind."

"Sorrow is sorrow, pain is pain, death is death for black as well as white," Jock said.

"Indeed." Bombarda sipped his drink. "I begin to see on you an Anglican collar, like Newton's. Too bad."

"That I doubt," Jock laughed. "Not Anglican, anyhow. In Scotland we were just as shy of Anglican collars as Roman."

"How odd," Bombarda said. "I have difficulty remembering that the sects which have separated from Rome have also separated one from another."

"I am not very religious," Jock said, "and I certainly can't straighten you out on a question as big as that."

"Spiritual values have occupied my thoughts much of late," Bombarda said. "I'll give you Dolores for that thing around your neck."

Jock took off Apoko's odoriferous talisman and tossed it on the table. "Take it and welcome! I'm glad to be rid of the stench."

"Thank you," Bombarda said greedily. "Thank you so very much!" and he put it on.

"I'd have thrown it away before now except that Apoko would have got his feelings hurt."

"Oh no, no, no."

"What's it made of?"

"Life," said Bombarda.

"Oh, very well."

"Dolores will be in your room tonight."

"Don't bother about that."

"Have you considered that such an arrangement might be thoroughly acceptable to her? Have you noted the gangrene-green look with which she favors Leyla?"

"I thought her eyes were yellow," Jock said.

Bombarda smiled craftily. "I thought you'd seen them. Enjoy her."

"Enjoy Apoko's little nosegay," Jock answered.

"They are hardly the same." He touched on something else. "Have you observed the condition of the Ashanti prisoners of war, Senhor Paul, their gaunt and haggard look? Not prime, not prime."

"I suppose Apoko couldn't feed so many."

"They must be fattened up."

"Yes, I should think so."

"Will you stay and help me fatten them for market?"

"Can't you do it alone? Why do you need me?"

"I am fatigued, sick and beside myself. I need help. I have not forgotten my offer of a partnership, Captain Paul."

The image of Dolores merged and identified itself with Jock's lusty ambition for gain. "Is there food, space, medical care? I agree they are scrawny; they ought to be fattened so they can make the trip to market with a minimum of wastage in transit."

"Everything is here in abundance, but it needs a strong hand to direct. I am not up to myself; I need supervisory assistance. Will you stay?"

Jock hesitated. He was dimly aware that the tug to remain was sensual, hot and red as the wasting harmattan wind. Bombarda sensed his scruples and glossed them over with gold. Who would know, he demanded; not his brother in America, not his parents in Scotland, not the lady in Virginia —

"Her!" Jock scoffed.

No one whose opinion he valued. What was the harm? Wasn't there time? Above all, wouldn't staying be profitable? "Will you stay, at least for a while, till I am in better health?"

"All right, I'll stay."

Don Jesu was all for sailing at once. He would simply trot the cargo aboard and pack it in. If they were scrawny, they would take up less space. He would weed them out as they died and throw them overboard. Result — as many would reach Bermuda as if fat ones had been loaded in the first place.

"No, no, my friend," Jock laughed. "That would truly be an example of the law of diminishing returns. A hundred healthy are worth two hundred moribund on any auction block."

"*Servidor!*" Don Jesu shrugged. "I am willing to learn."

"A week, two weeks, and then you shall sail."

"Meanwhile I am to crisp in this heat and expire of boredom?"

"Maybe I'll give you Leyla to lighten the tedium."

"I'd rather crisp."

"He can't have her!" Bombarda retorted. "Give her to me! Let him crisp."

Bombarda still hoped for physical rehabilitation and fondled Apoko's charm. Chima shook his head dolefully. Chima, the Ibo, had been watching Onumba, the Ibo, and suspected where the trouble lay and doubted the power of Ashanti magic to ward it off.

"Then crisp I must," Don Jesu said, "but my patience is not inexhaustible. Pray fatten them quickly."

Door to door in the residence that was becoming crowded Bombarda had installed Leyla and Dolores.

During many nights Dolores crept into Jock's room, bringing with her such fire as agonized Chima when he looked on his master next morning, fearful that his master was being consumed; he shared Jock's soul and hence in a way he could share Jock's transports, but he felt a concern which Jock could not feel: she who was empty was emptying him who was full, as must be true, for Dolores had begun to strut and preen herself and wear clothes. The ultimate outcome only the spirits of evil could foresee; the white man remained undiminished, his strength stood firm: but Chima had seen grubs in the soil which gnaw at the roots of mighty trees till a little storm uproots them. He sweated and prayed, and wished it were possible to pump his own blood into the body of his master. Unfortunately the process was not reversible.

Meanwhile, under Jock's discipline the population of the barracoons fattened, took on a gloss and stored up strength for the long ocean voyage, while Bombarda relaxed, slept with Apoko's repulsive little bag on his breast and dreamed of the time when he could sleep with Leyla. Nay, he would do more, for as his weakness increased, his thoughts grew more daring and he fancied them practicable. He projected another assault upon the Ashanti. He would lead it in person. He could not be wounded; his blood could not be shed; was he not protected by an Ashanti charm, to say nothing of all the saints? His mind flagged, and he took it for cleverness; in this new venture he would need no help, not even Captain Paul's. He kept his project secret, fondling it late at night like the charm.

Stealing from Jock's bed as Jock, numbed, succumbed into sleep, Dolores was happy, hopeful: "The soul I lost I gain again, and the belly that was drained is replenished." For the belly was where the soul dwelt, if one had one. "Who could have told me it would be pleasant? He has taught me to say in English, 'I love Jock.' This is white magic, and I am whole again." She spat on Leyla's door.

"I doubt if this is good," Chima puzzled, working his low brow, "for without Leyla she would not have desired him. Or would she, since he desired her first?" Forest pools reflect nothing but empty sky till the thirsty animal stoops to drink, and then they reflect the animal. That is the essence of emptiness. He weighed in his mind the relative advantages and disadvantages of killing Leyla, whose presence had troubled the empty pool. Chima's bulging shoulders sagged under the burden of the dilemma. In ordinary circumstances he would have consulted Onumba, the fellow Ibo, the medicine man who communed with the spirits and knew their secrets; but Chima did not trust Onumba.

Dolores had no one else to trust, and she went to Onumba one night when Jock was asleep and the residence was quiet. In the teeming barracoons the fattening captives snored and scratched in their sleep, full of good food, dreaming of the paradisiacal servitude that Jock promised them in America, where white man's chains did not strangle and everyone wore shoes.

Onumba said from his hut, "I am very busy. Go away."

"I have brought a roast chicken and rum."

"Enter, daughter," Onumba said and laid aside his mask. Stretched over the wooden frame of the mask was a transparent filmlike substance with whiskery tufts where the chin had been, vastly enhancing its potency.

"That is a white man's face," Dolores said.

"Do you come to me for guidance, daughter, or to instruct me in my craft?"

"For guidance," Dolores said, awed at the art of one who worked spells with a white man's skin. "Was it cut living?"

"It was."

"You are very powerful," she said.

"Very."

"I am gaining a soul."

"I know," Onumba said, softening shreds of chicken with noisy swigs of rum in his toothless mouth.

"I wish to keep my new soul."

"That is natural and laudable."

"How can I keep it?"

"By keeping him who bestows it."

"How can I keep him?"

"Let me see you." Agile, knowledgeable fingers examined and probed. "Give me more rum," he said.

She had anticipated his demand and produced another bottle. Onumba drank deeply, eying her. "You are clever."

"I think. I plan."

"You must give him a child."

"I strive, answering his strivings."

"How strong are the loins of the white man?"

"Strong — I think."

"Don't you know?"

"I lack experience to compare."

"That can be remedied."

There was an interval, while she submitted.

"Stronger than that?"

"Oh yes."

"Then it is frenzy," Onumba said, "and the white man must be calmed. Does the white man drink?"

"More heavily all the time."

"Put this in his drink." He gave her a nutshell full of powder.

She frowned. "How calm will it render him?"

"Do not question that which you do not understand, or it will calm you too. But more."

"I do not desire that."

"Only in his calmness will his seed take root, and then with his child you will keep him."

"Oh loved; oh desired; oh desirable!" Her breasts swelled with yearning, foresavoring the ecstasy of the babe — it would be white, it would look like him, it would hold him; she smiled. Already thinking of something else, Onumba patted her belly impersonally, professionally.

"Then you will hold him forever," he promised.

"Thank you for your wisdom."

"Bring me more rum tomorrow."

"Must you do again all that you did tonight?"

"Bring me rum every night and I shall not."

"I will bring the rum."

Onumba put on his horrible mask and began to croon over a small bleached object in the shadow of the corner of his hut.

"Whom do you conjure against?" Dolores gasped. "It is white!"

"Go away," Onumba muttered. "It is not Captain Paul."

"Then I do not care who it is."

Those who engage in the meat trades know that a certain period ensues in the yearly business cycle when nothing much happens: no cattle, no sheep, no pigs are born or bought; neither are they slaughtered or sold. This is the quiet critical period when the stock are coddled, examined for disease, the unfit separated from the fit, the marketable majority brought up to prime. And so it was with nearly three thousand Negroes, daily putting on weight under Jock's watchful eye in Bombarda's barracoons. Don Jesu all but expired of boredom.

"When I was engaged in my former profession," he said impatiently, "an hour's activity made me a fortune for weeks. Now the reverse is at hand: weeks must be spent to gain the gold that I used to get in an hour."

"Think how respectable you are."

"Respectability be damned."

Slow for Don Jesu, the weeks had passed with ecstatic swiftness for Jock. "It hasn't been long."

"I want to get out of this wretched place."

"Soon now."

"It is all very well for you," Don Jesu said. "You have Dolores."

"Indeed I have."

"But what have I?"

"There's always Leyla."

"Thank you, no."

"I agree with you there," Jock laughed.

"Give her to the factor. He wants her, I don't."

"He hasn't spoken much of her lately," Jock said thoughtfully. "I wish he would. She might do him good."

"Nothing will do that madman any good."

"I don't think he's mad; just scared."

"Isn't it the same thing?"

"I don't know; I truly do not know."

"Why is Bombarda scared, behind all his sneaking treacherous cannon that immobilized even me?"

"I don't know that either, poor man."

"Poor man indeed! He's rich as a prince. This establishment —"

"Establishments have to be managed to be worth anything."

Bombarda spent his days on his porch, looking sicker and sicker but protesting that he never had felt better in his life, cheerful, hospitable, but weak and forlorn.

"It is difficult to understand Bombarda," Jock said.

"It would probably be easier if you knew his history."

"Who knows that?" Jock laughed.

Don Jesu shrugged, "Who does indeed?"

Jock said, "Probably the quinine infusion he drinks will put him on his feet. Till he's better, he's asked me to stay here and help. I'm going to."

"The more fool you."

"I don't see it that way. If he falls to pieces so will his factory, and if his factory falls to pieces where will you and I get cargoes?"

"That's true," Don Jesu said, "That's very true. You are farsighted, Señor Paul."

"Would you agree to convoy *Two Friends* with your ship to Tubman? The blacks are nearly ready for shipment."

Don Jesu looked very serious. "Would you trust me to escort your property all the way to America, deliver it to Tubman, trust me to render a true accounting?"

"I sincerely wish you would."

"You 'wish.' You 'request.' You 'suggest'! No, by God! That is *caballero* speech. You seek to put me on my honor, knowing that I would not sully my honor for all the gold in the world. You want my parole. I will not give it."

"You could, you know, and break it. I am a gardener's son."

"True, true," Don Jesu said. "There is no dishonor in breaking parole with the son of a peasant."

"Just keep the ship in sight as much as possible; confer with Webb frequently on the way over; lay in a supply of coconuts for juice — cheaper than scurvy grass."

"You trust me without my parole?"

"Yes."

"I think you were raised by a Jesuit!"

"I was raised, sir, by a Presbyterian dominie who had no use for Jesuits."

"He must have been worth knowing." But Don Jesu's lip curled suspiciously, exposing the diamond. "Maybe you have no other means of transport, no way to get rid of them but through me."

"Haven't I?"

"I see none in the lagoon."

"Do you recall how, in your boredom, you went hunting a day or so ago, and shot one small monkey?"

"O-of! It reminded me of Onumba."

"While you were hunting, I sold three hundred of Bombarda's leftovers to the captain of an unprepossessing ship of 'Swedish' nationality, whose crew looked surprisingly Spanish. He sneaked in; he sneaked out; he paid me in emeralds. But emeralds like his are more likely to come from Brazil than from Sweden."

Don Jesu laughed heartily. "He said he was Swedish, eh? It is an old trick. Emeralds? I probably know him."

"He looked at your ship, asked no questions and sailed hurriedly on the first tide."

"An old friend," Don Jesu said airily. But he was now convinced that he was not the only slaver on the Guinea Coast and that Jock would sell to anybody. "How much did you cheat him?"

"Bombarda's leftovers, the ones he had before we got Apoko's captives, were worth exactly as much as your friend's cracked and colorless emeralds. Some of the jewels were no better than beer-bottle fragments. But then, some of Bombarda's leftovers —"

"Even I follow you," Don Jesu laughed.

"I'll use them for trade with the Ashanti."

"I suspect they'd prefer beer."

"No, they make their own. Trade rum is their aristocratic drink. I wish I could civilize the Ashanti and teach them to drink decent Scotch whisky."

Don Jesu said with a sudden friendly smile, "I'll bring you some when I come back from Tubman."

"You *will* escort the *Two Friends?*"

"Yes. With my speed and her armament we could withstand the Invincible Armada."

"That got lost, as I remember."

"By fire, by water, by wind, not by British guns."

"Any Scotsman would agree to that."

"And I'll render you a faithful accounting!" Don Jesu said. But he added, nudging Jock playfully in the ribs, "You know, you peasant, I can sail circles round that tub of yours. What is to prevent me from simply appropriating her?"

"I don't think you will."

"Maybe you are the Jesuit," Don Jesu said. There was subtle solid sense in Jock's statement that Bombarda's establishment ought to be kept open. It was extensive, reputable, profitable, and Don Jesu would have liked to possess it. Unfortunately, being in honest trade, he could not simply take it like a prize; and even if he could, he knew he lacked patience to manage it. Captain Paul seemed to know how.

Weighing the factors against him, Don Jesu said sententiously, "Captain Paul, I give you my word of honor."

"Fare swiftly." Jock shook his hand. "Farewell."

Alone in his bed, hot with fever, tortured by an all-consuming hatred of black men, sure that his blood could not be shed, fondling Apoko's charm tight-clutched to his breast where it protected and stank, stank and protected, envisioning golden limbs that entwined and enchained Jock Paul, lasciviously straining to peer through the holes of the bamboo partition into the dark room where they lay, loathing her, loving her, lusting for her, Bombarda stuffed his fist into his mouth lest he shout aloud, "Now is the time! Now, while he is bewitched!"

And in truth Captain Paul had paid little attention to Bombarda since Don Jesu's departure. If he had, he would have stopped him.

Bombarda failed to appear one morning at breakfast, and the residence was strangely quiet.

Chapter 18

THE ASHANTI, being a neutral tribe of traders, were courted by all sides in the native wars and could camp anywhere. They were not liked; their "customs" were the most savage in Africa, where savagery was taken for granted; but they were feared, and no tribe ever quite gave up the hope that they might be won over as allies. It was disturbing, perhaps, to think of one's sons and daughters, one's warriors and wealth falling into their hands; but since the Ashanti bought prisoners indiscriminately from all sides, no one construed such behavior as personal animosity. As for the freedom with which they passed through the territories of neighboring tribes, no infringement of sovereignty was involved: Africa was not Europe, and African economy was not agricultural. The Negro thought of his land not as real estate, since it contributed no wealth, but as a sea which was common to all. Hence the shifting frontiers of the native nations, and the prosperity of the Ashanti.

Like much in his long African life, Bombarda had absorbed these alien concepts little by little, year by year. African standards of morals, African notions of government, which had set him to roaring with laughter when first he came to the Guinea Coast, pronouncing them "Ludicrous! All hind-side before!" now seemed to him natural and logical. In all but the color of his skin he had changed. And even in that he had changed a little, not to black, indeed, but to yellow.

He had stripped his factory of guards, both native and Portuguese, and set himself at their head in his traveling chair. From this vehicle he now led them, like the searching head of a long snake of which he was the eyes, into the jungle. He felt strong enough to walk, but at the last minute he had taken Leyla, like Darius his wife in a chariot, to witness his exploit.

"I am monstrously clever," he said to her.

"Clever," she echoed, smiling, trying to learn his language, thinking she must be his.

"I am more clever than Captain Paul."

"Paul?" softly.

"Damn you, don't say his name like that!"

He struck her.

"Paul?" in a still smaller voice. Perhaps it meant "I like you," and she had said it wrong.

This time he doubled up his fists and beat her till she moaned.

His major-domo, trotting alongside, succeeded in attracting his attention. "Master, we have taken another scout."

"Huh? What tribe?"

"A Fulani, master."

"What was the last?"

"An Ibo."

"Oh yes." Bombarda was all captain again, leading his host on a punitive expedition against a perfidious enemy that only he, in his monstrous cleverness, could humble. Fierce passions drove him: revenge against Apoko, who had neglected to "dash" him at the *dantica;* the prospect of easy booty; the cancerous hatred of all whose skins were black; and fear. "We didn't get much information out of the Ibo, did we? You never do; they're too tough. The Fulani have more feeling. Question him."

"No scout will divulge information, especially to you."

"Question him thoroughly."

It was essential to learn where the fighting was, for there the Ashanti would be; and a clever man could creep up on Apoko's barracoons with certain success in the relative absence of guards.

The Fulani scout was questioned; Leyla supposed he must have committed some crime of unusual wickedness to deserve such treatment, and she turned her bruised face away so as not to watch. Just before he expired, a whip, a needle and a knife had drawn from him all he knew.

"Well?" Bombarda demanded.

His major-domo answered, "The fighting is two days' march to the north; it is finished now; Apoko returns with many prisoners to the same camp."

"Who won?"

"The Fulani, or so he said. But he was a Fulani."

"When was the battle?"

"Yesterday."

"Then I have a whole day in which to strike and retire!"

"Does my master believe the words of the Fulani?"

Bombarda looked at the condition of the body.

"In such circumstances it is very likely that he told the truth."

"Shall we bury the body lest it be used for evil?"

"Why bother?"

"There are Fulani among our men, master; some of them will be afraid if it isn't buried."

"Forward!" Bombarda roared.

The snake resumed its tortuous progress towards the Ashanti camp. Bombarda drew the curtains of his chair and settled back with Leyla. "The air is invigorating up here away from the coast," he said, fondling her. She spoke nothing but Circassian and did not understand his words, but she could not mistake his intention.

"How strange that I please you now when I did not before; and after the terrible thing we have witnessed!"

"You have a beautiful voice."

"I am glad you are going to be kind to me."

He hurled himself upon her like a hunger-mad beast, voiding the pent-up passion of years. "You are the first white woman I have had since —" It was ever so long ago, and his mind drew a merciful curtain over the last: he could actually see the curtain: the color of it was black: black was the shameful thing that lay behind it, the thing he refused to see.

The black curtain trembled and merged with real ones, behind which a silver light was shining. He drew them aside and looked out from his chair. Moonlight flooded in, and in the distance he saw the faint outline of the Ashanti camp. There were few fires. He was in plenty of time.

"I think I have never beheld so beautiful a night." He sighed and gazed at Leyla. He felt cleansed. "Soon I shall teach you Portuguese so you can talk to me." It would be comforting to sit with Leyla and hear again his beautiful native tongue from the lips of a beautiful white woman. He would dress her in European clothes. White servants would wait on her. He grudged the little hour the assault on Apoko's compounds would take. But he had planned too cleverly and marched too far to go back now.

Leyla thought, "I hope he will always be gentle like this."

The quiet of the residence that morning struck Jock as curiously wrong. He had not been conscious of Bombarda's smoothly run, somewhat effete domestic service until it stopped. Like the beat of surf or a cicada song in the trees, he did not miss it until it no longer was there, and then its absence was ominous. Chima, not Bombarda's faithful major-domo, was laying the breakfast table and doing it very clumsily, although he was doing his best.

"Where is the factor? Where are the servants? Why hasn't the place been swept?"

"I will sweep," Chima said brightly, "I do everything. Oh, Jesus-God-damn!" He had spilled the lukewarm ill-brewed coffee, and his needle-toothed grin disappeared. "Forgive!"

"Why is no one here?"

"I am here," Dolores said.

As their liaison had blossomed, she had loaded herself with more and more jewelry and trinkets.

"I don't think you ought to wear three watches at once," Jock said not unkindly, "especially at breakfast."

Dolores removed them, wondering why. They were gifts from him. And if one was good, why were not three better?

Onumba was also there, knocking at the porch door, complaining that no one had brought him his breakfast. He was thirsty, too, he said; and he stuck out his tongue in a sneering malicious grimace at Dolores.

"What is this?" Jock asked.

Dolores did not answer.

Chima said uncomfortably, "She takes him a bit of rum every night to strengthen him in his invocation of the spirits."

"I should have thought one of Bombarda's own people could do that," Jock said severely. "I don't like you wandering about at night alone. Let someone else take Onumba his rum from now on."

"They would refuse," she said. "His magic is directed against a white man."

"But not you!" Chima exclaimed. "Not you, dear-master-John-Paul-God!"

"You poor creatures," Jock murmured to himself; but aloud, impatiently, "For heaven's sake, give the old scarecrow whatever he wants and send him packing."

Chima piled Onumba's arms with food and rum.

Onumba said, "I have whatever I want, and I burn whatever I don't."

Dolores said, "What he burns is not you."

"That's very comforting," Jock said. "Chima, go out and find the factor. Find out where everyone is."

But Chima already knew, and told him.

The seriousness of the situation put a different face on Bombarda's disrupted household. "I've got to get him back, Chima. See what force you can round up. I've got to go after him."

"I thought you did not care," Chima said, bewildered.

"Well, I do. He's sick. Hurry."

"I don't see how that affects us," Dolores said. "Come back to bed."

Jock pushed her roughly aside.

The force that Chima could round up was a sorry lot, composed of kitchen hands and cleaning women and boys too young to fight. Bombarda had stripped the factory clean, the Portuguese guards with their muskets and swords, the native guards with their spears.

"Leyla is also gone," Chima reported.

"The fool! He could have had her any time he asked."

"He liked her better stolen," Chima said.

Jock said soberly, "Chima, the factor Bombarda is not himself. He suffers here, do you understand?" Jock pointed to his head.

"Oh yes!" Chima said. "I understand that."

"Better than you do," Dolores said.

Jock frowned. "Take Dolores to Onumba and let him look out for her while we are gone."

"I will," Chima said.

"And then I'm afraid you and I shall have to go looking for Bombarda alone. The people he left behind would only impede us."

Dolores looked at Jock with veiled rebellious eyes. She would not let him go alone.

"I will take her to him," Chima said.

"When we find Bombarda, I shall reason with him and coax him back, lest something bad happen."

It had already happened.

The Fulani scout in his dying breath had lied and had had his revenge. Not a day's march away but already back at the camp was Osai Apoko, king of the Ashanti, as monstrously clever as Bombarda himself. Thousands of white eyes glinted expectantly from concealing shadows. The few fires were snares.

Bombarda emerged into the clearing before the Ashanti barracoons only to find himself instantly surrounded by an overwhelming force of feathered Ashanti warriors. All but his immediate entourage took flight, screaming with terror, into the jungle. His carriers and major-domo only remained. They were instantly thrust through with spears to facilitate and simplify what was to follow. In a solemn silence Apoko strode up. "Well, Bombarda?"

"God save me!" Bombarda prayed.

Leyla supported his sagging shoulders and marveled at this new and violent turn of events. "Let him alone!" she screamed, shielding him with her body.

An elder approached the Osai and whispered to him, "That is Hakim's slave girl, given by Hakim to Captain Paul."

"It is," Apoko said. "Bombarda stole her."

Rough hands pulled Bombarda out of his chair. Spears were raised to take his life, but the elder spied something hanging from Bombarda's neck, bobbling upon his panting breast.

"Hold!" He held up his hand.

"Why?" Apoko asked.

"See!"

"He stole that too," Apoko said. "Strike the spears home!"

"We can not!" the elder declared.

"See! See! See!" Bombarda shouted, waggling the talisman at them. "I am safe! You are powerless! My blood can not be shed!"

"This will require consultation," the elder said thoughtfully.

"He's a liar and a cheat and a thief!" Apoko said, stamping his foot. "There is no reason to consult. Kill him! I command!"

"Softly, softly," the elder purred. "You are young and impetuous. Your father, the great Osai Tutu, always consulted his ministers before important decisions."

"Consult all you please, so long as this criminal dies."

"He shall die, but his death must be in accordance with custom."

Apoko said, "Good!"

The "customs" appealed to him; he had had a fatiguing day and would have liked to partake of brave sustaining food in which dwelt the soul of a fearless man, as Bombarda had been, until lately at least. Something had recently sapped him of strength, but still he was strong.

There was now no reason to conceal their presence. Cooking fires blazed up everywhere; the white man's expedition had been spotted, reported, routed, and the leader caught. While prisoners poured into the barracoons, the Ashanti roasted their meats and stewed their stews in large communal cauldrons and awaited with interest the decision of their ecclesiastical elders now squatting on feathered haunches around their king, advising him and resolving a talismanic difficulty.

It was the unanimous decision of the elders that Bombarda's blood could not be shed since he wore an Ashanti charm.

"But he stole it!" Apoko said. "Just as he stole the girl."

"Just so."

"He shall not escape me!"

The council of elders were not beyond a solution. "No, he shall not escape, neither shall his blood be shed."

"That is a mystery."

"Yes, but see."

"Anything, so long as he dies."

"See."

Bombarda, already tied hand and foot, was now carefully bundled up in all his clothes, clothes being absorbent. His jacket, which he had laid aside during his amorous encounter with Leyla, was put back on him. They buckled on his shoes and adjusted the ruffles of his jabot. They found his wig and slapped it on, pasting it tight with mud. Then, beginning at the feet, they applied layers of mud till he looked like a brown cocoon up to the neck. Then the head.

"Captain Paul will want his charm," Apoko said.

"It still protects Bombarda," the elder said. "Later it can be retrieved."

They put hollow straws in his ears so he could hear; in his nostrils, so he could breathe; they left a little open space at the mouth so he could speak.

Before a campfire they turned him like a roast till the mud was thoroughly dry. The cocoon was now white, all the moisture having dissipated under the action of the slow heat. From its depths came strangled noises, "Jesus! Mary! Joseph! Help me!"

"He is still alive," the elder smiled. "He knows, hears everything."

"God damn the fiends!" moaned Bombarda from his grave. "God damn them to hell! Hell! Hell!"

"A strong man," Apoko declared. "A pity we could not partake of his strength in the customs."

"There are others."

They placed Bombarda in one of the iron cauldrons, now clean and dry after the evening meal, and put it over a bed of glowing coals, fanning away the fumes lest he smother instead of roast to death; he was a slow time dying. The sheath of caked mud fulfilled its purpose. When the body was removed, not a drop of blood had been shed.

"Where are the others?" Apoko asked.

"Yonder; stronger, braver than he, since they stood by him when cowards fled: his major-domo, his carriers."

"They are not yet cold?"

When the body is cold, the spirit has departed.

"The major-domo actually still breathes."

"Good."

The Osai Apoko was to have his brave ceremonial meal after all, and so would his weary warriors, in the fantastic practice of the Ashanti "customs" which faraway Europe had dimly heard of, shuddered at, and disbelieved. This was not cannibalism as the Spaniards had found it in the West Indies and Captain Cook was finding it in the South Sea Isles, not mere gross eating of human flesh, but a delicate consumption in very small pieces of all those parts of the body which had contributed to the prowess of the enemy, in order that that prowess might be transferred to him who consumed them: all that which made for clear sight, sharp hearing, keen scent, strength of arm to strike, strength of leg to pursue, strength of heart, and the strength that lives in the loins to beget fresh generations of warriors.

When the ceremony was announced, a shriek of delight went up from the Ashanti; fires were kindled higher; the drums began to pound, and the elders got out their knives, which were not iron but flint in accordance with tradition that had not changed since the Stone Age.

The jungle was full of the stealthy noises of flying feet and snapping twigs on every side, with an occasional burst of nervous gunfire deep in the gloom; but when Jock called out, as he constantly did against Chima's advice, the noises would fall silent. Bombarda's men were in full retreat, disorganized and terrified, panting for the safety of the Coast, both Negro and white. They mistook him for one of the Ashanti scouts who infested the area and crouched motionless till he had passed.

"It's too late," Chima said.

"Maybe not," Jock said, and urged him on.

"We have been followed," Chima spoke again, but uncertainly. "I *think* we have."

"Let them catch us then!" Jock said.

"Yet it was a soft, soft step," Chima demurred, not trusting his own ears. There were so many distracting sounds. "Perhaps it was only an animal." Later they heard a shot and Chima said, "Whatever it was, I don't hear it any more."

Then they heard the drums.

"Master!"

"What?"

"It *is* too late!"

Jock looked at him. Could fear make a Negro turn pale?

"You've a ghastly countenance in moonlight," he grinned.

Chima said, "It is the Ashanti 'customs'!"

Jock remembered vaguely that Newton had mentioned them, but Newton had not explained. Neither did Chima explain, following doggedly as Jock pressed forward. Nor was any explanation clear when they came upon the Ashanti camp. Standing behind the bole of a giant bombax tree, Jock looked out and saw nought but a ceremonial dance, much like the one he had witnessed at the *dantica*, but less lively; the drums beat a deeper slower note and some gorgeously befeathered medicine men were passing out little rice bowls of sweetmeats. Apoko sat on his green mat as before, his arm resting on the black-draped Golden Stool. The only fearsome thing that struck Jock's eye was Bombarda's chair, overturned and burning in a fire.

"He may be still alive," Jock said.

A voice behind them said, "Welcome."

Both whirled to defend themselves and were instantly overpowered. While a dozen strong Ashanti held them fast, the pleasant voice said, "Do not be alarmed. We have been escorting you. The forest is full of scoundrels tonight. One we would have slain, but that was done for us."

Jock and Chima were conducted to the edge of the green mat. Apoko said, "I expected a brave man like you to come after his property. But it was foolish to venture out alone on such a night. That is why I gave orders that the space around you be kept clear. Welcome."

"Where is my friend, Bombarda?" Jock demanded.

Apoko was puzzled. "Friend?"

Chima said in English, "For God's sake, hold your tongue. He is dead. Look yonder."

"No friend steals, as he stole from you," Apoko said. "No true merchant steals, as he tried not once but twice to steal from me. I put him to death. You shall see."

Bombarda's body was brought forward. A medicine man with his flint knife tapped off the crusted mud at the throat, exposing Bombarda's chest and drew out the charm. It was charred and brittle like the body beneath it, which was crumbling away from white ribs.

"My gift can now be returned to its rightful owner," Apoko said.

Jock retched uncontrollably on the ground.

"Burn that carefully," Apoko reminded the medicine man. "Some enemy might obtain it and through it do harm to Captain Paul."

"He is trying to be kind," Chima whispered.

The medicine man placed the still-warm charm in a bag of new skin that seemed to have been grown for the purpose and strung it to a wet white tendon and held it towards Jock, smiling; but Jock's belly was empty and he could retch no more.

"Put it on," Chima pleaded.

Jock could not move.

"Come here, my friend," Apoko said, and he hung it around Jock's neck. "It is stronger than ever now."

199

Chima sighed. His master at least was safe, and probably so was he. "Thank him," Chima said.

"God help us all!" Jock said in English.

"He renders you heartfelt thanks," Chima said to Apoko. "He is overcome and he cannot find words to express his gratitude."

"He is welcome. But there is more. The slave which Bombarda stole is also safe. I return her."

Leyla was brought forward.

Jock found his voice. "I am glad she is safe," he said to Apoko.

"There is still more," Apoko said. "A Fulani sorceress was following you, weeping and tearing her hair. No doubt she had seen what Bombarda did to the scout, who was one of her nation, and meant to do you harm. She had a speaking charm upon her which moved, though it was made of gold and gold cannot move. My escort would have protected you, of course, but one of Bombarda's Portuguese fugitives shot her. He deserves your gratitude."

In proof they now brought forward the body of Dolores. On her breast, close to the bullet wound, Jock's golden watch still ticked.

Jock wept.

"You must thank him again," Chima said.

"No, by God!"

Chima said in a low voice, "He weeps thanks for all the dangers spared us. But he wishes now to retire."

"We have all had a trying day," Apoko replied. "Good night."

Near to swooning, Jock permitted Chima to lead him away to one of the Ashanti huts, which Apoko had courteously made ready for them.

Chapter 19

JOCK LAY all day and all the next night in the Ashanti hut, burning with thirst, fever-tossed and conscience-stricken. Chima would not sleep but, like a dog whose master is not himself, watched out the long hours squatting at his side, whisking away mosquitoes with a leopard's tail and waiting for his master to rise up again and command; like any dog who, even though his master is dead, never doubts that he will recover. "I wish my last words to her had not been brusque," Jock muttered as his scattered senses wandered slowly back.

Chima said miserably, "I was at fault. I took her to Onumba. He promised to keep her safe, but he did not. If you kill me, you will be strengthened; kill me quick."

"It is Onumba's fault, not yours."

Chima set his teeth and resolved not to die; another's fault was greater than his.

A helpful Ashanti medicine man, sent by Apoko, stooped down and entered the low door of the windowless hut, and rattled a gourd full of dried things to frighten away the spirits of evil. He looked at Jock, knowing that Jock was a patient of importance, a friend of the Osai, and if he did not cure him he would lose prestige, maybe more. But the white man was strong, his malady was common; he was yellow of countenance but only a little. Faugh! The whites took sick in Africa even when no one was conjuring against them! It was nothing, nothing but shock and fatigue and a touch of fever.

"It is serious," the medicine man pronounced, "but my magic is equal to the emergency."

He closed the door of the hut, sealed the cracks, burnt a lion's liver over a slow fire of eagle feathers and mumbled incomprehensible words; and Jock, almost suffocated by the fumes, sat up and chased him away.

He left Jock a bitter infusion of quinine to drink, which Chima also partook of on the sly, to strengthen in himself that little part of Jock's soul which he shared; and went off to report to Apoko that Captain Paul was better.

In great weariness and depression of spirit Jock came to himself, aware of all that had passed and his present surroundings but eager to put it behind him, like a man awakening from a nightmare. As never before, he was conscious that the slave trade differed from other trades, but in what and wherefore he would determine another time, when he had leisure, when it was not so close, nay, when it was far away in space and time.

The hut smoked as if meat were curing inside. The medicine man received plaudits from his tribesmen and a kindly word from his king and great advancement in reputation that day. Jock Paul ran out of the murky interior coughing and cursing. "See!" said the medicine man, "the white man's stride is firm, his wind is strong, and his skin is restored again to that pink which renders them so unattractive and in which they take such pride."

"You have done well," Apoko said, "and he cannot help the color of his skin."

Cheerfully Apoko relinquished to Jock the body of Bombarda, not wishing it around to infect his people. He was less inclined to surrender Dolores: the Portuguese musket ball could be put to good use. But the medicine man had already extracted it and added it to his pharmacopoeia of charms to be employed against white men in case of need. As for the golden watch, Apoko did not want that mysterious object at all.

So Dolores too was turned over to Jock.

"Why do you want them?" Apoko asked.

"To bury."

That was a wise precaution, Apoko said. Buried, their spirits could not wander and do harm.

Apoko gave him an escort to the Coast. "But I do not think you will need it," he smiled, "for all is quiet now." It was a gesture of friendship: a guard of honor, noisy, festively feathered, drumming and singing and skipping, that accompanied him back to Lagos, bearing the silent bodies of the dead.

Surrounded by his guard, Jock did not notice that Chima no longer walked beside him. Chima had hurried on ahead, anticipating an opportunity to serve his master; the privilege would be his alone if he could arrive at the residence before the others. He gloried in the thought, and as he ran he smiled, and as he smiled the light glinted on his teeth.

Twenty miles from Bombarda's factory in a crumbling fort erected a century before, Dom Sebastiao de Serpa Pinto, governor of the Portuguese Province of Lagos, maintained his official residence and sought against unimaginable odds to maintain the dignity of the Portuguese Crown. His district was extensive and his responsibilities were heavy. Westward lay the gold mines of Elmina and numerous establishments along lost little rivers from whose auriferous sands gold was extracted by a panning process. Eastward lay the mighty river Niger, down whose broad and turbid flood floated barges laden with ivory. Before him lay the hundred-mile-long Lagos Lagoon, where all this wealth collected and was shipped, not only ivory and gold but thousands of slaves, the most valuable commodity of all.

All this territory and all this activity lay within the governor's jurisdiction, and in it he was charged with the maintenance of order. It often seemed to Dom Sebastiao that if African affairs were conducted so as to afford the police protection that any decent fishmonger in Lisbon had a right to expect, Lagos Province could be, as it potentially was, the brightest jewel in the Portuguese Crown. But his garrison were underpaid and some-times not paid at all; there were not enough of them, and many of them were transportees with criminal records, serving out their sentences. His appeals for better soldiers and adequate supplies were ignored, lost in piles of similar requests from India to the Azores that went unanswered on the desk of the colonial secretary at Lisbon until they were thrown away. Only in demands for revenue was the government at home efficient. It was an age when colonies were milked, not nursed. Dom Sebastiao did his best with what he had, though he knew that his wretched soldiers stole from the supply house, gold production figures from the mines were falsified, gold dust leaked from the pans into the private pockets of his overseers, and ivory mysteriously disappeared into smugglers' ships. Things had never been any different; Dom Sebastiao was not a man to change things; his blood was noble and stanchly conservative. But he was adapt-able. The world-wide practice of bribery, called "dash" in Africa and "gratuities" in the English-speaking world, smoothed the way for that kind of official corruption which, when nothing else would work, had kept the Roman Empire alive during the long twilight that preceded its final eclipse and descent into the Dark Ages. Like every other colonial official, the gov-ernor of Lagos pieced out his rarely paid salary with bribes from the local factors, looking forward to the time, not too long hence, when he could retire to his estates on the banks of the Tagus, secure in fortune and rep-utation. "Everything proceeds in normal fashion," his reports to the colonial secretary invariably stated, and a gift would accompany the report.

But when serious trouble occurred in his province, he was forced to be-stir himself and put it right, especially when the trouble affected his own "dash." The native wars had been fought with extraordinary bitterness this year. Such a situation would, as a rule, have been welcome to the governor since it assured a plentiful flow of slaves to the traders along the Coast. But the word had come to his ears that one of his most dependable sources of in-come, the veteran factor Bombarda, had permitted a misunderstanding to arise between himself and the Ashanti. Dom Sebastiao respected Bom-barda's solidity as a trader and had known him in Portugal; he regretted his old friend's lapse into friction with the natives, and he determined to pay him a personal visit.

There were of course no roads through the festering mango swamps that lined the Coast, and the paths through the interior were long, circuitous and dangerous. Fortunately the smooth waters of the lagoon provided a safe highway. The Portuguese flag at his mast and his gubernatorial flag on the bow of his yacht identified and protected him. No one, not even a privateer, would fire on the governor of Lagos, from whose death nothing could be gained and from whose lax, conniving administration so much might be expected. Comfortable and confident, regretting only the break in the quiet routine of his life, Dom Sebastiao sailed up to Bombarda's landing and stepped ashore.

The factory looked much as it always had. Smoke rose from the barracoons where fires were cooking food for the captives; to judge from the bustle and hum they must be numerous. Native and Portuguese guards patrolled the high stockades, arms at the ready.

He was met at the door, however, not by Duarte Bombarda but by a sandy-haired stranger with a strong lean chin and a remarkably humorless smile. Jock tried him in English and Ibo; the governor spoke no English and his Ibo was bad; Jock spoke no Portuguese; after some floundering they discovered that they were both at ease in French.

"Soyez le bienvenu," Jock said.

"C'est extraordinaire," said Dom Sebastiao.

Bombarda's tragic story unfolded.

"Where did you bury him?" the governor asked.

"I will show you."

Within the enclave of Bombarda's residence Jock had buried him where the cannon overlooked the lagoon, marking his grave with a cross.

"He always liked this spot," the governor said.

Hard by was the grave of Dolores, marked by a headstone inscribed with her name. Jock thought she might have been a Moslem.

"Who was she?" the governor asked.

"A member of the household for whom I had great regard."

"I see."

They left the somber place and returned to the residence. Chima served them wine. There were whip welts on his back, but his manner was anything but sulky. He served Jock first; Dom Sebastiao raised his eyebrows slightly. Leyla moved in the background, but Jock showed no interest.

A shrewd appraisal of Captain Paul convinced the governor that conditions on the Coast were not beyond repair.

"You say you are friends with the Ashanti chieftain, Captain Paul?"

"I am sure of it. He could have murdered me too, charm or no charm. Remember, Bombarda was wearing it."

"But instead he sent his witch doctor to make you well. That is significant. Ashanti prosperity rests on trade; their commercial standards are high. Apoko sees in you an honest trader."

"I can honestly say I have always been that."

204

"But more than that he senses no hatred against his race in your heart. You will find that the savage is curiously sensitive to hate."

"Hate them?" Jock said thoughtfully. "No, I do not hate them. You could no more hate an exasperating child."

"You have found very quickly the golden key that unlocks their nature and assures success in Africa," the governor said. "Do you have children?"

"I am a bachelor," Jock said.

The governor smiled. "Yes?"

"I have no children, sir."

"Ah. Permit me to beg your pardon. I have several; all white, I may add; soon I shall see them again. Their mother sent me some miniatures by the last packet only two months ago. I hardly recognized them, so big have they grown. I shall show them to you when you visit me."

"I shall be delighted," Jock smiled.

"You don't care a fig," the governor said, "but it is polite of you to show interest. A family man grows lonesome in Lagos."

"I suppose so."

"When the children were little," Dom Sebastiao resumed after a pause, "they used to exasperate me with their wickedness: they quarreled without cause and made senseless noises. They were afraid of the dark. Their self-ishness was naked and unashamed: once the girls put a live frog in their nurse's soup just to hear her shriek; the boys were continually tearing the wings off flies and racing them to a line, or pulling off a spider leg to see if it really would wiggle till sundown. As for broken windows, alas, how many I paid for; but neighboring boys broke mine as well, and I in turn was paid by their fathers. As I remember the score, however, I fancy my boys were a little more accurate at hurling their stones.

"We punished my little savages and taught them their manners, their mother, their nurses, their tutors and even I, if the offense was grave. And every night they would come to my study and kiss my cheek and say, 'Good night, Papito,' little aware that they had done anything genuinely repre-hensible and equally unaware that they were being taught a civilized code of behavior necessary to transform them into ladies and gentlemen.

"At the time I learned that I had secured my appointment as governor here I watched my children closely, knowing that I should be separated from them for a long time. Never had my children's faces seemed so beauti-ful as just before I left them." He looked at Jock. "I note that you are clean-shaven. No doubt you shave yourself."

"I always do," Jock said.

"Picture to yourself a miracle, Captain Paul. Picture to yourself a

205

magical shaving mirror which reflects both your own face and the face of a beloved wife, mysteriously merged into one smaller fresher face with smoother skin and brighter eyes and softer lips that no one yet has kissed in passion, though Love it was who fashioned that little face: so shone for me the beautiful faces of my children. Do you find my paternal reminiscing sentimental? Tedious? Illuminating?"

"Not illuminating, sir."

"Let it illuminate you, Captain Paul. In Africa I discovered the same unsophisticated cruelty, the same senseless noise, the same superstitious fears; the same delight in fighting; the same greed; the same deep untaught total centering on self. You will concede that these are human traits; one finds them in infants. But in the African savage everything is exaggerated. He lives beyond the pale of religion, science, courtly codes of honor; he cannot read; he cannot write; for him there are no books to transmit the accumulated wisdom of thousands of cultivated minds preserved over thousands of years. His childishness is exasperating; but it is understandable. If it requires prolonged and patient effort on the part of devoted fathers and mothers and nurses and tutors to civilize little Portuguese children, how much more effort will it not require to civilize the Negro! Yet he possesses a wondrous capacity for love."

"That would explain my manservant," Jock said. "Chima murdered a man in circumstances of great barbarity. I was inclined to gloss over the incident when I found out why he did it, but his deed struck such terror into the hearts of these people, just when I was getting things under control after our return from the Ashanti, that I was forced to punish him. Discipline demanded it."

Chima heard his name and brightly approached the table. "You can fill our glasses," Jock said, "and this time serve his excellency first."

Chima had run through the forest with giant strides for so stocky a person. The fugitives from Bombarda's expedition, having nowhere else to go, were filtering back to the residence. In the utter lack of leadership Chima set them about their accustomed duties, cunningly exaggerating the likelihood of an Ashanti attack, to keep them busy, far from Onumba. He was not to be cheated of his opportunity to serve. He asked oblique questions: No, Captain Paul had confided to no one else that Onumba's fault was great, greater than his. His, then, would be the glory. He skulked around Onumba's hut and peered in. Onumba lay drunk amid empty bottles and flyblown garbage, the remains of a feast. In a corner Chima glimpsed the charred remains of the object that had represented

Bombarda, and understood Bombarda's fiery end. But in the same corner another white object had been newly set up, and Chima's legs went weak with horror. He fled to the residence and swept it vigorously, remembering that Captain Paul had desired that the place be neat. When not a speck of dust remained and no excuse to linger longer, Chima returned to Onumba's hut, never doubting that death would strike him for what he was about to do.

He shook Onumba awake. To kill a sleeping, drunk, or mad man kills only the body.

"Onumba!"

Onumba looked at him with bleary bloodshot eyes.

"Chima?"

"Onumba, do you hear?"

"I hear, pig."

"Onumba, do you hear, see, smell, taste, feel?"

All the senses.

Onumba recoiled.

"Go away!"

"I brought her to you. You let her go."

Words tumbled out of Onumba's mouth in panic.

"She was cunning. She gave me rum. She ran after him when I slept. She loved him. She thought she could save him. But he is dead. Is he not already dead?"

Chima answered, "I am dead. You are dead. She is dead. He is alive."

Chima hurled himself upon Onumba and tore out his throat with his teeth. As Onumba died he spoke. "I didn't mean her to die."

Chima buried Onumba, the bottles, the garbage, the image, under the floor of the hut; he smoothed the ground and marked it with all-conquering magic, the Christian cross of the white man, and washed himself in the lagoon, marveling that he was still alive. When Jock returned, he had him whipped.

"Discipline demanded it," Jock said to the governor.

The governor said, "You did right. You are different from Bombarda. Your discipline is impersonal. His was tinged with hatred."

"I knew that; but I never knew why."

"He is dead now and I can tell you. He had his reason."

Twenty years ago, the governor said, when slaves were more common in Europe than now, there was a fashion among Portuguese nobles of giving little blackamoors as gifts to their ladies. They would serve as page boys, and the women would vie with one another in devising gorgeous costumes for them: Turkish pashas, Indian rajas, Damascene caliphs and the like. They provided endless merriment and a constant source of conversation among the ladies. It was all so exotic and amusing. But Bombarda misjudged the maturity of the pretty little Negro he gave his wife, or perhaps she taught him; the governor had never much cared for Senhora Bombarda, a beautiful feather-witted creature who lacked solidity. "However it came about, Captain Paul, he found them together, you fancy how, and slew them on the spot." Of course there was a terrible scandal. Probably it would have died down in time, since no one really blamed poor Duarte. But his wife's family were powerful and stubborn; they refused to let the matter decently drop. They hounded him through the courts till a friendly judge hinted that unless Bombarda left the country he would undoubtedly hang for murder. On that he exiled himself to the Guinea Coast and set up his slave factory, bringing with him all that remained of his pride and his love: his furious hatred of all who were black. "I think he would have been happier hanged," the governor said. "Hatred kills."

"It killed him," Jock said.

"Tomorrow we shall speak of pleasanter things," the governor said, smiling engagingly. "Much pleasanter things, for both of us."

Chapter 20

THE GOVERNOR spent the night at the residence, leaving his personal guard on his yacht, a mark of honor coupled with a show of trust such as the oldest member of the household could not remember his having accorded the late factor. Under its mellowing influence the staff did their utmost to please him, serving him hot chocolate as soon as he stirred in the morning and filling Bombarda's bath with hot water, since it was not to be supposed that his excellency would swim in the lagoon like Captain Paul. Jock loved the cleansing sting of salt water, especially if he had drunk too much the night before, as had happened often of late; but even if he had not enjoyed the swimming, he would now have avoided Bombarda's bath, which was one of the Ashanti cauldrons.

"You keep an efficient ménage, my dear Captain Paul," Dom Sebastiao exclaimed. "I was not better served in Portugal!" His manner was brisk and extremely friendly.

He expressed a desire to inspect the factory. Jock took him on an extended tour.

Chima, whom the natives now looked on with awe, had ordered Onumba's hut torn down and thrown into the lagoon, where the tide would wash it away. Over the floor he had had them pile up a cairn of heavy rocks, each so big that no living man could lift it alone, far less a dead one. Hidden in a crevice between two rocks was a small wooden cross, tied with a tendon that ants were already attacking. The governor's sharp eye spotted it at once and he sighed; but he did not disclose it to Jock; he did not want ruffled tempers today. Captain Paul just might get angry; true, he had shown no religious tendency, but those were usually the ones who made much of slights that were actually trifles. Dom Sebastiao was no theologian, but he deemed it likely that if savages trusted crosses to frighten away demons, even in conjunction with dead stones and filthy charms, that was a very good start towards something better.

The governor praised the condition of the grounds, the alertness of the guards, the dryness of their powder. He praised the repair of the stockades and noted that sanitation was even better than Bombarda had been able to achieve.

"How in the world do you manage that? That is always one of the worst problems."

Jock grinned. "I honestly hate to tell you."

"Oh come, sir! I can bear it."

"To tell the truth, I had to consult Chima on the matter. He simply lines them up at a certain hour and commands them to use the latrines."

"Suppose they can't?"

"Maybe he scares it out of them. Then everything is carted away and buried. Of course, if one of them is really sick, I isolate him and have him looked after."

"I have heard that sanitary discipline of much the same sort is enforced on British men-of-war. Have you ever served on a British man-of-war, Captain Paul?"

"Not I, and not many Scotsmen would. But the story you heard is true."

"Well, they certainly seem a healthy lot!"

He praised the supply house which, under Bombarda's regime, had been left to a slovenly native storekeeper: the last supplies to arrive were continually the first to be consumed because they were always on top, with the result that everything on the bottom disintegrated with mildew or was eaten by ants. Jock put the stores on shelves, waist high, so that no one would have to bend down, and the legs of the shelves he placed in buckets of salt water, which drowned the insects. "I owned a provisioning agency in America," Jock said.

"Do you still own it?"

"I wish I did. But I sold it when I went into this business."

"There is surely more profit here."

"That is true enough, though I never lost money on my agency."

"There will be even more profit now, I expect. You were Senhor Bombarda's partner, were you not?"

"I agreed to work with him on a share-and-share-alike basis, temporarily at least. No contract was ever signed."

The governor waved technicalities aside with his hand. "No contract is necessary between gentlemen."

"He simply trusted me and I trusted him."

Dom Sebastiao had witnessed the rise and fall of many slavers on the coast. Rum, women, disease or assassins' bullets usually made off with them. Even the good ones, like Bombarda, were likely to possess secret seeds of ruin. The loss of a good one was serious: his factory fell to pieces. But here was a hard young healthy ambitious man, a shrewd successful merchant who had dealt in perishables before, captain of a ship, an expert in navigation, who could command not only men but affection, no lecher, resourceful, brave, and best of all he could get along with the Ashanti! It seemed almost too good to be true.

Perhaps it was too good to be true. Captain Paul also possessed a conscience, and from his manner that conscience was tugging at him. Perhaps the hardness was only on the surface, or perhaps it ran deep, but was melting. Souls did sometimes grow, though not often in Dom Sebastiao's experience. If such was the case with Captain Paul, he would have to be approached cautiously or he would not stay long on Lagos Lagoon.

"It would seem to me," the governor said pleasantly, "that in view of your oral contract with the late factor, which is perfectly binding as far as I am concerned, the Portuguese Crown is not justified in stepping in and seizing the property. In default of heirs, and Bombarda has none, you succeed to the whole." Dom Sebastiao could not help adding, "Subject to the usual conditions, of course."

Jock said, "This is nothing I foresaw or expected, and I am puzzled about what you mean by 'usual conditions.' "

"Mere trifles."

"But what?"

Dom Sebastiao shrugged. "Oh, transfer title fees, license fee to trade, accreditation with the colonial secretary —"

"And the governor's 'dash'?"

"My dear Captain Paul!"

Jock laughed. "Till one ends up without a sou!"

The governor took him by the arm. "I detect a note of scorn in your voice, Captain Paul. The sun is very warm; I do not wish it to heat your temper. Do not laugh off the tremendous value of a place like this. Good men are hard to come by on the Coast, and I am prepared to make great personal sacrifices in the matter of my 'dash' to keep you. It will be cooler on the porch of your delightful residence."

It was true, the governor conceded, that a *strict* interpretation of all the laws that regulated the collection of taxes and fees could beggar a man, "an undesirable man, Captain Paul," who attempted to set up as a Coast trader, so much so that not only would he end up without a sou but he would actually be in debt before he started. But for a desirable man (with liberal "dashing" of the local officials who issued the papers and kept the records) the laws could be interpreted less strictly. "I'm afraid that will still amount to about twenty per cent of your income for the first year, Captain Paul."

"I have not made up my mind to stay at all, sir."

"Haven't you?"

"I am a little weary of trafficking in human bodies. I thought it would be different."

Conscience. A bad sign. The governor wavered.

"Twenty per cent is the least anybody has ever paid. It is less than one shipload, you know. I have practically overlooked my own 'dash.'"

Jock did not want to stay. But his trader's blood was up. "I consider twenty per cent an unconscionable gouging, sir."

"I really do not see how —"

"Tell me, did Bombarda pay his tax?"

"Why, of course."

"Then it would seem to me," Jock said slyly, "in view of the fact that I was his partner on a fifty-fifty basis, that my own tax is already fifty per cent paid."

"*Madre de Dios!*"

"Wouldn't you say?"

"It is a point of view. But Captain Paul, only ten per cent! That is practically piracy."

"Of course," Jock said, "I am unacquainted with all the local officials who will have to receive gratuities. Would it be possible for me to make over the ten per cent to you *personally* and let you take care of 'dashing' them?"

The governor visibly brightened. His "dash" had suddenly assumed ponderable dimensions again, while half a dozen others shrank to the vanishing point. "That would be a genuine pleasure," he said. "I assure you, Captain Paul, not a penny shall find its way into improper hands."

The governor would willingly have remained to enjoy Jock's hospitality and get to know him better and find his weak point, if he had any besides conscience; but three ships appeared on the horizon, standing in for Lagos and traveling, apparently, in convoy. His presence sometimes embarrassed the Coast factors, who were supposed to deal only with British buyers.

"It has been all too short a visit, Captain Paul," he said amiably, extending his hand. "But it strikes my memory that I have another mission at the opposite end of the lagoon. *Au revoir; à bientôt;* come and see me and I will show you the miniatures. And do bear in mind, my dear resident factor, that *all* your customers are British; list them as such in your records. You do — you do know how to write?"

Jock laughed. "Yes, I can write."

"Then you must be all the more careful about slip-ups and lapses of memory. When my factors can't write, I provide their records myself. In many ways that simplifies things."

"I'll be careful."

"Caution ships to display the British flag when entering and leaving my waters. One never knows when the Portuguese packet will arrive, invariably accompanied by some cursed inquisitorial British man-of-war to make sure the treaty provisions are being honored. You can imagine how awkward a situation would arise for me if my province were to be caught in illegal trade."

Jock shook the proffered hand, smiling. "I'll caution the customers," he said. "But these ships are quite legal. They have already run up the British conglomeration of crosses."

"You didn't use your glass," the governor said.

"Can't you see them?"

Jock could never understand why everybody could not see as well as he did.

"Frankly, no."

"Well, they're there, big and bold and haughty."

They were; but the governor, departing without delay on his yacht, was more convinced of Jock's eagerness to trade than of his acuity of vision.

Jock was just as glad the governor was leaving.

Leading the convoy was the sinister black ship with the rakish masts; behind her followed the broad-beamed *Two Friends*. And behind *Two Friends* followed a mystery, with rigging slack and sails in shreds and broken spars askew.

"I wonder what story Don Jesu will concoct to explain away *this?*" Jock muttered to himself, and ordered his establishment to continue on a guest footing but to pack away the vintage wines and set out something stronger.

"By my mother's soul," Don Jesu said, lifting in solemn oath a hand on which glittered several new finger rings, "we ran into a frightful storm! Hailstones big as cannon balls went sailing over the waves. I sighted this unfortunate ship in distress. Naturally I sped to her rescue."

"Naturally. How big did you say the hailstones were?"

"Big as can — what are you accusing me of, sir!"

Jock sighed. It was too late to help matters. "Oh, nothing, Don Jesu."

"No one ever saw such hailstones."

"That I thoroughly believe."

"My own ship suffered slightly from them."

Jock nodded. It stood to reason that the ship must have put up some resistance.

"Were you able to save the crew of the ship you rescued from the storm?"

"Alas, at the height of the tempest the cowards took fright and launched their boats and rowed towards shore."

"The African shore?"

Don Jesu said hesitantly, "No. It happened just out of Jamaica on the way across. That rather bothers me. They'll all be in Kingston by now, telling everybody my friendly signals were cannon fire."

"What nationality was she?"

"British, worse luck."

"Worse indeed. Now there will be a frigate after you, won't there?"

"I wouldn't mind one frigate; what worries me is a squadron. There are heavy units of the British navy in American waters just now, trying to browbeat the colonists into paying their taxes."

American politics were far away from Jock after a stay in Africa that seemed long and had been so crowded; but he had always admired the American colonists' attitude toward British authority, especially when it touched on their taxes. It reminded him of Scotland's resistance to tyranny over the centuries; but Scotland had lost.

He grinned. "Don Jesu, I know, of course, exactly what you did."

Don Jesu's diamond shone momentarily, sheepishly. "I am not a very good liar. Come, *amigo mio,* do not scold me. I have something for you." He presented him with some cases of Scotch whisky. "You said you wanted this. I am forced to confess, however, that I bought them through an intermediary — a sort of merchant — well, what he actually does is smuggle the stuff. British taxes on whisky are positively unchristian."

Jock laughed heartily. "They certainly are. I thank you, Don Jesu. It's an excellent brand. I'd never scold you for evading some British taxes. But it was foolhardy to seize a British ship."

"My men practically forced me into it. Incidentally, *Two Friends* didn't take part in the engagement, which was short and easy, though she may have stopped a ball or two."

"I have seen a great deal of bloodshed here recently," Jock said seriously. "I'd like to feel that you did not butcher the crew of your prize or walk them off the plank to drown."

"Walk the plank?" Don Jesu looked at him with scathing professional scorn. "A legend! Absurd stage theatricals! Nobody does that any more. It brutalizes one's crew, and they're hard enough to manage as it is. No, you hold a fair trial and hang the rascals in a civilized manner just like at the Old Bailey, except that Old Bailey hangs women and children, even pretty women.

No gentleman of fortune would sink so low. And how tenderly the little darlings show their gratitude afterwards! You don't even have to ask. Yet it is true, I made a mistake. I should have destroyed the British crew. If I had, they wouldn't be swearing out warrants against me in Jamaica."

Jock knew that he was telling the truth.

"For you I suggest a long stay in Lagos," he said. "Things will blow over, or somebody else will do something worse, or there'll be a war and your little lapse will be lost in a welter of bigger affairs. Meanwhile, you'd better paint out the name of your prize and alter her rig so no one will recognize her."

Don Jesu said, "You are truly a friend. Her name, of course, I have already ripped off, smoothed over and painted out. But to alter her rig touches on genius! Come to me when you join *my* profession, and mine will be the gain!"

Their evening started merrily, but Jock's aversion to Africa deepened as he related the story of Bombarda's death, the pitiful unnecessary slaying of Dolores and Onumba's horrible end.

"If your dagger-toothed ape were mine," Don Jesu said hotly, "I'd have rewarded him. I'd certainly never have whipped him."

"I had to, to preserve discipline."

"You set altogether too high a store on discipline, Captain Paul."

"If you did the same, your men could not have dragged you back into piracy."

Don Jesu shrugged. "Perhaps."

In the days that followed, while the prize was altered, Don Jesu rendered a fair and faithful accounting of the sale of Jock's cargo to Tubman. "He bought mine too at a very good price, but he remembered our meeting at Madame Louise's and I cannot pretend that he likes you. As for me, of course he would dagger me in the back if he could. Nevertheless, he knows a good cargo when he sees one and he wants more."

"I suppose he'll get them from somewhere, me or you or somebody else."

"I promised them in your name. But I should hesitate to deliver them. There are times when it is prudent to disappear for a while. I think for me the time is now."

"Where will you go?"

"Eastward, round Good Hope. The Indian Ocean is delightful."

"Why not stay here," Jock said, "and set up as a trader?"

"Compete with your establishment? What chance would I have?"

"Suppose it weren't mine?"

"But it is."

"It needn't be. I tell you it needn't be! I detest this traffic, Don Jesu."

"It isn't the slightest bit different from any other honest trade," Don Jesu said. "If I have learned nothing else about commerce, I have learned that."

Jock did not try to convince him to the contrary. "If you will agree to take this cursed body-mart off my hands, my friend, I shall feel as if a stone were lifted from my heart."

"On what basis?" Don Jesu asked suspiciously. He had always coveted Bombarda's factory, and now more than ever it was desirable because it could afford him a safe haven; but Captain Paul outgunned him as a merchant. "How shall we share?"

Jock spoke heatedly. "I want nothing but to be quit of it. Take it, just take it!"

"You do not beguile me," Don Jesu said stiffly. "I refuse to be put on my honor. Share and share alike, like gentlemen, or nothing. Will that do?"

"That will do," Jock said.

"And you will deliver to Tubman? Remember, I have promised cargoes."

"How many?"

"I did not specify."

"I will make one crossing, one way, in *Two Friends*."

"Then what?"

"I don't know."

"Then I shall never see you again."

"And then you shall be the sole resident factor of Lagos."

Don Jesu said with shining eyes, "If you are serious, Señor Paul, if you desire to leave this trade, which seems so eminently honorable to me, nay, wonderfully legal and profitable, or if you are in trouble — can I help you there, my friend? No, you would never ask — or if feelings I cannot fathom forbid you to stay, know that I value this sanctuary you offer with a heart overflowing with gratitude!" The flowery Spanish rhetoric torrented on. "If ever you need Don Jesu de Silva y Villanueva, you have only to whisper the word and my sword will take wing like an avenging angel's and fly in the face of the foe of my friend!" To Jock's considerable embarrassment he embraced him warmly and kissed him on both cheeks.

"You'll probably have to 'dash' the governor ten per cent or so to transfer the license from me to you."

"Did you 'dash' him when you got yours?"

"Yes, I did."

"Then we won't transfer any license. I wouldn't understand it anyhow. We'll leave the factory in your name, and I'll say I am acting for you. And we'll both be five per cent richer."

Jock could not help smiling.

"With a mind like yours for percentages I've a notion you'll do well as a factor."

"I am used to calculating shares," the gentleman of fortune replied.

Shortly before the harmattan wind veered round from the land to the gulf, bringing with it no longer gritty air but low clouds and spits of rain, harbingers of months of deluge to come, wetting Jock's sails and serving no end but to speed him more swiftly forward, Jock left Don Jesu and Lagos Lagoon. Never had he felt so light of heart.

His excursion into the slave trade had not lasted long enough to make him a fortune, but he was by no means poor. Snugly stowed under his bunk was his old mahogany sea chest, heavy with three thousand pounds in gold. Delivery of his new cargo to Tubman would augment handsomely that considerable hoard. Africa lay behind in space and time. Ahead, nearer and nearer every day, beckoned Jamaica and Tubman and all the opportunities that a not-too-poor young man might look forward to, and grapple with, and make pay.

But Tubman did not meet him in Kingston Harbor. The police did.

Chapter 21

THE EVIDENCE against Captain Paul was strong. Survivors from the *Bristol Nell,* a British merchantman, had rowed their boats into Kingston and marched in a body to the authorities, solemnly deposing that their ship had been viciously attacked and in spite of valiant resistance compelled to surrender after a prolonged battle. It was not to be expected, they pleaded, that a meager merchant vessel could compete with the swift-sailing black ship and the formidably armed *Two Friends,* between whose crossfire they had had no choice but to save themselves if they could.

"You saved yourselves admirably," the governor of Jamaica said, hearing the evidence. "You sustained no casualties, as I gather."

"Providence held us in His hand," they declared.

"One would have thought you might have had casualties. These are times when revolutionary notions infect the colonies and spread to the vermin that always infest these waters and multiply in times of unrest."

"We were outgunned, outmaneuvered, caught in the middle," they said.

The *Two Friends,* examined from stem to stern for evidence of fighting, disclosed some battle scars: here and there a sail had been punctured; there were pockmarks on her side where spent cannon balls had dented her planking and bounced off into the sea. Jock guessed she had stood off out of range, waiting to see who would win.

But there was also evidence in favor of Captain Paul. Webb swore: "*Two Friends* was almost out of sight when the engagement took place. We took no part in it, Your Excellency. As we closed, to see what was happening, we were struck by shot from both ships. By then it was all over, and since nobody was hurt I deemed it best to proceed to Africa. Captain Paul's entire crew are ready to swear we had nothing to do with this act of

217

piracy, if piracy it was. Don Jesu insisted that *Bristol Nell* fired first. I did the only thing that could protect the owners of *Two Friends*, which might otherwise have been seized by Don Jesu." Captain Paul's entire crew so testified.

The governor of Jamaica, weighing the situation, said to Jock, "You would seem to have chosen a disreputable associate in this Spaniard, whose unsavory history is well known to us." But Don Jesu was also a most profitable rascal to pardon, the governor remembered, thinking back to the last time he had sold Don Jesu his freedom. If Don Jesu had been at hand, the governor might not have fined Captain Paul. But Don Jesu was far out of reach, snugly engaged in legal trade in the Portuguese Province of Lagos in Africa. In England's need for friends and the growing unsafety of West Indian waters, with New England in revolt and the southern colonies ever more truculent towards King George, with political parties fiercely divided on colonial affairs at home, with bribes dangerous to accept because of political spies, with one's very governorship liable to be swept away overnight if one made a wrong move, threatened both from within and without, with smuggling rife and privateers daily more impudent around one's isle, it was not a time to make mountains out of molehills. But something had to be done.

Balancing his position like an expert tightrope dancer, seeking the likeliest victim to supply funds, which had always smoothed his way out of dilemmas, the governor decided, "I am prepared to exonerate *Two Friends* from participation in an act of piracy, but restitution must be made to the owners of the *Bristol Nell*. And though you seem not to have been present in person, Captain Paul, the conduct of your ship was suspicious to say the least, and you must bear your share of the blame. I therefore relieve you of command of the *Two Friends* until her owners can be consulted. That may take some time."

It assuredly would, Jock knew, recognizing how few of Colonel Fielding's business partners would dare to come forward and avow ownership in a slaver. Like the governor of Lagos, the governor of Jamaica was seizing on a fortuitous incident to enrich himself.

"I have also decided," the governor said, "to sequester *Two Friends* temporarily, together with her cargo, as compensation to the owners of *Bristol Nell* and to relieve the distress of her unfortunate crew."

Tubman, who had testified at the hearing and painted Don Jesu as black as possible, whispered to Jock, "At least you are not going to be hanged. You can thank me for that."

Jock was not hanged; but all in one hour, less time than it took for one sun to set or one night to come on, he saw himself legally pillaged of command and a ship and a cargo, and, as it turned out, of something more. When a police officer delivered Chima to him, along with his mahogany chest and some other few personal effects, while the crew of *Two Friends* were scattering into oblivion, Jock found that only ten guineas remained of his three thousand pounds, apparently overlooked at the bottom of the chest under some books and an old Scottish kilt. The governor's agent in his haste to "sequester temporarily" the ship and everything of value aboard her had not considered books or a Scottish kilt assets: the kilt was moth-eaten and old; the books had suffered much through disuse and the African climate. Jock was minded to toss the rubbish away; but his mother had woven him the kilt, he could not remember when, he seemed always to have had it; and Henri had given him the books. He dusted them off and he kept them.

Tubman consoled him. "You would only make trouble for yourself if you tried to get your money back," he said. "The governor would deny all knowledge of it. But you can soon make it up and more. We must not lose touch with each other, Captain Paul; we can be of great value to each other. What is to prevent you from instructing Don Jesu to consign more cargoes to me, and you and I shall share in the profits?"

"I couldn't even get a message to him," Jock said.

Tubman laughed till his fat perspiring body shook like pudding. He had had a delicious revenge: he had outwitted the Spanish pirate who had outwitted him, and he had brought down a peg this scheming Scottish merchant. "I think you can get a message to him. I purchased *Two Friends* from his excellency before the hearing."

"*Before* the hearing?"

"Naturally. So you can send your message through me."

"I'll see you in hell first!" Jock said.

With ten guineas to his name Jock took lodgings in a cheap boarding house.

On ten guineas a gentleman might live one week. A disgraced nonentity might exist a month; could he stretch it to two? Jock could not remember; on the lowest level it could hardly be made to last longer. He surveyed his reversal of fortune; it was complete. The kilt made him think wistfully of home, where his parents might be in need. He had heard nothing of them during his stay in Africa, nor from Willie, for he had not cared to disclose his whereabouts or what he was doing. Now pride restrained him from taking passage to Fredericksburg, where Willie would at least provide a roof over his head: the flamboyant younger brother could not bring himself to crawl back a suppliant to the elder. Iron bit into his heart; his spirit drooped and brooded; the rooming house reeked of frangipani and fried potatoes. He fell asleep and slept the clock around, and when he woke he was ashamed of his dreams.

In his dreams Dolores was white and alive again, impossibly merged with Kitty in feature and form, and both-in-one adored him; he had just shot Geoffrey Tubman through the heart, and Tubman had gasped in his dying breath, "Thou hast conquered, O Caledonian," in a monstrous parody of Julian the Apostate. King George III was pinning on his breast an order blazing with diamonds while highborn gentlemen scowled with envy and fine ladies whispered behind their fans, "That is Captain Paul; he saved the day; how handsome he is!" And he was immensely, fabulously rich.

"Is this what I am made of?" he cried to his lumpy pillow. "Am I truly so daft for glory? Not from King George!"

Glorious sunlight flooded his cheap little room. The day was fine and he was alive and healthy; he was ravenously hungry; even the stale odor of last night's fried potatoes smelled good, and the red-jasmine perfume of frangipani was strong and provocative. *That* was no leftover from his dream of the highborn, the glory. No lady used frangipani. He had smelled it at Madame Louise's and suchlike places on water fronts. From the yard below rose homely sounds, distantly remembered, of squawking chickens and a grindstone grinding an ax. From farther off in the streets, which were not Kingston's best, came shrill voices of troops of children, romping or quarreling or playing a game, it was hard to tell which and Jock was no expert. From closer by, through flimsy partitions, he heard a man and wife in a room down the hall beginning their day with an argument. These were not sea sounds or African sounds, and it was good for a change to hear English. He yawned and stretched and went to the window to breathe in the air and let the sun shine on his face before he dressed.

The shortest of knocks thumped on his door, and before he could say "Come in," in came his landlady with a tray of steaming coffee and half a cold chicken with thin slices of ham ranged alongside. He recalled that he was dressed in his sailor drawers. "I hadn't expected a lady to call on me so soon," he grinned, "or I'd have welcomed her more decently attired."

She was a harried motherly soul of considerable girth and determination. "You're decenter than most I've got," she declared, "and *you* paid in advance." On this, having set down his tray on a rickety table, she warned, "If you do not get up earlier, the theatrical people won't leave you a smidgin for breakfast, not a smidgin."

Like many other terms Jock had encountered in the lusty speech on the

American side of the Atlantic, "smidgin" was new, but its meaning was at least as clear as Ibo.

"And you're skinny enough as it is," she pronounced.

Jock said, "Thank you very much," but already she was gone. From down the hall came another thump as the landlady banged on the door of the quarreling couple with the force of a well-aimed cannon ball. "Shut up, you two!"

"Thou wretched, rash, intruding fool, farewell!" the man's voice boomed.

The woman mocked in a throaty voice, "Out, damned spot! Out, I say!" But the domestic controversy subsided.

"Those would be the theatrical people," Jock smiled over his breakfast, and the source no doubt of all the frangipani perfume.

It was certainly different.

In a week they were less mysterious, or at least identifiable by face — when the make-up was off — and by name, though only the good Lord knew what names they had borne before they had entered the arts. James Moody, the manager, probably used his own: strolling companies of actors had to be licensed and, like vagabonds, they were under constant official suspicion. Less probable, but melodious, were the names of the others: Lydia Hart, the leading lady, she of the "Out, damned spot!"; Joseph Hightower, her husband, who had called the landlady a "wretched, rash, intruding fool"; some pretty soubrettes, whose appetites were Gargantuan; a pallid, sunken-cheeked young man who coughed a great deal and whose name was alleged to be John de Gaunt — "His complexion is perfect gallows," Moody said amiably, while the young man nodded in return, acknowledging the compliment, "and I always give him the villain's part; extraordinary talent!"; a Negro slave-handyman who shifted scenes and ate apart; and a superannuated transportee who had once been employed by the banking firm of Baring Brothers in London. "A wizard at keeping accounts," Moody said, "but one dark night he absconded with a carpetbag full of securities."

"They were nonnegotiable!" growled Sterling Gould, the same defense he had used without effect on the lord justice who sentenced him.

"Mr. Gould was transported anyhow," Moody laughed. "He now keeps my accounts, a thoroughly dependable man."

"You can't be transported from here," Sterling Gould muttered. "I wish to God you could." He turned his head and vented his disgust of the whole colonial New World on the floor.

"Do not spit!" said Joseph Hightower. "It isn't refined."

"Joe does it all the time on the stage," said Lydia Hart brightly. "On

Shylock's beard," she explained to Jock, with wonderfully informative eyes.

"Spitting like mine, madam, is an art," her husband said.

"We are all Shakespeareans here," Moody said proudly. "I studied under the great Garrick himself at the Drury Lane, and now my people learn from me, in a sort of apostolic succession as it were. Indeed, I may say that I rose so high in Garrick's esteem that I advanced to a footing of intimacy where I did not hesitate to address him as 'David,' *sans peur et sans reproche.*"

"That's French," Lydia Hart said.

"It means," Moody explained carefully, " 'without fear and without reproach.' "

"You said it very elegantly, Mr. Moody."

"Of course I did, sir. How do you know? Bless my soul. Do you mean to say you understood?"

"I was taught a little French once by a Marquis d'Hauteville de Beaujeu."

"I was given to understand by the landlady that you were some sort of mariner, Mr. Paul."

"So was the Marquis d'Hauteville de Beaujeu."

"He hissed you down, he whistled you off!" the leading man said laughing.

"Joseph," Moody said severely, "you are drinking too much again!" Then, stiffly to Jock, "It was not my intention, sir, to probe into the privacy of your affairs, but you need not have countered with a line like that. We try to be friendly here."

"I was only telling the truth, Mr. Moody. Henri was a marquis and he was a sailor."

"Maybe Mr. Paul is a Frenchman too," Lydia suggested. "Paul is a French name, isn't it? I knew a Frenchman once."

Her husband scowled. "It does not amuse me, my dear, to suffer the interminable recital of how many fools you once knew."

"I tried so hard with such poor success to better the breed," she said, with a mock little shudder of fear which set off her beautiful bare shoulders to their best advantage. "He beats me every night, Mr. Paul."

Jock said as impersonally as he could, "I was born in Scotland, Mrs. Hightower, and a Scotsman I shall die," giving it a good broad Scottish burr.

"Do not die too soon," she said softly.

"Now that," Moody broke in, "is an accent no one could counterfeit!

222

What a wonderful innovation it would be to introduce real Scottish brogue into a Macbeth!"

"Nobody would understand it," Sterling Gould said dismally.

"No, I suppose nobody would. Only a fool would try. I myself am an Irishman, Mr. Paul." Some seats away the palefaced player of villainous parts took out his handkerchief to hide a smile and succeeded only in laughing into it till he coughed. Moody looked concerned; the man was sicker than he knew. To encourage him Moody accepted the joke, which was on himself, in good humor by asking in exaggerated Irish brogue, "And would ye be thinkin', Mister John de Gaunt, that a mere little mention in one little breath of 'Irish' and 'fool' could ever suggest they are one and the same? Never, me bhoy!"

Then they all caught the joke and enjoyed it together.

"Scotchman and Irishman," Sterling Gould said, coming as close to a smile as his lugubrious countenance would permit, "both Gaels, both foreigners."

"Mr. Sterling Gould was so British," Lydia Hart said in a loud aside to Jock, "that they deported him."

"Security reasons," said Sterling Gould.

"Black sheep, black sheep! A whole bag full!" they chorused.

Jock had never been thrown with such people before. They were frothy, nimble-witted and far too personal in their remarks. They spoke too loudly and laughed too shrilly at too little. Jock got the impression that they continued to play to an audience even when the performance was over. Yet they never seemed happy unless they were talking about themselves, often in long monologues, two or three going at once.

But if they were rude and personal towards one another, they were curiously delicate towards an outsider like Jock. After the first tentative queries, which he had seemed to put off so brusquely, they asked him no more questions about himself for a long time. "They must think I have more to hide than they," Jock mused. It was odd that they should accept him on such a basis, but they did. The little soubrettes flirted brazenly, even though, as he knew, having heard them through the thin walls, they had entertained gentlemen in their rooms till dawn. Everyone brimmed with energy.

Jock had known for as long as he could remember that actresses, especially the young ones just beginning their careers, were little better than water-front prostitutes. Leading ladies aimed somewhat higher. Tradition required that they take a fashionable lover from the upper classes, nobility if they were able, royalty if they were geniuses like Dorothy Jordan, the vivacious magnetic London actress who had attracted His Royal Highness the Prince of Wales, who would one day succeed mad George III as William IV, and had already borne him a royal bastard. "It's half Irish!" Moody chuckled, rubbing his hands. "Now that is something to give our royal family nightmares!" She would never stop, Moody predicted, till the well-known fruitfulness of the Irish had presented the prince with a dozen.*

Joseph Hightower and Lydia continued their domestic bickering. In time, by common consent, the little soubrettes stopped flirting with Jock, since Lydia had so obviously set her cap for him.

"These islands are small and gossipy," she said one night. "One cannot help hearing that you have large African interests, *Captain* Paul."

"Drop it," her husband said.

She persisted, resting her dimpled chin on her shapely shoulder, looking up at him. "You can surely trust *us* not to gossip, sir."

"Lydia, behave yourself."

"He's terribly possessive," said Lydia, pouting.

Jock said, "Who wouldn't be?"

"I think she thinks you're rich," Joseph Hightower said unpleasantly.

She said, "What a gross outlook he has."

Meanwhile Jock's ten guineas had dwindled to eight and then to six, and then one night he treated the company to wine and found he had three left. Chima was costing him nearly as much as he cost himself.

Not all the conversation of the theatrical people was frothy or personal. It became apparent to Jock that James Moody was something more than an aging impresario, exiled to the outskirts of the Empire because he could not compete at the heart, which was London. Moody had a deep and genuine respect for the stage. From time to time he would lecture them seriously at table, warning them against ranting, posturing, stealing applause from one another. He labored tirelessly to weld the company into an artistic whole, deploring the sentimentality of the French stage, which Marie Antoinette was peopling with cardboard milkmaids who never saw a cow and effeminate shepherds who never saw a sheep: "Passionless, false, impossible!" was Moody's verdict; and deploring also the Italian stage, which was degenerating into endless soli and monologues interpolated into a context to supply an excuse for the prima donna to show off her voice or her ankles; returning with patient persistence to the massive integrity of Shakespeare, where the whole is greater than the sum of its parts and each part shines with reflected glory from participation in the whole.

Once he recited Hamlet's directions to the players in the "dumb show,

* The final score was ten.

224

wherein he caught the conscience of the king." It sounded odd to Jock, a sort of paraphrase; not as he remembered it taught by the dominie in Arbigland. But that was long ago and perhaps Jock had forgotten.

Said Moody (and, as at all such times, his company listened with respect), "Speak the speech as I, James Moody, pupil of Garrick, pronounce it to you, easily and with understanding: for if you mouth it, I'd as lief the town crier spoke the lines. And do not saw the air with your hands, for you only distract your hearers with wild gestures; be moderate, speak clearly when you declaim; the passion is in the words, which gain strength from your clarity of delivery. Oh, it offends me to hear a robust periwig-pated fellow tear a passion to tatters, to very rags, to split the ears of the audience who, for the most part, are stupid as swine. One need not sink to their level to move them, nay, if one does, one moves them not; for whoever heard of a pig raising another pig above his piggishness! But be not too tame either: suit the action to the word, the word to the action. And above all, do not strut or bellow, for it is enough to mirror humanity. Do not deform it; it is already too much deformed." And he ended, as Hamlet had, "Go, make you ready."

He praised them that night after the play. "But tomorrow is *Julius Caesar*," he reminded them. "Have your parts well in mind, especially the Cassius. You stumbled somewhat in your lines tonight, Mr. de Gaunt," he said to the villain.

Lydia said, "John isn't here," and pointed to De Gaunt's empty chair.

"Oh, so he isn't," Moody said, squinting down the table.

"He went to bed right after the performance, coughing."

"Is he worse, poor lad?"

"I'm afraid he is."

"Then I shall have to play Cassius," Moody sighed. "Oh well."

Hightower said, "That will require some alteration in the part, won't it? *You* 'lean and hungry'?"

"Oh, I'll fix all that."

Jock asked, "How? *Caesar* is the one play I remember well."

"You do?"

"That one, anyhow."

"That is interesting," Moody said. "Come to my room, Mr. Paul, about the witching hour if you are still awake. I will show you something I learned from David Garrick."

Jock suggested slyly, since Moody was sleek and well fed, "Did he teach you, perhaps, to melt the too too solid flesh and resolve it into a dew?" Everyone laughed and applauded.

225

"Bless my soul," Lydia exclaimed, "Captain Paul quotes the Bard. He has missed his profession."

Moody said with dignity, "I did not hear him. Ladies and gentlemen, you shall have your new parts by sunrise, not that you'll be awake."

"He'll 'improve' them beyond all recognition," Lydia pouted, leaning toward Jock; the pout pursed her full lips much as if they were about to receive a kiss.

"Can such perfection be improved?" Jock asked, smiling.

Hightower scowled; Lydia beamed.

Jock knocked at Moody's door at midnight, in good humor though now he was penniless. His board and lodging were due next day and he could not pay. That would have worried him once. In the company of these lighthearted people it no longer did. He could always find employment as a common sailor if nothing better presented itself.

"Come in!" Moody called, but did not look up when Jock entered. He sat at a table, an open book at his elbow and some pages of foolscap in front of him; two cheap tallow candles cast a murky light on his shell-pink pate; he had laid aside his wig and was industriously writing with a quill pen that looked as if, for it too, the molting season was at hand. He wore a pair of spectacles, which Jock had not seen on him before.

"I've brought you a bottle of good Scotch whisky," Jock said; he did not say it was his last.

Moody's look of intense concentration relaxed into a smile. "I am too fatigued to call immediately to mind the dozen Falstaffian lines that would best thank you for it," he said pushing his spectacles up onto his forehead. "Scotch whisky is nearer to usquebaugh than anything I can think of."

"We call it usquebaugh sometimes at home, too."

"Naturally," Moody said, savoring it, holding it up to the light, "one sees in it only Highland mist, not the deep sweet smoke that caresses the peat bogs of Ireland. You will have observed, Captain Paul, that I am a perfectionist in everything."

Jock stretched his long legs onto a chair. "I wonder what a perfectionist would do if he found himself on the beach in a lovely West Indian isle, stony broke."

"An academic inquiry of course, Captain Paul."

"Of course, Mr. Moody."

"Sterling Gould assures me that I am not broke."

"I didn't mean you."

"Then I do not ask you, sir, who you do mean."

Jock said, "I shouldn't really mind except that it has been pleasant here in the company of your people — 'healing' would be a better word. I shall hate to say good-by."

"Must you?"

"Yes, very soon."

"May I ask without presumption — it is a thing to which no shame attaches — how often it has happened to me! — whether you find yourself temporarily short of funds?"

Jock smiled. "Like a cowrin' mouse, that squeaks in th' dark o' the crypt!"

"That scans," Moody said. He had juggled pentameters all evening.

Jock laughed heartily. If Moody had been anything but an actor, lower than a beggar in the social scale, he could never have made so frank an avowal of poverty. "Scan or no, it's the truth, Mr. Moody." He lifted his glass. "Your health, sir; you have restored mine!"

Moody chuckled. "Your financial situation would astonish Lydia Hart and delight her husband."

"I shan't tell them."

"Neither shall I. What will you do?"

"Go to sea, I suppose."

"Let us not make our adieus prematurely. You have a saw-toothed man-servant, have you not? Why not sell him?"

"I ought to, of course. I can't afford his keep. But I cannot bring myself to."

"I'd buy him. I need another strong back to shift scenes and pack properties and clean up after battle scenes. They like to see things smashed in the provinces."

"No, I don't think I'll sell him."

"Then why not set him free?"

"Cast him adrift? He'd starve without me!" Jock was shocked. He had bought them and sold them; it had never occurred to him to set one free. It seemed like a cowardly way out, shirking responsibility. "That would be inhuman. What would he do?"

"Oh, he'd find employment — dockhand, porter, gardener. I've seen Negro freedmen. They get along, like the rest of us poor mortals. I never yet heard one curse his master for freeing him."

"Yes, I suppose even poor savage Chima could be a gardener," Jock said slowly. In his mind's eye he saw his father trimming the hedges on the estate of the laird of Arbigland, and his father's skin was black as coal. And so was his. "I'll think about it."

It was a sobering thought.

Seeing him pensive, Moody said cheerfully, "Come, sir; Fortune's a fickle mistress. Do not be moody; *I* am Moody; ha, ha, ha! What the Bard could have done with my name!"

Jock grinned. "What a pity he never thought of you."

"He has me now. Wouldn't you like to hear what a sea-change Cassius has suffered? As you mentioned earlier, to the applause of my company — I'll be bound, sir, I was a little incensed at that or I should have shattered you with a quotation — it is painfully evident that I cannot look as lean and hungry as the part requires in time for tomorrow's performance. Ergo, the lean and hungry Cassius must be made over, and put on flesh and look like James Moody. Attend. Caesar is speaking:

> "Yon Cassius hath a fat and porkish look;
> He eats too much: such men are dangerous.
> I fear him not.
> Yet if my name were liable to fear,
> I do not know the man I should avoid
> So soon as that fat Cassius. He reads much;
> He is a great observer, and he looks
> Quite through the deeds of men. . . .

"I must confess, Captain Paul, good as it is, that the original is somewhat better, and far more like you than my Procrustean alteration has made him like me. I cannot do this sort of thing as well as David Garrick. *He* changes everything, expands, deletes, puts in whole scenes and nobody knows the difference. But even the Jamaican colonials won't believe a fat Cassius."

Behind his weary eyes the slow light of inspiration began to dawn.

He reached out and tore up the foolscap sheets.

Nobody would have to learn a new part.

He could leave Shakespeare intact.

"My dear Captain Paul!"

"Yes?"

"*You* shall play Cassius!"

Chapter 22

HE ONLY took up acting to be near you," Joseph Hightower said belligerently to his wife. "He isn't like us."

"Who would want him if he was?"

"He's some younger son in trouble, or some embezzler in hiding like

228

Sterling Gould, or a Royal Navy officer who sold the guns off his ship for the coiners to melt down. That happens, you know."

She knew.

"He has hidden assets somewhere."

"On that score, dear, I will not argue with you." She smiled and combed her long hair idly, drying it after the drowning she had just sustained with enormous success and to thunderous applause.

In the James Moody redaction of *Hamlet* Ophelia did not die off stage. For colonial audiences that would have been wanton neglect of the possibilities in the situation and an unpardonable waste of Lydia Hart's voluptuous figure. Moody had remedied all that. The brook was a clever little tank sunk in the boards close to the footlights. In it she would expire in full view of the audience. Too late, her brother, Laertes, would rush on and pull her out, wet as a fish, the filmy gown she had rent in her madness clinging like skin.

"I didn't think Laertes' embrace was exactly brotherly when he kissed the corpse of his sister farewell tonight," Hightower said.

"It brought down the house, didn't it?"

"You breathed."

"Damn it, do you want me to stop breathing too?"

"Do you have to do it so enticingly?"

"They like it that way."

"So does Mr. Paul."

"I think Mr. Paul has become a very competent actor in a very short time," Lydia said primly.

Hightower could only hope that Mr. Paul was truly a younger son. It would degrade him in the opinion of the entire company if his wife, a leading lady, should accept a lover who was not nobly born.

Shortly thereafter John de Gaunt died, not violently, as he had died a thousand times on the stage, to clapping hands and stamping feet that cheered the villain's demise, but quietly smiling, burnt away to a shadow, among comrades who mourned him. They buried him in the churchyard on King Street on a sunny day that he would have approved. His wasting disease had caused him often at the last to ask to lie in the sun. They paid little heed to a different name that marked his grave, and remembered him as John de Gaunt, a cheerful, friendly and talented player. Then, uneasy as actors always are when death strikes down one of their number, the troupe ceased to speak of him and wanted to move on. Moody felt the same, and agreed.

"I was satisfied with you before," Moody said to Jock. "I really need you now."

Jock had saved a little money during his weeks of apprenticeship. Moody now gave him de Gaunt's old salary.

Sensitive to a mood of death, of which he had seen so much in so many forms, Jock now broke his silence, the more readily because he was no longer entirely destitute.

MY DEAR BROTHER: [he wrote to Willie]

A touch of malaria, contracted no doubt on my voyage, has enforced upon me a period of idleness in which I convalesce — "play" would be nearer the mark — in this beautiful island. Thanks to buchu and the Bark, however, I am now perfectly restored, though still not quite what I was when you saw me last.

I am sorry to say that my illness has eaten heavily into the funds I had set aside for the sustenance of our dear parents. What do you hear from them? How do they fare? But I send you a Bank Draught in the sum of twenty pounds for their use. Nota bene: Permit no discount above ten per centum. Your banker will want more, pleading the uncertainty of the times, but bankers can always find an excuse to enrich themselves.

There is little evidence of political tension here, though I do observe a certain slackening off of shipping in the harbor and I hear reports of high prices and some scarcities among imported goods. On the other hand, I note that the theaters are crowded every night; people seem to have money to spend for luxuries, at least. In fact, it is said that persons who never set foot in a theater before attend them regularly now.

I hope the tailoring trade goes well and that the plantation prospers and that Bessie and you keep in excellent health. Write all the news and soon, to be held for call at the Post Master's here, where your letter will be eagerly looked for every day

By your Affectionate Brother,
JOCK

This letter was not entirely candid, Jock knew, and more than a little tongue-in-cheek. It revealed nothing about himself except his whereabouts, and it suggested that he might be ill, whereas actually his malaria was long cured and he had never felt sounder of body or lighter of heart than he did at the present time. But he could not bring himself to confess what he was doing. He had hidden the fact that he had engaged in the slave trade, which was sufficiently disreputable. To act on the stage was to sink even lower in the eyes of the world. If slaving must be hidden, how much more deeply must he hide his participation in the world's most contemptible profession! Nothing but anxiety for news of his parents, coupled with knowledge that Moody would soon take the troupe on tour, which would leave him without an address, could have moved him to write Willie even a line while he remained an actor. He was ashamed of himself for enjoying the stage, but he did. The applause above all elated him; and, as Moody shrewdly surmised, appeased a hunger for recognition as strong as a tiger's to kill or an eagle's to soar or a fish's to swim, an excellent trait in an actor.

Moody, judging the material with which he had to work and pronouncing it good, had proved a puristic tyrannical master. "First we will remove the Scottish burr, Mr. Paul. The function of speech is to convey intelligence; the audience must not be aware of a regional origin when absorbing a message that is universal," and he drilled him in elocution till Jock's tongue grew skilled and his ear grew sharp for accents that deviated from standard English and his brogue disappeared. "And now we must teach you to walk." Walking was more than a means of locomoting oneself across twenty feet of boards, which to an audience was temporarily the world. Walking, no less than speech, was a vehicle which served to convey a message: the good strode; the bad skulked; the coward dodged; the conspirator minced, dark and alert in the shadows. "It gets to be part of you," Moody encouraged when Jock sighed that all this was sham. "I merely strengthen that which everyone does naturally. Lydia Hart used to drown like a log, stiff and unlovely, till I taught her to drown beautifully, still supple, still woman, still desirable. Concede that she has learned how."

He taught him the stance of command, which was not difficult for a man who had captained a ship, and the trick of projecting the voice so that even the back row of the top gallery could hear and comprehend above the hubbub on the stage. "The trick is not loudness — your voice is admirably loud — nor even clarity of diction, though that is important. The trick is an almost imperceptible pause before the critical word, then out comes the critical word like a cannon shot. Try it. You will find that I am right." Jock tried, and Moody could compliment him, "Good lad! How you *carried* tonight!"

There were drills of a subtler sort in facial expression. "The actor is small on the stage; his face is smaller still, no bigger than a clipped farthing to the back row. It is permissible, nay, it is necessary, to exaggerate a little. The ancients used masks to overcome this difficulty; we use make-up. In gentlemen especially the features tend to freeze into immobility; I fancy

231

it's another side effect of British repression. Forget you are a gentleman; loosen your forehead and your mouth. Nature prompts you; do not stifle her; let her go!" The parallel-furrowed brow of perplexity; the sudden-shot-up eyebrows of astonishment; the classic "horseshoe stamp" of pain — all these on the forehead. The twisted snake-lip of contempt; the wide-open mouth of terror, that rigid screaming rectangle (witness the tragic mask) — all these below the cheekbones. These Moody taught him. He had only to permit them to appear and, by a little, to exaggerate them; they would feel natural.

Moody related a parable, the origin of which he did not know, remembered only because it was of value to an actor:

"There lived in ancient times," he said, "a man whose face was ugly as sin, and he fell in love with a beautiful girl. To win her he wore a handsome mask which fitted him like a skin and transformed his repulsive features into features a woman could love. Thus masked, he gained her affection and married her. But a rejected suitor sought revenge and said to the girl, 'Your husband has deceived you; I will show you what he really is,' and he reached up and tore off the mask. And behold: when the mask was removed, there was no difference between it and the features beneath."

And he taught him the polished deportment of a gentleman, which encompassed the entire body and was not a study in exaggeration but elegant restraint, which came easiest of all to Jock.

There were also the animal analogues. Mankind had petted his pets since time out of mind and fled from his foes in the elemental world of beasts: animal reactions were deeply embedded in folk memory and signified immemorial emotions: how the cat arches her back and rubs against your legs when she wants something or feels affectionate; how, by contrast, the dog lowers his spine towards the ground and fawns, looking up into your eyes, ready to lick your hand for forgiveness or for very love. Had Jock noticed that no cat ever looks you in the eye? No matter. That was a lesson more suited to female players.

The sinuous, sinister, belly-creeping serpent, cursed by the Almighty in the very first act of the Bible — learn how a tempter conducts himself. The head-erect, nostril-flared, mane-flung, proud-stepping horse — learn how the strong and guiltless march gloriously forward to fame. And the pitiful, futile flutterings of moths, fated to burn in a paltry candle, the doom of the indecisive.

Nothing was too little or too big in the animal world of nature to teach a lesson to the actor; for the actor, if he would but learn, would learn he was part of nature. That, Moody said, made acting natural. He was intensely sincere. "I repeat to you, Jock, it becomes part of you."

One night in an elevated mood after a successful performance, Jock said, "Your theories work, and acting comes easier to me now, so much so that I have difficulty distinguishing when I am playing a part and when I am being myself."

"It's all the same," Moody said, "not a whit different."

"But over the theater shine the stars. A sailor sees them."

"Stars, Jock?"

"Fixed and immovable."

"I'm afraid I don't —"

"It seems to me that your art stops short at the pit."

"Oh, I see. Maybe so. Well, we have an excellent roof to shut out the stars so they never distract the audience. An actor does not aim that high. Don't let a few inaccessible stars spoil a promising career."

"There are so many," Jock said.

"Enjoy them."

As Jock won for himself more important parts, Lydia's interest in him rose. Hightower was acquiescent, certain by now that Jock was a gifted younger son whose true name must be listed in Jacob's *English Peerage* and whose prospects were as good as any that could be expected in the provinces. He counted himself not only not shamed but positively advanced in the eyes of the company if Lydia should accept him as her lover, which indeed seemed at hand. She was working hard at it, and Jock was beginning to respond.

To Jock there was no blinking the fact that Lydia was superlatively attractive. And had not James Moody recently read him some pertinent lessons concerning the animal world? He also saw her every night, and he was not yet twenty-five.

Meanwhile Jock went every day to the postmaster's, distressed that Willie had not as yet answered his letter, and dispatched another. "I shall be loath to leave this place till I hear from you," he said, thinking how soon the troupe must depart, "though commercial opportunities in some of the other islands attract me. I beg you, write fully and soon."

Meanwhile also the Kingston *Gazette* carried the news, and the theatrical posters announced, that the James Moody Company of Players would offer their farewell performance the following week. The local critic commented, "It is the opinion held by this reviewer that Ophelia's death scene, portrayed with such artistry by Madame Lydia Hart and second to none, as we deem, but the great Jordan's of London, will be presented not once but twice if, as is confidently expected, applause demands it on the final night." (It was not at all unusual to repeat whole scenes, even death scenes, if an audience liked them.) After that, the reviewer pronounced in a valedictory vein, the Moody Company would move on to delight the audiences of Nassau in the Bahamas, St. George's in the Grenadines and Rockley Bay in Tobago, and other West Indian islands before embarking on a European tour that was certain to be no less than a Royal Progress. The European tour was pure fiction, but it served to convince the colonials of the high caliber of their entertainment.

Thus Ophelia went mad not once but twice on the final night and drowned not once but twice in the clever little brook sunk in the boards next the footlights. There was so little interval between the scenes that she had no time to stitch up the rents in her gown and perforce must tear it anew at her second death. This, since there was very little left, rendered her virtually nude, her beautiful torso bare in the arms of Laertes, who pulled her out and kissed her farewell for the second time that evening, a trying moment for Jock but an artistic triumph that assured enthusiastic audiences next season.

Sterling Gould was counting the receipts and professing himself satisfied.

The little soubrettes were buzzing, "She's got him now, or he's bloodless."

Moody was working on the itinerary.

Hightower had obligingly absented himself.

She said in her dressing room, "Dry me, Jock."

No one else was there.

Conscience stands off at such time, like a tide held back by a contrary wind; but when the wind subsides, the tide comes flooding in. Jock's Presbyterian scruples smote him. No one, not even Dolores, had ever afforded him such unalloyed sensual rapture. But with Dolores, poor savage, it had not been adultery. Complaisant as Hightower obviously, unscrupulously, self-seekingly was, for reasons that Jock could understand, Lydia still remained his wife, the wife of another man.

"I doubt we've been fair," Jock said.

"Is Joe fair?" she asked, crooking her little finger in a fine-lady gesture as she held her glass. "He's been warming the bed of one of those dirty little dancers for months. Is it my fault if I prefer a gentleman?" It annoyed her no end when men, having got what they wanted, placed things on a high moral plane. It put her in the wrong. Then next, when liquor

234

and lust would restore them, they'd come back raging like bulls; as Jock too did, to a perfectly played serpentine embrace that left him slain with pleasure.

"What is your real name?" she whispered, close, in his ear. He would tell her now; she would tell her husband; the noble gossip could be breathed abroad, and Hightower could strut like a lord and Lydia Hart could put on airs like Dorothy Jordan in London,

Always the lady, she drew a dressing gown modestly over her ankles. "Shame on you for looking, you naughty, greedy whoever-you-are."

"I would not have you suppose I am something more than I am," he said.

"I know what you are," she giggled. *"Mon Dieu!"* and explained, "That's French."

"No, you don't know," he said.

A compulsion to tell her the truth gripped him and conquered. Words tumbled out of his mouth. John Paul was his name, he said, no other, no nobler. No younger son, but the son of a Scottish gardener who labored all day with hands black with dirt. Once he had risen to head a ship chandlery, but then he had sunk into slaving; and now he was poor: the short unvarnished facts of a small career lived on a low level, far removed from the glittering world from which she assumed he had come and in which, by his silence, he had let her believe he belonged. "I am sorry, Lydia."

At first she did not believe him. Then, as the facts mounted, she began to cry. "You might have told me this before I yielded to you. A gentleman would."

She had not, he thought, put up much resistance; but he merely said, "I did not want to continue under false colors, Lydia."

He bent to pat her shoulder. She snatched away.

"Don't touch me! Liar! Whoreson! Coward! Cheat!" Her face corded with fury, went livid for shame. The fine-lady airs fell away. The mask of Venus dropped, and the ugly visage of Medusa glared and writhed. She railed at him like a fishwoman, screaming such gutter abuse as up to that time he had heard only in the mouths of drunken sailors. There was no calming her, and he hastily withdrew under a hail of rouge pots that followed him down the hall.

Doors opened, pert faces peeked out, simpered, and ducked in. One little soubrette whispered, "You'll be out of range in here with me, Captain Paul."

Moody opened his door and said, "I wonder if you'd step in here for a moment."

Jock slumped into a chair. "Everyone knows now, I suppose."

"Knows what? I asked you in to get your opinion on some little changes I've made in *Richard III*. I'm thinking of giving you the part. I've taken off his hump and made him less of a monster, added suspense to his lines —"

"Everybody knows what happened."

"How could they? I don't."

"Didn't you hear?"

Moody sighed. "My position is a peculiar one. I try to keep peace in my little family. Sometimes I close my eyes and sometimes I close my ears to things that happen. I am an artist, not a shepherd of souls. But I assure you, sir, that even if my eyes and ears had been screwed to the sticking point I could have witnessed nothing through a closed door. And as for the dialogue, only half of it was audible; your voice, if you spoke, did not carry. All that was heard was another of Lydia's tantrums. We've heard them before, but I must say her diction is usually clearer. I doubt if anybody understood a word — a few of the fouler ones, perhaps. How did you set her off so? How can I help smooth things over?"

"I told her," Jock said, "I was the son of a gardener and poor as a church mouse myself."

"Told by an idiot," Moody said sternly. "It would have been kinder to let her build castles in Spain."

"I told her I do not like to sail under false colors." Yet even as he repeated to Moody the words he had spoken to Lydia so short a while ago, he realized that he had *not* told her the truth about himself. The truth was quite different. He saw it clearly now. It was not a thing he would have cared to avow. The truth was, Jock Paul was still daft for glory and could take no pleasure in a prize he had not had to fight for. That was why he had humbled himself before her, deeper than actually was true. No wonder she had reviled him.

"I suppose Hightower will challenge me," Jock said soberly. "I shall regret that."

"I wouldn't be alarmed," Moody said.

"I'm not alarmed for myself. I like him."

"Ah, I forget. A sailor no doubt has experience in genuine arms. Ours are all harmless. But Hightower won't challenge you. Why should he?"

"After what happened —"

Moody held up his hand. "No, no! Do not tell me. I know what happened. You knocked at her door to light your candle; the wind had blown it out; you found her in deshabille, and she grew angry. You wanted to borrow a curling iron for your wig; your man had misplaced yours. At the very worst you took too much wine after supper and entered her room and threatened her virtue: she threw you out. Something of the sort she will tell us tomorrow, and the only wonder will be that she wasn't more gracious. Lydia is proud. She would die of shame if it should be known that she has flirted for weeks with a gardener's son. And her husband would never forgive her."

Jock said, "This is the maddest crowd I have ever encountered."

Moody replied, "Our values are eminently sound; we do tend to exaggerate *just* a little, perhaps. Only the stars, which you seem to admire so much, possess fixed and unalterable values. One does well to forget them. For reasonable people values vary. Come now. Let me read you a few of the lines of the Moody redaction of *Richard III*."

"I am a trifle fatigued," Jock replied, "so I readily concede that *Richard III* was the gentlest, kindest, sweetest monarch that ever drew breath, eight feet high and he never hurt a flea, and the Pope of Rome is going to saint him tomorrow at six o'clock in the morning. Good night, Mr. Moody."

Moody chuckled. "Good night, Mr. Paul."

Next morning at breakfast Lydia mentioned ingenuously, "Captain Paul passed by my door last evening to borrow a flame for his candle, which the wind had blown out."

"Oughtn't to open your windows," Hightower said. "Night air's bad."

"What a fright he gave me! I pelted him roundly, I'm afraid."

"I cannot conceive, my dear," her husband reproved her, "why anyone should take fright at our Captain Paul. Sir, I trust you will excuse Lydia's unmeant and unmannerly reception."

"I wasn't injured, sir," Jock said, "and I didn't take the reception amiss."

Moody's glance and Jock's met in the briefest flicker of understanding. All was well.

No one had anything to add.

Within a few days James Moody embarked with his Company of Players for Nassau, but Jock was not among them. They crowded the rail of their ship to wave good-by to him as they drew away from the quay. Hightower shouted merrily, "Farewell, thou trusty villain!" and murmured to Lydia, "Pity you let him slip." Lydia fluttered a big lace handkerchief, gift of a former admirer, and cried, "*Au revoir, Capitaine!* That's French." Moody alone of the entire troupe breathed a secret sigh of relief. The impresario possessed a keen ability to foresee threats to the calm and tranquillity, always precarious, of his temperamental little family. Jock Paul posed such a threat: he was too intense, too unformed, fluid at the moment but likely to freeze into some sudden mold when he had lived a little more, a freezing that might take place quite unexpectedly. It might take the form of uncompromising idealism; Jock had shown an alarming ambition to reach for the stars; he might take it into his head that he truly loved Lydia Hart, which would have been a shame, since Mrs. and Mr. Hightower, for all their bickering, had genuine affection for each other. He might decide that life was a fraud and drink himself to death, or, more likely, shoot out his brains.

If a theatrical career could be likened to life, and Moody firmly believed that it could, during which one toils up a slow ascent to the top of a mountain, breathes the thin air at the summit for an exhilarating moment or two, and rapidly slips down a steep decline on the other side, then most of his players were well on the downgrade. But Jock had just begun to climb through many twistings and turnings towards a summit still hidden in cold ice-crystalline fog: somewhere up there he would freeze. It was important that actors should never grow up. Jock had not as yet, but he was the kind that did. After that nobody could ever learn to play a part. He could only be himself, whatever life made him, plasticity lost forever.

Jock had been somewhat put out by Moody's acceptance of his resignation, which he had made with great firmness, expecting protests. Moody did not protest.

"No doubt it's for the best."

"I assure you that it is. You must understand that my family comes first."

"I understand."

Willie had not as yet answered Jock's letters.

With his salary paid, Jock was now possessed of perhaps sixty pounds. Chima had lately been shifting scenes, Moody had generously made an allowance to Jock to pay for his keep, and his great strength had proven of help in the final packing before the company left. But now Chima was a burden again, and Jock was unemployed. He thought of seeking a cheaper lodging, which would have been possible. But the landlady halved his rent and let Chima do odd jobs in the stables: with the company gone, it would take some time for the rooming house to fill up again.

"I am grateful," he said, "but a fortnight hence, if I do not hear from my brother, I shall have to take ship for Fredericksburg."

"There was nothing at the postmaster's again today?"

"I'm afraid not."

There was nothing at the postmaster's the next day either, and then suddenly Willie's answer came, though not through the regular channels.

Willie wrote:

Do not wonder at my silence, dear brother. The sad fact is that the mails are insecure. Conditions may be normal in Jamaica, but I assure you such is not the case here. American smugglers — pirates would suit them better — prey on British ships throughout our colonial waters. No punishment, in my opinion, is sufficiently severe for such rascals; but it must be admitted that others hold contrary opinions and applaud this flagrant breach of the laws. The culprits are seldom brought to justice.

Willie was taking an oddly un-Scottish attitude, Jock thought. Willie continued:

Thanks to Colonel Fielding's patronage, I have been able to purge my clientele of disloyal persons like Patrick Henry. Mr. Henry, since the death of his wife, seems to have gone quite daft, doing nought but stir up trouble with rebellious speeches about liberty, as if that were denied us. Even Dr. Franklin's paper, which I no longer read, is tinged with liberal political notions. And I hear, though I cannot credit, that Colonel Washington himself has retired to his estates and takes no part in putting down this traitorous disaffection. It may be difficult in your sunny isle to imagine the strength of the mounting passions here. As for me, thank God, I take my stand loyally for King and Country!

More and more odd in a Scotsman, Jock thought. But the next explained the financial basis for Willie's pro-British sentiments:

Colonel Fielding has sold his estate and gone home to England with his daughter Kitty, whom surely you remember. She was recently married to a major of impeccably loyal character. Colonel Fielding let me have many tons of most excellent tobacco at so low a price that I should have suspected it spoiled till he told me how anxious he was to return to his duty in England. Nearly all his friends, gentlemen of the highest distinction, patronize me now. It was quite surprising that he should have rented his place to the Dandridges, a family almost as disloyal as the Henrys. Little Dorothea Dandridge is quite grown up, by the way.

Prices continue high; my tobacco reaps me grand profit in England. I have especial hopes for my latest cargo, which I bought so cheap and which you yourself shall shortly see.

So much for the good news, Jock.

The rest is bad. As your eyes will have told you by now, I have all but lost the use of my hands through a crippling assault of the gout, and the complaint threatens other limbs. My hands are afflicted with arthritical sclerosis and I no longer can hold the needle to sew. I must hire tailors now. But I do not complain for myself. There is news far worse.

Our father is stricken, if indeed he still lives. Were I able I should fly to his side, but my health will not allow that. You and I know that he would wish to see us if, as I fear, he is nearing his end. Your letter told me little except that your convalescence is complete, for which Providence be thanked. I hope you can do what I cannot do and go home to him, discharging the duty for both of us and telling him why I cannot be there.

Not certain of your financial situation and suspecting from the meager amount of your last remittance for our parents, duly dispatched some time hence, that you may be worse off than your pride will admit, I have arranged free passage for you across the sea directly to Kirkcudbright!

The man who delivers this letter will be from the brigantine *John,* the same ship which put into Fredericksburg with the sorrowful news of our father's sickness. The *John* is now loaded with tobacco, most of it mine, and she sails for Scotland the instant she takes aboard that other valuable item of cargo, my brother Jock. Her Captain MacAdam is greatly beholden to me for the very high carriage he demanded, sailing as he will without convoy, and which I paid.

In our haste, alas, we may have omitted some few minor details with regard to clearance papers and tax manifests. It would therefore be best not to seek convoy on the way over. I hasten to protest that nothing is actually illegal — just hurriedly drawn and a bit slipshod; but the inspectors have eyes like hawks these days. The *John* is a good tight ship, owned by Currie, Beck and Company, whose sign we used to throw stones at on the quay.

This is set down to acquaint you with the ship and bid you watch over my cargo. Tobacco should be ventilated but not in wet weather: MacAdam is old and may forget this detail.

Bessie keeps well and sends fondest regards.

Yr. Aff't bro.
WILLIE

Thus Willie to Jock, mixing love with a canny care for a penny, professing British political leanings and yet probably by-passing the British tax collectors completely. Jock smiled: *that* was good Scottish sentiment anyhow. But Jock was distressed to note that Willie, doubtless through pain, had been driven to abbreviate at the end.

The sailor who brought the letter said with a burr that was straight out of Solway Firth, "We hac better be gettin' aboard, Mr. Paul." It sounded rough but it sounded good.

Jock scribbled a reply to Willie, which said little else but "I'm off!"

Chapter 23

AN EVENT of extreme unlikelihood now occurred. It was sudden and unexpected. It defied the canons of art. For months Jock had been deeply immersed in the never-never land of the theater, where things march in orderly fashion, where the unities are preserved and chance is rigidly excluded: in art everything is logical. He had come almost to accept that in life, too, things could be logical and chance play no part. Now he was abruptly jerked back and brought face to face with the fact that he was no longer acting a part on a twenty-foot stage, speaking beautiful pentameters set down long ago by a genius, but living the lone little life of one small man in the real and present world where chance continually intervenes and disrupts the march of events; and order, if it exists at all, exists only in the mind of God.

Half way across the Atlantic Captain MacAdam died. True, he was old, but not old enough to die. True, he was ill, but his illness should not have killed him. Jock had suffered from the same illness — all sailors who went into tropical waters were likely to contract malaria — and Jock had recovered. But with Captain MacAdam alarming symptoms soon made their appearance. Chills, fever and night sweats came on every four days, leaving him yellow and listless, but hopeful between their attacks. Then the attacks intensified, both in frequency and duration, laying him low every three days; then every two. A surgeon, but there was none aboard, would have recognized the ominous progress of the disease from quartan to tertian, from tertian to quotidian fever. They did what they could, dosing him massively with the Bark. It did no good. Shortly there appeared a symptom no surgeon was needed to recognize: the fatal onset of black urine. Captain MacAdam died in mid-ocean of blackwater fever, malaria's most malignant form.

They buried him hastily, the *John* halting only a moment, sails not furled but only set aback while the body slipped out from under the Union Jack and sank into the sea. Then the spars were swung round to catch the wind, and the *John* sped on again away from contagion. From the point of view of art, MacAdam's death was fortuitous and extraneous. Moody would have drawn through the entire incident a heavy line of deletion. "Pointless," he would have declared; and his critical dictum (from the artistic point of view) would have been most proper. The first mate took over, and the *John* sailed on.

Hard on the death of the captain there followed another, which would have irritated Moody even more. "This is still worse," he would have said, and sent the play back to the author with a notation: "Quite unacceptable; contrived; unsuitable for the stage, just as a fat Cassius is unsuitable." But the author's address was unknown, for the author's name was Chance.

For the second time in ten days John Paul stood bareheaded on the deck while the crew tipped up the plank and another dead body, the body of the first mate, who had also succumbed to the blackwater fever, disappeared beneath the waves. Jock, the only man left aboard who could read, read the burial service. The sails filled again and the *John* sailed on, with plenty of men who could steer if someone would only tell them whither, but no one left who could understand a barometer or use a quadrant or read a chart, far less write down the most meager facts in a ship's log.

This scanty complement of navigators on a merchantman the size of the *John* was not unusual even when officers could be hired cheaply, as now in the present shortage was no longer the case. It was not in the nature of things that the master and first officer should both die on the same voyage, let alone within the space of a fortnight. That there should be a passenger aboard equipped to step into the breach was unlikelier still, and it was this that would so forcibly have offended an impresario's conception of the believable. But so it turned out, and Moody, when he heard of it, as later he did, would be forced to shrug his shoulders and say, "Life, sir, is totally incredible; art dares take no such liberties. They'd whistle us off the boards."

It had been novel and pleasant, this role of a passenger. Jock had never played it before. All day long he could read and relax and listen to sea sounds and breathe keen salt air, taking his meals in the great cabin and enjoying the sharp high-flavored fare that he loved and landsmen abhorred, leaving to the constituted authorities the navigation of the ship. But now perforce, in the absence of others, he was obliged to assume the role of commander, for the crew turned to him as the one man to bring the *John* to port.

They were a sorry ignorant lot, dirty and lazy. The best men were all in the Royal Navy these days. Jock placed hogsheads of wine on the deck till the sun soured it into vinegar and swabbed the holds with it. He cut off their allowance of grog and set them to washing the ship's timbers with it, a highly alcoholic liquid. And he forced them to wash their filthy clothes in soda and their bodies in sea water and made them drink powerful purgative doses of castor oil. He wasn't very popular, but he saved their lives. And before the coullins of Scotland rose above the horizon, he made them paint the ship, which further sealed in the infection. The *John* arrived spruce and taut in Solway Firth, smelling sweet as a forest of pines, with everyone carping and complaining but healthy, grudgingly admitting that Captain Paul knew his business and was a most uncomfortable commander to sail under.

As the ship stood up the narrowing waters of the Solway towards the quayside of Currie, Beck and Company, Jonathan Beck, the firm's executive head, was called by a clerk to the "captain's walk" atop the building, and through his glass he descried the well-known rigging of his small but dependable *John,* under full sail racing home. The sky was lowering; the sea was choppy; the shifting cross currents of the Firth counseled caution. "It's lucky MacAdam knows the channel," Beck muttered, not without satisfaction. *John* had made a swift crossing. "But what does a man of his age expect in port that makes him crowd on sail in such weather? Strutting and capering like a painted trull in the High Street, that's what he is!"

The company functionaries laid down their pens and left their high stools and crowded the quay to watch the *John* come in. All canvas still spread, she advanced to a cable's length of the wharf, till they shouted and beckoned her off as if she would crash into the embankment. Then suddenly all the spars swung round, the wind caught the sails aback, way dropped off the ship and she stood still. At once, in perfect unison, up went all the sails together, to sharp commands in a big deep voice that had never belonged to Captain MacAdam, and were clewed up tight in a manner that only long practice and strong discipline can effect, leaving bare poles. The sudden halt was somewhat theatrical; it was good to look at, but it appeared to some that a mistake might still have been made. The *John* was stopped, but sixty feet of water still lay between her and the quay, farther than anyone could heave a line. Men on shore made ready to row out in boats to get the shore lines from her so the capstans could slowly warp her in. But Jock called, "Stay still! I'll come to you!" and an on-shore eddy, which he had noted and calculated to an extreme degree of nicety, took hold of the ship and bore her gently as a feather against her home berth. There was an element of luck, Jock had to admit, grinning to himself, in such perfect timing. But no one could deny that it was a superb maneuver, and would have called it expert seamanship even if the *John* had fallen short or overshot the mark a few feet. They tied her up and made her fast, the men on the wharf and the men on the deck of the *John* so close they could shake each other's hands.

From the men on the wharf to the men on the deck: "What's old MacAdam been drinking to hurry him so?"

Soberly the reply, "Captain MacAdam is dead. It was Captain Paul."

The name Paul was known in the little seaport of Kirkcudbright. "Not Willie Paul, him that was pressed?"

"His brother, Jock."

"That wee laddie?"

"He's nae wee laddie nae more."

In the offices of Currie, Beck and Company the anomaly was quickly explained.

Beck said, rubbing his chin reflectively, "I shall have something to say to you, Mr. Paul, when you will have visited your mother. Grateful as I am for your services, 'twould not be right to dwell on what I have in mind at this moment. Perhaps you already know what she will have to tell you." His kind manner seemed to indicate that he hoped Jock already did know, for then he would not have to tell him.

"I know only what my brother told me in America," Jock said, a tightness gripping his belly. "My father was very low. How is he now?"

Jonathan Beck looked at him compassionately. It fell to him often to announce hard tidings to families of sailors lost at sea, or to seamen whose loved ones had died ashore during the long months of separation that every voyage entailed. By many trials and through many approaches he had learned to break bad news softly, but the look on the face of the stricken hearer was always the same. "Three weeks ago," he said gently — and Jock gazed at him, recognizing the pause that comes before the critical word — "your father passed away. But I hasten to add that his end came quietly and without pain. He died at peace with God and his neighbors, in charity with all the world and enjoying the highest esteem of his employer, proud of his sons in America." He sighed. "It would serve no purpose, nay, it would border on meanness, to hide from you what

244

everyone knows in the village, and what you will learn the instant you mingle in the street."

"I had a fear that I might be too late," Jock said. "It was gracious of you not to conceal this news. I cannot take comfort in it, but I should be less than candid if I did not avow gratitude for your forthright discovery of it."

They parted, and Jonathan Beck, executive head of Currie, Beck and Company, found himself rising like one who bids farewell to a guest of equal standing. Somewhere Jock Paul, this son of a local gardener, had learned to speak like gentry; what is more, to do it naturally, without affectation, in a solemn moment when true self rises to the surface; it was part of him. And what was of even more interest to Currie, Beck and Company, he had become a ship's commander of extraordinary skill. Granted that Jock had a motive far stronger than Captain MacAdam's for getting ashore quickly, his wharfing of the *John* was still a superlative maneuver. In the scarcity of competent officers Jonathan Beck made a mental note that if Captain John Paul — the title already sounded right — did not shortly return to his office, he, Jonathan Beck, would seek Captain Paul.

This mental note required no action; Beck did not have to seek his captain; interest and opportunity coincided and strengthened each other: within the month his captain sought him, as surely as the needle seeks the pole. In the best of times Jock's interest would have led him towards the sea, the profession nature had fitted him for and in which he now excelled; and these were not the best of times ashore. Great Britain, still paying for the last war, was blundering into another. Taxes were high, prices were high, people were poor. William Craik, the laird of Arbigland, continued a sort of paternal affection for the widow and son of his dead gardener and went so far as to ask Jock, "Will you stay on in your father's place?" Jock learned that he would receive no wages if he did, merely the use, rent-free, of the house in which he had been born. To a man who had owned, and perhaps still owned, a factory worth thousands on Lagos Lagoon the arrangement was not attractive. "I think not, sir," he said.

To the laird's undisguised satisfaction Jock rented the cottage for a year, exacting a promise that he might have it in perpetuity as long as the rent was paid, and made over the rental deed to his mother. "I can pay another year if you wish, Mother," he offered. The rent was very low; Craik had never expected so much as a farthing for this little corner of his estate. "'Twould be a sinful waste," she said, still in her mourning dress, the nearness of death still real and unnerving. "Who knows how quickly I may follow." On a sudden impulse, knowing it would cheer her, not quite trusting Willie, having the money, not knowing when he would have it again or indeed where he would be a year thence, he paid over to the delighted laird another year's rent, and tumbled into his mother's lap all the gold guineas he had to spare, with a personal guarantee that she would live to be a hundred and that, till she should reach that age, he would provide for her. He lifted her mood and her natural good humor reasserted itself.

She posed him astonishing questions which betrayed how seldom Willie had corresponded with her.

"What does Willie do these days?"

It was hard to answer. Patently, Willie had concealed his prosperity.

"He tailors, and does a little farming."

The widow Paul sighed. "I hope he isn't too poor. His letters are full of money worries."

"He manages to keep body and soul together," Jock said, and did not sneer, as Moody might, "A biggish body, a smallish soul."

"He keeps well?"

Here Jock could be truthful. "He seems to suffer a chronic complaint in his joints, especially in his hands. It has greatly lessened his activity."

"Poor laddie."

"Aye."

She would, of course, have liked Jock to remain; but she fancied Craik's offer no more than he did, and when he said, "Mother, I think I shall go to sea again," she answered, like any Solway mother or wife to her menfolk, "Aye." But, unlike them, she had a roof over her head for two years, gold guineas in a tea jar on the shelf and a man who she knew in her heart would take care of her.

Jock had left home a boy and returned a man; and as he had grown in stature and experience, just so much had everything at home seemed to shrink: the Scottish hills were not so high as the distant mountains that had formed the horizon westward of Willie's plantation; the cottage in which he had been born was not so big as his residence at Lagos; the Bight of Benin was broader than Solway Firth. He cherished his Scottish homeland, but his vision was enlarged, the hills hemmed him in, and his feet itched to feel beneath them a deck that rose and fell to majestic ocean swells on the mighty highway that girdles the planet, not jiggling and jouncing in a landlocked firth. No sailor lives but can detect in his sleep, in the darkest cabin, without once thrusting his head through a port, whether his ship is in shore-smothered seas or riding the vast free main.

The widow Paul had had no funds, and Willie had neglected to provide any, to place a headstone over the recent grave. "Of course," Jock said wryly to himself, "Willie could not know for certain that Father would die before I reached home." But Willie had unquestionably kept their mother on short rations.

Jock arranged with a local mason to chisel out a headstone. It was not finished when he went to sea again. When he first set eyes on it, it had lain in the grass for more than a year, watered by his mother's tears. It contained an odd misspelling. Jock let it lie. Not many of the good people of Arbigland would know the difference. As for other people, no inquisitive biographers, no antiquarians of a future age were likely to prowl among weathering gravestones in an obscure Scottish churchyard to seize on an orthographical lapse on the granite that marked the grave of an obscure Scottish gardener, placed there by his equally obscure son. So the tombstone read:

IN MEMORY
OF
JOHN PAUL SENIOR
WHO DIED AT ARBIGLAND
UNIVERSALLY ESTEEMED

———

ERECTED BY JOHN PAUL JUNEOR

And now indeed his purse was flat as a flounder, and he presented himself at the offices of Currie, Beck and Company. He was immediately offered, and he immediately accepted, command of the *John*.

Chapter 24

THE PARTING WORDS of Jonathan Beck to his new captain were significant. "If you bring back tobacco next time, for God's sake provide me with tax receipts, or else arrange to have all the ship's papers lost overboard in a gale. One or the other, proper order or nothing." He had been most embarrassed by Willie's papers, not because they evaded British taxes but because they bore on their face positive proof of the evasion. The printed forms indeed were the correct ones, the cargo was accurately weighed to a pound: but on every sheet where the British tax should have been entered and signed for by a British agent, a big blank space appeared. "Under the circumstances I was forced to burn the papers," said Jonathan Beck, "and dispose of this illicit cargo in a quiet manner." Jock rightly guessed that Beck had seized on the occasion to evade the import taxes on the Scottish side as well. Officially the cargo of the *John* had never been purchased, had never been sold, had never, in fact, existed.

"Under the circumstances," Jock said, "I think it would be best to remit to my brother in gold, don't you?"

Beck hemmed and hawed but finally agreed. A bank draft in payment for a nonexistent cargo would remain a permanent record of something very like smuggling if Jock cared to call an inspector's attention to it. "You take a very high hand with me, sir," he said, and paid.

To the gold guineas of his own in his mother's tea jar Jock added a handful of Willie's gold sovereigns, stating that Willie had long meant to send her this little present but, being cautious with money as she must know by experience, had been willing to trust it only to him to deliver. Jock cautioned her to change them into silver a few at a time through Mr. Craik, lest too much gold in the village cause comment. Thus Willie contributed his share after all to his widowed mother's support. Nor was Willie robbed; the cargo had brought a good price. Beck indeed had been forced to accept a smuggler's rate, but he had dealt tax-free in a costly commodity, the price of which was rising every year.

"Next time, I promise your papers will be in order," Jock said to him, "or the log of the *John* will report the biggest gale in the annals of seafaring."

Beck guessed it would probably be the gale, and grinned. No captain had ever demanded such a store of gunpowder or so thoroughly worked up to efficient performance the armament of the little *John*. In the growing difficulty of obtaining convoy such precautions were laudable. The two Scotsmen understood each other and trusted each other not to cheat themselves as long as there were Englishmen to cheat.

Procuring a crew was not so easy. There were the usual number of ne'er-do-wells who quit after every voyage, forever seeking and never finding a better ship; for when discipline was as lax as they liked, conditions were frightful. When discipline was as strict as Jock's, they deserted clean healthy ships to die like rats of disease in stinking filthy holds. A sturdy body of good tough men stayed with the *John,* content to grumble and make the best of a very good thing; but the ranks of the ne'er-do-wells had to be filled, and, in the present state of affairs, could be filled only by other ne'er-do-wells. One of these was Mungo Maxwell, who had kept the tavern at the time when Willie was pressed and Jock had kicked the lantern. He was balding now, but still in his early fifties, big and strong. He had supported himself in recent years by rough carpentry, occasionally going to sea. Specialists, like officers, were scarce. Jock took him aboard in the carpenter's berth, and Maxwell, enjoying the best life he had had since his tavern failed, immediately began to put on airs, taking advantage of the acquaintance he had had with Jock's father and vaunting about the intimate friendship he pretended to have had with Mr. Craik, stealing pickles from the officers' mess and boring holes with a gimlet in grog butts. This bit of carpentry, at least, he did well, and the holes could not be found. He was unpopular with his shipmates because he never shared the spoils of his thievery with them, and the only evidence of it was a foul breath and a rolling gait in a dead calm. Soon nobody talked to him.

Mungo Maxwell's surliness and incompetence, his slovenly appearance and dirty habits continually irritated Jock, who would have punished summarily anyone else. But Mungo was a townsman, he had known Jock's dead father, carpenters were essential to a ship, and a poor one was better than none at all. He forbade him access to the liquor stores and hoped that the working of time, the lengthening voyage and the contempt of his shipmates would cure the carpenter's faults, as sometimes happened when a member of a crew was incorrigible. Sometimes, however, the bad example infected others. If Jock had been possessed of the "second sight," that gift of foreseeing the future that many Scots were reputed to enjoy, he would have flogged Maxwell soundly at the beginning of the voyage instead of at its end and thereby saved himself a chain of troubles that were to haunt him to the end of his life. Lamentably Jock was not so gifted; he put up with him throughout an entire Atlantic crossing.

In Kirkcudbright the *John* took aboard a part of her cargo: Scottish woolens and whisky destined for aristocratic American planters. A few days later she sailed up the estuary of the River Mersey in England and anchored at Bridgewater Quay to take on more cargo. This anchorage with a nautical name, seemingly so appropriate, had nothing to do with a bridge and little to do with water, for there, in fact, deep water ended. Bridgewater Quay was named for the third Duke of Bridgewater, who, desiring cheap coals for his lordshiply fireplaces to warm his lordshiply toes of a winter's night, had caused to be dug a small barge canal from the headwaters of the estuary through easily excavated ground to the city of Manchester, on which his estates bordered. The canal, once dug, proved a ducal bonanza. About this time the cotton trade received an enormous upsurge of activity. Cotton, spun a thread at a time for a thousand years by hand, was now spun by an ingenious new machine that produced twenty-four threads simultaneously, and was powered by a mule that walked round and round in a circle, turning a power wheel. There was even talk of harnessing these "spinning jennies," as they were called, to water wheels in Manchester's river. But there was more. Not only the spinning of thread but also the weaving of thread was becoming mechanized. The shuttle, long wont to be passed laboriously by hand through the woof of the loom, was now hurled by a mechanical lever faster than the eye could follow from side to side, and was aptly called "the flying shuttle." All over Manchester the spinning jennies hummed and the flying shuttles clicked, and the characteristic sounds were heard of a great new industry destined to characterize it forever afterwards. Old handcraftsmen had murmured against these innovations; but a generation of "websters" was passing away, following the long-lost generations of "fletchers," whose very occupation was forgotten. Who in the eighteenth century remembered when a fletcher once placed the feathers on the arrows of the dreaded English longbowmen? English warriors now won their empire with gunpowder. Manchester's textile activity changed even the English language, and so common a word as "factory," the place where goods were sold, now came to be understood as the place where goods were made.

But for every webster who had been put out of work a dozen new workers had been hired. Anyone could run the new machines. Little girls of six could augment the family income two shillings a week by standing all day long at the mechanical monsters, arriving at the factories while it was still dark in the morning and never leaving until it was dark at night. In Manchester no one need be unemployed or go hungry, though some softhearted mothers worried because their children never saw the sun, had little time to play, grew slowly, ate poorly and were pale while enjoying the immense boon of universal employment.

The price of cotton goods was now so low that even American Negroes could be clothed in it. Tons of the new fabrics poured out of prosperous Manchester. Through the Duke of Bridgewater's canal the laden barges passed at a nominal fee, enriching the duke, to Bridgewater Quay and, after this minimum of handling, the stuffs could be hoisted directly aboard the ships, to be sold at astonishing profits in the colonies. English mercantilists could now point with pride to the fact that the labor of a little Manchester girl could profitably compete with the labor of a full-grown Bengalee in his own country fifteen thousand miles away; and if there were seeds of disaster in this nobody detected them, for the Industrial Revolution and the monstrously swollen British Empire were as inextricably interwoven as the threads in the wonderful new textiles; and wise indeed would have been that man who, seeing a bright sun upon the horizon in his lifetime of only a moment, could have answered whether his eyes beheld a dawn or a twilight.

The quarter-deck of the *John* was small, but it afforded ample area for reflection: it was in a special way his precious personal prize. "I could be bounded in a nutshell," so went the lines of Hamlet, fretting over his troubles, "and count myself a king of infinite space" — except that poor Hamlet had suffered bad dreams. Jock's bad dreams were behind him. He had successfully hidden a double shame: the shame of the slave trade, which he had outgrown and lived down; the even greater shame of acting on a stage. From each encounter with fate he had learned, and grown, and been molded. He was not the only young man in the world, nor would he be the last, who had learned deep truths and risen to a high standard of conduct through certain experiences to which he would later never make reference. He recalled another fine Shakespearean line, "scorning the base degrees by which he did ascend." Jock had ascended to a quarter-deck by virtue of merit distilled from events he now wished to forget. Jock was unlearned in philosophy; theologically he was a child; but as he proudly paced the quarter-deck of the *John,* that personal reward of rank on which a common sailor dared never venture a step, casting an appreciative eye on the pyramiding taut white canvas that swept upward towards the stars, his practical mind joined many profounder thinking minds that had busied themselves through the ages with philosophical riddles and come to the conclusion: "From evil good can sometimes spring." The hidden things, the reprehensible things, the things he was ashamed of, had matured his judgment, clarified his values and fitted him for command.

Having reached the quarter-deck by so difficult a route, he was fiercely determined to be worthy of the honor. This was the first command he had held that was thoroughly respectable, authorized by officials ashore who trusted him to keep their records above reproach if scrutinized by the Crown inspectors, and who depended on his skill and ability in half a dozen fields.

More was required of a captain of a merchant vessel than merely to bring a ship swiftly, safely, in good repair and in reasonable health, from port to port. His employers were always far away, in space and time, sometimes a year, sometimes two years, sometimes halfway round the world. Jonathan Beck had no means of informing him, "Captain Paul, a cargo of sugar lies in Saint George; pick it up and take it to Boston, and take on tar and rosin for immediate sale in Rockley Bay." Nor could he inform him, "Algerian pirates have grown active following the death of the Sultan of Turkey, whose power in North Africa has lapsed; take special care in the Mediterranean." All this help was denied the merchant captains, who sailed alone, seldom speaking a ship, never reading a newspaper, cut off from the sources of information that guided men ashore. They were on their own. The wonder was that they did as well as they did; and they did many things: they battled the sea; they nursed their crews; they sniffed out cargo from port to port, bought it wherever it was to be found and disposed of it wherever it could be sold; they were expected to make a profit on every transaction, to keep accurate accounts, and bring home a cargo that could be sold at a profit in the home port. Much was allowed them, but even more was demanded of them. Since they acted on their own, subject only to vague and general orders, absolute kings in their little floating, isolated domains, it was natural that they should feel some resentment when, at the end of a long and perilous voyage, the ship's owner took all the profit. Hence it was every captain's ambition to own his own ship. Few of them ever did. Jock's earliest ambition had been to rise in the world and make a name for himself. In him ambition burned with especial brightness and heat. But calculate as he might, he did not see how he could put his hands on the five, or seven, or twelve thousand pounds that a ship would cost.

Surely the first step to rise in the esteem of his employers was to sail fast, buy cheap, sell dear, keep a taut ship, an open ear, a searching eye, and suffer not an hour to be lost or a farthing wasted through laxness on the part of any of his crew. No one who takes his responsibilities seriously can have much sympathy for persons who refuse responsibility altogether; there were many such in his crew. Jock Paul was a driver, a cold commander, quick to take offense at slackness, long to remember a fault and only grudgingly admitted to be fair; and Mungo Maxwell refused him even that. Yet many ships' captains were worse. Some seemed to take positive pleasure in frequent and bloody floggings. Jock seldom flogged, and never to blood: it put a man out of action for days. But if a mile could be gained by taking advantage of a gale, he would send all hands aloft for days at a stretch, continually making and taking in sail, when less of a driver would have settled down to reduced canvas and comfortably jogged on through the storm with everyone enjoying a normal quota of sleep, including himself. The long hours Jock spent on the quarter-deck caused whispers that Captain Paul never slept at all. This gossip was not, indeed could not be, true. But it was true that the captain had preternaturally sharp eyes. On the darkest night, let a man but stand too long without moving, or sit on the deck, or spit over the side, and a big voice from the quarter-deck, trained to carry to the topmost gallery, would call him by name and recall him sharply to his duty.

But he brought the *John* to Fredericksburg across the Atlantic quicker than MacAdam ever had done.

Willie had expected a letter; he had not expected his brother in person, far less that his brother would turn up captain of the ship that had carried his cargo of tobacco to Kirkcudbright; he greeted him affectionately and congratulated him on his appointment. Bessie gave him a good warm sisterly hug: "We had almost begun to fear we would never see you again. How is dear Father Paul?"

"Did my cargo sell high?" Willie asked.

"I'll show you," Jock said.

But first he told them the sad news. Bessie, who had never seen her father-in-law, dabbed dutifully at her eyes and went inside to supervise a dinner to celebrate Jock's homecoming. Willie sighed, "It was not unexpected. We all must go in time." His appearance was shocking to Jock; he had lost a great deal of weight, and he moved slowly as if movement caused him pain. Presently Jock saw his hands.

"Your cargo sold," Jock said, opening the lid of his mahogany sea chest, "like this."

"God bless my soul!" cried Willie Paul. The candles shone down on a spread-out layer of good round heavy gold sovereigns. "A thousand at least!"

Jock laughed. "You've an excellent eye. Eleven hundred and seventy-three, and three shillings sixpence in there somewhere, probably under the kilt. Mother made me another, and she could not understand that you mustn't wear a kilt aboard a ship that flies the British flag."

Willie had bent and begun to count the coins with fingers stiff as claws, cruelly swollen in all the joints. "I'll count it later," he sighed, hiding his hands. "No, of course I'll not count it. I'm satisfied."

"There was a little more," Jock said, "but I gave Mother some, along with some of my own to pay her rent. She's without support now, except for us."

253

"Good, good," Willie said. He probably would not have done it himself, but now that Jock had done it for him he was glad. "Did Mother move away?"

"I arranged it with Mr. Craik to let her stay on at home. He rented her the cottage very cheap. We paid two years."

"She'll be happier there," Willie said, nodding. His disease seemed greatly to have lessened his interest in everything, even in money. Food too had lost its old appeal, and Bessie eyed him sadly at dinner, where he ate very sparingly. The only thing that could strike a spark of emotion from him was the political situation, especially the recent doings up at Boston.

"Damned rebellious colonials threw stones at the soldiers!" Willie complained.

Jock asked, "What soldiers?"

"King George's soldiers, sir, sent to keep order up there. Damned colonials wouldn't even quarter them!"

"I don't think I'd like British soldiers quartered in my home," Jock said. "Would you?"

Bessie shot him a warning glance. Politics was a touchy subject.

"I am a loyal Englishman," Willie said heatedly. "I hope I shall always know how to do my duty."

"Be calm, my dear," Bessie said, but Willie went on.

"Damned mob threw stones, called them 'lobster-backs,' wounded them, knocked them down in the streets."

Jock frowned. He would have liked to hear the other side, but he could say with conviction, "People in authority certainly ought not to be stoned."

"In self-defense," Willie said, "the soldiers finally opened fire. They shot the rabble down. I say, 'Hurrah for the soldiers. Hurrah for the Boston Massacre!'"

Bessie said evenly, "It wasn't a massacre, Jock, though the people in Boston call it that. But there was a riot, I'm afraid, and five of the mob were killed. Then things quieted down, and later the soldiers stood trial for the shooting. A Boston jury found them guilty of manslaughter."

"That's hanging," Jock said.

"For doing their duty?" Willie smiled grimly. "Not with a good loyal defense lawyer! They were permitted to plead benefit of clergy. Jock lad, if you ever kill a man, remember that you can read. Punishment was reduced. They were only branded on the left thumb. Even that was all too severe, I think."

"It appeased the Bostonians," Bessie said. "It's been quiet up there ever since."

"It's been quiet here too," Willie said, glancing apprehensively over his shoulder, "but only on the surface. Under the surface the same traitorous disloyalty runs deep and sour. A good loyal man cannot feel at ease." He disclosed a remarkable fact. "In the past, Jock, like many another born Scotsman, I've considered the British tax collectors fair game and evaded them if I could. But now, in England's need, with every rascal plundering her, I'd be ashamed to. I should willingly have paid my tax on my cargo to Kirkcudbright, but if I had there wouldn't be a windowpane left in Bessiwill! It's got so it's respectable to smuggle. It's dangerous to pay. They'll break your windows. The planters have banded together to withhold tobacco from England. Spain can get it. France can get it. But not the mother country. They'll let it rot in the sheds rather than sell it to England. The confounded colonials want to be represented in Parliament."

It seemed to Jock that representation in Parliament might be a very sound notion in view of the fact that there were three million Americans, but heeding Bessie's warning eye he tried not to upset his brother. "I hope your planters haven't lost their taste for Scotch whisky," he said. "I've a lot of it to sell."

"Whisky isn't political," Willie said, and smiled.

In addition to the whisky, Jock disposed of his Scottish woolens, which bore no English taint; but when he cast about for a cargo of tobacco none was to be had. He was met with surly shrugs or evasive answers or told that the crop had failed. He went to his old ship chandlery, where some of the men remembered him. They frankly told him that the tobacco warehouses were bulging. A cargo of tobacco would be not at all hard to procure. Some dark night soon the customs sloop-of-war now watching in the harbor would go romping off after a smuggler; the instant she was out of sight Jock could load the *John* to the gunwales and slip out tax free, like everybody else. Just better not sell it in England. There would be reprisals on Willie. Jock was too recently respectable to risk having his first command confiscated as a smuggler; nor did he want Willie to risk more trouble than he already had.

Nor could he get a decent price for his English cottons, and rather than sell them cheap he resolved to sail on to some market less sensitive to the strong political winds that were blowing. He knew such a market; he had been there. The West Indies, he judged, were sensitive to nothing. What besides cotton could one sell in the West Indies? Pots and pans and ladies' bonnets, to be sure; but everything he could think of was bulky and common or outside his trading experience. Jock was no judge of ladies' bonnets. He continued to search, however. It went against his grain to waste a single cubic yard of space that might be put to profit.

In a warehouse on the water front his eye fell on a stout shelf piled high with broad steel knives, each about a yard long and fitted with a handle like a sword. They looked very much like sailors' cutlasses, but broader and heavier. The warehouse attendant said with a wink, "They're making some pretty fine cutlery up in New England. Cheap, too." Ironmongery of this sort was just barely legal. The cheapness of the articles meant only one thing: New England had greatly increased her iron production and had edged as close to the manufacture of weapons as she dared; a little push would send her over the line. There is nothing like the sight of a sharp gleaming knife to portray the anger of a people. The Romans had won battles with swords of poorer temper than this bright American steel. It took little effort to imagine the superb American long rifles being also produced in rising quantities — for hunting purposes, of course. Meanwhile these excellent "machetes," as they were called, were eminently peaceful agricultural tools; they could be sold in the West Indies to cut sugar cane. Jock bought a quantity.

Jock would willingly have sailed the instant his ship was full, but Bessie took him aside and pleaded, "It would cheer Willie up if we gave him a ball," and Jock agreed to stay on for a day or two, though his mind was full of the pounds and shillings and pence that the *John,* lying idle, wasted at anchor. Willie, observing their whispers and Bessie's busyness at her desk penning cards that could only be invitations, fell in with the little subterfuge and pretended great astonishment when every candle was lighted one night in the drawing room and a band of musicians arrived and unpacked their violins.

"Upon my soul, pet, what a delightful surprise!" Meanwhile he had quietly arranged for a *perruquier* to curl and powder his formal wig and, as Bessie saw with a sigh, to have new lace cuffs, much longer ones, sewed onto his formal shirt. They hid his hands.

But the tailor who no longer could sew had not lost his eye for fine dress; Willie made a good appearance. Bessie and Jock could be proud of him. With a face as straight as if he experienced no pain he went through several dances, with his wife, with a painted wealthy old widow, and with the prettiest girl of the evening, before he retired to a seat by the fire with gentlemen twice his age to talk politics and commiserate with them, as they did with him, over the miseries and vagaries of the gout, sipping Scotch whisky without water. This was the company he liked: good solid men who brooked no rebellious nonsense in colonials. They were colonials themselves, but in the present troubled times they identified themselves wholly with England, which many of them had never seen. Americans were dividing; new words were heard to distinguish the contending parties and were universally understood, "loyalist" on the one hand, "rebel" on the other, and a more ominous word was whispered, "revolutionary."

Jock avoided the political conversations, though the more he heard of the rebels the more he sided with them, and the more he heard of the loyalists the more shortsighted he thought them. Part of this feeling was rooted in Scotland, which had struggled for centuries to be free; part was rooted in Africa: he had left the most profitable trade in the world, he who yearned to be rich, because he had come to believe that even a black savage deserved some measure of freedom. Americans were not savage. On a less emotional level he knew from experience as a sea trader, subject to countless exasperating restrictions, that England's navigation laws were galling or stupid or both.

But he was a guest in a loyalist house; he was a British merchant sea captain; he did not wish to irritate his ailing brother, and he held his peace. It was ever so much more pleasant to dance with Dorothea Dandridge, the prettiest girl at the ball. She seemed glad to smile at him. At least he didn't talk politics, or smell of snuff, or weigh twelve stone like most of the loyalist worthies who stepped on her little feet.

At one point her mother reproved her behind her fan, "Dotty, my dear, you are paying entirely too much attention to this Captain Paul."

"He dances like an angel," Dorothea whispered excitedly.

"Angels do not dance," her mother said sternly, "and if they do, Captain Paul didn't learn steps like that from them. He dances like — like — well," she sniffed, "like a naughty Frenchman. I do not like that."

"I do," Dorothea said gaily, and Jock whirled her away again.

"Then I've taught her badly," the ambitious matron muttered to herself, and grimly resolved to repair the damage. In Fredericksburg John Paul was something of a mystery, much gossiped about, but about whom very little was known any more. He did not talk about himself, he put off inquisitive queries with an ingenuous smile and some apt remark that soon led the busybody astray till the query was forgotten — he left one wondering why indeed he spoke without a burr. His brother's speech was Scotch as the liquor in his glass. Jock would have writhed with shame if anyone had suspected that behind his good manners, behind his faultless accent, lay an intensive career of Shakespearean acting. He might indeed have denied it, so natural had accent and manners become. But just as natural was 'his resolve to drive the *John* south and get rid of the confounded English cottons aboard her and pick up a cargo, and drive the ship back across the Atlantic to Scotland with all possible speed.

The guests departed; Dorothea Dandridge bade him a melting good night; the mother looked down her nose; the musicians packed up their violins.

"I've got to be off now, Willie," Jock said.

Bessie said, "Tonight? But it's dark."

"It's a clear night; I've got to go; there are plenty of stars."

"But I thought we could have such a pleasant chat at breakfast."

"The tide changes at two, and we're set to sail."

"I've invited the Dandridges over for tea tomorrow, Jock," she said dimpling.

Jock smiled.

"If that won't tempt him, nothing will," Willie grunted. The whisky had eased the pain in his limbs and he was feeling fine.

"She is perfectly charming," Jock said, but he made no move to stay.

"I'll order the coach," Willie sighed, and sent a man to fetch it round. "Perhaps it's all for the best. I'll be flat in bed tomorrow, foul-tempered and creaking in all my joints. But we had a jolly ball your last night ashore, didn't we, Jock lad! I'll remember it."

With Bessie smiling beside him under the high white portico of the house, Willie waved his brother farewell, his wig a little askew on his head, his long wrist-ruffles fluttering in the lantern light, and on his face, no longer plump and round, a hint of that something which had burned so white in the face of John de Gaunt in his last days. So Jock remembered him.

Some of the crew were drunk after a last-chance round of the taverns. They had dirtied the deck. Jock set them to scrubbing it, down on their knees, pushing fifteen-pound holystones over the planks through a cleansing abrasive of soda and sand. The rough stones had no handles and had to be grasped with bare fingers. The soda bit. Periodically buckets of salt water dowsed the grinding mixture. It was March, the wind was raw and the sea water was cold. They cursed him heartily under their breath and bent their backs to the task. But they sobered up speedily. Mungo Maxwell, unconscious with drink, had sprawled himself into his bunk. Jock fined him a week's pay, since there was nothing reasonable that could be

258

done to punish him that night. The helmsman was tipsy. Jock pushed him roughly aside and set him to heaving the heavy lead. "If you fall overboard, I shall not stop to pick you up, depend upon it!" he shouted.

In white stockings, knee breeches and dancing pumps he took the wheel himself and did not relinquish it till noon next day. The estuary lay behind, the sea spread deep and green ahead, the red-eyed carousers were sober. The deck shone like snow, and all was safe. He turned the *John* south on a course for Tobago.

Chapter 25

RICH AND populous islands, excellent markets, lay along the route — Cuba, Hispaniola and Puerto Rico — teeming with fruitful plantations. The temptation was strong to stop and unload his cargo all in one day at any one of them. Unfortunately these great island possessions were not British and suffered under restrictive commercial laws as foolish as Britain's own: Cuba and Puerto Rico could legally trade only with Spain; Hispaniola only with France. Anything else was smuggling.

But Jock knew that these islands would welcome a smuggled cargo of good English cottons and keen American machetes. He had only to run up the Spanish or French flag, to distribute a few nominal bribes: official eyes would blink, official hands would be extended; smiling port officers would forge an excellent set of bills of sale to nonexistent British planters on any British isle Jock cared to point out on the map. Everyone would profit. The thing was done every day.

But sometimes such forged papers got one's employers into trouble at home; sometimes a spy in one's crew denounced the transaction to the authorities; sometimes a British man-of-war just happened to put into port and catch the culprit red-handed; sometimes the opposite occurred: a Spanish or French customs vessel might suddenly appear on an inquisitorial mission of inspection.

And sometimes a man rigidly obeyed the law simply because it was the law, no matter how oppressive. No captain ever had stronger motives for doing what was right than Captain John Paul with his first command on his first voyage. He would not sail under false colors.

Therefore he did not stop at these tempting smugglers' ports but struck far to the south, contenting himself with the British Lesser Antilles that stretched like beautiful green stepping stones in an arc on the eastern edge of the Caribbean Sea. The southernmost of these markets was Tobago, hard by the big and forbidden Spanish island of Trinidad. He planned to work his way north through the little British islands and then, if he had any cargo left, to dump it all at cut prices in Britain's one big Caribbean possession, the island of Jamaica. Such a voyage would require more time and a great deal more labor, but it would be absolutely legal. Nor need it, with care, be unprofitable: smaller communities must always pay a premium for their supplies, while larger markets like Jamaica, where ships put in often and competition was keen, bought cheap. On the whole, his plan was well conceived.

In Rockley Bay, the port of Tobago, lovely and lost on the outskirts of empire, the governor himself was a small-townsman. In a wig three years out of date he came to the quayside in person to meet the incoming *John*, like a provincial mayor whiling away the tedium of uneventful country life by riding down to the market place to watch the stage go through.

Traffic was light in Rockley Bay; the narrow waters were more than ample to shelter the scanty shipping. A small packet lay at anchor. A customs sloop with a rusty swivel gun (mounted aft, as if she never chased but always turned tail) rose and fell on the sleepy swell, exposing a well-barnacled bottom.

One unexpected ship caused Jock to start and stare: surely in all the world there was only one vessel so slim, so sleek, so black as Don Jesu's unnamed, ex-piratical full-rigger. But now she bore a name in big gold letters painted on her bow: *Virgen de la Paz*. That didn't sound like Don Jesu. Jock concluded he might have sold his ship, having no need of her in his prosperous slaving factory on Lagos Lagoon. Whoever might own her now, Jock had not time to row over and pay her a social call and ask after his old friend. He brought the *John* alongside the quay and went ashore.

A local dignitary presented him to the big-wigged governor, Sir William Young, and identified himself as James Simpson, judge advocate of His Majesty's vice-admiralty court, in and for the Province of Tobago Plantations. They bade him welcome, they wished him well, they expressed interest in the character of his cargo. They were hungry for news, and little as Jock had, it was news to them; they deprecated the attitude of the colonists on the seaboard of North America; they invited him to dinner. Jock thanked them, swept them a respectful bow, tickling their last-reign ideal of fine manners, and accepted.

Then he set himself to the business of striking deals with the island merchants who swarmed around his ship. Having inspected the quality of his cargo and seeing him in favor with their governor and their judge, the buyers were not disposed to haggle. If the other West Indian markets proved as active as Tobago, Jock guessed that not a yard of goods, not a single machete would be left to dump at cut prices in Jamaica. He could look forward to a swift and prosperous voyage and the commendation of his employers. Always ahead of the present, he saw himself walking the larger quarter-deck of a bigger ship than the *John*, a ship all his own. Then the mathematics of the situation stood out in their naked impossibility, and the daydream faded. But he had made an excellent beginning.

"Indigo!" Sir William exclaimed amiably after supper. "Indigo will make your fortune, Captain Paul. We swim in it here." The governor was in a mellow mood. He held in his hand a pear-shaped palm-filling goblet of crystal, at whose bottom sparkled a shallow pool of honey-colored Scottish liqueur. Jock had made him a present of it; it was Bonnie Prince Charlie's personal drink, the consolation of his exile; it was rumored to keep the prince, who still lived, still wandered, still pretended to the British throne, in a perpetual state of addled benignity; it was suave on the tongue and slow fire in the brain. Its Gaelic name was *drambuie*, which meant "the drink that leaves nothing to be desired." The governor was answering a question of Jock's which dealt with cargo procurable in Tobago and likely to sell at a profit in Scotland.

Indigo, a beautiful fast blue dye, grew wild in the highlands around Rockley Bay. The natives gathered the plants and threw them into tubs of water, where the hot sun fermented them. Nature did the rest. The dye settled down to the bottom; the natives scooped it up and dried it and pressed it into barrels for shipment. "The blue in half your Scottish tartans is pure West Indian indigo," Sir William said with satisfaction.

"Indigo is very dear in Europe," Jock said.

But it was very cheap in Rockley Bay, and the *John* took on a lighter-load of it. Jock sent the carpenter to inspect the condition of the barrels. If there should be the slightest crack, the damp would get in and the dye would ooze out, a brilliant costly mess. Maxwell pronounced the barrels tight as a virgin's — he used an expressive obscenity — and Jock, seeing him drunk, examined the barrels himself, white-faced with fury at the fellow's presumptuous language to his commander. But Jock had borne much from Mungo Maxwell and could bear a little more.

Next day the *John* took on much bigger barrels full of sugar, the heavy West Indian staple of trade. These barrels also had to be inspected to make sure they were watertight; sugar into which salt spray had leaked was hard to sell. During the morning Maxwell discharged his duty satisfactorily. But late in the afternoon when the laborers were tired, when accidents had to be especially guarded against because fatigue made them likely to occur, the carpenter began to take secret furtive nips at a bottle he had hidden in his shirt. He staggered against a Negro dockman who was easing a barrel of sugar from the top of the pile into position for the sling, which would hoist it aboard. This was an everyday feat of cargo handling, requiring strength and skill but ordinarily perfectly safe. The carpenter's drunken lunge, however, upset the dockman's delicate balance. The barrel toppled off the pile. It carried the dockman with it, pinioned him underneath and killed him.

Although he was drunk and scarcely felt the whip, Mungo Maxwell was instantly trussed up to the ratlines and flogged at Jock's orders. For once Jock was tempted to flog to blood; he knew he was well within his rights; the law set no limit to either the number or severity of the lashes; the law merely stated a sailor was not to be ill used. But Jock had made it a rule not to incapacitate his men, and he stopped the punishment short of a dozen blows, which many of the crew, drawn up at attention to witness, would have been glad to see more severely applied. "Bloody bastard didn't even bleed!" one of the crew complained. Record of the punishment was duly set down in the *John*'s log with the number of lashes, eleven, and the reasons therefor: first, for drinking whilst on watch; and second, for negligence of duty which resulted in loss to ship's cargo, viz., one barrel of sugar which could not be salvaged by reason of its being soaked with blood.

The sugar barrel had split open when it crushed the man to death, and the sugar had spilled out.

To the owner of the slave Jock made restitution at the dead man's full value and charged it to the same account as the barrel of sugar; both constituted accidental damage to property.

The corpse of the laborer was buried; his owner was satisfied; the sugar his blood had reddened was swept into the sea, and a crowd of chattering little pickaninnies swooped down on what remained and scooped it up by double handfuls and wrapped it in banana leaves and carted the little bonanza bundles off to their delighted mothers. The incident seemed at an end, with no one the worse but the dead man. Jock prepared the *John* for departure.

But Mungo Maxwell awoke in his bunk with a splitting headache, caused by the drink, and a sorely smarting back. He groaned that he was slain, and when his shipmates scoffed at him, he stamped ashore in a rage. He elbowed his way into the chambers of the judge advocate of His Majesty's vice-admiralty court, tore off his shirt, exhibited his back and swore he was ill used. Judge Simpson obligingly examined the rapidly disappearing welts and summoned Captain Paul. Jock told what had happened.

The judge scowled and ordered Maxwell to get out. In his opinion the punishment was slight and amply deserved by the provocation.

Then Mungo Maxwell deserted the ship. His bunk was found empty; he, his sea bag and all his belongings, except some lice and some empty bottles, had disappeared. Jock was glad to be rid of the troublemaker, but the thought struck him that Maxwell might get into mischief ashore and he made inquiries. The judge would be likely to know if Maxwell had caused further trouble.

"You can easily get him back if you want him," Judge Simpson said laughing. "He's gone aboard the packet in the bay. I know her captain well. He gave him a carpenter's berth. Shall I speak to Captain Eastament?"

"I can't say I want him back," Jock said. "I'm relieved that he's shipping out and won't cause trouble here. But I shall certainly need a new carpenter."

"If carpenters could be had for the asking in Rockley Bay," Judge Simpson said with a shrug, "Captain Eastament would never have hired him. Perhaps you can buy one from one of our planters. Many of our Negroes are excellent craftsmen."

But Jock knew they did not like the sea, and white sailors objected to working alongside of them, fearing to be classed as slaves. Besides, the cost would be very high. "Thank you, no," he said. "I'll pick up a carpenter in Grenada or Barbados or Antigua."

"More likely Jamaica," the judge said.

"I'll have to risk it."

The entire Mungo Maxwell incident cast a gloom on Jock's spirit. He especially disliked having to sail without so important a crew member as a carpenter.

"It's a pity you didn't arrive a bit sooner," Judge Simpson said. "We might have made your visit more entertaining. We had a troupe of players here some time back. They put on a very creditable Shakespeare in one of the empty warehouses. Do you enjoy the theater, Captain Paul?"

263

"Occasionally," Jock said warily.

"Come to think of it," the judge said, wrinkling his brow, "I met the manager of the troupe, in a purely business capacity" — he seemed to be apologizing — "a man named Moony or Moody or something of the sort. He said he once knew an actor fellow with the same name as yours! Played villains' parts, he said, and did it superbly. What a curious coincidence."

"Oh, I don't know," Jock said. "John Paul is almost as common a name as John Smith or John Jones."

"So it is, so it is. I've a frightful memory for names."

Jock's gloomy thoughts continued. That night he thrust the sugar bowl away and drank his coffee unsweetened. It wasn't his fault that the dock laborer had died; but the dead man might, just *might,* have been one of the hundreds of blacks Jock had herded into his barracoons and watched disappear in chains into holds of ships that transported them across the Atlantic, full of the glowing dreams he had painted of all the joys that a black man would experience when he became a white man's slave. This one had met his death on a white man's wharf because of a white man's drunkenness. How many others had died more painfully, more slowly, under cruel white masters, their bodies broken, their dreams shattered, cursing the name John Paul? There was blood on the quay, blood in the sugar bowl, blood on his hands. "Ha! They pluck out mine eyes! Will all great Neptune's ocean wash this blood clean from my hands?"

"Nonsense!" he cried aloud to the empty cabin.

And again, contemptuous of himself, "Actor fellow indeed!"

At such a rate he'd go daft. He opened his great-cabin door, strode across his quarter-deck, and leaped up onto his ship's rail and down to the wharf, firmly resolved to cure this wretched oppression by stepping firmly on the very spots where the Negro had bled. That blood was paid for out of ship's funds, it was ship's property now, just as legally as her timbers.

It was impossible for him to commit so utterly cruel and inhuman an act. Sighing, he walked around the stains. He returned aboard his ship. His thoughts were black as before.

He ordered the *John*'s launch set down in the water and had it rowed across the bay towards the place where the *Virgen de la Paz* was anchored. He would pay her captain a visit and ask for news, discreetly to be sure, of her former owner, Don Jesu.

As the distance lengthened between him and the wharf where the accident had occurred, his mood lightened somewhat. The smooth surface of the bay and the palm-fringed shore were bathed in the long slow tropical twilight, glorious, golden. Sounds carried over the water to his ear, as sounds do at evening, clear and audible but curiously mingled, like things seen through rippled glass. Somewhere children were laughing; someone was singing; a dog was barking, a guitar twanged out its steely notes: the rhythm was reminiscent of Africa, but the tune was a popular dance. Africa was at least a generation away from the fingers that plucked that guitar. So they didn't all die. Some of them lived happy lives and begat children, and some of the children grew up and sang and made music. He was just as likely to have caused happiness as to have caused pain; in any event he was only one man, he had been only one part of a monstrous system: one man could not change the world. But just the same, he was extremely glad he was captain of the *John* and not the slaver of Lagos Lagoon.

His launch was now close to the big black ship. He glanced up towards her bows. Unless the golden glow of the sinking sun deceived his eyes, and Jock's eyes were sharp for the precious metals, the long name *Virgen de la Paz* was actually gold-plated!

A straight-backed man with lace at his throat and a portly lady with a high Spanish comb in her hair, flashing with many jewels, paused in their leisurely walk around the deck to peer over the rail. Suddenly the man smiled. There was no mistaking that diamond smile. Jock had no doubt now that the ship's name was gold-plated at least. It might even be solid.

"*Amigo!*" Don Jesu cried. "My agents seek you everywhere! They cannot find you! I find you myself!" With a whoop of glee he tossed his fifty-guinea cocked hat into the air. It fell into the sea. "Blind pigs! I shoot my agents!" He sank the hat with a pistol shot. "Come aboard! Come aboard! Come aboard!" He roared an order at his men, who jumped as if a lash were at their backs. Indeed it would be if they didn't step lively. They let down the Jacob's ladder.

Laughing for the first time that day, Jock scrambled aboard. Some extremely libidinous remarks were exchanged among the British rowers of the *John*'s launch below when the fiercely mustachioed, pistol-discharging Spaniard threw his arms around their captain and kissed him on both cheeks.

"How happy I am to find you! How do you look, let me see?" He held him at arm's length a moment. "Lean as a hound, all chin as usual. But there I have the better of you, for mine begins to double." He turned to the woman beside him. Jock saw with a start it was Leyla. "My dear," Don Jesu said in a voice that was brittle with embarrassment, "perhaps you remember Captain Paul, who was with us for a time in Africa. Captain Paul, I present you to my wife, the Marquesa de Silva y Villanueva." In the brittle tone there was a warning, "Not a smirk, you rascal!"

She said, formally offering a hand that looked like a jeweler's exhibit, "Indeed I do remember the captain. I trust you have prospered since you left Lagos, Señor Paul?" She might have been greeting a casual acquaintance, not the man to whom her Arab owner had given her in exchange for an American long rifle. Clearly the Circassian slave had risen in the world since Jock shot the dish out of her hand.

For once Jock was glad he had been an actor. He knew precisely the role demanded of him. He bowed, lightly took her proffered hand, sought a bare spot among the heavy jewels and brushed her fingers with a formal kiss. "Permit me to felicitate the marqués on his happiness," he said very gravely, his face perfectly straight. In view of the unexpectedness of the situation he gave a magnificent performance. "May God prosper his union and shower him and his marquesa with every blessing."

Don Jesu was now sure that Jock would treat Leyla with the dignity he exacted from everyone, and relaxed. "He already has," he said with a smile. "We'll show you the little marqués presently. Tell me first what you are doing in this forsaken place."

"I am captain of the brig yonder," Jock said pointing to the *John*, "trading among the islands for a Scottish firm in my home port of Kirkcudbright."

"Is one permitted to ask the color of your cargo?" Don Jesu asked slyly.

"White sugar, blue indigo, gray steel."

"I only asked, my friend." Jock's tone had been severe.

"I hope to pick up tobacco in the Grenadines, Barbados, Antigua, Jamaica for sure."

"Nothing darker?"

Jock sighed. "I cannot bring myself to that again."

"And I shall never have to," Don Jesu said proudly. "I can now retire. Come. I will show you my son!"

Leyla consulted a flamboyant gold watch bestudded with many diamonds hanging on a purple ribbon which was attached by a ruby buckle to her pink belt. The combination of colors screamed for mercy, but Leyla liked rich colors. "It's his bedtime," she said, "I really don't think he ought to be disturbed."

"It's quite all right, my dear," Don Jesu said. "Tonight is exceptional. We have a guest."

"Oh, very well," the marquesa replied, compressing her lips.

"We shall be very quiet," Don Jesu promised, looking meaningfully at Jock and holding a finger to his lips. "In we go! Quiet, now."

He opened the door of the great cabin. The fragrance of scented soap, women's clothing, talcum powder and perfume assailed Jock's nostrils. He sniffed, startled. It was oddly incongruous aboard a ship. But what, he asked himself, did he expect in a nursery? Gunpowder? Following the marqués and marquesa, he tiptoed in.

A toothless wrinkled old Negro nurse was crooning the child asleep to a drowsy Ibo lullaby: no beauty *here* to tempt Don Jesu out of his conjugal felicity!

"How many times have I warned you not to speak African in front of the marqués!" Leyla said sharply.

"Yes, ma'am," the nurse replied, cringing back.

Little Don Jesu woke up, beheld his father and mother and, gurgling with delight, rolled out of his bunk.

In unison Don Jesu and Leyla uttered a horrified, "Oh!"

But the child stood up unhurt and wobbled on uncertain ten-month-old legs towards Don Jesu. He had Don Jesu's eagle eyes and his mother's fair Circassian skin.

"You forgot the rail again!" Leyla snapped at the nurse.

"Forgive! Forgive!" cried the nurse. "I did not expect anyone to come in."

"He isn't hurt," Don Jesu said.

Leyla slapped the nurse's face.

"Next time you forget I will punish you," she said.

"Yes, ma'am. Oh please, ma'am. Oh yes, ma'am."

The youngster was now crawling up Don Jesu's leg, aiming, apparently, for the brilliant velveteen breeches above the buttoned gaiters which were not, it would seem, worth chewing on.

"Adorable age, the toddling age," Don Jesu said.

"It is indeed," Jock said.

"You don't really know how to appreciate them till you have your own," Leyla said to Jock.

"I'd wager Captain Paul has a dozen all over the world," Don Jesu said.

"Jesu! Stop it at once!"

Don Jesu sighed, "All right, my dear."

"What nasty talk!" the marquesa said. "Did you ever hear the like, Captain Paul?"

"I confess I am penetrated with astonishment that would be almost impossible to describe," Jock said.

"Caught on a lee shore so to speak, weren't you, Captain?" Don Jesu grinned. "You clawed off superbly. I wish I had you for an agent."

Sea metaphors were a bit too much for Leyla. She chattered on. "The marqués would be far steadier on his feet, *far* steadier," she said reproachfully, "if he had solid ground under him to learn to walk on instead of a deck that is forever bouncing up and down, this way and that like a camel, so that even grownups stumble when they try to walk across a room. I must say I think it's frightful training, and I haven't the slightest doubt in the world that the marqués' progress will be retarded all his life because of it, if indeed he ever survives at all, and for a child of his birth with the station he has to assume some day, which is only his right, I think life on a ship at this early period, when so much depends on what we do, is inconsiderate and not at all what he's entitled to. Don't you agree, Captain Paul?"

"I regret that I am not in a position to hazard an opinion on such an important matter, madam," Jock said.

Don Jesu suggested, "Wouldn't you like a drink, Captain? I'd like your opinion on some whisky that was — hm — that was presented to me."

"On a matter like that," Jock said smiling, "I think my opinion might be of more value."

"Just don't *you* go swigging the wicked stuff," the marquesa said to Don Jesu.

"Good heavens no, dear, not a drop, on my honor."

"Well, I hope not," she said, picking up her son, tucking him into his bunk and firmly snapping up the rail that kept him from falling out. "And you," she said with a baleful glance at the nurse, "remember that rail!"

"Yes *sir*, ma'am! Yes sir, señora marquesa."

Leyla kissed the child good night. "Isn't he darling, Captain Paul?"

Jock could honestly answer, "He certainly is."

"I want so much for him!"

She was intensely, unfeignedly sincere in her simple motherly wish for her little boy's good. All her silly affectations dropped when she spoke of her ambition for him. In that moment Jock caught a glimpse of why Don Jesu had married her.

In the chartroom Don Jesu closed the door and slid the bolt, which was freshly oiled and shut them in without a sound. He opened the flag locker with a private key — one flag was inky black, belonging to no nation. It was rolled, and the design was not visible; but presumably it was the "no quarter" flag. This skull-and-crossbones banner was not the exclusive flag of piracy; many legitimate ships of war carried it, though privateers used it most. It was a signal that could be run up by any commander who became so furious in battle or so outraged by the unchivalrous tactics of an adversary that he proclaimed his resolve to fight till one of them sank, expecting no man of his own to be saved if he lost and promising no mercy to any man if he won. From the flag locker Don Jesu took a bottle of trade rum. From a more orthodox liquor cabinet he took a bottle of whisky and poured Jock a glass. He himself took a long pull at the bottle neck. *"Por Dios!* I wanted that!" he said after several swallows, which counted themselves as they went down, setting the ruffles at his throat to rippling with little wavelike motions.

Ashamed, he set a glass for himself. "The marquesa doesn't like me to drink trade rum," he said, "so I hide it."

Jock nodded.

Don Jesu tried several times to speak, but each time he stopped, unable to find the words. Finally he said, "No Spaniard, not even a peasant, far less one nobly born, gossips about his wife; but the circumstances surrounding the marquesa are not ordinary, and one may be pardoned a breach of etiquette. No doubt you have said to yourself, 'This Don Jesu stayed so long in Lagos that he grew to be like Bombarda, admiring a face and figure more suited to Orientals than civilized persons, and married a slave because she was the only white woman available.'"

That was exactly what Jock had said to himself.

"That is not wholly true," Don Jesu said, and added with candor, "though it must be admitted that daily association and constant propinquity tend to make a woman more beautiful. And no doubt you have counted months, observing my son's age. God sent him to me early, I confess, some weeks before a priest solemnized our marriage. But you greatly err if you think that Don Jesu, Marqués de Silva y Villanueva, could confer on a slave his nine-hundred-year-old name merely because that slave had borne him a son. No. I considered the matter long. I found in Leyla such companionship, such cheerfulness, such noble ideals, such spirit, such strength of character, all attributes of gentility, that I considered no favor too great for such a lady. Who knows indeed that she may *not* be noble? What do we know of the princely families of the Tartars except that they are brave, wild, unconquerable even by the Russians? Her name may be as old as my own!"

Jock nodded. Don Jesu was protesting too much. There was nothing to say. It was incontestably true, however, that Leyla had strength of character.

"How intelligent she is! How quickly I was able to teach her Castilian, Portuguese, English, the civilized Western tongues! I forbade her the African dialects, but she picked them up on her own. Think what an out-pouring of talents into the blood of our son! And try to imagine, if you can, a more loving devoted mother!"

"That I cannot," Jock agreed heartily.

"How fearlessly she slapped the face of that careless nurse!"

Jock looked at him.

"Do not stare. One must maintain discipline," Don Jesu said defensively.

Jock nodded agreement in principle.

"And how she treasures the little trinkets I give her. 'I must always be lovely in your sight,' she says to me often, 'and so I adorn myself.'"

"You are very generous," Jock said.

"I can afford to be. Of course later on, when she has seen more of the world, I believe she will not wear quite so many all at once. Not that I care. I rather fancy jewelry myself, as you may have noticed."

Jock smiled.

"It started," Don Jesu said, "when I — hm — took to the sea after a mi-nor disturbance at Salamanca when I was a student there. The student body at Salamanca has always been noted for lawlessness. There was a regret-table death or two during a town-and-gown brawl. I was held responsible, though I could not remember a thing next day. I was advised to absent myself for a while. At first I was starving poor, but soon, by strenuous effort, I was able to make my living. My very first diamond I still retain. Till I lose the tooth I can never starve again."

It was less embarrassing to hear Don Jesu talk about himself than about his wife.

"The student fracas must be long forgotten," Jock said. "You could return to Spain now if you wanted to, couldn't you?"

It was the wrong remark.

"Oh yes, I could," Don Jesu said uncomfortably. "Even the British have pardoned my slightly irregular nautical activities. The last pardon I bought was in Jamaica, I believe. But the marquesa would be ill at ease in Euro-pean society. It has been very difficult to find a place where people would value her at her true worth."

"I should have thought Lagos ideal," Jock said.

Don Jesu glared at him, but he saw that Jock had not been sarcastic.

"No, Lagos was almost *too* primitive. And besides, the governor there conceived a very low estimate of my business methods. I am not the natural-born merchant."

A story came out that Don Jesu, demanding an outrageous price for a shipload of slaves, meeting objections, had trained not only the guns of the residence but also the guns of his powerful ship on a French vessel in Lagos and sunk it in the lagoon. Those of the crew not slaughtered by gunfire or drowned he had chased into the African forests, which promptly swallowed them up and obliterated their memory. "The governor of Lagos took a very high hand with me after that," Don Jesu admitted. "But by that time I was thoroughly bored with commerce anyhow. I sold the factory." He gulped down a tumblerful of rum.

"I'm delighted you're out of the trade," Jock said.

Don Jesu leaned back in his chair and began to roar with laughter. "Never, never, never shall I understand the British! Or are you Scotch? That would be even less understandable. Or are you a red American Indian? They are reputed to be the silent ones. Do you recall, my friend, how we saved all the title-transfer fees and such when you left? The property remained in your name. *You sold the factory.* You demanded and received for your African interests, the residence, the barracoons, the stock, the license to trade, to say nothing of the good will of the Ashanti tribe, the sum of eighty thousand pounds. Captain Paul, I owe you forty thousand pounds. There is a little more, ten thousand or so, due you in accordance with our agreement to share and share alike, from payments made to me by purchasers of our slaves. I wrote it all down in a little book. I think the marquesa has it somewhere. She keeps the accounts. Shall I pay you now? Here? In this room?"

Jock said, "You are simply incredible."

Don Jesu's command of English, ordinarily so good, was slipping a bit under the influence of the fiery trade rum. "Does not 'incredible' mean 'not to be believed'? Are you calling me a liar, sir?" His face flushed scarlet.

"In your case," Jock said, " 'incredible' means honesty deserving only of an angel! You could have disappeared with every farthing and I should never have known the difference."

"Why in blazes do you suppose I've had agents searching for you in every port in America for months?"

Jock's head was in a whirl, his thoughts confused, not with whisky — his glass was still half full — but with the prospect of sudden wealth, wealth to make him independent, wealth to buy a ship of his own, wealth to achieve the dreams he had nursed since childhood.

"It is hard, hard to take," he muttered, his head in his hands.

"Hard to take? Fifty thousand pounds? Do you question the sum? I am sure of the forty; perhaps the ten is inexact, it may be eleven, it may be twelve — the marquesa has the little book —"

"No, no, friend. The source! The source!"

"The source!" Don Jesu spat out a lurid volley of Spanish curses. "I defy you to find anyone in the world who has earned, *earned*, Señor Paul, fifty thousand pounds more honestly than you did. Come, come, you crazy man! It isn't so hard. Take it quick like castor oil and be done with it."

"I shall have to think it over."

Don Jesu struck his forehead with his open palm. "I am drunk. I hear him say, 'I shall have to think it over.'"

Jock rose to go. "My rowers will be tired waiting so long."

"And now I hear him say, 'I leave for my paltry brig, which a thieving shipping firm lets me command so they may grow rich while I stay poor.' There is no logic in this man."

"Yes, I have to go," Jock said.

Don Jesu shook his head resignedly. He was more than a little tipsy. "Are you not afraid I shall slip out of the bay while you decide whether to be rich or poor?"

"Then I shouldn't have to decide," Jock said wearily; but in his heart he knew he had already decided.

Don Jesu did not rise from his chair. Jock slid back the bolt of the chart-room door. Don Jesu said, "Forgive me, friend; I cannot see you to the deck."

"I know the way. It doesn't matter. Thank you, Don Jesu."

Thinking him already gone, Don Jesu murmured a complaint under his breath to himself, an utterance his fierce pride would have stifled had he been sober, a confession which even drunk he would never have allowed to pass his lips if he had imagined Jock still within earshot: "I can't sail the confounded *Paz* out of here anyhow till that confounded Leyla decides the confounded ocean is flat as a confounded flounder and little Jesu won't stub his confounded toes! *Sic transit gloria piratica!*"

Chapter 26

Jock HAD long recognized that the sea, which enforced an unnatural life upon a man, was a mighty magnifier of human traits. One day in ten on the average the sailor might spend ashore. The other nine were spent on a featureless expanse of water with fifty or sixty other men, no women at all, in a crowded floating structure smaller than many houses. With his shipmates the sailor would soon exhaust the novelty of conversation; often he did not like them; if he did, his conversation took the form of interminable yarns, usually imaginary; no one could tell a whopping big lie with so straight a face as a sailor. For long periods he looked forward to his brief stay ashore, anticipating how he would spend it; for long periods thereafter he would look back and wonder how he might have spent it better. Landsmen saw the sailor during these short periods on land and judged that his activity everywhere must always be as strenuous. Actually no profession in the world offered a lazy man such an opportunity to slip through life with so meager an expenditure of mental and physical effort. By contrast, alert and ambitious men had ample occasion to show their talent: much time to plan, much time to perfect their skills, much time to analyze their mistakes; for storms came seldom, ports were infrequently touched, and one did not often have to defend the ship against a pirate. But just as the magnifying glass could magnify only what lay beneath it, so the life of the sea could magnify only those traits which a man already possessed: the lazy became lazier, the coward more cowardly, the lecher more lecherous, the drunkard more drunk; but also the good became better. Jock could never forget that Captain Newton had become a priest of God. Thus sailors tended to become confirmed individualists, sometimes to a warped and abnormal degree. One thing they all possessed in common, a marked and unusual tolerance. If they did not knife each other, they learned to live at peace with each other, granting the same freedom of action to others, even of eccentricity, that they demanded for themselves. It was very easy for the notion of personal liberty to take strong hold of a sailor. This notion of freedom for others as well as for himself, already deep-rooted in Jock's Scottish nature, had gradually matured, had shown itself in action when he left the slave trade, and had risen to a conscious ideal when he forced himself to shun political conversations in the loyalist home of his brother lest he speak out in favor of the "rebellious colonials."

But ambition also was magnified. The desire to rise in the world, to own his own ship, could not be put down. Jock had accepted the money Don Jesu had offered him. He had known he would before he left the *Virgen de la Paz*. Only a qualm of conscience, not to be argued away on short notice, had prevented him from accepting the proffered wealth at once, "now, here, in this room."

During a sleepless night the arguments had come: would refusing the wages of sin wipe out the sin itself? Patently not. *Was* it a sin? No, it was perfectly legal trade. He was merely averse to it. Was anyone else averse? Well, the Virginia Assembly had attempted to regulate the traffic with a view to decreasing the importation of slaves, probably not for humanitarian reasons. England, for obvious reasons, had declared the Virginia Assembly incompetent to legislate on the matter and encouraged the importation of all the blacks the New World could absorb, and more, so long as they were imported in British bottoms. Would he engage in the slave trade again? No, or he'd still be in it. Would Don Jesu put the money to better use than he? Jock doubted that. Could he not, then, in conscience, accept it? He did.

Early next day he had taken his launch to the *Virgen de la Paz*. "I thought you would come to your senses," Don Jesu had said. "But did it have to be so early in the morning? I am not going anywhere."

He and the marquesa were retiring to an estate in Trinidad, he said, which an agent had purchased for him. Terra firma would be better for the little marqués to learn to walk on. But he deemed the weather inclement.

It was the calmest time of the year, midway between the rains and the hurricanes. Trinidad was only twenty miles from Tobago; one could actually see it. Jock had declared that he understood perfectly.

Don Jesu's method of payment had somewhat surprised him. Jock had supposed it would be in gold, and his mahogany sea chest was ready to receive it. Don Jesu had scoffed. Gold there was for the asking, he said, but would gold be wise? "Once you suggested I habitually walked my prisoners off planks! How absurdly old-fashioned!" Was it not better to take payment in paper than a muleload of gold, which was certain to cause gossip and might cause mutiny among one's crew? But something had to be found for the chest, else why had it been brought? Don Jesu picked out an assortment of foul-tasting medical stores, chiefly purges, and some painful astringent ointments for those nagging skin afflictions so likely to be contracted on water fronts, and packed them ostentatiously into the chest. "That's for your crew to goggle at!"

In an oilskin package which could be sealed against the damp he stuffed a package of bank notes issued by the Bank of England. They were neatly tied in a string. "The marquesa counted it out; I'd wager my life it's correct. Till the war comes, they're good as gold." There was also, astonishingly, a good-sized purse with coins in it. "I suppose this is the money she couldn't find bank notes small enough to cover."

Don Jesu had then retired, to sleep off the headache caused by a full quart of rum the night before, with a scowl and a growl at the barometer, which continued to indicate "fair" as it had for days, with some prudent words about putting one's money in safe banking establishments and many a heartfelt invitation for Jock to visit him and his marquesa in his new Trinidad estate where he expected to expire of boredom, "if ever I can convince certain people it's safe to sail."

During the slow voyage to the northward, while he traded among the islands, selling cotton and machetes, buying sugar, tobacco and indigo, Jock had leisure to reflect on Don Jesu's pithy parting remarks. Don Jesu, sensitive as a weather vane, had caught the threat in the political winds that were blowing over the planet; war was surely coming, perhaps a very great war. Don Jesu had deposited large funds in a dozen different banking institutions in a dozen different countries; no matter who won, Don Jesu could never be poor. The fiscal habits of pirates had certainly changed, Jock mused. Only the stupid ones still buried specie and jewels on desolate sandy beaches like Long Island off New York. Farsighted ones like Don Jesu deposited their wealth in national banks. Then let the cannon roar! They founded elegant families and grew to gouty old age, secure and respectable.

Jock could follow no better example. The Bank of San Giorgio in the Republic of Genoa was six hundred years old. In six hundred years it had never defaulted.

There was a bank in Barcelona founded in the year 1401, now nearly four hundred years old. The Bank of Barcelona also was solid as a rock; Don Jesu greatly favored it.

There was the Bank of England, secure during two dynasties and five reigns of British monarchs. Though Don Jesu had voiced suspicion that British credit might suffer during the war that was coming, the notes of the Bank of England were as good as gold for the present at least.

As for the French, one should not trust French, or American, banks. Those people were volatile and unpredictable, their thinking shot through with the philosophical teachings of Locke, Rousseau and Voltaire, which did not make for solidity.

In Jamaica there was a street which in Renaissance days would probably have gone by the name "The Street of the Money Changers." It was now called King Street. On it were found branch offices of modern eighteenth-century European banking houses. When Jock reached Jamaica, he took his oilskin package to the Spanish and Italian branches of the oldest and soundest financial establishments in the world. He was met by sharp-eyed polyglot Mediterranean gentlemen in faultlessly curled wigs. His deposits were somewhat large; his appearance was obviously sailorish; but not a dark eyebrow fluttered. Far more suspect sailorish clients than Captain Paul often made deposits in the banks of San Giorgio and Barcelona; his money was as good as theirs; no questions were asked. He was thanked for his patronage and given a dish of tea while functionaries in thick spectacles on high stools engrossed receipts in the form of letters of credit, good from the Sandwich Islands to Ultima Thule.

Then he breathed easier. In the oilskin package he kept some crisp large-denomination Bank of England notes and hid them on his person. These would buy his ship.

This would be his last voyage aboard the *John*. Oddly, the prospect of independence made him sharper than ever as a trader. He haggled like a fishwife over the last purchases he made in Jamaica, personally scrutinizing each bale of tobacco as it was hoisted aboard. He was determined to leave Currie, Beck and Company with a reputation his employers could point to and say, "Captain Paul was our best."

Storm, death, rumor of murder and a disagreement between the faraway partners, Currie and Beck, stepped in to alter his plans.

The short dry Caribbean season of perfect weather, with cloudless skies and the thermometer at a constant eighty degrees, between the April rains and the summer hurricanes, had passed. As he prepared to leave Jamaica, the *John* full laden, the hatches battened down and not to be opened again till he should sail up Solway Firth, the barometer began to fall at an alarming rate. The air was sticky, sounds could be heard farther than they ought, pet monkeys looked frightened, and old men complained of rheumatic pains. Nature was brewing a thunderbolt. The storm came raging out of the south and lashed the island cruelly. The *John* rode out the hurricane in Kingston Harbor with double anchors fore and aft. There was damage to repair in the rigging after it roared away, with abating fury, over the Atlantic towards Europe. The same storm that held Captain Paul harbor-bound for a week propelled Captain Eastament towards England, and aboard Eastament's packet Mungo Maxwell died of malaria, his back long since healed. But two Scotch sailors from the ship carried the story to Kirkcudbright that the carpenter had died as a result of John Paul's flogging.

The storm was a present experience; Jock lived through it and surmounted it, fretting at the delay but shrugging it off: those were the hazards one took when one went to sea. The hazards of Maxwell's death and the rumors to which it gave rise lay in the future and were to be learned. That Currie and Beck were about to dissolve partnership was equally unknowable.

While the *John* was repairing, Jock sought out his old boarding house to while away the time. It was mid-season in the Shakespearean world. Moody was there with his company preparing next season's repertoire. He was busily rewriting *The Tempest* into a Caribbean setting, using as a guide a newspaper account that had just arrived from the neighboring island of Nevis, which the hurricane had utterly devastated. Jamaicans, whose island the storm had merely brushed, read the report with horror. "It is fascinatingly penned," Moody said with professional admiration. "What observation! What an eye for detail! I think I met the author once when the company played in Nevis. He's a Scotsman like you, an accountant by trade. His name is Hamilton, Alexander Hamilton. But he has one advantage over you in that he's Jewish-schooled — after all, there is only one school on Nevis and it's run by Jews. Hamilton can recite the entire Decalogue in Hebrew! One is not surprised that a Scotsman educated by Jews should be good at accounting, nay, even perhaps become a financial wizard when he grows a little older. But who would expect such a man to be a writer too! I can use whole portions of his account, with a little improvement of course. Next season I predict packed houses every night to hear *The Carib Tempest* by William Shakespeare!"

He exulted at his find.

But he was afraid he might lose Lydia Hart. She had taken up with a wealthy official of the East India Company and would probably go, with her husband in self-effacing attendance, out to Calcutta. There, under the iron hand of Lord Clive, the most ruthless empire builder Great Britain had ever produced, the memory of the Black Hole was all but forgotten, and India almost as orderly as Oxford. "And what, sir, have you been doing? Navigating, I'd say, from your Moor-of-Venice complexion."

"And so I have," Jock said. He related Captain MacAdam's death, the death of the first mate and his rise to command of the *John*, which he had commanded ever since. It was then that the impresario who was improving on Shakespeare sighed, "Life, sir, is totally incredible; art dares take no such liberties; they'd whistle us off the boards." He eyed Jock thoughtfully. With John de Gaunt dead and Lydia Hart about to depart for India, the personnel of the Moody Company of Players would be sadly depleted. But he sensed in Jock an independence that had not been there before. He could wish, but he could not ask, that Jock would rejoin the company.

"Do you remember when you played in *Caesar*," he asked, "and the powder misfired during the storm scene, and everyone laughed because the thunder came but there wasn't any lightning, and a soothsayer plucked at Caesar's sleeve?"

" 'He is a dreamer; let us leave him,' " Jock quoted.

"I have a melancholy soothsayerlike premonition that I shall not see you again. You will go on to greater things."

"These islands have proved better trading than I should have expected. I shall be back."

"I hope so," Moody said. "But the soothsayer's prophecy came true."

"That was art," Jock said. "I shall be a trader all my life."

Chapter 27

MUNGO MAXWELL had numerous indigent relatives in and around Kirkcudbright; they had never been proud of Mungo. But now that the scamp was dead, they professed to mourn him and resolved, if possible, to profit by his loss. John Paul had steady employment; his mother had spent some of her gold pieces publicly and local tradesmen had noted them; her son was known to be thrifty and now was assumed to be wealthy.

The two sailors from Eastament's ship were easily prevailed upon to swear on their oath that Maxwell had told them that he had been "most unmercifully, by the said John Paul, with a cudgel or baton, beat, bled and bruised and wounded upon his back and other parts of his body," of which wounds and bruises, the sailors declared on oath, Mungo Maxwell soon afterwards died.

Having sworn their swear, with beer in their bellies and a bit of "siller" in their pockets the deponents forthwith returned to their profession, shipping out of Kirkcudbright, to show up again someday or to disappear forever, as chance and the vagaries of their wandering life should decide.

A constable appeared in the offices of Currie, Beck and Company while Jock was going over his ship's accounts with the partners. Both were pleased with the cruise of the *John* and the profits she had made for the company.

"I think it is safe to promise," Jock was saying, "that with the greater experience I now have I can do even better next trip, if you keep me in command."

Currie and Beck exchanged glances. "There have been changes in the ownership of our firm, Captain Paul, which take that decision out of our hands."

The constable broke in gruffly, "He'll no' be sailin' nowhere on nothin', not for a while, he won't," and served Jock with a warrant for arrest on suspicion of murder.

Jock had been in singular surroundings before, but never in jail. It was now November; he had just returned from a voyage among tropical islands; the winter wind of Scotland was cold; the jail was unheated. The stones of the walls of his cell sweated with a damp that was near to congealing; the straw pallet on which he would lie was sodden with moisture and filthy with lice. Near the ceiling was a small window barred with a few iron bars. It seemed to have been designed with a view to economizing on iron: no man could quite slip through. The same thrift of construction also let in a maximum of cold wind. Summer prisoners had blessed its cooling breeze, but this was November and Jock did not think of them. He was furiously angry.

But for the fact that an oilskin packet lay under his shirt, he would have pounded on the door and raged at the turnkey, in choice quarter-deck language, "Go tell those blasted Maxwells to charge me with murder outright and let me stand trial! I won't stay locked up on *suspicion* of anything." But he controlled his temper. The cold was actually wondrous good luck, and he knew it. The constable had casually examined him for weapons, found none, and humanely permitted him to retain all his clothes, grunting that it might be chilly where he was going. The turnkey, taking the constable's word, had not searched him, signing a routine report, "No weapons."

The news of Jock's imprisonment had swept through the town. His mother arrived with a blanket and a good plump haggis, still hot. Chunks of haggis carried in a pouch had kept the lifeblood surging lustily through many a Scotsman's veins when he found himself lost in his freezing mountain mists. Elegant Englishmen sometimes attributed the wild bravery of Scottish warriors to haggis, and shuddered at its components: blood, heart, liver and lungs of a sheep with a dash of tripe thrown in, minced with heavy suet and oatmeal, massively seasoned with pepper, onions and salt, then boiled in the gut of the beast whose highly nutritious organs went into the makings.

"I'd have brought you a dram of whisky too," she said, "but the turnkey would have drunk it."

"Thank you, Mother, but you'd better go home," he said, "and drink the dram yourself. Your pretty face is blue with cold. I am quite comfortable."

"I will," she said. She kissed him through the bars. "I'm afraid the laird isn't coming to see you. He pleads a sore throat."

That angered Jock; he would have liked to see Mr. Craik, who might arrange bail for him. But he did not wish to set his mother against her landlord, who had it in his power to make her life miserable by countless little slights and who shared, apparently, the prevailing opinion in the town that Jock was in the wrong.

"They can't hold me long on 'suspicion'; I'll be out soon and pay my respects to him."

"Tomorrow I'll put up bail for you."

"No, no!"

"Why not?"

"Then people will think you are rich, and you are not."

"I'm not so poor I cannot go bail for my son, thanks to my dear son himself."

"I've lots of money due me on my wages. I'll go my own bail. For your own sake you must not do it, Mother."

"Very well, if you're sure you have the money."

"Don't whisper!" the turnkey barked.

She kissed him again through the bars. "Don't freeze, Jock, lad."

"Sailors get used to all kinds of weather," he laughed.

She walked away, her feet tapping smartly on the cold flagged floor, proud, erect, only a little grayer. She favored the turnkey with a fiercely contemptuous glare. He touched his knitted woolen cap and said, "Good night, Mrs. Paul."

The spicy aroma of the haggis filled the cell and wafted out through the door. The turnkey appeared and looked in.

"A wonderful woman, your mother," the turnkey said, fixedly eying the haggis: the widow Paul made the best in the parish. Jock had fallen upon it with his sailor's knife; already he felt better; it filled his belly with sunshine straight out of the Caribbean.

"All right, all right, I know what you want. Come in and I'll give you a slice."

"You've got a weapon," the turnkey said.

"It was your duty to search me and take it away. Why didn't you?"

"I forgot."

It was a sturdy knife of no great value, but it had a handle of mother-of-pearl and looked costlier than it was. Jock snapped it shut and tossed it through the bars. The turnkey caught it handily and fingered it covetously, turning it over and over. "I'll have to turn it in," he said at last.

"I don't see why. I didn't have it on me, did I, when you searched me for weapons? Didn't you make a report?"

"We always do."

"What would the warden say if you turned in a weapon now?"

"I'd catch it proper."

"Obviously I did not give it to you, and you do not have it," Jock said.

"I do not," the turnkey said grinning, slipping it into his pocket. "Thank you kindly, Captain Paul."

"But now it would seem that I have the haggis and you have the appetite," Jock said, taking a savory bite. "I can eat and you cannot. Why don't you come in?"

The fellow looked scared. "Maybe you've got other weapons. They say you killed a man."

Jock was pleased. His thoughtless exposure of the knife might have caused a thorough search of his person. He said with a villainous scowl, "I do not need weapons to kill my victims," and went over to the bars. "Here," he said, holding out the haggis, "help yourself."

The turnkey did and thanked him respectfully.

"Is there anything I can get you?"

"No, I think not."

"Maybe a candle?"

"There's not much to look at."

"It would keep you warmer."

"Yes, that it would. I'd like one."

Cautiously the turnkey handed him one through the bars. Towards morning Jock was glad of its feeble warmth. In spite of the haggis the cold struck in; the stinking pallet repelled him; he sat all night on the three-legged stool, the blanket around him, his teeth chattering, his temper rising with every passing hour, conscious of his innocence, furious at his degradation, sick with shame. A resolve as cold as the prison walls hardened like flint in his heart to clear his name.

Next morning he had a visitor.

There lived a Scotsman in Kirkcudbright whose name was Smith and whose Christian name was James. He was of local origin, but the Smith family had long been as poor and obscure as the Pauls. Recently James Smith had prospered, no one quite knew how except that, as always on the coast of Scotland, prosperity came somehow from the sea. He was widely rumored to have got his start smuggling to the nearby Isle of Man. What he had done thereafter, why his skin was permanently tanned, and how it happened that he had suddenly turned up after a long absence with funds to buy ships of his own and set up a trading company, no one questioned or cared. Slavery and piracy might both have lain in his past. Now, like Currie and Beck, his ships engaged in the profitable and legitimate West Indian trade. On the other side of the Atlantic, in Edenton, North Carolina, he had a brother who handled the company's affairs from the American end.

With a view to buying the *John*, Smith called on Jock in prison. He wanted a firsthand report on the ship's condition from the man who should know her best, her late commander. Smith had a cutlass scar on his cheek, a sailor's stride, sharp eyes and a confident manner.

"Before I make an offer to Beck," he began brusquely, "I thought I would talk to you. What shape is your ship in? Is she tight? How bad is her normal seepage? How often did you pump bilges? How close can she sail without broaching to? Her standing rigging looks good, but I saw some cracked deadeyes. What is the condition of her canvas?"

Jock's temper was raw; he was numb with cold and pent-up fury. He pretended not to know his visitor. "Pray who may you be, sir? I was not aware that I asked you in. Go talk to Currie or talk to Beck if you want to buy a ship. No doubt they will offer you a chair, a glass and a fire. My own amenities are somewhat limited."

"God bless my soul!" Smith said, taken aback at Jock's tone. "Are you not Jock Paul, son of John Paul, the gardener?"

"I am," Jock said, "and only courtesy to a stranger forbids me to guess out loud what sort of son *you* may be."

Smith gaped and absorbed the insult. The gardener's son talked better and bigger and bolder than he had remembered in the gangling lad that had gone to sea some years ago.

Smith's manner wholly changed. He strode to the door and rapped noisily on the bars with a handsome gold-headed cane. "Ho, there, you!" he shouted to the turnkey. "Will you leave a gentleman shivering and shaking in a drafty cell on a morning like this?"

The turnkey ran up. Into his pocket, clinking against Jock's pearl-handled knife, slipped some coins from the outstretched hand of James Smith. "I did not recollect that you might feel the chill," the turnkey said. "I'll fetch something directly."

"Not for me, ye sumph! For Captain Paul!"

The turnkey brought an iron scuttle full of live coals, and another stool. Jock had not left his own; Smith had had to stand.

Smith eyed him half in good humor, half in uncertainty as to his reception. "May I sit down, Captain Paul?"

"Please do," Jock said rising and extending his hand. "I remember you now, Mr. Smith. Perhaps I may be forgiven for my surly welcome in view of the long time I have been away and my present surroundings."

"A damned outrage, sir," Smith said. "Have you got a good lawyer?"

"I'll get one today. They can't hold me on suspicion."

"My dear Captain, permit me to offer you mine. You can render me a service, and the least I can do to reciprocate is to offer you my lawyer. Damned scallywag doesn't earn his keep any more anyhow. He used to, though." A look of nostalgia twinkled in Smith's hard eyes. "Did you really flog Mungo Maxwell dead?"

"I did not, sir!"

"Even if you had, sir; even if you had!" Smith said, holding up a restraining hand. "I should count it a favor if you would let me go bail for you. Now as to the *John,* is she shipshape?" He repeated the searching expert technical queries, which Jock now, smiling, answered fully.

The *John* was in excellent condition, he said. Some few minor details of maintenance like the cracked deadeyes indeed required attention, but a decent carpenter would soon put them right. For the rest, she was sound, tight, dependable and obedient.

"Currie and Beck are splitting up," Smith said, "dissolving their partnership. Currie thinks that a war is coming and wants to pull out and retire to England; Beck thinks that if war comes, now is the very time to stay in the shipping business. What do you think?"

"I think Currie is daft."

"My sentiments exactly," Smith said; but he probed him further: "Currie thinks that the war will eliminate profitable trade with the New World; Beck holds more liberal views and thinks that a company with colonial offices could very well carry on in spite of the war in the colonies alone. What do you think, bearing in mind that Beck is a thoroughgoing Scotsman with no love in his heart for the British?"

"I still think that Currie is daft."

Smith grinned. "That is what my brother Robert in America thinks, and my brother Robert is a canny soul. They say he has the second sight."

Jock said, "If England fights her huge American colonies, no second sight is required to predict that we will win. The tail cannot wag the dog."

"You said 'we,' Captain Paul."

Jock fumbled a moment for an answer; the "we" had slipped out without thinking. "I too have a brother in America," he said, "and I dare say I think of America as my adopted home."

Scotsman to Scotsman, James Smith declared frankly, "America's certainly better than England," and spat in the coals. "I am going to buy the *John*," he continued with an air of decision. "Will you command her for me?"

Jock became acutely conscious of the oilskin packet under his shirt. "If I cannot obtain a ship of my own, Mr. Smith, I'd like nothing more."

"Come, come, sir! No one climbs up that fast."

"You did."

"My opportunities were exceptional," Smith said cautiously. "I was able to make profitable deals both in Africa and the Spanish Antilles."

Jock smiled. "Nevertheless, I shall try first to lay my hands on a ship of my own."

Smith looked at him keenly, suddenly noting that Jock too had a trace of that deeply burnt skin such as only the African sun can impart. "God bless my soul!" he said with a touch of awe. "I should have guessed by your confidence. I have failed to recognize my own kind! But the trade is chancy. Give it up."

"I did."

"In case you do not buy your own ship, Captain Paul, consider my offer of the *John*. In any case I will write my brother Robert about you. Gentlemen of fortune," he said, extending his hand in parting, "ought to hang together."

Smith had done Jock more than justice; Jock had been a slaver but never a pirate. It seemed expedient to accept the compliment, however. "Not hang, I hope," he said laughing.

Smith bought the *John*. From Currie, Beck and Company, now dissolved, she passed to the ownership of Hewes and Smith, Joseph Hewes being an American partner with great and growing influence among colonial leaders.

Jock was released from prison on bail, secured by James Smith's bond. But his name was not cleared, and humiliating conditions were attached: in case anyone ever showed up to accuse him directly of Mungo Maxwell's death, Jock must present himself within six months to stand trial for murder. Jock would gladly have stood trial at once, but the venal talebearers with their hearsay evidence had disappeared, no genuine witnesses were likely to come forward, and meanwhile the Scottish law, the only law in the world that still in the modern eighteenth century could hand down the niggling archaic verdict "Not Proven" instead of a forthright "Guilty" or "Not Guilty," cast a shadow over his name.

"You'll never be brought to trial," Smith said. "Isn't that enough?"

"Neither will I ever be cleared," Jock said. "It is not enough."

"I know how you feel," Smith said.

Smith was a member of a lodge of Freemasons. Once they had been a band of Christian knights, crusaders against the infidel Turks, dating their founding from the Middle Ages. They numbered their martyrs and their saints. At the time of the Reformation they had taken their stand stanchly against the corrupt and worldly popes of Rome. But religious heat had cooled by the eighteenth century; no Freemason now denounced the pope; no pope denounced the Freemasons. Indeed, the pope had just suppressed his own Society of Jesuits, deeming them, for the moment at least, too militant for a world in which zeal for religion had shrunk to the vanishing point. Science and philosophy were in the ascendant; liberalism was in the air; Voltaire was applauded; Rousseau, mad as he was, was read with enthusiasm and his words fired men's minds with an ideal of freedom that was higher than the author's own. In such a tepid religious climate the Freemasons had lapsed into a fraternal body of nonsectarian gentlemen who professed belief in a God of some sort, who wore rings with secret Hebrew squiggles to prove it, and who stayed out late and enjoyed good talk in masculine company. Jews were admitted to their society; Catholics could join if they pleased, and some did. In America Benjamin Franklin, the skeptic, was a Freemason; so was George Washington, the austere High Anglican. In this tolerant society of freethinkers one common trait prevailed: they were exceptionally well-mannered, well-educated and well-behaved. They were also quite likely to be wealthy.

To erase some of the stain caused by his sojourn in jail, Jock petitioned the local master for membership in this highly esteemed body. Smith sponsored him. A single black ball cast into the cup during the secret vote would have excluded him. But Jock was not blackballed. He lingered in Kirkcudbright some weeks and rose from the first to the second, from the second to the third degree, a Master Mason. The gentry of his home town accepted him again. Jonathan Beck gave him a letter of recommendation, praising him for his handling of the *John* and his honesty as a trader. Mr. Craik now greeted him pleasantly on the street.

It was something, but it was not enough for Jock. He provided funds for his mother, just as much as before but this time in silver, and took leave of James Smith, wringing his hand and thanking him from the heart. He took passage on the stage to London, the home port of Eastament's ship. He was determined to seek out that captain and get from him a statement disclosing the facts of Maxwell's death, whatever they might be.

"I don't see why you bother," Smith said. "The chances are thousands to one against your ever being indicted."

"My good name means everything to me!" Jock said.

Smith could understand that. "Good hunting!" he cried, and Jock knew that Smith did not mean "for Eastament." He let it pass and waved him a cheery adieu.

In London he went to Lloyd's and quickly ascertained the registry of Eastament's ship. If lady luck had gone against him before, she was making amends now; the ship was in port; Eastament was aboard, and he proved a most honest fellow. "Maxwell? Maxwell? Oh yes, the lazy lubber who died of malaria on my last trip."

"Would you testify to that, Captain?"

"Certainly, since it's only the truth."

Before a notary Captain Eastament swore out an affidavit; the phrases were formal, massive and strong: "Mungo Maxwell, carpenter, formerly on board the *John,* Captain Paul, Master, came in good health on board his, this deponent's said vessel, then lying in Rockley Bay in the island of Tobago . . . he acted in every respect in perfect health for some time, after which he was taken ill of a fever which continued for four or five days, when he died on board the said vessel. And this deponent further saith that he never heard the said Mungo Maxwell complain of having received any ill usage from the said Captain Paul but that he, this deponent, verily believes that said Mungo Maxwell's death was occasioned by a fever as aforesaid, and not by or through any other cause or causes whatsoever."

Of this valuable paper Jock had several copies made and sent to his mother, to Craik, to Smith, to the Masons, and one to Lloyd's of London, where his name as a shipmaster would be watched. For Jock was about to do something all sailors dreamt of and which could be done better in London than anywhere else in the world: to pick out a ship of his heart's desire from the multitude of vessels there lying in port and buy her for his own. Almost it was like taking a bride.

His eye fell on a beautiful slender brigantine, larger than the *John,* fresh, sweet, taut, clean, with speed in all her lines.

He bought her.

He sailed her straight into disaster.

Chapter 28

FROM FORECASTLE to quarter-deck was a giant stride, but Jock had made it with ease; from the quarter-deck to actual ownership was an even greater leap. For now his responsibilities were the heaviest that anyone who wrested a living from the sea could assume. He had but one ship; he could not spread the risk; he remembered *The Merchant of Venice* and wished he could say with Antonio, "my ventures are not in one bottom trusted." Jock's were.

To function efficiently, an independent company consisting of only one ship needed agents in port to watch out for its interests exactly the same as for a firm of twenty ships. This was especially true for Jock, since he captained as well as owned his single vessel.

He lacked another asset of most shipping companies: he had no partner ashore. Before he had owned his beautiful *Betsy* many weeks, he began to understand why so many shipowners never went to sea. They liked the managerial duties ashore; he loathed them as time-consuming and dull.

Yet he knew he was forced, and, as a former ship chandler, competent, to discharge these tedious essential duties. He appointed a London agent, bought gunpowder, ship's stores and a cargo, interviewed applicants and signed on the best crew he could find, considering the times and his impatience to get to sea. Then the *Betsy*, Captain Paul, master and sole owner, set sail; and it seemed that the wind itself must have conspired with the god of the weather to smile on Jock's maiden voyage and give him a honeymoon with his beloved *Betsy*. It was just the sort of strong blow that Jock liked; one could get speed out of it; one could leave the miles behind in a hissing long white wake; a prosperous wind, wind made for a driver.

It was also the sort of wind everybody else hated and cursed, along with the man it so pleased. It kept the men constantly aloft in freezing temperatures, handling stiff ropes from which splinters of ice cracked off when you bent them with bare blue hands; it rendered footing hazardous on the spars; it stole your sleep and put out the galley fire and gave you a cold supper.

Of all these hardships Captain Paul was apparently oblivious, his young face perpetually wreathed in adoring smiles at the speed of his ship and her phenomenally excellent behavior in the dead-of-winter wind. Sometimes he frightened old hands with the chances he took. But his beloved *Betsy* seemed to return his love and bore all his driving as if nothing he demanded was too much for her. The *Betsy*'s superb performance under stress only caused the exhausted sailors to hate her as much as her master. If only she'd broach to or spring a mast! Not the *Betsy!* If only the bloody captain didn't steer so often himself, as if he hadn't a helmsman aboard! Not Captain Paul! The helmsman, twice as heavy as Jock and therefore entitled to be twice as strong, was particularly humiliated when Jock, after a protracted and seemingly easy spell at the wheel, would permit him (the wind moderating) to resume his duty — only to find himself forced to exert all his strength to keep from getting kicked by the fighting wheel with the force of an angry mule.

In such weather with such a captain there were bound to be grumblings, rumors and much dissatisfaction: "They say he's a Jew, he buys so cheap." "No, he's a bloody Kiltie." "They say he's a slaver; look at his cabin man with the teeth." "They say he's a rich Freemason, Master's rating." "Him being rich don't help us." "They say he flogged a man till his ribs stuck out and his liver split wide open." "Aye, I heard that one; finished the count on the corpse; two hundred."

Exaggerations always occurred among the men when a captain was new. Ordinarily they died out when captain and crew had lived together awhile. But Billy Perkin, the hulking helmsman, proud of his skill at the wheel and continually ordered to stand aside, would not let the rumors die.

But as yet the crew had had only a taste of Captain John Paul. A worse and more personal grievance was to come in Tobago, and hit them all alike.

For the rest, when the ship rode out of the wintry Atlantic and entered the blue Caribbean, when they were warm and dry again, they had to admit that the meat was red and fat, no weevils squirmed in the biscuits, no mildew soured the duff, there was plenty of molasses and cheese, and Captain Paul didn't water the grog. "It's only to get more work out of us," growled Billy Perkin, "and he makes us drink lime juice first so we won't eat much."

Only a few sea captains as yet, and none in the conservative Royal Navy, forced sailors to drink lime juice to keep their teeth from falling out with the scurvy. In this Jock realized that he was following theorists like Captain Cook; scurvy seldom appeared on the relatively short Atlantic crossing. But the disease was mysterious; lime juice certainly did no harm, and the theorists reasoned that if it could largely ward off scurvy on a long cruise it might completely ward it off on a short one.

Recent experience and knowledge of the West Indian markets alone would have shaped Jock's course towards Tobago; but another and stronger motive urged him on. In Rockley Bay he could procure affidavits from a judge and a governor that would further clear his name.

With high hopes for the future and great affection for his ship which was now tried and proven faithful, with a crew who thought they were ill used and a troublemaker to remind them that they were, Jock brought the *Betsy* up to the quayside where the docker had died in the port where Maxwell had been flogged. Jock was not superstitious, but he could have wished that the memories were happier.

Instantly the crew demanded their pay. Custom entitled them to half (less, at the master's discretion), the other half being held back until they reached home. Only thus would they go ashore after a voyage of months or years not entirely penniless. But Jock had made a spectacular crossing. The little they had earned so far would scarcely support a single night of proper carousing. To stretch it to two would require an effort of will, penny-pinching unthinkable in a jolly openhanded mariner who did not wish his entertainment restricted to the oldest, ugliest and cheapest of the water-front women. After such a crossing they felt entitled to something more. They demanded their full pay.

Jock gave them half.

Perkin led them grumbling ashore. On the wharf he said, "This is where he pushed a sugar barrel on top of a tired docker who didn't dance when he whistled. He killed him too." They muttered agreement, "Aye, he's a hard master." Long before Jock had finished his business in Tobago, they were stony broke, demanding the other half of their pay with increasing impudence, their ringleader egging them on.

In other circumstances Jock might have given them a sympathetic hearing, for he understood the helplessness of the man before the mast who steps ashore, prey to the harpies and sharpers. But this was no time to show laxness: lose the respect of your crew at the beginning of a voyage, and before it ends they'll be laughing in your face if you venture to give an order and spitting on the deck. He was inattentive and abrupt with them. When a deputation, headed by Billy Perkin, knocked at his door with a formal petition of grievance, he refused to admit them and ordered them off the quarter-deck. This, as he reviewed the tragedy later, had been an error of judgment. Sailors had a right to present petitions even when they abused that right and used it as an excuse for shirking and dodging. He should have made time to hear them.

An error of judgment, too, was his habit of wearing his sword whenever he went ashore in Tobago. True, it was part of a gentleman's dress, no more conspicuous than silver shoe buckles, white stockings or a gold watch fob, and Jock was dressing to call on gentlemen: the judge of the admiralty court and the governor of the province himself. But to his crew a dress sword was an insufferable affectation of elegance, or else, as Perkin darkly sneered, "We've scared him! We'll get our pay."

Jock was engaged in an activity vital to his honor. Judge Simpson, with his frightful memory for names, recalled that Captain Paul had disciplined a lazy rogue on his last voyage, looked up the minor incident in his records, discovered that the name of the malefactor was Mungo Maxwell and readily agreed to swear out a deposition exonerating Jock from all taint of ill usage. Jock wanted a formidable document, sworn in the presence of Governor Young. "With the whole world springing to arms," Judge Simpson said, "it is hard to see why his excellency, now so busy, should be bothered with such small matters."

But nothing less would satisfy Jock. It took several calls and much persuasion to secure the sworn statement that would lift the reproach of murder from his name.

Meanwhile he spent the few hours that remained each day selling cargo, buying cargo, appointing a West Indian agent, watering and provisioning the ship, purchasing crates of limes, even building a pigsty and chicken coop on *Betsy*'s beautiful white deck so his men might eat fresh meat, a custom to which he deferred but for which he felt like lifting his hat and saying, "My love, I blush to treat you so." And at night, weary and tense, he could carefully audit his purchases and sales in the *Betsy*'s book of accounts. "But at least I will work so hard and trade so sharp I shall never lose you."

At length, persuaded that only their joint names would satisfy Captain Paul's touchy sense of honor, Judge Simpson and Governor Young took time from their larger affairs, met together in a room and affixed their signatures to the document on which he set such store.

This time the wording was even stronger. The judge, "being duly sworn upon the Holy Evangelists of Almighty God, deposeth and saith" that "a person in the habit of a sailor" came to him complaining that Jock had flogged him, "showing deponent his shoulders which had there the marks of several stripes but none that were either mortal or dangerous, to the best of this deponent's opinion and belief," and further that Jock had appeared on a summons before the judge and "in his vindication alleged that the said complainant had on all occasions proved very ill qualified for, as well as very negligent, in his duties, and also that he was very lazy and inactive"; on which the judge had "dismissed the complaint as frivolous." But the said complainant died afterwards, the ponderous document recorded, on board of a different vessel, and Captain Paul, "as this deponent is informed, has been accused in Great Britain as the immediate author of the said complainant's death, by means of the said stripes hereinbefore mentioned."

And then at last Jock's good name was cleared, for if the language of the law was long, it was also unmistakably explicit. Judge Simpson swore, and Governor William Young witnessed, that "this accusation, this deponent, for the sake of humanity, in the most solemn manner declares and believes to be in his judgment without any just foundation as far as relates to the stripes before mentioned; which this deponent very particularly examined, and further this deponent saith not."

So, happily, ended the matter. Jock had copies made of the precious exculpatory document and gave them to his newly appointed agent with instructions that the first fast ship sailing for England or Scotland might bear them to the people he loved or whose opinion he valued or who might be interested: his mother, Lloyd's of London, his London agent, Jonathan Beck, Mr. Craik, the Masons, the Maxwells of Kirkcudbrightshire.

In time the papers arrived, and even the Maxwells were satisfied that Jock had murdered no one.

But by that time he had — or something very near.

Even Judge Simpson had frowned, pursing his lips and shaking his head, "This was most ill-advised."

Not once but now twice Jock had refused to talk to his men on their grievance of full payment for wages earned to date. Custom prohibited it; they weren't entitled to it; he would not hear them.

A group of them, mustered behind their ringleader, marched up to him, set foot on the quarter-deck and, Billy Perkin acting as spokesman, demanded money.

Jock was in good spirits; he had just sent off the Simpson-Young deposition. "Don't speak of it now," he said amiably to them. "I know how you feel, but we're leaving Tobago today. Ask me a bit later on in the voyage. Isn't Kingston better than Rockley Bay anyhow?"

"We want it now," Perkin growled, "and we mean to have it now."

Jock saw with a start that the follow was armed with a fid, the two-foot, ten-pound version of the marlinspike, used only for splicing the heaviest of cables, needle-sharp on one end, hammer-heavy on the other, a vicious weapon.

"God damn your eyes, get off my deck!"

Perkin advanced and raised the fid threateningly.

Jock whipped out his sword.

Next morning he said to the judge, "The rascal advanced upon my point; he lunged at me, and ran himself through. It was self-defense."

But the judge took a different view. A dozen witnesses were ready to swear that Jock had lunged first, with a face like the devil's, crimson with rage and yelling a curse that was heard from stem to stern on the *Betsy*. Moreover, compounding the difficulty, the death had occurred in port, where a captain's authority might be questioned, not on the high seas where a captain's authority was never questioned.

"Whatever the facts of the case, Captain Paul, one fact is plain: William Perkin is dead and your sword it was that pierced his heart. This is beyond my jurisdiction; the full admiralty court will have to sit in judgment on this action."

"Then indict me and let them judge me forthwith! My conscience is clear. Has not a man the right to defend himself?"

"Assuredly he has," Judge Simpson said, "and when the judges complete their circuit of the islands and reconvene to sit again in Tobago, I have no doubt they will find in your favor."

"When will that be?" Jock said.

Judge Simpson said, "Six months hence, as I believe. But do not worry. Though the matter is grave, rest assured they will clear you."

It was a comfort to know he would be cleared. But it was maddening to face the onset of bankruptcy that must inevitably come if *Betsy* lay idle six months in Rockley Bay, growing a lush crop of barnacles on her hull while the learned justices completed their leisurely circuit back to Tobago. Next day he went to see his newly appointed West Indian agent. "I'm afraid the situation is awkward, Captain Paul, but by no means irretrievable. I really do not know what to advise at the moment." The agent smiled and bowed him out with every mark of respect. Jock had now been formally charged.

The next day a bailiff served Jock with a warrant that confined him to his ship pending trial, and Tobagan constables with muskets patrolled the wharf lest the *Betsy* sail. Jock was lucky, one of the sentries said, to be allowed such commodious quarters; he should see the local jail!

Jock's heart broke. Discipline was impossible. For the crew, mutinous, unpaid (Jock would not budge an inch), unemployed — what work was there to do? They would not do it anyway — had a strangle hold on their captain: the men and the ship degenerated.

One morning Chima showed him a butcher knife, obviously stolen from the galley.

"Where did you get this?"

"The man let it drop."

"What man?"

"The man who was at your door last night."

Jock was not overly surprised.

"Was he sober?"

"Oh no, master."

"Did you hurt him?"

"A little bit."

And the next day Judge Simpson came down to the wharf and went aboard to talk to Captain Paul.

"I fully realize your difficulties, sir, but it's no good compounding a felony. I cannot counsel you too strongly to await your trial with patience and not to bring upon yourself more trouble than you already have."

"What am I supposed to have done now?"

"My dear Captain, I am sure you did not do it. In fact, I doubt whether any human being could have done it. But one of your men appeared in my chambers and exhibited a curious wound. This man said —" The judge paused, at a loss for words. "He alleged that you had bitten him. It looked like the work of the fangs of a beast. He was drunk, and I summoned a physician to treat him and took no judicial action. But it would be wise for a person in your situation to act with great circumspection."

"Maybe a wolf bit him," Jock said, "and maybe he deserved it."

"There are," said Judge Simpson, "no wolves on Tobago."

"I shall act with circumspection," Jock said. "Am I permitted to see my agent?"

"My dear Captain," the judge assured him, "you may see anyone you please. The only thing required of you is that you stay aboard your ship until the court returns."

"I am most grateful for your visit," Jock said.

His face, Simpson thought, was that of a man sick with the fever. "Are you feeling quite yourself, Captain Paul?"

"Yes, thank you."

"Then I shall say good day to you. Remember my words. They are kindly meant."

"I understand."

Jock knew what he must do.

Order and discipline were at an end. The men had stolen from persons ashore or got into the grog butts or both; somehow they had found the means to make themselves drunk without money. The decks of the *Betsy* were fouled with spittle, her rigging drooped, her cargo was rotting, uncared for. Every disease that a ship can suffer when her master is discredited now afflicted the *Betsy*. What would she be like by the time her captain was acquitted?

He knew he must lose her. What is it like to lose an arm, a leg? Men had been caught in mantraps and severed such members to save their lives. What is it like to lose your heart? And yet there was a chance that by paying a very high price he might save her.

He summoned his agent aboard. "I find myself in a difficult quandary," he said.

The agent smiled toothily. "Aye, Captain, we know. The whole town knows."

"I should like to hear what you have to advise for a man in a situation like mine."

"Well, Captain —" The agent looked over his shoulder and sunk his voice to a conspiratorial level.

No sympathy existed for Captain Paul in Rockley Bay, the agent said, where he was considered a tyrant if not a murderer. He ticked off the deaths: Maxwell, the docker, Billy Perkin. "Of course *I* know that these unfortunate accidents cannot justly be laid at your door. But not till the court reconvenes will everyone else know. That is six months hence."

"The time is exactly five months and two weeks. It is not necessary to remind me, sir, that my ship will be reduced to a hulk and my cargo eaten by worms long before that time."

"It is a pleasure to watch over the interests of a client who is a realist. I was coming to exactly that aspect of the situation." His eye glinted greedily. Jock braced himself to pay the price.

The situation was not unprecedented, the agent said. Many ship captains in West Indian waters availed themselves of the services of their friends ashore, their agents, when difficulties arose. What were friends for but to give advice? And the advice in this case was certainly to disappear for six months, then return, stand trial, be acquitted and resume one's normal activity, whatever it was. Others had done it; why not he?

Meanwhile the *Betsy* would not rot. One's agent would take her over, keep her shipshape and operate her till her owner should return.

"When I do, and when I am acquitted, my greatest concern will be that she be returned to me."

"If you do return," the agent said smiling, "and if you are acquitted, I do not see how I could possibly *not* return her, do you?"

"During my absence I expect you will demand all the profit she earns."

"I should think that only fair. It is very expensive to run a shipping company," the agent said. "There will be, in addition, certain gratuities I shall have to make to the authorities lest their irritation at your sudden inaccessibility should lead them to confiscate your ship as the property of a felon condemned in advance *in absentia* by his flight."

Jock was prepared for that too.

"Just so I get her back! Just so I get her back!"

"Sir, I give you my word."

"You'll wash her clean? You'll stone her decks? You'll sun her canvas? You'll sweeten her bilges?"

"Sweeten the *bilges?*"

"Boiling vinegar, sir; and if the mold is bad, burn sulphur!"

"Oh yes, of course. I've heard of such steps. Yes, indeed, I'll attend to all that."

"Then take her till I return."

"Where do you plan to go?"

Anywhere was possible, the agent said. He had several clients who would be glad to take him aboard secretly. Had Captain Paul ever visited Africa, India, Madagascar? Delightful places, hard to reach. One need not fear molestation.

"They are somewhat remote. I expect to return to stand trial. I intend to go to Trinidad."

Perhaps, the agent thought, Captain Paul really did mean to return: he wished to depart only twenty miles distant!

"Nothing could be easier. I have an excellent associate in Trinidad. A launch will draw alongside your ship at any time you decide. Would three o'clock in the morning be convenient? They will be Tobagans, thoroughly dependable, but it would be best not to discuss your plans with them. The sentries should be tired at that hour, and a little gratuity, which I shall provide, will put them quite asleep."

"I shall want to take my man."

"That would be a kindness. I doubt if he'd live very long after your departure."

The boat was late, but just before dawn it appeared, a silent smudge of blacker black against the black water. Jock let himself over the side on a line, as if he were a thief escaping from a house he had robbed. Men with dark faces, speaking no word, dressed in black, rowed him and Chima out to a Spanish fishing smack that was anchored outside the bay.

The violent sun of the tropics arose; in the distance a spit of land hid all but the masts of the *Betsy*, slender and tall and beautiful. It was too far now for the spidery tracery of her rigging to be visible. Jock was glad that his parting glimpse was not to see slack lines.

At her peak the British flag drooped mournfully.

Jock stood a long time watching her from the taffrail of the smack, which was wearing a little to the southward. As the smack gathered speed and his eyes remained riveted on the motionless *Betsy*'s masts, a queer and distressing optical illusion took place: neither he nor the *Betsy* was moving, but the spit of land seemed to slide in between them and grow and separate them with cruel finality; then, as the spit of sliding land rose slowly along its length to a very great height, the *Betsy* seemed to be sinking, sinking into a hideous wave of solid rock. The British flag was the last to go down. It must have been left out all night; certainly he had not seen it hoisted at dawn; it had hung there sodden and forgotten at the moment the dark had begun to dissolve into half visibility.

Jock wondered whether the court would really convene a half year hence. He wondered how long thereafter he must wait for acquittal. He wondered how long a time must pass till once more he would walk his own quarter-deck, and whether the learned justices would permit him to discipline the lubber who had left the flag out overnight. He wondered if he would sail again under that drooping ensign or whether it would have rotted at the mast before he regained his ship.

Perhaps he had wondered out loud.

An oddly familiar voice at his shoulder spoke, "If I were you I'd shoot the confounded rag off its confounded stick!"

Chapter 29

JOCK TURNED to find Don Jesu's eyes compassionately upon him. "I know how it feels to lose your ship," he said.

296

Jock would not have recognized him. Don Jesu was heavier in the face, his skin was pale from lack of sunshine, and he was rapidly growing a paunch. Gone was the fine gentleman of the *Virgen de la Paz* with his superelegant marquesa on his arm. Here was a Spanish fisherman, barefooted, lank hair bound up in a yellow bandana, and round his belly a screaming-purple cummerbund which served as a holster for a brace of pistols.

But the fisherman's disguise did not deceive Jock's eye, which was trained along with its other skills to see through defects of costume: the fisherman's rags were too clean, the pearl-handled pistols were perfectly matched and worth over a hundred guineas. And the irrepressible Don Jesu wore all his rings.

In spite of Jock's deep affliction of spirit he could not keep back a smile. "For a moment I feared you had fallen on evil days," he said. "I thank Providence that you have not."

"In a way I have," Don Jesu grunted. "Come below, Captain. I could do with a drink, and so could you."

On a handsome teakwood table Don Jesu set out two bottles, the violent pitching of the little boat making glasses impracticable: whisky for Jock, rum for himself. "We haven't much time," he said, glancing resignedly through the solid paneling of the cabin in the direction of Trinidad. "I am not permitted to drink at home." And lest he cast a reflection on the temperance dictates of his strong-minded marquesa he hurriedly added, "A bishop is coming to dinner; so is the viceregal lieutenant governor and the mayor of the town. Alas! I am borne down by such a burden of provincial respectability as no man has ever suffered before! I am moon-faced. I am fat as a poisoned cow. I am pale as a corpse and as motionless. My dear Captain Paul, you behold in me the woefulest gentleman of fortune that ever drew breath. The only fun I have had for months was coming over to save you. *Por Dios,* but we sailormen are helpless ashore!"

"What angel informed you of my troubles?"

"Angel, sir? That sharping trickstering devil of an agent of yours! And the British authorities connive along with him. What a golden opportunity you gave them to lay hands on your property! England needs ships now as she never did before; in three weeks your *Betsy* will be a sloop of war in the Royal Navy. King George wants fast vessels like yours. The best way is to steal them under the guise of lawful confiscation. Did you suppose for an instant that you would be brought to trial? Never! In a very few days you would have been removed to die quickly of rot in the jail-house of Rockley Bay."

Jock's face grew grim and wretched.

Don Jesu said, "Of course, there *is* a way, if you want her back so sorely. I could sink their stupid customs vessel, and we could make off with her. Would you like me to do that, my friend? It presents a tempting adventure."

Jock stared at him. "Sail your *Virgen de la Paz* into Tobago, shoot up the harbor, seize my ship? Good God, no! You'd start a war."

Don Jesu sighed. "No, not a war, not in the present posture of the world. But it would certainly cause a scandal, and the marquesa would be highly irritated. She'd scold me for days. Ah well; there is no escape that way."

"Even my ship isn't worth all that," Jock said.

"The world," Don Jesu declared sententiously, his tongue loosening with rum, "is as full of ships as of women. It is my considered opinion, sir, and I have had months to do nothing but consider opinions, that one is as good as another. My advice to you, sir, is to change both often. Become a slave to none. I drink your health!" He tipped the bottle and toasted Jock in a pull that lowered the level a full inch. "Oh dear me," he said, "this must stop. The marquesa — I mean, the bishop — would never approve." Cursing, he corked the bottle and locked it away.

"We shall have to settle one small social matter before we go ashore," he resumed in a businesslike tone. "Since you prefer not to cause an international incident it might be wise to adopt a different name. The viceregal lieutenant governor is liberal in his views, but it would embarrass him to sit down at the dinner table with a fugitive from a murder charge. He might feel compelled to return you to Tobago. Who shall you be, sir? An American, I should think. We prefer them to Englishmen. And a sea captain, of course, *Santísima!* What else could you be? How shall I present you? Captain John Smith? There was one, I believe, in American history. That will sound most distinguished, and yet Smith is so common a name that you will be respectably anonymous."

"No, I've a friend named James Smith," Jock said. "He has misfortunes to hide in his own life; I should not like to involve him in mine. He has a brother in North Carolina; both are in the shipping business. Smith strikes too close, I'm afraid."

"By all means we must not make enemies of Smiths who can aid you," Don Jesu said, "especially the Smith in North Carolina. Smith is quite out of the question."

"I never heard of anybody named Jones," Jock said.

"Neither did I. Jones it shall be. John Paul Jones, I salute you."

"You've still kept the John Paul," Jock said grimly. He had lost his ship. Now he must lose his name.

"So I did; from force of habit. Let it be simply Captain Jones. But no, that is a bit *too* insignificant for his excellency. You just do not look like an insignificant person. At least you must have initials. You are Captain J. P. Jones."

And as Captain J. P. Jones Jock met the bishop, the viceregal lieutenant governor and the mayor, who questioned him politely on American affairs about which Jock had no recent information. But since he knew only such Spanish as any sailor picks up from foreign crewmen and since the entire conversation had to filter through Don Jesu, who interpreted it and amplified it, Captain Jones learned a great deal. Revolution in America was brewing fast.

England was sending more troops to cow her rebellious subjects. New York, that thriving metropolis of twenty-five thousand, offered plenty of buildings that could be used as barracks, but the soldiers were quartered in homes, a great nuisance and expense to the householders, to whose womenfolk they were intentionally rude and to whose owners they were purposely arrogant, just to show who was master.

In retaliation, state after state in their local assemblies voted formal resolutions to export nothing to England, to import nothing from her. Legal trade languished. Smuggling now grew to the stature of a respectable profession, encouraged by colonial law.

Retaliation followed upon retaliation. The port of Boston was closed and blockaded by British frigates; other ports were threatened with similar paralyzing punishment. Fights developed between ships at sea; whole crews who had never set foot on British soil were impressed as deserters from the Royal Navy. Smuggling became privateering, and privateering became piracy: British ships were the usual victims, but no flag was safe.

The one strong man who might have brought order out of such chaos and lawlessness, a man who had successfully done it before, was not available. Lord Clive, the ruthless empire builder who had crushed the natives of India, was approached by the king to crush the colonists of America by his well-tried tactics of terror. But the king was informed that Lord Clive, having taken to eating opium, was now discovered to have blown out his brains.

Then in one stunningly shrewd maneuver England surrounded her nasty colonial children with deadly enemies. Canada, alien in race and religion, was only recently part of the British Empire; Americans had helped much in her conquest; she disliked the British, but she hated her American neighbors. Suddenly England, by an Act of Parliament, declared that loyal Canada henceforth should extend from the Allegheny Mountains to the Mississippi River, and from the Gulf of Mexico to the North Pole. The colonial states hemmed in by Catholic Canadians and savage Indians!

This was an act which the bishop highly approved, for it squeezed the Protestant Americans into a thin long indefensible strip between their mountains and the sea: he looked sternly at Jock, for Captain J. P. Jones had been at a loss how to cross himself at grace and was probably a Protestant.

The viceregal lieutenant governor, on the other hand, went out of his way to be pleasant to Jock; for he saw in Captain J. P. Jones one of those angry Americans whose quarrel with the mother country had opened the first small crack in the mighty British Empire. It was a crack which Spain, together with half the world, would like to see widened so they could rush in and rend that Empire to pieces. "Let your people just go a bit further," his excellency said, "and I dare say you will be surprised how many friends you have."

At this point Don Jesu asked something in long and fluent Spanish which he did not translate for Jock. Leyla, at the other end of the table, looked at her husband reproachfully and lowered her eyes. She was very close to tears, Jock thought, but her face was difficult to read.

The governor replied to Don Jesu in equally mysterious Spanish but with shrugging shoulders and brilliant smiles. It was perfect pantomime. Whatever Don Jesu had asked, the governor was answering, "My dear sir, it is not that I disapprove; I simply cannot approve officially."

The bishop also seemed to approve, and at the end of the supper his grave Latin benediction seemed to extend to Jock, at whom he now nodded and smiled.

"I have been permitted," Don Jesu said excitedly to Jock, "to play my part against the cruel British oppressors of liberty. *Amigo!* I can fight again! Will you come with me?"

"All the confounded bishop required," Don Jesu said, scurrying happily about his ship, "was that I remove her name. He deemed *Virgen de la Paz* unsuitable for a privateer. Ha! Ha! Ha! His reverend lordship did not know I had ripped it off three weeks ago. Before he left last night I presented the letters to him. 'For your chapel,' said I. 'Very heavy,' said he.

'Pure and solid,' said I, 'like the True Faith.' 'Bless you,' said he, and sent his servant off for a brace of his monks to lug them up to his church. He would not trust my men for some reason."

Don Jesu had made other changes too in his ship. Gone were her square transocean sails: she was now clipper-rigged. A glance at the ship's new trim would have revealed to Jock the waters in which she would sail even if he had not already known: square sails sent one bowling down the wind with the steady trades or a dependable monsoon astern: the Atlantic, the Pacific, the Indian Oceans. But a fore-and-aft rig like a schooner's was best for close in-sailing of American waters where one habitually cut across the prevailing westerlies. And the coast of colonial America, Don Jesu said grinning, was now where all the fun could be found. One could also, he stated practically, add to one's fortune there. Troops were paid in specie, especially the hard-headed Hessians whom England had begun to import: mercenaries always demanded cash.

Don Jesu's commission from the governor was not in writing. Relations between Spain and England were not as yet sufficiently strained to warrant the issuance of formal letters of marque. Hence Don Jesu's position was not that of a properly commissioned privateer; he could claim that distinction only by courtesy; if things went wrong, Spain could always repudiate him, and England, if England caught him, could hang every man aboard his black ship as a pirate at Execution Dock, and many such in these troublesome times were so hanged.

Don Jesu was not worried. The ex-*Virgen de la Paz*, now once again nameless, could sail circles around most British warships; and to those too heavily armed she could simply show her heels.

Manned, armed and provisioned, the sleek craft slid out of her Trinidad base, with Leyla standing gray-faced on the quay, a fantastic pink lace parasol held over her head by a slave and the little marqués beside her waving his chubby hand and piping a childish treble, "*Adios, Papito, adios, adios, adios . . .*"

"Motives are never unmixed, Señor Jones," Don Jesu said, swallowing a stubborn lump in his throat and waving good-by to his son, "but I think that if I were asked I should be forced to confess that I have never felt freer in my life than I do at this moment. It is said in America that only to be free is to be happy."

"That I verily believe," Jock said.

There followed the things Jock never told, the things he would like to forget, the things he had to forget, things that in time to come he himself could never believe had occurred. Sanity is a kindly mistress, he would muse, to those who possess her; only a mental scavenger roots among rotting events of the past which she mercifully buries. Things probably happened in the lives of all men at which Honor and Sanity shuddered; but if at the end of life the average was not too bad, perhaps the All-Wise might not judge one too harshly. So might one think at life's end; so might one hope when the sordidness was actually happening, recalling how one's gardener father had mixed with the soil stuff that stank but out of which growth was achieved.

There was the time when Don Jesu fell in with the British frigate. She was three times his size and she heavily outgunned him. At close quarters she could have blasted him out of the water. Not the slightest advantage could be expected from an engagement with her. But since her heavy guns could not reach him, since she was slower than he and no other ship was in view, she presented an excellent target to practice on. Don Jesu felt he could do with a bit of amusement and at the same time give his men some drill.

All day long, standing just out of range, laughing at the fountains of spray her short-falling broadsides sent up around him, he peppered her with chain shot. "The great thing is to destroy the rigging," he said. Jock saw British sailors dropping like spiders from broken webs as they bravely attempted to repair the damage under the leisurely target practice. It was a fine clear day, the wind was light. They fell, presumably, sixty feet to the hard deck below. At length a lucky shot cracked the frigate's foremast; it teetered a full harrowing minute before it fell toward the bows; from a distance it looked as if a giant had crushed a handful of match sticks and tossed them carelessly over the fore parts of the ship.

"Who laid the gun that did that?" Don Jesu cried gleefully.

"I did," Jock said.

"A beautiful shot, sir."

"It was a lucky shot."

"Didn't you aim for the mast?"

"Certainly. A miss either side would have done damage."

"Then it was not a lucky shot, Señor Jones. What an eye you have!"

"What a gun."

"Yes, I am proud of my guns."

Having had his sport, Don Jesu sailed round the cripple twice and took off with an impudent parting shot, leaving her to unsnarl her upper works and bury her dead.

On another occasion he fought a brig in a fair fight and sank her, letting those of her crew who still lived go free, giving them his longboat and launch and plenty of provisions, and a chart to guide them to land.

"She was French!" Jock protested.

"That's why I set her crew free," Don Jesu said, grinning.

"We have no quarrel with France."

Don Jesu shrugged. "I did not believe her flag."

But though he had freed the French crew, to survive if they could in the open boats, he savagely hanged one sailor, a member of his own crew. A powder monkey had fainted, perhaps through fatigue, perhaps as a result of malaria, for he had a yellow skin. This cut the chain of powder-passing and delayed for a moment the servicing of a gun. For a week the slender youthful body dangled from a yardarm's end. Then seagulls attacking the carrion, the neck ripped apart, and head and body splashed separately into the sea, sweeping rapidly astern with a cloud of shrieking gulls circling and diving upon them. "When will your son, the marqués, reach the age of fifteen like the powder boy?" Jock asked. Don Jesu snarled, "Discipline must be maintained. The marqués will never go to sea."

He brooded and sulked and would not speak to Jock for days. Then, the mood lifting, he remarked defensively, "I was not born like you with salt in my veins. At heart I hate the sea. Ships were no love for me at first, only an escape. Did you know, sir, that for years I was seasick?"

There was the incident of the Yankee smuggler. A British man-of-war had engaged a small American ship and, having disabled and looted her, left her to sink at her pleasure with all aboard. Somehow she had managed to plug the holes in her riddled hull and, with a makeshift mast and a tattered sail, was wallowing in the general direction of the American coast, sluggish as a sick sea turtle. Don Jesu did not waste time.

"Shoot me down that stupid stick, Señor Jones. I want her boats. I foolishly gave away mine."

Jock aimed well above the hull so as not to injure the men, and missed. "Use chain!"

"I might puncture the boats," Jock said, and loaded again with solid shot. Chain scattered.

"You ought to be a priest!" Don Jesu said disgustedly. But he slapped Jock's back and shouted for joy when Jock cleanly severed the mast with his next ball.

Behind the bulkheads the desperate Americans, cruelly and overwhelmingly attacked not once but twice in two days, took cover, took aim with long rifles and prepared to die fighting.

Drawing near, while cutlasses began to glint aboard the little American craft, which expected instant boarding and death, Don Jesu said, "Speak them, Señor Jones. They'll believe your Scotch accent quicker than mine," and ordered the friendly flag of France run up. Till then he had attacked under British colors.

Jock shouted, "We want your boats, na mair! We are friends!"

Under the muzzles of their rifles he set out alone in a small workboat and rowed himself over to the American ship. "They won't fire on one lone man," he had said. "Not Americans."

"Nobody would," Don Jesu had said. "Not if the one lone man had my guns behind him."

Grateful to be permitted to live, the Yankee smugglers gave up all their boats, of which they had several for the purpose of sneaking ashore on dark nights to pick up contraband.

"I doubt you've need for your rifles," Jock said. "Permit me the loan of a dozen or so."

They would willingly have surrendered the lot.

"Why did you bring back these things?" Don Jesu asked.

Jock said, "They shoot farther and sharper than any that our men have. Even an African trader, if my memory serves me, coveted one and was willing to exchange for it an object of priceless value."

"You've a very impudent tongue," Don Jesu said.

In return Don Jesu liberally supplied the Americans with medical stores to treat their wounded and gave them new timber and canvas to rig another jury mast. Then, leading his men in a cheer, *Viva los Yanquis!* he treated the Americans to the third flag they had seen on his black ship, ran up the skull and crossbones and left them in a state of understandable perplexity.

There was the time when, after a storm, they found a British merchantman separated from her convoy. She was big, but heavily laden and poorly armed. Don Jesu fired at long range, shredding her sails. He skipped round her and raked her fore and aft. Her spars crumpled and splintered; a mast split, toppled. Jock silenced her forward deck gun with grape, uprooting it from its base. The gun crew already lay slaughtered around it. The ship was soon reduced to utter helplessness.

"I want her rudder," Jock said.

"She can't maneuver now," Don Jesu said.

"It's a fearsome thing to lose a rudder," Jock said.

"As you please."

Don Jesu took his ship in a swift close swipe past her stern. Swiveling the forward gun, Jock pumped solid shot into her after parts till her rudder-post burst asunder, then sent a volley of grape and chain into her great cabin. This was one engagement he did not regret. There would be cargo and specie aboard the merchantman.

She struck, and Don Jesu's crew with cocked pistols leveled at the heads of the prisoners, forced them to row back and forth between the ships, transshipping the prize's cargo: powder, arms and provisions; grog, water, canvas, sail-needles and twine; tools, pump gaskets, the quadrant, the charts; all the excellent and essential equipment that England knew so well how to provide. With a little luck a privateer need never go back to home port. And some fascinating chests of money that had been destined as pay for the Hessian troops. During this time, while Jock oversaw the transfer, Don Jesu went aboard the prize and chatted amiably with her commander, praising his sherry and giving him much friendly advice on the shortest course to a safe haven.

When the transfer was completed, Don Jesu said, "Señor Jones, would you go below and see to the storing of the stores? You are so much more expert at that sort of thing than I."

While Jock was below, he heard cannon fire. Fearing another ship might have come up, he hurried to the deck. The merchantman was just disappearing below the surface of the waves, her commander awash to his knees in his grave on his down-tilting quarter-deck, screaming curses at Don Jesu.

"Prisoners are awkward," Don Jesu said. "How can one feed them properly?"

Jock could not bring the dead back to life.

"And now, Señor Jones," Don Jesu said, rubbing his hands, "let us count the specie. I fancy a great many British soldiers will not get their pay this month."

There was the incident to which Don Jesu referred afterwards as "the day we took the explosives aboard." And yet, but for that incident, he might have remained at sea two years instead of one.

They came across an unescorted ship flying the little-known blue-and-white flag of Greece. "There is no such thing! The blackguard is under false colors!" Don Jesu scoffed, who flew none of his own. Jock sent a warning shot across her bows and the Greek hove to. Down dropped her mysterious colors; up shot the white flag of surrender, begging for quarter. On her poop deck occurred an extraordinary waving and fluttering of kerchiefs, petticoats, lacy nightwear and other mysterious female garments. She was full of women.

Boarding her, Don Jesu discovered her to be French, returning with a cargo of young colonial girls whose American fathers no longer desired their daughters to remain in fashionable English schools. He sank her, taking aboard the girls, some brandy, gunpowder and other essentials.

The girls caused trouble. It had been a year since Don Jesu's Spanish crew had set eyes on a woman. Don Jesu was forced to set sentries night and day on the cabin in which they were locked. "If only my foolish men could imagine the fate that I save them from!" he said.

But chests of silver and gold were piling up in the great cabin. The crew could claim their share. To add to this close and tempting treasure, now came the women.

"It is too much for flesh and blood to bear," Jock said.

Don Jesu said, "God damn the flesh and blood!"

But he put about and shaped his course back to Trinidad, setting the troublesome females ashore on the coast of Long Island near Patchogue, a desolate sandy waste where no one ever went or ever would go, but where there were no Indians and from which even a girl could find her way to safety with many an exaggerated tale to tell, no doubt, of the perils through which she had passed.

In Trinidad the piled-up chests of treasure speedily dwindled; there were so many to divide the treasure among. The men had their shares, which reduced it by half. A gratuity, very large, had to be presented to the viceregal lieutenant governor, who in turn must present a gratuity to the governor, who said he must split his with the viceroy of New Spain himself. Nor must one forget the bishop's charities. And the ship required a thorough overhaul.

But even so, something remained. In the name of John Paul Jones, Jock made deposits in his European banking accounts. Don Jesu said, "Surely one name or the other will serve you in times of distress, which I pray will never afflict you. I see no reason now why you should not live like a gentleman, of some fortune indeed, all your days. But never," he warned, "disclose the source of your funds."

"It isn't likely I shall," Jock said.

"I meant," Don Jesu said stiffly, "the fact that you possess assets in safe Italian banking establishments of which no one is aware."

Don Jesu's marquesa had grown very devout and strait-laced in his long

306

absence. She entreated him not to go to sea again, but she seemed prepared to accept the fact that he would, prompted by the viceregal lieutenant-governor, who praised her husband's doughty blows against the British oppressors of liberty. It seemed to Jock that Don Jesu, especially when he was with his son, wavered in his resolve; but the marquesa found out about the shipload of girls and returned to the subject again and again with the searching persistence of a Grand Inquisitor: Had he actually kept them under lock and key? Who had the key? Didn't they ever eat? Who carried in the food? Had he kept close watch on the carpenter's tools? Wasn't a saw ever missing to saw through a deck from below? What, not even a gimlet to bore a peekhole?

"By God, madam," Don Jesu exploded, "the next time I salvage a cargo of confounded females I shall give them the run of the ship, personally service every damned one of the cats and throw them into the sea!"

During this exchange Jock had left the room, for by now he had picked up enough Spanish to catch the import of the conversation, and he was aware that the rift between Don Jesu and Leyla was deep. Don Jesu's pride would not suffer an outsider to know of it. As for Leyla, she would have expired of shame or performed some startling Circassian act of vengeance or self-destruction.

It was good to remember later that Don Jesu and the marquesa had made up their differences during their last few days together, walking arm in arm in the gardens in the evening or holding the hands of their son between them, listening to the bells of the bishop's church on the hill, drinking the chilled fruit juice that the marquesa believed was so much better for one than rum. And in truth Don Jesu drank it very bravely. He did everything bravely.

He died bravely.

Strange flags had begun to appear in American waters. There was a flag exactly like the British flag except that large white letters of the word LIBERTY were sewn onto it. There was an extremely confusing white flag with a yellow pine tree in the center and across the top, almost too small to be legible, the long phrase AN APPEAL TO LIBERTY, which could be read only when the wind blew so hard as to hold the flag stiff as a board. There was a flag with a rattlesnake, a flag composed entirely of red and white stripes counting up to thirteen; another had thirteen blue and white stripes. There were long-forgotten flags of the states that had not been used for a century, now resurrected and flown again in the face of England. For these were the flags, however makeshift and hard to recognize, that Americans of many states were inventing, independently of one another, to show their abhorrence of Great Britain. But as yet there was no war. Anything wild, strange and confusing, Don Jesu at length concluded, probably designated an American ship; and unless he was prepared to hang his first mate, the best gunner he had ever had, it was prudent for him not to fire on her.

These strange flags had to be approached with caution, for they were quick to fire first. Of all the flags in his own commodious locker Don Jesu found his French one the most respected when he approached to ask the nationality of some ship that flew queer new colors. Somewhat fretfully he agreed to steer clear of these vessels, many of which presented tempting prizes, and hunt only those that flew Britain's flag, which had at least the merit of being recognizable. "What I especially dislike about the situation," Don Jesu complained, "is that it presents such an opportunity for deception."

One day Jock sighted through the glass a ship about the size of Don Jesu's own. She was hermaphrodite rigged, hence a tolerable sailer both on and before the wind, but Jock judged her a little too broad in the beam to have quite the speed of Don Jesu's. To Don Jesu, who stood beside him and trusted his eyes, Jock relayed his description.

"Hermaphrodites maneuver slower than I," Don Jesu said, liking his chances already.

"Some of her ports are painted on. It is very well done, but some at least are false."

"Good, good," Don Jesu said grinning, his petulance fading fast at the prospect of a fight. "Well, Mister Tender Conscience, is your captain permitted to give his men some exercise, money, fun? What flag does she show, sir? What flag?"

"Nothing yet."

"We'll force her to."

Don Jesu ran up the British flag.

Instantly the stranger responded with the same.

Don Jesu roared a torrent of rapid orders, the ship sprang to action, the men shouting and laughing. In these many-flagged days they had not taken a prize for a long time and were beginning to grumble how small their shares might be at the end of so cautious a voyage.

Don Jesu presented a much-changed aspect from the pallid paunchy landsman who had got the lieutenant-governor's connivance and the bishop's benediction to sail as a privateer months before in Trinidad. Now he was lean, lithe and brown as when Jock had first met him. Today his diamond and his smile sparkled as they had in Africa. On the quarter-deck in front of all his men, who shouted applause and cheered him, he threw his arms around Jock and kissed him on both cheeks.

"At last you permit me to fight, Captain Paul!" In his jubilation he had forgotten that Jock had a new name. "For a time I was afraid you were trying to reform me like — no matter like whom." He crowded on sail and approached the stranger. The featureless shore of Long Island was in sight. There was a light onshore wind. The stranger was to leeward, between Don Jesu and the land; he wanted to keep her so.

She recognized her inferior fighting position and tried to improve it, taking a tack to seaward to give herself room to maneuver. This presented her bow. She had not counted on the black ship's range.

"Fool, fool, fool!" Don Jesu exulted.

Just within gunshot he raked her, his guns charged with grape and chain. Her ugly foresail began to show rents and holes, but even more serious, the shot passed through and cut critical rigging behind. Suddenly she came aback. In a stronger wind she would have snapped her foremast. As it was, she simply stopped dead in the water. "Sexless monstrosity!" Don Jesu yelled. "You cannot even hug a wind!"

He gave her one broadside of solid ball; then, while she struggled to sheer off and make way, he swooped round her, returned, and emptied the iron of the guns of his other side into her hull. The ships were now very close. The stranger was snarled above and leaking below, Don Jesu's familiar pattern; the pitiful false ports, so ingeniously painted on, had opened at last, from the outside, burst in by shattering cannonade.

She struck; Don Jesu's crew cheered. Jock left his post at the forward guns, which had wrought such havoc in the stranger's rigging, and ran to the quarter-deck. Don Jesu ordered cease fire.

But she struck in a strange and abnormal manner. Not only did the British flag come down; the azure-lilied banner of Bourbon France went up.

"She has chosen a peculiar moment to change her nationality," Don Jesu observed in a puzzled tone.

Then an overwrought sailor on the surrendering ship, young or untrained or unnerved by perhaps his first fight, did a monstrous thing. He was stationed by the chasing gun on the forecastle head of the ship, a small caliber, long-range piece. By accident or otherwise he touched his match to the vent. The gun fired.

Don Jesu was standing directly in line of the ball, which was about as big as those croquet balls that were so fashionable among young ladies and gouty old gentlemen, which Don Jesu would now never live to be: it neatly severed his right arm, not as a surgeon would have amputated it, but arm and shoulder too. Where his shoulder should have been was a clean-cut concavity, exactly fitting the roundness of the ball. The force of the impact spun him bodily thrice around like a ballet dancer before he fell. His arm dropped twenty feet away; another inch would have carried it over the side. It chanced to have fallen against the quarter-deck rail. In a brainless muscular contraction the hand with all its jeweled rings was closing on a stanchion of the rail.

To slow the horrid gush of blood if only a little, Jock lifted Don Jesu to a sitting position, while horrified crewmen rushed up, pressed arteries with their fingers, attempted to tie a tourniquet round his chest.

"I can't breathe," Don Jesu said. "You're stifling me. Take off that confounded rag."

Out of habit they obeyed; it was useless anyhow.

Looking at Jock, Don Jesu said, "I am a dead man, am I not?"

Jock tried in vain to reply.

"Answer me, *amigo*."

"Aye," Jock said, "I fear so."

"Bless you for not lying. But I knew. I knew when I could not see my shoulder. Where is my arm?"

He turned his head and saw it gripping the rail.

"See how fast I hold!" He smiled. "I do not fall overboard!"

He tried to raise his rapidly failing voice to its old roar of command. "You there, ho! Bring me my arm!"

A sailor took hold of it. So white did the bloodless knuckles appear, so firm had he thought the grip to be, that he wrenched at it forcibly, as if it would resist. It did not; it meekly relinquished its hold.

"Treat me gently!" Don Jesu commanded. "Well, fellow? Give it to me!"

How does one present to a man his severed arm when he demands it? The sailor gaped foolishly.

Don Jesu reached out and took his arm and hugged it to his breast.

"Thank you," he said courteously.

He was motionless for a moment except for his labored gasping, silent perhaps for the eternity of silence that lay some few heartbeats away. Then a last passion shook him. He stirred and muttered, "Sink me that scoundrel who flew false colors!"

The men growled fiercely, "Aye!"

"*Amigo?*"

Perhaps his glazing eyes no longer saw.

310

"I am here," Jock said, holding him tighter.

"Pickle me in a butt of rum and take me home to my son. Let my marquesa bury me in holy ground. The bishop will not deny me that."

"I will, Don Jesu."

"I hear in your tone that you will not."

"I will. On my sacred honor I swear I will."

"No, do not swear. It is better otherwise. I shall present a fearsome sight for a child by then. The marquesa could never abide the smell of rum. But do not bury me at sea. *Do not bury me at sea!*"

He bled to death rapidly.

Book Two
The American Dawn

Chapter 30

DURING THE TIME that Don Jesu had lain dying on the deck, a chorus of pleading voices had risen from the stranger: "It was an accident! We shot the gunner who did it! See! His body! Quarter! Quarter!"

But no one had listened and no one had looked. The ships slowly drifted apart.

When Don Jesu died and Jock's stricken senses returned, he heard the anguished cries from the French ship floating over the water. No Englishman spoke with so sure an accent; there could be no doubt that she was French.

"Your black ship is known!" came the cries. "We saw your flag; we flew the same; we did not want to fight! Look here!"

They held up the limp body of the offending gunner and, lest the pistol wound in his face be invisible across the widening distance, they thrust cutlasses through the corpse to prove that it was dead.

"It was an accident!" Jock cried. "Accidents happen!"

The crew shoved him aside. Without a command, animated by a single desire for vengeance, as if Don Jesu were still alive instructing the gunners, organizing the boarding parties, the men leaped to their arms and grappling hooks and brought their ship alongside the Frenchman.

Now Jock learned something that Don Jesu had known by instinct: when a hundred and twenty men know exactly what they want, no officer can hold them back.

Screaming like maniacs, scorning firearms as too merciful, with cutlasses in their hands and dirks in their teeth, with butcher knives, crowbars, pump handles and boat hooks, they swarmed over the Frenchman's side; they battered and hacked her men to pieces. There was a woman aboard, the wife of a junior officer. Standing in line, reeking with blood of the slaughter, they raped her till some of them, feeling her cold, said, "She must be dead," and kicked her and spat on her. But cold she was not to be buried. They set fire to the ship, starting it in the woman's cabin. The Frenchman went down in a pillar of smoke and fire, exploding at the last when the flames reached her powder. Not a bottle of brandy had they looted from the ship, nor a sou.

Sorrowing, they returned to their ship. Chima and Jock had laid out the body of Don Jesu, his arm in place, in his bunk in the great cabin.

"We will bury him in Martha's Vineyard," Jock said.

They said, "Who are you to say where?"

"It was his last desire. Everyone heard it. Martha's Vineyard is the nearest island. The ports of the mainland will not take kindly to our sinking French ships."

"It wasn't our fault."

"It will be hard to convince the Americans of that."

"You are not our captain!"

In the bloody democracy of a pirate ship, the most perfect in the world, without even the vague show of governmental sanction that letters of marque conferred upon a privateer, a captain ruled by the force of his character, his fair treatment and understanding of his men. If he slipped, they voted him off the quarter-deck and out of the great cabin. If he resisted, they murdered him. And what power could say them nay? *Hostis humani generis,* the common enemy of mankind, a noose awaited the pirate anyhow if his luck went bad.

Death of a captain created a vacuum. A new one had to be chosen.

Jock understood his position perfectly. "If you disagree with my choice of his burial place," he said, shrugging, "you can decide otherwise. If you dislike me, you can set me ashore. If you hate me, you can kill me; I doubt if I am a match for the lot of you. But I think if you do I shall take one or two of you with me to hell."

Moody, he thought, would have applauded this speech. But Moody could not have appreciated the deep emotion which prompted it. Jock was sick at heart at Don Jesu's death; he was sorry for the Frenchmen whose timidity had brought on their massacre, and he was appalled at the fate of the woman.

"We do not hate you, Mr. Jones," the men said. They were sentimental. "You loved Don Jesu."

"That I did."

And they were practical. Jones was literate, an experienced navigator and a deadly gunner. From the point of view of a gentleman of fortune there was nothing wrong with him except that he was distant in his manner, read poetry and never got drunk, thus putting on airs. But so had Don Jesu.

They spoke among themselves. "I heard Don Jesu say, 'Don't bury me at sea.' "

"Aye, so did I, so we won't."

"Maybe they'd hang us in New York and Boston, just like Jones says."

"Boston is full of Pilgrims who hang Catholics, and in New York the British will hang us because Don Jesu was known."

"Aye, he was known."

"We shall bury the captain in Martha's Vineyard," Jock said, as if there were no question about the matter.

"Yes, sir," they said.

There was nothing else to say.

He did not move into Don Jesu's great cabin, as some of them expected and some would have approved. In his state of depression and disgust he wanted only to quit the cursed black ship and go anywhere, do anything else. But the little marqués in Trinidad and the marquesa, his mother, deserved an account of Don Jesu's death and return of valuable property, the ship, to which they were rightfully heir. Whether the crew would return it to them, no matter how much they had loved Don Jesu, was problematical.

"He does not put on airs," some said, "or he'd have moved into the great cabin. Mate's got a right to it till we choose a captain."

Many favored an immediate election with First Officer J. P. Jones as the only candidate for captain. Had Jock been interested, he might have learned that opinion strongly favored him. He played no favorites, distributed no mourning ration of grog, and encouraged none of the sly crewmen who approached him with sidling glances and thinly veiled hints that an extra share in the next prize would buy him a favorable speech in the forecastle, where groups of men continually debated the question of the succession. He grimly charted a course to Martha's Vineyard to get him there in the least possible number of hours.

The rustic inhabitants of Holmes Hole on that windswept sandy island were exceedingly startled when a swift black ship with canted masts, flying no colors, dropped anchor in their quiet secluded bay.

The local parson said a prayer. The local constable went hunting in the interior, developing a taste for pigeons. The tavern keeper dug up a barrel of buried rum, untaxed and smuggled in. Some girls grew pale; most girls crushed rose petals and rouged their cheeks, and perfumed their

317

hair with vanilla. A goodly body of fishermen, whose boats these days carried more contraband than fish, observed the marks of fighting on the ship, concluded there might be vacancies in her crew and decided to ask for employment. For even in this isolated community it was known that privateers were active; the closer a privateer was to a pirate the higher would be the shares. As a rule the prizes were British; one could always call it patriotism, and often it was. The ship, for all her battle scars, was in excellent trim to a fisherman's eye, which was critical; and since she was there, she had won. All in all, her welcome at Holmes Hole was cordial.

But there were no vacancies aboard her. All her captain desired of Holmes Hole was six feet of holy ground to bury a comrade who had died. The Americans scratched their heads: there was plenty of ground for such purposes, but holy? Catholic holy? Not likely, Captain Jones. There wasn't a papist on Martha's Vineyard except the old Canuck who lived alone and ate lobsters on Friday in a shack on the other side of the island.

Jock consulted his crew. "Well, men, what do you say?"

In and out of the great cabin, mumbling a prayer or saluting or simply standing awkwardly with stocking cap in hand, the men had visited Don Jesu. The changing features, the pallor, the bloat of death decided them.

"It's time to dig him under," they said.

Jock found a place where the wind blew strong on a sandy slope with a view of the sea. They were going to stitch him into a bag.

Jock's temper flared. "He's a marqués, you dolts! In Spain he'd be buried in marble! If I could have got him home in time, the bishop would have said Masses for him for a month! We can do better than canvas."

The instant he had uttered the words he regretted them. These were the men who must sail the ship back to Trinidad and give it up freely to Don Jesu's rightful heirs.

To his astonishment they cheered him. *"Viva el Señor Jones!"* and among the *Señors* were some *capitans,* which nobody took amiss.

Jones walked through Holmes Hole inquiring for metalsmiths. There were none. "I want only sheet lead enough for a coffin, copper if I cannot find sheet lead."

Lead was in great demand for bullets, they said, and there was no sheet copper on Martha's Vineyard. Hulls were sheathed on the mainland, not here. But an excellent carpenter was available to fashion a coffin, even to pitch it inside and out if — an extraordinary demand — it had to be watertight.

The young carpenter who made the coffin was Thomas Chase, a handyman, fisherman and, most recently, a smuggler in these troubled times when law was lax, when traditional authority was breaking down, when few questions were asked and ambitious men rose fast. He was an engaging fellow; Jock liked him. He said, "There's good shooting, Captain Jones, in the hilly parts of the island. Even a few deer left if you plan to stay long." The inhabitants, especially the candy merchant and the tavern keeper, had been impressed with the importance of displaying hospitality towards the black ship's crew, who spent so much money and behaved themselves with such decency. And so they had, there being no loot on the island, few girls to upset them and Don Jesu's death still so recent and depressing. But more moved them than these considerations, Jock knew: the pirate's practical desire to gain for himself a safe haven where he would not be hanged in the time of need which always came.

"I like to hunt," Jock said, "but we'll sail as soon as our comrade is buried."

With torches smoking in the wind they tramped up the hill in silent procession. Tears found the creases of old scars and dropped from bristled chins unashamed. The local pastor read a psalm, startled as a hundred and twenty swarthy Spanish ruffians crossed themselves, and stood aside quaking while shovels dropped sand with compassionate gentleness, never a thump, only a swish like the whisper of water along a hull, on the coffin of Jesu, Marqués of Silva and Villanueva, late of Spain.

Jock did not sail at once.

A wedding followed.

In Holmes Hole the tavern keeper's daughter fell in love with the flashing black eyes and as yet unscarred face of one of Jock's gunners, dimpling and laughing and trying in vain to pronounce his Spanish name, which he assured her was most distinguished. He won her heart, she his.

"I wish to stay ashore and marry," he said to Jock.

"Then stay," Jock grinned.

"It was Don Jesu's custom to require permission to leave the ship."

"I am not your captain."

"You ought to be."

"I don't think the men will object," Jock said, laughing.

"But one cannot desert or one loses one's shares," he stammered.

"Oh, I see. Well, if the men object, I'll take care of your shares myself." He said, "You ought to be captain."

They did not object. They made a fiesta of the wedding. They voted him his shares and contributed a handsome bonus out of their own to set him up in the smuggling business, with many a pointed anatomical reference to what would happen the instant the Protestant pastor tied the knot,

especially that slippery ridiculous knot with the intimate name, absolutely
no good, which all sailors blushed to tie and not one landsman in a thousand had ever heard of; but since it was all in Spanish not even the bride
took offense. Gravely the pastor set down in the parish register the name
of *Joe Frederick*,* the nearest that anyone in Martha's Vineyard could
come to pronouncing whatever the groom had been christened in Trinidad.

Sudden marriages were commonly speeded through on Martha's Vineyard for reasons that everyone understood and charitably winked at; but
in the case of Joe Frederick the usual consideration did not apply, the
groom having arrived so recently in Holmes Hole. The urgency of tying
the knot was owing in great part to Jock's determination to sail quickly,
before the restraint imposed by Don Jesu's death wore off and the crew
became objectionable. But even so, three or four days were required to
complete the arrangements, and during that time Jock hunted deer with
Thomas Chase, the coffin builder, who voiced a wish to join Jock's crew.
"I too am engaged to be married," he said. "I do not need a fortune, but
I'd like to lay hands on a modest sum to set up my new household."

Dissuading him, Jock found he possessed a fertile imagination for spinning a fabulous yarn. Putting on a murderous stage-scowl, he confided
darkly, "You little know who I am. I am actually the bastard son of the
Duke of Queensberry" — the duke being a bookish octogenarian gentleman whom Jock had once glimpsed on the Earl of Selkirk's estate in Scotland — "and my noble kinsfolk seek me everywhere to slay me and wipe
out the stain of the family scutcheon. All of my crew have much to hide,
nothing to lose. Truth to tell, my friend, we're a parcel of cutthroats
and scoundrels. Unwise to join us, unwise!"

Rejected, Thomas Chase could only reply, "If you won't have me, I'll
manage to get a ship and privateer on my own!"

Then Jock sailed.

On the voyage to Trinidad the crew chose as their captain First Officer
J. P. Jones. He accepted the honor and bore south with all speed. In
Trinidad he delivered the ship to Leyla, who wept and said, "When I was
a child and a drought came, the headman said to my father, 'You must
sell her,' and my father said to me in Russian, '*Nichevo*, it cannot be

---

* Mrs. Joe Frederick lived to the age of ninety. A Congress yet to assemble
in a nation yet to be born would one day record in its permanent archives, for
all posterity to witness, payment to her of prize money and a pension. She had
on her wedding day more to look forward to than she knew, a not unusual state
of affairs.

helped.' When Hakim owned me he said to me, 'What Allah wills will be; what he willeth not, will not be.' And now that I have learned the True Faith, the bishop tells me, 'God's will be done.' Thus I know that God holds us all in His hand, so my husband's death must have been in accordance with God's will."

She continued stoically, "Since he sailed away, I have sometimes thought I tried too hard to make him over, for sometimes he reproached me. But he never said I was a bad mother to his son." Her son, she said, was henceforth the pivot of her life; and Jock, recognizing her strength, had no doubt that the little Marqués de Silva y Villanueva, a tiny mite for so sounding a title, would be brought up to bear his nine-hundred-year-old name with dignity and honor, particularly since Leyla, now Dowager Marquesa, possessed ample means. The viceregal lieutenant governor, indeed, suggested that Jock stay on in her employ and sail the black ship, delighted with the gratuities it had brought him, promising proper letters of marque which the heightening tension in the world would very soon, in his opinion, warrant issuing.

But Leyla had a letter which she gave to Jock. It had come, much traveled and stained, circuitously from his Tobago agent. It was from Willie, but not in his hand.

> He is very low, [wrote Bessie] not only in body but in spirit, depressed by conditions which neither he nor I can understand. Many friends are departing. Business is falling off. Mr. Henry makes treasonable speeches. A maid spoke insolently to me the other day, and some drunken rebels threw stones through the tailor-shop windows, though our dear Willie was not there and indeed was confined to his bed. Other planters find markets, but no one will buy from Willie. Dr. Read visits him almost daily, taking a pint of blood or more each time, purging him repeatedly and raising blisters on his limbs to ease the pain; but even with Dr. Read's treatment poor Willie does not mend. Rather he grows weaker and weaker, and I fear he is sinking fast. But he never complains, not even at the blisters, which he will suffer no one else to dress but me, though I must turn my eyes away. He speaks constantly of you, wondering where you are and when you will return, if ever. He greatly desires to see you again,
>
> Which is also the fondest wish of
> Your all-but-sister,
> BESSIE

Jock seized the opportunity to cast off an association which had become abhorrent to him. The atrocities committed aboard the French ship weighed heavily on his conscience. Now, like so much else in his short life, he must bury that hideous memory too, never refer to it, try to forget it. Little loath and not very warmly, he bade his piratical crew farewell.

His sudden departure, just when they had voted him captain, offended many of them. He knew that the secret he sought to hide would leak out: too many pirates had known him too long as a pirate captain. More even than his Shakespearean acting this scandal would rise to plague him as long as he lived, continually nourished by scattered rascals from the black ship who, in after years, down on their luck in water-front taverns and sponging houses, would grin drunkenly and roll a bleary eye and mutter, "John Paul Jones? Jock *Paul*, by God! One and the same. I was with him."

With sober skill Leyla paid off the crew, who quickly dispersed: the viceregal lieutenant governor had let it be known that pirates were unwelcome in law-abiding Trinidad. Forthwith, the ship having been reconditioned, Leyla manned it with another crew. They were just as bad and their mission was identical; but they were different men, and they were not so likely to steal her ship as the men whose devotion had centered on her husband.

Meanwhile Jock took passage to Fredericksburg in a Spanish packet ship, very swift, very innocent and full of nothing but asphaltum, a curious substance that bubbled up out of the earth and formed a great lake in Trinidad. Asphaltum was entirely useless for anything but surfacing a gentleman's garden walks and unpopular on account of its smell. But it was a safe cargo. By no stretch of the imagination, not even by the British frigates now blockading the American coast, could asphaltum be considered contraband or war material. Leyla, in her gratitude to Jock, furnished this passage, which in any case was cheap.

But there was yet no war. Indeed, how could there be a war? War was a state of belligerency between two sovereign nations. America was no nation, possessed no sovereignty. The colonies were provinces, disgruntled at the moment and deserving of punishment; but they must not be punished so severely as to become useless and unprofitable to the mother country. Most Englishmen and many Americans sincerely believed that with a bit of paternal chastening they would come to their senses and return again to the status of loyal Englishmen, which they always had been until very recent years.

Realizing that many loyalists still remained in America, Jock grew a fine red mustache to disguise his features. He was known in Fredericksburg as a former local merchant of some prominence. He was a fugitive from a murder charge in the West Indies. He had buried a pirate captain from a pirate ship on an American island. He was Scotch, hence suspect to any good Englishman. In a community where national passions were rising, there would be many who would scheme to advance their own fortunes with the British officials (who still were in charge) by denouncing a man with so much to hide.

But Bessie's plaintive letter wrenched at his heart. Willie was dear to him; he could not desert at a time of great need when mobs threw stones through shop windows, when customers would not buy, and a brother lay sick of a long wasting progressive and now perhaps mortal illness. Jock could only hope he would arrive in time.

He did not.

Willie was dead and buried with no stone to mark his grave. Bessiwill was dark. A dozen windows showed splintered shards where stones had gone through. The grounds were deserted, the lawns uncut, the gardens high with weeds. The house needed paint, as if its master had had no money to paint it, yet Bessiwill was the pride of Willie's heart. At the sight of the rundown plantation John Paul Jones felt no sympathy for the American cause.

He walked around to the slave quarters. Smoke came up from the chimney of a single cabin.

"They ran away," said Patrick. "All but me."

Jock recognized him as Willie's coachman.

"Why didn't you run away too?" Jock snapped at him with bitter resentment.

"Oh, no, sir. The mayor's going to sell the big house and I'll be butler to the new owner."

"We'll see about that," Jock said grimly. "Where is your mistress?"

The coachman said, "Mis' Paul went off with some ladies and gentlemen in the big coach. It took four horses to pull; it was plum full, and trunks on top. They was all fine people, all scared and crying. I was afraid they'd have trouble, crowded like that; mebbe break an axle. But Mis' Paul wouldn't let me drive. She wouldn't let me come. There wasn't room. A fine gentleman drove. It was sad."

"Where did they go?"

"I don' know, sir. New York, they said, mebbe Canada. They didn't tell me. But I heard."

"Why didn't they go by sea?"

"No room in the ships; they tried. Ships is crowded. All fine ladies and gentlemen are going away."

Jock said, "The river is full of ships."

"Oh yes, sir; but those stay here."

Patrick had revealed much that he did not himself fully comprehend: the flight of the loyalists to New York, which was the stronghold of the British troops; the further projected flight to loyalist Canada; the press of frightened people boarding the few ships which still carried passengers, probably at exorbitant rates, other ships being converted to men-of-war; the tightening naval blockade of American harbors.

A tobacco warehouse had been burned, all but a couple of horses were missing, Willie's excellent cellar had been looted. But not much in the house had been stolen.

"Police came and chased the rebels away," Patrick said.

Presumably the mayor had not wanted the property destroyed, so it could be sold to a new master. There was no use asking Patrick how it happened that a mayor could sell a plantation which did not belong to him. The times were assuredly out of joint.

"Take me to your master's physician," Jock said. "His name is Dr. Read."

"I know, sir; I know. Dr. John K. Read, and he talks just like Master Paul. But it's mebbe twenty miles."

"Hurry up."

"There's nothing but a dirt wagon left, sir."

"That will do."

Patrick still hesitated. Jock was dressed like a gentleman, in sword, white wig, cocked hat, ruffled shirt, knee breeches, silver-buckled shoes. It was common enough attire, but out of place in a dirt wagon with nothing to sit on but a hard plank where a black slave driver also sat.

"It ain't fittin' f' you to sit with me," Patrick said.

Jock said, "You will do as I say."

As the wagon jolted over the road, which was little more than wheel tracks with grass in between, towards the house of Dr. Read in its quiet country surroundings, Patrick mused, "Things is certainly changing."

"They certainly are," Jock said absently. "Changing dangerously, chaotically, wildly, incredibly, universally."

"Yes sir; yes sir, Master Paul," Patrick said uneasily, drawing away so as to put as much distance as possible between himself and the man who sat with him on the buckboard. Perhaps the man was conjuring magic words. "Yes sir, Master Paul. I didn't mean no harm."

"You must not call me 'Master Paul,'" Jock said sternly. "You must call me 'Captain Jones.' I have changed my name. Everything is changed."

"Yes sir, Captain Paul."

Jock sighed. "Not Captain Paul. Remember my name, or I shall see to it that you do not become the new master's butler."

"Yes, sir, Captain *Jones!*"

Jock had no choice but to present himself under his true name to Dr. Read, since he came to inquire after a brother. The doctor eyed him keenly for a moment, then welcomed him into the house. Read brushed some pamphlets and newspapers off a chair and said to him, "Sit down, sir; sit down. Company is a pleasure. You will find a pipe somewhere, maybe in my desk. Pray excuse me for a moment, and then I shall listen to what you have to say. Your man and your horses will be hungry."

Jock heard him in front of the house directing Patrick around to the rear where animals and a slave might find rest and refreshment.

The room smelt strongly of drugs and tobacco and looked unswept. Over the mantel hung a portrait of a woman, but there was no other evidence of female presence in the house. Jock glanced at the pamphlets, which were inflammatory political pieces, and at the newspapers, which reported more dumping of tea in Boston harbor, the arrival of more British soldiers in several American ports and the scalping of a dozen settlers on the western frontier in Pennsylvania. "It may come as a surprise to many Americans," the paper said bitterly, "that a great part of Pennsylvania is now declared to be Canada." It asked in a bold editorial, "How long can a house stand divided against itself? Some will wonder, indeed, whether such a structure *should* stand." These were strong words, Jock thought, and strong must be the spirit of the people who dared to print and wished to read them.

He glanced back to the plain, rather angular features of the woman in the picture. "My wife was very beautiful," Dr. Read said, sighing, coming in. "She died two years ago. The house has never been the same. It is not good for a man to live alone."

"I do not know," Jock said.

"Not good at all."

Read was still young; Jock guessed that not too long hence the woman's picture would probably be taken down and replaced by another.

Read's burr was as Scotch as Jock's once had been, and as Willie's had been till he died. Like most Scottish doctors, Read had been graduated from Edinburgh. Even native-born Americans, he said, like Benjamin Rush, exactly the age of Jock, had gone to Edinburgh to be educated. "Rush has started a society for the abolition of slavery," Read said with satisfaction and some pride. "A daring, farsighted humanitarian."

"That would be a good thing," Jock said. It was curious that many ideas

325

which he had thought peculiar to himself had long since taken root and blossomed on free American soil.

Read was talkative, like a friendly man who had lived alone longer than he liked. But though he seemed to talk only of himself, he would drop a shrewd question from time to time and Jock would realize that he was under sharp and intelligent scrutiny. What did Jock think of the pamphlets? What did Jock think of the renewed dumping of tea in Massachusetts? There had now been not one Boston Tea Party but a dozen. Did Jock think a war was coming? What did he consider the colonies' chances?

"On the map the American military position looks hopeless," Jock said. "We're outnumbered, outgunned, and worst of all surrounded."

"I see you class yourself with us."

Jock grinned. "I would not class myself with England."

"One might fancy from your estimate of the situation that you know something of strategy."

"I have had some experience in fighting," Jock said.

"I have heard gossip, but no one knows for sure."

Jock said, "I can confess to a brother Scot that I have sunk more British ships than even the British realize." Candidly he avowed his twenty months aboard Don Jesu's pirate ship, suppressing only such crimes as he himself was trying to forget.

Read chuckled heartily. "I know several high-minded — not to say high-handed — gentlemen who would like to make the acquaintance of a man like you. These are times when anyone with fighting experience is welcome; yours seems to have been considerable; nobody's past is too closely scrutinized. Uncle Ben will be glad to hear of you."

He did not immediately disclose Uncle Ben's identity. He wanted to settle, he said, "the unfortunate business that brought you here, the death of your late and deluded brother."

Willie had died, Dr. Read told him, of a fatal dropsy attendant upon the terminal stage of a progressive arthritical condition that had troubled him for years. "In the end I eased him all I could with laudanum, noting in him a weakness of constitution which rendered him extremely sensitive to pain; there are such men. Perhaps that is why he was a timid loyalist and you, sir, were a pirate."

"Willie was stouthearted!" Jock said, flushing. "When the time comes for me to bear pain like Willie's, I do not know how I shall take it; I have never sustained even a scratch in battle."

"I spoke as a medical man," Dr. Read said calmly. "I suggest that you

326

smoke another pipeful, Captain, and relax that apoplectic countenance of yours."

Willie had been buried in great haste, the doctor said. Immediately afterwards, confused and frightened, Bessie had fled. "But my cousin William did the same thing," Read said shrugging, "and Cousin William was the governor of New Jersey. The thing is happening all over America."

Cousin William, he said, answering the query on Jock's face was William Franklin, son of Benjamin Franklin, who was Read's "Uncle Ben."

"When Cousin William sailed, it nigh broke Uncle Ben's heart. How strange it is that the son was a bigoted loyalist and the father, whom all the world reveres, is a stanch American! One is reminded of the Scripture: 'The father shall be divided against the son, and the son against the father; the mother against the daughter, and the daughter against the mother.' That is the heartache of the civil war that is coming: families themselves are breaking up."

But there was more. William Franklin, the governor of New Jersey, had a son, a boy of eighteen. "And that boy," Read said, "split bitterly with his father just as his father had split with *his* father, my Uncle Ben. The boy refused to leave America for England; Uncle Ben took him in. All this in one family."

If families, united by the ties of blood and natural affection, could thus be riven asunder by the political passions now rocking the colonies, what chance was there of averting a war between the colonies and England?

Several other Fredericksburg loyalists had fled with Bessie, taking with them as much money and concentrated valuables as they could carry. "The flight of wealth is more harmful than the flight of persons," Read said. "It weakens the banks and undermines what little financial credit we have."

Jock said, "I am surprised that Willie chose you for his doctor, and that you were willing to treat him."

"Sir, I am a physician," Read said with dignity. "Had I hated your brother, which I did not, I should still have treated him."

It was owing to Dr. Read's intercession, indeed, that Bessiwill still stood. It was he who, on Willie's death, informed the mayor that the plantation should be guarded lest the rabble, who were eager to loot empty loyalist houses, destroy it.

"Perhaps my Scotch aversion to waste prompted me," the doctor said smiling, "but even that provident action of mine acted in reverse. The loyalist mayor took flight with some other British bigwigs in your brother's coach; and now the deputy mayor, who is as fiercely American as his predecessor was English, threatens to 'sequester' your brother's property. In times like these sequestration means confiscation and illegal sale, which will be legalized, no doubt, if America wins."

"America will win," Jock said.

"If that is how you feel, I think you had better see the deputy mayor. Declare your sentiments and demand your brother's property as sole heir."

Jock said, "It isn't mine. It's Bessie's."

"If America wins, as I too have faith that she will, Bessie will never get a penny."

"Then I'll take it and keep it safe till she returns."

"I think," said Dr. Read, "they will never return, any of them."

Jock now entered a humiliating period of dual identity. Sometimes he was John Paul; sometimes he was John Paul Jones. Both identities were smirched. Not all Don Jesu's victims had drowned; some had made their way to shore. Unexpectedly on the street, despite his disguise, someone would recognize him and shout, "Pirate! Murderer!" Sometimes in a water-front tavern, where sea gossip ran riot, someone would whisper to a companion, "That is Captain Paul who ran the British sailor through with his sword!" And the companion, according as his sympathies were rebel or loyal, would smile and lift a glass, or mutter threats under his breath. The world, Jock discovered, was very large until you tried to hide yourself; and then it was very small, full of everyone you wished to avoid.

But in a country that had become half rebel, half loyalist, dual in personality no less than Jock, a split-personalitied man could survive. In more orderly times, Jock knew, he would have been hanged long since at Execution Dock in London.

"He is not at all like his brother," said Dr. Read to the deputy mayor. "He is one of us."

On this the deputy mayor gave up his scheme to sequester Bessiwill. Captain John Paul was declared universal heir to his brother's estate, to the tailor shop, the plantation house, all; and poor Bessie, being a loyalist and having fled, was unmentioned. Legally she was beneath notice. Jock set up a stone on Willie's grave. "I shall find her and give her what is hers, brother," he said to the silent earth.

On the stage a ghost would have risen from the boards, a voice would have answered from the wings, or a soothsayer would have plucked at his sleeve to give him some hint of the future. But this was a speechless stone on a rainy day in a graveyard where no one but Jock came to honor the dead loyalist, and the future was veiled.

But he caught a glimpse of the future nonetheless. Dating back through a period of many months Willie had sold nearly all his acreage. Bessie, just before she left, had made large withdrawals at the bank and taken the proceeds with her in cash. Little remained of Willie's once extensive property but the house, and that was in disrepair. A plantation house shorn of its supporting plantation would have been useless even to an experienced planter. Jock had been many things but never a farmer. He knew he would have to sell.

When the estate was settled he found he had less than a thousand pounds to deliver to Bessie if ever he found her, which he deemed increasingly unlikely.

Swift and momentous events began to swirl around him. The long-brewing, long-pent-up storm was now bearing down fast upon the American colonies. A sailor could sense its nearness.

Chapter 31

EACH DAY brought new rumors: of Indian raids on the frontier with frightful atrocities; of ships boarded at sea, American cargoes confiscated, American sailors kidnaped as deserters from the Royal Navy in spite of the fact that they had never set foot on a British deck, never set eyes on the island of Britain. The rumors ran that these sailors were transported to England, where English juries hanged them.

There were rumors more sordid: of American householders insulted and American women dishonored; and the women, no matter how willing or unattractive, were always reported as angels of innocence, beauty and youth, whereas the soldiers, no matter how gentlemanly and restrained (as indeed they had standing orders to be), were always reported as fiends of brutality and lust.

Jock cried, "I would give my life for a good fast ship to blast the British to hell!"

In Jock's queer and unpleasant position, never knowing when someone would denounce him as a murderer or fugitive, pirate or brother of a loyalist, with Bessiwill sold and no house, no ship of his own, he had grown fast friends with Dr. Read, who welcomed him as a house guest into his secluded home for the fellowship he brought, for the tales he had to tell (when he unbent to tell them), which lightened the tedium of a lonely man whose broad interests and philosophical mind seemed natural in one whose uncle was Benjamin Franklin; but above all because he liked him.

Read said, "In my view there is probably some exaggeration; I never yet heard gossip that did not grow in the telling. But whenever I treat a patient with a fever, I know there is sickness in the body to cause that fever. So it is with the body politic. Hence there is truth in these rumors, much truth, for the fever is high. Patience, Captain; you will get your ship."

Chima had promptly cleaned up the house and made it livable.

"Chima isn't as good as a wife though," Read said one night, very comfortable after dinner, his mind running on his widowerhood.

"He possesses a quality of fidelity," Jock said, "which I have not observed in women."

"My dear Captain," Read said, through a fragrant cloud of tobacco smoke such as no longer could be enjoyed in England, "you do not know our American women. A quarter of a mile away lives one who may alter your views."

Jock grinned. "I hope she likes sailors."

"Alas, what woman likes sailors? Sailors are perpetually absent from home."

"So are doctors, are they not, on their rounds?"

"True, very true. Both our professions sorely try the softer sex. But sailors are longer absent and hence try them more sorely. Which do you suppose you would choose, sir, a lady or a ship, one or the other, given the choice?"

"You must equate the choice, Doctor. Am I to suppose them of similar virtues?"

"I shall try to equate, if I know the nautical terms. Let me try. Suppose them both slender in the middle —"

"Waist. A ship too has a waist."

"Slender in the waist, then; spirited but obedient —"

"Virtues, virtues in both, sir."

"Smooth bottomed —"

"One would shudder at barnacles on either."

"Tall —"

"No, there I part with you. Tall ships, little women."

"Dorothea must take off her heels."

"Aye, off with her heels."

330

"She isn't really so tall."

"I know."

"How could you possibly?"

"I know an American Dorothea."

"It cannot be the same. We are now above the waist, are we not?"

"Say rather 'forward' to be strictly nautical; 'above the waist' is anatomical."

"Anatomy is my profession. But 'forward' let it be. Forward, then, without fear. Consider now the upper structures, billowy, swelling —"

"Sails to catch the wind; I follow you."

"To catch the man, my dear man."

"Oh aye, oh aye; I deem that the best of all; let the upper structures be white and tight and let them billow, billow."

"I get a distinct impression," said Dr. Read, glancing at the picture of his wife above the mantel, "that Abigail would have disapproved of this bachelor conversation. Forgive me, my dear. We are speaking of ships. Well, sir, which would you choose?"

"The ship," Jock said positively. "One cannot blow the British to hell with a lady."

"I think you may meet the lady sooner than you meet your ship," the doctor said doubtfully. "Many men who could give you a ship live hereabouts, but they are all in Philadelphia now, framing a humble petition to the king."

"Humble petition to that tyrant, that madman?"

"Softly, softly, Captain! Is your servant to be trusted?"

"Like my guardian angel."

"Then I can tell you in confidence that there is now meeting in Philadelphia a congress without a name, the first assembly to which all the states have ever sent representatives. They will petition the king in most humble words to grant extremely unhumble liberties: freedom to lead their own lives without interference from the mother country, freedom to assemble and debate, freedom to choose a representative government of our own whose decrees neither parliament nor king can annul, trial of Americans by American courts under American law; and above all, no standing armies quartered on us. Every British soldier in America will have to pack up and go home. This congress, which some have named the Continental Congress since it represents the whole British-American continent, will thus demand virtual independence — in most humble terms."
Read chuckled heartily. "Our demands won't be met, I expect. And yet who knows what a mad monarch will do?"

331

"Are you sure of your facts, sir? These will appear exasperating demands."

"We are an exasperating people."

"How do you know so much about things that nobody else knows?"

"From my uncle, Benjamin Franklin. Are you a Mason, Captain?"

The question was not properly phrased to elicit the secret affirmative reply. Jock simply answered, "Yes, I am; a Master."

"I noted the square and compass, or whatever the emblem is, on your watch fob. That should help with the local leaders. Colonel Washington, who was born nearby, belongs to the local lodge."

"I don't think my being a Mason will do much to get me a ship."

"Well, it won't hurt; and your record as a, ahem, a gentleman of fortune with a preference for British prizes won't hurt either. A little patience, Captain, a little patience till the delegates return from Philadelphia, and then I would wager my beautiful Edinburgh diploma you'll get your ship. I do not doubt you will soon tread a quarter-deck again."

But first Jock trod a dance measure.

Mr. Patrick Henry gave a ball to entertain the Virginia delegates returning from the Continental Congress, now just ended. Also invited were delegates from neighboring states within easy riding distance, including Uncle Ben; "but he has grown a bit heavy to keep up with the younger men on horseback," said Dr. Read, "and so he remained in Philadelphia."

Mr. Henry, superb politician that he was, knew that a bit of refreshment would be welcome to the congressmen after their arduous and somewhat frightening labors: it is no light thing to frame a petition that puts your head into a traitor's noose; it is valuable to meet together afterwards in an atmosphere of relaxation and unity, to cement your resolve and fortify your spirit. The "humble petition" had now been dispatched to King George. What his answer would be was unknown. Thought Patrick Henry, "I must keep them together lest they weaken, detached from one another in the isolation of their homes."

Foggy and damp, the Virginia winds of late autumn bit to the bone. The roads were impassable to carriages; the horses sank fetlock deep in the red Virginia mire and splattered the congressmen's boots with blotches that dried the color of blood. More than one delegate noted the color and silently pondered its implications. In the dry well-lighted Philadelphia hall, taking their snuff and warmed by impassioned oratory, united and rebellious, it had been easy to frame the bold document to the king. Now in the dark wet piny woods came the second thoughts, which were always

332

less bold. Hence the ball given by that firebrand Patrick Henry, who knew best of all men how to kindle a fire in others and who knew, as an inescapable corollary, how fire must constantly be fed. Pondering Mr. Henry's singular eccentric genius, Read said to Jock, "Twice he failed as a merchant, perpetually as a planter; his power lies in speechmaking; America needs him desperately — but in small doses. The coca leaf has no function but to stimulate: too much is poison. You are invited to the ball, by the way."

"Me?" Jock was astonished.

"Your own Scotch self," said Dr. Read, a twinkle in his eye.

"As John Paul or John Paul Jones?"

"As my guest, ostensibly, but I suspect that the real attraction in you is the corsair who sank seventeen British ships."

"It wasn't nearly so many."

"It was quite enough to reach the ears of Lord Dunmore. He has complained about you to everyone in Virginia and to the home government in London."

Read saw in Jock's face that Lord Dunmore was a name unknown to him.

"Dunmore is His Majesty's governor of Virginia. I need hardly say that his lordship will not be present at Mr. Henry's ball. Let me give you a small sartorial hint, Captain: no wig. Wigs are going out of fashion as the badge of loyalists, symbol of British oppression. Fortunately you are well supplied with hair."

"I am well supplied with names also," Jock said uneasily. He was half inclined not to go.

"The pretty lass I mentioned is sure to be there," Read said.

"So may my ship," Jock said, "so I'll go."

The doctor was in a mellow anticipatory mood; he looked forward to seeing a lady he greatly admired and hoped, if she would have him, to marry. "How a man can think about ships at a ball is beyond my understanding," he said.

Read started enthusiastically early; they arrived almost the first of all the guests; Jock did not wish to be conspicuous. "There is no harm in a final pipeful before we go in," he suggested.

"None at all," Read said, "if you want to freeze."

A servant took their horses while they strolled for some minutes under the trees in front of the house. It was not at all unusual for gentlemen to finish their smoking out of doors; many fastidious matrons complained that tobacco smoke could not be got out of the upholstery and clung to the curtains and made them smell like red Indian blankets. Taking snuff, on the other hand, with its sniffling and sneezing, its tapping of boxes and snapping of lids, its dusting of waistcoats with breezy lace handkerchiefs, was a fashionable ritual, altogether acceptable. "Smoking is a cleaner habit," Read said, "but poor Mrs. Henry actually suffers, chokes up and gets red in the face when she breathes the fumes. She is ailing, I fear. Mr. Henry does not smoke, naturally."

"Naturally," said Jock.

"I think he would not in any case. He's convinced it would ruin his speaking voice."

Shortly the guests rode up, most of them in their town carriages since they had brought their wives. Read identified them: Mr. and Mrs. Thomas Jefferson. He was very tall, his clothes fit ill, his face was angular, ruddy and strong. "He has an enormous brood of children already," Read said, "and you need no doctor's eye to detect he is adding to it." Jefferson handed his wife down the steps of the carriage with tender solicitude, his fierce hawk eyes momentarily soft, and helped her into the house.

Mr. and Mrs. James Wilson, Latin professor, lawyer, "holder of almost as many diplomas as Uncle Ben," said Dr. Read. He added with pride, "He's a Scot. Got his diplomas at Glasgow and Edinburgh."

A slender lad with a high intelligent forehead and a good strong chin that made him look older than he was galloped up alone on a high bay mare and tossed the reins to the lackey. "Another Scot," Read said, "at least his father is, though he is native-born. James Monroe. He reads law in an office here in town. Mr. Henry predicts a brilliant future for him."

"They look amazingly young, all of them," Jock said.

"So they are; and so are you; and so is America."

Dr. and Mrs. Mercer, the doctor a Fredericksburg physician who kept an apothecary shop and once had treated Colonel Washington during one of his many illnesses and who still treated some of the Washington family. "A profitable clientele," Read remarked wistfully, since the colonel was the richest planter in Virginia, perhaps the richest man in America, whose two hundred slaves worked a plantation so big it was measured not in acres but in whole townships, vast, far-reaching and fertile.

One man in his middle years, the only one so far who wore a wig, alighted alone from his carriage. "Mr. Peyton Randolph," said Dr. Read. "He's bald. He lives at a distance, so comes alone. But his presence is necessary since he headed the Virginia delegation to the Congress."

Two merchants arrived on horseback. One of them looked familiar.

"There comes the shipping firm of Hewes and Smith," Dr. Read said.

"Robert Smith?"

"Aye, another Scot."

"Brother of James Smith of Kirkcudbright?"

"The same."

"I know James Smith. It was James Smith, you remember, who got me out of jail. He promised to recommend me to Robert."

"Then by all means let us go inside and make Robert's acquaintance. He carries your ship in his pocket. Hewes and Smith are here not only to demonstrate their love for America but also to make sure their shipping firm will get its share of prizes in the war when it comes. Hewes is a congressional delegate; Smith manages the Philadelphia office — a Scotsman can always mix duty with profit. But a Scotsman can also freeze, my friend; and if you do not go in I must go in without you." The doctor was shivering. They walked toward the door.

Just as they were about to mount the steps, a coach-and-four with a footman and a driver on the box drove speedily up and came to a sudden halt, balancing gently on tempered steel springs. Jock was reminded of a large ship being expertly maneuvered to a dockside. The entire equipage was a study in elegant black: a quartet of perfectly matched black horses, a brace of perfectly matched Negro servants sitting very straight on the box, the black coach with its costly paneling of *vernis Martin* lacquer, obsidian-brilliant in luster. The footman leaped down, lowered the steps, removed his hat, bowed, and opened the door.

"I did not expect *him* to be here," said Dr. Read. "I heard he was ill again. I expected him to rest up at his mother's place, Ferry Farm, a mile or so away and then go on to Mount Vernon."

For this important guest Patrick Henry himself appeared at the door.

"Who is this one?" Jock asked.

"You can tell by his welcome. It is Colonel Washington."

Out of the coach stepped a man in white stockings, white wig and a velvet suit as black as the coach.

"He's bald too," Read said. "He's only forty-three, but he looks sixty."

Washington was even taller than Jefferson, and massive of build. By contrast his cheeks were hollow and his thin-lipped mouth was stern and unsmiling. He handed his wife down the coach steps with the reverence due a queen; and when she stepped into the light, she was as pretty and vivacious as he was austere and forbidding, with hazel hair and a friendly smile and a little lace headdress distinctly pert and coquettish. She was,

Read said, exactly the age of her husband: "The colonel has lost his youth; the colonel's lady keeps hers."

But Jock was not looking at the Washingtons.

Next to descend from the coach was a portly, prosperous-appearing gentleman in sober professional dress. His smooth and well-remembered features took Jock back in memory to that day of the terrible tide in the Solway Firth, that night when poor Willie fell prey to the British press gang, that night when the boy Jock Paul kicked the lantern.

"Jamie!" he cried, rushing up. "Jamie Craik!"

Craik looked round in amazement, saw him, forgot the pretty kinswoman of Mrs. Washington, the young girl he was about to hand down the coach steps, turned, ran and collided head on with his oldest friend. To the amazement of the onlookers, while heads turned to watch, the two men, having forcibly arrested each other's onrush, ended in an embrace that was far more Spanish than Scottish, hugging each other and shouting each other's Christian names: "Jamie!" "Jock!"

Mrs. Washington took her husband's arm and said smiling, "Dr. Craik seems to know someone here." Washington smiled too, more with his eyes than with his mouth, nodded pleasantly to Jock and walked with his wife up the steps to be greeted effusively by Patrick Henry and ushered into the house.

In an unintelligible dialogue, which Moody would never have permitted on the stage, Jamie Craik and Jock spoke simultaneous lines: "I didn't know you were in America! What have you been doing? Where have you been? What are you doing now? *What* are you now?" and as a consequence obtained no information whatsoever and imparted none. They ended by laughing and pumping each other's hands.

The girl in the coach door said, smiling, "Is it your intention, Dr. Craik, to send me round to the stables with the horses?"

"Good heavens," said Craik, "I was so startled I forgot my manners!" He handed her down, and the coach set sail for the anchorage to the rear of the house. "Miss Dandridge, permit me to present to you the oldest friend I possess in this world, Mr. John —"

"Captain Jock," Dorothea corrected, smiling warmly.

The stern voice of Dr. Read interposed, "Captain John Paul Jones!"

This jumble of identities required clarification, and quickly. The motherly form of Mrs. Washington could be seen hovering behind the sidelights of the door, waiting for Dorothea to come in. Mrs. Washington was not afraid of Dr. Craik, who was happily married and the colonel's physician, and she knew Dr. Read by sight, eminently respectable, Dr.

336

Franklin's nephew. But the bronzed young man with the nautical look about him had not been properly introduced, and until he was (maybe not even then), he was certainly questionable company for Dorothea, whom tonight she had promised to chaperone. Chaperoning Cousin Dorothea was always something of a problem; the colonel considered her overly bold, and once when a toothache was torturing him had asked tartly, "Are we not seeing altogether too much of your cousin Dorothea?" "Don't you like her, George?" she had asked. "My dear, everybody loves her. The trouble is, she loves everybody." He had also muttered, "flibbertigibbet!"

Dr. Read said hurriedly to Craik and Dorothea, "I could not guess that you both knew my guest. I am glad that you do. I like him too. But certain circumstances, nothing dishonorable, nay, rather the contrary, have made it expedient for him to drop the name John Paul."

"Are you in trouble, lad?" Craik asked, his honest face suffused with sympathy.

Dorothea smiled archly. "No lady who ever danced with him would need to ask such a question. She'd know the answer by instinct."

Jock said, "I am, or may be, in very great trouble."

Craik said stanchly, "Everyone is these days, one sort or another. We'll get you out of it."

"The only trouble he's in," Read said, "is with the British, like all the rest of us. The plain truth is, he sternly put down a murderous mutiny aboard his ship in the West Indies, and now a British admiralty court is looking for him demanding an account of his actions. I need not tell you what sort of justice an American or a Scot can expect in a British court."

Jock was glad Dr. Read had stopped there.

Dorothea's lovely eyes grew big and round.

Dr. Craik nodded hearty agreement. "Not a jot, not a tittle of justice."

"Unless we're to lose him — even here there may be a sneaking loyalist spy among the servants — we surely ought to associate ourselves with his reasonable effort to elude his enemies and call him, as he calls himself, Captain John Paul Jones, or better yet, simply Captain Jones."

Laughing, Dorothea said, "We certainly don't want to lose him, do we, Dr. Craik?"

"We certainly don't —"

"Cousin Dorothea!" The door opened a crack. "Isn't it terribly cold outside?"

"Coming, Cousin Martha," she cried, and whispered to Craik, "I'd better go in on your arm," and whispered to Jock, "I'm not a bit cold, are

337

you?" and whispered to Read, "You won't lose him on my account, I assure you."

Inside the door Dr. Read said, "Madam, here is a friend of mine, a friend whom Dr. Craik has known since they both were boys in Scotland: I present to you Captain Jones."

As deeply buried as Willie Paul, the name Jock Paul was now buried.

To be buried is not to be forgotten, merely to suffer a permanent stoppage of career: nothing more is expected of the man or his name, and his past becomes static. *Nil nisi bonum de mortuis*, Jock discovered, was more than a pious resolve to remember nought but good of the dead; it was a sigh of relief that their dynamic activities trouble us no longer.

Thus there were some at Patrick Henry's ball who were perfectly aware that Captain Jones was John Paul; Robert Smith was among those who knew. But an unknown Captain Jones was less embarrassing to deal with than a known fugitive from justice; Smith actually welcomed Jock's pseudonym; it smoothed the way for the hiring of a much-needed captain.

"It is true, Captain Jones," Smith said, "that America is in dire need of masters with fighting experience. Did you happen, by any chance, to have occasion to fight the ships you commanded?"

Knowing he knew, Jock could smile and answer, "Yes, sir, it happened often."

Smith said to Hewes, "Mr. Hewes, shall we not soon require a new master for the *Alfred?*"

Hewes, the congressional delegate who also knew Jock's history, answered, "If His Majesty spurns our petition as everybody thinks he will, the *Alfred* and many others will need new masters. Captain Jones, we are delighted to make your acquaintance."

And to those, like Colonel Washington, who knew nothing about him, Jock started fresh without a taint as Captain Jones, sure of the friendly welcome that anyone with a valuable skill could expect.

During the early evening Mr. Henry, a perfect host, circulated among his guests, making them welcome. He had a knack of saying exactly the right thing. He was elegantly dressed, but (without seeming to speak of himself) he soon managed to convey that not an item of clothing in the entire Henry household was imported from hated England.

To fathers of large families, like Thomas Jefferson, he spoke of the new generation of Americans whose birthright was freedom and ever such should remain, glancing dramatically up to where his own six children were

338

safely asleep abovestairs. Here was the master lawyer swaying the jury, with the art of advocacy born in his blood.

To childless men, like Colonel Washington, he did not mention families but spoke of the military posture of the world, the colonel's favorite subject, and the influence of the moon on the tobacco crop, knowing the colonel firmly believed that one could predict rain by observing whether the horns of the moon pointed up or pointed sideways.

To Dr. Read (who had found his lady, a handsome widow) he mentioned the new lightning rods he had installed on his barns, "thanks to your Uncle Ben," and hoped Uncle Ben would tell him where he could buy one of those new musical instruments the prolific old philosopher had invented: an extraordinary device composed entirely of drinking glasses tuned to a scale by varying amounts of water: turn the crank and touch the rims of the glasses with a moistened finger and behold! — ethereal music like angel voices mysteriously floods the room. It had enchanted the Philadelphia ladies. "But then, your Uncle Ben enchants all the ladies!"

"Does he?" the widow asked Dr. Read.

"As a matter of fact, he actually does," Read said.

She smiled fondly. "I am persuaded, Doctor, that the trait must run in the family."

"My dear lady," he replied, "it would be difficult to convey at this time, when so little privacy is granted us, how highly I treasure your esteem."

To the ladies, with whom he was a great favorite and who asked after the health of his ailing wife, Mr. Henry was exceptionally gallant, paying them subtle but proper compliments. Mrs. Henry was improving every day, he declared; but when he spoke of her, his worried visage belied his words. Dorothea Dandridge chatted at some length with him, Jock being busy with the men, especially Hewes and Smith, though just before the dancing started he had drifted over to hold a long conversation with Jamie Craik, whose title of "Doctor" was just as difficult for Jock to get used to as "Captain" was for Dr. Craik.

For Dr. Craik the host's conversation turned on the subject of Colonel Washington's health in genuine solicitude: the health of America's best, America's only, soldier of renown was of critical importance to America's cause. "*Aut Caesar aut nullus,*" Mr. Henry said significantly. "How actually does he fare?"

"Aye," Craik said, "it's the colonel or nobody. Oddly enough, almost incredibly, he's in excellent shape. He thrives on adversity. He is indestructible."

For a man whose countenance the smallpox had deeply pitted at the age of nineteen, who once had contracted tuberculosis from his brother (who died of it), a man whom at various periods dysentery and malaria had brought to the brink of the grave, whom ague, pleurisy, soaking night sweats and a host of fevers had ravaged, who suffered from chronic shortness of breath, whose chest pained him often, whose digestion was shaky, who took a cold easily and threw it off slowly, George Washington was a phenomenon of survival. "He has been through so much," Craik said, "and come through it so strong that I doubt whether Nature has any thunderbolts left in her arsenal of sickness to hurl against him. If I were to hazard a prediction, I'd say Colonel Washington would live to be a hundred."

But when Mr. Henry had passed on to speak to his other guests, more of whom had arrived, Craik confided to Jock, "The colonel may live to be a hundred, but constantly in pain. We never mention it, but his teeth are in frightful condition. Of course, it's not so painful to extract the front ones when they cause him trouble; it's the big deep-seated molars that torture him. One day I'm afraid they'll all have to come out."

"No wonder he never smiles," Jock said.

"Aye, he's sensitive about his appearance. I've seen his portraits as a boy; handsomest lad you ever set eyes on."

"You've got a son of your own, I hear."

"Aye," Craik said, "the laird of Arbigland is a proud grandfather now."

"You've a good clientele in the colonel."

"Well," Craik said thoughtfully, "if he stays as well as he's been this last year, I doubt if I'll ever send him another bill. His patronage helped a great deal, however, when I first set up practice in Alexandria. It would be a sad thing for us if the colonel should fall sick this year."

Jock had told Jamie much of what had happened to him since he left Scotland; he could not quite bring himself to avow the Shakespearean interlude. "How exciting your life has been," Craik said enviously. "How stodgy my own seems by contrast." He patted his embroidered waistcoat, tight over a comfortable belly. "You'll never have one of these!" he said, laughing.

"I envy you your solid secure career," Jock said.

A voice with bells in it said, "I do not believe *that* for a moment." Dorothea rustled up. "If you will not come to me, Captain Jones, I must come to you. I can always tell Cousin Martha I was asking Dr. Craik for a draught of febrifuge."

She was charmingly frank, Jock thought, though Craik, who knew her better, chuckled cynically; ladies did not commonly admit even in fun that their blood was feverish. But fun or no, he noted how strongly her allure was working on Jock. Rose petals or rouge or the music of the violins, which had now begun, had suffused her cheeks with an enticing flush.

Bowing himself away, Craik said, with a sally that proved to Jock what a fashionable clientele he must have, "I would not discomfit my friend, Miss Dorothea, by extinguishing so lovely a flame."

"You Scots are unnerving at times," Dorothea said to Jock. "You're so terribly impudent in the nicest way."

Dr. Read, smiling fondly at his own plump partner, bethought himself in a bit of his philosophical mind not yet anaesthetized by the music how much could be read in a dance to distinguish the temper of a people: this was no slow, courtly minuet, no cold evolution of figures better observed than enjoyed. This was no cheerless bloodless drill on a dance floor dictated by a Beau Nash to please a Hanoverian-British king who delighted in German inflexibility, always devoid of imagination and fundamentally gloomy. This was a lively spirited dance, based on the naughty French *valse à deux,* with much laughing, joking, calling to friends across the floor, completely relaxed and informal. The promenade with which it started soon broke up into individual units of dancing couples, arm around waist and scarcely a foot of space between male and female, an intimacy that would have been scandalous in England. This was the dance of a society in rebellion against the stiff conventions of England, as indeed it was against all things English. "Lord Dunmore would call us depraved," Dr. Read said slyly to his partner, who answered him, "Oh, Dr. Read, *you* depraved!" Actually, Lord Dunmore and other Europeans had said they detected in American dancing an echo of the Americans' uninhibited African slaves and their savage Indian neighbors.

"Colonel Washington has danced every dance!" Jock said to Dorothea. "Somehow I'd expected him to strike an Olympian pose and glower like Jove at the foibles of us mere mortals."

"Cousin George is a little old dear," Dorothea said. "He loves to dance and never misses a chance. He's not half so stern as he looks. He's a very good dancer, too."

"He danced nimbly with you. I watched you."

"I'm glad," she said softly, "glad you watched."

"Everybody watched you," Jock said jealously.

"They were watching Cousin George, you silly. He's a very important man." She was looking up at Jock with wide-open innocent eyes, and if they saw how he melted under their subtle heat they did not betray the fact.

"Mr. Henry also danced with you. Two dances."

Her hand, which appeared to others to rest so decorously on his shoulder tightened against him in an invisible squeeze that shot through his body like an embrace. "Now I know you really were watching. But a host has to dance with just everybody, doesn't he, no matter how painful the duty?"

"Not two dances."

"Greedy," she whispered.

"Aye."

"Poor Mrs. Henry," she said after a while.

Mrs. Henry had sat smiling wanly, shawl on shoulder, patiently throughout the evening, too ill to dance.

Some of the bachelor guests had frowned because Jock had managed to dance with Dorothea more often than any other man at the ball. But since Colonel and Mrs. Washington seemed to have set their stamp of approval on him, since Dr. Read had sponsored him and Dr. Craik had hugged him, and Smith and Hewes, with their powerful shipping and financial interests, had been observed to slap his back and roar over the punch bowl at some private joke of their own, there was little her disappointed suitors could do except grumble that America was being taken over by Scotsmen, bag and baggage. "But concede," said one wag, "that the baggage is beautiful."

Jock hated the evening to end. "Shall I see you again?" he asked.

"If a sailor can ride horseback a quarter of a mile."

"Soon?"

"Aye." She tried to say it the way he did. "To think that a Scot should have chosen the name of Jones."

"Sailors say 'aye' too," he said.

"Ladies do too. I just did."

That night Dr. Read was in an elated self-congratulatory mood. The widow had accepted him. "Some time back I posed you a question, Captain: 'A lady or a ship, which would you choose?' Well, sir, how do you feel about that question now?"

"I hope I shall not have to choose, sir."

The doctor saw how deeply he was smitten, and dropped his bantering tone.

"I should hate to see you get hurt, my friend," he said.

342

Chapter 32

JOCK DID NOT think he would be forced to make a choice between a ship and a wife. Hewes and Smith were married. Most sea captains were married, and up in New England, that other focal point of colonial rebellion, famous and respectable families had been founded by seamen and were carried on by seamen to this day: many indeed had made fortunes as whalers, and a whaler's voyage often lasted three years.

Nor did he think he would "get hurt," for there was nothing to hurt a man in Dorothea Dandridge. Witty, beautiful, high spirited, wellborn, she represented all he had ever hoped for in a wife. Her ancestry was English nobility on both sides, and whatever a Scot might think of the English, he could not deny that a long line of distinguished forebears bred gentility and manners into the girls. Sometimes he was willing to concede that the men had virtues too: they were good fighters, good merchants, good craftsmen and good sports. They were abysmally maladroit in colonial administration, of course.

He suspected that Dr. Read did not trust Dorothea simply because she was utterly unlike the placid widow who had captured his own philosophical heart. From Socrates to Samuel Johnson, philosophers had always been notoriously inept at choosing their wives. Jock smiled at the thought; maybe that was what made them philosophers. If Dorothea had been spiteful or thoughtless or unkind, Read's warning might have had some foundation in fact; but the fact was quite contrary. Dorothea was thoughtful and kind even to a disturbing degree. It would happen not once but very often that she could not see him because she was going over to sit with Mrs. Henry, to chat and cheer her up, or go into the kitchen and brew her an invalid soup or help with the children, washing the little boys' faces and braiding the little girls' hair. "They're adorable children," she would say to Jock.

"No one would fuss over six children of somebody else's," Jock would say, "if she did not love children!" and he loved her for it.

"Of course I do," she said, her eyes big and soft. "Any woman does, any decent woman."

343

"I would too," he said. "My own, anyhow."

"None of your own?" she said, laughing. "Not anywhere, in all the ports you've touched? I thought sailors —"

"I'm serious, Dorothea."

"You're nicer when you're not," she said.

It was galling not to be able to say to her, "I love you with all my heart, as I thought I could never love anyone, wholly, devotedly. I would do anything, give up anything for you. If you do not want a husband who will be absent on voyages, I'll give up the sea." Would a woman know what that would cost him? No, but never mind. "I will turn merchant; I've been one before. I'll buy a plantation and build you the biggest house in Fredericksburg — I can — I can afford it —"

But here the yearned-for imaginary proposal stopped dead. Here was precisely the ugly thing in his past that sealed his lips. Even an ordinary man kept prudently silent concerning certain details of his bachelorhood when he asked a woman to share his life; Jock's life had not been ordinary, and he had more to hide.

Dorothea would only ask with innocent wondering eyes, "How, Jock? How can you pay for such expensive things?"

And he would be forced to answer, "With pirate gold, Dorothea, and with certain substantial sums I laid by during a period when I sold men, women and children, children as young as Mrs. Henry's, into slavery. And now that you know I can afford you, which of my two names will you choose, Madam Murderer or Madam Pirate, knowing in advance that someone sometime will fling it into your beautiful aristocratic face?"

She would freeze with fury and shame and reject him.

Until he could make the name Jones a name that even a Dandridge would not be ashamed of, it was better to let her take the lead and not appear serious outwardly. Patience was difficult to learn; he had never been patient with the Biblical story of Jacob who waited seven years for Rachel and was saddled with seven years more before he got her; only so precious a prize as Dorothea made patience tolerable.

But things moved faster now, especially in America.

In England King George spurned the "humble petition" presented by the Continental Congress, declaring it an unauthorized assembly incompetent to legislate. Four hundred useful colonial laws, framed by Americans and under which Americans had lived and solved their own problems for two hundred years, were swept summarily aside and declared void by the home government.

344

Blood began to flow.

In New England at Lexington, Concord and Bunker Hill British and American forces fired upon one another. The Americans fought like Indians, loading on their bellies, skulking behind trees. The British fought like European gentlemen, in full view and well-ordered formation, winning all the battles; for the Americans simply disappeared afterwards into their forests, laughing. But a third of the British invariably lay dead on the field, their red coats now doubly red.

The great undeclared war now burst into being, bitter, impossible to stop, growing daily in scope. The chancelleries of Europe looked on, weighed America's chances and prepared to take sides.

Lord Dunmore took flight with his family aboard a British frigate in Norfolk harbor and, in retaliation upon the rebels, summoned a British fleet around him and bombarded the city with merciless intensity.

Norfolk burned for three days and three nights, while thousands of homeless fled into the wilderness and the winter's cold. When the fires burned themselves out, nothing remained standing, not a house, not a shop, not a stable, nothing but one small church, saved by its stone construction and isolated from the flames by its graveyard. All else was reduced to ashes.

While yet the ruins smoldered and smoked, a second Continental Congress rode angrily up through the piny woods to Philadelphia.

Gone now for Jock were the pleasant rides, the carefree picnics, the intimate hours with Dorothea in pastoral scenes by romantic brooks in Virginia's beautiful countryside, where she had alternately encouraged his suit with a boldness that fired his blood and discouraged him because, as she said, he was getting too serious too soon: she was young, she said, and so was he; they should wait, wait, wait. It had been difficult to wait under kisses like hers. But she never said a flat Yes, she never said a flat No; never rejected him out of hand and never accepted him fully, till he almost burst. "Wait," was what she said.

Equally uncertain was the very roof over his head: the widow's trunks had begun to arrive well in advance of her wedding day, she being a practical soul; and the widow herself (no nonsense about *her*) had surveyed her future home with a gimlet eye, running her finger over the mantel top and murmuring fondly to Dr. Read, "Oh, you poor dear!" if so much as a speck of dust remained visible on her glove afterward.

"It isn't that she dislikes you, Captain," Read said uneasily. "Actually, she's very fond of you."

Jock chuckled. "I should have left long since. You know what keeps me here, abusing your hospitality."

"I know; a quarter of a mile's ride to the Dandridge girl. Hasn't she kept you dangling long enough?"

Jock scowled, and the doctor shrugged helplessly and changed the subject back to the widow.

"What she really objects to," he confided, lowering his voice as if the widow, twenty miles away in Fredericksburg, might hear him, "is that saw-toothed servant of yours. He frightens the life out of her."

"I'm afraid Chima frightens most everybody."

Most uncertain of all was the murky political state of affairs between America and the mother country. "The war is real now," Read said. "Blood has been shed and battles have been fought. Yet not one American in ten realizes that the issue is independence, not merely redress of abuses. Many people are uninformed, living on the frontier, far from the centers of information; some still want a compromise. It takes a Scot, a merchant like Smith or Hewes, or an enthusiast like Mr. Henry or a philosopher like Uncle Ben to see clearly that only complete independence from England will satisfy us now."

One night a newsy letter arrived from Franklin in Philadelphia, where the Congress was sitting and debating. Read scanned it and couched its contents in medical terms as was his habit before giving it to Jock: "There is always blood at a birth," the doctor said, "and the process is agonizing to the mother. Sometimes she dies. No one knows how the infant feels; probably it is still too new to feel anything; it certainly does not know what is happening. Sometimes the mother does not die; she is only woefully weakened like poor Mrs. Henry. Read this letter, my friend. The whole world knows that Benjamin Franklin takes a cool and balanced view of things. You can believe my Uncle Ben when he states that we in our generation are witnessing the birth of a nation, a free nation, Captain, saucy as pepper. Now it would appear that we have done a thing that will frighten King George out of his wits."

"He's out of them anyhow," Jock said.

"Only half, to date. This news will put him into a strait jacket!"

Jock read the letter.

That was the last night he spent under Dr. Read's hospitable roof; next day he took horse for Philadelphia.

When the news in due time passed over the Atlantic and reached the king, a distressing scene took place in the royal residence. It was quickly hushed up by the four doctors who were in constant attendance. Pity and shame sealed the lips of the royal family. Servants were banished belowstairs. Close relations and the medical men cared for him. It was hoped that the tragedy could be hidden, like many another in the ancient palace that Cardinal Wolsey had built out of grinding extortions and Henry VIII had stolen out of love for a serving girl. But of course the secret leaked out.

Behind closed doors in his private apartments King George III, the Britannic Majesty on whose world-girdling empire the sun could not set, fell into a fit, lost control of his most primitive bodily functions, befouled himself like a babe, babbled nonsense and was forcibly confined in a strait jacket lest he injure himself and those who loved and restrained him.

Before his wits cleared, the attack had lasted some weeks, the most serious that ever had struck him. At this critical juncture William Pitt, America's friend and England's most beloved statesman, died, a mental and physical wreck.

In the chancelleries of Europe ears pricked up and greedy eyes began to shine. Never had chance, madness and death so conspired to cripple the British lion. When would arise again such a golden opportunity to tear to pieces so rich an empire!

The news that produced this adverse effect on King George's health was a reliable report of unprecedented nature. One of his American colonies, led by those archscoundrels Smith and Hewes in the maritime province of North Carolina, had met in a rebel assembly. They had voted a resolution declaring complete independence from England. They had sent up their draft to that other rebel assembly the Continental Congress, as a model and a guide.

One Declaration of Independence was on paper.

Would the colonies unite? Would a second Declaration signed by all thirteen be forthcoming?

"Be calm," his keepers soothed him. "It cannot happen."

He babbled, "What? What? What?"

Chapter 33

ANYONE BRED to the sea must perforce feel at home in a forest. There is a lack, and there is a presence. Lacking are buildings and highways, the artifacts man spreads on the land to display his mastery over nature, first fruits of civilization and culture. Lacking also is man himself, as he is on the sea. Spurring towards Philadelphia (with Chima at his side, who grinned and breathed the free air as he had not since Africa), Jock encountered no one, saw nothing but the faint path overgrown and winding towards the north. This the lack, with its loneliness and peace.

Present was all he knew best and loved best: innumerable trees, which he saw as masts; giant boles, which he saw as planking and ships' ribs; branches he saw as spars; and enveloping him like a cloud was the fragrance of pine, which his senses interpreted as turpentine, paint, oakum, tar, resin to slush a line and calk a seam. Here was the freedom he knew and of which he was a part, elemental and vast.

The magnitude of America was like a sea: beyond the Alleghenies, lying like a reef, stretched unthinkable miles of the Mississippi valley; and beyond that, on the other side of a distance which staggered the imagination, lay another ocean, the Pacific. All this was known to intelligent Europeans, but they could not comprehend it. No more could they grasp the concept of infinity or the astronomical remotenesses glimpsed through the telescope Mr. Newton had invented and Sir Frederick Hershel was perfecting.

Here was a bigness which Americans accepted as their birthright but which Europeans could not feel and hence neither feared nor judged aright. Only Russia possessed such vastnesses, and Russia like America puzzled the European mind. Sailor and ever more convincedly American, Jock felt at home. So did the savage, Chima.

Precisely because he felt at home Jock experienced no awe, no surprise at the splendor surrounding him. He accepted it as he accepted the sea and merely wished that this overland voyage were less long.

Near Philadelphia he passed some Indian villages and formed a low estimate of the red men he saw. These were tame Indians, stolid, vacant-faced, who farmed a little and hunted a little and drank a lot. It had been a long time since he had thought of Henri de Beaujeu, the marquis turned sailor, whose doctrinaire mind had dwelt romantically on the "noble savage" pictured in the writings of Jean Jacques Rousseau, who never saw one. Probably poor Henri had long since been scalped.

He thought of his name, Jones.

The utter lack of distinction in the monosyllable he had chosen when he wished to become anonymous made him smile wryly now that he again coveted glory. "Dandridge to Jones will seem a step down," he muttered to the flying trees. "Why the devil didn't I hit on something like Cameron or Barrington or de Beaujeu?"

He murmured the possible combinations: "Mrs. John Jones. Mrs. J. P. Jones. Dorothea Jones."

They were insipid, flat.

He would have to rise very high to gild a name like Jones with a luster deserving of Dorothea Dandridge.

Shortly the peace of the forest gave way to a scene of bustling activity as Jock rode into Philadelphia. This was the national capital of America insofar as a loose congregation of colonies could boast of a capital. Certainly it was the biggest city in America, and in America bigness was a national delight. Even families were big, and a famous prediction of Uncle Ben's, according to Dr. Read, was that England was already doomed to defeat even without a war. Americans were breeding so fast that in a few years population alone would swamp her; England would go down under the sheer weight of America's huge and exasperating vital statistics. Commenting on the enormous baby crop was one of his sly parlor entertainments, along with his "hydro-harmonia" (the singing glasses) and his game of "the shocking kiss," in which a lady and a gentleman would each hold a metal wire attached to an electrical machine, the handle of which Uncle Ben would turn: and when they approached their lips to each other's, a spark would be seen to leap between them, to much squealing, much clapping of hands and not a few scandalized eyebrows raised at such carryings-on. In the faraway twentieth century, Franklin predicted that more than a hundred million people would live in America, "the pleasantest possible way," he observed dryly, "to outnumber our enemies. The method already is known." "Sir," said a pretty young girl to him, "such a figure is almost incredible." "My dear," replied the irrepressible old gallant, tilting his head a bit so as to observe her more closely through the bifocals that he had invented, "I might say the same of yours."

Franklin had lived in Philadelphia many years; Dr. Read had told

Jock much about him; the stamp of his personality was on the city, broad-visioned, cultured, practical. The paved streets, the lighted street lamps at night, the fire engines, the printing plant, the hospital, college, library, theater, all were his projects. Here was the home of the American Philosophical Society as well as the home of the Continental Congress: it was natural that both the wisest and the most rebellious minds should gather in the city that was Uncle Ben's home.

But there was more to the city. There were manifold activities, awesome in their scope and vitality, in which Franklin had had no part, for they reflected the genius not of one man but of a whole people: docksides laden with outgoing merchandise manufactured here: carpets, paper, cordage, canvas; ironmongery, blown glass, knitted goods; and from the surrounding countryside, grain, lumber, meat, horses and fine white flour.

And if all the ships loading at the water front could not handle such plenty, there were more ships abuilding in cradles nearby. They were sleek slim craft with clipper lines that made a sailor sigh for possession, as at the sight of a lovely girl. The French knew how to build such ships but could not sail them. The British knew how to sail them — they could sail anything — but could never quite trust such delicate hulls. England had bludgeoned her way to empire with bottoms so thick that cannon balls bounced off, and would not sacrifice security for speed. But America could both build and sail the clippers.

Jock would have been glad to pay his respects to Franklin immediately. He had a letter of introduction to him, and he was the bearer of another letter from Dr. Read apprising his uncle of his continuing good health, his forthcoming marriage and mentioning with concern the breakdown of the postal system. Franklin had long held the position of postmaster general from the Crown: the Crown had now dismissed him, and communication between the colonies, like everything else, was in a state of utter chaos.

Jock was met at the door by a suspicious servant who said that Dr. Franklin was not at home and, no, he did not know where he was or when he would return.

"I have letters for Dr. Franklin," Jock said.

"I will give them to him when he returns."

"They are from his nephew in Fredericksburg," Jock said.

But the tight-lipped servant was not to be disarmed by a friendly smile or a couple of letters purporting to come from a relative of his master. He closed the door quickly, and Jock heard the bolt click shut.

In another part of the town overlooking the Delaware water front Jock met with a warmer reception. Here was the spacious residence of Robert

Smith of Smith and Hewes, the shipping merchants. Here the door opened wide, smiles greeted him, and Smith wrung his hand in welcome. "You come at an opportune time, my friend," he said.

He laughed at Jock's chilly reception at Franklin's home. "Apparently the butler took you for a British spy. They are everywhere. Every stranger is suspect."

There was no mystery about Franklin's whereabouts. He was up in Boston conferring with the New England leaders of the revolution. New Englanders were a hardheaded stubborn lot, Smith said, proud of their leadership in the fight against England, jealous of the southern colonies, and likely to be extremely self-righteous about the southerner's peculiar institution of slavery, which New Englanders did not need and did not like.

"Nobody likes it," Jock said with conviction.

"Aye, but never express yourself so to a southerner," Smith said.

Franklin had gone north with a double purpose: to smooth out the differences between North and South, and, a project dear to his philosophical heart, to devise a national American flag that would signify to the British, to the world, and to the colonies themselves that America was united. It was a difficult diplomatic assignment.

"Did he ride all that way?" Jock asked, thinking how a saddle must have chafed the old man.

"Plenty of men would have volunteered to carry him up in a sedan chair like a French nobleman," Smith said, "but he took my word that the sea route was safer than Indians, and we sent him up in a fast little cutter. He got through the blockade."

Smith chuckled. There were two thousand ships of all sizes, ranging from undecked fishing smacks to strong armed clippers, now buzzing like hornets around the blockading fleet. Like the leather-clad frontiersmen with their deadly long rifles, these predatory Americans would dash in unexpectedly, take pot shots at the British, do what damage they could and fade away. "They united long enough to create a diversion and drew off the frigates till Franklin slipped through. He met General Washington on the heights above the town."

"*General* Washington?"

This was news for Jock's ears. Events had moved swiftly in the Continental Congress.

It had recruited an American army.

It had appointed a commander in chief: Colonel Washington of Virginia was now a general, empowered by the Congress to create, if he could, a unified fighting force on land and sea from the uncoordinated, undisciplined, ill-informed, highly individualistic man power of the thirteen colonies. They came from all sections of the land; they had little in common but their spirit of rebellion, a strong but unstable element in their character bred by lonely, self-sufficient and isolated lives. They would be slow to obey; they would have to be persuaded, not ordered. How different from the British, used to command and to take commands. How different from the precision-drilled Hessians, who fought like machines. Only the massive patience of a Washington, by common consent of the Congress, could possibly transform Americans into a unified fighting force.

It had appointed governors of the states, the royal governors having fled home to England without, however, resigning.

It had begun to assemble a navy which, unlike the free-booting privateers, would obey orders and submit to discipline.

Thus a double government prevailed in America, in its cities and forests, in its municipalities and fortifications, in its arsenals, harbors, rivers and ports, on the western frontier and on the eastern seaboard: everywhere throughout this sprawling American land, eveywhere that sovereignty ought to be exercised, sovereignty was dual. Mr. Patrick Henry, for example, was now governor of Virginia; but so was Lord Dunmore.

"There will be a lot of hanging if England wins," Smith said grimly, "and I would be one of the first."

"So would I," Jock said. "But we won't hang."

Smith mentioned in passing that Governor Henry had appeared in a new suit of elegant mourning on the occasion of his latest speech before the Congress. Mrs. Henry had just died.

Jock had not heard from Dorothea; nor did he, though his stay in Philadelphia lengthened. Doubtless her time was filled with neighborly duties attendant upon the death of her close and good friend, selflessly tending those six little children whom she loved so much and who now stood in such need of care and affection. Still, he would have treasured a line from her.

He wrote her enthusiastic letters: "Never," he said, "have the prospects of raising the name Jones to a higher status looked brighter than now; if love and resolve can still aught avail in a troubled world and a troubled life" — he wrote in a vein of exaltation, for his pen had a habit of soaring on paper — "I will make Jones a name that any man might be proud to bear, and no lady — be she as lovely and beloved as yourself — need be shamed to share." Thus Jock, from his heart; and no answer.

He thrust from his mind the vague apprehensions that troubled him, assuring himself that she must have written, her letters must have miscarried, the fault must lie in the breakdown of the postal system.

Shortly, in a sassy little cutter, in a storm that had lashed the Atlantic coast for several days, Dr. Franklin returned, with a new theory in his head for forecasting weather and under his arm a new flag. Whatever touched him inspired him, and whatever he touched he changed.

He had heard in Boston, he said, that a storm had first struck the frontiersmen in Pennsylvania; next day there was a storm at Fort Ticonderoga, which Benedict Arnold had captured from the British, dragging its cannon and precious powder overland through the woods to General Washington, who was certain that now with this heavy artillery he could blast the British from Boston. And next day a storm had struck Boston itself. Could it be, Franklin wondered, that the three storms were one and the same? Storms had always been believed to spawn and expire in one spot. But was it not possible — nay, logical — that storms moved like whirlpools on a river, flowing from west to east? And if it were true, might there not arise, to the general good of mankind, a system of forecasting the weather and bringing one more unknown into the purlieus of natural science?

Next day, among the spectators in Carpenters' Hall, with Smith beside him joining in the general applause, Jock had his first glimpse of Benjamin Franklin, who presented the new flag to his congressional colleagues. He was a powerfully built, ruddy-faced man, looking far younger than his seventy years, with a large balding head and an aureole of snow-white hair: the flag was a measure of his almost immeasurable genius.

Thirteen bold red and white stripes, signifying the thirteen united states ("One day we printers will capitalize those words," Franklin said), ran lengthwise across its substance. Jock had seen similar striped flags and admired their visibility at sea.

But there was something more to this one, something that would overcome the scruples of conservative Americans who demanded freedom but still hesitated to take the final step to complete independence, that awesome irrevocable declaration the Congress was still debating. In the canton of the new flag, in the upper left corner nearest the staff, reduced in size but still there, were the British crosses on British blue, the ensign intact of the imperial mother country.

It was unanimously approved and authorized.

Smith said excitedly, proudly to Jock, "And it's fallen to a Scot to raise it for the first time! I couldn't get you a captaincy. There are too many New Englanders ahead of you. But I got you a command, and I got you the honor of hoisting the new Congress Colors on her!"

The charged atmosphere of Carpenters' Hall worked strongly on Jock. He had not seen before this freely elected assembly of a whole people who desired to be free. He had fallen doubly in love, with a woman and with this land of the limitless sweep and the limitless ideal. The two loves mingled in his heart to nourish the growth of something that had always been there, inborn and vital, a legacy of his turbulent Scottish blood: the notion of freedom.

Small at first, applying only to himself as an individual, it had led him into the slave trade where a man could "make rich," and win freedom for himself.

Growing, it had led him out of that trade when he came to see that black men were also men and no man ought to be a slave.

Now, growing bigger still, the notion of freedom had blossomed into an ideal, applicable not to one man, not to one race, but to a whole nation — and if such an ideal could expand to encompass the entire world, Jock was not conscious of it nor could he foresee its personal peril to him. Growth is slow; ideals will claim their martyrs; tragedy was far from his thoughts.

It was enough and it was good that Americans in their struggle to be free had chosen him to hoist their new flag.

In moments of deep emotion like the present Jock had a tendency to express himself melodramatically. He considered it a weakness, a failing left over from the stage.

Only a stern effort of will kept back the words that leaped, swaggering and hot, to his lips: "I, Jones, will so comport myself that this flag of freedom shall become the terror of the seas!"

Chapter 34

THE CONGRESS COLORS flag was short-lived.

It never became the terror of the seas. What little glory it gained was owing entirely to the man who first hoisted it over the *Alfred*, flagship of the American "fleet" of eight paltry vessels which gathered on the Philadelphia water front to receive the cheers of thousands of spectators on the shore. The spectators were at one with the Congress in unity, like the thirteen stripes in the flag; but all but a few retained in their hearts a stubborn remnant of self-identification with England like the canton in the flag. There was not only blood, there was pain at the birth which physically was a separation; no one who ever has witnessed one ever has said that the process is speedy.

The winter of 1775 was at its peak, gray, foggy, cold. Life slowed down all over the world, following the rhythm of its immemorial cycle; vegetation suspended its growth; animals dug themselves holes in the ground and went to sleep; even among humans where conditions were extreme something similar occurred: Siberian peasants banked fires in stoves big as beds, lay down on top and drowsed away the dark and cheerless months, hibernating like bears.

Having run up the flag with a swelling heart, Lieutenant John Jones of North Carolina retired below to the gun deck, which was his special responsibility, to drill his gunners. North Carolina! But he had to come from somewhere. His captain and all the captains of the Continental "fleet" were New Englanders, most of them with near relatives on the newly created Naval Committee. Smith and Hewes, who had sponsored him, who themselves came from North Carolina, had said to the Committee that Jones (who had never set foot on its soil) was also a North Carolinian.

Of the eight vessels which comprised the fleet, three deserted before it cleared the Delaware, which was jammed with floating ice. They had been privateers before, and to privateering they now returned as soon as they learned that the "navy" was under orders to carry out a mission from which not a penny of profit could be got for themselves.

A shortage of cannon and gunpowder was plaguing the Americans.

Congress had learned in secret session that a large quantity of powder was stored at Nassau in the Bahamas. To capture it and bring it back was the thankless mission assigned to the fleet, three eighths of which had romped off in the quest of easier richer prey before their hulls tasted salt water.

New Year's came, the new year of 1776, a year of unmitigated disaster: the year Benedict Arnold, having marched against Quebec, was defeated and marched back again; the year a British fleet defeated Arnold's American fleet on Lake Champlain (for the sea war spread to the inland waters also); the year General Washington lost the Battle of New York, which the British then burned, and the Battle of Long Island and the Battle of

White Plains. It was the year the British turned triumphantly on Philadelphia itself, and the Continental Congress was forced to flee or be hanged.

But it was the year Lieutenant John Jones of North Carolina rose from the gun deck to the quarter-deck; for, incredibly, the little fleet accomplished its mission, and for a day the Congress Colors floated over the citadels of Nassau.

At times, as the fleet bore south, Jones thought wistfully of the sleek trim privateers. The *Alfred* was sturdy but cranky and slow, a clumsy sailer as was to be expected of a converted merchantman. But he had been a privateer, nay, he had been worse and had had his fill of it. His outlook had expanded and so had his heart through the miracle of a double love, in whose warmth was now shrinking smaller and smaller the wholly normal emotion of selfishness; he took a dim view of the selfishness of a privateer. He wanted to rise — that was part of him — but he wanted to rise in a legitimate navy that could beat the British, an American navy which one day would outnumber, outgun and outsail the imperial British flotillas that now patrolled and terrorized the seven seas. He wanted it so much that he did not consider it an impossibility, as he never considered impossible anything he wholly wanted.

He was not very logical, his gunners thought, when he set them to shaking barrels of powder to keep it properly blended and sighting their guns all day long, drilling them, shouting commands and demanding instant obedience when there wasn't anything to shoot at. His captain also considered him something of a freak.

The island city of Nassau lay in those beautiful tropical waters where Jones had traded when he still was Jock Paul. He knew them as a merchant. More, he knew them from the charts of Don Jesu who sometimes had stopped there to water, provision and afford his men some amusement. Nassau had been a haunt of buccaneers for a hundred years and possessed an unsavory population except for the British garrison.

Nassau was protected by two forts flanking the town, a strong one named Fort Nassau and a weaker one opposite named Fort Montague. In the sea before the town ran a long island; it was this island which gave to Nassau its excellent roadstead in which, safe from gales, a score of ships might anchor.

But the eastern entrance of the anchorage was treacherous, full of shoals and hidden sunken rocks.

The American fleet had bold orders and little information: they were to sail straight up the deep water of the western approach to Fort Nassau and capture it. Jones on his gun deck was appalled when they started this maneuver in broad daylight. But he was not consulted; no one knew of his intimate knowledge of the alternative approach, and he was too strict a disciplinarian to expect that a captain would permit a lieutenant to desert his guns at a moment when an attack was impending, appear on the quarter-deck and question a plan of battle.

A signal roared from the walls, warning of their approach. Soldiers from Fort Montague could be seen running to Fort Nassau to protect the powder and repel the attack.

The element of surprise now lost, the enemy now concentrated and ready, the American fleet reconsidered, withdrew out of gunshot and held a council of war. Now and only now could Lieutenant Jones make his voice heard.

In the great cabin of the *Alfred* with five captains attending him — five earnest honest men who had sailed themselves into a predicament — he unfolded a battle plan so full of snare and deceit that, as they congratulated him after all was over, it would have cheated the Father of Lies himself: how much more misled were the fair-thinking straight-shooting British, who expected the blow to fall in a logical spot.

The rock-ridden shallow approach *was* passable, Jones contended. One had only to wait for the evening and then, with God's help and a foot or two of the scanty Caribbean tide, the fleet might slip over and in. Once in, they would fall on Fort Montague, weaker by nature and now further weakened since most of its garrison had rushed to defend the stronger fort where the powder was. And once Fort Montague was gained, they would train its guns, together with all the guns of the fleet, on Fort Nassau and blast it to bits if it did not capitulate.

Jones spoke with the authority of certain knowledge, but also, for he drew on all he had, in the deep persuasive voice that once had moved audiences in theatres and now moved this cabinful of captains.

His plan was well conceived, they agreed. It was always a part of British strategy, deeply ingrained and now grown rigid through years of success, to attack the strongest adversary first; and what they did themselves they would probably expect others to do. Moreover, the movements of the American fleet certainly presented every appearance of a descent on Fort Nassau. But the channel that Jones proposed looked unnegotiable, and no native pilot was available to guide them through, "especially in the dark," they said.

Jones knew the channel, he said; he had sailed it before in ships of even greater draft. He himself would pilot them through if they would trust him.

They had to trust someone or abandon their mission. Perforce they trusted Jones.

Jones perched himself in the crosstrees of the foremast of the *Alfred* and shouted his commands down to the deck. Captains were always a little jealous when pilots took over; momentarily they must stand aside, as brimful of authority as buckets with water but just as immobile and speechless. Five captains now had to stand silent and follow the lead of one lieutenant.

The sinking sun shone in the eyes of Fort Nassau's gunners and set on the sails of the American fleet, which bore to the east and appeared to give up their absurd enterprise. Then in the quick tropic twilight the line of ships turned about and came back, as if madly determined to pile themselves up on the rock-strewn suicidal shoal. Presently they were observed to weave and twist in snakelike file, and a trumpet voice carried to the shore, as if a demon with cat's eyes were piloting the snake. Then, not a timber scraped, they sailed into the smooth roadstead.

A hundred American Marines scrambled ashore under the shelter of a blistering cannonade that shattered the coral battlements of the weak and virtually undefended Fort Montague. The British flag came down. A white flag of quarter went up. Unopposed, the Marines marched in. All night the Congress Colors floated over the fort.

Fort Nassau was now in an untenable situation. Next morning it surrendered without firing a shot, while the half-Spanish population of the town looked on apathetically, enjoying the show and wondering if the good old days of the rollicking buccaneers, always so profitable to the islanders, might not have returned. The Americans' tactics had been like the buccaneers', certainly as wild. The islanders did not much care who governed them and would have welcomed back the lax old Spanish rule.

But they were informed that the flag now flying over the forts was the flag of the United States of America, that the Americans would not stay long, this was only a raid, and a liberal donation of money and rum (which had been found in the forts) would be given to anyone willing to help manhandle the cannon and powder into the ships. There was much native aid cheerfully given in this laborious transfer: seventy-one heavy cannon, fifteen brass mortars, flints, cutlasses, matches, sea stores and money: but alas, only two dozen barrels of gunpowder. During the night the British had dumped a hundred and sixty-two barrels into the sea. At least, it could not be fired against Americans.

For good measure the Americans took into custody the person of Nassau's royal Governor Browne, observing flippantly: "His Majesty seems to afford you little protection here. Perhaps you'll be safer with us." He would be useful in an exchange of prisoners which, now that the war was lengthening, were piling up on both sides.

The governor came aboard meekly enough when he discovered that the raid was not, as it seemed to be, the work of ingenious Spanish pirates who had adopted the confusing flag with England's ensign in its canton: these were merely those turbulent Americans, almost Englishmen, as civilized as Americans ever had been or ever were likely to be.

"You would not have had so easy a time of it," he said with great truth, "if our fleet hadn't been busy blockading that damned thousand-mile coastline of yours!"

"It's longer," they said.

Glancing at the Congress Colors he said, "It's hardly fair play of you rebels to fly a sneaking device like that."

They did not explain it to him.

"Well anyhow," he shrugged, "it won't last long."

It did not.

But its disappearance into the limbo of forgotten standards round which brave men have died did not take place in quite the manner that Governor Browne envisioned.

By the time Jones returned to his captaincy, America, whose generals were losing battles and whose Congress was in flight, firm in their faith no matter how dismal the present prospects, had put to paper another Declaration of Independence, signed by all thirteen states in Congress assembled, to give King George nightmares and to be weighed word by word in the chancelleries of Europe; to stand, if America stood, forever before the bar of world history. On this bold document, to immortalize or hang them, friends he knew had put their names and men he had seen and admired: Thomas Jefferson, who wrote it; Benjamin Franklin, who polished it; Joseph Hewes, whose *Alfred* he had piloted through Nassau's shoals; Robert Morris, associate of Hewes, who once had owned the *Alfred,* who was rich and rising in the Naval Committee; John Hancock, who had signed his commission and then, turning it over and writing anew on the back, his new commission as captain.

Absent was the greatest name of all, George Washington, who was with the troops. Absent too was the name of Patrick Henry, since a governor could not sit in Congress.

He wrote to Dorothea, "They are sending me off again, this time with a command of my own!"

359

But the postal system must still be in turmoil; he had received no word from her on his return.

Chapter 35

AND NOW INDEED he began to achieve his heart's desire. The name of Jones began to be heard in America. Shortly it would spread round the world, for such was his resolve and such were the hidden cards that Fate dealt, grinning.

On land the armies marched and countermarched; the tide of battle ebbed and flowed; he heard of the land war only at intervals; he was out on the sea, scanning the horizon for enemy sails and, when he found them, living through fateful hours of battle, short in retrospect, but eternities when they were happening and when all hung in the balance. During these eternities the air he breathed was gunsmoke, and the voices he heard were screams, and the noise was the roar of explosives, and the light by which he steered was the burning of enemy ships that went hissing down into watery graves made hot from the heat of their flaming deaths. It was an awesome, a fearsome time.

His orders from the Naval Committee gave him great liberty of action: "You are to embark," they read, "upon a cruise against our enemies so long as water and provisions last." It was exactly the sort of order he relished. He made the most of it.

Two months later the Naval Committee received an astonishing report from Newport, Rhode Island, where Captain Jones, having run out of water and provisions, had put in to refit. They had expected much of him, but not this:

> HONORED SIRS:
> I have taken sixteen sail, manned and sent in eight prizes, and sunk or destroyed the rest. The list of prizes is as follows:
>
> | | | |
> |---|---|---|
> | 1 — The Brigantine | *Britania* |
> | 2 — " " | *Sea Nymph* |
> | 3 — " " | *Favorite* |
> | 4 — The Ship | *Alexander* |
> | 5 — The Brigantine | *Success* |

6 —	"	"	*Kingston Packet*
7 —	"	"	*Defiance*
8 —	The Sloop		*Portland*

— These I manned with prize crews and sent in.

9 —	The Ship		*Adventure*
10 —	The Brigantine		*Friendship*
11 —	The Schooner		*John*
12 —	"	"	*Sea Flower*
13 —	"	"	*Ebenezer*
14 —	"	"	*Hope*

— These, being unseaworthy after the engagement, I burnt, setting their crews ashore as I was already encumbered with more prisoners than I could feed.

15, 16 — Two small schooners which beached themselves being on fire. I did not pause to ascertain their names.

Thus far the neatly penned report read like an impersonal inventory of some merchant's stock in trade. The Naval Committee strongly suspected it was a hoax. Captain Jones would not have been the first commander to falsify an impressive record of victories that existed wholly in his imagination. But there was more. His report continued: he permitted himself a rebuke to the selfishness of the privateers.

It is [he wrote] to the last degree distressing to contemplate the state and establishment of our Navy. The ordinary sailor is strongly moved by motives of self-interest, and while this is the case, unless the pay of our sailors and their share of our prizes is made more attractive, our Navy can never become more respectable. And without a respectable Navy — alas! America! Give the sailors *all* the prizes! The privateers do.

The Naval Committee did not like being lectured; they had problems aplenty on their hands. But Jones had friends on the board. Hewes said, "He wouldn't lie; the prizes will show up unless the British recapture them." Robert Morris, the cultured millionaire, observed, "He writes with a facile pen; note how he ends his report."

Jones had written: "The situation in America is new in the annals of mankind; her affairs cry *haste,* and speed must answer them!"

Shortly all eight of the ships he had taken appeared in ports up and down the coast still held by Americans. His prizes were real; they were not figments of his imagination.

They were promptly refitted, their battle damage repaired, and they were sent out again to prey upon the British. Every vessel gained from England was a double loss to England: it could no longer fight for her, it could now fight against her. The Naval Committee noted with pleasure that Captain Jones's eight prizes added up to exactly the number that Congress had originally authorized as the entire American fleet. In two months he had doubled it. They rewarded him.

They gave him two more ships to join the *Alfred*.

He wrote proudly to Dorothea: "They are sending me off again instanter, after some successes which may have come to your ears. I long for your letters, but perhaps it is natural that I do not receive them. Many ports are burnt or in British hands, and I never know where next I must put in to refit; I move about fast. It would be surest, I think, if you should write to me, to address your letters to the Naval Committee. Mr. Hewes will send them to me, to command my heart, by the same postal rider he employs for the orders which command my ships. *Ships*, Dorothea! I am to lead a squadron!"

To make absolutely certain the letter reached her — she too, like the Congress, might be in flight — he sent his letter sealed to Joseph Hewes to be forwarded to her wherever she was. Hewes opened it, read it, sighed, and then compassionately held it to a candle and burned it in the flame. Hewes was weary and sick and getting old. Like Robert Morris, he was expending a fortune in America's cause. He was burdened with high duties of office and exasperated by the ineptitude of the fledgling American Navy. Everyone wanted to be an admiral, and almost no one (except the privateers) could sail a ship. Jones was too valuable to lose. Let the letter be lost in the ashes of some American town that the British were burning. Letters were being lost, and so were lives. Let Captain Jones continue to work his prodigies of seamanship without private grief at the head of the little force he so glowingly described to the girl he loved as his "squadron."

Jones drilled his three-ship squadron as if it were a national fleet, forcing them to execute difficult maneuvers again and again, devising a set of signals, flags by day and lights by night, demanding that the signals be learned and instantly obeyed. It was a tedious business, irksome to men unaccustomed to discipline. Nor could they expect reward: the mission was unprofitable, the weather was cold, the course was north.

Captains were disgruntled and crews were listless, for now in these terrible times even payment of wages had become uncertain.

One ship clumsily ran aground in a fog, sprang a leak too big to be repaired and was forced to limp back to port.

The other ship simply deserted. When Jones looked for her on a morning following a heavy blow, she was gone. He thought she might have foundered, though the storm had not struck him as particularly dangerous. Still, she might have developed some structural weakness and gone down. He had watched her laboring during the night; then suddenly all her lights had gone out. Only a captain's order or an all-engulfing wave could have extinguished them so quickly. He cruised in the vicinity some time, hoping to pick up her boats, which might be carrying survivors. He would learn, as he would learn much else, that her captain had deemed the strength of the squadron now so depleted by the loss of the other ship as to render its mission impossible of success and, on his own authority, had returned to the Naval Committee for assignment to duty elsewhere.

Jones, in the *Alfred,* pressed on alone.

In his weakened condition he knew there was only one chance of accomplishing his mission now: to explain its supreme importance to his men and make them fight like demons. If he could not offer them gold, he at least could offer them glory.

He ordered a pirate-sized ration of grog passed out to all hands and summoned them to the quarter-deck to hear him while they drank. When so strict a commander as Captain Jones unbent so far, they knew there was something special in the wind. There were mutters at first, "He talks big, don't he!" but rum and the strength of his passionate faith spread to them and warmed them, won them over to him and infused in them a conviction of success as great as his own. Before he had finished, they cheered him.

They were bound for Nova Scotia, he said. It was cold, yes, but not so cold as the state of Maine, which was even farther north, and he'd see they had plenty of what they held in their cups to keep them warm.

Nova Scotia was on the mouth of the Saint Lawrence, that big Canadian river that ran like a highway to invasion to strike at the heart of the United States. Up and down the Saint Lawrence river sailed the British warships, transports, supply ships, with food and supplies for the British armies. Three American vessels, his squadron, had been sent to interrupt these supplies. Now there was only one ship, the *Alfred;* but the *Alfred* was the biggest and best. To his own men, the *Alfred's* crew, had

363

fallen the honor of striking at the enemy where they were certain to be found, the mouth of the Saint Lawrence, before they could get in and stab America in the back. There was plenty of sea room to maneuver. There would be plenty of prizes. He could not promise them money like the privateers, but he could promise them names, pensions, recognition, freedom, advancement in the Navy of a nation whose flag had flown for the first time over the very ship on whose deck they now stood and still flew triumphant.

He paused and let them look at it, privately noting that the wind and sun were just right to display it to advantage.

He gave them a laugh, for he knew the power of a laugh.

Who, he asked, was this formidable British general for whom all the supplies now pouring into Canada were destined? Who was this man who planned to march south and invade America when he got them? Gentleman Johnny Burgoyne, they called him. Gentleman! Did they know that this so-called gentleman was a whoring, high-living, high-gambling soft-bellied rake who actually wrote plays for the London stage? Did they know he had taken his mistress, another theater creature, with him to Canada? "Cut off the good food, good wine and warm clothes of *such* a man," he said, "and Gentleman Johnny will quickly lose heart and go back to his playwriting!"

He made it sound logical, noble and not too hard. He believed what he said, but he also knew his power of persuasion. It was not likely, he thought, that many of these sturdy Americans, who still revered if they did not live up to the code of the early Puritans, had had occasion to attend West Indian theaters and see their captain acting upon a stage.

He ended on a sober note.

There were a hundred American prisoners of war toiling in the coalpits of Cape Breton, cold, naked, starving, subjected to all the brutality that the British knew so well how to inflict upon their slaves. It was their mission to set them free.

A curious incident occurred on the voyage north. He came across an American privateer, the *Eagle,* in Tarpawling Cove near Nantucket. He hove to and went aboard and sought to persuade her captain to join his expedition. The privateer captain laughed in his face.

Among the crew Jones saw some defaced and ill-disguised naval uniforms.

"Am I deceived, Captain Field, in my apprehension that some of your men are deserters from the Navy?"

Insolently the privateer answered, "Oh, that. They must have picked up those old uniforms somewhere, bought them maybe."

"Unlikely, sir; the Navy is still so new that its uniforms have not had time to wear out. They are in short supply; they cannot be bought. These men are deserters. I demand, sir, the instant delivery of every American Navy man aboard your ship!"

"You'll have to come and take them off," sneered the privateer.

Jones answered quietly, "I did not entirely trust your flag, Captain Field, and I took a certain precaution in case you were flying false colors. Would you care to look out of your cabin window?"

The privateer looked and stared straight into the muzzles of the *Alfred's* guns.

"Would you like me to give the signal? I have only to wave this handkerchief," Jones said.

The privateer said, "You dare not fire upon an American ship."

"Yes, I do."

"Your men won't shoot."

"Yes, they will."

"You'll be killed."

"So will you."

"God damn you for a pirate!"

"God damn you for a privateer!"

Forty deserters were rounded up and delivered to the *Alfred*. Some of them had to be routed out of the bilges in which they had hidden themselves.

Stronger in man power, if not in quality, the *Alfred* bore north. Jones lectured the deserters severely but not unkindly. "It isn't as if you had deserted to the British," he said.

They growled they would never do that. They had only wanted more money.

He promised to put in a good word for them if they did their duty, and hoped that the excellent spirit of his own crew would spread to them by a sort of contagion.

It did.

Off Nova Scotia he fought and captured the British ship *Active,* manned her and sent her in to refit and repair and be joined to the Navy. Her prisoners were placed in one of the American prisoner camps to be exchanged or to wait out the end of the war.

In a thick fog he came across a stumbling convoy of merchantmen under the protection of a single British frigate. He stood off till the frigate had passed and then swept in and cut four ships out of the convoy, forced them to strike and took them out to sea before the fog cleared and the frigate returned looking in vain for her lost wards. He manned them and sent them in, full of arms, powder, blankets and winter provisions.

His crew ate better after that, and Captain Jones was liberal with the captured British rum. It had long been a legend that he could see in the dark, dating from the perilous passage at Nassau; now it began to be whispered that he could see through fog as well — fog had contributed enormously to his success in capturing the four merchantmen.

But every ship he took depleted his crew by the subtraction of a dozen dependable sailors and one good officer who composed the prize crews.

All of these actions involved shooting, though not very much. He was playing a cat-and-mouse game. He darted in; he hit; he fled. Nevertheless there were wounded aboard his prizes and wounded aboard the *Alfred*. But he himself never sustained a scratch in battle. It began to be rumored among the other legends that were growing up about him that the safest place during an engagement was where the captain was. It was invigorating to serve under a man who appeared to bear a charmed life.

He changed his tactics now, conscious that every prize diminished the number and fighting strength of his crew. He led an unexpected raid ashore: he burned a fleet of Nova Scotian fishing boats and the warehouses where the fish were dried, so that Gentleman Johnny's army might be spared the discomfort of eating salt cod; he burned an anchored transport laden with munitions, which exploded in a spectacular display of pyrotechnics, adding a touch of drama to the gloomy winter sunset; and he sternly lectured the French-speaking fishermen in their own language on the folly of serving the British, who, at heart, really hated all papists. He left them confused and irritated, which was his effect on most men; but they remembered him.

Then he fell in with the greatest prize of all.

One aspect of his mission he had to abandon. Ice had begun to block the Nova Scotian harbors. He could not get in to free the Americans from the mines nor, if he had been able, could he have accommodated them aboard the *Alfred*, encumbered as he now was with prisoners.

But the *Mellish* made up for all that.

He sighted the merchantman sailing alone without convoy. She was very large and deeply laden, riding low in the water. Her heavy load meant sluggishness; her solitary situation meant big guns and a powerful fighting crew. She was tempting, but she would be mean. He watched her through his glass, taking her measure, while some of his British prisoner captains (who dined with him in the great cabin) permitted themselves to smile, "You will never take *her*, Captain."

They believed their liberation at hand, and the fact that they might be killed in the engagement that was about to take place troubled them not at all, or if it did they did not allow it to show on their faces. One had to admire the British officer. One reason the prizes got safely to American ports was that the British parole was as good as their bank notes. Once they had given their word, having surrendered, that they would not attempt to retake their ship, they did not break it. Only a nation with a long history of good sportsmanship bred men like that.

But Jones did take her.

Because of her sluggishness he was able to outmaneuver her, crossing her bow and crossing her stern, raking her with gunfire. He did not attempt to burst her sturdy hull: he ripped her rigging to shreds with chain and grape; he cut her sails to tatters and splintered her spars. He immobilized her.

"Your French tactics will not avail you in the end," the English officers observed, white-faced with anger.

He did not ask them why; they would have cut out their tongues rather than disclose why; anyhow, he knew.

He closed in as if preparing to board, and instantly the *Mellish's* decks swarmed with an entire company of British soldiers in addition to the crew who stood by to repel the attack. Her great guns could not reach him. Jones was approaching down wind on the slower ship towards her bows, just out of reach of the deadly sector through which her guns could fire. Only the swivel guns on her deck wrought some damage to the *Alfred*.

Then, unexpectedly, scores of hidden riflemen lurking in the *Alfred's* rigging opened fire with their deadly American hunting guns, picking off the British soldiers on the deck who were armed only with muskets of half the range and not half the accuracy. Presently the slaughter on the deck was so great that the British captain struck.

That night, with Jones as host at the head of the table in the great cabin of the *Alfred*, there was considerable discussion of American firearms among the captured British captains, to which company was now added the captain of the *Mellish*. Forlornly, ahead of the *Alfred* where Jones could keep an eye on her, the beaten *Mellish* led the way to Boston and her own internment.

In addition to her soldiers, in addition to great quantities of powder, muskets, medical supplies, tools, tents, bullets, and bayonets, in addition to substantial sums of money for payment of troops, the *Mellish* carried ten thousand warm winter uniforms for General Burgoyne's army.

"General Burgoyne is going to be very cold," the *Mellish's* captain said, staring disconsolately into his plate. "I did the best I could."

Jones would not let so valuable a prize out of his sight. He convoyed her to Boston himself.

He prepared a report of his cruise to the Naval Committee. Concerning the *Mellish* he wrote: "The loss of the *Mellish* will distress the enemy more than can easily be imagined, as the clothing on board of her is the last intended to be sent out for Canada this season. The situation of Burgoyne's army must soon become insupportable. I will not lose sight of a prize of such importance but will sink her rather than suffer her again to fall into British hands."

In Boston at last there were letters. One was from Dr. Read. One was from Dorothea. He opened hers first.

She had always called him Jock, or sometimes in fun Captain Jock, or sometimes those tenderer names that had promised so much happiness; now suddenly they grated, hollow, empty, meaningless, forever lost.

This letter began:

> DEAR JOHN:
> You have been away so long and so much has happened to both of us that I hardly know how to begin this, but it is only fair and better for us both if I tell you frankly that my sentiments toward you ——

The writing swam together.
Dr. Read's letter read:

> You have told me from time to time that you were under some expectation of purchasing a Virginia estate; but some more agreeable idea will, I fear, call you off and deprive us of you. Miss Dandridge is no more — that is to say, she a few months ago gave herself into the arms of Governor Patrick Henry.

Dazedly he spoke to the emptiness of the great cabin, while the harbor noises carried through the timbers and the smell of land, always unclean at first, drifted in: "But it was the children, those six little children she loved, not the father twice her age! I thought it was. But she married him."

Chapter 36

NOW, TO ADD to the private grief of the letter beginning "Dear John," there came a flood of professional exasperations.

One by one, seven bailiffs appeared to serve him with court subpoenas demanding that he present himself to answer charges brought against him by seven of the forty deserters he had snatched from the privateer *Eagle*.

Then one more subpoena arrived: the commander of the *Eagle*, Captain Field himself, was suing him for ten thousand pounds damages for "illegal action against an American ship of war."

"Philadelphia lawyers have a reputation for ability," he thought wearily, and sought to engage one to defend him; but just then Philadelphia fell to the British.

He appealed to the Navy Committee, but his letter came back as improperly addressed. The Naval Committee no longer existed. It was now the Marine Committee. It could perhaps be reached, for the moment at least, in Baltimore, Maryland, whither the Congress had fled.

He appealed to Joseph Hewes. Hewes replied he had just been defeated in a campaign for re-election to Congress, had lost his seat and was now a private citizen again. His fortune was spent, his health was failing, his influence was nil, he could not help.

His letter contained an ominous hint which Jones did not grasp at first: "You would be surprised to hear what a vast number of applications are continually making for officers of the new frigates, especially as regards their command. The strong recommendations from those provinces where any frigates are building have great weight."

Where were the provinces where frigates were building? Jones asked himself. Why, in New England. Who then would command them? Why, New Englanders. And who was he? He was Captain John P. Jones of North Carolina, a "southerner" in the madding chaos of the politics of a revolution. 'Twas a topsy-turvy world gone sair agley when a Scotsman from Kirkcudbright was accounted a southerner! But it was good that America was building frigates. To command a frigate pulled at him like a physical desire, strong as the pull of hunger or thirst or love.

Shortly a dire communication arrived from Baltimore from the Marine Committee. He had been degraded, it informed him, from third to eighteenth in the list of American naval captains. The *Alfred* was to be taken from him and assigned to a newly commissioned captain who had just entered the service.

America in her distress could not do without him, but neither could she do without the new men who, later than Jones, now came forward to serve her. His loyalty was proved; theirs must be rewarded at once.

Without a ship, and forced to defend himself in eight court actions for damages, he left the *Alfred* and went ashore.

While engaging a Boston attorney who undertook to represent him as defendant, Jones suddenly received orders from the Marine Committee that he was to sit as one of the judges in a court-martial on the commander of the ship which had deserted the *Alfred*'s squadron.

Thus, heartsick and fuming with resentment, he found himself called to appear simultaneously in nine separate naval court actions: in one as a judge, in eight as the defendant. Irony could go no farther.

Irony could go farther.

A sure and friendly hand reached out to cut through the desperate tangle that enmeshed and immobilized him.

It was the hand of a privateer.

Chapter 37

HIS LAWYER riffled through the sheaf of subpoenas and said to him, "I think you'll have time to go up to Portsmouth and see Mr. Langdon. These instruments" — he indicated the pile of accusations — "are legally full of holes. Some of them actually indict you in the name of King George, using the old printed forms. I can stave off your enemies, at least till they indict you in proper form. Fortunately the new American forms change every day. For the moment at least you are safe to leave Boston."

"Safe!" Jones cried. "I don't want to be safe. I will not run away. I want to be right. I will prove I am right."

The Boston lawyer said, "You raise an interesting question of ethics, sir, which has nothing to do with your present predicament: to be safe and to be right are happy conditions which cannot always be enjoyed simultaneously. America is right, but is she safe? If she were safe, would she be right? To me my heart dictates the answers. To you *a fortiori* yours must do the same. Take the bull by the horns, Captain Jones, and ride up to New Hampshire. Langdon has heard of you; he wants you for a new ship of his. If you will permit me a literary quotation: 'There is a tide in the affairs of men which, taken at the flood, leads on to fortune.' Perhaps I ought to explain the allusion: it is a line from William Shakespeare, the great poet. Sail on that flood, Captain Jones, and let me take care of the legal matters, you in your province, I in mine."

Suppressing a grin, Jones said, "I shall be guided by your excellent advice, Mr. Tillinghast. This Shakespeare sounds like a very sensible fellow. Is he an American?"

The polished lawyer saw the rough sailorman to the door.

Once more along the American coast that he had seen from the sea from the Antilles to Nova Scotia, Jones took horse and rode northward toward a meeting with a man who had heard of his name and toward, as he hoped, another command. Jones was used to the smooth powerful forward surge of a ship; he disliked the jerky earth-bumping sensation of the saddle; sometimes in moments of abstraction he would draw up with a start, "By God, the clumsy beast has run himself aground!" and then laugh and be off again. Only a gallop was smooth enough to put him at his ease, and at a gallop he passed from Boston to Portsmouth in one day.

"Chima," he said as they rode, "we are going to Portsmouth, New Hampshire. It's a seaport in New England, and you're going to be pretty conspicuous up here."

"Will that displease you?"

"Good Lord, no! I never care if I am conspicuous."

"Then why should I care?"

"We shall not see many Negroes, and those we do will all be free men."

"Capture them," Chima advised.

"No, no. Don't you want to be a free man?"

"Master, I am, if you are."

"But don't you want to be free of me, not have any master?"

"No," Chima said.

"Chima, I used to think that slavery was right. Now I know that slavery is wrong. Therefore you ought to be a free man and serve yourself instead of me and be your own master. Do you understand?"

Chima looked sick, as if he had been struck in the face. "How have I

371

offended you? What have I done to displease you? Please, please, please do not cast me adrift, oh please."

"Promise me, Chima, if you ever change your mind, that you will tell me, and then I will legally set you free."

"With subpoenas?" Chima looked sideways, suspiciously, at him. His master was full of tricks. "I promise," he said, resolving to be on his guard in the future against any repetition of the unknown offense, whatever it was that had caused his master to threaten to "set him adrift." Chima's speech was as nautical as Jones's own.

Portsmouth was a distinctly racy place, sporting the biggest dance hall in America. The fine old American practice of bundling had died out here only lately, and indeed in the cabins of the hinterland during the long cold winter nights was rumored to still survive in a state of vigorous activity. Pirates and privateers had been welcome transients in Portsmouth's harbor for as long as could be remembered and had not yet worn out their welcome. The consumption of rum was noteworthy. In the better houses, however, it was consumed, by the ladies at least, in the elegant form of a punch that would stagger a grenadier.

To the best of these houses overlooking a busy shipyard Jones and Chima rode, to be greeted by a big black smiling boy who spoke hardly a word of English, obviously a newcomer just over from Africa. He took the horses and Chima round to the rear. Jones heard them laughing and chattering in Ibo.

This was Jones's first whiff of the strong, eccentric and independent personality of John Langdon, who owned the shipyard and the stableboy. In Langdon's household there were plenty of Negroes who were not free men. Shortly Jones got to know him better. He was young, almost as young as Jones, and tremendously vital. There was much in common in their joint careers, probably more than Langdon would admit, for Langdon had been a sea captain himself for some years prior to the recent time when, with vaulting ambition and sudden wealth, he had set himself up in the shipbuilding business and gone into politics.

"Commerce can be extremely rewarding financially," Langdon said.

"Indeed it can," said Jones.

"At the beginning of the war I built and operated only privateers," Langdon said, "and I've still got a few of them busy. My captains do very well for themselves."

"There's no doubt about that, but they fight alone, and if we're to win we must fight in fleets."

Langdon smiled and said good-naturedly, 'I have come to agree with you. You are not to be tempted by the offer of a privateer, are you, sir." It was not a question; it was a statement of fact.

"No, sir. Just now I'm bedeviled by rather an opposite course of events."

"The *Eagle* incident?"

"Yes."

"I don't own her any more, but I built her."

"Her mainmast is three feet too far to the fore."

Langdon chuckled and let it pass.

"Do not worry about your lawsuits, Captain. I am building a ship for the Navy now. That gives me a certain influence with Congress. I'll get the whole batch of your troublesome legal actions nonsuited. Or if I can't, I'll see that they're all brought here for trial in Portsmouth; a change of venue can easily be arranged in times like these. Then I'll simply heave them out of my court. By a singular good fortune I am also a judge, you know."

The busy, busy privateer was judge of New Hampshire's court of common pleas, member and speaker of the New Hampshire House of Representatives, colonel of the New Hampshire militia, and had just resigned his seat in the Congress to become the Navy's prize agent for New Hampshire, a far more profitable enterprise. There was no doubting his patriotism; but while Hewes had spent a fortune aiding America, Langdon was piling up a fortune. America needed them all; fortune was fickle — lavish here, niggardly there — and did not matter anyhow: they would all be bankrupt and worse if England won.

"It was largely owing to your incessant prodding of the Naval Committee that Congress has finally loosened up and made it possible for a prize agent to turn an honest penny," Langdon said.

"The sailors are beginning to get some share in the prizes too."

"Yes, yes, of course. Everyone admires your efforts in their behalf. But is it not true, sir, that a captain is also a sailor and that his share is somewhat greater?"

Jones flushed. It was enormously greater. "I wasn't thinking of that when I fought for the rights of my men!"

"I did not say you were, but since you have demonstrated that you are not afraid to die — Great God! How you have demonstrated that! — I merely suggest that while you live you've a right to live well. *I* do."

Jones, in his present frame of mind, was not averse to living well. "I'll bear that in mind when I get my next command," he said, smiling, "and I'll make it a point to take some valuable prizes."

Langdon said, "I saw that list of prizes you took with the *Alfred:* sixteen in six weeks! That's why I asked Congress for you for my *Ranger.* She's yours, Captain, if you want her."

If he wanted her! She was slender as a sylph, trim-tapering astern, with the swift American-clipper bow that overrode the waves, never brutally bludgeoned against them. She looked fresh; she smelled new; she felt smooth under his hand. There was speed in all her delicate lines. Yet she was tough. Her ribs were New England oak that had been two hundred years agrowing, two hundred years of victories already won defying the fierce New England storms. Her hull was deep and sharp; this was no barge-bottomed trader. Her freeboard was low as a yacht's; here would be a difficult target for the hull-bursting British to shoot at. Her three whip-limber masts shot up to a dizzy height which, to the uninformed, looked dangerously top-heavy. Surely so slender a ship would capsize with such masts under a full press of sail. Jones knew she could carry her sail; the stability of her hull was enormous; her strength was deceptive. Only a privateer or a pirate could have built her.

"Like her?" Langdon asked.

Jones said, "I love her!"

"She will carry twenty-four guns."

"No, give her eighteen! Why burden an angel? Give her wings!"

"Most of my captains want both, both speed and a heavy battery."

"They are wrong, wrong! You can never have both."

The two strong-minded men struck fire from each other more than once while the *Ranger* was fitting out.

Langdon reduced the battery to eighteen, shrugging, "You are the man who will have to fight her," but he refused to dig out the mainmast and place it some feet farther aft where Jones wanted it: "Captain, you'd spin like a top! You've got to have *some* stability!"

Jones let it pass with a sharp remark, "I don't have to be drawn like an oxcart. I teach my men to steer."

Jones would have liked to set sail at once, but Langdon stubbornly refused to deliver the ship to the Navy till every penny due him on her was paid. The Congress, still in exile, was slow to pay, not from niggardliness but from cruel lack of funds.

While the *Ranger,* half rigged, awaited delivery, Jones lived well in a handsome house that a loyalist had abandoned. Langdon in his capacity as a judge had confiscated the property, renting it to Jones.

The court-martial on which Jones would have sat as a judge never convened. Congress had not the power, nor was it in a mood, to censure anyone who would fight, even languidly, against England.

The hand of Judge Langdon reached out and easily quashed the lawsuits in which Jones had been summoned to defend himself.

Up in Canada General Burgoyne, without uniforms or supplies, waited for warmer weather to invade the United States.

In the hinterland behind Portsmouth trappers trapped as usual, and youths and maidens bundled, and Benjamin Franklin's theories of American increase took on tangible form in a rash of early spring marriages. "Mother Nature," the philosopher observed in his French château, whither the Congress had sent him to woo the French over to America's side, "hath mysterious means of Her own to compensate for the awful losses in war that Her foolish children bring upon themselves."

Langdon's parties had always been gay. His household staff, all slaves, with their bright liveries and deferential behavior, gave his social functions a touch of the exotic. The music was lively, the punch was hot. The New England coast was rock-bound, but not stern, not in these days of revolution.

Captain Jones, who never talked about himself but who seemed to have been everywhere, known everyone, and who had taken more British prizes than anyone else in the war, was much in demand as a dancing partner and much gossiped about. Whispering into each other's curls, the girls would warn, "He'll dance you into a dark alcove, man you and take you in! Take care!" Frowning over their teacups, the watching mothers would wonder, "Something must have happened to him: he's hard as an iron nail! And he looks like such a nice young man, such excellent manners," and then cruise off over the shiny ballroom floor to convoy their daughters back into safety and light. A pretty cousin of Langdon's quite lost her heart and her head and told her mother that if Captain Jones did not propose to her she planned to propose to him. When this reached Langdon's ear, he wished that the currency crisis would pass and Congress would pay for the *Ranger*.

Shortly the crisis passed. The printing presses began to roll. Paper money flooded the country. The Continental currency depreciated almost at once; no foreigner would touch it; but Americans took it, even John Langdon who loved hard money. It was the measure of their faith in the future. The *Ranger* was paid for, rigged and readied for sea.

With the warmer months had come the long-delayed and much-dreaded invasion from Canada. General Burgoyne marched south with eight thousand men, ill-clothed and ill-provisioned. He never had quite made up the supplies of which Jones's descent on the Saint Lawrence Gulf had robbed him.

In a series of nibbling battles which wasted his strength he lost many men, but still pressed south.

Then in a fierce engagement at Saratoga, New York, the American forces converged; Burgoyne was surrounded and soundly trounced. Gentleman Johnny gave up. He surrendered himself and his entire army. Americans breathed one mighty sigh of hope. It was the turning point of the war.

And now to make the most of the victory, the only ponderable demonstration of strength America yet had made in the war! How full were the military annals of the world of great wars lost because victories had not been pressed home! To win friends, to woo the world and let it be known that the British were not invincible, was now the first care of America.

Congress, in exile, grew bold; their native American reluctance to hide a light under a bushel came strongly to the fore. This American brashness might offend polite Europeans but it could not be minimized: no one could deny the astonishing fact that Burgoyne had surrendered.

Congress, in exile, ripped the British crosses from their victorious flag, cutting the last tenuous ties with the mother country. Henceforth in the canton appeared thirteen stars, matching the thirteen stripes.

On the same day they adopted the Stars and Stripes as the flag of the United States, Congress formally appointed John Paul Jones to command of the *Ranger*.

Now came the race across the sea to win those friends.

Other swift vessels took part in that race to carry the news to France; it was news too vital to America's cause to commit to one man or one ship.

So superbly did the *Ranger* behave that Jones fell prey to temptation. He itched to blood his beautiful new ship. Near the coast of Europe he turned aside at the sight of two British sail bearing up from the south. Skipping nimbly round them, first the one and then the other, he captured them both; manned them with prize crews and sent them home to Langdon. Tongue in cheek and in high good humor, he penned a note:

Honble. Sir:
Please to accept and dispose of, I hope to your profit, the first fruits of the *Ranger's* first cruise. Examination of the cargo, or what may remain of it, of these two brigantines will reveal what I mean by *first fruits*.

The cargoes were nothing but oranges, lemons and grapes, loaded at Malaga and destined for London: some casks of Malaga wine Jones removed for better use on the *Ranger*. The brigantines themselves, of course, would be of great value, but the pulpy fresh fruits would likely all be spoiled.

The *Ranger* lost the race to France by one day. Jones glared furiously at the mainmast: "I told that damned privateer he'd placed that damned stick too far forward! I'd have had those two prizes in one day if the *Ranger* had answered the wheel quicker!"

Now he met Franklin. The sturdy old man walked out of his château, not yet a recognized embassy, and said, "Is Philadelphia retaken?"

"Not yet," Jones said.

"Alas!" Franklin said and clasped his hands together and walked slowly back into the house.

"Soon, sir."

"I know."

He knew so much. But Philadelphia was his home.

At this time the American Commissioners in France, headed by Franklin, lived in a queer half-world of nonacceptance. The glittering society of Paris shunned them like poor relations of questionable morality, fascinating but not quite respectable. Their dress was homespun, their political creed was extreme. They represented a people in conflict with the doctrine of divine right of kings, this in the premier monarchy of Christendom ruled by His Most Christian Majesty Louis XVI, who, when he ascended the ancient throne of his ancestors, had been anointed with holy oil from the *Sainte Ampoule*, a miraculous crystal vial flown down from heaven itself in the beak of a pure white dove for the baptism of King Clovis, first Christian king of the Franks, ancestor of fabled Charlemagne, remote ancestor of His Present Majesty, thirteen long long centuries before. The United States was one year old. Intruders in an old house, upstarts in an established community, the Americans were decidedly not company one liked to be seen with.

Their château at Passy was located in an isolated section of a gloomy wood outside of Paris where their presence would not embarrass the better element of the capital and where its activities would not be spied on by agents of foreign governments, especially Great Britain, with whom France was still at peace.

Thither flocked a motley array of dreamers, impostors, self-seekers, adventurers and charlatans: Count Cagliostro with alchemistical powders to sell, elixirs of youth and a mixture guaranteed to make ugly women beautiful; the aging Casanova with a scheme for a national lottery that would make everybody rich, who, dismissed, pinched all the chambermaids and set up a cheating game of cards in the stables; self-styled poets who greatly desired that Dr. Franklin would please to print their epics in praise of America, he having so many presses; British traitors attempting to sell British military secrets, which everybody knew, in return for an American regiment; a fur-capped Pole with a ring in his ear who said he knew how to freeze the river Thames into one solid block of ice; a man with a map of Montezuma's treasure; a "mason" who knew where the gold in the pyramids was hidden; and there were wild-eyed French revolutionaries who wanted pistols in a plot to assassinate the French king.

Thither came also, but furtively, powerful French ministers of state, finance and marine, cloaked and masked and at night in coaches with lights extinguished, as if their owners were stealing off to attend some naughty nude theatrical presentation or some assignation with a mistress. The unorthodox Americans had power; no sober statesman could afford to dismiss them lightly. In the cynical chess game of European politics their friendship might tip the scale against England. Hence in the dark they were courted, and in the light they were shunned.

Now the tremendous news of Burgoyne's surrender swept all this subterfuge aside. The château at Passy, like the temple purged of the money changers, became respectable. Light shone in; the vermin crawled off to darker holes. In broad daylight the better elements of Paris openly visited the Americans. The president of *l'Académie Française* in a spectacular uniform blazing with literary honors endorsed Dr. Franklin's view that Captain Cook, the Englishman, returning from the South Seas with priceless scientific data, ought not to be molested. "It warms the heart that Your Excellency's broad humanitarian outlook does not limit itself to the exigencies of war against your enemies;" and he added with a knowing smile, *"et ceux de nous autres de la France!"* Already a promise of aid! The minister of marine, equally sparkling with military decorations, engaged to instruct the French fleet that Captain Cook might pass through. Nobody knew that poor Captain Cook had been eaten by cannibals in the Sandwich Islands and his ships were returning without him.

Openly now the chancelleries of Europe revised their estimate of America's might.

France signed a treaty of alliance, commerce and perpetual friendship

378

with the United States, thus recognizing her not as a colony of Great Britain but as an independent sovereign state. Holland, Spain and the Scandinavian countries followed suit. Imperial Catherine of Russia associated herself with the movement in what was called "the armed neutrality of the North."

No one declared a war, but all prepared to shoot and no one was neutral now.

The whole world pounced on England.

While these great events were shaping, Captain Jones dug out the *Ranger's* mainmast and stepped it farther aft, where he wanted it. He added some tons of lead to her keel, to further increase her speed and emerged with the raciest, trickiest ship of war afloat.

Franklin glowed. He said to Jones, "Something of benefit to our country has been on my mind, a means to simplify and make known to the world all these involved and diplomatic developments, such as the favorable treaties that lately have been signed. The common man will best understand them by something as simple as they were complex, something that can be seen like a banner and heard like a shout. Nothing will prove so convincing as a salute to the new United States flag. I shall prepare the ground at court and make certain the salute will be formally approved by the highest authorities. You, who speak French, shall arrange the details with the French admiral at Quiberon Bay."

"You do me a precious honor, sir."

"Since you were the first to raise the Congress Colors on an American ship, I conceive it only your due to be first to receive a salute to the Stars and Stripes."

In Quiberon Bay the French admiral saluted, the minister of marine approved and the king countersigned.

Next day, just to make sure, Jones tricked the admiral into repeating the salute by appearing suddenly and giving him an unscheduled salute; the admiral was forced to answer. Again the minister approved and again the king countersigned.

And then, outstripping his orders, sailing up to the big French naval station at Brest, Jones fired an unexpected salute to the flagship there; he was met with smokeless silence.

He had himself rowed over to the flagship and went aboard in his newest dress uniform and sternly addressed the bewildered French commander.

"Is it not customary, sir, to return the salute of a visiting ship of war of a sovereign nation and ally?"

One would have thought that the United States was going to the aid of France instead of the other way round.

"I have no orders, sir," the Frenchman replied, astonished at being addressed by an American so fluently in his own tongue.

"Did you not know, sir, that I took the salute to the Stars and Stripes not once but twice from the admiral himself in Quiberon Bay but a few days since?"

"I'm afraid I did not. Perhaps my orders are coming overland; sometimes there is a delay."

"I came by sea," Jones said. He showed him the beautifully engrossed copies authenticating the two salutes, signed by the ministry of marine and the king. The Frenchman apologized handsomely.

Amiably Jones said, "I shall be delighted to repeat my salute, sir."

This time the Frenchman roared out his recognition in a thundering return, with marines standing smartly at attention and officers saluting with their swords.

Franklin had asked one salute; Jones had got it, and had stolen two more.

In England the admiralty muttered that everywhere along the French coast, wherever the paltriest American vessel appeared, the French Navy outdid themselves to salute her.

Shortly that paltry vessel embarked on a cruise that sent shivers down their spines. It was now to happen, not in old legend, not in some faraway Indian port, but in this very present year, in this now-occurring war, in their own British waters, nay, upon their own British soil where no enemy foot had stood for seven hundred years, that a terror would descend, so fantastic that mothers would literally frighten their babies to bed with the name of John Paul Jones.

Chapter 38

HIS ORDERS from the American Commissioners read:

We rely on your ability as well as on your zeal to serve the United States, and therefore do not give you particular instructions as to your operations. We advise you, after equipping the *Ranger* in the best manner for the cruise you propose, that you proceed with her in the way you shall judge best for distressing the enemies of the United States, by sea or otherwise, consistent with the laws of war.

Franklin, who wrote this order, was protecting as well as commissioning the young man, so unlike his son, whom he had liked and befriended on sight and who was his guest at the château at Passy. Under the seemingly innocent phrasing of the order, as always in everything Benjamin Franklin ever wrote, lay deep thought and compassionate understanding.

"After equipping the *Ranger* —" Jones could have been court-martialed and dismissed from the service for tampering with her mainmast.

"Why did you incur expense and alter the structure of a vessel built for the United States Navy and duly approved and accepted by Congress?"

A pink-cheeked lad in his nineteenth year, the Marquis de La Fayette, one of the better element who now openly visited the château at Passy, leaned forward to catch the reply. What reckless presumption in a subordinate! thought the marquis.

"Sir, this is why," Jones said, looking around the dinner table for an object to use as a demonstration. Franklin was not a sailor, but he understood the wind.

There was a crystal dish near at hand, oval in shape, with olives and celery in it.

"Here is a hull to explain," Jones said, smiling, half in French for the benefit of the marquis. "But first to dispose of her cargo."

He emptied the olives and celery onto his plate.

"And now to pump her dry."

He poured the melted ice into his finger bowl, swamping the rose petals.

"And now to rig her — off balance."

With his finger for a mast he pushed the dish from the rear end. Instantly the crystal "ship" veered wildly off to one side and collided with a wineglass. "With the driving power too far astern you have no control, you cannot steer."

Then, to demonstrate the opposite extreme, he hooked his finger under the lip of the front end of the dish. "This rig is conventional; you can steer, but your rudder continually must fight the mast which drags you along like a wagon in the wake of a stupid ox. Roughly, that was my difficulty with the *Ranger*'s rig: the drive was too far to the fore. So this, sir, is the simple change I took the liberty of making."

He placed his finger firmly in the balance-center of the dish and propelled it forward. "Now see how sweetly she sails!" The lightest touch of a finger at the "stern" — the rudder, he explained — swiveled her unerringly wherever he wanted her to go, darting in and out among enemy porringers and dangerous decanters, skillfully avoiding the silverware reefs and shoals.

"The drive must come from the heart," he said.

The intense young marquis, brimful of the new notions of liberty that had captured the imaginations of half the nobility of France, cried with shining eyes, "Captain, the force of your allegory is not lost on me!"

Franklin said dryly, "It is also good engineering. Captain, you have demonstrated your point in a practical fashion that I can understand," and in his order, so that Jones would not be disciplined, gave him retroactive authority to do what he had already done to the *Ranger*.

That Jones could sail a ship was to be expected; that he was capable of proposing a broad strategy which corresponded exactly with Franklin's own was likelier in an admiral or a statesman than in a simple captain; but propose it the captain did.

Some means must be found to break up the blockade that was strangling the life out of American ports. True, America now had friends in Europe, but their fleets were not yet effective. American sea power was far too weak to challenge the British fleet en masse. Therefore some subterfuge must be tried to do the work. The recall of even a few of the British ships of war that were now ravaging and burning American towns would prove of tremendous value to American morale as well as demonstrate America's resolve to Europe.

Suppose, Jones had suggested, some American ship should appear unannounced on the British coast and burn a few British towns!

"You will be all alone, one ship in enemy waters," Franklin said thoughtfully, weighing the terrible chances against him.

"Sir, I have sailed those waters from my youth! Let me try."

It was a time to try, and a time to take chances.

Hence, in Jones's orders, the phrase, "by sea or otherwise."

La Fayette raised his glass and toasted Jones, "À l'Amérique!" and murmured to himself, "Incroyable!"

But into the order, remembering his own wild youth and wary now of passion, Dr. Franklin inserted the qualifying phrase, "consistent with the laws of war."

"But of course!" said the Marquis de La Fayette, whose young ideals were at high pitch and who could imagine nothing devious or expedient, far less anything piratical. Smiling at him with understanding eyes over half-moon spectacles, the aging philosopher remembered that at nineteen the things of this world are very black or very white.

"Naturally," said Jones, who was no longer nineteen, "consistent with the laws of war." Whatever they were.

Franklin now loosed the scorpion, to sting the British lion in its lair and drive the beast half mad with rage and shame.

With the flag locker well stocked with the national flags of all nations and some that did not even exist, and canvas flaps concealing his gun ports, Captain Jones slipped out of France disguised as a peaceful merchantman and sailed for England. Off Cape Clear on the Irish side of the Irish Sea he fell in with a brigantine and sank her, not pausing to ask her name or to pick up survivors, who floundered in the water among overturned boats and floating debris in a blanket of flaxseed which had apparently composed the ship's cargo. It drifted slowly in the directon of Ireland; presumably so might they; he wanted no prisoners.

He steered north into Saint George's Channel, captured, manned and sent to Brest the ship *Lord Chatham,* and sailed north again.

The success of his plan depended on no one's suspecting his presence; no one yet did. He was now very close to Scotland.

Off the Mull of Galloway he chased a small British schooner making for Solway Firth, overhauled her and smashed her to kindling wood. It could not be said that the schooner sank. Rather she disintegrated and spread out like broken straw over the surface of the sea. Cruising momentarily through the wreckage, he was delighted to find no single survivor to pick up, none to swim ashore and betray his presence.

A sloop on a course that might have warned England he likewise wholly destroyed with all hands.

But an Irish fishing boat so small she excited his pity gave him pause in his murderous forward rush. "Damn you!" he yelled. "What are you doing here!"

They were fishing, they said.

He spared their lives and took them aboard and sank their boat with a single shot.

The *Lord Chatham* had carried a full cargo of strong port wine, the drink of British lords. Jones let the impoverished Irishmen drink themselves drunk from a cask of it.

There was in the vicinity, the drunken Irishmen told him, a big British man-of-war, the *Drake,* twenty guns; why not sink her? They liked the British no better than did the Americans. They would show him where she was.

383

Jones crept up on the *Drake* in the night, but at dawn he found himself in a bad position down wind of her; a squall was rising and dangerous waters were close. He ordered the British flag run up; she answered with the same; the ships exchanged friendly salutes, and Jones steered north towards the British city on the south bank of Solway Firth from which had set out the press gang who captured Willie Paul his brother so long, so very long, ago.

He had determined to burn Whitehaven.

In blackness at midnight, with only faint starshine to guide him, Jones took the wheel himself and piloted the *Ranger* into the harbor. There he dropped anchor, not in the usual noisy fashion, with cable free and whipping through the hawsehole, but furtively, silently unwinding it in a reversal of hoisting, the frightened men tiptoeing backwards around the capstan, easing the anchor down to the bottom he knew and they did not. They did not, they could not, share the confidence of their commander. They found themselves on an alien shore in utter darkness surrounded by enemies on a wild and thankless mission from which they could gain not a penny if it succeeded and for which if it failed, as seemed likely, they could all be hanged. With imaginations full of the terror of the unknown they pictured the hundred ships, the two forts, the city of ten thousand Englishmen poised and waiting for an oar to splash or a dog to bark — for any suspicious noise that would give the alarm and doom them to death.

He called for volunteers to burn the ships, which were tied up side by side like sitting ducks. It was Saturday night, he said: the ships would be deserted, their crews would all be ashore getting drunk. The tide was at the ebb, the ships were immobilized, grounded. He proved it; he pointed to the British masts. Dimly against the stars his crew could discern that they all did in truth slant a little away from the perpendicular. Their keels were stuck in harbor mud.

Thirty-one men reluctantly came forward. They agreed to attempt to set fire to the ships, they said, if he would lead them. But they protested that his scheme was impracticable. Arson was an art; ships never burned when you wanted them to, only when you didn't. How could they set fire to ships with only a lantern? How did he know the ships were deserted? What about watchmen? What about the forts on the shore that even they could see, ugly and low and blackly threatening? Would they not open fire the instant a flame appeared?

Of course they would, Jones said; that was what forts were for, to open fire; that was why he proposed to silence them; and that was why he would not be available just at the moment to lead the two boatloads of volunteers,

384

who must devise some means of burning the ships without him. He and two men, he said, would now proceed to incapacitate the shore batteries and join them later in case their lanterns blew out.

He was taking a very casual view of the matter, the volunteers murmured among themselves. The leader of one of the boats said, "He's mad, stark raving mad!" The other said, "I'll fight a ship, but I'm damned if I'll swing for a pirate for *him!*" Some of the men at the oars whispered to each other, "He was a pirate; he's never forgotten." Others grumbled, "Damned Scotch Kiltie!" "Wants company in his noose!" "It is hopeless." "What's in it for us?" and "Bloody pirate!"

As Jones disappeared with his men in a small work boat, the volunteers, taking their cue from his sarcastic remark, blew out their lanterns, rowed a little distance away from the *Ranger* and then returned. They tied their boats to her cable and waited for the sounds of the alarm that must certainly come. Jones would be dead; they would hurry aboard and escape with the ship.

For hours the oily waters lapped at the hulls of the boats, full of the fear-frozen motionless men. In their straining ears the sound of those little waves was magnified; surely the telltale noise would be heard and betray them. "He is dead; let us go home and report he died bravely," someone giggled hysterically. Someone slapped his mouth, "Shut up, you fool." "Sh-h-h!" everyone else whispered. The slap seemed to have cracked like a pistol shot.

But Whitehaven slept on. One by one during the long and anxious hours of the night the lights on the shore blinked out. Here and there some faint candle still outlined a square of windowpane behind which some old person perhaps lay dying, some infant perhaps was being ushered into the world. Everywhere else blackness piled upon blackness. One house indeed remained brilliantly alight, the public tavern on the water front.

Overhead, as the earth spun, the awesome bowl of the sky turned like a solid thing, fraught with the warning of passing time and spangled with lights that beckoned to safety; westward the stars dropped into the Irish Sea, whither the crew could escape; eastward the stars rose over the British hills where their enemies waited to hang them.

Then, creeping up behind those hills, a lighter blackness outlined their summits with firmer, more terrifying lines. Dawn was at hand.

"He's been gone all night."

"He is dead."

"Let us go."

They tensed at a sound like a frigate descending upon them. It was the

385

work boat with muffled oars and greased locks creeping silently back from the shore.

Never before had they had to withstand such a cursing. A lifetime of seafaring, a poet's imagination and a tongue skilled to declaim from the stage had given their captain an extraordinary command of invective: cowards, traitors, incompetents! lily-livers, renegades, rogues! slow-bellies, liars, gallows bait, skulkards, thieving cheats! and a great many others of a more personal nature which were even more resented.

"Captain, for God's sake do not raise your voice, sir! You'll bring down the British upon us!"

"Idiots!" he yelled. "They're asleep! I said they would be asleep. Why didn't you burn the ships?"

"Our lanterns blew out," they said.

He struck his forehead with the palm of his hand. "My God, I showed them the cowards' way out myself!" He could have cut out his tongue.

Why had they not rekindled their lanterns? he demanded.

The air was damp, the steel would not strike a spark from the flint, they said.

Had they tried?

The sparks would have been seen from the shore and betrayed their presence. They had left the flint and steel aboard the *Ranger*.

He saw what had happened. He pleaded with them. He swept his arm towards the sleeping shore. In the gathering dawn they could see him now. His eyes were wild but his face was utterly composed and confident.

It was not too late, he said.

He and his two men had rowed over to the forts. The garrison were all inland or at the public tavern. The walls were low. Standing on each others' shoulders, they had gained an embrasure and entered. In a guard-room they had tied up some sleepy sentinels, too old and too frightened to require killing. Armed with hammers and iron spikes, they had run through the fort and spiked its guns.

Repeating the operation, they had rowed to the other fort, surprised the old pensioners who were delegated to watch it and spiked its guns also. Thirty-six cannon pointed at the *Ranger* could now no longer shoot. "And unless I've forgotten how to tie a knot, those old gentlemen won't get the gags out of their mouths for three hours and won't move a limb."

He made it sound easy. For him, in his exalted mood, it had been easy. He shamed them.

"Come now, men. They burn our homes. Let us burn their ships!"

They said they would go and kindle the lanterns.

386

"No, let's get the British to give us a light. Upon my word, gentlemen, from the looks of your faces I fancy you could do with a drink. Row me over to the tavern. It's likely to close once the sun is fairly up. We must not make the good barman work on Sunday."

He laughed and settled himself in the stern of one of the *Ranger's* boats. They rowed him to the shore. The other boat followed.

"You'd better not come in," he said to them. "Too many early morning customers might look suspicious. Besides, you don't look prosperous." They had changed their naval uniforms for odds and ends of work clothes as a disguise.

They were glad to stay on the beach, but they thought he might have spared them the slur on their poverty, which was their only grievance.

He called to them cheerily, "I'll bring you back a dram."

He presented his two lanterns to the sleepy-eyed barman, who obligingly lighted them for him. Jones and his officers tossed off a whisky or two and bought a jug of grog. They were fishermen, he said, from the other side of the Solway and had missed their way in the dark to their boat. He pretended to be a little drunk and put on a broad Scotch burr.

No wonder they had gone astray, the barman agreed, taking their pay, counting it carefully.

Where were the armed ships that usually patrolled the Firth, Jones wanted to know.

Over in America, the yawning barman supposed. He did not like Scotsmen. He wanted to close up.

With the lighted lanterns Jones returned to the beach.

The *Ranger's* two boats rowed over to a fat-bottomed merchantman, the *Thomson*. They might have been her own crew returning in the early morning light after a rollicking night of carousing ashore. Unopposed they went aboard. A single watchman greeted them, amazed. They bound and gagged him and lowered him over the side into one of their boats and descended into the hold of the ship. They kindled a fire against a bulkhead and watched it take hold, pouring a barrel of tar over it to speed it on its way.

Fire at sea was a perpetual menace, feared by all sailors. Jones expected the torch once kindled to spread to all the vessels in Whitehaven Bay.

When smoke and flames belched up through the grated hatchways of the *Thomson's* main deck, he imagined he had succeeded.

He sent his two boats back to the *Ranger* and, with a skiff from the burning ship, put the watchman ashore on the mole, untying him and removing the gag, covering him with a cocked pistol.

"Go back and tell your people it isn't safe to burn American towns! For every one you burn I, John Paul Jones, will burn three of yours. Behold! Your harbor is in flames!"

"It isn't," the watchman retorted, and ran for his life.

It was now eight o'clock in the morning. The sun was an hour above the horizon. Churchbells began to ring for Morning Prayer and continued to ring, warning the town of an emergency.

People rushed down to the water front in their Sunday clothes, curious spectators, unarmed and unsuspecting. A big ship was burning. The flames had reached her rigging, and there could be no doubt that she would become a total loss. But the lines that moored her to the other ships had burned through and extinguished themselves in the water; the wind was calm, the smoke went straight up, no other ship was in danger.

Then shortly the change of guard appeared at the forts; they found the cannon spiked and the night watch trussed up and gagged. The *Thomson's* watchman ran through the town, screaming that an American pirate was burning a ship. The people panicked and milled about, some taking horse to spread the alarm, some pressing forward, unarmed though they were, to tear to pieces the blackguard who stood on the mole, a lone and insolent figure laughing at them.

He fired a pistol into the air to show he was armed. He tucked it into his girdle and drew out another, cocked it and leveled it at them.

They fell back astounded, disorganized, unprepared and more than a little disbelieving the evidence of their own eyes. For some minutes the crowd and the man stood still and watched the *Thomson* burn.

Jones wrote in his report: "I still remained for some time on the mole to observe at my leisure the terror, panic and stupidity of the inhabitants, who in number of at least ten thousand remained motionless like statues or ran hither and thither like madmen to reach the hills on the other side of the town. But I was not able to delay longer my retreat, which I made in very good order. What was done, though not all there might have been done with a bit of wind instead of a calm, is sufficient to show that all their boasted navy cannot protect their own coasts, and that the distress they have occasioned in America can soon be brought home to their own door."

And yet as he rowed himself away from the mole, which instantly filled with a fist-shaking cursing crowd, he felt himself a failure. White-haven had not gone up in flames. The holocaust he had pictured in his imagination, more real than reality, had not materialized. Hard on the heels of his great expectations he now experienced an extreme depression:

388

he cursed his men for not having set more fires. They in their own defense replied that they had been victims of a not unwarranted apprehension; they did not know the coast as he did, they did not know that British forts and British ships were deserted on Saturday nights; they reminded him that they had not proved utter cowards: wherever he led them had they not followed?

"Can't you lead yourselves?" he complained irascibly. "Must I be everywhere at once to show everybody what to do?"

"Mad," was the verdict of the forecastle, where sailors off watch debated the vagaries of their commander. It was far more profitable, they all agreed, to ship aboard a privateer than a vessel of the United States Navy.

Smarting under his reproaches, conscious of their own passive part in the raid, slim in their purses and hurt in their pride, one of them wrote a round robin, and all who could write signed their names and those who could not made their mark.

Let the captain but give them a profitable venture, they petitioned; one and all, they would demonstrate their loyalty to him.

"Good!" he said, for his own failure smote him like a knout. "I will give you a profitable venture."

It was madder still, that venture.

In Paris Benjamin Franklin read the British newspapers. French fishing boats with contacts on the other side of the Channel smuggled them in for a nominal fee. For a nominal fee in the opposite direction British fishing boats smuggled the French newspapers into Britain. During this war, fresh news, like fresh fish, rose to a height of unprecedented value, profitable to their purveyors. No statesman attempted to stop the exchange; the power of public opinion was now recognized, and means to shape it by propagandistic news articles were becoming known.

It did not appear to Franklin that Jones's descent on Whitehaven was a failure.

He read from the *Morning Post*: "John Paul Jones, the privateer, has done an infernal incendiary business in a scene too horrible to mention."

From the *Daily Advertiser*: "An American pirate last night landed near the head of Old Quay at Whitehaven, proceeded to a public house and drank much liquor, then set fire to and greatly damaged a collier."

From the *Morning Chronicle*: "The inhabitants of Whitehaven are very much alarmed and in daily expectation of being plundered by American privateers. The people on shore keep guard every night, and the inhabitants mount watch in rotation. There are great preparations making, everyone fitting up and repairing their old rusty guns and swords, making balls and mixing powder, resolved to give the raiders a warm reception if they should attempt another landing."

The accounts were reticent, chary of details; but whatever Jones had done, he had certainly done something that greatly alarmed the British coast.

The conservative *Gazette* was more enlightening. Its account was curt and factual. It reflected an astonishing upset in British financial circles. "Such a dampening effect on commerce," the *Gazette* reported, "has the American privateer *Ranger* made, that yesterday insurances were five guineas percent that lately were one and a quarter."

Overnight John Paul Jones had raised the rate on British marine insurance four hundred per cent!

From the Whitehaven *New Daily*: "We are all in a bustle here from the late insolent attack of the provincial privateer's men, who seemed not in a hurry to leave the coast."

Another from the *Morning Post*: "We hear that Wadrington Castle, the seat of Sir George Warren, K.B., was early last Friday morning burned to the ground and, it is strongly suspected, by the crew of an American privateer who was seen cruising off Druridge the evening before."

But in a later edition of the same paper: "Sir George Warren, K.B., distinctly resents that his seat is rumored to have been burnt. Sir George instructs this paper to inform the public that no Americans have landed anywhere near; and his seat, so far from suffering damage, is actually in a state of being substantially enlarged by the addition of a ten-stall new stable."

Franklin chuckled. Jones was getting credit for things he had not even done.

But he frowned at another item. It was no more than Britain deserved, but it was inconsistent with the laws of war and it did not sound like Jones. The *Morning Chronicle* and *London Advertiser* printed a letter from Edinburgh, which spoke of "alarming intelligence that an American privateer had appeared off the coast of Kirkcudbright and that the crew had landed and proceeded to Castle Douglas, the Earl of Selkirk's residence, and pillaged it. The absence of British ships to protect our Scottish waters from pirates and murderers, who seem able to land at their pleasure, no English force preventing, cannot be too much deplored."

Was it possible that Jones had actually ravaged the Scottish coast on which he had been born?

"I will give you a profitable venture!" Jones said. Behind them in the distance the smoke of the burning *Thomson* was turning white. Perhaps they were pouring water on the flames; perhaps she had burned to the water line and the flooding tide had extinguished the embers in a cloud of steam. But the rolling horizonful of smoke he had imagined billowing up from a whole harbor burning was not there, and he was sick at heart.

Across the Solway, thirty miles from the cottage in which he had been born, where his father had died and where, perhaps, his old mother still lived, lived the Earl of Selkirk. Jones remembered the isolated residence on the wooded promontory by the River Dee. Even in those days the earl had been a member of Parliament; likely he still was, likely grown in influence.

He explained his plan to his men; it was instantly to their liking.

Britain habitually ransomed her prominent noblemen taken in war, he said. She had done it for centuries. Once she had ransomed a king, King Richard the Lionhearted. She had bought him back by beggaring her national treasury for three whole years. The custom was traditional. Even now the piratical Dey of Algiers raked in a huge sum every year in return for British captains so clumsy as to get themselves captured on the Barbary Coast.

He proposed to kidnap the Earl of Selkirk and hold him to ransom.

At the very least, he said, the British would exchange the earl for American prisoners at the rate of five hundred to one, and they, his crew, would assuredly be rewarded by Congress.

"We just want money," they grinned.

The more he thought about his suddenly formed project the better he liked it. It could hurt no one, not even the earl; it would quiet his men; best of all it would lift from his conscience the shame he felt for the failure at Whitehaven.

That evening he anchored at the mouth of the Dee and led a small raiding party ashore. He needed few men; he was unopposed.

He asked some casual farmers on their way home whether the earl was in residence. They all said No, but he wanted to make sure.

He inquired of a tenant who lived so close to Castle Douglas that he was certain to know.

The tenant was friendly enough to a man with an accent not only Scotch but the Scotch of Kirkcudbrightshire, but he looked suspiciously at Jones's man, whose pistols bulged in their girdles and whose cutlasses could not be hidden. They were only fishermen, Jones explained, and anyone who did not carry a dirk or a pistol with American pirates lurking about the coast was daft.

The tenant agreed and hurriedly walked off to his cottage, calling over his shoulder that the earl was in London, everybody knew that, and the residence was full of nothing but servants and women.

Jones's shoulders slumped. He had failed again.

"Was he telling the truth?" his men asked.

"I'm afraid he was."

"But there's still money in the house, jewels, silver, gold!"

"Good God!"

"And only some women to protect it!"

"You damned pirates!"

One of them, safely to the rear, said, "Weren't you a pirate?"

"Who said that? Come out and face me! Who said that?"

Nobody answered, but he saw their smirks and heard them choking back the guffaws.

He knew when an audience was hostile. He had learned long since that no one man could stop a greedy unruly crew when they had decided exactly what they wanted to do. He himself was responsible; he had led them to expect gain from the earl's ransom.

"Very well," he said. "Four or five of you go up and rob the place, since that is what you demand. I will stay here with the others. But if I hear one woman scream, if I hear one man shout, if I see one spark of flame, I will go aboard the ship and abandon you to be hanged. So help me God, if you do not comport yourselves like American gentlemen, I'll rouse the whole countryside and abandon you all to be hanged!"

"Captain, we just want money," they said.

"All right. Go get it. Silver is the best, especially spoons and forks and tea things, which are always sterling. Plate is good too. But stuff that looks like gold is likely to be copper-gilt, especially in Scotland. Make haste!"

"Thank you," they said, impressed. In some respects it was valuable to sail under an ex-pirate even if he had reformed.

Between Castle Douglas and the shore he waited with the others. There was no sound of violence. Before the twilight quite faded, the raiders came hurrying back, laughing, and dragging two big sacks that rattled with a good clear solid sound.

"We got it!" the leader said.

"Got what, Mr. Wallingsford?"

Wallingsford was his first lieutenant.

"Every ounce of sterling in the house!"

"How do you know?"

"She said so."

"Who?"

"The countess herself. The butler was trying to hide some of the stuff in the apron of one of the maids. The countess was angry and scared. She made the maid stand and deliver. She even gave us sacks to pack it in. We treated her like a lady and she treated us like gentlemen — of fortune." He laughed.

"I am glad you behaved yourselves."

"But a curious thing. When it was all over and she saw nobody was going to get hurt, she offered us a cup of tea. 'Madam, Americans don't like tea,' said I. 'So I have heard,' said she. I said, 'We dump it into harbors.' Then she asked me to sign a paper."

"She *what?*"

"Maybe she wanted to prove to the earl she hadn't pawned the stuff. It was an inventory of the silver. She wanted a signed receipt."

"Did you sign it?"

"Of course I did. She had been so very civil, considering the circumstances."

"When we get aboard, Mr. Wallingsford, I suggest you count the pieces of silver and try to remember what it was you signed a receipt for."

Back on the *Ranger* Wallingsford counted and knocked at the captain's door. His face was flushed and angry. "She tricked me into signing for at least ten times what we got, on my honor she did!"

"Now you are ten times the pirate you tried to be. That happens."

"I never called you a pirate, sir."

"And the next time you rob a Scot, remember to count. Count fast."

It was not an episode that would reflect much glory on the United States Navy, Jones thought gloomily. But it won his men over to him, and it was well for them all that it did.

Wallingsford said threateningly to the crew, "The next man I hear speak of the captain as a 'damned Kiltie' or a 'bloody pirate' will have to answer to me. Remember."

Lieutenant Wallingsford had been in command of one of the boats that had failed so signally to fire the ships in Whitehaven and had been the first to extinguish his lantern.

One day later he had led the raid that stole silverware from a woman.

One day later he died gloriously for his country.

Chapter 39

MEN DIED for England too that day. Those who did not die were court-martialed when next they saw their homeland: their crime was the loss of His Majesty's Ship *Drake*, an excellent vessel, twenty guns to the adversary's eighteen. She was the first British man-of-war ever to surrender to a ship of the infant United States Navy, a stunning, undreamt-of, unbelievable phenomenon.

Her Captain Burdon could not be court-martialed; he was dead with a bullet in his skull. Her Lieutenant Dobbs, second in command, could not be court-martialed; he too was dead. So were forty others.

The court exonerated the *Drake's* survivors; it was not their fault: the Americans had not fought fair.

Some Englishmen with broad minds and a deep understanding of their own history thought back to the age when their island had stood in mortal peril from Philip of Spain, the age of the Invincible Armada, when all that mattered was England's survival by fair means or foul, the age of the great Elizabeth and her poet who put in the mouth of a madman, "Kill, kill, kill, kill, kill." Americans in this present war were fighting like the Englishmen of that older war.

War was taking a nasty turn. Such things boded ill for the future. Good manners in war were dead, dead as poor Captain Burdon; the wars of the future might march from terror to terror and end God knew where.

The average Englishman, however, simply despised the name "American," and turned white with fury at the name "Jones."

When the Irish fishermen sobered up, they told him the *Drake* had been some three weeks in Belfast Lough and would likely still be there. If he proposed to engage her, an enterprise any good Irishman would applaud, would it be asking too much if Captain Jones would please to set them ashore?

"I regret that I cannot spare you a boat," he replied. "You must remain my guests for a little longer. You may stay below deck, however, if you like."

"That we will!" they said, but they did not expect him to lock them up.

The North Channel was narrow here. If one sailed from Scotland to Ireland, one was never out of sight of land. Having robbed Castle Douglas at sunset, Jones was off Belfast Lough at sunrise.

He lay off the point some time, displaying no flag. The *Drake* was anchored within the waters of the estuary, her captain observing him through a spyglass. At length the *Drake* signaled, but Jones did not answer. He had no intention of fighting within narrow waters.

Towards middle morning Wallingsford called his attention to a swift little packet on a course from the Solway to the Lough. "Shall we take her, sir?"

"That will be only the news of your little escapade, mister, spreading to Ireland. No, no, let her go. She's too small. Anyhow, I'd like a higher sun. I don't like sun in my gunners' eyes."

On this he ordered the British flag run up.

It gained him some time, but the *Drake* hoisted anchor, cleared her decks and pointed out of the estuary, suspicious of him, preparing to fight.

Jones edged away from the shore, keeping the *Ranger*'s stern towards the *Drake*; she was getting close now; she might see the canvas flaps that covered his gun ports. He coaxed her out into mid-channel where there was room to maneuver.

"Now we'll see if he does us the honor to ask who we are," Jones said. "Keep the men below, Mr. Wallingsford; we're a peaceful British trader; no one must answer when he hails."

Shortly the *Drake* called out, "What ship is that?"

Receiving no answer, her captain sent out a boat with an officer and five sailors to investigate.

"Drop them a ladder, Mr. Wallingsford."

Wallingsford relayed the order; a Jacob's ladder clattered down the *Ranger*'s side. A British officer with an angry face clambered smartly up, set a beautifully polished pair of boots on the quarter-deck, saluted the British flag and demanded of Jones, "Why don't you answer signals?"

"Kindly take this gentleman into custody," Jones said.

The officer, to his extreme disgust, was locked in the cabin with the Irish fishermen.

Leaning over the rail, Wallingsford shouted, "You, down there! You come up too!"

"Why?"

"Up, I say!"

"But we've got to row him back."

Wallingsford leveled a cocked pistol at them. Up they scampered, and the empty boat was veered aft and taken in tow.

Through a glass the *Drake*'s captain had watched this singular course of events and guessed, but could not quite be sure, with whom he had to deal.

Coming very close, he demanded, "What ship is that? Can't you hear me? What ship is that?"

Jones glanced at the sun, sails, set of the tide, position of the ships. He judged that the moment now favored him. He was upwind of the *Drake*, bearing down swiftly. In perhaps twenty seconds he would cross her bows. His men knew what to do.

"If I have correctly understood you, sir," he answered slowly, deliberately, stalling for time as the *Ranger* raced forward, "you have just inquired of me the identity of my ship; that is to say, you wish to know who we are, as is only natural when encountering a stranger in one's home waters, one might almost say in one's own front yard —"

He had used up fifteen seconds. The *Ranger* was charging across the *Drake*'s bows at pistol-shot distance.

"What? What? What did you say?"

"Now!" Jones commanded.

The British flag came down; the Stars and Stripes shot up; the flaps disappeared; the *Ranger*'s guns glared out of open ports.

"The American ship *Ranger!*" he yelled, and raked her with a broadside from which she never recovered during the hour-long battle that followed.

Having crossed the bow of the *Drake,* he still might have sustained severe damage. The classical maneuver was now for the *Drake* to deliver a broadside of her own that would hit him when his tail was turned while he was downwind and rake him from the rear.

Not Jones. Not the *Ranger.* In an almost impossible maneuver that made him look as if he were about to capsize, Jones swiveled the *Ranger* in a sharp turnabout; he did not complete his run; he did not continue downwind; he did not expose himself to a raking. Still in front of the *Drake,* he brought the guns of his other side to bear and blasted her with a second broadside. He had managed to rake her twice before she could fire a shot. He was not only unfair; he was nonclassical.

The *Drake*'s upper works were a shambles. Having hamstrung his prey, he now closed in to devour it.

He wrote in his report: "The action was warm, close and obstinate. It lasted one hour and four minutes, when the enemy called for quarter. Her fore and main topsail yards were cut away and hanging down at the cap, the topgallant and mizzen gaff both hanging up and down the mast. The second flag which they had hoisted, the first being shot away, was trailing in the water. The sails and rigging were entirely cut to pieces; her masts were severely wounded and her hull very much galled. I lost Lieutenant Wallingsford and one seaman, with six wounded, five of whom will recover. The loss of the enemy in killed and wounded is very much greater, that is to say, forty-two. The captain and lieutenant were among the enemy wounded, the former having received a bullet in the head the minute before they called for quarter; he lived and was conscious some time after my people boarded the prize. The lieutenant survived two days. I buried them with honors due their rank and the respect due their memory."

Jones now released the Irishmen, gave them one of the *Drake*'s tenders, a bigger boat than the one they had lost, and set them free.

He took the *Drake* in tow and proceeded to Brest without incident.

Chapter 40

BENJAMIN FRANKLIN came down from Passy to view the prize. The *Drake*, with men busily repairing her battle damage, lay anchored in the harbor. On her foremast flew the British Union Jack upside down. In the universal language of the sea a national ensign in such a position spoke a message: "We are in distress. Help is requested."

But above the Union Jack there fluttered a victorious, almost unknown flag, the Stars and Stripes of the United States. In such a combination of flags the one beneath must speak a more doleful message: the Union Jack was saying, "I have been beaten by the flag that flies above me." In the thousand-year-long history of England nothing quite like this had ever happened before.

The effect was as startling and dramatic as one of the sparks from Dr. Franklin's electrical machines. America was proving that England could be worsted on her own element in sight of her very own shores, as astounding an idea as the idea that a lightning rod could ward off a thunderbolt. Myths were disappearing: the myth of God's anger in a storm, the myth of British invincibility on the sea. The *Ranger* and the *Drake* lying side

397

by side in the harbor told the story in clear, simple but highly theatrical terms that everyone could understand and that everyone could see.

Jones, in action, was incapable of doubting the outcome. He always wanted, wanted so very hard, to win that he could not imagine defeat. But after an action he could look back and remember technicalities, possibilities of slip-ups, split-second decisions that might have proved wrong and ended in disaster.

He had never been beaten in a fight. He had never suffered a wound. He believed with all his soul that he fought for the right. Right would prevail, he was sure of that. Without being particularly religious he felt himself on solid ground in his conviction that the opposite could not possibly be true: the proposition that evil might triumph no man in his right mind had ever put forward. It must follow, therefore, not as a matter of blind faith but as a matter of incontrovertible logic, that as long as he fought with all his devotion and skill for what he sincerely believed to be right he was fulfilling a destiny as high as a man could aspire to. Personal ambition by no means was lost; it had not even shrunk; but relatively it was smaller now in his immeasurable ambition for America. And not for America alone; the liberty that America was certain to win — anyone could see the proof by a glance at the monstrous humiliation of the Union Jack — would spread in time to oppressed peoples everywhere, everywhere round the whole wide world. Yet he did not view himself as a star-touched immortal whom destiny had singled out for glory. Pistol balls had gone through the skirts of his coat; men had been killed at his side. Chance might have altered the aim of the enemy cannon; a fraction of an inch one way or another in the hands that aimed the pistol might have snuffed out his life on any number of occasions. He was intensely practical, realistic. But so long as Death missed him he could live and he could dream.

The Selkirk silver weighed on his conscience. It had been sold at auction, the proceeds being distributed among the crew of the *Ranger* as prize money. Jones had bought it back; he now determined to return it to the countess.

In a soaring mood he wrote to her: "I am not in arms as an American, nor am I in pursuit of riches. My fortune is liberal enough, having no wife nor family and having lived long enough to know that riches cannot ensure happiness. I profess myself a citizen of the world, totally unfettered by the mean distinctions of climate or country. I am ready to sacrifice my life with cheerfulness if that forfeiture could restore peace and goodwill among mankind." He hoped that the war would soon close, he said, but until it did he was determined to retaliate upon the British for their "barbarous and unmanly practises," in America, their burning of towns and their cruel treatment of prisoners. He was glad he had two hundred prisoners of his own, taken from various prizes, to exchange for suffering Americans. Meanwhile, "since I do not war against the Fair," he begged her to accept the plate from him. He would esteem, he could not help adding, a note from her hand acknowledging its receipt.

He sent the silverware by a circuitous route through the few countries that still remained neutral in Europe, and after much journeying it arrived at Castle Douglas, the tea leaves still in the teapot. Lord Selkirk sent him a handsome reply, but that was after the war, and Jones received it in circumstances wild beyond anything he could yet imagine, and Jones's imagination was uncommonly vivid.

Meanwhile, a bundle of British newspapers arrived which he and Franklin chuckled over. Jones was caricatured in scathing cartoons in the costume of an Algerian pirate, black as a Moor in the face, perpetrating incredible cruelties, setting fire to the hair of recalcitrant members of his crew who refused to obey his tyrannical orders, decapitating others with a slash of his cutlass, always twelve pistols stuck in his belt.

"I had always imagined I dined with a man of unusually fair complexion," Franklin said, smiling, "and if my eyes, being somewhat dim with years, had deceived me, I feel sure Madame de Chaumont would have undeceived me, her eyes being fifty years younger and brighter."

"They are certainly bright," Jones said.

"Perhaps these newspapers have aroused in her an interest in you. Take care, my friend."

Other reports related to British girls ravished by Jones and his pirates. "You could scarcely have spent *that* much time ashore," Franklin said. The papers screamed at the murder of scores of husbands, brutal raping of their wives and the defloration of beautiful innocent British maidens by wild, piratical, lascivious Americans, especially Jones. "When I witness the sordidness to which freedom of the press can sink," Franklin said, "I could wish for a British censorship, such as they have here in France." But later he said, "No, freedom of the press is one of the good things we inherited from England. I could never condone a censorship of newspapers even in the camp of our enemies. I do not forget that for a long time I strove for a reconciliation, speaking before Parliament, trying to make them remember that we Americans were only Englishmen demanding our traditional English rights."

"I was never an Englishman!"

"I failed to effect that reconciliation. Now, of course, we must fight and we must win."

"We will."

"I do regret extremely that the press is used as a weapon of war, cynically twisting the truth and inventing all sorts of lying horrors which undoubtedly are effective in winning over weak minds. Perhaps that is only to be expected, bad along with the good, in a world where someday all people will learn to read."

"Truth ought never to be warped to seduce a mind," Jones said. "Truth can win on her own."

"At any rate," Franklin said, smiling, "the important thing is to win." He knew how often Jones had sailed under false colors to steal a technical advantage over an enemy. What a complex of contradictions this Captain Jones was, with such soaring ideals and such brutally realistic methods of achieving them. The Marquis de La Fayette too had flaming eyes, but the marquis had a softer chin. Sometimes Franklin felt a little old and longed wearily to go home. Once he too had professed himself a citizen of the world, going so far as to state he could be perfectly happy anywhere, even in Edinburgh in spite of Edinburgh's frightful municipal sanitation. But that was in his own wild youth. Now his work was done. After a long rich life he had succeeded in his last and most difficult service: he had accomplished the signing of the alliance that had brought France into the war on America's side. America was home; Philadelphia was especially home, sunny and sweet and beautifully paved, and he did not think he would care for Edinburgh now.

"Truth sets a man free, and man ought to be free. A Scotch dominie said that when I was in school."

"Jesus Christ said it," Franklin said.

Abashed, Jones said, "Truth and freedom will win in the end, sir. I propose to play some part to further that end, whenever, wherever I can."

Franklin smiled, remarked that he in turn proposed to invent a substance that would preserve him to witness the process; and, suddenly struck with the novelty of the notion, wondered what caused old age and whether anyone would ever make a study of it; it deserved study. But he suspected that the eventual triumph of freedom and truth lay far in the future, if not for America at least for most nations, which Jones now included in his vision. For America, with fighters like Jones winning her battles, freedom seemed as certain as the certainty that dawn would rise to high noon. Franklin thought he could afford to grow old, without regrets.

While the *Ranger* and the *Drake* lay at Nantes, a stream of highborn statesmen, admirals and generals drove down in brilliantly lacquered coaches with liveried postilions astride the horses and perfumed ladies with beautifully applied rouge on their smiling lips and soft smooth cheeks. For a Scottish-American this exquisite polished continental nobility was dazzling. The silky-white wigs of the ladies sparkling with jewels were theatrical, but not of the stage: these were worn with the perfect poise of centuries of breeding, and the jewels were real, ancestral. The ladies lionized him; he was strange, new and original; he personified a cause that was all the rage of the youngest, handsomest and most daring of the men of their class; and he had won. They smiled with their eyes, and spoke praises with their lips close to his face in subtly turned flattery: how greatly he must condemn, they supposed, the poor weak sex that had nought to offer in the brave new cause to one who so richly deserved so much, anything, all!

It was heady stuff for a sailor, thought Franklin, and never yet had he known a sailor immune to a woman's wiles. Actually — for in Franklin one thought swiftly begat another — who was? Well, *he* was; by now, at any rate. It was high time Captain Jones was off again on another cruise.

Even the French men wore rouge on their cheeks and beauty patches. It astonished Jones to observe such things at first. But often the rouge covered a malarial yellow that some admiral had got fighting the British in India, and a patch often stood squarely alongside an old cutlass scar. The king set the style for the men; Marie Antoinette set the style for the ladies. It was simply the high fashion of the court; Franklin saw through it; Jones would too in time; in time the strong lean chin would prevail over the impatient eyes. But before he was hopelessly dazzled by so much attention, it would be well to get him to sea again, and Jones, for his part, declared he was thoroughly anxious to go.

There would be no difficulty there. Everyone asked for him. The château at Passy was owned by an extremely wealthy manufacturer of ceramics, M. Ray de Chaumont. Seven times he approached Jones with the offer of a privateer, and when Jones said No, put his offer in writing in seven letters, which Jones did not answer. Jones said, "I detest privateers on principle. That is no way to build a navy." De Chaumont replied, "They are an excellent adjunct to a navy, as witness the success of your own American privateers in their glorious exploits against our enemy."

The French minister of marine asked for him. "I am used to the *Ranger,*" Jones said. "She's as sweet as a frigate."

"Would you give her up for a frigate?"

Jones's desire for a frigate shone in his face.

"I have a frigate for you," the minister said.

She was the *Maréchal de Broglio,* seventy-four guns, swift, powerful, new.

Jones tried not to let the delight he felt show on his face. "I have always wished for such a ship," he admitted, "but I should want to enlist my own crew."

"*Mon cher Capitaine,*" the minister replied, "nothing could be easier of arrangement. In fact, anything else would be impossible."

Delicately the minister let him know that one of the requirements of the French Navy happened, alas, to be that no Frenchman could be an officer who was not first a nobleman. The *De Broglio* would, of course, require officers. Personally they might be willing to subordinate themselves to the great American captain, but the king's regulations, alas again, forbade such a degradation of class. As for the men of the French Navy, they were all at sea. Two great fleets had sailed, one for America, another for the western shores of France to harry the British; only sufficient French ships remained to protect the shores of the homeland; French sailors were accordingly in extremely short supply.

Just at this juncture the crew of the *Ranger* got homesick for America. They were weary of Navy regulations and dissatisfied with their prize money. Their period of enlistment was up. In Jones's frequent absence from the ship Franklin feared that her crew would simply slip off with her and sail back to New England; he signed the order that let her go.

Jones regretted her loss but consoled himself with the beautiful *Maréchal de Broglio* and set about to man her. He met with utter failure. Not one good officer, not one competent seaman came forward to sign on. Shuffling groups of water-front loungers, fugitives from justice, offscourings of jails, ex-galley slaves, peasants who had lost their farms and hordes of beggars, blind, maimed and sick, presented themselves as recruits. This was his first glimpse of the horrifying misery and poverty that lay submerged under all the glittering nobility of France; there were ships like that, brightly painted on top while underneath all was wormy and rotten; they never withstood a blow. He pitied the creatures and sent them away.

The minister said pleasantly that Captain Jones was a long time manning his ship. The need for her was great. When did Captain Jones expect to sail?

Angrily Jones answered that he could not man her with wharf rats.

"Alas, monsieur le capitaine, then I must man her myself," and almost at once a full complement of French naval officers and men marched aboard her. "My hands were tied," the minister said. "I had orders from the king."

Jones rode up to Passy and asked for Franklin's help. Franklin shrugged heavily. "When our Navy is as old as theirs, it too may be hamstrung with regulations and top-heavy with tradition. In its present youth its difficulty is the other way round, and everything is too lax." He was thinking of how he had had to let the *Ranger* go because her crew were homesick, homesick in the midst of a war. "General Washington himself has lately gone on record as saying, 'The plague, trouble and vexation I have had with the crews of all the armed vessels is inexpressible. I do believe there is not on earth a more disorderly set.' We cannot always get all we want in a minute."

The old man's views were too broad to apply to Jones's present predicament. "If I had a mistress," Jones said petulantly, "I have more than time enough now to show her attention."

"I doubt if she'd hold you long," Franklin laughed. "Do not fret yourself unduly; you will get your ship."

Jones looked at him keenly. "I think you are teasing me, sir. Is there hope of a ship that I do not know about?"

"Monsieur de Chaumont spoke to me today. He wants you to head a squadron with the *Duras*."

"But Monsieur de Chaumont outfits privateers!"

"Not entirely; not any more."

Now that the war against England was full-fledged and openly declared, the French government had granted De Chaumont a semiofficial position midway between an owner of privateers and an officer of the fleet. He was at liberty, if he chose, to buy ships and fit them out for war; he might man them with anyone he wanted, including royal marines and noble French Navy officers, if any volunteered to sail for him. The government actually encouraged enlistments by granting a somewhat greater percentage of prize money than regular Navy men could expect.

"Do I understand that an American can now give orders, say, to a noble French captain?"

"In De Chaumont's squadron, yes. The French are a flexible people."

"Discipline him if he doesn't obey?"

"I'm afraid in that case he would be at liberty to tell you he had decided to go home."

"Good Lord, flexible indeed!"

"It's the best I could do."

It was better than nothing.

"I'll take it! I'll take this — this —"

"*Duras.*"

"She shall bear your name, sir, if you will permit me the honor."

"Oh no, you'd better not do that," but Franklin smiled and seemed to relish the idea. "You see, nobody can pronounce my name over here."

"Then I'll Frenchify it, to honor the great, good, wise man who is my friend! Do, sir, permit me!" His spirit rose, his cheeks flushed at the thought of another command even though he had not seen the ship. It would be a shame, Franklin thought, to dampen such ardor.

Jones said, "I will call her the *Bonhomme Richard*. They can surely pronounce that."

"Hm-m," Franklin nodded. "Yes, I think they are familiar with my little *Almanack*. They've been reading it twenty years. Very well, if the minister permits the change."

The minister did.

She was thirteen years old, but that was merely the strong middle age of a ship. Jones went over her timbers with a gimlet in his hand, testing for rot. She was dry, but she was sound; she had been well cared for; her ribs and planking must have been pitched every year; pitch even preserved Egyptian mummies. Her masts and rigging were new; De Chaumont had given her all the sail power safe to carry. There were forty-two gun ports but as yet no guns, the heaviest potential battery Jones had ever commanded. Less to her credit was her fat-bottomed hull; she was a converted merchantman. You could not fall in love with a heavy middle-aged matron, Jones said laughing, but you could not deny that she had power.

De Chaumont and his beautiful wife, who was rich enough to copy the dress of the fine court ladies and constitutionally inclined to copy their fashionable habit of taking lovers, accompanied him on his tour of inspection.

"You'll bring me luck," De Chaumont said, adding to himself, "and prizes!"

"'I was never interested in my husband's ships before," Mme. de Chaumont said.

De Chaumont said, "I'm adding more ships; you shall have a splendid squadron and you shall command it!"

"You need never lack for agreeable company," said Mme. de Chaumont, with so melting a glance that her husband looked sharply at her. She hurriedly added, "The Marquis de La Fayette is joining you."

"Yes indeed," said De Chaumont, "and five fire ships. This time no one is going to stop you when you start burning things up!"

"No one," his wife said.

Jones was not in the least embarrassed. He rather enjoyed the pompous merchant's scowls. Mme. de Chaumont was bold and vivacious, slender and mischievous as a kitten; M. de Chaumont was built a little like the *Bonhomme Richard*.

The squadron began to gather in the harbor of L'Orient. The *Alliance*, an American frigate, just launched, thirty-six guns, a gift from America to France and named to honor the alliance between the two nations, slid across the ocean. Jones contrasted her clean low lines with the tubby bottom and preposterously high poop of the *Richard*. But the *Richard* was his flagship.

A captain named Landais, who had been discharged from the French Royal Navy for not obeying orders, asked De Chaumont for command of the *Alliance* and got her. Jones hoped Captain Landais's orders might have been so unreasonable that they justified disobedience. Shortly all De Chaumont's ships had French captains; Jones was far too busy to waste time objecting to things he was powerless to prevent. The *Richard* at least was his to arm and man.

A cartel of American prisoners, exchanged for the *Ranger's* prisoners, arrived from England. Fresh from prison, poor food and ill treatment, they hastened to enlist under Jones. Jones took all who looked able to fight. One was a Richard Dale who had gone to sea at twelve, twice been in British prisons and twice escaped, and now, once more free, was lusting to fight again. Jones sent him down to Brest to pick up one of the small vessels which De Chaumont described as ready but which Dale found out was not. Writing to his commander, Dale said:

SIR:
I shall make all haste imaginable to git everything ready to com round. I shall have been every glad to had things in radiness to com round amidiatly, but as they was not I hope you will not think hard of me, for it would give me a great deal of satisfaction to pleas you if lay in my power.

Humble Servant,
RICHARD DALE

Dale arrived with the vessel only half a day late; he had exhausted himself to "pleas" his new captain and "com round" in time, though to do so he had had to resort to some ingenious temporary expedients in the half-ready state of the rigging. Jones grinned and made him second in command of the *Richard*. The man was good.

Two faces appeared out of the past: Joe Frederick, who had sailed with Don Jesu, and Thomas Chase, who had built Don Jesu's coffin and who, after shipping as a privateer, had lost her and fallen prisoner to the British. Their eyes twinkled with remembrance, but they saluted him gravely as "Captain Jones" and he promptly signed them on. With many veiled hints and mysterious winks they would sometimes refer to the terrible past and the diabolical prowess of the captain, thus elevating themselves in the eyes of their forecastle comrades and, in return, toning up the spirit of all the rest of the crew. Everyone knew that Captain Jones could burn British towns, but the rest of the things he had done — aye, went the hints of Joe Frederick and Thomas Chase, they were written in water long since sailed, blood that was long since shed and fires that nobody lived to tell of.

Still there were not enough men to sail or fight the *Richard*. Nathaniel Fanning, an intelligent youngster, one of the exchange prisoners whom Jones had made a midshipman, wrote home to America describing his captain's methods of enlistment: "His smoothness of tongue and flattery to seamen when he wants them are persuasive, and in which he excels any other man I was ever acquainted with. In fact, I have seen him walk to and fro upon the quay at L'Orient for hours together with a single seaman in order to persuade him to sign the ship's articles." By ones and twos and threes he got them, all healthy, strong brave men. If there were time, he thought wryly, he could fill the ship, but by then young Fanning would be sporting a long white beard. One likely recruit was a devil-red American Indian who, for his fierceness of countenance, went by the sweet name Red Cherry.

Shortly a company of a hundred marines in the person of a French Colonel de Chamillard offered itself to him. Jones needed deck fighters, even though he disliked the short range of French muskets, and accepted at once.

"Permit me to introduce my lieutenants," Colonel de Chamillard said.

Lieutenant McCarthy smartly stepped forward, saluting, followed by Lieutenant O'Kelly, Lieutenant O'Donnell, Lieutenant O'Neill — the French marines were all Irish volunteers, eager to fight against England.

Jones could have hugged them. The *Bonhomme Richard* might be slow, but her growing crew were priceless. He strove to get more.

Cannon were a separate difficulty. The minister of marine had obligingly offered to cast an entire new battery for him, and the order was actually sent to the royal foundry at Angoulême. But naval orders of greater urgency continually superseded it; the guns were delayed so long that Jones feared peace would come before they did. He went out on his own and begged and bought one here, one there, some from the king's own ships of war, whose captains often seemed willing to sell them. These were the best, and how the French captains might explain away the disappearance of their armament Jones left to them.

An unexpected windfall presented him with a peculiar choice, a gambler's choice. The *Bonhomme Richard* had sixteen ports on her lower gun deck, eight on either side. Now suddenly the minister of marine found eight monstrous cannon in an arsenal and made him a present of them. They were long and old-fashioned, but their length gave them range and they fired a hugely destructive eighteen-pound ball.

"How delightful! Now you can use them on either side!" Mme. de Chaumont exclaimed. She was visiting him on his ship again. The dark caverns of the lower decks fascinated her, and she held his hand tightly for protection in case a mouse should squeak.

"It is your innocence that is delightful," he laughed. How to explain to a woman the awful carnage these iron monsters on wheels would inflict on a crew in a sea, with the deck slanting back and forth, unless they were securely tied. If ever they once got loose!

"Innocence, *mon ami?* Monsieur de Chaumont would be ravished to hear you attest to it. The silly old darling actually suspects me. What a pity he isn't here!"

Perhaps at that moment a mouse did squeak. She cried, "Oh, *mon Dieu,* what was that!" and threw herself into his arms.

"Nothing," he said, holding her tight, "nothing, nothing, nothing at all." He said it slowly against her lips. It was delicious to console so tempting and yielding a prize. The consolation deserved some little drawing out; it seemed complete.

"But assuredly it was something," she said softly as Chima served them a glass in the great cabin, smiling broadly.

Reverting to the cannon, he explained, "Prudence would dictate placing four of those guns on either side, since I cannot change their position at sea, thus dividing my fire to meet an attack from any quarter."

"Capitaine Jones is not prudent," she said, "and the whole world knows

407

it is he who attacks, I most of all." From a little bag she drew forth a tiny jeweled rouge pot and painted her lips with a finger end and dusted a powder puff over her cheeks.

"I will put them all on the side where the mouse squeaked," he laughed. It happened to be the starboard side.

That night M. de Chaumont said to his wife, "What were you doing so long aboard the *Richard* this afternoon?"

"Inspecting the guns of Capitaine Jones."

"Are you not spending a good deal of time in the company of Capitaine Jones?"

"No more than you do."

"The case is not precisely the same. People are beginning to talk. Is it possible that you have conceived a liking for this American pirate?"

"No more than you have."

"But he isn't *noble*, my dear."

"Neither are we," she said, patting his cheek fondly, "but noblemen court him. The Marquis de La Fayette is going to sail under him, isn't he? The marquis never noticed us till Jones came. Jones is a very brave man, and highly connected. Why, he told me he was going to put all those big new guns of his on one side, the starboard side!"

"Yes, he is brave to do a thing like that." Apparently the conversation had consisted of nothing but marine technicalities, for Mme. de Chaumont had never before known starboard from port. Nevertheless, M. de Chaumont continued uneasy and expedited the outfitting of the squadron in every way that he could. He even contrived to find a quantity of American long rifles which Jones had begged for.

"Where in the world did you get these beauties?"

"Oh, I think they must be things one of my privateers must have purchased a year or so ago from some American ship."

"Perhaps in the Caribbean," Jones said. He could imagine the terms of the purchase. De Chaumont's men had simply looted and sunk some luckless American, probably also a privateer; but he put on a smiling actor's face and the grim thoughts did not show.

"Very likely," De Chaumont said.

The guns were in excellent shape. The Americans caressed them like pets till they gleamed. Jones was exceedingly fond of this beautiful American small arm. It was totally unlike the conventional smoothbored musket, which quickly fouled because the ball touched every part of the barrel. To load a fouled musket was so difficult that a man had to hammer the ball down against the powder with repeated blows of a ramrod, a time-consuming operation that often proved fatal in battle. At their best muskets were inaccurate; their bullets wobbled in flight. But the long rifles never fouled; the ball touched only the ridges within the barrel; the ridges gave it a twist that kept it from wobbling and sped it unerringly to its target.

No one knew why a rifle ball struck so true, but then nobody knew why a spinning top did not fall over. Hunters liked to measure the powder charge from a powder horn to vary the range; but Jones used paper cartridges with a standard measure, a method faster and less dangerous when one was under fire. One hunters' trick he approved and taught his men. They sewed the balls into tight little fittings of soft leather. The fitting improved the range and automatically cleaned the rifle every time a man loaded it. It did not destroy the aim, for it disintegrated the instant the ball left the barrel.

As the squadron gathered, he drilled his men daily in sight of the other vessels, hoping they too would drill; but the French captains were seldom aboard ship, and the lieutenants said they had no orders to drill.

Jones's full complement was still not made up, though a great many British prisoners, for pay and prize money, said they would be willing to join. He resolved never to accept them except as a last resort and redoubled his efforts to recruit dependable men.

John Adams came over from America for a visit to Franklin and saw Jones's men drilling. He also saw Jones. He hastened to write in his diary: "Walked out to see Jones's marines, dressed in the English uniforms, red and white; a number of very active and clever sergeants and corporals were teaching them the maneuvers. This is the most ambitious and intriguing officer in the American Navy. Jones has art and secrecy, and aspires very high. You can see the character of the man in his uniform and that of his officers, variant from the uniforms established by Congress — golden buttonholes for himself, *two* epaulettes — marines in red and white instead of green! Eccentricities and irregularities are to be expected from him. They are in his character, they are visible in his eyes."

A captain was entitled to only one epaulette, an admiral had two. But all the French captains had two; no one else took the regulations of Congress very seriously, so neither did Jones, especially not in so ludicrous and ugly a matter of dress. "I should have developed a permanent list to port, walking off balance like that!" he said to Franklin, who only smiled. The old man was in excellent humor these days. The Americans had driven the British out of his beloved Philadelphia.

As for the red and white uniforms, a great many red coats were available now from captured Englishmen. They were economical, and they would serve in action as a useful disguise.

At any rate, no one reprimanded him.

Even in the rain he continued his recruitment of men, with Chima holding a large pink umbrella over his head. If an otherwise likely-looking prospect stepped under its shelter to escape from the rain, Jones would politely pass on and try some fellow who wasn't afraid of getting wet. He became extremely conspicuous, and he did not seem to care if his methods appeared, to say the least, bizarre. He knew his methods worked, worked fast.

But there was not enough time. The squadron was complete; De Chaumont pressed him to make up the rest of his crew with British prisoner-volunteers, and in the end he did. Franklin had written him, "The Marquis de La Fayette will be with you soon," and sent him his sailing orders, orders with a daring triple objective. La Fayette had written in a burst of warmth, "Be certain, my dear sir, that I shall be happy to divide with you whatever share of glory shall await us, and that my esteem and affection for you is truly felt and will last forever."

But now the news of the squadron's objective and the squadron's unorthodox character reached the ears of the king of France. The king positively forbade such a venture. Action followed swiftly.

It was intolerable that so prominent a nobleman as Marie Joseph Paul Yves Roch Gilbert Du Motier, Marquis de La Fayette, should place himself under the command — nay, on the very ship — of an American pirate. La Fayette was sternly ordered back to his regiment, the excellent regiment of the regular French Army which he maintained entirely at his own expense and with which he had hoped to aid in the descent upon the English coast, which was one phase of the triple objective of Jones's squadron. Reluctantly La Fayette obeyed and gave up his part in the adventure.

Jones was sorely disappointed. He greatly admired the high-minded young man. He had counted on La Fayette's soldiers to infuse a spirit of obedience and orderliness into the squadron, which now, all but the *Richard,* lacked discipline. "I shall miss him very much," he said to Franklin, "but the king himself has given the order recalling him." His respect for authority was too great to permit him to complain.

"I can alter your sailing orders," Franklin said. They were impossible of accomplishment now, as Franklin very well knew. "I can make them a little less all-inclusive."

They were:

First, to seize and hold to ransom as many British towns as, in the opinion of Captain Jones, could be captured; burn them if they refused to pay.

Second, to capture the Baltic fleet, a large convoy of merchant vessels which every year brought to crowded England vital supplies of overseas food.

Third, to capture as many British ships of war as could be found in English waters, including the Baltic fleet convoy.

"Let the orders stand, sir," Jones said.

"Very well," Franklin said.

To De Chaumont the withdrawal of La Fayette was a heavy blow, political, social and financial. With the great name of La Fayette to lend prestige to an expedition sponsored by a merchant of ceramics, that merchant might hope to find favor at court, perhaps a peerage. But now the contrary had occurred: La Fayette was gone and the merchant had lost favor with the king.

With loss of favor went loss of social standing, which in turn meant loss of rich government contracts. De Chaumont blamed Jones and retrenched. The five old fire ships he withdrew from the squadron; he reconditioned them as privateers and sent them out under rascally captains on desperate voyages, the details of which he did not confide to his American friends, especially the American commodore, as he now called Jones, smiling to his face and behind his back withholding all chance of success.

"My dear Commodore," he said, "since we shall not now have the honor of including the Marquis de La Fayette in our enterprise I am sure you will agree with me that the sea force ought to be strengthened. I am adding two more ships, the *Monsieur*, forty guns, the *Granville*, fourteen."

Jones was exceedingly grateful. "I shall do my best to bring honor to your squadron, Monsieur de Chaumont."

"One can do a great deal with seven ships, Commodore."

Jones nodded, mouth grim.

"We cannot permit the commodore to sail without a ball," said Mme. de Chaumont.

"Quite so," De Chaumont said, smiling. He had lost La Fayette, but he was not easily discouraged. He had fought his way up through the commercial world from obscurity to riches. La Fayette could not join his squadron, but the merchant could boast that another marquis would honor his ball.

It was a festive expensive affair. Mme. de Chaumont was at her prettiest. M. de Chaumont appeared with not one but two emerald watch fobs. Mme. de Chaumont took Jones by the arm and said, "Commodore, you must meet our guest of honor. Do not be alarmed by his forbidding exterior; he is ever so much younger than he looks. Once he was in disfavor, a *lettre de cachet* exiled him for a while; but all that is past now, and he is back on his estates, and the king showers him with attentions." Her face changed a little. "I do hope you and he get on together."

Jones grinned. "I shall try not to disgrace you, Madame de Chaumont."

"It's just that our guest is so frightfully conservative, and you're not."

"I am with men."

"Monsieur le marquis," she said, "permit me to present to you the commodore of my husband's squadron, Captain Jones."

The marquis looked at him coldly. Jones recognized him at once. Mme. de Chaumont remembered that the marquis did not particularly like Americans and prepared to withdraw the commodore as discreetly as possible.

Suddenly a change occurred in the face of the marquis. The taut lines softened. Years dropped from it. Half-recognition illuminated his oddly sunken eyes. He raised a diamond studded lorgnette. "No!" he breathed. "It cannot be!"

"I think it is, monsieur le marquis," Jones said.

"Jacques! Jacques Paul!"

"You never could pronounce 'Jock,' monsieur le marquis."

"God bless my soul!"

After that the ball of M. and Mme. de Chaumont went smoothly and gaily. It fell into an accepted social pattern. Men who had waited for the marquis to snub the American now pressed forward to wish him well; handsome wives and pretty daughters took pains to make themselves noticed, to mention a husband angling for a contract or a cousin in search of a command.

Though how it came to pass that Commodore Jones was smiled upon and greeted as Jock Paul by the guest of honor, Henri Armand Marie Hippolyte Victor de Beaujeu, Marquis d'Hauteville in Poitou, was a mystery to everyone.

Jones and the marquis spoke together for some minutes. Henri had resumed his icy calm; Jones had adopted his formal mood.

Mme. de Chaumont observed to her husband, "What we lose with one marquis we gain with another! Jones seems to know everyone of influence!"

"I do not understand," De Chaumont said. "La Fayette is a wild young dreamer; it was to be expected that he and Jones would see eye to eye. But d'Hauteville is the most cynical, most disillusioned man in France! How is it he knows and likes this Jones, or Paul, or Jacques, or John or whatever the rascal's name is?"

"How do I know, my dear?" She was overjoyed at the success of her ball, and laughed, "I hardly know him myself."

"Hm-m," said M. de Chaumont.

"But he's brought us luck."

"It will certainly be easier for me at court with d'Hauteville behind me," De Chaumont said.

The marquis was saying to Jones, "I should like to talk with you before you sail on this curious mission of yours."

The room was uncomfortably warm, but the marquis retained his ball-room dress and his formal powdered wig. His cheeks were gaunt, and under his white silk stockings his calves were thin as an old man's.

Jones loosened his jabot, tossed off his wig and lighted his pipe. The marquis did not complain, but smoking so obviously distressed him that Jones knocked out his pipe.

"Thank you," he said. "The memories associated in my mind with Indian tobacco are painful."

The habit of smoking by civilized men was, the marquis said, symptomatic of the troubles that beset the world. The war between France and England was perfectly proper, traditional, a conflict between gentlemen; but the war between England and the American colonies was wrong from the moment of the Declaration of Independence. "Evil forces are loose on society," he said, "and mankind is drunk with a dream of liberty. A fantasy! A fallacy! You at least, my friend, I fancied safe from this monstrous delusion. You were so simple, so natural, so profoundly and understandably selfish when I first knew you."

"Delusion, monsieur le marquis?"

"The delusion so fashionable just now that everybody is exactly as good as everybody else regardless of race, color, creed, capacity, breeding or birth! *Mon Dieu*, how clearly I see the heresy now! The delusion that princes and peasants are equal, that *all* men are created equal! You recognize the words, 'all men are created equal'? They are from your own absurd Declaration of Independence."

"But Henri, princes and peasants *are* equal," Jones said.

The marquis stiffened at the familiarity, then sighed. "Alas, it is my

413

own fault; the son of a Scottish gardener calls me by my Christian name! I taught him to, in my youth and folly, on the selfsame voyage where I taught him to read Rousseau in the original — Rousseau, that madman!"

Jones reminded him, smiling, "We were all being taught in those days. You were taught to coil a rope clockwise."

"An inconsequential accomplishment."

"It was important then."

"That was long ago. I was a boy, a fool, an enthusiast, an idealist like La Fayette, crazy as Rousseau, as visionary as you are now."

"Rousseau's ideals are not crazy. All Americans follow them, fight for them."

"Rousseau is mad, and so is Voltaire, and so is Locke, and so are all the crackbrained apostles of egalitarianism. When I knew you first, it was I who was the deluded liberal, and you were the canny individualist looking first and solely to advance the personal interests of Jock Paul. Now the scales have dropped from my eyes; I see things as they truly are. But you have changed. You have even changed your name."

"Perhaps we have both changed," Jones said.

"No, no! I have cast off the follies of youth. You have put them on. Your eyes are dazzled by the so-called 'enlightenment' that beguiles even the La Fayettes of this world — his innocence excuses him. Innocence no longer excuses you, Captain Jones. How do I see you? Deluded man, I see you in the forefront of the crazy Americans who subvert the natural order of things. I see you leading an upstart people in a revolution against centuries of authority, denying the right of kings, undermining a way of life that has been abuilding since Caesar's time, sapping the foundation of an edifice of culture that will surely collapse into rubble unless you and rebels like you sheathe your swords and adjust yourselves to an orderly society that has served mankind well for two thousand years. Oh, my friend, my friend, how foolish I was to imagine that savages could be gentlemen and gentlemen could be savages!"

"I've a manservant who is a gentleman," Jones said.

"That is a contradiction in terms. You reason nebulously, like everybody else nowadays, especially Americans."

"My manservant is a Negro who saved my life in Africa."

"No doubt he expected a reward."

"He received nothing but slavery."

"Slavery for Negroes is proper. It is in the natural order."

"He can have his freedom any time he likes; I've repeatedly offered it; he refuses."

"He knows his place; that too is fundamental to the natural order."

"Is he still a savage?"

The marquis shrugged, "Savage, peasant, bourgeois, serf, what does it matter? Each in his place."

"What am I?"

The marquis smiled tightly. "Let us say that you became my friend at a time when I was temporarily out of my mind."

"What is my place?"

"Surely not at the head of a piratical squadron that is setting out to burn the towns of your rightful king!"

"I'm amazed that you spend so much time on me," Jones said. They were so far apart in their thinking that further discussion would surely be fruitless and might become unpleasant.

The marquis's face softened as it had when he first eyed Jones through his lorgnette in the ballroom. "I do not forget how you permitted me to escape from your brother's plantation in Virginia. That was a kindly act. It proved my salvation."

"I remember. Your ideas were different in those days."

"Much the same as yours are now."

"As I recall your words, you wanted to join 'the beautiful savages who possessed neither money nor manor houses; who were subject to neither laws nor kings'; and you wanted to 'live in glorious natural simplicity amongst golden sons of the golden sun.' Did you do so?"

"Yes. And my dream turned into a nightmare."

"What proved your salvation then?"

"Kindly close the door," the marquis said.

"It is closed, monsieur le marquis."

"Lock it."

Jones obeyed.

"Is it locked?"

"You saw me lock it."

"My lorgnette is not an affectation, sir. I see somewhat dimly since the Indians burned my eyes."

"Good Lord!"

"I dare say you have never witnessed the torture a tribe of savages is capable of inflicting on someone they dislike."

"I never saw a man survive it," Jones said, thinking of Bombarda's white ribs beneath their sheath of mud.

"The door is locked?"

"Yes."

The marquis removed his wig. A tonsure such as no priest had ever suffered revealed itself. An empty area large as a man's hand glared white with old scar tissue.

"When I fainted, they thought I was dead and they took my scalp. This is the portal through which dreams of equality flew out of my bleeding head, through which sanity entered in. This, sir, was my salvation."

He put on his wig.

"I still smell your pipe," he said.

Jones jumped to open the window and door.

"If you must fight for the wilderness of your adoption, do not fight to win. Americans are extreme and uncompromising. There is a savagery in them that they learned from the savages who surround them. Fight to redress your grievances, if you feel you have any, but let the fight be inconclusive, temperate, a draw. For if America wins, there will come a wave of anarchy upon the world such as Europe will never survive, nay, civilization itself."

Resentment flushed red in Jones's face. He stifled the retort "I always fight to win!" Poor Henri's eyes were still seeing nightmares.

"I am only one small part of the American war," Jones said.

The war was going better for America now. The mighty empire Great Britain had won a piece at a time she now had to defend as a whole. She had not enough ships, not enough men, not enough money, not enough powder and shot to wage the stupendous struggle everywhere at once. Her fleets and armies were at war to retain a belt of possessions that circled the planet, in a conflict that flamed round the world, as bitter and as fraught with slow doom as the girdle of Nessus that Hercules wore, whose hidden poison tormented the giant till he built his own funeral pyre and burned himself to ashes rather than endure the agony.

Gradually the pressure on America was lessening. In England there were mounting fears of a French invasion. The coastal towns were alarmed and called on the admiralty to send home the fleets. Such ships as could be spared from the world-wide conflict the admiralty set to cruising the home waters in a state of constant readiness. Into these troubled and ill-patrolled but watchfully waiting waters Jones now sailed at the head of his squadron.

One could be pardoned a moment of self-satisfaction, Jones mused as he surveyed his squadron from the *Bonhomme Richard*. The gardener's son had come far in the world. He had risen to tread the quarter-deck of a flagship. Round him in perfect formation sailed six vessels of war, all his to command. He had only to address a request in a conversational tone to his lieutenant Richard Dale. Mr. Dale would order a signal. A flag would streak up to a masthead. The commodore need not look to assure himself that the signal was there; it would be. The commodore would look at his ships. And lo! the distant ships, far beyond hail, subject to his will by an invisible chain of command, would alter course and take up a new formation, would sail in file or sail in line or sail in another direction, all this because he had wished it so and had spoken a word to Mr. Dale. At another signal those ships could be made to converge on a prize. Another signal and the squadron's hundred and eighty-six cannon would open fire. He could create a pattern of battle in his mind and see it take material shape on the sea around him; he could destroy at will, at a word, at a distance. To create and to destroy was the very stuff of power, an attribute of gods.

"Pray remind the *Monsieur* to keep station," he said to Dale. "She's a full cable's length out of line," and went below. From his cabin he heard Dale give a command; he heard through the deck above him the running feet of a midshipman — it would be Fanning, the youngster would have the signal flag under his arm. He could not forbear peeking out of the cabin window aft: over the blue, white-crested waves he saw his file of ships in the wake of the *Richard: Pallas, Vengeance* and *Cerf, Monsieur, Granville* and *Alliance,* and all but *Monsieur* as precisely placed as a ballet troupe on a stage, beautiful ladies, deadly ladies, beautiful in motion in a dynamic world where all was motion, wind, waves and clouds. He saw the *Monsieur*'s yards trim a bit to the wind; the ship fell in line and took up her appointed station. It was an extremely gratifying experience.

His moment of self-satisfaction was short-lived. Discipline faded almost as quickly as the cheers of the crowds and the bark of the salutes that had bade the squadron farewell from France.

A few days out of L'Orient Jones sighted a British ship, the *Verwagting*. He judged her about right for the forty-gun *Monsieur* and signaled the *Monsieur* to engage, standing by in case the *Monsieur* needed help, anxious to give the captain of the *Monsieur* credit for a singlehanded capture, since he had so recently reprimanded him, and prudently desirous of avoiding accidents. Nothing seemed easier to a parlor tactician, given seven ships opposed to one, than to form a circle round the victim and all cannonade her; but usually some shot flew over the prize and injured friends.

The *Monsieur* roared in and handily beat the *Verwagting*.

"Well done," Jones signaled, and ran up a clutter of flags. "Man her with a prize crew and send her back to Monsieur de Chaumont."

The captain of the *Monsieur* was a privateer and could not read signals. He ran up a duplicate signal that repeated to his commander, "Well done."

Jones hailed him aboard the *Richard.*

"Man her with a prize crew and send her home to Monsieur de Chaumont," he said. "You have done the squadron great honor today, Captain."

"Squadron?"

"Monsieur de Chaumont will be delighted. Send her in and let us be on our way for more quarry."

"But she's mine! I took her!"

During the night the privateer captain looted the *Verwagting,* transferring all her cargo to his own ship.

At dawn Jones saw the captor and the prize making off like a couple of guilty lovers on a course towards L'Orient.

Jones put the *Richard* about and chased his subordinate. The *Richard* was a slow sailer, but so was the *Monsieur,* another converted merchantman. About midday Jones overhauled and hailed the two ships, snatching a megaphone from Dale.

"If you do not heave to, I will sink you!" he roared.

Sulkily the *Monsieur* hove to; the *Richard's* ports were open.

The *Verwagting's* cargo was laboriously re-transferred while the English prisoners laughed and the Frenchmen aboard the *Monsieur* swore. Jones manned the prize with a crew from the *Richard* and sent her in to L'Orient.

And the next night the *Monsieur* deserted. The squadron of seven was now reduced to six. Jones pressed on towards the western coast of Ireland, where British ships from America and Canada might be expected returning home.

Two rocky shoals lay off Cape Clear in Ireland. They were called the Blaskets and the Shallocks. In this treacherous water Jones sighted a British brigantine, the *Fortune.* He signaled the squadron to stand clear of the rocks and, knowing the shoals, chased her with the *Bonhomme Richard.* The *Fortune* struck, and just as she did so, the wind dropped dead and the ocean surface went smooth as glass, glass on which oily waves still moved and under which currents still ran. Captor and prize drifted towards shipwreck.

Jones ordered a bargeful of British prisoners from the *Fortune* to tow their ship off shore. They cut the cable and rowed madly to the Irish coast, bent on escaping.

He ordered out his own barge to tow the *Bonhomme Richard*, which was now dangerously close to white water, manning it with some of his volunteer-prisoners. They too cut the cable and rowed to Ireland, where they stated that they had been forced to fight against their will.

Jones manned another barge with Americans, who succeeded in towing the *Richard* a mile to deeper water and safety, helped by a changing tide and a breath of wind that was scarcely sufficient to lift the sails.

Light as it was, the wind was enough to move the cutter *Cerf*, the slim little ship from the regular French Navy. He sent the *Cerf* to look for the bargeful of British prisoners, not wishing them to escape.

The *Cerf* mistook the American barge for the British barge and opened fire upon it. To escape the fire, the Americans followed the British, rowing for their lives towards the Irish coast, where they were captured and interned.

Too late the *Cerf* recognized her mistake. She turned south, deserted, and sailed back to France.

Jones now let the *Fortune* go and, in a strengthening evening breeze, sailed north.

During the night Captain Landais of the *Alliance*, deeming that Commodore Jones had mismanaged the action — which Landais had viewed all day from his frigate in deep water and at a safe distance — sailed off in a pique to commune with himself.

The *Cerf* was gone, the *Alliance* was gone, the *Monsieur* was gone. The squadron of seven was now reduced to four and the commodore did not know why. But even with four, Jones fell in with some prizes, manned them and sent them in. He was still on the westward leg of his cruise round the British Isles. His hopes were still high that the ships which had disappeared had simply lost contact and would rejoin the squadron. Meanwhile, though he was not strong enough to burn Liverpool, he was strong enough to disrupt coastal shipping, and he continued to send back to France a respectable series of prizes.

Off the Hebrides the squadron captured a ship with an extremely valuable cargo of Canadian furs. Jones ordered the *Granville* to man her and send her to France. The captain of the *Granville* was delighted with the charge. He not only manned her, he personally conducted her to France with the *Granville*. Thus another ship deserted, and the squadron of seven was now reduced to three.

Then suddenly it grew to four again. Captain Landais reappeared with the *Alliance*, having taken a prize of his own, a good West Indiaman.

Jones's spirit soared. The frigate *Alliance* was the best ship of the squadron. Perhaps the others would turn up too.

He called a conference aboard the *Bonhomme Richard*. Present were the captains of the *Pallas*, the *Vengeance*, and, after a wait of most of the day (lest he appear anxious to attend), Landais of the *Alliance*. Jones waited with all the patience he could muster; the *Alliance* was too valuable to lose.

When Landais heard that the prize he had captured was not to become his personal property, he became extremely agitated. He was inordinately vain of the prowess he had exhibited all on his own in his unauthorized absence from the squadron. "I took her without any help from you, monsieur le commodore," he said defiantly.

Jones tried to soothe his ruffled feelings. Landais had been dismissed from the French Navy. It was natural that he should wish to rehabilitate his name as well as his fortune by claiming all credit for the prize.

"No one will dispute that you have won glory in your single-handed capture of this rich merchantman," Jones said affably, noting in his thoughts that a twelve-year-old with a frigate under him could have cowed the sluggish trader. "But you will recall that our standing orders state that all prizes are to be shared in common by the entire squadron. Now pray, sir, sit down and let us talk. I propose a descent upon the Scottish city of Leith. I know the place. It is ill protected. I will lead you into the waters of the Firth of Forth, and under our guns the city will disgorge a ransom of at least two hundred thousand pounds sterling. Think what the distribution of so much wealth will mean to us and our men! Think of the shame we will put upon our British foes! Think of our reception in France when we return successful from this victory and all the other victories that still await us. Our cruise has only begun!"

"Am I to have my prize or am I not?"

"No," Jones said.

Jones manned her and sent her in.

During the night Landais in the *Alliance* disappeared again. Jones searched for the ship all next day and could not find it.

Once more the squadron was reduced to three.

With these three, Jones took two more prizes, manned them and sent them in, coasting slowly down the eastern shores of Scotland, scanning the horizon each morning for sight of his four lost ships, never sighting them.

It was now mid-September. Good weather no longer could be counted on. He had been absent from France for a month. Time was growing

420

short. He had weakened the crews of his three remaining ships by constant withdrawals of officers and men to form prize crews. He could scarcely afford more victories.

The rich Baltic fleet was due; it was part of his mission to take it. Leith was at hand; it was part of his mission to ransom British towns.

He took to pacing the deck at night, peering into the darkness for the *Cerf*, the *Monsieur*, the *Granville*, at least the *Alliance*. At least the *Alliance* would return; she had returned before. He reproached himself. Why hadn't he given that imbecile Landais his damned merchantman? No, he couldn't have; his orders forbade it. Well then, why hadn't he taken him aside and made a private deal? No, that wouldn't have been fair to the faithful captains of the *Pallas* and the *Vengeance*. He cudgeled his brain. What *could* he have promised that damned Frenchman that would have kept the beautiful American-built frigate in the squadron? Nothing.

His head ached with sleeplessness. Sometimes his superb eyes played him false, and he would think he saw the *Alliance's* sleek low lines and tall white sails at dawn on the horizon. It would be a patch of mist; he would feel the dampness on his skin, and he would remember how wet and wild the weather of Scotland can turn in autumn.

He decided to make the attempt with what he had, three ships.

He dressed his marines in red coats, his officers in British naval uniforms, donned a British admiral's uniform for himself, pinned a British decoration on his chest for good measure and ordered up the British Union Jack. Then he sailed into the Firth of Forth, penning a furious demand for ransom to the provost of Leith.

"Leith and its port now lie at our mercy, and were it not that humanity stays my hand, there would fall upon you the just retribution that you deserve; for I solemnly declare that I have it in my power and do now propose to lay your city in ashes." But he promised to spare the port the horrors that the British had visited on American towns in similar circumstances in return for a reasonable ransom, one hundred thousand pounds sterling, payable in thirty minutes. (In the absence of Landais he did not deem it wise to demand two hundred thousand.) If the ransom were not forthcoming, Jones's letter continued, then the bearer, Colonel de Chamillard, would instantly set fire to the place with the formidable regiment of Irish marines who were under his command.

That Leith was actually defenseless proved true.

A shore boat set out from the town full of happy shouting Scotsmen. Jones's three warships, swarming with redcoats and flying the Union Jack, were the first evidence of English protection that the inhabitants of Leith had witnessed in months, doubly welcome in view of the fact that an American squadron had been preying upon shipping all round the coast for weeks.

Jones invited the leader of the group aboard the quarter-deck of the *Bonhomme Richard,* and generously accepted his speech of welcome. What could His Majesty's Navy do, Jones asked in his best Shakespearean tones, for His Majesty's brave and loyal subjects of Leith?

"For God's sake, Admiral, give us some powder and shot!"

"Have you nothing to shoot with?"

Nothing; perhaps a barrel or two of old powder, caked hard as a brick from twenty wet winters' absorption of mist. The admiral had no idea how misty the winters of Scotland were.

"Ah," said Jones, and glanced at Lieutenant Dale, who prudently held his American tongue, trying hard not to grin. "I think that can be arranged. Lieutenant, pray see to this brave man's wants. The best powder for the shore battery of Leith is in charge of Corporal Cuffee."

"Aye, aye, sir!" Dale replied.

Cuffee was the cook, and Cuffee's "powder" was sand, on which the galley fire was built. Dale had a cask of it slung into the Scotsmen's boat.

"Take care not to open it till you deliver it to the shore battery," Jones said severely, adding some well-chosen words on the virtue of keeping one's powder dry.

"Oh aye!" said the grateful Scotsman.

But Jones regretted that he had no shot small enough to fit the shore cannon and recited their likely caliber: was he not correct in their size? Aye, the Scotsman agreed, the admiral was correct; and he left with his sand and his boat, telling his comrades that the Royal Navy of England had the interests of Scotland at heart after all, and that the admiral was marvelously well informed.

Jones then disembarked his marines, pulled down the Union Jack and hoisted the Stars and Stripes on his squadron, training his guns on the town.

A mile away from Leith was Edinburgh, set on a hill. From its ancient castle walls, through dozens of spyglasses the dignitaries of Scotland's capital city watched the astounding change of flags and beheld with horror a regiment of armed marines scrambling into landing boats. Nowhere within miles was a force sufficient to stop them. No British ship was in sight. No cannon could shoot. By now the deception of the sand was known in Leith. There was panic. Messengers rode frantically in all directions with pleas for help. Householders buried their pewter and loaded their wives and children and mattresses onto carts and fled into the hills.

On the shore a throng of pious folk bared their heads in prayer, and a worthy man, the Reverend Mr. Shirra, besought the good Lord to raise the wind and confound the invaders.

And the good Lord raised the wind.

All during the morning Jones had noted the low barometer. He had seen with apprehension a bank of black clouds approaching upon a sudden southwest blow. He had hoped to outspeed it. He failed. The gale struck and raged for a week. With difficulty Jones re-embarked his marines. The gale blew him out of the Firth and into the North Sea, to the salvation of Leith and the everlasting reputation of the efficacy of the prayer of the Reverend Mr. Shirra.

Still there was Newcastle-on-Tyne, close by; and after the storm the wind was favorable. While some damage to the main-mast of the *Richard* was being repaired, Jones called another conference and proposed a new venture.

Newcastle supplied London with coal; winter would soon be here; without coal Londoners would freeze, from the king in his palace down to the lowliest shopkeeper. The spirit of the enemy would flag, numb at the heart.

The burning of Newcastle would be simple, Jones said, trying to infuse his own spirit into his captains. They had been greatly disappointed in the cargo of a prize, a schooner taken just after the storm, too small to be worth manning and sending back to France; she was full of nothing but pine lumber and barrels of unrefined pitch. Jones pointed out that the sorry vessel could be transformed into a weapon of war. She would make a perfect fire ship.

He proposed to send her flaming into the midst of the fleet of colliers anchored in Newcastle harbor, some full of coal, some waiting to be laden. He painted the devastation of the coal ships, their cables burnt, drifting hither and thither over the harbor waters, bumping against wharves, setting fire to warehouses; the conflagration spreading unchecked throughout the town, its buildings destroyed, its piles of coal burning for weeks and sending up pillars of black smoke that would be visible for miles and terrorize whole townships. When his captains objected that the fire ship might miss its target, he offered to sail her in himself and row off in a dinghy at the last moment when he was assured that the target was struck and the mission would succeed.

But they refused. They were weary. Wealth had eluded them at Leith. The burning of Newcastle, even if it were successful, would be utterly sterile of profit to them. Moreover, their sensitive pride was touched; the destruction of a miserable fleet of dirty coal barges lacked the element of glory so dear to the heart of a Frenchman.

Jones fumed in his practical soul. They would have gladly hazarded their lives in a venture less substantial but more spectacular.

He begged, but they were adamant. He threatened, and they threatened in return. They threatened to leave him. Darkly they asked him where he supposed were the *Cerf,* the *Monsieur* and the *Granville*. Where above all was the *Alliance?* Had he not guessed by now that his squadron had deserted him?

He asked, "Are you saying that you will leave me too?"

Politely they replied that they would. The burning of Newcastle was unprofitable and undignified.

That the last of his ships should sail off and repudiate him was more than professional pride could bear. Franklin had praised him as an apostle of unity, preaching the doctrine of fighting in fleets when all other Americans preferred to be privateers fighting alone. Was he proving so difficult a commander that he could not hold even a squadron together? Four out of seven ships had already deserted him.

Hiding his disappointment, he put on a cheerful smile and abandoned the burning of Newcastle.

Then Landais turned up with another fat prize. Inwardly raging, Jones counted the critical hours he had lost, first waiting for Landais to consent to attend a conference to which his superior had summoned him, then the full day during which the superior had searched for him: a day and a half of lost and wasted time. If Landais had obeyed orders, the squadron could have appeared at Leith thirty-six hours earlier and beaten the storm and accomplished its mission. Not one hundred but two hundred thousand pounds sterling, instead of nothing, would now be piled up in chests in the great cabin of the *Richard,* waiting for distribution to the officers and men of the squadron, and an immense humiliation would have been inflicted upon the enemy.

"You have done wonders alone," he congratulated Landais. And he said to the captains, "Now again we are strong enough to proceed to the faithful discharge of the last phase of our mission: the attack on the Baltic fleet, the capture of her merchantmen and the annihilation of her convoy!"

To this the Frenchmen agreed.

The Baltic fleet was coming down the North Sea from the ports of Germany, Poland, Finland, Scandinavia and Russia after trading all summer throughout twenty-five hundred miles of coast. It comprised scores of ships, and they carried cargoes, principally foodstuffs, that were absolutely essential to the sustenance of England, which never raised enough grain or caught enough fish to feed its millions of mouths. Jones was informed of the fleet's movements from the statements of captured prisoners from many prizes who had seen it and observed its course. Its interception, capture, or even its disruption would vastly and adversely affect the food economy of Britain.

Having emerged from the Baltic, it would cross the North Sea and make for London.

With the *Bonhomme Richard,* the *Vengeance,* the *Pallas* and now again, to his immeasurable joy, the strong and swift *Alliance,* he lay in wait for the quarry, hidden behind a spit of land called Flamborough Head.

His squadron could be seen from the shore. It was now too late to disguise his identity. His presence was known, and the British coasts were alerted from the Hebrides to the Channel Islands. But every cutter that tried to dart out from England to warn the Baltic fleet he pounced upon and sunk, and there were no admiralty ships at hand to retaliate.

The afternoon was clear and fine but full of the threat of change. A southwest wind was blowing, favorable to Jones since it put him to windward of enemies from the north. Over the sun-warmed land mass of the British Isles this wind gathered warmth into itself and, continuing its sweep over the cold North Sea, mingled with the dry air that pressed down from the pole at this time of year and gave rise to a smoky haze on the northern horizon from which he expected the Baltic fleet to emerge at any moment. The day was the twenty-third, the month September, the year 1779. It would be a night of full moon.

During the afternoon he sent out a boat to reconnoiter round the point. It returned with a report that a mass of sail could be observed to the north and east. He signaled his squadron to remain hidden behind Flamborough Head and had himself rowed out to confirm the report, which seemed almost too good to be true.

It was true. He counted upwards of forty ships in a long slow-moving line, crawling down the hill of water whose crest was the horizon, the tail of the convoy stretching over the rim, hidden by mist and the curve of the earth and the shadow of twilight the planet already had cast on its atmosphere like a giant eyelid, closing.

To protect this rich and helpless fleet, which so far had sailed in safety and now required but a day to reach London, the admiralty, in its confidence and overweening pride, had detailed only two ships of war.

Jones examined them carefully through his glass. He could not make out their names, but one was a small frigate with only eleven ports on each side: that meant a battery of twenty-two guns, probably six-pounders in view of her smallness. She had probably accompanied the fleet throughout its entire voyage. She was not formidable.

The other was a much larger frigate, swifter of sail and more heavily armed. She was copper-sheathed, and she had two gun decks, the lower of twenty, unquestionably eighteen-pounders, the upper, twenty more, lighter of caliber but deadly. She was formidable.

The most formidable detail of her aspect, however, was not her armament; it was her paint. It was builders' yellow, from stem to stern. Even her masts were yellow, the builders' original, gaudy, spectacular paint, chosen with a view to impress the admirals who witnessed a new ship's launching and accepted her for the Royal Navy. She was obviously just off the stocks. Her timbers would be at their strongest; her guns would be new, fresh-cast, accurate. Her sails shone white as newly bought linen that had never yet seen a laundering. In all likelihood she had gone out within the last week in her spanking newness to meet the fleet and give it confidence and escort it home to London.

He chose her for himself. Against her he pitted the brittle-timbered slow-sailing *Bonhomme Richard*.

Smoke signals rose up all along the coast. Unable to send messages by sea, the inhabitants ashore were attempting to inform the fleet that danger was lurking nearby. But the convoy sailed serenely south, misinterpreting the signals or unable to see them by reason of the setting sun that shone in their eyes.

As the ships in the van of the fleet sailed round Flamborough Head, Jones signaled his squadron to a general chase.

Pallas and *Vengeance* instantly obeyed him, making for the smaller of the British escorts, which identified herself as the *Countess of Scarborough*.

Captain Landais in the *Alliance*, however, set his topsails aback and dropped far behind to a safe distance, to the fury of Jones, who needed him sorely, and to the utter bewilderment of the other British escort, which identified herself as the *Serapis*.

The highlands above the shore were thronged with thousands of spectators. At every moment more people came running to witness the impending battle, like the crowds around a gladiatorial arena, fascinated by the prospect of death at a distance. Some, it was afterwards said, cooked their suppers on the embers of the dying signal fires.

The spectacle was worth their attendance.

The list of dead was to be so large that neither side, for very shame, would ever publish an accurate accounting. But the spectators would experience the thrill of cannon flashing and toppling masts; they would hear a roar like close and continuous thunder, interspersed with the barking of rifles; they would smell gunpowder smoke and hear the high-pitched screaming of dying men while a blood-red harvest moon rose over the gently rolling surface of the sea.

The merchant ships of the Baltic fleet dispersed at a signal from the *Serapis*, each merchant captain taking individual action to save his own ship, some running for the safety of the Humber estuary, some doubling back on the course from which they had come. The escorting British frigates sought to place themselves between Jones's attacking squadron and the merchantmen whose safety was their charge; but the *Countess of Scarborough* was already heavily engaged, and Jones was bearing down on the *Serapis*. In such a situation the fighting ships paid little attention to the merchant ships; only the spectators ashore saw them lumbering off in all directions, leaving the moonlit waters clear for the men of war.

Jones took care to approach the *Serapis* head on so as to hide his ports, which were fewer than his adversary's and betrayed his inferior armament. But the *Serapis* had only to look at the *Bonhomme Richard*'s high poop and rounded bows to recognize her as a converted merchantman. Therefore the *Serapis*, confident of quick victory, did not press on with all the speed she had but allowed Jones to come abreast, to great shouts of applause from the shore.

Lying abreast fifty yards apart, the ships exchanged simultaneous broadsides, wounding each other severely; but whereas the *Serapis* was new and tough, the *Richard* was thirteen years old. Thus the shots of the *Richard* merely made holes in the hull of the *Serapis*, while the cannon balls of the *Serapis* broke down large areas of the hull of the *Richard*, crashed clean through her and burst out the other side with enough force still behind them to ricochet off the sea, like stones that schoolboys skip over ponds.

On the starboard side of the *Bonhomme Richard*, the side away from the *Serapis*, gunners stood aghast at the sight of bulkheads blown outwards away from them, moonlight streaming in through great empty spaces that suddenly opened in the ship's side. Both *Serapis* and *Richard* suffered in their upper works, the *Serapis* rather more than the *Richard*, since destruction of an enemy's driving power was habitual with Jones. But so far the advantage was all with the *Serapis*. Her tactic was classical. The stronger ship was methodically smashing the hull of the weaker to bits.

With a faster ship Jones might have crossed the *Serapis'* bow and raked her from the fore, or her stern and raked her from the rear. Since the *Serapis* was the faster, it was only to be expected that she herself would attempt the deadly raking maneuver. Jones watched for it. Also, since the *Serapis* was between him and the shore, it was likely she would seek the advantage of greater sea room. The classical maneuver to anticipate was therefore a sudden burst of speed on the part of the *Serapis* and an attempt by her to take a tack that would cross his bow to the northeast.

He could not outsail her, but he might outwit her; he could not rake her, but he could ram her. Sustaining her murderous broadsides with his ship disintegrating beneath him, he allowed himself to drift closer to the *Serapis* till her captain thought he must have lost control of his vessel. Close fighting was out of fashion.

Abruptly the *Serapis* made sail and tacked on a course designed to round the *Richard's* bows. The ships were now so close that the individual outlines of human figures could clearly be distinguished in the rigging, on the decks and through the gun ports of both ships. Jones rammed. He brought the bow of the heavy *Richard* into grinding contact with the starboard quarter of the *Serapis*. The stern of the *Serapis* was sleek and low. The *Richard's* high old-fashioned jib boom overrode it, sweeping it clear like a monstrous broom handle, tumbling men and guns and deck works into the sea, splintering against the mizzenmast and collapsing in a tangle of lines and tackle blocks and shattered timbers and fallen canvas. Scores of the *Serapis'* men rushed to this scene of confusion to cut and clear away the heavy debris and throw it overboard, thinking Jones would sheer off. He did not. He made sail and ground the bows of the *Richard* deeper into the *Serapis*.

Seen from the *Serapis*, the *Richard* presented a deplorable aspect. Fires had broken out inside her; men could be seen through the gapes in her hull throwing buckets of water on the flames, and smoke poured up through her hatchways. Water was rising in her bilges; all her pumps were sucking, their streams were torrenting from her sides, but her masts no longer stood upright and it was apparent that she was developing a list. Her decks were strewn with dead and dying. Jones's flag had been shot away.

Jones had escaped a raking, that greatly feared and disastrous sweep of shot none of which could miss, all of which would wreak multiple damage; he had saved himself from being reduced to a helpless hulk in a matter of seconds. But even so, the *Richard* gave the appearance of a wreck. For a moment the cannon of both ships fell silent, for in the fore and aft position in which they now stood neither could bring her guns to bear upon the other. Captain Pearson of the *Serapis* was a brave and seasoned fighter; he saw his adversary's plight; he was a compassionate man.

"Have you struck, sir?" he called.

"Yes! Yes! Quarter! Quarter!" a sailor cried from the *Richard*.

Some said Jones shot the man.

Jones always averred that he merely threw his pistol into the hysterical fellow's face and stunned him.

"No, sir," Jones called in a trumpet voice. "I have just begun to fight."

Jones was genuinely perplexed by the query, which seemed to demonstrate to him that the British captain totally misinterpreted the situation. Jones was answering with what he considered a sober statement of fact, the only reply possible, far from vainglorious, anything but desperate. To Jones the facts of the engagement were simple:

Item: His ship was by no means sunk.

Item: The training in which he so long and sternly had drilled the faithful crew of the *Richard* had as yet had no chance to come into play, and now could.

Item: He no longer required speed to win.

Item: Contact had nullified every factor of the *Serapis'* superiority.

Item: He had clutched his prize and he did not mean to let her go.

Item: In his mind's eye the vision of triumph shone so clear that it quite blotted out the apparent disadvantage of the moment. To everyone else the *Richard* was *in extremis;* to Jones she had just begun to fight; all that had gone before was mere preliminary to the victory he saw as certain.

He knew exactly what he would do now; soon the *Serapis* knew; soon the thousands on the shore would know, and then all England, and then all the world, for before their eyes a new tactic of close infighting was being born, a tactic so effective and successful that it would become a fashion traditional before it was old.

In the silence before the resumption of the cannonading he shouted to his riflemen in the *Richard*'s tops. Every fighting ship carried a few men armed with muskets aloft; the range was normally great and they seldom had much to do; but Jones had scores of them, not only in the tops (which he had enlarged for the purpose) but on the yards, in the crosstrees, in the ratlines; and they were not musketeers: they were sharp-shooters, armed with American long rifles. Now, at pistol-shot range, the whole upper works of the *Richard* began to spit death from unexpected and unorthodox places, and the swarm of men laboring to clear the stern of the mass of debris on the *Serapis* began to die, slumping over their axes and knives, adding their dead bodies to the litter and confusion.

Jones drove the *Richard* harder against the *Serapis*. Slowly his pressure on her stern swung her round, and the ships lay in contact against each other, length to length, starboard side to starboard side, their heads reversed, so that the bow of the *Richard* clove to the stern of the *Serapis* and the stern of the *Serapis* lay entangled, now inextricably, with the *Richard*'s bow. Pearson dropped anchor, hoping to pivot on it and sheer off, a seamanlike decision. But it failed. The anchor fell on the *Richard*'s deck and served only to draw the ships tighter together.

There was a line in Shakespeare uttered by the rebel Jack Cade in one of the *Henry* plays. It was whimsical and apt. Jones laughed and shouted it: "Now have at them!"

Jones's behavior uplifted his men, though some thought him a trifle mad; his madness colored their own thinking, set a pace and led a way for energies loosed by the mighty stimulus of battle, by death all around, blood bursting from bodies destroyed at one's elbow, and by the ear-splitting palpable volume of noise of the enemy cannon erupting ten feet away, for in the present position of the ships the broadsides had started again.

Jones had now brought his starboard battery, the ponderous eighteen-pounders, to bear on the *Serapis*.

Simultaneously they fired.

Simultaneously three of the monsters burst, fragmenting throughout his lower gun deck, from which all gunners not instantly slain deserted. The high poop of the *Richard*, its sides blown out, now resembled one of those primitive cattle shelters, a roof with no walls, upheld by weak and crooked timbers; but these were in flames. More and more it was possible to look straight through the hull of the *Richard*.

The failure of his lower battery was a serious setback, but the guns on his main deck were all in action.

The battle was now so close that the ports of the *Serapis* and the ports of the *Richard* rubbed, open, against each other. To charge their guns, which required first a cartridge of powder, then a cannon ball inserted at the muzzle, then ramming the ball against the powder by means of a long iron ramrod, Jones's gunners were forced to extend their ramrods into the ports of the *Serapis* within reach of the *Serapis'* gun crews, who attempted to seize them.

Here again Jones's unorthodox methods came into play. Instead of allowing the *Serapis'* men to seize the ramrods, hidden riflemen suddenly appeared from behind the *Richard's* cannon, took aim and fired, and the grasping hands of the Englishmen clutched only the empty air, which supplied one last breath to the bodies to which the hands were attached.

Captain Landais in the *Alliance*, observing the night to be fair and the moonlight exceptionally lovely, noting that no other British warships appeared to disturb him and that the *Countess of Scarborough*, her fire slackening, was at the point of surrender, now deemed that his intervention might be opportune. He fortified himself with a draught of vintage wine, screwed up his small store of courage and cautiously crept within cannon shot of his desperately struggling commander. He placed the *Alliance* in a position that evoked murmurs of amazement from the crowd on the shore. He stood well off from the *Serapis* and the *Richard*. He loaded his cannon with chain and canister, small shot certain to scatter, incapable of penetrating a hull, lethal only to soft human bodies at such a distance; and having so charged his guns, he delivered broadside after broadside which struck both ships indiscriminately. *Serapis* wondered which side this hitherto-inactive ship was fighting on; curses arose from the *Richard*, "Don't sink us, damn you!" and even some of the British muttered, "Shame!" On this, well pleased with himself, Captain Landais again withdrew and took no further part in the action. His fire had taken especially deadly toll of the corps of marines who were firing in close-fighting formation from the poop deck of the *Richard*.

Both the *Serapis* and the *Bonhomme Richard* had now lost so many dead that either captain could have surrendered with dignity. As the combat had lengthened, the thought of striking his colors had occurred more than once to Captain Pearson. No military court would condemn him; all military commanders knew that once a fifth of your men are dead you may withdraw with honor.

Every general and admiral, poring over the accounts of the great battles which constituted the bulk of the recorded history of man, was aware that an army armed only with spears — nay, only with stones — could fight to the last two furious men, their comrades all slain around them, if such were the animal resolve that impelled them. But a decent respect for the awful machinery of destruction which man's busy brain had concocted and a deeper instinct of common humanity stepped in at a certain point to call halt to mass murder. Honor was

431

satisfied. Pearson decided to haul down the Union Jack, since his American adversary possessed no better sense than to immolate them all.

Just then a curious incident occurred. Some scores of Jones's prisoners, their locked quarters being now shattered by continuous riddling of cannon balls, found themselves at liberty and swarmed out of confinement. They stepped from the *Richard* to the *Serapis* through the gaping sides of the ships. "Hold out, Captain Pearson! Hold out but a little longer! The American is sinking!" And so he was.

Encouraged by their report, Captain Pearson continued to fight and the slaughter also continued.

Hard on the heels of the British prisoners, through the same avenues, came Americans with cutlasses and small arms; and hand-to-hand fighting among groups of men swung back and forth from one ship to the other.

In a square-rigged ship, of course, the long yardarms far overhung the hull. With hulls in contact the yards of the *Richard* now stood over the *Serapis*; in fact, the hull-to-hull contact pressed the upper works of each ship into the other's so that the rigging aloft was one vast and confusing tangle of sails, ropes and timbers, most of it broken and unmanageable.

Here again Jones's unorthodox methods prevailed. The men in his tops had long since cleared the men from the tops of the *Serapis*, shooting them down. Now the projecting yardarms of the *Richard* served another purpose, an absolutely novel maneuver in which Midshipman Fanning distinguished himself, for he led the first assault, being agile, small and young.

Men crawled out on the yards of the *Richard* with buckets filled with incendiary bombs and started to drop them one by one on the decks of the *Serapis*. These dropped into clusters of men and, when their fuses burned down to the powder charge, exploded with killing effect, the more awesome since it was new. Who had expected a rain of missiles from above! Morale dropped and casualties mounted within the *Serapis*, and those who lived grew faint with fatigue. The fight had gone on too long, and still the accursed American refused to sink. On fire, listing and riding ever lower in the water, Jones continued to keep his guns in action, answering the broadsides that were destroying him.

Shortly his broadsides became heavier than those of the *Serapis*.

One of the incendiary bombs fell into a hatchway. It exploded in a powder train that the servers of the *Serapis*' guns had laid to supply the cannoneers. Nothing was hotter or more fearsome than the searing *whooosh* of prime gunpowder burning unconfined in open air. It ran like a multiple snake of white flame through interior passageways that led from the magazines to the guns, and all along its course sweating men were busiest and most crowded. Those who survived for a moment ran screaming to the deck in their shoes and collars, their clothes burnt off, their naked bodies charred and their hair in flames; and those who could muster the strength hurled themselves into the sea to cool the fierce burning.

Now the *Serapis* too began to burn.

Valor demanded no more.

Captain Pearson struck his flag.

Jones stepped from the sinking *Bonhomme Richard* and took command, by right of conquest, of the *Serapis*, accepting Pearson's sword.

Book Three
The Russian Night

Chapter 41

AN ERA had ended. Another had opened, and the whole civilized world drew breath and thankfully relaxed, to enjoy — like a man awakening from the chaos of a nightmare — the almost incredible relief of universal peace, orderly, normal and sane: to savor release from the tensions of war, to relax from the fear of the unknown, free at last from the dread of the personally unexpected. Once again Americans slept deep and undisturbed at night: no minuteman now came riding at midnight to rouse them with warning that the redcoats were coming: the redcoats had long since departed: America had won.

Similarly, on the coasts of the British Isles, no one now kept watch on the cliffs with torch in hand to fire a barrel of pitch that would blaze a signal that meant that the ships of John Paul Jones had been sighted.

John Paul Jones, with an American passport in his pocket, had actually made a friendly visit to his former London agent just after the formal signing of the peace treaty between a new nation, the United States of America, and Great Britain. The London agent, recalling the profitable voyages of the *John* in the West Indies, hoped that Captain Jones would again go into commercial shipping and, should the captain decide so to do, would again designate him as his agent. Jones was affable but noncommittal.

Some of the older clerks in the office scurried for cover at the approach of so formidable a client; but many were new and merely gaped in youthful awe that the head of the firm had greeted so casually a man with the reputation of being the bloodiest pirate in existence and who, but for a passport stamped with an American eagle, would have been apprehended by the nearest policeman and hanged to the nearest lamppost.

"The war is over now," the head of the firm said to his youthful associates. "Perhaps some day we shall get the colonies back, but until we do let us trade with this new 'United States' with all our might. America is a far more profitable customer now than she ever was before."

Above this commercial plane, on the higher level of statesmanship, rational Englishmen consoled themselves. "Oh, indeed we *shall* get back the colonies, depend upon it. But it must be borne in mind that if Great Britain were to nurse a grudge against every nation after every war she ever fought there'd be nobody left but the Hottentots to be friends with. Name me one single nation, sir, that we haven't warred against at *some* time or other since William the Conqueror!" No one could name such a nation.

But deep down under the smart of defeat, under the stanch good nature with which the British accepted it, under the sterling good sense with which they rationalized the absolute necessity that impelled them to trade with their recent American enemies, ran a proud tradition, shining as chivalry, that a gentleman beaten in a fight does not complain. It was a sporting instinct shared by the Americans, the French, the Spanish, the Scandinavians; by the Mediterranean nations where it had started; it was the instinct of fair play and good manners, born at the Renaissance out of the ashes of classical Greece and Rome. It was the ethos of Western culture, unknown and inexplicable among peoples whose cultures were different and in whose thousand alien tongues there existed no word for "sportsmanship." On British and American playing fields where youths engaged in athletic contests spectators would often cheer a losing team who had made a good showing against insuperable odds. No nation that had missed the Renaissance could have understood those cheers.

One by one, beginning with America, Great Britain had made peace with all her enemies.

On the highest level of all King George III received the first American ambassador. The king said to John Adams, "I will be very frank with you. I was the last to consent to the separation; but the separation having become inevitable and having been made, I said, as I say now, that I would be the first to meet the friendship of the United States as an independent power." The king, who had recovered his sanity, accepted the American's credentials, adding, "Let the circumstances of language, religion and blood have their natural and full effect." Nothing he ever did so put the stamp of "gentleman" upon him; nothing anybody ever did so epitomized the concentrated essence of chivalry in defeat, that precious possession transcending all animal instincts, which only the heirs of the Renaissance possessed.

The English-speaking world settled back to work, to trade, to build, to repair, to meet a series of currency crises and claw back to a plateau of peace after their awful descent into the vale of divisive and fratricidal war, burdened with debts but determined to discharge them with honor.

A generation was growing to manhood which could not remember the battles of the American Revolution; a generation of philosophers whose pens had incited it had passed away: Rousseau was dead; Voltaire was dead; and Benjamin Franklin, feeble and old, was tottering on the brink of the grave. But what of the generation in between? What of the generation of young men, now in their vigorous prime of life, who had fought and won the war? Like the Macedonian, they wept for more worlds to conquer.

They were carried forward on the crest of a wave of revolutionary ideals that still continued, spreading out from the New World to engulf the Old and beyond the Old to the older still, to distant and baffling areas of tundra and steppe of incredible vastness, where the wave would spend itself.

There lived and ruled in Russia an extraordinary human being, German by birth, female of sex, and by education Oriental. The German in her was apparent to anyone: whatever she did she did thoroughly; she possessed an enormous capacity for tedious detail; she worked at her *métier du roi* — she herself would have designated kingcraft by the French phrase, French being a fashionable language among the nobility of Russia — as hard as the lowliest of her serfs at their tasks. Amongst a people who never bathed, nay, in whose costly furs, the most beautiful in the world, lice leaped and the odor of urine clung, she exemplified the German passion for personal cleanliness and bathed daily. German too was her personal bravery. While the common people of literate England hesitated to submit to inoculation for smallpox, lest they turn into cows, she, the Autocrat of All the Russias, bared her dimpled arm to the knife, and not only her own but the arm of her son as well, whom she loved dearly, having first, with Teutonic foresight, had the operation tried on several of her ladies in waiting. When it neither disfigured nor killed them, she rewarded them lavishly. She was too intelligent to expect them to turn into cows, but she was mortally afraid of disease. Disease might ruin her beauty, which she had preserved far beyond the expectation of most women of middle age. No one could deny that the Empress Catherine of Russia was not only beautiful but enormously, preternaturally attractive to men. Dr. Anton Mesmer, the Viennese physician (whom Benjamin Franklin, heading a commission to investigate his astonishing psychic cures, had failed to explain by any known system of rational science) had remarked wistfully, "Her Imperial Majesty possesses the 'animal magnetism' to a superlative degree. How happy I should be to see her!" The remark had become known in Russia, for Catherine's spies were everywhere and flattery was

439

always welcome. But Catherine called for his picture and found him much too thin to arouse interest, and Dr. Mesmer remained in Vienna.

German too was her hunger for land — not all the land of Russia was enough to sate the lust of Catherine the Great. One of her wars with Poland had already sliced off a third of that ancient kingdom, which Russia was now digesting. German too was her clarity of vision and, having hit upon a project, the stubborn tenacity with which she adhered to it. Having humbled Poland and set a discarded lover as king over the Poles (lest he become jealous of her next, as was very likely), she now turned her glance to the south.

Russia needed an ice-free port. An excellent one lay on the Black Sea, which connected with the Mediterranean and through the Mediterranean with all the world. The name of the port was Ochakov. Long Russian rivers debouched at Ochakov into a broad and beautiful lagoon, a perfect roadstead capable of sheltering vast fleets of merchant shipping situated at the natural terminus of cheap and easy trade routes that penetrated deep into Russian territory and down which, at a minimum of cost, the products of the Russian heartland, especially the elegant furs, could be floated.

Ochakov, however, belonged to Turkey.

With German logic, realistic and thorough — heavy Teutonic volumes had been written to prove a point less demonstrable — the empress reasoned that Ochakov was more useful to Russia than to Turkey and hence should be Russian. Besides, it wasn't fair. Turkey had scores of ice-free ports and little to sell; Russia had not a single one and bulged with products that everyone wanted. Was it fair to be strangled by a weakling? She scorned weaklings with the fierce contempt of a woman who had conquered strong men all her life and who, in her personal rise to power, from a petty German principality to absolute rule of the biggest nation on earth, had stuck at nothing, neither wars of aggression nor extermination of rebels, nor even incitement to murder, for Catherine had come to the throne through sweet cajolery of a regiment of palace guards who abducted her husband, the emperor, and strangled him. The first act of her reign was to decree a long period of mourning for the "apoplexy" of the emperor, who lay in state in a high collar that hid swollen welts on the neck, while candles burned and incense rose and priests chanted Masses and long lines of mourners filed swiftly past the coffin. She sternly forbade the slightest malicious whisper against the late emperor, punishing with the knout the gossip which everyone knew to be absolutely true: that Russia was well rid of him, that he had been a drunkard and a half-wit whose only pleasure was torturing the dogs which slept in his bed, hanging rats with a string for treason when they made nests in his mattress, which he fouled like a babe, and drilling a regiment of toy tin soldiers in the company of a valet whom he dressed up in the uniform of a field marshal. For it was not to her interest that the office of emperor should be degraded. And having thus exalted the institution of a monarchy during the day, keeping a prim court and permitting no racy stories even in French, she would put off her mourning weeds and retire to her private apartments at night with the colonel of the regiment who had strangled her husband. Here her personality seemed to change, though actually, with German precision, it merely exhibited another facet of itself. Her mind — and it was always exceedingly clear — was neatly compartmented. There was a proper time and a proper place for kingcraft; the codification of a universal corpus of law for all Russia, never before attempted, was an example. There was a proper time and a proper place for directing her wars, which she waged with success, astounding her field marshals with her understanding of the art of conquest. Also for religion: she set an example for rigorous attendance at Mass; her clergy's prayer that God would bless her was from the heart. And for charity: she built countless cathedrals and hospitals. For public works: she built canals and factories and shipyards and even tried to improve the wretched Russian roads. For learning: she founded libraries. For architecture: when Russian architects continued to build their stocky kremlins (every Russian town had a "kremlin," or castle) with their bulbous towers to shed the Russian snows, she imported Frenchmen who showed them how to erect edifices with classic Greek columns of pure and pleasing design. For literature: she maintained a voluminous correspondence with Voltaire for many years; Voltaire sang her praises, making a reputation for her as a liberal humanitarian which long outlived him and still was current when, needing an admiral, she asked for John Paul Jones.

And there was a proper time and a proper place for love. In her it was strong. In her everything was strong. But her multiple drives never obstructed one another; they worked together in neat and harmonious unity. Driving and driven, this genius of a woman held absolute sway over a sprawling empire of millions of square miles and millions of polyglot peoples. They breathed by her sufferance. The diamond that blazed on the tip of her scepter, not cold like ice but yellow and hot like flame, had been given her by the lover who slew her husband; and the lover had bought it for ninety thousand pounds from a ship's captain who had stolen it from a French soldier who, in turn, desecrating a Brahmin temple, had wrenched it from the eye of an Indian idol. Yet Catherine the Great, Imperial Autocrat of All the Russias, was perfectly charming.

Her skin was fresh and fair. Her eyes were blue and possessed a peculiar depth that was singularly magnetic. Many of the princesses who attended her had equally brilliant eyes, but their brilliance was shallow; it stopped at the surface: theirs were eyes to look at. Catherine's were eyes to look *with;* and through them all the fires that consumed her flamed out to consume the beholder.

The majesty of her presence inspired awe. She was fragilely boned, and she walked on delicate little feet with entirely feminine steps, graciously smiling on those who pleased her, whose fortunes were instantly made: nobles fawned on such favored courtiers, whose credit with tradesmen was immediately good for a year.

The opposite also was true. One day at court she inquired of a wealthy landowner why it was that so little good painting was produced in Russia. The landowner owned a serf with a harmless artistic bent who painted sunsets on shingles with a horsehair brush of his own making for his own amusement at night by the light of a tallow candle. He could not paint by daylight since he worked from morning dark to evening dark. The landowner said, "Indeed, Little Mother, good paintings *are* produced in Russia, nay, by one of my own men." The empress was delighted and expressed a desire to view an example. Gleefully the landowner dispatched his major-domo to the only art-supply shop in Moscow, an establishment run by a Frenchman. (There were hundreds of foreign specialists in Russia.) The major-domo bought a huge supply of brushes, paints and canvases. The landowner took horse, with a bare dozen of his retinue in the interest of greater speed, and spurred home sixty versts in a blizzard to his estates.

"Now paint!" he commanded.

"Paint what?" said the lout.

"Paint art."

"What is art?"

"Obey!"

The terrified serf stared at the confusing welter of tubes of color, long-handled brushes, empty white canvas squares and the easel, not one item of which had he ever set eyes on before. He fumbled among the mysterious objects and found a tube of red. He did not know how to unscrew the top so he bit off the bottom end. He chose the biggest brush and searched for something to paint on. His glance lighted upon the pallet. It was probably a shingle. Holy icons were painted on beautifully smoothed shingles like this. A priest had once shown him the wooden back of one in a church. He started to paint a sunset on the pallet.

The major-domo who had bought the art supplies was standing by. "Master, that is the pallet," he whispered.

"Idiot, that is the pallet!" the master shouted. "Don't you know what the pallet is?"

The serf dropped it in terror and sank to his knees, searching for the hem of his master's robe to kiss.

"I do not know."

Since it was obvious that the master did not know either, the major-domo said severely, "You squeeze a little paint from all the tubes onto the pallet, and then you dip your brush into the colors you want and then you paint on the white canvas."

Clumsily the serf attempted to obey, but he was so frightened that the sunset which he managed to put on the canvas was wretchedly drawn and hideously colored.

"I never painted in daylight before," he said.

Even the landowner could see that this was not art.

He ordered the serf trussed up to the easel and flogged. He was not a vicious master, and the knout was the common kind: a nine-inch handle of hard wood to which were attached strips of rawhide interwoven with wire and ending with loose wire ends. The serf received only three or four lashes and bled very little.

But the next day, when the serf painted no better, the master, fuming at the delay and fearing disgrace at court, ordered a dozen more.

Suddenly under the lash the painter stiffened, gasped, grew red in the face, rolled up his eyes, and died.

In utter bewilderment the landowner strode up and peered into his face, suspecting a ruse. To faint at twelve blows, not even harshly applied! He had not meant to incapacitate him. How could the fellow paint if he were incapacitated? He had only wanted art, Russian art, for the Russian empress. He put his hand on the dead man's heart; he could feel no beat. Still suspicious, he pinched the dead man's nose and held his palm over the open mouth to shut off the breath: surely now the fellow would make a show of recovering consciousness in order to breathe. But the painter no longer needed to breathe.

"He was so strong, too," the landowner muttered.

"He ran away, Little Mother," the landowner said. "Many serfs run away nowadays, to the detriment of Your Majesty's stanchest supporters."

"It is the fault of the times," the empress replied. "There are rebel forces afoot which displease me, especially in America." She smiled pleasantly on the landowner lest he lose face.

Gone were the days of her happy exchange of "freethinker" letters with men like Voltaire, whose ideas she now saw as a threat to the power of monarchs, her own above all. After the American Declaration of Independence she had issued a ukase, a decree which doomed the serfs of Russia (who had achieved some small measure of freedom) henceforth to a bondage more severe than ever before. Henceforth they became chattels, like Negro slaves. He who owned the estate on which they lived owned them as completely as a crop, a barn, a bull or a spadeful of earth, and their children were his also, like the increase of his fields and his farm animals. The Russian serf became absolute property.

By enriching the nobles of her empire in this fashion she engaged their loyalty and bound them to her. This was the exact opposite of the trend toward the liberty, equality and fraternity of mankind which had made one revolution in America and was well on the way to making another in France. Catherine of Russia feared only two things: one was disease and one was revolution. Liberal books that she herself had ordered printed in the first years of her reign she now ordered publicly burned, deeming them subversive, and punished anyone in whose house they were found.

One aspect of her great attraction, in which she took deserved pride, was her hair. She wore her own; it was snow white, and it shone with a luster that was the despair of the beauties of her court who vainly tried to equal her. Sometimes she would smile at the way fashion favored her. How cruelly the years would show except for the fact that everyone wore white wigs! Seventeen-year-old ladies in waiting, eighteen-year-old cadets aspiring to a command, youth with full lips and fair cheeks, wrinkled old age — one and all their heads were coiffed with white false hair, powdered, curled, beribboned and perfumed, but how dull and lifeless in contrast with her own! She was lucky in that, as she was lucky in most things, and she improved upon the quirk of fashion which permitted her to compete with the youngest and prettiest of the women who surrounded her by letting it be known that anyone who appeared without a wig would assuredly incur her displeasure. The displeasure of Catherine the Great could assume grotesque forms.

The rule was relaxed only for General Field Marshal Prince Gregory Potemkin, whom Jones met on his arrival in Russia. But no rules applied to Potemkin. His usual wig was brass wire tightly coiled, since his own hair had been fiery red before he became bald and he liked to preserve the ghost of the only thing about him that ever had been handsome.

Potemkin still shared Catherine's confidence but no longer her bed, that being lately reserved for an empty-faced captain of the guard named Zhubov, twenty-five years old. Twelfth of her favourites, Zhubov was the only one Potemkin had ever thoroughly disapproved of. It was only to be expected, Potemkin supposed, that as Catherine grew older her lovers should grow somewhat younger; that was in the nature of things; but all the others had been men of ability, and this Zhubov was stupid as a statue and just as beautiful. Potemkin was not jealous; power was his passion now; but it hurt his pride that Catherine, who once had chosen himself and after him a succession of able men, had hit upon this amiable fatuous youth as her favourite. It disturbed his sleep and reduced him to fits of melancholy during which he would shut himself up with only his nieces to attend him and stare at the ceiling for days with his one eye, the eye patch that hid the other's empty socket being thrown aside since it irritated him. What would become of Russia if Catherine, in choosing her lovers, should lose her good sense? What would become of him and his ambitions? How could he supplant that contemptible mass of male beauty with something more respectable — or at least of more value to Russia and himself? The shifty eye and the empty socket stared long at the ceiling, scheming.

Mingled with the schemes to supplant the favourite floated in reverie schemes to capture Ochakov. General Field Marshal Prince Gregory Potemkin was Commander in Chief of all the armed forces of Imperial Russia. In the present necessity for gaining control of the Black Sea an admiral of proven ability was required.

Zhubov had said brightly to Catherine, "Little Mother, if war is to come, declare it at once and let me be the first to fight for you against the Infidel!"

She had smiled and patted his head. "Such courage! How often you display it. But you are needed here."

Nor could she declare a war of aggression quite so simply as that, not with all these new notions of freedom and equality and right-to-determine-your-own-government and God only knew what other nonsense. Her education in Oriental subtlety warned her that any declaration of war in the present posture of men's minds required that she champion a Cause, something plausible and acceptable to decent men. What better Cause than a crusade against the Unspeakable Turk?

"Zhubov has suggested," she said to Potemkin, "that the Turkish war take the form of liberating all the poor oppressed Christians now groaning under the yoke of the sultan. I think he is absolutely right."

445

"It is you who must have suggested that, Catherine. It is far too good for Zhubov."

"Nothing is too good for Zhubov," she replied archly.

"Alas, how you torture me, Little Mother."

"Flatterer," she laughed. "Dear flatterer, dear counsellor. Now to the business."

"In that, at least, we always agree."

They always agreed when the interest of Russia was at stake; and the interest of Russia required the acquisition of Ochakov, the ice-free Black Sea port.

Catherine had reached out her small white immensely powerful hand to grasp an admiral who could insure her success in the war and sent for John Paul Jones. She got him, as she got most else. But at first he had hesitated. He wrote to Jefferson, who had replaced old Benjamin Franklin as American minister to France: "I have not forsaken America, which has had many proofs of my steady affection," and he added, underlining the words, *"I can never renounce the glorious title of a citizen of the United States!"* How much more readily he would have unsheathed his sword again for the Stars and Stripes than for the Russian flag, that oddly deceptive device which faced two ways, the double-headed eagle! "Yet America," he wrote, "is independent, is in perfect peace and has no public employment for my military talents."

Idealism and proven ability pushed him to action. The action he envisaged, the action he begged Congress and President Washington to give him, was an American expedition against the pirates of the Barbary states of North Africa. He was refused.

Commerce to him was a forgotten art, linked in his memory with the youth he could now successfully forget. Yet America had sent him on a succession of thankless missions as a prize agent to European capitals to handle the tedious commercial details, dragging out from year to year, that dealt with enemy ships captured in the Revolution, most of them his own prizes. It had been galling, it had hurt his pride, to haggle over dollars due the United States Treasury with the memory of battles that won those ships still green in his mind. Now came a call to action from another nation which needed him, a call flattering to his pride, offering release from tedium, a new opportunity to add glory to his name; and it came not only from the most aristocratic monarch on earth, it came from one of the world's most fascinating women.

President Washington, writing to Jefferson, approved. "I am glad our

446

Commodore John Paul Jones has got employment, and heartily wish him success."

The Comte de Ségur approved. He was a Frenchman who had known Jones during the American Revolution. He was now ambassador to Catherine from Louis XVI of France. It was he who brought to Jones his commission in the Russian Imperial Navy, saying: "My sovereign will learn with pleasure of the acquisition of Imperial Catherine of your great talents. I have her commands for your acceptance of the grade of captain-commander, with the rank of major general in her service, and that you should proceed as soon as your affairs permit, the intention of Her Imperial Majesty being to give you a command in the Black Sea, under the orders of Prince Potemkin. The immortal glory with which you have illumined your name cannot make you indifferent to the fresh laurels you will gather in the new career which opens to you. I have the honor of being on this occasion the bearer of those sentiments of esteem with which your brilliant exploits have for a long time inspired Her Imperial Majesty. Under a sovereign so magnanimous you need not doubt of distinguished rewards in your further pursuit of glory. Every advantage of fortune awaits you. Go to her!"

Thus counseled the polished Frenchman to John Paul Jones, rusticating in Denmark, thirsting for action, daily more impatient with the petty commercialities America had thrust upon him, prize agent for the paltry kingdom of Denmark. Thus came release, his commission in the Imperial Navy of the biggest nation on earth.

It read:

> *Order to Our Admiralty College.* Having admitted Captain-Commander John Paul Jones to Our service, We have graciously commissioned him as captain in Our Navy with rank as major-general and We have ordered him assigned to Our Black Sea Fleet; and to that effect We have issued an order to Field Marshal Prince Potemkin.

It was signed *Ekaterina,* the Russian rendering of *Catherine.*
He went to her.

The manner of his going was the measure of his release, like a gun hammer let loose by the trigger, reacting with the pent-up drive of a powerful spring long compressed, and the result was nearly as hazardous to life.

To pass from Denmark to Russia, the fastest route, the only route Jones would consider, lay through the sea lanes: to Stockholm in Sweden and thence across the Baltic and into the Gulf of Finland, landing at length in Saint Petersburg, the Russian capital — a comfortable voyage of two or three days. The bitter winds of winter were past. The month was April; the sun climbed higher now, and at noon there was warmth in it.

But April in the Baltic was different from April in the Atlantic, and the difference lay in the salinity of the waters. Jones had sailed so long on the salty Atlantic that he had forgotten the comparative freshness of Baltic sea water: so many rivers drained into its all-but-landlocked expanse from Sweden, Finland, Germany, Poland and Russia that ice lasted longer there.

When Jones reached Stockholm, he was courteously informed that conditions were unfavorable, the Baltic was full of icebergs, the Gulf of Finland was jammed with grinding floes and passage was impracticable. No ship was expected to make the attempt for at least three weeks.

Overland, then, Jones suggested.

The Swedes shook their heads and smiled at his inexperience. The overland routes were wild and desolate even in summer. In spring, with the frost oozing out of the ground and the rivers rising, the roads were bottomless quagmires.

Could not one ride horseback?

No, the forests were infested with robbers and runaway serfs little better than brutes. And if one escaped the human brutes, there were nature's brutes, stirring at this time of year: bears coming out of their winter's sleep, thin, vicious, savage, hunting food for themselves and their newborn cubs; there were howling packs of famished wolves. One man would assuredly die on the overland trip, and no escort could be found foolish enough to go with him.

In that case, he said, he would charter a boat of his own. The Swedes shrugged; no one would rent him one.

"I should not care to spend the next three weeks in utter inactivity," Jones said blandly. "I shall find a fishing boat that I can hire and explore the nearby waters for my own amusement till regular service between Russia and Sweden is resumed."

That indeed was possible, the Swedes replied.

"I used to be something of a sailor," he said.

Respectfully they answered, for no one had forgotten the *Serapis*, "Captain Jones, the whole world knows that."

"I have been rather too long in countinghouses and in the anterooms of embassies."

They understood.

448

He hired a fishing smack and a crew of four, almost too few to man it even in a leisurely cruise for pleasure.

A small crew suited his purpose. Jones had secretly resolved on a daring scheme to get himself to Russia: four men were all that one man could conveniently hold at bay with a brace of pistols.

Once out of sight of land his holiday aspect suddenly changed. He grew grim of face and his scowl became fierce. He ordered a course to the Gulf of Finland and, when they sighted the white and grinding fields ahead, he forced them into the ice, leveling cocked pistols at their heads. When the wind dropped, he forced them to row. They thought him mad and humored him, plotting to tie him up and take him back like a maniac bent on destroying himself and them; but whispers of his piratical past had reached even Sweden, and so perforce they rowed, cursing him, scheming to fall upon him while he slept.

At night the white ice crunched and cracked and boomed, breaking itself to pieces, thudding against the hull. Jones threaded a twisting course through the lanes of black water that only he could detect until, like many a crew before them, they discovered with awe he had eyes that could see in the dark.

He spelled their labors, relieving them two by two, permitting them to sleep so they would be strong to row, keeping them well to the fore of the boat so no one could reach him. He himself did not sleep at all during the entire voyage of four days and four nights, and he ate with a sandwich in one hand, a pistol in the other.

Sometimes the passing ice loomed high above the hull of the little craft. Over it, sweeping down upon them, whined the cold night air, laden with moisture, penetrating through his greatcoat, causing him to shiver.

One of the Swedes, a sailor who had spent some time in the tropics, said, "You might as well shoot me now. I had malaria once. Do you know what it does to a man, being wet and cold and tired after malaria?"

Jones was thoughtful. He had heard some such rumor long ago and forgotten. He let the sailor sleep more than his share after that.

When there was a wind he let them all sleep, guiding the boat by the stars, occasionally opening the slide of a dark lantern a hasty chink to consult the chart on his knees. Each dawn his crew looked down the muzzles of pistols pointing directly at their heads.

Sometimes he changed the priming, lest they suspect the damp air had rendered it incapable of firing. Once near the end, when they were particularly surly, he shot at a sea gull and brought it down.

"I am very anxious to reach Saint Petersburg," he said. His voice had a rasping quality by now. He looked wide awake, wider awake than when they had left. His eyes were unnaturally bright, and his cheeks were pink with a flush that was not sunburn.

But they did not reach Saint Petersburg.

Deep in the Gulf of Finland the ice ahead stretched out one solid growling ocean of floes, barring all passage. Jones steered for the port of Reval, capital of the Russian province of Estonia.

On the shore the rustic inhabitants regarded the approach of his boat as a miracle. No one had crossed the Baltic all winter. No one would cross it again for a month: so long did the ice last that year.

The Russian governor, viewing his credentials, dispatched a mounted courier at once to the empress, foresavoring the prospect of favor which he knew would come to himself for being the first to inform her imperial majesty that the devotion of her famous captain-commander had impelled him to perform a quixotic passage of the icebound sea in four days.

The empress responded immediately with a generous gesture, triple in purpose, neatly compartmented like her soul, imperial in its display of absolute power: she tickled the sensitive vanity of her American captain-commander; she flattered her Estonian governor; and she achieved a grotesque retaliation upon an exceptionally lovely young lady in waiting who had been rash enough to appear at the court of Saint Petersburg without a wig to conceal her beautiful blond hair.

To her Estonian governor she sent a decoration for him to pin on the breast of his military tunic, remarking with the combination of majesty and feminine allure that she knew so well how to commingle (the technique that never had failed to serve her from the beginning of her spectacular rise to power through all the intervening years during which she had kept it): "It was sweet of you to think of Us and to be the first to tell Us of the exploit of Our Captain-Commander Jones, of whom great victories are expected in the war against the Sultan, to the end that Our unfortunate coreligionists in Turkey may be liberated from their onerous yoke." And the governor pinned on his ribbon, secure in his knowledge that his star was in the ascendant and that the empress would shower him with favors thereafter.

As for Jones, she positively outdid herself. She had been apprised of the hazard to his health that the passage of the Baltic had cost him. She did everything in her power to ameliorate its consequences: she sent him a fashionable French physician with orders to build up his health. She mingled maternal with imperial solicitude: Rear Admiral Jones (he

450

heard the new title with amazement) must not lapse into a sickness that would render him careless of glory, into a fatigue that would vitiate the drive he always had demonstrated and which she so greatly admired.

None of her lovers, none of her statesmen but had drawn their drive-to-excel from herself, from herself as the font of power. She knew the inspiration she spread, like the dark and blinding sepia "ink" which a cephalapod emits by instinct to becloud the area in which it lurks and feeds.

"Rear Admiral?" he asked. He was lying in bed, still feverish.

The physician was measuring him a draught. The courier, having delivered the greeting from the empress, stood at attention, a Tartar hat of astrakhan wool at a jaunty angle on his head, an open smile on his handsome face — the empress's couriers were invariably handsome. The governor held in his hand the new commission which the courier had brought, along with the doctor, an admiral's uniform precisely fitted to Jones's measurements, Jones never knew how . . . and a something else of which Jones was not aware till next day.

"Let me read to you this!" the governor exulted, unrolling the beautifully engrossed parchment. "It will warm you quicker than the physician's draught."

The parchment read:

> We graciously command that as soon as Captain-Commander John Paul Jones shall present himself before Our Commander-in-Chief General Field Marshal Prince Potemkin that the said John Paul Jones shall be given the rank of Rear Admiral."

Not twenty-four hours on Russian soil and already rewarded! His spirits rose and his fever disappeared.

"It will nevertheless be necessary for monsieur l'amiral to refresh himself with much sleep to be strong in Her Imperial Majesty's service," the physician declared, a long forefinger uplifted in warning. "We Russians must not lose our new amiral in the same moment we gain him, now must we!" and he clucked like a motherly old hen.

"Oh no indeed, monsieur le professeur," Jones answered, grinning, taking his cue from a constellation of stars on the doctor's long, richly embroidered Russian tunic. This doctor was obviously a personage of some importance in the imperial household. "We Russians must guard our health with great care."

"Parbleu!" said the doctor, "but monsieur l'amiral speaks French!"

"Your linguistic talent will stand you in good stead," the governor said wistfully. "All the nobility speak French if they can. Me, alas, I have never been able to learn it."

"*Tiens!*" the rear admiral said.

The doctor smiled to himself.

Under the influence of the draught, which was largely vintage brandy, the resounding new title and forty uninterrupted hours of sleep, Jones woke to a glorious spring sunset, a feeling of perfect health and an invitation to a ball.

"It is our Easter season," the governor said, "different by a few days from yours because of our calendar, but it is the same high holiday time of rejoicing that you papists celebrate in the West."

It was new for a Scotch-Presbyterian-American to be called a papist. But then, everything in Russia was new.

"I feel like celebrating," he said; and after a moment, with an air of concern, "Where are my men? Are they provided for? Is the boat safe?"

"What men, Admiral?"

"Why, the good Swedes who sailed me here."

The governor looked embarrassed.

"Oh, them. Oh yes. I shall inquire after them."

"I did not have a chance to pay them. It was my intention to reward them for the service they rendered me."

"I shall inquire."

In Russian, of which Jones did not understand a word, the governor gave a rapid order and received a rapid answer from an aide.

"They are still close by, Admiral. Is it actually your intention to reward the Swedish serfs?" He looked incredulous.

"Still close by? Good! They did not attempt the perilous voyage home alone?"

"Oh no. No indeed. We saw to that. We were not sure you wished them to return."

Jones, in a grateful mood, told the governor how anxious he was to recompense the seamen who, however unwillingly, had obeyed his orders and fought their way through the Baltic and delivered him to his new responsibilities. "I have no American funds to give them," he said, "but I am determined to make amends for their hardships out of my own pocket." (More than once in recent years he had had to draw on his secret funds.)

Russia was big, Russians were lavish, their attitude towards money was otherworldly: it irked them to think of it at all. In this they contrasted sharply with Westerners.

The governor's stolid face betrayed the pique that he genuinely felt.

"You wish to pay them *yourself*, Admiral? But that is impossible. We shall pay. What is their due?"

Jones struck on a figure.

The governor multiplied it by ten, and the delighted Swedes, who had been held in strict confinement, were released, toasted in all the public houses of Reval and, when the weather cleared, sailed back to Stockholm enriched beyond their dreams, with praise for the man who had forced them at pistol point to perform a fantastic passage and harboring confused opinions with regard to the Russians, who first had cast them into jail for no reason and then for no reason had paid them far more than their service was worth. "There are two colors in Russia," one of the Swedes remarked, shaking his head in mystification. "One is black and the other is white, and you never know which you are."

But John Paul Jones did not hear and could not benefit from the ruminations of his crew. He went to the ball.

Chapter 42

TO PENETRATE the secret recesses of Catherine's mind would have been an impossibility. Only an intelligence more than human could have performed such a feat. Nay, even a more-than-human intelligence would have found itself at a loss unless possessed of a knowledge of good and evil vouchsafed neither to angels nor devils, whose very perfection of nature delimits their knowledge. To penetrate the secret recesses of Catherine's mind would have required the more-than-human perception not only of an angel but of a devil as well, so complex was the Autocrat of All the Russias.

On Easter of the year 1788 an angel of the Lord flying from Saint Petersburg to Reval, singing to the cathedral bells, would have noted the following:

Item: A certain Princess Anna Kourakin will be sorely tried this night. The princess is vain by reason of her great beauty, but otherwise blameless; I will stand by her side and comfort her in her pain.

Item: Four rollicking guardsmen have been given unexpected leave to celebrate the Easter holiday away from the capital. They are drunk with vodka and laughing with anticipation, spurring along the military road from Saint Petersburg to Reval. They have learned through whispered gossip, which started with an apparent slip of the tongue of Prince Potemkin, who never is wrong, that a "runaway female serf" of exceptional loveliness has been captured in Reval. Her punishment will be unusual and entertaining. The Guardsmen are excited at the prospect of witnessing it. They will remember it and relate it to their envious companions for weeks to come. One of the Guardsmen is her husband, Prince Kourakin. But I, being an angel, will blind him with drink so he never will suspect that the runaway "serf" is his wife; and though he will later observe the condition of her head, he will never guess that the empress went further than shaving her hair as punishment for not wearing a wig.

Item: Admiral John Paul Jones, who is about to change his name again, does not require my assistance at this time, his time of trial being yet a little while away.

Item: Alas for poor humans! What an effort to keep them out of trouble!

But the angelic itemization would have fallen short of the whole.

Flying beside the angel flew a demon, and he noted the following, cringing and cowering at the music of the cathedral bells:

Item: A certain Princess Kourakin will be tortured tonight. She is smooth and slender and built to tempt a man. I will stand by her side in her trial and increase her pain. I will visit her with a fear that shall never leave her so long as she lives. I shall find means to inform her that one of the men responsible for her shame was her husband. I shall put in his mouth, "My dear Anna, I happened to be present at a most extraordinary celebration of Easter while you were safe at home, in which a runaway serf was punished. It would be difficult for you to imagine how absurd it was, how uproariously ludicrous!" Anna Kourakin will never be sure whether her husband did not recognize those pretty dimples in the secret place. She will fear to make mention of them even if he does; and she will say, "Oh, everybody has those, even serfs, I expect."

Item: The interesting matter of the new admiral must receive some attention as soon as I finish with this princess. Already his vitals burn. How cleverly he concealed that trace of pink in his urine from the physician who attends him, grooming him for even higher rank. Later he will amuse me.

Item: Long live the race of Adam and Eve! How lonesome hell would be without them!

In Saint Petersburg in the premier cathedral of Russia the Empress Catherine graciously attended Easter service, bestowing her imperial smile on her loyal clergy who, in golden vestments and jeweled crowns, praised equally God and her, which to her seemed quite as it should be.

Shaving her head with a surgeon's skill and a Frenchman's appreciation of the beautiful, the physician remarked in a kindly tone, "It was rash, *mon enfant*, to precipitate yourself into this predicament." The blond locks fell to the floor; later he would burn them; it was a private room. "May I observe that your cranium is exquisitely modeled, that a sculptor would delight in it?"

"I am hideous, horrible!"

"Poor child."

"Lost," she said.

"Oh, not at all. Perfect for the occasion. Even better than I had expected."

"What occasion?"

"When the occasion arises, just do not make a move, no matter what happens."

"What more will happen? Is this not all?"

"This is all that need be known, so long as you do not betray yourself by a shudder, a tear or the slightest motion."

Terrified, she begged, "In God's name tell me what more is to come." She was now bald as an egg.

Seriously, kindly, he said, "To inform you would cost me my place, but I promise that no one will recognize you. You will keep your secret and preserve your good name if you can be strong."

"My good name?" Princess Anna Kourakin had wondered why the empress had lowered her voice, had spoken almost generously, had reprimanded her lightly and had said she planned to make no public disclosure of displeasure — and then had whisked her off, bound and gagged, concealed in the baggage compartment of a coach that had hurriedly left from Saint Petersburg. "Doctor, shall I be permitted to keep my good name?"

"So long as you do not raise your head or expose your face to the assembly who will be dancing in the ballroom your anonymity will be entirely complete. No one will even suspect you are human."

"Prepare me! Help me to be strong! I cannot stand not knowing! I cannot bear the thought that my husband may see me subjected to some horrid public humiliation!"

He sighed and patted her head. "Only *this* will be visible to the dancers in the ballroom. As for the rest, *hélas!*"

455

She shuddered. "Now I thank God that my husband is in Saint Petersburg."

During the day while the governor and the admiral attended church services, while the great iron bells of Toompea Citadel boomed out a discordant paean of Easter joy, a carpenter with a saw cut a hole in a wall. It was just the proper height from the floor so that a delicate woman, kneeling like an animal on all fours, could insert her head through it if her head had been slightly reduced in size by shaving her hair. Like the measurements of the admiral's uniform, the measurement of the hole was perfect. The wall separated the governor's ballroom from the wardroom, a sort of common room where the sentries customarily relaxed between watches, gossiped, drank and amused themselves.

The hole completed, the carpenter, who was a serf, found himself instantly rewarded by being presented to a new owner nine hundred miles away in the province of Ulianovsk, where the beer was excellent, life was easier and where, favored, he soon rose to the position of overseer. Each Easter in church, recalling his good fortune, the overseer would raise his voice and answer along with the happy congregation, "He is risen indeed!" when the priest would intone the immemorial joyful chant, "Christ is risen!" and thank God for the strange and wonderful workings of His providence: to have received so much for so little, for cutting a hole in a wall that had something to do with an Easter egg that was part of the decoration of the governor's ball!

The governor's ball was a lengthy affair; it started at ten o'clock at night and ended at five in the morning with dawn creeping in at the windows. It was on a monumental scale; everything was big.

The toasts were generous, frequent and strong; the speeches of welcome introducing "Admiral Pavel" were interminable; the music was loud and the musicians were apparently inexhaustible, sawing and sweating at their violins.

The court physician, who hovered round him throughout the evening, observed, "You do not recognize the honor Her Imperial Majesty does you: in Russian *Pavel* is *Paul*."

"I am used to variants of my name," Jones said.

"The honor is personally significant," the physician persisted. "The Czarevitch, her son, is also a Paul, that is to say Pavel, like you." He lowered his voice and glanced apprehensively around him. "One does not mention him any more; his mind is as weak as his mother's is strong. His excesses startle even the Russians. Not till you came has Her Imperial

Majesty spoken the name Pavel with pleasure. One fears that the poor crown prince will never live to reign."

Jones shook his head in sympathy.

The physician passed his arm through his in a friendly gesture. "But *you* are not to die, *mon brave!* I have explicit orders to the contrary. In fact, you are my special charge. Come, let us examine how our Russian hosts enjoy themselves. In France such decorations for a ball would border on the fantastic, would they not, barbaric in their exaggeration? But never call a Russian a barbarian, never! Nothing so incenses them as to be called barbarians."

"Oh, I shall be very careful," Jones laughed.

Eagle banners and colorful bunting hung on the walls. A life-sized painting of the empress smiled down from a place of honor above an immense fireplace; tapers burned before it as if it were some holy icon in a shrine. A huge fire blazed on the hearth, and a dozen Easter hams kept hot on a hob as big as a bed. To add to the heat caused by the fire and the throng who crowded the room, an enormous brass samovar brewed a hogshead of tea, mingling the suffocating odor of charcoal with the smell of the strong black drink. The governor's ball in Reval was less prim than the stately minuets being danced at the imperial court in Saint Petersburg, and long before dawn many of the guests were tipsy. Then they would drink the tea, stronger and blacker than ever by now, placing a cube of sugar between their front teeth and sucking the tea noisily through it while the sugar dissolved.

"Try it!" the governor said. "This is the only way to drink tea."

"It might put some weight on you," the physician smiled. "Slenderness like yours isn't the style in this part of the world," and, since he had to translate for the governor, who did not speak French, he added, "I was telling Admiral Pavel that the Russian method of tea drinking will do something to amend the alarming Lenten figure of his and give him a build like Your Excellency's."

"I am a big man," the governor said, placing a beefy hand on his paunch and solemnly acknowledging the compliment with a bow. "A very big man."

Jones tried a cup, fumbled badly, and was immediately surrounded by a gay and chattering group of gentlemen and ladies who sought to help him perfect his technique: "This way! Like this! Suck harder! More noise!"

Laughing, he said, "It will take me a little time, I'm afraid."

Behind a long serving table against a wall liveried servants prepared the new and immensely fashionable sandwiches, the invention imported from

457

England, slices of meat between slices of bread which one could eat dancing! But most of the guests soon tired of the foreign novelty and, having proven their skill with ham sandwiches, went back to a less exotic buffet of smoked salmon and caviar. The heaps of caviar on the giant platters were constantly renewed.

Against this same wall, as a decoration, were scores of brightly colored Easter eggs — eggs of all sizes, swallows' eggs, hens' eggs, ducks' eggs, ostrich eggs, all beautifully gilded and painted. Artists traditionally spent weeks in their preparation. Nowhere in the world were Easter eggs so prized and elaborately decorated as in Russia. Some at the governor's ball were obviously artificial, since they were larger than any known bird could have produced. The governor was particularly complimented on one artificial example that lay in a golden beribboned basket. A railing kept the guests away from the display lest someone by accident break the costly and fragile objects.

"I am going to present the one in the basket to the empress," the governor said to Jones.

To Jones it looked like all the rest, just as motionless, just as alien, just as fantastically painted.

To himself the physician said, "Brave girl! She is holding up! Or perhaps she is dead by now." But no, his practiced surgeon's eye caught the throb of a vein on the surface of the egg. She was alive.

In the room on the other side of the wall, exposed to the drunken sentries and Guardsmen, among whom was Prince Kourakin, the body of the "runaway serf" lay naked and helpless to their insults. Tight iron bracelets had been fitted to her elbows and knees and firmly attached to the wooden floor with iron spikes. Her head disappeared in a hole in the wall. She was so motionless that they thought a fraud had been perpetrated upon them, some ingenious statue substituted, till they touched her flesh and found it warm, felt her heart beat and discovered, as one after another they ravished her, that she was real.

As they became drunker, they became rougher.

Kourakin struck her across her hips with the flat of his sword.

"Insolent pig!" he shouted. "Act alive! This one's a prince!"

Her body tightened, though she could hear nothing through the wall; her fists clenched, she sweated in agony as the welt on her hips rose and throbbed; but otherwise she remained as motionless as before, hiding her face in the golden basket. In the ballroom at that moment the physician noted the pulsing of the vein.

"Oh, let her alone," said one of the others, who had had his fill of her.

"It's not so much fun when you can't see their faces," another complained, going back to his bottle.

They tried to pull her away from the wall but discovered that an iron clamp around her neck made withdrawal impossible.

"Damn you all, don't strangle her!" another said. "I haven't had my turn!"

Kourakin said thickly, "I can usually drink more than this," and vomited violently.

"Me too," said another sleepily.

"You got her dirty," said the man who had not had his turn.

One, who had drunk somewhat less, observed slyly, "If this is punishment, she ought not to complain."

Another muttered, "Oh, it can't be much pleasure after so many."

"Serfs don't mind how many," said Kourakin, who was rapidly losing consciousness.

It had been no part of the physician's orders to drug the Guardsmen's vodka. But a Gallic sense of honor had told him enough was enough; a physician's conservatism had warned him that there were limits to what the human body could stand. Shortly after midnight, when the lights of the ballroom were dimmed so that the assembly could watch a Tartar entertainer swallow swords and eat fire, the empress's handsome courier quietly substituted another egg for the head of the Princess Kourakin and dragged the unconscious Guardsmen and sentries away from her slack and fainting body. That same hour he took her back to Saint Petersburg in a coach with drawn shades and covered lamps, driven by men who did not know who was concealed in the muffling cloak.

In the ballroom Jones danced till dawn and looked forward with anticipation to his presentation at court.

Chapter 43

THE PREVALENCE of princes confused the new admiral at first; virtually everyone he met bore the title; he associated it with royalty. But in Russia princes seemed almost as common as lairds in Scotland and marquises in France. Then he discovered that in Russia anyone with any claim to nobility, no matter how vague, was entitled to be called a prince.

Prince Potemkin, however, was none of this common herd. Potemkin was triply a prince: prince by reason of his noble birth; Prince of the Crimea, by reason of a military campaign he had conducted in that province; and Prince of the Holy Roman Empire, by reason of Catherine's diplomatic pressure on the feeble Austrian emperor, who feared Russian reprisal if he did not grant the ancient, much-tarnished but still-revered title that he alone of all Christian monarchs could bestow.

Ever since Easter the court at Saint Petersburg had been in good spirits, taking their cue from the empress, who seemed in a happy mood. She spoke enthusiastically of the Turkish war; her courtiers mirrored her confidence and talked of nothing else, predicting easy victory. Zhubov begged her daily for a regiment, and she indulged his military ardor so far as to let him have a beautiful new colonel's uniform, which no one could deny made him more handsome and dashing than even he had been, and danced with him at receptions enjoying the envious glances her ladies could not hide — but she gave him no command.

"For the time being, this is a sea war," she explained to him fondly. "You will serve us better here."

Potemkin's nieces, who knew him best and managed his eccentric household, were overjoyed at the change which the prospect of war and the coming of the American admiral had wrought in their uncle. For weeks he had sulked in his study, dressed in a sacklike dressing gown which exposed his grotesquely bowed hairy legs, eating virtually nothing, poring over maps of the Black Sea, drinking quantities of tea, alternately caning and coddling the Kalmuk slave who brought it, and showing no interest in his diamonds, always a bad sign in Prince Potemkin. Now, however, he changed, and they knew that his restless mind had found the only peace it was capable of experiencing: action and a plan.

He recovered his Gargantuan appetite, put on his eye patch, his brass wire wig, his uniform of Commander in Chief and shaved. Jones found him completely at ease, relaxing with his diamonds.

He possessed an enormous collection of them. Admirers and sycophants, seeking for favors, who presented other jewels, no matter how valuable, found that they displeased him; he would dismiss them with curt thanks, deny their favors and later they would find he had given the jewels away. But diamonds delighted him. They were all unset. If they came to him mounted in emblems or rings, he would dig them out of their settings and put the naked stones in a chamois bag in which he kept all his others. He neither knew nor cared what the value of his collection might be. Sometimes he would let them drip idly through his fingers, like a child playing with a double handful of sand, delighting in the fire they presented to the eye and the curious feeling of coldness that diamonds, especially by the handful, seem to impart to the touch.

But most of the time he would arrange the collection in geometric patterns on a large square of black velvet, taking infinite pains that their color and size be harmoniously contiguous and that the lines of the figure — circle, star, polygon — be rigorously exact.

He had fashioned a star and crescent the day he admitted Admiral Pavel into audience.

"One moment," he said, not looking up when Jones was ushered in.

Jones watched, alert, amazed at the man.

"It isn't quite right," Potemkin said, knitting his brow.

Jones was silent.

Potemkin raised his head. His piercing eye was bright as the jewels; the eye patch on the other was black as the velvet.

"Well, is it right?"

"No."

"Do you know what it is?"

"Yes."

Jones was long since aware of the appearance of the Turkish flag, the flag that would identify the ships it was now his duty to search out and sink. Perhaps it was natural that his Commander in Chief should be thinking of the enemy too.

"Why isn't it right?" The eye drooped cunningly. Jones felt he was being tested.

The colors, crystal on black, of course were wrong, but Jones sensed that Potemkin would not be satisfied with a small criticism: the man was big, his projects were big, no little answer would suffice.

"If Your Excellency will permit the suggestion of a change in the design you have traced of the enemy flag, I believe I can improve it."

"By all means," Potemkin said.

Jones stretched out his hand and rubbed out the star and crescent, leaving the diamonds a scrambled mass.

"Eliminate it," he said.

Potemkin stiffened; no one was permitted to touch his diamonds; he glared at the admiral. Then he gave him a thunderous clap on the back, crying, "Bravo!" and roared with laughter. "The empress will not be dissatisfied with you, mark my word!"

Nor was she. The admiral's reception at the Winter Palace was a sensation. Behind him was the tremendous prestige of Potemkin's friendship.

461

His world-wide reputation for valor was known: the French king, after the successful American Revolution, had presented him with a ceremonial sword; the American Congress had voted him a gold medal commemorating his victories; the sculptor Houdon had immortalized him in marble. At Jones's formal reception the British ambassador took refuge in frigid reserve, and smiled painfully at mention of his name. Poor Zhubov looked sick at the sight of him. Without question Admiral Pavel was the most controversial, most interesting and most gossiped-about figure to be presented at court in the Easter season of 1788.

"We are happy to receive you, Pavel," the empress said, smiling. "We are persuaded that the trust we have placed in your talents and the devotion you bear to our person is not misapplied, nor will the faithful discharge of your duties go without recompense."

He kissed the hand she extended and answered, "Madam, the zealous desire I experienced to enter your service and place my sword at Your Imperial Majesty's command, a pull that drew me across an icy sea, now tugs at my heart in the opposite sense and bids me exile myself from the warmth of your welcome, to the end that a quick and decisive victory over Your Imperial Majesty's enemies may render me the worthier to hasten again to your side for such recompense as Your Imperial Majesty may consider my due."

It was a fulsome and flattering reply. Potemkin, standing at his side, his face enigmatic, thought to himself, "Mussing up my diamonds was nothing compared with a speech like that! Where does he get his gall? How did he know exactly how to treat her? The man is rash or a consummate actor or both." But, noting that Catherine allowed her hand to rest longer than protocol required in the admiral's, he was not displeased, for Zhubov was turning green with jealousy, and the empress was smiling like the Mona Lisa.

Oddly, Jones meant every word. He was not calling upon his Shakespearean experience. The imperial hand he kissed was the hand of a young girl and as warm. Well had Dr. Mesmer pronounced, "She possesses the animal magnetism to a superlative degree."

"Since you must leave us," the empress replied graciously, "fare swiftly hence, fare well, and fare swiftly home." And to the universal astonishment of the court, before she withdrew her hand she actually patted his. It might have been motherly. But then, it might have spelled the doom of Zhubov. To a court accustomed to rapid changes in the personal life of the empress, one never knew when an old favourite would be dismissed and a new one installed. During the remainder of the reception, after the empress had retired on the arm of a crestfallen Zhubov, Admiral Pavel was surrounded by a throng of well-wishers tendering him a flood of invitations to boar hunts and shooting parties and month-long sojourns in country estates the instant war should be won and he should return from the total annihilation of the Ottoman Empire, which everyone seemed to take for granted. They were a friendly people, the Russians, Jones thought, with a sovereign who brought out the best in them, understandably, it seemed to him, for he himself had responded to her personal charm. One of the courtiers who wished him well and regretted that his duties as a Guardsman prevented him from enlisting in the admiral's enterprise was a Prince Kourakin, whose wife was exceptionally pretty and who clung closer to her husband's arm than most of the courtiers' wives. Jones was told that the princess had suffered a bout of fever on Easter day which seemed to have wasted her strength; her eyes had a haunted doelike look as if she were afraid that the fever might return. Jones admired Prince Kourakin's solicitude for his ailing and lovely young wife, and he knew from old experience, now reasserting itself in an irritating manner, how harmful fevers could be and how long they could trouble one.

Late in the spring, in good fighting weather, Admiral Pavel arrived at the Black Sea and assumed his command. Behind him simmered a witches' brew of intrigue. Before him lay the cruelest of all his victories.

Chapter 44

THE SULTAN OF TURKEY had massed a powerful fleet in the Black Sea for the defense of Ochakov, knowing that if the port could be provisioned by sea it could withstand a protracted siege from the armies that Catherine was sending overland to attack it. At the head of the land force rode the one-eyed Commander in Chief, Prince Potemkin. The sultan knew Potemkin's tactics: frantic attacks, long periods of indecision, sulky retreats, and frantic attacks renewed. The two potentates, Asiatic in outlook, were evenly matched, understanding each other.

But Admiral Pavel was a mystery, and the Captain Pasha who commanded the Turkish fleet had orders to spy out his methods, reconnoiter his position and above all to build up strength before attacking him, for all that was known of the admiral in Asia was that whenever he fought he was outnumbered and whenever he fought he won. Patently, the only safe course was to build up the odds so heavily against him that even his genius would be forced to give way to sheer weight of numbers. In addition to heavy ships of the line the Captain Pasha concentrated a force of galleys, propelled by long oars, a type of craft never seen in the Atlantic but common in the Mediterranean since Phoenician times and still useful. They were manned by Christian and Negro slaves who were chained to the oars.

Surveying his fleet from his flagship, the *Vladimir*, Admiral Pavel felt a surge of confidence. The vessel was stanch, well constructed and heavily gunned. His other capital ships, sturdy frigates copied from European models but Russian built, had good lines and looked shipshape. Their crews, a polyglot mixture of Russians, Greeks, Germans and Poles, were obedient, healthy and cheerful. Reinforcing his heavy ships was an auxiliary force, a flotilla of sloops and schooners of lighter draft, well armed and newly equipped. The empress had expended huge sums on her Black Sea fleet.

But on closer inspection ridiculous deficiencies turned up. Admiral Pavel, to the disgust of his gorgeously uniformed subordinates, stripped off his crested boots and bemedaled tunic, rolled up his shirt sleeves and personally climbed into the *Vladimir*'s rigging. Everything was wrong. Critical lines of the running gear intended to trim the spars ended abruptly tied to a mast or a shroud and were thereby rendered functionless, whether through carelessness or ignorance Jones could not tell. He found brand-new canvas sails so loosely attached to the spars that they would assuredly have ripped free and carried away at the first good blow.

He commanded the deficiencies be made good. To his surprise the crew, laughing and joking and spitting on the deck, clambered aloft and rapidly set things to rights. "So they *did* know how!" he mused. "Then why in the world didn't they do it right in the first place!" For a ship's driving apparatus to be in perfect condition when she went into battle was a matter of life and death to every man aboard her. What sort of madman takes his own life so casually that he ties a mainsail halyard to a ratline? If the bravery of the Russians should equal their carelessness, there would be surprises ahead when the ships went into action.

He ordered the decks cleansed of the spittle and filth, but the good-natured crew so quickly fouled it again that, in disgust, he ordered the decks sanded each day and had the sand swept over the side each night.

464

Below decks he made another discovery. The pumps had no hoses attached to them. A set of new hoses lay nearby. But the chief engineer had stubbornly refused to take the new ones out of their packing, having been reprimanded when the old ones leaked and had to be renewed. He had firmly resolved that the new ones should be given no chance to wear out.

But the worst deficiency was in the matter of the shot. The magazines were brimful of gunpowder of German manufacture, excellent in quality. The cannon balls, however, were all too small for the *Vladimir's* cannon.

Scowling, tired and powder-stained, wearing his own hair, looking like one of his own gunners instead of the admiral in charge of Black Sea operations, he had himself rowed from one ship to another, clambered down into a dozen magazines and discovered a similar state of mismanagement, and raged in French and English at his subordinate captains. Shrugging and smiling, they protested that the situation was by no means unprecedented; things always happened like this. Was it not enough that they were ready to die for Great Catherine and Holy Russia? Must one insist on perfection in details as well?

"Is it not preferable," said one affable captain, "that the shot be too small than that it be too large? One can always expel the too-small ball from the too-big cannon. Suppose it were the other way round?"

Admiral Pavel experienced a sinking feeling in the pit of his stomach. He directed his launch to the lighter ships of the flotilla and hurried to inspect their magazines.

And here he found the cannon balls for the *Vladimir*. The shot for the big ships had been loaded aboard the small ones, which could not possibly fire it, and vice versa. No one had bothered to inspect.

This error too he ordered rectified. It was a tedious and delaying business, requiring scores of small boats rowing back and forth between the ships. After many hours and much labor the shot was matched to the guns and the guns to the shot.

In giving his orders and questioning his men the admiral was greatly hampered by a linguistic difficulty, since he could speak no Russian. Many of the captains and officers were noble, and they of course spoke French; but the more noble they were the worse seamen they were, and the less they knew or cared about the mechanics of the vessels they commanded. With the gunners, carpenters, sailors and engineers who were not noble and spoke nothing but Russian, the admiral conversed through an interpreter named Bahl, a pimple-faced German who had been assigned to him as an aide. In the company of this shifty-eyed person, who served him also as a valet, Jones often regretted the simplicity and single devotion of Chima, lost like so many others on the *Bonhomme Richard,* a world away in space and time.

Then an extraordinary and dangerous inadequacy turned up in the charts. They were newly drawn, expensively mounted and beautifully colored. Someone, however, had forgotten to mark in the sounding figures, those all-important little numbers that speckle a navigator's chart and tell him at a glance how deep the water is under his keel.

Jones blinked his eyes in disbelief and angrily ordered a signal run up to summon his second in command aboard the flagship. Half an hour later he found the signal man fumbling in a code book, searching which flags to display, scratching his head and muttering a jumble of apologies. Jones countermanded the order and sent his launch for the noble subordinate, who, after a suitable interval in which to wax his elegant little mustache, appeared in the admiral's great cabin.

Prince Charles of Nassau-Siegen was the bastard son of a powerful Dutch nobleman, who acknowledged but greatly disliked him and had cut him out of his will. In his early youth he had been profligate and wild. He had sailed round the world with Bougainville, the great French geographer, mathematician and explorer, who had immortalized the name Bougainville by giving it to some beautiful South Sea islands. But all the young Dutchman had learned in that notable three-year voyage was to drink *okuliha* and tell tall tales: other adventurers into those delectable isles had returned with recitals of amorous exploits under the tropic moon; nothing so unimaginative for Prince Charles of Nassau-Siegen! He returned with a smirk on his handsome face and a solemn declaration that in June of the year 1769 he had seduced not a hula dancer, not the daughter of a chieftain of the islands, but no less a personage than the Queen of Tahiti herself under a palm tree close to the beach. To relieve his poverty, which he found irksome, he had charmed and married a wealthy Polish noblewoman, whose family Catherine had favored; thus he found himself lord of an estate. Shortly he appeared in Saint Petersburg seeking a position in the service of the empress, making himself popular not only with sprightly recitals of his adventures as a navigator but also as a loyal Polish subject of Her Imperial Majesty bent on agrarian reform. Russians loved Poles who were interested in agrarian reform; modernization and Westernization were all the rage. "Once when a band of Tartar robbers attacked my estate," said Nassau-Siegen, "I loosed sixty trained bears against them. The loyal brutes fought brilliantly for me, and after they had routed the bandits they picked up stones in their claws and hurled them after them." The empress found his manners engaging and, believing he was a sailor since he had sailed round the world, appointed him second in command of the Black Sea fleet under Admiral Pavel.

Jones knew that Nassau was a liar, would do anything to enhance his own reputation and was a contemptible fop, but not until now did he recognize the depth of his ignorance.

"Have you seen these charts?" Jones demanded.

"But of course, monsieur l'amiral!" He sensed that the admiral was displeased. "Do you object to them?"

"Confound it, man, look at them!"

Nassau-Siegen examined them, squinting in concentration. "Perhaps they were hurriedly prepared, sir, but concede that they are beautifully executed. Such artistry! What an exquisite blue here in the north!" He pointed to the south.

Jones changed his tone. There was no use badgering the fellow. He could not read a chart; he thought that the compass rose in the corner was merely an interesting decoration, and did not know it was placed there to orient the surrounding shores and enable a navigator to shape his course.

"I was only a little concerned," Jones said, "that these charts seem to lack sounding marks. It would be a help to know the depth of the water under our ships."

"But the Black Sea is so big," said Nassau-Siegen. "There is so very, *very* much water all around that I'm sure there must be plenty underneath."

Jones sighed.

"Thank you very much."

That night under cover of darkness, concealed from the eyes of the Turkish fleet which was growing more formidable every day but still made no move to attack, Jones had himself rowed out in a boat with muffled oars and greased locks and personally took soundings of the lagoon. He repeated the reconnoiter the next night and the next, and after a week there were accurate sounding marks on all the charts of the Russian fleet. The Russians wondered why he bothered with such details, why he demeaned himself with such serflike labors: he was certainly not like an admiral in his behavior. He was totally unlike Dutchmen, Frenchmen, Germans and other Westerners whom their rulers had placed over them. Perhaps he was merely a madman, like Potemkin; and at that their Russian hearts opened in understanding, and they began to love him.

Then Jones drilled his fleet, and taught them a few rudimentary signals and compelled them to sail in formation. The Russian crews responded heartily and worked like slaves to perfect their gunnery and seamanship, handling the sails with skill and serving the guns with promptness and economy of motion, though as yet the admiral permitted no firing, even for target practice, lest he precipitate a Turkish attack before he was ready.

Word came meanwhile that Potemkin was approaching Ochakov with the Russian land forces. Nassau-Siegen told the admiral that the delay in the movements of the Imperial Army was owing to a desire on the part of the Commander in Chief to receive a shipment of perfume from Paris for his nieces, a shipment which had not arrived when promised. Now, however, it had been received and Potemkin, out of his sulks, was on the march again.

Jones had watched with increasing concern the continuing build-up of the Turkish fleet during this protracted period. It would have been foolhardy to have struck before he had forged his amorphous force into a coordinated fighting unit. Now that he was ready he found himself opposed by a vastly superior strength.

But he knew that he possessed one immense superiority over the enemy. He now possessed charts of the lagoon which had been prepared within the last ten days; the Turks' were assuredly older; they might be as inaccurate as the Russians'. He based his strategy on the presence of a sandy shoal he had discovered near the mouth of the River Bug to the east of Ochakov.

During the night in the *Vladimir*, with an escort of three heavy ships of the line, he made a rapid foray against the Turkish fleet, firing broadside after broadside upon them, not of grape shot and chain as was his custom, but of eighteen-pounders, massive shot that wrought great damage to their hulls. It was not his intention to smash their sails; he wanted the ships mobile; he left them their driving power. Jones was inviting attack and proposed to lure them to destruction.

There was an immense uproar and hubbub among the Turks, with beating of monstrous alarm drums and, after an interval, a thunderous return of fire. But by that time Jones had slipped away into the darkness.

The Turks formed line of battle and bore to the northeast after a string of lights that appeared to be frigates. But the lights were lanterns stuck high in the masts of smaller ships.

Following these decoys, the Turks pressed on towards the treacherous

468

shoal at the mouth of the river: in water where frigates could go, they reasoned, frigates could follow. But the decoys were ships of lighter draft. Suddenly one, then two, then three of the Turkish men-of-war ran aground, including the flagship of the Captain Pasha, with such force that they buried their keels irretrievably in the sand of the bottom, deeper than the scant tides of the Black Sea could extricate. Listing at a sharp angle, their masts canted crazily against the stars, their guns became useless, since they must now fire either into the sea or at the sky. Simultaneously Jones signaled his heavy ships to attack the rest of the fleet from the rear and flashed an order to the flotilla not to molest the ships which had run aground and were now out of action but to lend what help they could against the light units of the enemy.

The Captain Pasha saved himself in a swift, slave-driven little skiff and boarded another vessel and signaled a general retreat. Jones followed, still chasing at dawn, leaving two more battered Turkish wrecks behind to capsize and sink and inflicting damage on dozens more. Driven by panic, the swift Turkish ships evaded him, racing for the Sea of Marmora and the protecting forts of Constantinople. Reluctantly Jones gave up the chase and turned about.

Suddenly he was aware that Prince Charles of Nassau-Siegen was nowhere in sight; he had not followed the admiral in pursuit of the enemy. He wondered what had happened and was reminded of the insubordination of Landais.

When Jones again approached the spot where the three Turkish men-of-war had run aground, he saw smoke in the distance. As he drew closer, he saw the three ships in flames and smelled the stench of burning flesh.

During the night Nassau-Siegen had methodically bombarded the helpless vessels with a particularly cruel variety of fire bomb called brand-cougles, which were so fiercely flammable that they would continue to burn even when immersed in water.

The Turkish sailors knelt on the decks and begged for quarter, but Nassau mowed them down.

Worse still was the fate of the Christian slaves below deck. Each ship carried about a thousand of them and, as was customary with so many prisoners who might otherwise revolt, they were chained to their posts of duty. There, chained, three thousand of them burned to death. Some Turkish galleys which had not been able to escape Nassau also bombarded with brandcougles in order to increase the number of enemy vessels that he could boast he had personally destroyed. Christian rowers died chained in this holocaust also.

469

Admiral Pavel penned a factual report of the battle to the empress, disapproving the needless slaughter, especially of the Christian slaves whom the war was supposed to emancipate from Turkish oppression. In addition he wrote a letter to Jefferson in America renewing his old request for a command against the Barbary pirates.

Potemkin intercepted both letters, read both and burned both in the portable brazier that warmed his tent at night: the admiral's report of the battle contained political matter, since it seemed to reproach Russian methods of waging war; it was also too modest to suit the taste of the man who had made "Potemkin Villages" a legend. As for the admiral's personal letter to America, it betrayed a wish to leave Russia; Potemkin wished him to remain.

Potemkin then wrote his own report of the action to Catherine: the Turkish fleet was utterly annihilated, he announced, with eighteen capital ships sunk, scores more damaged beyond repair, and the remnant dispersed and in flight.

Within the week he could pen her another, and this time without exaggeration: Ochakov, surrounded by land and blockaded by sea, had in truth surrendered.

The empress commanded Admiral Pavel to return to Saint Petersburg and present himself at court and receive his reward.

Chapter 45

THE SURRENDER of Ochakov marked a turning point in the history of Turkey, which shortly came to be known as The Sick Man of Europe, signalizing its inevitable demise. The sultan heard first of the burning of his ships; then hard on the heels of that somber intelligence came a report of the massacre at Ochakov, for Potemkin's army marched in and butchered the population indiscriminately, including women and children, till Russian muskets grew too hot to shoot and Russian arms too weary to wield a saber. The victory of Ochakov required no exaggeration. Russian triumph was complete.

On this the sultan, whose mind had never been strong, went mad and died. His empire began to disintegrate. From Baghdad to the Atlantic a shock ran through it like an earthquake, disrupting its unity.

And then came the rush for the spoils. It was not to the interest of Western powers that a vacuum should exist too suddenly in the critical Middle East, since into that vacuum Russia, already a colossus, would flow and grow more colossal still. Each Western nation wanted its share. A throng of European ambassadors appeared at Constantinople with offers to Turkey of treaties of trade and perpetual friendship, for wheresoever the carcass is, there will the eagles be gathered together. Active hostilities ceased; if Catherine pushed too hard, she might find all Western Europe allied against her. There was indeed no formal peace, but the Russo-Turkish war lapsed into a period of quiescence, and the thunder of the cannon gave place to the purring of diplomats.

It was a suitable period for Catherine to reward her victorious warriors. In Saint Petersburg she bestowed upon Field Marshal Prince Potemkin the Order of Saint Andrew, the highest distinction Russia had to offer.

Prince Charles of Nassau-Siegen and Admiral Pavel of America, kneeling at the imperial throne, as handsome and likely a brace of young men as the court had beheld for some time, had pinned on their breasts the Order of Saint Anne, less resplendent than the Commander in Chief's but accompanied by so warm a smile from the empress as to make up for the difference. Poor Zhubov, in his barren colonel's uniform, stood by and tried hard to hide his chagrin.

Potemkin beamed. It seemed to him that the sparkle he knew so well in Catherine's eyes had been especially brilliant when she congratulated Pavel.

Shortly he had reason for even greater complacency. His informers brought him daily reports of the empress's solicitude for the admiral's comfort and health. She had lodged him in a luxurious villa; she had personally provided for his diet, rest and care; she had sent him her personal physician again to watch over him. Potemkin smiled, remembering. This was the pattern, twelve times repeated, that Catherine had followed whenever she chose a new favourite. Zhubov would soon be thanked for his services, and good it would be for Russia. Imperial Catherine was herself again.

Jones conceived a great liking for the physician, who indeed was a professor and an Academician and a witty raconteur, though on reviewing the conversations afterwards he noted that the professor seemed to have disclosed very little and asked a great many questions.

"It is a pity, monsieur l'amiral, that ships carry no doctors."

"Oh, we have them on warships, you know."

"Of course, of course. I was thinking of all the young men on merchant vessels, smaller ships, especially those that trade in the tropics and in the waters of the New World."

"Yes, we could use them."

"Think what mankind would have been spared if Columbus had had a good doctor aboard! The infection his caravels brought to Europe has added one more scourge to poor suffering humanity. How insulting it is to my Gallic ears to hear on every side 'the French disease' to describe a malady that is so patently West Indian in origin. The date of its appearance in Europe, if nothing else, proves where it comes from."

Jones said, "All I know is that it is prevalent everywhere now."

"But still epidemic in the West Indies, if my study of the subject is correct."

"Epidemic everywhere, I'm afraid."

"You yourself sailed in the West Indies for a long time during your youth — *Mon Dieu!* Not that you are old! — did you not?"

"Yes, for some years."

"And you never contracted — hmmm — you were very young at the time, you know—"

Jones laughed heartily. "I never cared much for red Indians, thank you; and as for the rest of the women I knew, I should never have needed your services even if you had been available. Though I should have liked to have had you aboard to treat some of my crews. Faugh!"

It was hardly the rigorous examination that the physician usually made, but the admiral's attitude towards the subject was so casual and frank that the physician sensed he had nothing to hide. He was clean, clean as Zhubov.

He made his report to Potemkin. "The admiral has no idea why I questioned him about his private life, which seems to have been uneventful from a medical point of view."

"Then he's a fool."

"No, I don't think so. His mind is full of other things: liberty, fraternity and the equality of man; he has the *idée fixe*. He talks of nothing but war against the Turks, and he cannot understand why you do not give him a fleet at once for a descent upon Constantinople."

"Did you examine him?"

"Excellency, how *could* I in his uncooperative frame of mind?"

"The dolt! Does he not see the prestige, the power, the glory that are his for the asking?"

"It seems not. He speaks only of ships, battles and a vague and impracticable ideal of freedom; his thoughts are doctrinaire and run to the theme that wrought the revolution in America and tortures my own native land in these days, but which Her Imperial Majesty keeps safe from these shores."

"It is some ruse. He is clever. I will talk to him."

But when Potemkin talked to him, subtle as a snake, the admiral replied, "Excellency, everything you say is true; my devotion to the empress is profound; her ideals inspire me, since they are my own: liberation for the oppressed. I yearn to please her, and I am flattered that I have found favor in her sight. I am proud that she calls me by the name of her own dear son, Pavel. I am new in her service, but I understand how a Russian feels: one would willingly lay down his life for her, as one would for his own beloved mother. I have learned that it is permissible in Russian to address the empress as 'Little Mother.' I should like to learn the word, so that when this great and majestic little old lady receives me again I too may so address her and express my affection."

Potemkin eyed him searchingly; the American was incredibly dense; it would take some time to bring him to his senses; but Zhubov's overthrow was worth the effort.

"Russian is hard to learn," he said. "I should not advise you to attempt the familiar address just yet. In Russian 'Little Mother' and 'Little Old Grandmother' sound very much alike. When you know her better, I am persuaded that you will understand how quickly Her Imperial Majesty would take offense at being called 'Little Old Grandmother' by a man she favors so greatly as her new admiral. Do I make myself clear, Pavel?"

Jones said seriously, "I shall labor incessantly to make myself worthy of her favor."

Potemkin grunted. It irked him to deal with such blindness. He thought, "I see more with my one eye than this American with two!" Aloud he said, "That is all that Imperial Catherine desires," smiling engagingly, biding his time.

But weeks passed. Catherine too could bide her time; not for nothing was she Catherine the Great. To outwait, outwit and outmaneuver Potemkin, ablest and wiliest of her lovers, was no small feat, comparable in its duplicity with the skill with which she outmaneuvered the diplomats, and the skill with which she neither warred against nor made peace with the Ottoman Empire. Imperial Catherine never gave up what she had without getting something better. Calm and imperturbable, smiling, majestic, sure-footed as a cat, she ruled, reigned over, and managed all she touched.

It soon appeared that Zhubov was not to be supplanted. Yet at the same time Admiral Pavel continued to rise in favor. "What?" Potemkin thought, mentally gasping. "Two at once?" It had never happened before.

The empress presented a huge estate to Zhubov and nine hundred serfs to work it. (Each year she bestowed on the average a hundred and twenty thousand of these human chattels on courtiers who pleased her.) Had the estate been situated in some distant province, everyone would have been certain that Zhubov's day was done; but such was not the case: it lay on an excellent carriage road a scant two hours from Saint Petersburg. As if riches were not enough, she raised him in military rank. Zhubov was suddenly a brigadier general.

Never had the Russian court been so gay. Never had the empress given so many balls, receptions and concerts. The court neatly balanced their attention between General Zhubov and Admiral Pavel, as did the empress. Foreign diplomats, following the lead of the court, seeking the imperial ear, would draw the favored men aside and whisper a suggestion of high import to their own governments, often coupling the suggestion with thinly veiled promises of rich rewards if the empress should look with favor upon it. But Zhubov was afraid to accept bribes from anyone but his sovereign, and Admiral Pavel seemed incorruptible: both men reported faithfully to the empress, however. She would smile and murmur her thanks, noncommittal.

And never had Potemkin so thoroughly enmeshed himself in a web of his own weaving. Not only had he failed to supplant the favourite; he had placed one more obstacle between himself and Catherine. He went into a fit of depression and shut himself away from the world, brooding.

In the midst of this self-imposed isolation a courier arrived from the empress with a friendly note in her own handwriting informing him that the Turkish war was still in being and that the defense of the Russian frontier in the Turkish sanjak of Rumania required the personal presence of the Russian Field Marshal Commander in Chief.

He hastened at once to the palace and demanded an audience in a loud and peremptory tone. His wig was on askew and he had not shaved for several days. To his surprise Catherine received him at once. He did not kneel. He did not bow. He ranted.

"If you are determined to exile me, exile me to Siberia! If you are determined to humiliate me, strip me of my commands! If it pleases you to punish me, punish me with the knout! Any incompetent fool can defend the Rumanian frontier, even Zhubov! But why send me away from you?"

She took him by the hand and led him to a chair and sat him beside her, humoring him like a petulant, much-beloved child. Listening servants, ears glued to doors, marveled at her understanding. Potemkin's Asiatic extremes of mood were to be expected; the patience of Catherine was always something new. She let him rant his rant, and then she soothed him.

"I did not say you must depart tomorrow, Gregory; I did not say you must depart next week. I merely said you must depart. When you study your dispatches, which I am told you have not opened for many days, you will agree with me that Jassy in Rumania is the spot where the Turks will strike next and where we must be on our guard. I have already strengthened the area. Some time not too long hence you must go there in person and take over, since no one else is competent for the command. Where Russia is concerned, you and I always agree, do we not, dear friend, dear counselor?" She reached up and patted his cheek. "Gregory, you need a shave."

"General Zhubov's cheek is smoother, I expect," he said unpleasantly. "Yes it is."

Jealously he retorted, "And so is Admiral Pavel's, no doubt."

Catherine laughed. "No doubt."

Potemkin experienced a sudden sensation of panic; he had always been able to manage one favourite; never before had he been forced to face the possibility of contending with two at a time. He was convinced that he had undermined his own position of power.

He struck like a viper, hidden and hissing. He put on a smiling ingenuous face and remarked casually, "The admiral was telling me recently how deep is his devotion to you."

"Was he?" she asked coquettishly. "What did he say? Tell me everything he said."

"He said you were the most lovable old woman he had ever seen."

The empress drew in her breath sharply. "Is that what he said? 'Old woman'?"

Potemkin enlarged, exaggerated. "Indeed he did. 'Little old grandmother' was what he said, his exact words."

She muttered in German under her breath, "Schwein!"

Potemkin hid his smile. When Catherine lapsed into her native German, she was deeply shaken.

"Shall I go on?"

"Yes," she said, her face a mask. "Go on."

"He said the 'grandmotherly affection' you aroused in his heart made him willing to lay down his life in your service."

"He doesn't understand," she said. The Autocrat of All the Russias seldom permitted her lip to tremble.

Relentlessly Potemkin pursued his advantage. "Of course he does not understand, Little Mother. He is a stupid insensitive pirate, a hybrid Scotch-Englishman" — Catherine instinctively disliked the English, as did all Russians — "most recently a revolutionary, plotting the downfall of legitimate monarchy everywhere, America, France — who knows where it will stop? How *could* this revolutionary understand my sovereign, my princess, my Imperial Catherine!"

"No one has ever understood." Her voice had a desolate quality like the soughing of wintry winds in barren branches of bleak and empty forests. "Only you, Gregory, and even you only a little."

He waited, his one eye veiled, while she continued to hold tight to his hairy paw of a hand. He watched her white face regain its composure, the majesty flow back. "But he was a glorious admiral," she said.

The Russian language, complex, expressive and subtle, possessed a tense which denoted "that which is finished now."

Potemkin was secretly jubilant and remarked, "Assuredly he was."

In that hour the Russian night, insidious and inexorable as freezing to death, closed in and enveloped the admiral who did not know he was finished.

Chapter 46

AND NOW behind the scenes the intrigue began to brew that was fated to poison the life of Admiral Pavel. Nothing appeared on the surface, but the viper's fangs had struck home, the slow venom began to kill.

To his great relief Jones found the inquisitive attentions of the imperial physician withdrawn: he felt perfectly well and he was glad to be rid of the chatty charming Academician. At the same time a prominent European ambassador was lodged in the villa which Jones had occupied, and Jones was permitted to take bachelor lodgings more suited to his taste. With him went Johann Gottfried Bahl, his valet-interpreter: the admiral was so busy with charts of the Sea of Marmora and maps of the defenses of Constantinople that he had no time to study the Russian language; he who had mastered the intricacies of African Ibo in his youth now depended more and more on the services of subordinates, like all generals; and indeed he never learned the difference between Russian *nyet* and *da*. Bahl took care of all that.

Bahl took care of his bachelor rooms as well, engaging and paying an old servant who made up his bed, swept the floors and kept the place tidy. Someone, Jones did not bother to ask who, cooked his meals; Bahl served them while the admiral perfected his campaign plans. Dispatches showed up on his breakfast tray in the morning. He read them assiduously and penned long reports to his Commander in Chief, who would smile and burn them, unopened. He also wrote to America requesting replies to his numerous letters: Potemkin impounded and burned this correspondence too, having read it.

"Admiral Pavel is inactive and lazy," Potemkin reported to the empress, who answered, "He is without imagination."

Thus with every mark of respect, surrounded by taciturn noncommittal associates, John Paul Jones lived in a vacuum, waiting for news that never came, shut off from the world as if couriers did not exist and Russia were no part of the civilized world. He did not even know when Gouverneur Morris replaced Thomas Jefferson as American minister to France, the journals that announced this appointment having been kept from him, not that the change affected Russia but because Potemkin, eternally suspicious, knew that information is power and that an uninformed man is helpless.

Into this vacuum of his life, while the admiral elaborated grandiose war plans which no one ever looked at, which indeed his Commander in Chief suppressed, there entered a creature of Potemkin's twisted imagining. A young girl, a peddler of butter and a mender of lace, arrived at his lodgings with a face like an angel's and a poverty that excited his compassion.

She was a blue-eyed German girl with a Russified name, Katerina Stepanova: the empress at this time was peopling her immense but sparsely settled empire with immigrants known as "colonists." The girl represented herself as the daughter of an immigrant named Frederica Sophia Koltzwarthen, wife of one Stephan Koltzwarthen who had come to Russia some years before to begin a new life far from his native land where chance and ineptitude had doomed him to mediocrity. In Russia he would rise, in Russia the promised land. The story of his rise, equally owing to chance, was intimately connected with the story of the American's downfall.

"Buy all the butter you please," the admiral said testily. "Since when do you trouble me with kitchen details? On the other hand, since you have

477

felt that you must consult me on this weighty matter, buy as little as possible. Russian butter is detestable."

"Rancid!" said Bahl. "The Russians like strong tastes. But this butter is something special, country-fresh and as sweet as the peddler who offers it; both deserve your attention, at least your inspection, sir." His pimply face twisted into an insinuating leer.

Jones looked up from his charts. "I suggest that you yourself inspect these sweet country-fresh products, Mr. Bahl, and purchase both or either in accordance with your own conscience and requirements," and he returned to the Sea of Marmora with a compass and parallel-ruler, charting an imaginary course, signaling an imaginary fleet into line of battle.

Bahl was being well paid for his office as tempter; he was not to be put off and he persisted, "I noted this morning, sir, that some of your jabots and wrist ruffles want mending."

"Buy new ones," Jones said absently.

"But it is wasteful to buy new ones when the old ones can be mended so cheaply — two kopecks — washed and returned in a day. I have seen samples of this girl's needlework."

Jones sighed. "Let her in, let her in; buy her butter, attend to my linen and leave me in peace."

But Bahl ushered the girl into the admiral's study and consummated the transaction like a court reception, interspersing his praise of her butter and needlework with praise of herself; and as for the girl, she was a remarkably pretty and friendly creature.

Shortly Jones began to enjoy the diverting and unexpected interlude. She returned several times, each time dressed more suggestively than the last, till any man, sailor or no, would have perfectly understood how she made her living and how little a part in it butter and needlework played. On several occasions the admiral, who was much alone these days, his invitations to court having become oddly infrequent, kissed her and gave her a glass of wine; and finally, as stated in the "confession" extorted from him when the affair became public and assumed disastrous proportions, dallied with her behind closed doors.

On the night that this happened, as Katerina emerged from the admiral's quarters, Bahl stopped her and told her to stand still.

Still as a statue she stood, knowing what was coming, the thing for which she already had been paid.

Bahl ripped her blouse and her scanty underclothing, exposing her. Then he struck her in the mouth, cutting her lip.

"Thank you," he said, noting the exact time and date in a little book.

"It was not in the agreement to ruin my face!" she cried, choking back the tears.

"Hush, little treasure! For that you will be paid something extra. Go now; the American must not hear. Go to your 'mother.'" He laughed.

"I won't be able to work for a month; the men won't look at me now; when I heal I'll have a big ugly scar."

"After this you won't have to work for a year. Go now, go, go, go!"

She took to her heels and ran crying to her "mother."

"Quick!" the old woman said, "while your tears are still fresh and the blood still flows! It is much more convincing."

She whisked her into a waiting coach. The driver required no address. He drove off at a gallop in the direction of the Central Bureau of the Chief of Imperial Police.

Major General Nikita Ivanovich Ryleyev, distinctly sober for so late in the evening and consumed with curiosity, remained at his desk long after the hour when he usually shut up shop and went home; the Chief of Imperial Police had heard a whisper from a personage he could not ignore that something of interest would happen that night, something requiring his personal attention.

"Who will be guilty?" asked the Chief of Imperial Police.

The informant from the court responded, "That is surely in your province to determine, sir."

"I exist only to serve Her Imperial Majesty," Nikita said.

"So do we all, sir."

"It would be such a help to know what Her Imperial Majesty expects of me."

"Sir, if I were the Chief of Her Imperial Majesty's Imperial Police I have no doubt that — to cite a purely hypothetical crime that might happen tonight — I should look most sternly upon anyone, no matter how exalted his position, who should so far give way to his baser impulses as to insult, nay, to ravage beat and bruise, some helpless member of the sex which Her Imperial Majesty so gloriously represents and so vigilantly protects, especially if the poor girl happened to be a Russian subject and the assailant a foreigner."

"Thank you," Nikita said.

Within the hour, while he waited for the crime to be committed, it was reported to him. The old woman and the girl appeared before him, the old woman in tears, the girl unquestionably weeping and bleeding at the mouth. Her lip was deeply cut as a result of a severe blow and four front teeth were loose.

479

Secretaries took down the women's depositions.

Admiral Pavel, retiring for the night, found himself under house arrest, his bachelor quarters suddenly full of grim-faced uncommunicative soldiers who said in bad French, "Not speak," "Not evade," "We take paper, pens, no write," "Sleep now." But they placed lanterns around his bed and shone them on him all night, as if he should suddenly sprout wings and "evade" on the sly. As for Bahl, he had disappeared.

In this curious situation, cut off from contact with the outside world, without newspapers, without mail, forbidden to write to Potemkin or the empress, unable to communicate even with De Ségur, his friend, Admiral John Paul Jones lived for three weeks.

When he raged, his jailors fired pistols into the floor, into the ceiling, then leveled them at his heart; when he was quiet, they were quiet, impassive; when he asked them questions, they answered, "Speak Russian"; when fitfully, exhausted, he slept, a young man with a pencil and pad took down the words he uttered in his nightmares.

"What are you writing, damn you?"

The young man answered in faultless French, "I do not speak French."

The weather was turning chill. In his nervous exhausted condition Jones was now extremely sensitive to cold.

"I am cold!" he said.

"Open the window," the young man said. "The admiral is warm."

Jones banged it shut again, cursing.

A soldier broke out the glass with the butt of his musket, touching his head, grinning, signifying that the admiral was mad. He nearly was.

Then there appeared at his door a stocky man with an oily smile who announced, "I have taken upon myself your defense, Admiral Jones." Jones noted with apprehension that the lawyer did not use the intimate Russian "Pavel."

"Defense? What defense? What am I charged with? Who charges me? Who dares to charge me! Why am I treated like a criminal? Why am I kept under guard week in, week out, by this mob of uncouth barbarians?"

"Softly, tread softly," the attorney smiled, exposing front teeth much rotted from tea drinking, "Only the rustics consider madmen touched by the gods any more and humor them. Here in civilized Saint Petersburg we put the insane behind bars, lest they injure themselves and others."

"I am not yet mad," Jones said, "but much more of this cold and I shall be."

"It is ever so much colder in Schlusselburg," the attorney said.

At the mention of Schlusselburg even Jones's jailers looked grave. It was the Russian counterpart of the Bastille in France. It was a remote and gloomy fortress entirely surrounded by water where prisoners disappeared without a trace.

"What is Schlusselburg?" Jones asked.

"I do not desire to speak of unpleasant eventualities, Admiral. I am here to prevent them from occurring. I am here to defend you against the complaint of a certain ten-year-old sempstress who states — h-m-m, h-m-m," — he riffled through a sheaf of papers — "that on the night of the thirteenth of March you, Rear Admiral John Paul Jones, an alien, did lure with lascivious intent one Katerina Stepanova Koltzwarthen, a virgin, into your private apartment and there by force and against her will overpower, rape, brutalize and wound her by a blow or blows in her face and elsewhere, which blows resulted in cuts, bruises and loosened teeth —"

"Before God, you lie!"

"— and all of the said forcing, raping, brutalizing and wounding is attested and sworn to in depositions now extant in the files of Her Imperial Majesty's Chief of Imperial Police, Major General Nikita Ivanovich Ryleyev."

"Who swears to these damnable lies?"

Soberly the attorney read the names: Katerina Stepanova Koltzwarthen, the plaintiff; Frederica Sophia Koltzwarthen, her mother; Stephan Koltzwarthen, her father; Professor Jean-Baptiste Levasseur, Physician in Ordinary to Her Imperial Majesty, who examined the plaintiff."

"He? My friend? He examined the sempstress?"

"And another name, Johann Gottfried Bahl."

"My valet?"

"But a formidable witness, Admiral. He stood by, observed, heard everything."

Jones struck his forehead with the palm of his hand several times in rapid succession. "Why is this done to me? It isn't true, not a word of it! Why? Why?"

"It would be more to the point, sir, in the interest of your defense, to prepare a statement explaining how the criminal acts set forth in the depositions happened to occur." His oily smile reappeared. "We are both men, are we not? Do not men understand men? Can we not say, in extenuation of your acts, that a little vodka, a little wine, the presence of the girl, her beauty, her proximity — can we not say that the admiral lost his head for the moment — the girl weakly resisted his advances — he plied her with drink — she succumbed to the wine and the great man's charm — she lost her sobriety and her virginity — and then she fell drunkenly against the bed post, cutting her lip? I can prepare a defense, sir, that will put her thoroughly in the wrong. You need only confess a little of your part in the affair. Your punishment will unquestionably be less severe. In fact, I have already prepared such a confession."

"I will never confess to a lie!"

"I doubt if the single unattested word of an alien will stand up against the sworn testimony of so many Russians," the lawyer said, shrugging. He clapped on his hat. "I have reconsidered my situation, sir. You have had your chance. You refuse to cooperate. I regret that I cannot undertake your defense after all."

With that he left.

Jones attempted to bribe his jailers to appeal to De Ségur to procure a good lawyer to defend him. They pocketed the bribes, shook their heads and observed, "No lawyer would dare."

Shortly Jones was conducted to the Central Bureau of Her Majesty's Chief of Imperial Police. The interrogation was short.

"Are you guilty of the charges against you contained in these depositions?" asked Nikita Ivanovich Ryleyev. He spoke in Russian. An interpreter repeated the questions to Jones in French.

"I have not read them."

"Are you guilty or not?"

"I am not," Jones said.

"He says Yes," said the interpreter in Russian. Nikita Ivanovich Ryleyev wrote *Da* as the prisoner's response.

"Thank him," he said.

The admiral was thanked and dismissed.

Jones was returned to his quarters under the same confinement as before. His end was now known to all but himself: there awaited him a curious taste in his food, an inexplicable illness, a bullet in the back three thousand miles away in Siberia or death at the hands of some robber who would assault him on the street the moment he was allowed to go out for a walk: but death. And if some foreign government should evince any interest in the accident that had ended the admiral's career, there were always the files of the Imperial Police, producible at a moment's notice, to prove that John Paul Jones had led an irregular private life and, like many another, fallen into a pit that he himself had dug. The true cause of his death, however he might die, was already prepared for publication: "alas, it was all his own fault."

Potemkin could congratulate himself that he had triumphed, late and by a narrow margin, but completely. Only Zhubov, poor fatuous Zhubov, now remained. The stronger man, far far too strong, was eliminated. Imperial Catherine never spoke his name these days, and if by mistake some courtier would make mention of Admiral Pavel she would look stern and her lips would tighten. Soon no one mentioned his name.

But history marched, despite the cunning of Potemkin and Catherine's pique.

The Comte de Ségur, ambassador from the court of His Most Christian Majesty King Louis XVI of France, took a serious view of the troubles of John Paul Jones, his friend and the friend of his king. Time and again he presented himself at Jones's rooms, only to be informed by a surly sentry that the admiral was not at home.

"Then why are you guarding his door?"

Orders, the sentry would say.

"Whose orders?"

"My orders."

"Fellow, that is no way to answer a question from the French ambassador."

The fellow would lapse into silence.

Frowning, De Ségur would step into his coach and drive back to the French embassy.

De Ségur needed Jones. There was great restlessness in France. There were ominous rumblings among the peasantry and the petty bourgeoisie. Taxes were high. Harvests were poor. There had been bread riots. The Army and Navy, being largely recruited from the lower classes, were undisciplined, reflecting the discontent of the people. At the top, among the nobility, there was a sense of withdrawal and a hardening of solidarity: the gap between noble and commoner was widening. Even La Fayette had modified the revolutionary views of his youth and now stood stanchly allied with his class against the dangerous ideas instilled by the pens of Rousseau and Voltaire, ideas which had swept away monarchy in America and which many feared would sweep away monarchy in France.

Admiral Jones had sometimes expressed to De Ségur his dislike of the absolutism by which Russia was ruled, his disappointment at the savagery with which the Russo-Turkish war had been waged, his horror at the inhuman burning not only of Turkish enemies but also of Christian slaves, and above all the deplorable servitude of thirty-eight millions of human beings, the serfs of Russia. John Paul Jones had lifted a corner of the veil of Catherine's pseudo liberalism and caught a glimpse of what was underneath: the massive cynicism, the stark and absolute power, by which she dominated her complex and enormous empire. Perhaps, he had said to De Ségur, there was no other way to dominate; captains had to be severe disciplinarians on ships, as he knew by experience; but it never was right to permit subordinates to act cruelly. "Asiatics are cruel," De Ségur had said. "This is a part of the world which the Renaissance passed by. *L'homme universel,* the complete man, the good sportsman, good loser, the magnanimous victor, is here unknown, for he is the product of Western culture. But here, what? The Kaizaks still impale; Tartars still blind their prisoners with hot pokers; the Russian Commander in Chief still permits his armies to massacre women and children, as happened in Ochakov. True, the empress, a European not an Asiatic by birth, is struggling valiantly, manfully one might almost say despite the multitude of her amours, to instill a Western concept of fair play into Russia, and to some extent at the top she has succeeded. But it will take many monarchs and many years, generations perhaps, for such a concept to filter down to Ivan Ivanovich, the *Jacques Bonhomme,* the common man of Russia."

But most of all De Ségur wanted Jones back in the French Navy, counting on his personal integrity. Jones had received a testimonial sword from the king of France, and counted it among his most precious possessions. In receiving it he had sworn to defend the French king against all his enemies. Jones had never been known to break his word. France could use such a man in these times. It was not in the interest of France that an admiral with such a record of victories, who could discipline sailors yet gain their devotion, should be destroyed.

It was thus that the prestige of France was brought to bear in high places to extricate Jones from his troubles.

It ended in a compromise.

His release was quick; Potemkin sulked; the empress sulked; but released he was.

In all his medals, with his ambassadorial chain of office circling his shoulders and the Order of the Holy Ghost blazing on his breast, the Comte de Ségur presented himself to Imperial Catherine and pleasantly reminded her that Admiral John Paul Jones, now held incommunicado by the police, who were no doubt acting without Her Imperial Majesty's knowledge, was an officer in the French Navy as well as a commodore in the Navy of the United States of America: two sovereign powers protected him. He was a personal friend of George Washington; he was a personal friend of King Louis XVI. With particular reference to the French king,

De Ségur noted that His Most Christian Majesty would take a grave view of any infringement of the rights of a friend he had honored in the past and would undoubtedly honor again in the future.

"Do you dare, sir, to voice threats to our face?" the empress demanded, flushing hotly.

De Ségur's countenance went all diplomatic smiles. "Madam," he protested, "who could conceive of so despicable a thought! I had in mind only the treaty of friendship which exists between France and America, a treaty tried in war and sanctified by outpouring of fraternal blood! How highly these two countries value this man! How in this, as in so much, they think as one! How many millions would grieve at his loss and how angry they would be if he did not return! But threats, madam? I assure you, *non!*"

"We know nothing about the American," the empress replied, "except that certain follies which he has committed have got him into trouble. Admiral Jones is no concern of ours. He is free to come as he pleases, go as he pleases. We suggest that you speak to Prince Potemkin."

She dismissed the ambassador curtly.

Armed with sworn statements, De Segur now approached Potemkin.

De Ségur had spies of his own, since no ambassador could adequately discharge his duties at the Russian court without them, expending large sums yearly on their maintenance, a charge which was duly passed on to the French Treasury. De Ségur was able through the efforts of his informers to amass a formidable array of testimony in favor of Jones, including a statement from a clergyman, a Pastor Braun, whose flock consisted of a motley collection of shiftless German "colonists" in a poor section of Saint Petersburg.

Pastor Braun swore and deposed that Katerina Stepanova was a well-known prostitute, nineteen years old, not ten, who worked in a popular house of ill repute in his parish; and as for her "mother," she was not her mother at all but the madam who ran the place. The man who posed as her father acted as procurer for the establishment.

"And this Johann Gottfried Bahl, the admiral's valet," De Ségur smiled. "He appears to be one of Your Excellency's own agents."

"What if he is?" Potemkin said, shrugging. "Don't you employ agents?"

"Of course I do. How else would I know all this?"

Potemkin glared. "It is my agent's word against your agent's word, you know. You and your sworn statements! These miserable scraps of paper! You and they are a long way from home."

"I, sir, am a long way from home; but not my papers. I took occasion some days ago to send copies of them to France."

"Impossible! How?"

De Ségur did not answer; he merely remarked, "Imagine the consternation if they should be published, if the entire world should learn the truth of the plot against Admiral Jones!"

A gleam of respect glinted in Potemkin's eye. "You actually managed to smuggle information out of Russia? I must be getting old! And you will publish it, I suppose?"

"Oh dear no. I am sure that will not be necessary. Bear in mind that Her Imperial Majesty has just granted him leave to go."

"I know. She loathes him."

"And I am persuaded that Your Excellency will put no obstacle into the path of his going, since Her Imperial Majesty sanctions his dismissal."

"She wants him ten thousand miles away, and so do I!" Potemkin said; and muttered after a pause, "What a pity, what a pity he did not turn out otherwise; they could have been such good friends."

"May I then assume that I am at liberty to tell him that his arrest was a regrettable error, that he is free to come and go as he pleases?"

Potemkin shook his head violently. "No, by God! That would put the Imperial Police in the wrong; that would put me in the wrong. Worse, it would put the empress in the wrong. She has seen the police dossier; she read it with pain and disappointment; she believes every word of it. No! Imperial Catherine does not make mistakes. Neither do the Imperial Police. Neither does Gregory Potemkin! One way or another the American must go; but first he must make a full confession of the guilty conduct that led to his dismissal. Do you understand, my clever French friend?"

"I understand precisely," De Ségur said. "I will do what I can."

"If you cannot manage to get a confession out of him," Potemkin said, "I assure you that I can."

De Ségur remembered the "Potemkin villages," and answered, "Yes, I believe you could," and was silent a moment. Then, brightening, "Actually, Your Excellency, in a case like this, who knows? It would be incredible, contrary to nature, that nothing whatsoever should have passed between the admiral and the little sempstress, would it not?"

"Just be sure the signature is genuine," Potemkin said. "It must bear the scrutiny of generations."

"I am sure the admiral will consider it the part of wisdom to confess *something*."

"He had better."

486

As suddenly as they had descended upon him, the admiral's guards now disappeared. He was utterly alone when De Ségur drove up to the house where he lived. Even the servants had vanished. It was a metropolitan neighborhood, but people in the vicinity stayed within doors; a few stray pedestrians on the street hurried by, looking in another direction, as if Admiral Jones's quarters were plague-stricken.

Haggard and distraught, Jones opened the door himself. De Ségur was appalled at his pallor. The admiral had a cocked pistol in his hand.

"Come, come, old friend; it isn't as bad as that," De Ségur said smiling. "Let me in."

"How do I know you are my friend? How do I know anything any more?"

But he let him in.

Little by little, as the French ambassador unfolded the enormity of the intrigue against him, Jones lost the sense of unreality that had gripped him and grown during his weeks of isolation. De Ségur spoke quietly, factually. A healthy anger displaced the disorientation in the admiral's mind. "I see what they want! I see why they want it! But confess to a lie? Liberty in exchange for a lie? Never! I will not crawl through life a self-confessed rapist, a beater of women, a deflowerer of ten-year-olds! I'd rather die!"

"All men die," De Ségur shrugged. "Why hasten the process?"

"Whenever my honor has been weighed against my life, as has sometimes happened in the past," Jones said simply, "it has never occurred to me to question which was the lighter, nor do I ask that question now. The first duty of a gentleman is to respect his own character. I will not confess to a lie."

"What really happened, Admiral?"

"Why, this pretty little whore schemed her way into my rooms with the connivance of that rascal who posed as my valet, and — and — and —"

"Yes, Admiral?"

Jones flushed. "Does dishonor attach to a bachelor, a sailor without a wife, without a sweetheart, with no ties, in a foreign country — an extremely exotic country, sir, where the sovereign herself sets an example of laxity unparalleled in our Western nations — come, answer me, sir, does dishonor attach to such a man in such a situation of he dallies with a *fille de joie*?"

The Frenchman chuckled. "Admiral, I would not be burdened with your Presbyterian load of conscience for all the money in the world! There

487

is no dishonor! The affair was light as a feather. Confess only to the minuscule truth of this little matter and be free to return to Europe."

"Truth will not satisfy these people," Jones said dispiritedly.

"On the contrary, this time it will, since we negotiate from a position of strength, stronger perhaps than you know," De Ségur said smiling; and he told him how the whole history of the "complot," as he called it, would be published in every newspaper in Europe and America in the event of the sudden disappearance or accidental death of Admiral John Paul Jones. "France would be loath to lose you and so would America, my friend, for the sake of an overscrupulous conscience."

Jones said wearily, "I had begun to feel I possessed no friends; it is a comfort to be reassured that I do. If I *do* confess to a peccadillo, however, I will do it in my own way and in my own words."

"Good! Dictate! I shall take it down."

That is why a document of considerable importance appeared in the Imperial Russian Archives in the French language. Triumphantly De Ségur presented himself at the Central Bureau of the Chief of Imperial Police in Saint Petersburg and laid it on the desk of Nikita Ivanovich Ryleyev.

It read:

SIR:

The accusation hurled against me is a fraud, concocted by the greed of the mother of a depraved girl who came to my house a number of times and with whom I often frolicked, each time giving her some money. But by no means did I take her virginity. Never did I do the least violence to this girl, nor to any member of her sex. I thought her to be some years older than Your Excellency has been told that she is, and each time that she came to see me she was perfectly compliant in doing all that a man could desire of her. The last occasion passed like all the others. I may say that the girl left my abode thoroughly happy and content, without voicing the slightest complaint of any maltreatment whatsoever by me. If the girl's defloration has been duly authenticated I assert and swear that it was not I who deflowered her.

I have the honor of being, Monsieur,
Of Your Excellency, The most humble and Very Obedient Servant.
(*Signed*) JOHN PAUL JONES

To His Excellency, M. de Ryleyev
Major General and Chief of Imperial Police
Saint Petersburg

Nikita Ryleyev mopped his brow and clutched at the precious paper. It would do. His position was saved. His official head would not roll. "You have been most obliging," he said to De Ségur. "I shall never forget you for this. There would have been frightful retaliations against my department if my records had been discovered to be in error. Now all is well."

Potemkin was satisfied.

The empress was satisfied; again she was right, as she had to be and always was. She refused audience to the admiral, stating that she disliked to receive persons found guilty of moral turpitude. She struck him from the active list of her rear admirals and returned to the embraces of Zhubov, who was the most satisfied of all.

Yet Imperial Catherine preserved the amenities. She did not dismiss or degrade her American: she rewarded him for his services and graciously granted him a two years' leave of absence and ordered him instantly escorted from the country.

Jones left, alive, but not for long.

Chapter 47

HE RETURNED to a France he no longer recognized. A revolution more awesome than the American was in progress. This revolution concerned not some distant American colonies but the heartland of Europe itself, older than England, older than Spain, tearing at its vitals and threatening a thousand years of culture.

The Bastille had fallen. The Army and Navy were mutinous. The people were hungry; the king and queen were prisoners in their own palace; they attempted to escape; hooting mobs brought them back and shut them up again. Scores of political parties, some moderate, some prey to extremely bloody notions, sought to dominate the shaking state. The days were full of shouting parades, the nights were full of alarms and sudden panics. A constant stream of aristocratic fugitives fled over the borders, abandoning their ancient estates, convinced that the end was at hand.

In this gathering storm Jones found himself alone and confused. In other years, in better health, he could have seen the situation more clearly and played, perhaps, some significant part in the great events that were shaping. But he could not gain audience with the prisoner-king who once had honored him and whose Navy now refused to obey orders. De Ségur's influence had dropped to zero at Paris. Other noble friends had emigrated. He could not see La Fayette, now head of the National Guard and vainly trying to mediate between king and people and even more vainly endeavoring to preserve some semblance of internal security. The revolution marched inexorably towards an end that none could foresee beyond battle, murder and sudden death.

For Jones, who was seriously ill, France was chaos; he longed to return to America. He wrote long letters to Jefferson and Washington, hoping they would get through. For him time dragged with exasperating slowness, as with any sick man in pain, but for the rest of the world, stimulated by sharp and fundamental change, time flew.

His sickness lay deep in his past: the bouts of malarial fevers he had suffered in his youth, reactivated by his exposure during the crossing of the icy Baltic on his frantic dash into Russia and rendered chronic, with mounting malignancy, by exposure to constant Russian cold, especially during his cruel confinement.

But he was not cold now. He had no fever now. He imagined himself in perfect health, and it never occurred to him that violent extremes of temperature or a lifetime of violent demands on his strength could have wrought permanent damage to his kidneys. All he knew was that he suffered excruciating pains in his abdomen and back. He was impatient with the pain, not because it hurt but because it prevented him from thinking clearly.

A physician who treated him said, "A touch of the dropsy, monsieur l'amiral," and gave him laudanum to drink, which killed the pain and further befuddled his thinking processes.

In the alien atmosphere of revolutionary Paris, which grew less comprehensible to him every day, his thoughts turned more and more to America.

He renewed his request to President Washington for a command against the Barbary states on a day when he thrust the laudanum bottle away from him to keep his thoughts clear: the military situation of the Ottoman Empire vis-à-vis the tremendous might of Russia was poor, he declared, and as a consequence the Dey of Algiers, cut off from support by the Sultan of Turkey, was helpless. Now therefore was the time to sail against the Algerian dey and force him to stop his piratical practices, to parley from a position of strength, strike open his dungeons, liberate the Christian prisoners there, liberate all Christians, not only Americans, and bring to a halt once and for all the notorious custom of holding to ransom ship-wrecked and captured sailors, a custom as old as the Crusades and wholly at variance with American ideals. Why Great Britain perpetually truckled to the pirates mystified him and excited his indignation. Jones was very forceful that day in that letter. The President admired it, approved his spirit, remembered him. Jefferson thoroughly endorsed it.

But the pain returned. Jones again had recourse to the laudanum bottle. The period of lucidity passed and his old vigor faded, while all around him the fires of the French Revolution burned higher, and that cruellest of all social upheavals gathered like a boil to a hideous head, awaiting the lancet and the outpouring of blood.

Shortly he was aware that his uniforms no longer fitted him. His knee garters bound him; they were too tight and left white indentations on the flesh which persisted longer than they ought. He rubbed the spots and slowly, too slowly, the white would disappear. He thought the fabric of the garters might have shrunk and ordered his servant to set over the but-tons. But it happened again and he was forced to acknowledge that his knees, not the garters, had changed. His legs had begun to swell.

The swelling rose to his abdomen and thence to his chest. He who had "skylarked" in his youth, sliding down the bellying snow-white sails, whose agility had been proverbial and whose slenderness had been the envy of portly associates, now at the age of forty-four walked like a heavy old man, painfully and with a cane.

Yet he had seen men grow bloated with scurvy; he had seen many cases of gout; he assumed his condition would pass. That he was at the point of death did not once enter his thoughts. He sought to cure his scurvy with fresh fruits; he drank nothing but water to cure his gout; he ate sparingly to reduce the weight which oppressed his movements — it would have been difficult to eat normally in any case since the laudanum rendered him incapable of hunger.

Painfully one day he hobbled to the residence of Gouverneur Morris to inquire for news from America. Gouverneur Morris was not interested in ailing heroes of the American Revolution, a conflict now slipping so rapidly into the past in the face of the frenetic developments in France. Besides, there was death in the face of this John Paul Jones. What had *he* to do with the Barbary states, what made him think *he* could head a squadron in his condition, and why should America intervene in North African politics anyway, when all France was about to erupt? Gouverneur Morris sent him away: No, there was no news from America.

On the sixth of June, 1792, John Paul Jones observed his forty-fifth birthday, alone and in pain. It struck him as ironical that he should be so ill, so old and forgotten, at an age when most men are winning their first real solid success, some achieving appointments to their first command, setting foot on their first quarter-deck. How many he had trod! How many men in this vigorous prime of manhood first took to themselves wives, founded families and lived to see their grandsons! He seemed to have lived too fast; his star had risen too swiftly and sunk too soon. He was greatly depressed that night and he measured out a double dosage of laudanum, knowing that tomorrow his body would rebel and cramps would claw at his belly. But he would sleep in peace.

On July eighteenth, having sat for some hours in his study, he experienced a profound sensation of fatigue and an uncomfortable feeling of nausea. It would pass, he thought, if he should lie down and take a nap. He was irritated at the incident because he had planned to visit Gouverneur Morris that night and ask again for news from America.

He rose from his chair and walked into his bedroom. He attempted to remove his coat and take off his shirt, not only to breathe better — it seemed oddly difficult to breathe — but also because he wanted his lace to be fresh when the American minister should receive him. Gouverneur Morris was a great dandy and always frowned on limp or wrinkled lace in others.

But the effort was too great. He could not remove his coat, far less his shirt. For a moment he steadied himself against the bed post, then grinned and decided to take his nap fully dressed. What sailor, dead tired, undresses to catch forty winks of sleep? A sailor takes his rest whenever he can, anywhere, and goes on to what's next.

Fully clothed, he relaxed; and he thought he crawled gratefully onto a ship's bunk to snatch a moment's oblivion till some superior officer should rout him out again with a brash halloo and a shout that a blow was coming on, there was duty to be performed, work to be done. Lively now, laddies, step lively, I say!

Instantly alert, he answered the Superior's call. He heard a crashing about his ears and a roar like the thunder of bursting things, things smashed and destroyed. This was an emergency.

He answered swiftly.

They found him, not yet quite cold, lying athwart the bed onto which he had not quite managed to crawl. His feet, with his boots on, rested on the floor.

The moment of oblivion was forever.

They buried him in the Cemetery of Saint Louis.

And then an answer came in response to his many requests for an expedition against the Barbary pirates. American sailors were being captured and enslaved in increasing numbers. American indignation burned, and in solemn fury the American President turned to the man who had first counseled action.

President Washington acted.

John Paul Jones received the command he had sought.

There came, too late, the coveted commission. He never saw it.

It read:

GEORGE WASHINGTON, President of the United States of America: To all to whom these presents shall come, GREETING.

Know ye that, reposing special trust and confidence in the integrity, prudence and abilities of JOHN PAUL JONES, a citizen of the United States, I have nominated and appointed him, the said JOHN PAUL JONES, as Commissioner for the United States, giving him full power and authority, for and in the name of the United States of America, to confer, treat and negotiate with the Dey and Gouvernment of Algiers or with any person or persons duly authorized on their behalf, of and concerning the ransom of all citizens of the United States of America in captivity with the said Dey, gouvernment and subjects of Algiers, or with any of them, and to conclude and sign a Convention thereupon, transmitting the same to the President of the United States for his final ratification by and with the advices and consent of the Senate of the United States. In testimony whereof I have caused the seal of the United States to be hereunto affixed. Given under my hand at the city of Philadelphia the first day of June in the year one thousand seven hundred and ninety two, and of the Independence of the United States the sixteenth.

(Signed) GEORGE WASHINGTON

Epilogue

THE FRENCH REVOLUTION waxed, raged and waned. With the passing years the Cemetery of Saint Louis became no longer a place of interment. Its headstones disintegrated and the graveyard became a grassy park. Pleasant walks were laid in it, and new buildings began to encroach upon the greensward. But the old maps were never lost; and those who slumbered there could be found if patient antiquarians wished to find them.

One hundred and thirteen years after his death a squadron of steamships belonging to the Navy of the United States of America crossed the Atlantic and brought him home. It was a rapid crossing, albeit without sails. It must have pleased the man who said, "I wish to have no connection with any ship that does not sail fast."

Dat